Praise for *Peop*

W9-CFL-058

"A riveting novel... The Gears don't shy away from authenticism in depicting the violence that resulted."
                                                        —*Booklist*

"A lively tale of warring clans... Should leave readers hungry for more entries in the series."   —*Kirkus Reviews*

Praise for *People of the Raven*

"I haven't read a novel this good in a long, long time. *People of the Raven* draws you into a magnificent, sweeping world—America, circa 7300 B.C.—that is so real you can almost breathe in the air of it. It tells a big-hearted story of war and peace, love and violence, with a cast of richly drawn characters. This is a novel that will stay with you for years—I guarantee it."
                                        —Douglas Preston, *New York Times*
                                        bestselling coauthor of *Relic* and *Brimstone*

"*People of the Raven*, at one level, is the recreation of a lost and forgotten civilization by two noted archaeologists. But this story of Kennewick Man also involves an important legal battle pending in the U.S. Supreme Court and is a good read for those of us intrigued by the earliest Americans."   —Tony Hillerman

Praise for *People of the Owl*

"*People of the Owl*... cements the Gears' place in Jean Auel's genre of prehistoric fiction."
                                        —*Romantic Times BookReviews* (4 stars)

"Extraordinary... The Gears colorfully integrate authentic archaeological and anthropological details with a captivating story replete with romance, intrigue, mayhem, and a nail-biting climax."   —*Library Journal*

By Kathleen O'Neal Gear and W. Michael Gear
from Tom Doherty Associates

THE ANASAZI MYSTERY SERIES

The Visitant

The Summoning God

Bone Walker

THE FIRST NORTH AMERICANS
SERIES

People of the Wolf

People of the Fire

People of the Earth

People of the River

People of the Sea

People of the Lakes

People of the Lightning

People of the Silence

People of the Mist

People of the Masks

People of the Nightland*

People of the Owl

People of the Raven

People of the Moon

People of the Weeping Eye*

BY KATHLEEN O'NEAL GEAR

Thin Moon and Cold Mist

Sand in the Wind

This Widowed Land

It Sleeps in Me

It Wakes in Me

It Dreams in Me*

To Cast a Pearl*

BY W. MICHAEL GEAR

Long Ride Home

Big Horn Legacy

The Morning River

Coyote Summer

The Athena Factor

OTHER TITLES BY
KATHLEEN O'NEAL GEAR
AND W. MICHAEL GEAR

Dark Inheritance

Raising Abel

*forthcoming

PEOPLE
of the MOON

W. MICHAEL GEAR
AND KATHLEEN O'NEAL GEAR

TOR®

A TOM DOHERTY ASSOCIATES BOOK
NEW YORK

NOTE: If you purchased this book without a cover, you should be aware that this book is stolen property. It was reported as "unsold and destroyed" to the publisher, and neither the author nor the publisher has received any payment for this "stripped book."

This is a work of fiction. All the characters and events portrayed in this novel are either fictitious or are used fictitiously.

PEOPLE OF THE MOON

Copyright © 2005 by W. Michael Gear and Kathleen O'Neal Gear
Excerpt from *People of the Nightland* © 2006 by W. Michael Gear and Kathleen O'Neal Gear

All rights reserved, including the right to reproduce this book, or portions thereof, in any form.

Maps and illustrations by Ellisa Mitchell

A Tor Book
Published by Tom Doherty Associates, LLC
175 Fifth Avenue
New York, NY 10010

www.tor.com

Tor® is a registered trademark of Tom Doherty Associates, LLC.

ISBN-13: 978-0-765-34758-9
ISBN-10: 0-765-34758-X

First Edition: October 2005
First Mass Market Edition: November 2006

Printed in the United States of America

0 9 8 7 6 5 4 3 2 1

To Our Beloved Shetland Sheepdog

BEN

Born: May 1, 1999
Killed by Cougar: February 24, 2005

You gave us such joy.

Acknowledgments

We wish to thank the following people for their help in writing *People of the Moon*. First and foremost, Glenn Raby, of the Pagosa Springs District Office of the San Juan National Forest, not only gave us a personal tour of the Chimney Rock Archaeological Site but forwarded copies of vital excavation reports and out-of-print articles on the early fieldwork conducted there.

Public visitation of the Chimney Rock Archaeological Site would not be possible without the dedicated individuals who volunteer their time and resources to maintain the site and direct the tours. To each and every one of you, thank you for helping to make this site available to all people.

The Hot Springs County Library, Thermopolis, Wyoming, saved us weeks of effort and thousands of miles of travel by running down excavation reports by Earl Morris and Paul S. Martin on both the Aztec and Lowry Ruins. To Karen, Tracy, B.J., and the rest of the staff, we offer our heartfelt thanks.

As always we rely on our professional colleagues. Countless papers, articles, and monographs have contributed to our understanding of the prehistoric Southwest. We would like to specially acknowledge Dr. Steve Lekson of the University of Colorado. Coming from different directions, we always seem to arrive at the same place.

To all of our professional colleagues, thank you.

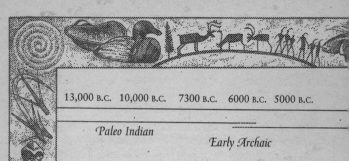

| 13,000 B.C. | 10,000 B.C. | 7300 B.C. | 6000 B.C. | 5000 B.C. |

Paleo Indian

Early Archaic

People of the Wolf
Alaska & Canadian
Northwest

People of the Earth
Northern Plains
& Basins

People of the Raven
Pacific Northwest &
British Columbia

People of the Nightland
Great Lakes Region

People of the Fire
Central Rockies &
Great Plains

People of the Sea
Pacific Coast &
Great Basin

People of the Lightning
Florida

Paleo Indian

Archaic

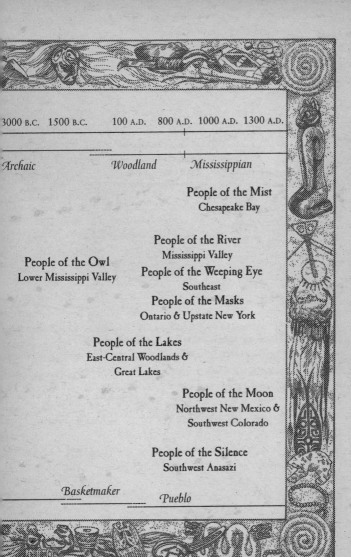

3000 B.C.	1500 B.C.	100 A.D.	800 A.D.	1000 A.D.	1300 A.D.

Archaic   *Woodland*   *Mississippian*

People of the Mist
Chesapeake Bay

People of the River
Mississippi Valley

People of the Owl
Lower Mississippi Valley

People of the Weeping Eye
Southeast

People of the Masks
Ontario & Upstate New York

People of the Lakes
East-Central Woodlands &
Great Lakes

People of the Moon
Northwest New Mexico &
Southwest Colorado

People of the Silence
Southwest Anasazi

Basketmaker   *Pueblo*

Foreword

It was during a visit to the Chimney Rock Archaeological Site outside of Pagosa Springs, Colorado, that writing *People of the Moon* became imperative. The site itself is one of the most amazing in the Americas because of its cultural value and stunning physical setting.

People of the Moon deals with the collapse of the northern Chaco frontier in the mid-twelfth century. Among the critical events are the spectacular destruction of the northern Chaco great houses; episodes of extreme violence, including cannibalism; and the relocation of the political center of the ancestral Pueblo world from Chaco Canyon to Aztec, New Mexico. (Please note: Aztec, New Mexico, has nothing to do with the Mexican Aztec civilization. Early entrepreneurs along the Dolores River were more interested in marketing the site than with any concerns about ethnohistorical accuracy.)

We like to think of the Anasazi as, well, the Anasazi. In reality what we now call the Anasazi, or ancestral Puebloans, were composed of numerous ethnic, linguistic, and tribal groups—each with their own distinct social or cultural identity. While they all practiced some form of corn-bean-squash agriculture, lived in similar styles of houses, and shared a common technology, we see local variations in pottery, artistic motifs, and skeletal traits. It was a multiethnic society.

That the Chacoans maintained hegemony over such vast and diverse populations for more than two hundred years is a testament to their military, religious, and political skill and ingenuity. They were doing quite well until the climate let them down.

We know from paleoclimatic studies that the Southwest turned colder and dryer around A.D. 1150. Crops failed and people went hungry. Of all the passions that motivate human beings, deprivation is the most powerful. Mix it with ignorance and hunger, and you get spontaneous combustion. In our modern world it is the root of terrorism, civil war, and holocaust. Deprive a human being of what he thinks is rightfully his—be it food, safety, or even a concept as abstract as justice—and he will respond passionately, violently, and most often, irrationally.

While the characters in *People of the Moon* are, of course, fictional, the sites, such as Aztec (Flowing Waters Town), Lowry Ruin (Tall Piñon), Far View, Pueblo Bonito (Talon Town), Chimney Rock Archaeological Site (Pinnacle Great House), the Bluff Site (Windflower), and Cowboy Wash (Saltbush Farmstead), are actual sites, many of which are open to visitation.

Saltbush Farmstead is based on the Cowboy Wash Archaeological Site, and no, dear reader, we didn't just make up the terrible events there. What the archaeologists discovered at the site is even grimmer than our fiction. See the article "Cannibalism, Warfare, and Drought in the Mesa Verde Region during the Twelfth Century A.D." by Brian R. Billman, Patricia M. Lambert, and Banks L. Leonard in Volume 65, No. 1 of *American Antiquity*. It's available through interlibrary loan.

Burned corpses were reported on the slope below Chimney Rock Pueblo. See Frank H. H. Roberts's "Report on Archaeological Reconnaissance in Southwestern Colorado in the Summer of 1923" in *The Colorado Magazine,* Vol. 2, No. 2, published by the State Historical and Natural History Society of Colorado. See Frank Eddy's "Archaeological Investigations at Chimney Rock Mesa: 1970–1972" in the *Memoirs of the Colorado Archaeological Society* No. 1 for details about the burning of Chimney Rock Pueblo.

Perceptive readers will note that we have relied heavily on Earl H. Morris's 1924 "Burials in the Aztec Ruin" in the *Anthropological Papers of the American Museum of Natural History,* Vol. XXVI, Part III. All of Morris's reports make fascinating reading.

Should you travel to any of the archaeological sites fictionalized in the novel, you will find no mention of many of the events portrayed in *People of the Moon*. Government personnel and volunteers are not allowed to mention violence, burials, witchcraft, or other "culturally sensitive" information.

The fact is, we are at heart a messy species, especially when economics, political philosophy, religion, military technology, and deprivation get mixed together. Atrocities occur with great regularity in prehistory as well as in our modern world. Sanitizing the past is every bit as morally irresponsible as whitewashing atrocities in the present. It trivializes and dehumanizes the victims.

We genuinely believe that in remembrance lies redemption.

Prologue

A light breeze whispered through the piñon and juniper trees, its melody the only sound that contrasted with the metallic ring of thin steel on packed dirt.

Dusty Stewart sat back on his haunches and laid his trowel aside to scoop loose dirt into a dustpan. He was a fit-looking man who wore a tattered straw cowboy hat jammed atop his sun-bleached blond hair. In a dust-streaked plaid shirt and faded Levis he looked as a South-western archaeologist was supposed to.

He squatted in a square delineated by a series of strings laid out to impose a grid over the buff dirt. Two squares away a trim dark-haired woman wearing Dockers, a loose white cotton shirt, and a boonie hat was on hands and knees as she worked at the dirt with a dental pick. She looked to be in her late thirties, athletic and tanned from days in the sun. Dark glasses concealed her blue eyes, but her dark ponytail was streaked with occasional gray.

Dusty took a paintbrush from the collection of tools just outside the string line and looked around. Two conical piles of freshly screened backdirt supported one-man screens: wooden boxes with handles to which quarter-inch hardware cloth had been tacked.

His Dodge diesel pickup was parked just beyond the strings; it sported a layer of grime atop its once cherry red paint. The truck sat on churned soil—a partially constructed road that ran back into the trees. Colorful flagging tape streamed out from white lath that the surveyor had used to mark the right-of-way.

A stone's throw to the west, the alluvial flat they worked on dropped off to a wind-scoured beach. Once waves had dashed against the shore, but only desiccated yellow sandstone remained. Drought continued to play hell with the Southwest; after winter runoff the reservoir was only half full, the closest water nearly a quarter mile away.

To his right, a broken slope dotted with trees rose toward a cracked sandstone-capped ridge. The grasses and brush had a dry and parched look.

Dusty bent forward and studied the rounded shape he'd uncovered with his trowel. He used the paintbrush to gently sweep dirt from the smooth brown curve of a human skull. The knife-sharp rim atop the eye orbits, along with the high rounded forehead, suggested that this was a female.

He grunted as he shifted, trying to keep his ankles from paining him. Squatting all day was for youngsters. He'd passed thirty too many years ago. Judging from the skull sutures, the woman he exposed may have been twenty. Where he'd used a dental pick to loosen the dirt around her slack jaw, the third molars were just erupting.

"I don't know," Dr. Maureen Cole murmured from her nearby excavation unit. She, too, worked to release a skeleton from its prison of loamy earth: a young man, probably in his twenties. Like the woman Dusty worked on, he was laid out on his back, almost entwined with another young man. Who in turn lay partially atop a teenager that Maureen had tentatively identified as a female based on mandibular morphology.

In all, they had four young adults, two subadults, and one infant crowded into the round depression of what had once been a shallow-basined structure of some kind. More than a wickiup, less than a pit house—was this a hunter's shelter? The few artifacts they'd recovered hadn't given Dusty the impression that he worked on a traditional dwelling.

"You don't know what?" Dusty finally asked when Maureen didn't elaborate. He rocked back on his heels, resting his arms limply on his knees. The paintbrush hung from one hand. Under the strings the skeletons rested as if placed, each one on its back, heads turned this way and that.

"Something I probably can't prove," Maureen said. "Just a hunch, mind you."

"Spill it." Dusty stared down at the young woman's partially exposed skull.

"It reminds me of Vilnius."

Dusty made a face. "Vilnius? Like in Litha . . . Lutha . . . Whatever. Way off in Europe?"

"Lithuania, dolt," Maureen shot back.

Dusty remembered. She'd gone off to work on the Napoleonic War dead. Something about a mass grave that had turned out to be troops and camp followers who had died on the retreat from Russia. The dead had been laid in a huge trench and covered up. The discovery had been a major coup for physical anthropologists.

"Okay, so what do Napoleon's dead in Lithuania have to do with a Bureau of Reclamation access road in northern New Mexico?"

She was frowning, staring down at the skeletons. "I don't know yet."

Dusty knew well enough to leave her alone, let her work on her hunches. She had an uncanny sense about human osteology. She'd driven him berserk one time proving the existence of a prehistoric serial killer. But she'd been right in the end.

He resumed his squat, careful of where he put his feet. Excavation was his thing. He'd been digging since he was three, or maybe it was four. Returning to his trowel, he made quick work of the sandy red dirt that covered the young woman's ribs. Here and there bits of clay from the old walls mixed in with darker stains that had been the wooden posts. He took a moment to extend his steel tape, measured in the stains, took depths along their lengths, and entered them into his pit notes. Then he sketched in the poles' locations on graph paper. If he was lucky, he might be able to reconstruct how the wall had been built.

When he took up his trowel and continued pulling the soil back from the circular ribs, it rang on something hard. A good excavator can tell what's in the ground by the trowel's sound. Stone makes it ring. Bone gives a hollow grate. Dusty eased up. This in-between sound had come from ceramic. A pot?

He used the tip to uncover the object—and stopped. It was rectangular, made from brownware, a low-temperature fired clay. The artifact sported six holes set into the clay at an angle, and the shape was convex, sort of like a curved bar of soap. He could see one of the woman's finger bones and yes, on the other side, was the terminal phalanx from her thumb. She'd been holding the thing.

Dusty resorted to his bamboo sticks, long slivers of sharpened bamboo that didn't scratch bone or ceramic. With them and his paintbrush, he exposed the ceramic object she had held through the centuries.

"Son of a bloody bastard," Dusty whispered.

"What have you found?" Maureen asked, straightening in her pit.

Dusty was measuring, drawing in the find. Then he reached for the GI ammo box that kept his Nikon safe from the dust and elements. Focusing the lens he took shot after shot.

"Stewart? Are you going to answer my question, or am I just Jell-O?"

"Jell-O?" he asked, having not heard a word she'd said.

She stood, smacked dust off her cargo pants, and stepped around the backdirt pile to look. "I don't get it. It's a piece of red-brown clay with holes in it."

Dusty carefully freed the object, making sure that the finger bones weren't disturbed. "It's a feather holder."

"Huh?"

"The first one was found in Pueblo Bonito by George Pepper back in the twenties. Most of the rest came from Chimney Rock. Mary Sullivan and Kim Malville determined they were originally manufactured at Chimney Rock. They could tell by the clay they were made from."

"That's just across the border in Colorado."

"Right. So, we've got a rare elite good, a painted feather holder. We know they were used in Chacoan ritual. Very high muckety-muck stuff. Always found in a religious context."

Maureen frowned. "So, what's it doing here?"

"Good question." Dusty straightened and walked back to the truck. There he pawed through the few sacks that held artifacts until he found a potsherd. The vessel, a water jar, had been crushed when the Cat exposed the first body. It was whitewashed, rather crude. "Arboles black-on-white," he whispered, stunned by the implications. He'd have to go back to the lab to be sure, but it just had to be. And that broken cooking pot that he'd found earlier, he'd bet dollars to donuts that with sectioning it was going to turn out to be Payan Corrugated.

At the sound of a truck he looked up. A white Army Corps of Engineers pickup wound its way through the piñon and juniper, puffs of dust rising as it followed the disturbed ground where the Caterpillars had been cutting the new road.

Rounding the last curve, Jerry Lummis could be seen through the dusty windshield. He pulled up, set the brake, and killed the engine, then slapped a white hardhat onto his head and stepped out, a clipboard under his arm.

"Hey, Dusty. How's it going? You get that skeleton out? I've got two Indian monitors coming down from Ignacio to pick up the bones. That, and the engineer's screaming bloody murder. He's got equipment sitting, and if we get another fire, he's gonna lose it till next spring."

Dusty sighed, rubbed his smudged face with a grimy hand, and said, "Uh, Jerry? You got a bottle of scotch hidden away in that truck?"

"Scotch?" Jerry looked confused. He often looked confused when talking to Dusty. It just happened that way. Something about the alignment of the planets when he was born. "You can't have booze in a government truck."

"I've got a bottle of rye in mine. You might want to chug a couple of swallows. After I show you—"

"I'm *working*! Government employees can't drink while they're working!"

"Tell that to the Congress." Dusty decided to give it to him stone-cold sober: "We've got seven skeletons, Jerry. The cat skinner just cut the top one."

"Seven?"

"Yep." Dusty stared across the hood of his truck to where Maureen's shapely bottom wiggled as she worked with a dental pick and brush to finish exposing the infant. "Come on. I'll show you what we've got."

"We've got a disaster, that's what!" Jerry looked ashen. "I gotta call the tribes. Wait till my supervisor hears about this. You didn't call the news, did you?"

"What kind of stupid question is that?"

Jerry took a deep breath. He'd been hammered hard by an Albuquerque reporter once when the Corps built a Rio Grande levee through the middle of a sixteenth-century pueblo.

"Hey, Maureen," Jerry greeted warily. He was the sort who didn't get along well with professional women.

"Jerry," Maureen said tersely. "I think I've got it."

"Got what?" Jerry asked nervously.

"Cause of death."

Jerry winced. "Tell me it's not cannibalism or anything violent. We can't take violent. It'll be so much damn trouble. I tell you, the politics in this state—"

"Starvation," she said firmly. "I'd just about bet on it."

Dusty said, "Wait a minute. I thought you couldn't prove starvation."

She sat back on her heels. Dusty could see the infant's tiny shape, the skull little more than flat squares of thin bone, the ribs curls on the dirt. The small pelvis was in three pieces.

"If it were just the adults, probably not," she told him, but pointed to the infant. "With the baby, I'd bet on it. We're talking about growing bone. I can look at the histology in thin section. Any growth abnormalities should show up on a stained slide. Additionally I can run spectroanalysis for trace minerals. Even the gross anatomy of the epiphyseal surfaces should demonstrate malnutrition."

Then she pointed to the teenage girl. "I'll bet I can prove thickening of the epiphyseal bone on her, too. Had she lived, it would have shown up as a Harris, or growth-arrest line in the long bones. I might be able to document an incipient hypoplasia in her teeth."

To Jerry, Dusty said, "In English, that means that the body leaves signs of stress while it's growing. During starvation the bones and teeth cease to grow."

She gave Dusty a grim smile. "That's why I thought of the Napoleonic War dead. They starved to death on the retreat out of Russia. It was the way the corpses looked."

Dusty held up his potsherd and feather holder. "And we know where they came from. They're from Chimney Rock up in Colorado."

"But what were they doing here?" Maureen asked.

Dusty shrugged. "We're on a direct line from Chimney Rock to the Gallina country. Maybe they were on their way there."

"Wait a minute," Jerry cried. "What about my road? I can't have controversial bodies in my road."

Dusty tried a placating smile. "Jerry, take a deep breath. Follow my lips. This is a very important site. If we can prove that these people came from Chimney Rock, we might be able to tell why they left."

Jerry stamped his foot, waved his clipboard, and paced in a small circle. He was looking around as if searching for a solution. In Dusty's experience, people who worked for the Corps of Engineers rarely found one.

"The question has always been why they left," Dusty insisted. "The Piedra Valley had water, arable land, and a large local population. Then at 1150 A.D. they walked away. Other areas wouldn't be abandoned for another one hundred and fifty years. Why Chimney Rock? Was it tied to the Chaco collapse? Jerry, we've got a chance to solve this one."

"Starvation wasn't chronic," Maureen added. "The teenager's incisors, the front teeth, are smooth and free of hypoplasias. I'd be thinking in terms of a single traumatic event."

Jerry was fluttering his clipboard. Too much coffee today? He stepped over, staring down at the neatly laid-out skeletons. A look of horror crossed his face.

"Oh, come on," Dusty said. "You've seen skeletons before."

"That's not it," Jerry muttered. "Look, according to the Corps of Engineers, I'm the authorized officer for this project."

"Yeah, that's why you've got the opportunity—"

"Cover it up."

Dusty stared dumbfounded. "Cover it up?"

Jerry swallowed hard. "Backfill it. I'll have a backhoe up here first thing in the morning. We'll lay a dirt pad over the top of it, then rehab the whole area."

"Didn't you hear *anything* I said?" Dusty thrust his face into Jerry's. "There's a good chance these people walked out of Chimney Rock during the abandonment! If Maureen can prove they starved—"

Jerry stabbed a finger in emphasis. "They starved here. We're a hundred miles from Chimney Rock!"

"They were passing through!"

"Dusty?" Maureen warned, rising and stepping over to place her hand on his shoulder. "Take a breath. Think 'Zen moment' before you regret it."

Dusty nodded, shot her a "thank you" grin and said softly, "Jerry, they weren't living here."

"What do you mean? It's a pit house! Key word: house."

"It's a shelter. I've been digging these sites all of my life. When the Anasazi lived someplace they had lots of pots, grinding stones, fire hearths, and they left midden, trash piles, laying around. So far I've found a water jar and a cooking pot. My guess is that they were traveling light, headed—"

"Cover it up." Jerry was adamant. "Do it. And they're Ancestral Puebloans. According to the Corps, we don't call them Anasazi anymore."

Maureen looked confused. "But these people can tell us—"

Jerry turned on her. "It's *culturally* sensitive. That's why. It's Bureau policy that we don't *talk* about dead Native peoples. We don't speculate about them, and we most surely don't *study* them. Not when it's *burials* we're talking about."

"You just cover them up," Maureen replied.

"Just like the Corps did with the Kennewick site up in Washington?" Dusty asked. "Pile dirt on top of it and hope it goes away?"

"Damn straight." Jerry nodded. "I can defuse this before it blows up. Tell the Indian monitors that we've left their ancestors undisturbed, rerouted the road."

It was Dusty's turn to reach out, laying a restraining hand on Maureen's shoulder. He'd seen that gleam come to her eyes before. When it did, she had the same volatility as crystallized dynamite. To forestall the explosion, he said, "So you'd rather they didn't even exist?"

"Got that right," Jerry growled. "We do dams and water. That's our job."

"Cultural resources are your job, too," Dusty corrected.

"Not when it involves dead people. Way too much controversy. And you archaeologists don't help. The last thing I need is some inflammatory declaration that these people might have starved to death. Cannibalism and warfare are bad enough!"

Maureen added, "History is controversy. People throughout history have acted like people. Why should the Anasazi be different?"

"Because they're in *my* jurisdiction."

"Yeah, and they really should have considered that!" Maureen had crossed her arms. "Whose heritage is it, anyway?"

Jerry took a deep breath. "Look, forget it. I'm not interested in science. I'm not interested in facts. We don't do anything here that's going to make anyone uncomfortable, or stir anyone's wasps' nest. Burials are political dynamite. I'm the authorized officer, and the burials get covered up. That's it."

"Jerry—" Dusty started.

"Stewart, if you ever want to work for either the Army Corps of Engineers or the Bureau of Reclamation again, you're going to cover them up. I'm going to take your film and field notes for 'curation' in my office so they don't show up at some archaeological conference. You're going to write me a one-page report detailing the fact that you found seven burials, that they were left undisturbed, and that the site was stabilized and avoided. It's 'No Effect' under 106 compliance. Period! Then you're going to send in your invoice, and we'll send you a check." He thrust a finger into Dusty's chest. "Got it?"

"Lysenkoism," Maureen said harshly.

"I don't care which archaeologist's theory is in vogue now."

"He was the Soviet minister of science under Stalin," Maureen added. "You would have liked working for him. He ensured that scientific results were compatible with the party line. Two plus two may or may not equal four—depending on those in charge." She pointed at the site. "In your system, these people never existed. Their story isn't as important as the official myth. They never starved, never loved, and never died under politically unacceptable circumstances. They just lived perfect little lives, and then had the grace and courtesy to fade into a culturally appropriate mystery."

Jerry smiled. "I can live with that. Meanwhile, cover them up. Right now. I'm going back to the truck to call my supervisor. Hell, I'm even willing to pay overtime to have this finished today."

Dusty turned to Maureen, "Well at least we've got the feather holder and the potsherds. With those we—"

"Put 'em back!" Jerry called over his shoulder. "You make good notes, Stewart. Lay them right where you found them."

"But, Jerry, there's only—"

"Cover it up!"

Dusty stared at the ceramic feather holder. This was the first one found outside of a Chacoan great house. His fingers traced its smooth surface. All those years, the young woman had held it just as he did now, feeling it between his thumb and fingers. *She knew how valuable it was.*

"It's going to hurt my soul," he said dully. "Why do I still do this job?"

"Because someone has to care who these people really were," Maureen added gently. "Someday it will change, Dusty. It will be the First Nations who do the changing. They'll want to know the facts about who their ancestors were as people in addition to the myths."

Dusty walked over, bent, and replaced the feather holder in the young woman's hand. "Maybe someday," he told her.

Heart heavy, he took his shovel from the backdirt pile and began easing the soil over the bones. The thought rolled around in his head: *They starved? Why?*

Shovel load by shovel load, he and Maureen covered up the answer.

First Day

The mountains are quiet and cold. The stone upon which I sit sends its chill up through my flesh, into my spine. Cold. The world is cold. Even this sunrise spilling across the landscape below me in a blaze of orange-yellow reflects its cold in the purple shadows cast by the buttes, canyons, and peaks.

I look into eternity. There, distant in the southwest, the light narrows to focus on a rising column, a pillar of billowing pink climbing into the sky: the Rainbow Serpent.

For five years now, it has been pumping steam and lava from the underworlds. Sometimes ash drifts down like brittle flakes of snow. At other times, it is a fine dust that catches glints of sunlight. Here, so far from the source, we observe it as a feathering of gray on open containers of drinking water.

Signs and portents.

They weave around me, and I no longer care. Once I fought against them, seeking to save the people. Now, I no longer seek to influence Power, only to let it wash over me, through me.

My lover is dead.

His name was Badgertail. He kept me safe for twenty summers—and it is still a miracle.

I see him as a young man, tall, with a squat toad face and the burly body of Grandfather Brown Bear. The blue spiders tattooed on his cheeks dance when he smiles.

I rock back and forth to ease the pain in my chest. Blessed Spirits, how I miss him.

For over a sun cycle, I had to watch my Badgertail grow more transparent each day, until he became a skeleton with kind and loving eyes. Even at the hard, lonely end, his love shone like a fire through his suffering. I keep that last glimpse of his living eyes.

When he died, it was as if some grasping force inexorably pulled the guts out of my souls, ripping away their essence and leaving me nothing but the painful hollow of memory.

Now I yearn for Death. We are old companions, more intimate than lovers. Sometimes in the midst of crowds, but more often among wounded or sick people, Death stands so close my legs will not hold me. I must sit down. Even when I am alone and warm, and my belly is full, I catch myself staring at the doorway, anxious, as though my heart hears Death's soft footsteps just outside. I long to reach out, to pull Death close, to feel it wind around my shoulders and tighten about my waist. I want its chill to cup my breasts, and stroke my throat. Death's cold thrust will spread from my womb through my hips and into my bones. As it slips around the base of my skull and lies metallic on my tongue, I can finally let go. Then, and only then, will I be free to find Badgertail again.

Meanwhile, I wait. And watch.

People have been coming to me for some time now, braving the "Mountain Witch" to ask if I know the Rainbow Serpent's purpose.

I tell them, "Look to your souls. The monster that lurks below is risen. Let loose, it brings death to those it bites."

They listen wide-eyed, sober, and chastened.

But they do not understand.

Some monsters rise from the depths. Others lurk just below the surface. Monsters are everywhere.

In the distant clouds, I see figures. They fly noiselessly over the morning-mottled desert below my mountain. Silent. Shifting. Cloud People. They are aptly named, for I see human forms there, winged, wearing masks that are at once beautiful and grotesque. They Dance with the trailing streamers of the Rainbow Serpent. Brother Sky mating with Grandmother Earth.

From the corner of my eye, I am aware of a misshapen form pirouetting through the dew-silvered meadow. There, in front of the white-barked aspens, he is but a flicker of movement, a sleight of the eye.

"What is being born, old friend?" I ask. Like me, his attention, too, is riveted on the Rainbow Serpent where it crawls upward to insert itself into the sky.

I hear his voice whispering to my souls. . . .

Ah, yes. Of course.

In the end, all human endeavor comes to this.

I am more than a witch. I Dance the darkness, whisper with the dead, and smile down upon the dying. I have witnessed the deaths of great kings and seen empires Dancing toward their dissolution.

That is why I was chosen. To see the signs. To know the future.

I rise on stiff legs and draw a deep breath into my aged lungs. My world is about to end. The signs are here. The future is here. And the Rainbow Serpent is the proof.

I lift my arms and step down from my rocky perch. Closing my eyes, I sense Brother Mud Head. He sways this way and that, his feet shuffling in the Dance.

I match his movement, my uplifted hands mirroring his. Together, in a state of lethal bliss, we Dance the death of a nation.

One

The day the world changed, three young hunters were gambling. They sat in the shade of a gnarled old piñon pine on the west side of First Moon Valley. With dry pine duff for a cushion, they had spread an elkhide, stained and frayed, but soft from years of use. It kept the sharp needles from sticking the gamblers, and ensured that the counters and gaming pieces didn't get lost.

The ancient pine dominated a flat that stuck out like a brusque shoulder from beneath the sandstone rim of what was locally called Juniper Ridge. Above them, in the swale behind the rimrock, Mid-Sun Town—a collection of pit houses, moiety kivas, and two-storied masonry structures—baked in the late-summer sun. They could just hear the periodic calls of children, the barking of a dog, and when the wind was right, the gobbling of turkeys as they ran about in search of grasshoppers.

Across the valley First Moon Mountain rose like a triangular wedge. At its summit twin pillars of rock marked the long-sealed opening where Sister Moon had been coaxed into this world by the Hero Twins. The inclined slopes of First Moon Mountain were covered with a patchwork of trees, scabs of exposed rock, corn and bean fields, and dotted settlements, many of which puffed lazy smoke into the hot air.

Just to the right, across the valley, they could see the promontory called the Dog's Tooth, where a stubby point of sandstone was separated from the base of First Moon Mountain by a low saddle. There, atop the peak, a buff-plastered two-story building, several pit houses, and two great kivas could be seen rising above their walled enclosure. The old sorcerer known as White Eye was reported to live there.

On the other side of First Moon Mountain, across First Moon Creek, they could make out the line of villages atop Pine Mesa.

Below them the valley bottom was a composite of fields dedicated to corn, beans, beeplant, peppergrass, and goosefoot, all resplendent in various shades of green as the plants matured. This was the true wealth of First Moon Valley—the verdant fields and the water that nourished them.

People worked in the floodplain fields, some pulling late-season weeds, others using hoes to channel water from sinuous ditches onto their crops. The workers were bare to the waist, brown skin contrasting to pale fabrics they wore belted about their hips. Sunlight glittered in threads where it reflected from the narrow ditches. Small gray-brown mud-covered frame structures had been built here and there between the fields. These were for storage of tools and sometimes shelter for people when the afternoon storms rolled through. Though there had been few of those this summer.

To the north, looking up the River of Stones, the gamblers could see the distant pointed peaks of the Spirit Mountains. Rocky gray summits, some still patched with white, rose above the dark green-timbered mountains.

A grasshopper clicked in the hot air as it flitted on silvered wings, and the young man known as Bad Cast rattled gaming pieces in a battered gray ceramic mug. He looked north again, then raised an eyebrow as he studied his two companions. "Think Ripple's having any luck up there?"

"This time of year?" Spots shrugged, then ran a hand down the scars that covered his arms and mottled his skin in colors from pink to brown. In his youth he had been called Bead, a name mostly forgotten since the night he and his sister had barely escaped the fire that burned their mother, father, and uncle to death.

"It'll be a miracle," the third, Wrapped Wrist, replied. "The animals are scattered throughout the mountains. And on a day like this, you can bet the elk are bedded down in the deepest, nastiest black timber they can find. Even if

Ripple kills one in there, packing him out is going to be a nightmare."

"Not to mention keeping the meat from souring," Spots added. "Weather like this can turn a whole elk in less than three hands of time."

Bad Cast rattled the gaming pieces again. "You know Ripple. Hunting is just an excuse to get him out of the valley and away from his sister. I swear, Fir Brush could be someone's mother-in-law, as grouchy as she's getting to be."

"You going to throw those pieces, or are you trying to wear them into dust?" Wrapped Wrist asked. He was made of muscle. It corded on his packed bones, bunched on his thick chest, and rounded his arms and legs. Slabs of it sloped out from his neck, ramping onto his broad shoulders. His stomach, bare in the heat, rippled and swelled even as he breathed. A faint smile lingered on his wide lips, a challenge in his eyes.

Bad Cast rattled the pieces again and tossed them from the cup. Six polished ovals of bone pattered on the tan hide, bounced, and settled. Gleaming in the filtered light, two were marked with hatching, the others with small crosses.

"Two and four!" Bad Cast cried. He reached out and took two counters from the pile in front of him, tossed one apiece to his friends while they groused. Each of his friends removed two counters from their own piles, and tossed them to his.

Having made a winning throw, Bad Cast recovered the gaming pieces and dropped them back in the cup. He grinned as he rattled them teasingly. "You want to bet double?"

"No," Spots growled. "The way you've been throwing, you'll leave me with nothing."

"Sure, but I'll give it all back when we're done." He hesitated. "Well, maybe after you give me that abalone shell pendant you've got."

"Toss the pieces." Wrapped Wrist gestured for him to hurry up.

Bad Cast rattled the thin bits of bone and tossed them out on the hide. Three hatches accompanied three crosses.

"Finally!" Spots cried, taking the cup from Bad Cast. "Even up." He rattled the bone pieces in the cup, cast, and groaned as two hatched and four crossed pieces landed faceup on the hide.

Bad Cast chuckled as he tossed a counter to Spots and received two more from the hunter's dwindling pile. As Wrapped Wrist took the cup and scooped up the gaming pieces, Bad Cast added, "I really want that abalone shell pendant. Have you seen how the light gleams in all the colors of the rainbow? Half the valley is talking about it."

"You don't have that kind of luck," Spots answered. His expression, however, was anything but confident.

Wrapped Wrist frowned at the piles of counters. Bad Cast had two-thirds more than either he or Spots. He set the cup down, cracked his knuckles, wiggled his fingers, and pressed the palms of his hands together, flexing his powerful muscles.

When he picked up the cup again, it seemed infinitely fragile between his thick fingers. With a cautious toss, he leaned forward to see the pieces land. He let out a loud whoop. "Six! Do you see that? Six! I doubled!"

All the pieces had landed with the hatched side up, automatically doubling whatever had been bid.

Bad Cast kept his smirk to himself. Spots howled mournfully as his pink-patched fingers counted out six of his little black stones and shoved them toward Wrapped Wrist.

Fortune would change. It always did. As Bad Cast thought that, he looked out at the valley he called home. Here, hidden away within the hills at the foot of the high mountains, his people lived in a paradise. They had water, good soil, and even though the land was gripped by drought, their crops would be good this year. Enough to see them through as well as pay the Blessed Sun's cursed tribute.

He glanced up at the heights of First Moon Mountain. From this vantage high on Juniper Ridge, he could just see Pinnacle Great House where it perched atop the knife-backed ridge below the twin pillars of rock. There the First People hid in their high fortress, living like blood-sucking ticks on the hard work of the First Moon People.

"Can't do much about it," he muttered.

"What was that?" Spots asked, a gloomy tone to his voice as he fingered his remaining counters.

"The First People," Bad Cast replied. "I was thinking how good the harvest is going to be this year, and how much of it they're going to take."

Wrapped Wrist shot him a sidelong glance. "The Traders say things are pretty grim out in the deserts. The First People just better hope they've got enough to go around."

"Why is it always us?" Bad Cast asked. "Why are we the ones to feed the whole rest of the world?"

"You don't think the Made People clans and the Deep Canyon folk and all the rest don't send their tribute? Look at what happened at Lanceleaf Village. This new war chief, the one called Leather Hand, killed most of the clan leaders, and stripped the ones left alive of their ancestral lands. Just gave the fields and holdings to others . . . left the survivors with nothing but the ability to beg for an occasional handout."

"Well, thank the gods we're here where we don't have to worry about food."

"Unless the First People send their Red Shirts in and demand our whole harvest," Spots muttered.

"They wouldn't do that." Bad Cast rubbed his nose.

"Oh, no?" Wrapped Wrist rattled the gaming pieces and cast. "Three and three."

As Bad Cast took the cup and scooped up the gaming pieces, he said, "Our people wouldn't just stand by and watch our winter food supply carted down the River of Stones and over to Flowing Waters Town."

"Is that right?" Spots shifted, squatting on his haunches as he watched Bad Cast toss the gaming pieces and take two more of his counters. "You think the First People would just walk away if the clan elders told them to leave us alone?"

"We can't fight the Blessed Sun," Wrapped Wrist reminded. "No one has ever beaten the Red Shirts in a pitched fight."

"Jay Bird has," Bad Cast reminded. "He not only

sacked Talon Town, he squarely whipped Webworm when he tried to recover the captives and retaliate." He lifted an eyebrow. "Doubles?"

"Done!" Wrapped Wrist agreed, then said, "The Fire Dogs are professional warriors. Chief Jay Bird spent his life as a war chief. Like the First People, he has warriors who do nothing but train." He turned, sweeping his arm across the valley. "Look out there. All you'll see is farmers and hunters like us. What do we know about war?"

"I didn't mean we'd go to war." Bad Cast threw, and cursed as five crosses came up. In resignation he counted out five pieces to each of the others.

"Then what?" Spots asked.

"I only meant that the Blessed Sun wouldn't seize our entire harvest. It would be stupid. We're some of his most reliable providers. He needs us."

Spots took the cup. "You're probably right. Besides, it wouldn't make sense to anger the elders. If there was unrest here the Blessed Sun would have to station even more warriors in the valley. He needs every man he's got to keep down the troublemakers over west and down in the Red Rock country." He rattled the gaming pieces. "Doubles?"

"Triples," Bad Cast cried. "With the right throw, I can break you."

"I don't know about that," Wrapped Wrist warned as he stared down at his little pile of stones. "Nope. Not me. I'm out, and you, Bad Cast, are a fool."

"Trust me. I've seen how Spots's luck is running today. Sometimes Power rides crosswise on a man's shoulders. Today simply isn't his day, and I'm going to own that abalone shell pendant by nightfall."

"I'm still out." Wrapped Wrist leaned back with finality.

"Triples, it is." Spots closed his eyes, sighed, and rattled the cup. Then he lifted it to his lips, blew softly on the inside, and cast. For a moment he couldn't look; then he squinted his right eye to a slit, daring to peek.

"Gods!" Bad Cast cried.

Spots let out a whoop, opening both eyes and leaning forward to savor the sight of all six pieces with their hatched sides to the sun. "Triples! And then doubled!

Let's see, that's how many?" He started counting on his fingers.

"Three tens and six," Wrapped Wrist said woodenly. He was watching Bad Cast's expression of complete horror as he added, "Yes, indeed. The gods are riding crosswise on Spots's shoulders today."

Bad Cast slumped sickly as he started counting out the round black stones. "Three tens and six?"

"You're three short." Spots held up three fingers defiantly. "Three! How're you going to pay up?"

Bad Cast looked at Wrapped Wrist. "Could I borrow three? I'll get them right back."

"Absolutely not." Wrapped Wrist crossed his arms. "I didn't think you were sane when you made the bet, and you're more crazy now."

"Ripple would loan me the pieces if he was here."

"Well, he's not." Spots leaned forward, jaw cocked. "So, let's see. You wanted my abalone pendant? Huh? What do I want of yours?"

"He doesn't have much," Wrapped Wrist noted. "Just that blanket back there."

"Soft Cloth made that for me. It was a gift!" Bad Cast reached back and pawed the blanket toward him. It was a beautiful thing, red-and-black striped and decorated with round shell buttons and patterns of tubular beads made from bird bones.

"You know," Wrapped Wrist added, "according to the rules, he's three short. That's three different things you could demand of him."

"Right!" Spots clapped his hands. "I want your atlatl"—he squinted at Bad Cast—"and that hunting shirt you're wearing."

"What? That's all I've got on!"

"A man shouldn't play if he can't stand to lose," Wrapped Wrist said idly, his eyes drifting off to the north, where the valley narrowed around the River of Stones.

Bad Cast stared in disbelief, seeing no give in Spots's eyes. Reluctantly he pulled his shirt over his head, wadded it, and threw it at Spots.

"Ah, there they are: the lordly males." Soft Cloth's

voice carried on the warm afternoon. Bad Cast winced, craning his head to look up the hill. Through the piñon branches he could see his wife—their three-moon-old daughter riding in the crook of her arm—as she picked her way down the trail. Gods, no! Of all the times for her to pick. . . .

Soft Cloth stepped around the tree, stopping short as she took in Bad Cast's naked body. Her shapely eyebrow lifted, a quiver at the corner of her mouth. "Let me guess. It's the heat, right? Things got a little too warm down there in the shade under the tree?"

Spots grinned up at her and raised the wadded shirt. "Your husband bet triples, and I rolled a six. He couldn't cover his bet. I've got his atlatl—and that pretty blanket you gave him!"

"I see." She said nothing more. Bad Cast winced as her knowing brown eyes met his—and spoke with a greater eloquence than any words.

She was a Bee Flower Clan woman of the Soft Earth Moiety. They had been married for over a year now. In all that time, Bad Cast had never done anything remotely like this. At least, nothing he'd ever been caught at before.

It was Wrapped Wrist who said, "You know, Spots, you might be willing to lend your kinsman a hunting shirt. You know, just for today so that his dangling man parts don't get too much sun. It would be a real pity if they got burned, sore, and started to peel."

Bad Cast glared obsidian spikes at his cousin.

Soft Cloth couldn't keep her lips from lifting with amusement. "My husband would appreciate that. Not that his man parts are high on my list of concerns right now."

"That hurts," Wrapped Wrist said.

Bad Cast threw his hands up in despair. "Woman, what are you doing here?"

She flipped her long black hair over her shoulder, amusement in her eyes. "I just came down to remind my husband that if he wants to eat tonight, he needs to bring me enough firewood to bake the corn cakes I've just finished making." She shot a look at the blanket before adding, "If he carries enough wood, it should protect certain delicate parts of him from the sun."

Bad Cast jumped to his feet, ripping the shirt out of Spots's hand. "All right, I'm going."

Soft Cloth dropped to her knees at the edge of the elkhide. With her free hand, she picked up the cup and dropped one of the gaming pieces inside.

Bad Cast pulled on his hunting shirt and stopped to watch as she rattled it back and forth, mischievous eyes on Spots.

"I'll play you for the blanket," Soft Cloth said.

Spots narrowed an eye. "Women aren't supposed to play this game."

"One cast. If it comes up hatched, I take the blanket."

"What if it's crosses? What do I get?"

"I make you another."

"Done."

Soft Cloth rattled the gaming piece around the cup and tossed it onto the hide. The hatched surface gleamed in the light. Spots laughed aloud and shoved the blanket across.

"It's a nice blanket, isn't it?" She plucked it up, carefully folding it under the baby. Then she gracefully stood. With a mocking smile she told Bad Cast, "I hope you don't freeze this winter."

"You know, I just—"

"Smoke," Wrapped Wrist said, his eyes fixed on the northern mountains. "It's high on Snow Mountain. Just down from Cougar Pass."

"Ripple," Spots cried, standing and staring to the north. "He's killed something."

"Not just that," Bad Cast added, "but he needs our help."

The amusement had left Soft Cloth's eyes. "I need firewood *before* you run off to help your kinsman."

"I think we can all see to it," Wrapped Wrist said as he climbed to his feet. Only then did it become apparent that for all the muscle packed on his frame, the top of his head barely came to the middle of Bad Cast's chest.

"What about my atlatl?" Bad Cast asked as Spots began rolling up the elkhide.

"I'd talk to your wife. Maybe she can win it back for you."

Two

Once, years before, lightning had struck the bulging shoulder of the high peak called Snow Mountain. The resulting blaze had burned hot through the old-growth spruce and fir. Ash had settled in a little hollow to nourish the grasses and a stand of aspen that found a hold in the fire's wake. Now the delicate white-barked trees skirted one side of the open meadow. Columbines, daisies, shooting star, and yarrow flourished. Fed from snowmelt and rain, a small stream cut through the bottom, gurgling and trickling over the rocks.

It was there, below Cougar Pass, sheltered from the prevailing winds, that Ripple had made his camp for the night. While a thousand stars lay like dust on the sky, a moonless night turned the surrounding spruce and fir into inky lances.

The portion of night-darkened meadow illuminated by the flickering fire was carpeted in grass. Flowers in night-washed dots lay dreaming. The stream, no wider than his open hand, trickled in its mossy channel to his left. Rounded boulders—like the one he leaned against—glowed in the firelight, as did the jagged branches of the fir and spruce that rose along the slope to the right.

Ripple, a man of the Blue Stick Clan of the Black Shale Moiety, sat before a small crackling fire. Muscles slipped under the smooth skin of youth. His face was composed of angles, a high forehead, and flat and wide cheeks. Under full lips his chin lowered to a point. Ripple's nose might have been sculpted, thin and slightly hooked. The firelight gleaming on his black eyes reflected a young man tormented by memories; they had etched lines around the corners of his mouth.

That morning Ripple had surprised a yearling elk with a

perfect cast. He had driven the stone-tipped dart into the young cow's chest. She'd no more started to run than she tumbled into a pile, kicked grooves in the grass, and gasped out her soul through bloody nostrils.

His day had been a hunter's: blessed and challenged. The flush of success had been tempered by the hollow sense of sorrow every hunter feels when he walks up to a dying creature. Life comes at a price. Coyote had seen to that when people first entered this world. Life was the prize sought by all.

The young hunter cast a glance at the piles of spruce boughs that protected his kill. Then he stared nervously at the timber. The other hunter was still out there.

Vigilance can be maintained only for so long. Braced against the reassuring stone of a boulder, fatigue lay warm on his bones. The muscles in Ripple's neck relaxed as he drifted, his head sagging. Eyes, anxious the moment before, clouded under heavy lids.

As he nodded on the fringe of sleep, the whistling memory of a stone-headed war club arced through a blue sky. He awoke with a jerk before it could land. Blinking, he stared sleepily at the fire, yawned, and shifted anxiously.

Ghosts. I am haunted by them. Is this, too, a place of ghosts?

He turned his attention to the stars that spilled across the black moonless sky like a frosty mist and wondered: *Do ghosts make the man, or does the man make the ghosts?*

Ripple forced the memories from his souls. He was here, now. Alive. Let the dead rest, no matter how unjust their fate at the hands of the Blessed Sun's warriors.

He shook himself and picked up another piece of smooth gray aspen to place on the fire. As flames licked around the weathered gray wood, he stared at the four piles of cut spruce branches. Bad Cast and Wrapped Wrist should be coming. His two friends must have seen the signal smoke he'd raised earlier that day and be on their way up the mountain. A man didn't just throw an elk over his shoulder the way he did a deer or—

Something stirred in the grass.

Ripple tensed and traced his fingers over the sleek wood of the atlatl and dart he cradled on his lap. Small feet skittered across the forest floor. What? A packrat? Perhaps a weasel drawn by the scent of fresh blood?

He reached up to rub his tired eyes. A cone fell in the forest, clattering from branch to branch before it thudded on the duff. A distant wolf howled; then came the hushed moan of wind through the conifers.

Ripple had been engaged in the process of skinning and quartering his dead elk when the bear arrived. Drawn by the scent of blood and offal, the bear was long of body, old, with a muzzle scarred by encounters with long-gone rivals. He had watched warily, prowling around downwind, sniffing, tearing at the ground with his claws, and making muffled groans of irritation.

Grizzlies and Ripple's people had an ancient relationship; over the years, each had learned to be cautious of the other. People who treated bears disrespectfully were lucky to escape with a severe mauling. Bears who acted too aggressively around people rarely managed to get away without being eaten.

For his part, Ripple had figured that the bear was just as hungry as he was, so he had grudgingly left the gut pile after shuttling the last of the quarters away from the kill site.

Now, as midnight neared, he hoped the bear had understood the agreement. But you could never tell about bears. The scent of fresh elk meat might be tempting after having had a little time to digest the first offering. For that reason, Ripple had resolved to stay awake, keep his fire going, and guard his meat.

He hadn't anticipated how long the night would stretch, how soothing the sound of the little brook could be, or how the soft sigh of the high-country wind in the trees could relax strained nerves.

Weary, he didn't feel his head wobble. Wasn't aware when his heavy eyelids lowered. In his mind, he was still staring at the leaping fire, though it only reflected on the backs of his eyes.

The soft fabric of sleep settled gently over his tired body and eased the strain in his taut muscles. His breath-

ing deepened, and flickers of Dream tugged at the edges
of his souls. In that between place, the souls were most
susceptible to Power and the call of the Spirit World.. . .

The sound of steps brought him upright. The fire now
burned brightly and cast a yellow light that shimmered in
the trees. The melodious trickle of water began to repeat a
cadence, rhythmic like the hollow clack of sticks. Where
it sighed in the branches, the wind muted to flute music
that rose and fell with each of the approaching steps.

A thrill shot through Ripple's body, and he blinked at
the bright yellow light. In the dark-domed sky above, stars
began to ebb and flow like waves. Here and there he could
see them floating softly down toward earth, turning into
snowflakes. His breath fogged, thick with each exhalation.
The growing cold made him shiver and hug himself.

A flicker of movement in the trees brought him alert.
White flashed in the shadows.

The bone-numbing cold intensified.

Ripple reached for the fire. To his consternation, frost
glittered on his fingers. Despite the bright light, no heat
came from the leaping flames.

He cried out in fear.

"Scared, are we?" The voice was an old woman's.

He raised his gaze from his frozen hands to the white
apparition that stepped out from the hoar-frosted trees.

No nose marred her blank white face. And those eyes!
Large red irises surrounded black pupils that gleamed like
polished midnight. Sharply pointed teeth glinted in her open
mouth, and a tongue as red as smeared blood lolled down
over her chin.

The cloak on her shoulder might have been spun of dusk
and blew about her like a storm. It blended with her di-
sheveled white hair. One hand held a long walking stick, the
tip of which she planted in the snow that deepened around
her feet. Belted with a corn-yellow sash, her long dress hung
below her knees. The swaying hem sparkled with lines of
delicate beads. Leggings, white as summer cloud, were dotted with gems of turquoise that reflected against the snow.
As she raised her hand in greeting, he could see the most extraordinary turquoise bracelet gleaming in the firelight.

"Who . . . What are you?" he stammered.

"Hard times are coming," the crone's voice told him. "You of all people know that, don't you?"

"Hard times? What . . . What do you *want* from me?"

Huge black pupils expanded in her red eyes. "I want the future."

"I don't understand."

"Don't understand what? The future? It's what will come. What can be." Her head tilted; ice crystals flashed in the cold yellow light. "That is, assuming you have the courage and skill hidden away inside that strong young body of yours to make it come true."

Ripple shivered, curling in upon himself like a ball. Gods, had he ever been so cold and frightened? When he looked up into those red-rimmed black eyes, he wanted to weep.

"I was married to him once, you know," she told him offhandedly.

"Married . . . to whom?"

"The Blessed Sun."

Ripple tilted his head. "You were married to Webworm?"

She jabbed at him with her walking stick, causing him to scramble sideways in the snow. "No, you wretched lump! What would I have to do with some incompetent and fragile man? At my touch he'd freeze solid! No, I mean I was married to the Blessed Father Sun. A long time back. Before your kind ever climbed into this world."

He tried to concentrate. "But I thought Sister Moon—"

"Later," she snapped. "Much later." Her body swayed slightly as snowflakes fell around her. Then she sighed and straightened. "You've seen the Rainbow Serpent?"

"To the southwest," he managed between chattering teeth. "Yes. It crawled up from the earth five summers ago."

"The fulfillment of prophecy, boy." She fixed on him again. "The Straight Path Nation is teetering."

"May the Rainbow Serpent devour them all!" he growled through clenched teeth. Then, realizing what he might have said, cowered back.

"Yes," she hissed. Her tongue shot this way and that as

did a bloody rope when jerked by a child. "Do they still talk of how the Straight Path warriors came to the First Moon villages?"

"It is said that they surrounded our people while they were assembled for the renewal. That they came in the night, trapped us on the heights, and took our elders hostage in return for allowing the rest of us to pass back down the mountain."

"And then?"

"Then they took every tenth person, and along with the elders, marched them off to Straight Path Canyon as slaves. They worked many of them to death, made them build the White Palaces. Those of us left behind in First Moon Valley were given orders, told to pack stone, mud, and water to the heights. Each clan had so many loads to carry or their people in captivity would be killed—and the red-shirted warriors would come and maybe kill the rest of us."

"To save yourselves, your people complied. You built their great Pinnacle House high on the spire just below the twin pillars." She paused. "The Straight Path Nation considers you to be barbarians, you know. They think you are little better than two-legged beasts—animals like this elk you've killed—meant only to serve them." A pause. "How well you, of all people, understand their ways."

"Yes." He swallowed hard, a fleeting image of a red-shirted warrior slipping through him. He remembered the flash of sunlight on the polished war club as it began its arc downward toward—

"I am older than the rest." Her words interrupted the image. "Wiser in so many ways. The time of the Blue God and the Flute Player is passing. Spider Woman waffles, unsure where her loyalties lie. Father Sun Dreams of miracles and events far beyond this world." She hesitated. "Did you know that I can grant wishes?"

A terrible shivering racked him. "No."

"If I could grant you one wish, Ripple, what would it be?"

Without thinking, he said, "To be rid of the First People."

"No matter the cost?"

He hesitated. "No matter the cost."

"If it meant pain and disfigurement, would you still pay such a price?"

A different cold filled his souls. "Yes."

Her mouth curled in a smile that exposed more pointed teeth behind her lolling tongue. "I have to know if you are the one I seek. Are you strong enough? Can you bear the pain and harden your souls?"

He winced at the violence in her voice, watched her panting breath freeze in the air like a white question.

"Oh, so your words desert you?" She turned slightly, a haze of frost following her cape. "Little wonder, I suppose. Not all humans are glib in the face of a god."

"I'll do it," he gasped.

Her black pupils grew against their background of red. "You and I have an agreement, then, Ripple. If you can take the pain, if you have the faith and strength locked away in those shivering souls of yours, you shall have your chance to destroy the First People. But you must know it will be fraught with danger. Many of the old gods will side with them. Are you ready for such a trial?"

"I am," he told her bravely, wondering what he'd just done.

"The threads of Power are being drawn tight across your world. Terrible dark days are creeping up on you. If they do not break you, seek the old woman you know as the Mountain Witch. The one who Dreams the One. She knows you, has watched you, as you have watched her. She Dances with Brother Mud Head and weaves the threads of the future from the turquoise cave. Allies appear in unusual places." The movement was so rapid he barely saw her cape whip around. She vanished in a swirl of bitter-cold white.

Her voice lingered in the frost: *"Do not disappoint me!"*

The Dream shattered.

With a cry, Ripple bolted upright in the night, his body possessed with violent shivers. Gods, he was cold clear to his core! How could he feel like this? It was the middle of summer.

He stared around, blinking, to find his fire burned down to glowing coals. Fumbling in the near darkness he placed his hand on another length of aspen wood before adding it to the fire. He placed another, and yet another, on the coals. Bending low, he blew, heedless of the swirling ash. A flickering tongue of fire curled up the smooth gray wood. Within moments the fire crackled to life again.

Ripple extended his shaking hands, grateful for the warmth.

A Dream! It had to be. As the flames leapt, he looked toward where he had Dreamed the old woman.

Ripple stopped short. There, in the growing light, he could see a frosty ring of snow lying thick on the grass, nodding the heads of flowers. When he stepped over, brushed at the snow, and pulled the spruce boughs from atop the elk, he found all four quarters frozen hard as stone.

Morning light grayed the sky as Bad Cast led Wrapped Wrist and Spots into the little clearing. His contested hunting shirt from the day before was smudged and dotted with forest detritus. They had been climbing for most of the night.

Kin helped kin—especially when it came to retrieving freshly killed meat. Bad Cast's First Moon People were divided into two moieties: the Black Shale—to which he, Spots, Wrapped Wrist, and Ripple belonged—and the Soft Earth, which laid claim to his wife and daughter. Within the Black Shale Moiety were four clans. Of these, he and his friends belonged to the Blue Stick Clan.

Bad Cast had known roughly where Ripple's signal smoke had come from, having hunted this mountain all of his life. Despite being familiar with the trails, no one liked climbing up through the forest in darkness—and last night had been particularly inky, with only starlight illuminating the faint paths that led up the steep slopes. In the black timber, they'd had to feel their way, tripping over deadfall and cursing. Talus fields had created their own nightmare of shifting rock and poor footing.

In midsummer, however, meat had to be immediately tended to or it soured rapidly. Bad Cast knew that Ripple would have immediately cooled the carcass and taken measures to protect his kill from crows, coyotes, wolves, and bears, but the first priority was to get it off the mountain and down to First Moon Village, where it could be cut into strips, dried, and smoked. It had been a long time since they'd had a kill good enough to risk traveling the mountains at night.

Despite yesterday's gambling disaster, Bad Cast considered himself the responsible one. While he had certainly made a "bad cast" in the game, his name actually came from an unfortunate incident when he was a six-summers-old boy learning the atlatl. The dart had slipped as he cast. He'd watched in horror as it sailed sideways. Old Chief Hard Clay had happened to be walking past—just in time for the errant dart to drive its way right into his stringy left buttock. The old man had walked with a limp for the rest of his life.

Bad Cast was average in height, unremarkable in looks. Some considered him to be the most boring man in his village. Of the four friends he was the only one who had married—as all responsible young men should. He and Soft Cloth had one child—a three-moon-old girl that he doted over to the point it irritated Soft Cloth and her family.

He glanced back at his companions. Wrapped Wrist wasn't just a mediocre gambler, but the shortest and strongest man in First Moon Valley. He was known for his amiable nature, his love of a good joke; but most of all his reputation with women had traveled the length and breadth of their territory. They fawned over him, not only for the size of his organ and its legendary endurance, but for his reputed talent when using it.

Spots was the irreverent one. The lodge fire that had left him hideously burned on the left side of his body and face had also wounded his souls. His parents had both been holy people, Seers and Healers, who had invested significant portions of their lives in the quest to understand the ways of the gods and Spirits.

After the fire, Spots had shied away from such things, aware of the injustice worked on his parents by the very Spirits they had tried to propitiate. The sleek patches of scar tissue, mottled against pink and normal brown skin, acted as a constant reminder of this betrayal. To his way of thinking, the youngster named Bead had died in that searing heat, so he had embraced the appellation "Spots" with a sense of inevitability.

Sniffing, Bad Cast caught the acrid odor of smoke. He climbed toward a fringe of aspen that skirted an old burn, feeling the weary looseness in his muscles. It had been a long climb, perilous and exhausting. For him, however, it had been much better than having to face Soft Cloth after the loss of his blanket and the embarrassing situation in which she had found him. The teasing dished out through the night by Spots and Wrapped Wrist had been merciful compared to the sarcastic wit with which Soft Cloth would have assaulted him.

Now, as they entered the flower-strewn clearing, he hoped that Ripple's kill was big enough to warrant his inclusion in the party. If he showed up at Soft Cloth's with a single partridge, or a couple of strips of venison, he'd never hear the end of it.

Smoke hung in a blue layer that stretched back into the fir trees. A fire smoldered beside a trickle of water that burbled its way down toward a patch of willows.

Bad Cast caught sight of Ripple and tossed a wave toward his still figure. His friend sat, back braced against a rounded boulder. The hunter might have been frozen in place, wide eyes staring vacantly at a ring of wilted vegetation beside a stand of aspen.

"He might show a bit of delight at seeing us," Spots grumbled from behind. "After all, we've only spent half the night running into things, tripping over roots, rocks, and being slapped in the face by branches."

Bad Cast slowed, frowning. "Something's not right." He could see it in the set of Ripple's shoulders, in the tight grip he kept on his atlatl and dart. Blood splotched his hunting shirt—normal enough after having processed a kill. From a quick glance at the pieces of carcass Bad Cast could tell it was a young elk. The hide had been rolled into a bundle and tied; it rested on the grass behind the four quarters. Spruce branches had been tossed this way and that, as if Ripple had rapidly pulled them from the meat.

"Hey! Ripple! We're here. Got breakfast ready?" Wrapped Wrist called, waving as he burst into the clearing. "Nice elk. That's meat for five families."

Wrapped Wrist pulled up, a puzzled expression on his face as he took in Ripple's stiff posture, wide eyes, and slack visage. "What's wrong?"

"Let's find out." Bad Cast stepped warily forward, head tilted nervously. "Gods, is he even alive?"

Wrapped Wrist muttered, "My father's brother was found just like that: sitting up in his lodge, dead as a rock. I wanted to keep him there. He was a lot easier to talk to that way. Wasn't nearly as picky about the food, and the odor would have kept my sister's in-laws away until he finally petrified."

"He was four tens and five winters old," Spots growled. "Ripple's just past two tens. He's young. Healthier than any of the rest of us."

Bad Cast crouched down, staring into Ripple's glazed eyes. He waved his hand in front of Ripple's face and got nothing in return. When he touched his friend's skin, he yanked his hand back. "He's like ice!"

"Hey! Ripple, stop it!" Spots punched Ripple's shoulder. At the blow, the hunter rocked slightly, then blinked and looked up. He was staring straight into Bad Cast's eyes when he said, "She was here."

"Looking for Wrapped Wrist, no doubt," Spots muttered, staring sidelong at his friend. "Women go a little flighty when he's out of the village for a night."

"Hush!" Bad Cast barked. "Who was here? What happened, Ripple?"

"She came to me." His brows lowered. "Cold . . . terribly cold. Snow on the ground around her feet. Her eyes . . . gods, so red and empty."

Wrapped Wrist squatted down beside Bad Cast, thick forearms on his knees. "Who was she?"

"Cold Bringing Woman." Ripple's whisper was awed.

Bad Cast cocked his head. "The god? The one the First People call Old Woman North? You're saying she came to you last night?"

The nod was ever so slight. Ripple swallowed for the first time. "She said I could destroy the First People."

"You?" Spots replied skeptically. "You? By yourself? When the wishes, curses, and prayers of everyone else in the world can't?"

"For a price," Ripple whispered. "I have to see the Mountain Witch, the one who Dreams the turquoise cave. She'll know what to do. What this means."

"The witch?" Wrapped Wrist said warily.

"She Dances with Mud Head and weaves the threads of the future." Ripple said it absently. "Allies will appear in unusual places."

"Sure," Spots added. "Whatever that means."

"I have to pass the test . . . watch for the signs."

Bad Cast stood, stepping over to the elk quarters. "Well, the signs are that this is going to sour if we don't get it down to—"

"It's frozen."

"Sure," Bad Cast growled. "It was hot as blazes last night." But he hesitated as if unwilling to find out. Then he stepped over and placed a hand on the meat: cold and clammy. Frowning, he punched it. The surface might have thawed, but when Spots pulled his belt knife and jabbed the sharp quartzite point into the flesh, he couldn't drive it in. With a thumbnail he widened the slit to expose ice crystals in the meat.

"I'll be," Bad Cast whispered. He let his hands run over the wilted vegetation. It looked as if it had frozen in the night.

"When did you kill this elk?" Spots demanded.

"Yesterday morning," Ripple replied.

Wrapped Wrist gave Bad Cast a worried look, lowering his voice. "What do you think?"

Bad Cast rubbed his jaw. "How do you freeze an elk solid in the middle of the summer?"

"Power." Ripple stared at them through haunted eyes. "I have the chance to destroy them."

"How can you destroy the First People?" Spots demanded. "You're nobody! Not even one of the Made People. The way the First People think, you're a barbarian orphan from a slave people the Blessed Sun doesn't think of but once in a sun cycle—if then!"

"I have to go see the witch," Ripple maintained stubbornly.

"Right," Wrapped Wrist agreed. "It's more likely that she and Mud Head will knock a hole in your skull. Then they'll suck your souls out with your brains and have them for dinner."

Ripple shook himself and stood. He wobbled on his feet for a moment. "I'm going. And I want you to go with me."

"Us?" Spots cried. "Why us?"

"Because you were on the way here. She had to know you were coming."

Bad Cast felt a shiver go through his bones. "Yes, well, let's get the meat to First Moon Village. Then we'll talk about it, all right?"

"Where's the gut pile?" Wrapped Wrist asked. "You know, the heart and liver and all."

"I shared them with Father Grizzly," Ripple whispered, eyes still seeing something terrible and distant.

"Of course you did. Cold Bringing Woman and Father Grizzly. Your new best friends." Spots lifted an eyebrow. The gesture created a frightening expression on his scarslick face.

"She chose me," Ripple said self-consciously.

Rotted gods! He really believes it! Bad Cast could see it in Ripple's face, in the set of his shoulders. A shiver ran down his spine, as if Cold Bringing Woman herself traced a frosty finger down his back.

Three

The sprawling cluster of buildings called Tall Piñon Town existed as a gift from the prevailing southwesterly winds. They carried streamers of white cloud from the distant oceans across the arid basins to shower life-giving summer rains on the high stone-scabbed mesa. In the beginning the gift of the rains had been thick forests of piñon, juniper, and ponderosa pine. Over the years the trees had sent their roots deep into the soil, changing it from stony to a sandy loam. The first farmers had denuded portions of the mesa top, ringing trees to kill them and then burning to clear fields. In that ash-rich soil, their crops had prospered. Steep-walled gorges—chiseled down through the underlying rock—gave the farmers an additional advantage. Fields could be planted along the canyon walls and in the narrow alluvial bottoms where check dams and ditches captured runoff.

As the population increased over generations, Tall Piñon had grown from a collection of pit houses at the canyon heads into a thriving Trade and ceremonial center. Blocky multistory buildings perched on the low ridges leading down to the south.

Two generations ago emissaries of the First People had arrived, and during the following years had built the Tall Piñon Great House in the northwestern corner of the dusty rectangular plaza.

The location was perfect for the First People and their far-flung empire. High on the mesa top they had an unob-structed view of the entire northern border: Distant towns like Juniper Edge and Lanceleaf Village were visible. So too was the Far View Town observatory atop Green Mesa, Thunderbird Mountain, and the spine of World Tree Mountain to the south.

The local Deep Canyon People made up one of the

largest populations in the region. The yield of their bountiful harvests was stored in numerous granaries and storerooms located in the lower floors of the imposing buildings.

In the beginning, the First People's influence had been minimal, but over the generations their grip had been tightened through judicious marriages, military alliances, and the subtle indoctrination of the local peoples into the intricacies of the Flute Player's religion. But a conqueror's hold, even if so softly applied in the beginning, is never secure. Not as long as the conquered can remember better days.

Carefully cradled within the arms of Tall Piñon's U-shaped settlement, the squat cylinder of the First People's great kiva hulked like a giant drum. Dug into the sloping ground on the west, the eastern side was cushioned by a thick berm of soil. While heat waves shimmered off the dusty surface, a ring of people waited anxiously, eyes on the white-plastered walls.

Inside, down in the cool depths of the subterranean structure, two men sat. One dressed in red, the other in a pristine white robe. The great kiva's interior was illuminated by a square shaft of blue light that slanted down through the smoke hole. It cast midmorning sun on one of the plastered masonry columns that supported the heavy soot-stained log roof. Reflected sunlight shone on freshly painted images of the gods where they had been rendered on the kiva walls. Bright colors had been used to create their Dancing bodies. From the perspective with which they had been drawn, the gods might have been staring curiously at the two men who sat silently on the northern bench, separated by the stairs that led up to the Priest's room at ground level. Both men studied the images with pensive eyes.

Deputy War Chief Leather Hand was seated to the right of the polished-pole stairway. During times of ceremony masked Priests entered from the ready room above, their bodies festooned with the colorful regalia of their office: feathered plumes; painted wooden headdresses, fans, and false wings; bustles of brightly dyed cloth; and shields decorated with symbols of the First People's gods and monsters.

For the moment, Leather Hand wasn't thinking of Priests. Of all the men in that northern reach of the First People's empire, he might well have been the loneliest. He braced his scarred hands on his knees, a serious look in his dark brown eyes. His crisp red war shirt hung loosely from muscular shoulders. The first faint traces of silver streaked his thick black warrior's mane, now pulled back in a severe bun and pinned with a single standing eagle feather. His heavy jaw was set, a weary tension around the lines of his wide nose.

He turned to the white-clad Priest. This man, Seven Stars, Deputy Sunwatcher for Tall Piñon Town, wore a Priest's flawless white robe belted at the waist with a deep purple sash dyed by larkspur petals. Long sleek hair, freshly washed with yucca soap, hung down his back in silken waves. His features could only be described as beautiful, more feminine than masculine. Soft doeskin boots shod his small feet. He absently rubbed his chin as he considered the paintings.

Leather Hand observed, "You look moody, my friend."

The Priest nodded. "We are in the midst of very dangerous times."

Leather Hand returned his attention to the newly decorated kiva walls. The old gods looked fresh.

Matron Featherstone is dead. The thought rolled around between his souls, and he didn't know how to feel about the news. Even as he sat there, her ritually prepared corpse was being borne south, through Straight Path Canyon toward Humpback Butte, where her breath-heart soul would fly into the sky.

Seven Stars murmured, "Since the death of the Blessed Crow Beard one tragedy after another has befallen the Straight Path Nation. It has been five sun cycles since his death. Our people have survived the disgrace and exile of Matron Night Sun. They have seen Talon Town—the grandest town in the Straight Path Nation—raided and despoiled. When the Blessed Snake Head assumed his father's throne he betrayed his people, was murdered by his own warriors. Declared a witch, he was buried in an unmarked grave. No sooner had that been done, than old Featherstone, a halfwit, was declared Matron."

Leather Hand tightened his grip on his knees. "She was of the Red Lacewing Clan. Next in line after Night Sun. Some Matron. You saw her. Most of her time was spent lying senseless on her sleeping mats, drool leaking from the side of her mouth. Of her waking moments, perhaps one in ten was lucid."

"May Spider Woman have pity on her souls," Seven Stars added solemnly.

"May she indeed," Leather Hand agreed. "Her son, the Blessed Webworm, has barely managed to keep the Straight Path Nation together. My warriors report that rumors pass from lip to lip that the First People are doomed. You know how many villages have revolted; others have turned on their neighbors. I am running my warriors ragged keeping the peace." In doing so, authority grudgingly had been shifted from the Matrons to warrior governors like Leather Hand. He had the muscle to ensure local obedience.

"Why does that worry you?" Seven Stars asked mildly.

"I have seen the reservation in Matron Husk Woman's eyes. I'm not sure if she dislikes my methods, or if it is just me she despises."

"Brutal times take brutal measures. It is the Blessed Sun's order that placed you in command here. She can do nothing but obey Webworm and Matron Desert Willow."

"Perhaps." A pause. "What do you think?"

Seven Stars smiled in amusement. "War and religion are one and the same. Your authority doesn't threaten me."

"But it is a change from the way things were."

"The world is full of change. Think no further than yourself. Have you not changed over the past five sun cycles?"

Leather Hand grunted in agreement. "My mother was a wonderful lady. I can remember the humiliation I used to feel when she called me 'such a gentle boy.'"

"And were you?"

Leather Hand nodded absently. "Most children are fools, Priest. It took me longer than most to discover how the world really worked. Lessons rarely come as painfully as mine did."

"A gentle boy?" Seven Stars's lips raised at the irony. "Is that why the Blessed Sun sent you here? To be gentle, War Chief?"

"Don't mock me, Priest."

Leather Hand looked across the freshly renovated kiva and into the eyes of the Flute Player. He had been painted in black, his eyes white with blue irises.

"Do you like the image?" Seven Stars asked.

"Yes. The blood no longer boils in my veins when I enter this place. Of all my duties, overseeing the reconsecration of the kivas has been the most rewarding."

Featherstone is dead. The thought intruded again. And with her, perhaps, so too was the thlatsina heresy.

"You never believed Sternlight's prophecy?" Seven Stars asked.

"Never." Before his death, Sunwatcher Sternlight had told of colorful ancestral spirits who lived in the distant high mountains. "In the end, Sternlight's new gods couldn't save him from being taken captive by the Fire Dogs and finally murdered by the great Chief Jay Bird."

"I've always thought the story about that was a little hazy, something about revenge. But to the common people, it has become a legend. Supposedly when Jay Bird's stiletto pierced Sternlight's heart, his soul flew out through the wound in a pillar of light and rode the Rainbow Serpent's column of rising smoke and ash to the heavens."

"A lie is just like using dog shit to paint a god's image, Priest. It may be pretty, but in the end it still stinks."

Leather Hand allowed himself to admire the images painted on the newly replastered walls. The four square roof support columns that rose on either side of the wooden foot drums interrupted his view, but he could appreciate the overall effect.

In an effort to remove the offending images, Leather Hand had ordered the local barbarians to scrape the walls down to bare stone. Then he had them carefully collect the scrapings and bear the baskets of flaked clay three days' walk over to the River of Sorrows. There they were cast into the current to be carried off to the distant north so their scattered remains couldn't pollute the soil under his feet.

For the base coat he had decided on a light brown plaster and required runners to carry in white, yellow, red, brown, and black clays. To these he had had the artists add mineral and organic pigments so that the colors were bright and fresh. He nodded as his gaze passed from image to image. Where just days ago Sternlight's accursed thlatsinas had blasphemed the walls, now the old gods once again reigned.

"Featherstone is dead," he said aloud. "And the thlatsinas are dead with her. The Blessed Webworm has ordered all trace of their existence to be obliterated. Any who practice their ways are to be punished."

A weight had been lifted from his shoulders. His souls had taken on an airy feel, floating and light. When he looked at the east wall, Spider Woman's image now Danced on the clean plaster. She wore a bright yellow dress and carried a feather prayer fan. In the south, the Flute Player cavorted, his burden basket riding high on his back. Three feathers curled up from his head. He held his flute to his mouth, and his enlarged penis protruded before him. In the west the Blue God thrust her arms out, seeking her next victim, her open mouth ready to devour the soul of any unwary prey. Finally, if he turned his head, he could see Old Woman North, dressed in white, as she lifted her staff to bring the cold winds of winter into the world. Between the figures, the spirals of Father Sun and circles of Sister Moon marked the southeast, southwest, northwest, and northeast. Cloud People sent rain from the skies; zigzags of lightning marked their passing. Finally, the Plumed Serpent hovered over the bench, his body bright blue, eyes hollow circles of turquoise behind a black forked tongue.

"It is a beautiful place now," Leather Hand said fervently. "I can feel peace here, as if the old gods are breathing from the very stone and plaster."

"I fear your peace shall be short-lived. The barbarians can smell the First People's weakness on the wind. At the first hint of vulnerability, they'll be ready to pounce."

"Not as long as they fear my warriors."

Seven Stars gave him a knowing look. "A whipped dog fears its master. Each time you beat it with a cudgel, it cowers back, ears lowered, tail between its legs. But with each blow, War Chief, it longs to bite back. Sometimes a bit of succulent meat and a kind word can succeed where a blow will not."

"I have no meat to give, Priest." Leather Hand leaned his head back, feeling the cool touch of the damp plaster. At least in Tall Piñon Town part of the world had been set straight. He could feel the lines of Power running through the great kiva, realigning themselves into the wonderful patterns of the past.

Succulent meat and a kind word? What had that ever accomplished except to create suspicion about one's resolution to follow a given path?

Closing his eyes he could imagine his brother's face. Those knowing eyes were staring at him out of the past, boring out from Leather Hand's memory. A faint smile hung on his brother's lips, a question in the arch of his eyebrows.

"Where are you now, Brother?" The words carried in the silence of the great kiva. The fire popped in answer, and the painted images of the gods watched him with a sober curiosity.

Seven Stars said nothing as Leather Hand asked, "Does your soul Dance with the Ancestors? Have they welcomed you with open arms?"

He smiled, imagining the scene. Mother, Uncle, their grandparents, all would be laughing, taking his brother's breath-heart soul into their embrace.

"Your brother was a great man," Seven Stars said softly. "He was taken into the realm of the dead with great joy."

By the gods, I miss him. A stitch of grief lanced his breast. In spite of himself, Leather Hand clasped a fist, the muscles of his arm knotting.

"Tell me about him," Seven Stars prodded.

"Wraps His Tail grew up Dreaming about being a warrior. He always told stories about the day he would assume the Blessed Sun's red shirt and take up his warrior's duties. He bragged of the battles he would fight, of the wealth he would accumulate, and the glory that would be his as he fought the Tower Builders in the north and the Mogollon Fire Dogs to the south.

"Wraps His Tail was accepted as a warrior just after his seventeenth birthday and rose rapidly through the ranks to the position of deputy under the great War Chief Ironwood."

Seven Stars nodded. "That was in the days after the renowned Beargrass stepped down for the sake of his wife and family. Yes, I recall. More than just one of Ironwood's deputies, Wraps His Tail was Ironwood's closest friend."

Is that why they murdered him? The old question rolled over in Leather Hand's mind. His brother's body had been found just outside the walls of Talon Town. He'd been attacked from up close, his skull split—apparently by someone who knew him. A severed badger paw had been placed in his hand along with the powdered remains of a corpse. A sure sign of witchcraft.

But why? Wraps His Tail had never had anything to do with witchcraft.

"Wasn't there some confusion over the events of his death?"

"The Blessed Sun, Crow Beard, was dying . . . and my brother was returning from some intrigue Ironwood had plotted. And there was plotting aplenty during those days. Witchery and deception were everywhere."

"Perhaps they still are." Seven Stars ran thin brown fingers down the seams of his fine white robes.

Leather Hand took a deep breath and willed his body to relax. "If you ask me, Matron Night Sun, War Chief Ironwood, and the Blessed Snake Head all had their part in helping to rot the First People from the inside out."

"And don't forget the false Prophet, Sternlight." Seven Stars added.

Yes. He and his accursed thlatsinas.

"False gods for false times," Seven Stars whispered.

"What was my brother's life worth to them? Just another betrayal along the way?"

"Perhaps those days are over." Seven Stars steepled his fingers. "The Blessed Webworm has begun the process of renewing our world. He has planted the first new root at Flowing Waters Town on the Spirit River. With the completion of Dusk House, construction has begun on Sunrise House. Our people will be rejuvenated, refreshed."

"I'm not sure renewal can be achieved by abandoning the lands where our ancestors lived for so many generations."

Seven Stars smiled. "I was one of the surveyors, War Chief. We marked the path most carefully on the route up from Northern House. The line that runs through the center of our world lies precisely between Dusk House and Sunrise House. We are now closer to the opening where our ancestors climbed from the Fourth World into this one."

"It's a land of gray," he said with a snort. "Gray dirt, gray vistas . . . and eventually we will be gray people."

"Perhaps." Seven Stars refused to rise to the baiting. "But unlike our situation in Straight Path Canyon, we will be gray people with a reliable and inexhaustible supply of water."

Leather Hand stood and pulled his long red war shirt straight around his muscular body. Retrieving his use-polished war club from where it leaned against the plastered bench, he slung his black chokecherry-wood bow and the quiver of cane-shaft arrows over his shoulder.

He turned. "I shall tell the others what I think about the work." The wooden rungs whispered under his sandals as he climbed up to the stone steps leading to the northern antechamber. He passed the Priests' dressing room and climbed the final ladder out into the sunlight.

Four

Heat poured over Deputy War Chief Leather Hand as he blinked in the searing brilliance. The midsummer sky had a brassy tone, and the light was brutal after the dim kiva interior.

Through the gaps between the surrounding buildings he could see the flat country north and east of Tall Piñon. Despite occasional stands of trees from which the town had taken its name, the land looked stark, baked, and dusty. South, out the open end of the plaza, hazy blue buttes shimmered on the distant horizon.

Wide roads running in either direction connected the great house settlement with two other nearby communities of the local Deep Canyon People. Like most of the northern barbarians they were divided into two moieties, the Yellow Stone, whose clans operated out of the westernmost town, and the Black Cup along the canyon rim. More than one hundred structures dotted the ridgetop within sight of Tall Piñon Town. He could also see terraced farm plots turning brown in the summer sun; a series of dry reservoirs, shrines, small villages, and isolated farmsteads were sprinkled among the trees and arroyos.

Leather Hand's ten warriors stood at ease, their red shirts sweat-darkened as they nodded greetings to him. The three Priests—subordinates of Seven Stars—wore white and waited with curious expressions on their florid faces. So, too, did the five artists who had painted the images. But their manners were wary, almost anxious.

Farther back—across the broad roadway and below the berm—a crowd of Made People stood in the plaza, some shading their eyes with the flats of their hands. Here and there among them were Deep Canyon People who served Tall Piñon Town. They wore drab smocks and had their hair pulled back in braids that were pinned with rabbit or deer-bone skewers.

With word of the rededication of the great kiva, a crowd had gathered—mostly farmers from outlying farmsteads. They had journeyed in from their shabby pit houses in the canyon bottoms, or from their cornfields along the mesa tops. Rudely dressed, and for the most part ignorant, Leather Hand despised them as filthy vermin. At sight of him or his warriors their eyes bugged out, and their mouths hung open in wonder. They might have been see-ing gods instead of mere men.

Beyond them, the irregular shape of the Tall Piñon Great House baked in the bright sun. Oriented with the long axis running north-south, the three-story edifice had been plastered with tan mud, the images of the old gods still visible on the walls. Unlike so many of the towns, Tall Piñon's great house hadn't been repainted. As much as Matron Husk Woman disapproved of Webworm and his policies, she'd disapproved even more of Crow Beard's thlatsinas.

Leather Hand fought the urge to snarl at the thought. While great houses were the symbol of the Straight Path Nation's political authority, the kivas were the real heart of their Power. How dare the Priests upset the fragile bal-ance by desecrating them on a false Prophet's orders?

"Well?" one of the Priests asked.

"Continue with the reconsecration. The kiva now basks in beauty."

Smiles passed between the Priests. Leather Hand could see the artists' visible sighs of relief.

He took no time for the others, but gestured his warriors to follow and headed for the great house. As Leather Hand crossed the road and passed through the crowd, they melted away from him and his sweat-damp warriors like fat from a hot obsidian blade.

Up the gentle slope he passed a line of black-on-white seed jars set close to the wall and climbed the pine-pole ladder to the first-story roof, then up to the second. He stopped before the third-story room block. Turning on the clay roof, he looked out across the flat with its blocky pat-

tern of buildings. In the southeast, Thunderbird Mountain
thrust up like a low dark triangle against the skyline. To its
left he could see the sprawling shape of Green Mesa. Far
View Town was up there—the peg that anchored the
Blessed Sun's authority firmly among the Green Mesa villages. That was the ancestral home of the Buffalo and
Coyote clans of the Made People. For that reason, Far
View was symbolic. Given its commanding view of the
vast northern frontier, it was tactically vital. More than
one hundred warriors lived there under yet another recalcitrant Blue Dragonfly Clan Matron. With its stone-lined
reservoir, tall towers, and remarkable canals, it reeked of
the First People's authority. Lose it, and suffer a blow to
the very heart of the Straight Path Nation—not to mention
line-of-sight communications with the Blessed Sun in
Flowing Waters Town.

He turned his gaze northeast to the Spirit Mountains.
All but a few patches of snow had melted from the high
peaks. On a scorching day like this, he could almost wish
he were up there in those cool heights.

Those rugged high mountains belonged to no one. They
were the refuge of desperate barbarians and slaves who
had fled the authority of the Straight Path Nation. Hunting
parties of the Tower Builders who lived up north fre-
quently prowled there. Sometimes those high peaks and
mountain meadows were the haunts of even wilder barbarians who drifted in from the buffalo plains and then
vanished back the way they had come.

Not all dangers were human. Rumors told how the high
country was the home of monsters, malicious spirits, and
witches. It was said that a man who died in the shadows of
the timber-cloaked canyons would lose his soul forever—
that it would wander lost and frozen, struggling through
snow in winter, confused and dazed by the dense stands of
trees in summer.

Turning his gaze to the northwest he could see the dis-
tant Salt Mountains: isolated peaks deep within the Tower
Builders' lands. To the west were the green summits of the
Cedar Mountains. They shimmered in the hot light. Just to

their south lay Windflower Village on the northern banks of the River of Souls. Beyond that lay the Red Rock lands, where the Blessed Sun's domain extended clear over to the Great Canyon.

Straight south the Bearclaw Mountains had a silvered look in the hot light, and below them, the fanglike projection of World Tree Mountain jutted skyward.

He could see it all: his province and area of responsibility as ordered by the Blessed Webworm.

"The first and foremost task," Webworm had said uncertainly, "is to reassure the people. The south is not an area of concern. Traders tell us that the Mogollon chief, Jay Bird, is happy to rest on the laurels of his victory. No, the problem is in the north. Some of the Matrons, Husk Woman at Tall Piñon and White Cloud Woman at Far View Town, along with their allies, are working against me. Seeing their lack of respect, the subject peoples under their rule may take this opportunity to break away. If they do, it could even spread to the Made People. That, or the Tower Builders might think us vulnerable and weak." He had looked straight at Leather Hand and said, "You will take as many warriors as you need to stabilize the north. Do not fail me."

That very night Leather Hand had called upon the pick of the Blessed Sun's warriors and begun his journey from Talon Town. He had followed the Great North Road past the shrines and watchtowers, trotted his forces up the line of great houses and over the trails that brought him to Tall Piñon Town with its large population, critical granaries, and resources.

Nor had he arrived at Tall Piñon any too soon. Within days, he had crushed rebellions and subdued threats at both Lanceleaf and Turtle villages. He had stopped a war party of Tower Builders, ambushing them at the crossing of the River of Sorrows, and ensured that every last vestige of the thlatsina religion was being erased.

Behind him a scratchy voice said, "Is that frown indicative of your normally foul mood, or are you truly displeased with something? Did the painters not meet your expectations? Or has the day just been too busy to give you the opportunity to pull some poor wretch's arms out of his sockets?"

Leather Hand bit off a curse as he turned to see Matron Husk Woman where she sat in the shade of her T-shaped doorway. "I'm actually very pleased with the painters; it's the treasonous inclinations of certain persons in authority who should know better that burns in my heart."

The old woman gave him a thin-lidded stare, distaste in the set of her wrinkled mouth. "I just wish Webworm and Desert Willow would keep their poison down south where it belongs. If they suck on it long enough, perhaps it will gag them and the rest of us can get on with our lives."

He leveled a hard finger. "You take too many liberties, Matron."

She arched on old eyebrow. "Beware, Deputy War Chief. I am a Matron of the Blue Dragonfly Clan. You would be wise not to forget it."

Sighing, he walked over and climbed down through the roof entrance into the quarters provided for him. The upper room was four paces long by two across, plastered in white with black zigzag lines for decoration. A fire bowl filled with cold gray ash lay in the center of the floor. Several corrugated cooking jars rested against the west wall. The larger black-on-white jars along the eastern wall held corn flour, beeweed leaves, saltbush, dried meat, and other foods. Stepping off the ladder, he removed his weapons and laid them to one side.

His slave, Meadow Girl, watched him warily as she ground yellow kernels of corn into flour. She hunched over the mealing bin in the northeastern corner like an oversized mouse. With each stroke she pressed the handstone down over the corn. It made a hollow grumble as it grated against the trough-shaped grinding stone. Corn flour dusted her strong brown fingers and mottled patterns on the backs of her hands. She was young, just eighteen summers. Sound, and firm of body, her breasts swelled the fabric of her brown garment as she knelt over the sandstone-slab-lined mealing bin. Her gleaming black hair was tied back out of the way.

"My cup. I would drink," he ordered. He had claimed her at Lanceleaf Village after executing her uncles and brothers for their part in the rebellion.

She avoided his eyes as she rose, found his tall cup—a beautiful thing, white with black hatched lines—and poured a cup of cool water from the large brownware jug. She kept her eyes averted as he accepted it and drank.

He considered her thoughtfully. She was emblematic of how the western half of his domain was under control, the people wary of evoking his wrath. He swirled the water in his cup. Sometime soon, he was going to have to make the trip to First Moon Village and see to the situation there. The lunar cycle was almost complete. The Priests who followed the path of the moon were going to want to begin preparing for their most sacred of nights. The Sunwatcher, Blue Racer, would be planning his journey north from Straight Path Canyon to First Moon Village.

It was Leather Hand's responsibility to ensure that no surprises awaited them. Not only that, Ironwood was alleged to be in hiding near there. And Leather Hand had old business with Ironwood.

I shall see that your ghost rests easy, Brother.

He had to remind himself not to crush the beautiful cup in his hand.

Inside the log-walled lodge, an old man lay beneath a pale white elkhide. His bed was made of moss covered with a thick winter buffalohide laid double to cushion his frail bones. An arm's length away in the exact center, a fire burned cheerily, sending smoke billowing up to the opening in the roof.

The outline of his skull could be seen beneath the old man's sunken skin. Wisps of white hair lay askew on his speckled pate, his nose like a wilted mushroom. Thin brown lips were pulled back, revealing receding pink gums that held but a few pegs of worn teeth. His right arm, a stick of bone covered with loose dry skin, had lost its muscle.

Only his eyes—deep within the skull's hollowing orbits—remained bright, gleaming as they watched the young man who fussed with a bowl of broth. The youth used a spoon crafted from a mountain sheep's horn to ladle thin venison stew past the old man's slack lips.

The young man wore a knee-length brown war shirt belted at the waist with a yellow cloth sash that held his belt pouch, a hafted chert knife, and a deer-bone stiletto. His thick black hair was drawn up tight against the back of his skull, held in a bun by a rabbit-bone skewer. Worry pulled at the young man's eyes and reflected in the set of his mouth. His hawkish nose and thin face weren't handsome, but he sat with a serious dignity that left the viewer feeling serenity.

The old man loudly swallowed the broth that trickled into his mouth; he gave a faint wave of his hand as the young man raised it again.

"Is that enough, Dune?" the young man asked.

"It is." What was meant to be a grin was a frightening rictus. "Don't waste it."

"But you need your strength, Elder."

The widening grin exposed more of the toothless gums and the rounded mound of the old man's tongue. "My body no longer has need of strength. It is now little more than a husk for the souls. I feel it."

"Feel it?"

"The breath-heart soul, it's slipping, Poor Singer. Coming loose . . . like cottonwood down . . . drifting ever so lightly in my chest."

The young man's head lowered, chin coming to rest on his breastbone. "Please. Don't go. I need you."

"For what?"

"To teach me."

"You know most of the things you need to know."

"I know nothing, Holy Derelict."

"Ah, then you know everything. The rest is illusion. Or deception." The old man's eyelids fluttered. "I have only one thing left for you to consider."

"What is that?"

"Tell me the story of how the people came into this world. Not just the First People, but all of them."

Poor Singer cleared his throat, beginning softly: "There are two kinds of 'People' in the world. First People and Made People. The First People were the descendants of those who bravely climbed through the four underworlds. They were led by a blue-black wolf and emerged into this world of light. Made People, on the other hand, have four main clans: the Bear Clan, Buffalo Clan, Coyote Clan, and Ant Clan. As well, many lesser clans exist, including the Redbird, the Buffalobeard, Badger, and the Canyon Wren clans. But each of these allies itself with the one of the four great clans, and so is considered part of it. Each clan was originally the animal its name implies. The Creator "Made" them. She breathed upon the animals and changed them into humans to provide company for the First People. For that reason the First People have always seen the Made People as inferior: They were once animals, whereas the First People have always been humans."

"And the others?" the old man asked. "How do all the other peoples fit in?"

"Other peoples, like the Mogollon Fire Dogs, the Hohokam, the Tower Builders, the barbarian tribes, and wild peoples are not human at all. Despite their humanlike appearances, they have the souls of beasts. The Fire Dogs—my mother's people—claim that they once lived as fiery wolves in Father Sun's heart and were cast out because they started chewing up his body. As they ran through the heavens toward earth, their blazing wolf bodies transformed into human shapes. That's why the Straight Path Nation believes that they have the souls of predators, born to kill."

"Do you believe that? Being Fire Dog yourself?"

Poor Singer shook his head, then realized the old man had closed his eyes. "No, Dune. I don't think my souls are different from anyone else's."

The old man's jaw slipped sideways, his mouth an irregular oblong. He wet his lips, gathered himself, and asked, "What is the purpose of the turquoise wolf?"

Poor Singer reached under the elk robe and pulled out the little fetish that hung from a thong around Dune's neck. "The turquoise wolf figurines are only made by the First People in Talon Town. Because the First People climbed through the Underworlds, they have secret knowledge of those places that Made People do not. They know the landmarks that lead souls to the Land of the Dead, and know the locations of the snares and traps that can catch a soul and hold it forever. For a price, First People will share this secret knowledge, and they might even provide a seeker with a turquoise wolf such as this one to guide him on the journey to the Land of the Dead."

The words were barely more than a breath. "Do . . . you . . . believe that?"

Poor Singer twisted the hem of his roughly woven brown war shirt. "I don't know anymore. That's why I need you. Any certainty is gone. I'm lost, Dune."

"That is the final . . . trial. To . . . lose yourself entirely."

The young man frowned. "Holy Derelict, as always, your words make no sense."

"Quite the . . . contrary. They make . . . all the sense . . . in the world."

Poor Singer stared at the old man.

After several heartbeats, the old man opened his eyes and said, "The wolf . . . give it to Matron Night Sun. She will . . . need it . . . soon."

"Yes, Dune."

"Take it . . . now."

Poor Singer gently removed the talisman from around the old man's neck, cupping the warm stone and leather thong in his hand.

Silence.

For long moments he looked into the old man's eyes as the brilliance faded into a dusky haze, and then to milky gray.

"You always did mock me, didn't you, old friend?" Poor Singer reached out and gently closed the old man's sightless eyes before he placed his hand over the smiling mouth. Like a soft caress the Holy Derelict's breath-heart Soul slipped from the body into the smoky night air.

For a long time, Poor Singer sat, just listening to the crackling of the fire as it consumed the pitch-filled piñon wood.

Five

With his back bowed by the weight of the heavy elk quarter, Bad Cast had to crane his neck to look up at the sky. Though Father Sun still cast a faint yellow light through the high heavens, evening shadows deepened into blue and purple in the canyon bottom. In the First Moon Valley ahead of them, smoke from a hundred fires added to the effect and muted ridge lines, patches of conifer, and the rounded slopes. It blurred the hard-edged outcrops of sandstone and shale. Behind them, centered in the valley, he could see one of the naked peaks where Cold Bringing Woman Danced. It blazed in orange glory.

They followed the worn path that paralleled the River of Stones. It was at this point that the valley opened; the high pinnacles of First Moon Mountain jutted against the southeastern sky while the length of Juniper Ridge could be seen extending southward on their right. They passed the first cornfields, those belonging to a Black Shale clansman.

The land around First Moon Valley was densely inhabited. Some people lived in farmsteads, while others occupied one of the ten villages, each with at least two great kivas for the moiety celebrations. While some dwellings were still ancestral-style pit houses that sheltered single families, many were multiroom, multistory masonry buildings that housed clans, lineages, or extended families.

No matter where a person lived, First Moon Mountain dominated the valley. Its Power filled the very air.

Bad Cast glanced up at it as he led his party down the worn trail at the head of the valley. He called a stop at the upper crossing of the River of Stones. There they laid their piles of still-cold meat onto the grass before bending and sucking up great gulps of water.

Drinking until his belly swelled, Bad Cast settled back

on his haunches and wiped a hand across his wet mouth. Water trickled down his chin.

One by one his companions copied his position, each thankful for the chance to rest. Sweat had tracked patterns through the grime on their bodies. Blood splotched their clothing where it had leaked from the meat, and flies still made a nuisance of themselves as they swarmed around their feast.

Bad Cast stretched his tired limbs. Every muscle quivered, and his joints—especially the ankles, knees, and hips—ached. His shoulders were raw where the pack straps had eaten into his skin.

He took a quick look at his companions, seeing fatigue reflected in their expressions. Ripple, however, looked the worst. Something brooding and terrible lay behind his eyes.

What did he really see up there?

Bad Cast leaned forward, cupped water, and splashed it into his hot face. Settling back, he considered the ramifications of Ripple's vision. Whatever it had been, it boded no good for the rest of them.

Before them the floodplain was filled with cornfields. These were fed by short ditches, giving way to other, smaller, dryland plots higher on the terraces. Here and there, as the slopes rose, small wattle-and-daub structures made rounded bumps on the land. These were field houses: huts built of wooden lattice, plastered with clay-rich mud, and fired to a hard finish. People kept tools there, used them for the short-term storage of harvested food, for shelter from a passing storm, and sometimes even slept inside when they needed to guard their fields.

Clan villages sat higher on the slopes. Clusters of single and multiple dwellings could be seen as fires twinkled and thin plumes of smoke rose into the evening sky.

Bad Cast let his gaze linger on the jagged spires, and the gap between them—could feel the Power of the place.

His uncle's words returned to him. On that long-ago evening he had just stepped from his boyhood initiation in the kiva and looked up at the familiar peak. Uncle had said, *"There are places, boy, passages where the Below*

Worlds emerge into this one. First Moon Mountain is such a place. Do you know why?"

"Yes, Uncle. What we see here is the top of the tallest mountain in the Third World, which is beneath us. It's so tall that it pokes up through our world."

"Is that important for our people?"

He had swallowed hard, nodding. "Yes, Uncle. In the beginning time, the People lived in the First World. Down in darkness at the bottom of the earth. One by one, they climbed through the three Below Worlds and finally emerged into this one."

"Is that different from what the First People teach?"

"They say that there are four underworlds, and that this is the Fifth World. They think they were the first humans to enter this world and that they are special, Blessed. They think their gods are the only gods because they came first. They think the Yamuhakto, the Warriors of East and West, were first led into this world by a blue Wolf."

"But you don't believe that?"

"No, Uncle."

"According to our beliefs, who were the first men to emerge?"

"The Hero Twins."

"And who led the Hero Twins?"

"It was Spider. When she led the Hero Twins out into this world, she cast her web into the sky and climbed up. Then, as the People died, she would pull the souls of the worthy up with strands from her web. They became the Star People."

"And how did Sister Moon come into this world?" Uncle had asked, his eyes boring into Bad Cast's.

"Spider Woman climbed down and told the Hero Twins that it was too dark in the night sky. The Star People needed some form of light, since Father Sun went to sleep every evening. She told the Hero Twins to go down into the Third World and to bring Sister Moon back to light the night sky."

Uncle had nodded his approval and gestured for Bad Cast to continue.

"The Hero Twins climbed back down into the Third World, which was illuminated by Sister Moon. They told her how the Star People spent their nights in blackness. But Sister Moon didn't care. She told the Hero Twins that her light was needed in the Third World."

"And how did the Hero Twins manage to get her into this world?"

Bad Cast had taken a deep breath, frowned, and looked around the kiva roof, where his relatives watched patiently. He said, *"They tricked her with corn cakes that Spider Woman had packed for them. They took them out of their packs and started to eat them. Sister Moon was hungry. She'd never eaten blue corn cakes, and the smell of them made her mouth water. Using the corn cakes, the Hero Twins drew her toward First Moon Mountain, where it thrust up through the sky of the Third World and into this, the Fourth World. The corn cakes were particularly sweet, spiced with beeweed and yucca blossoms. Sister Moon kept following the crumbs they trickled behind them. She would lick up the crumbs, and call out for a blue corn cake.*

"'Come a little higher,' the Hero Twins called back, trickling more crumbs. To each other they said, 'These corn cakes are the most delicious, sweetest corn cakes we have ever eaten.'

"And Sister Moon, hearing this, kept following, ever higher. The Hero Twins stayed just out of her reach, climbing and climbing until they climbed out between the twin pillars of First Moon Mountain."

Uncle had nodded sagaciously. *"And then what happened?"*

"Sister Moon climbed out behind them. When she did, the Hero Twins crumbled the corn cakes between their hands and threw them into the sky. Sister Moon leaped up after them, chasing the crumbs into the sky where they became the hazy star path that we can still see."

"And then what happened?"

Carried away by the solemnity of the occasion, Bad Cast's voice had risen. *"Sister Moon spent nine sun cycles seeking the corn cakes. Then, realizing she'd been tricked, she started back across the sky looking for the entrance to the Third World."*

"And the Hero Twins?" Uncle had asked.

"They saw her coming, and knew she would go back to the Third World and leave the Star People in darkness. To trick her they hid the entrance, piling up stone and dirt to make the entrance look like the ridgetop we see today."

"So that was it? Sister Moon is forever trapped in our night sky?"

"No, Uncle." Bad Cast had shaken his head. *"Sister Moon is always looking to go back to the Third World. That's why she forever searches across the sky, looking first for corn cakes as she heads south, and then for the entrance to the Third World as she comes back north.*

"The Hero Twins, knowing that she is forever searching, made stone images of themselves, one on each side of the hidden opening to the Third World. There, they stand guard to this day. We can see them anytime when we look up at First Moon Mountain."

As he remembered, Bad Cast turned his eyes toward the mountain, seeing the twin spires of rock, and relived that long-ago day when he had been made a man. Being initiated to the Blue Stick Clan kiva had been the most important event of his life. From the moment he had repeated the holy story and looked at the twin monoliths, his life had changed.

He shot another glance at Ripple. His friend sat wearily, his chest rising and falling. It was as if he had already set himself apart from them. The deep-seated anxiety that had lain behind his eyes remained, haunting and dangerous. He seemed oblivious as Spots and Wrapped Wrist studied him with hesitant sidelong glances.

It was Wrapped Wrist who leaned forward and whispered, "What do you think about his vision?"

Bad Cast shrugged, voice low. "How do you explain the frozen meat?"

"Maybe he found it in a cave?" Spots suggested. "You know, there are caves like that in the high country. Or at the edge of the snow fields. Places where ice doesn't melt even in the hottest of summers."

"Then how did he pack four heavy quarters that far without the meat thawing?" Wrapped Wrist countered. "And those wilted plants. They looked frost damaged to me."

Bad Cast muttered from the side of his mouth. "I went back to the place he said he killed the elk. The blood's still there. So, too, were the grizzly tracks. I stuck a finger in a pile of fresh bear shit. Not quite warm, not quite cold, but definitely last night's. It's just like he said."

Wrapped Wrist screwed up his face. "But Cold Bringing Woman? She doesn't come down from her mountains for moons . . . assuming you even *believe* in her."

Spots lifted a skeptical eyebrow. "Something makes it cold for half the year. Or are you saying the First People are right? They've been trying for tens of sun cycles to tell us our stories are false."

Wrapped Wrist shifted uncomfortably as he kneaded the powerful muscles in his thick thigh. "It's not that. I mean, not really. I think it's that Father Sun goes south. We all know that. When he's in the south it's colder, that's all. Just like when the Cloud People roll across a summer sky. The temperature drops. It doesn't mean that Cold Bringing Woman—"

"Why don't you go all the way and call her Old Woman North?" Spots used the First People's name for the terrible white-faced winter god.

"I told you, I don't believe in the First People's ways!" Wrapped Wrist scowled at Spots.

"Just in their warriors," Bad Cast grumbled. What people said aloud in public was closely tied to the proximity of the red-shirted warriors who enforced the Blessed Sun's will in First Moon Valley.

To Bad Cast's dismay, Ripple called from where he rested, "Think what you will. I'll tell you what I believe: We will begin the process of breaking the First People. You didn't see what I saw. Even the old gods are tired of the First People and their ways."

Bad Cast filled his hot lungs with a breath. "Don't forget what they did to your father, my friend. Or how you got your name in the first place."

Ripple smiled for the first time, but it was forced, almost

a grimace. "Perhaps that's why Cold Bringing Woman called on me. She knows the colors of my souls."

"Just so this madness doesn't end with you showing the world the color of your blood," Wrapped Wrist warned.

Spots had been running his fingers over the puckered scars on his left arm. "This must not be spoken of openly. You must promise, Ripple, that you won't walk up to the First People's great house and shout out at the top of your lungs that according to the gods, they're doomed."

Ripple lowered his head, eyes on the thick green grass that grew beside the stream. "I am no fool, Spots. The time isn't right for that yet."

"Oh?" Bad Cast asked. "You know when this magical blow to the First People is going to take place?"

Ripple shook his head. "No. I have to be tested first. I have to endure. Then, if I survive, I have to go to the Mountain Witch. Then, and only then, can I destroy the First People."

Bad Cast glanced from one of his friends to the other, sharing their unease. It didn't do for a man to let his mouth run off about the First People. Those who did were usually awakened in the darkness as red-shirted warriors dragged them out of bed, hustled them off, and dispatched them in the most gruesome of ways. It was said that a cup made out of Ripple's father's skull still rested on a shelf in the First People's kiva up at Pinnacle Great House.

As Bad Cast hitched himself wearily to his feet he glanced up at the high pillars of First Moon Mountain. Below the twin spires of rock, the square three-story structure of the hated great house could be seen. Visible for days' walks in any direction, the tan-plastered edifice hulked on his people's most holy ground. In the dusk it made a blot against the indigo sky.

Six

The growing community of Flowing Waters Town baked under a hot midday sun. The new capital of the Straight Path Nation had been placed on the first terrace above a shallow westerly bend of the Spirit River. Located by the Priests after a careful survey, the center of the community lay in direct line with the Great North Road, which ran up from Straight Path Canyon. That line transected the space between the Blue Dragonfly Clan's Dusk House and the Red Lacewing's Sunrise House. On the higher terraces the Made People clans were already at work building small towns. The entire area was a hive of construction as immigrants moved in, desperate to make a new start in the Spirit River bottoms.

Wind Leaf, war chief of the Straight Path Nation, stood atop the towering fourth-story roof of Dusk House. The giant building was a dominating rectangle of stone, its walls plastered with buff-colored clay carried down from the uplands a day's walk to the north.

Traders, hawkers, and others with goods to Trade had placed their blankets along the walls. For food, trinkets, or luxury goods, they engaged in the game of give and take, always in search of some sort of advantage.

At that moment Wind Leaf could have cared less about the exotic goods changing hands four stories below him. His attention was focused on the brightly dressed party that approached from the south. Like a thin worm the ragged line inched wearily down to the shallow ford.

For days he had been kept apprised of the party's progress after leaving Straight Path Canyon. Now he watched as the Blessed Sun's procession splashed across the Spirit River.

His lips bent into a wry smile as he thought, *So, it is finally finished. The Blessed Matron Featherstone's souls are officially gone, sent to join the Cloud People. Webworm is home.*

The world is changed forever.

Webworm's party emerged as it climbed laboriously up onto the silt-gray floodplain, crossed the feeder canal, and plodded wearily along the cord-straight road that ran between green fields of corn, beans, and squash. The Blessed Sun walked first. Then came the Priests followed by a large party of red-shirted warriors under the command of Deputy War Chief Ravengrass. After them walked four lines of Made People, one each for the Ant, Buffalo, Coyote, and Bear clans. Finally the slaves and servants followed, nearly empty packs swinging on their backs.

The war chief raised his gaze. Beyond the river, lumpy uplands rose in juniper and piñon-dotted hills. The worn trail across them led a half-day's run to the south, where Northern Town stood on the bluff above the River of Souls. Farther south, across the desert uplands, beyond Smoking Mirror Butte, lay Straight Path Canyon, now mostly abandoned.

At the hollow sound of wood knocking on wood, he looked to the east and snorted at the irony of it all. No more than two bow-shots away, the Blessed Sun's master mason, an Ant Clan woman named Yellowgirl, labored under the hot sun with a series of strings, pegs, and a level. On the ground, the first outlines of a new building could be seen in the lines of string, courses of stone, and the foundation ditches the slaves had dug into the soil. Toiling slaves marched back and forth between piles of sandstone that had been stacked during the previous winter and spring. More slaves brought large water jars perched like bulbous second heads on their thin shoulders as they trekked up from Spirit River.

Proof once and for all that the Red Lacewing Clan has fallen! The thought stuck in his head like a bitter thorn.

That building, too, was a constant reminder to all how the world had changed.

Wind Leaf heard light footsteps behind him, and smiled as a soft voice said, "So, my husband has returned?"

"He has, Blessed Matron."

"Then daft old Featherstone is nothing more than a memory."

"That is correct."

Desert Willow, Blessed Matron of the Straight Path Nation, stepped up beside him, her thoughtful eyes on the building project to the east. "They're making progress . . . despite their dead Matron."

"The Red Lacewing Clan is in decline. It shows in their building. Sunrise House is going to be much smaller than Dusk House."

She smiled at that, a cunning humor reflected in her full red lips. Her eyes were sharp, active, betraying a calculating mind behind her heart-shaped face. She wore a white skirt of softest cotton belted by a bright yellow sash. Strands of turquoise beads graced her slim neck and hung down between her round breasts. Though only twenty-three summers of age, Desert Willow's manner couldn't be mistaken. Anyone who had known Matron Moon Bright at the height of her authority in Kettle Town would have recognized her granddaughter's commanding presence.

"I think I shall go and see to the construction of my husband's house."

"Matron? You didn't come out to greet him?" Wind Leaf asked.

She shot him a sly smile. "I'm afraid I shall be spending way too much time with him as it is." Her shapely brown hand reached out, the fingers tracing the lightest of caresses down his arm. "If I should become . . . bored, will you be standing guard tonight?"

He chuckled under his breath. "Yes, Matron."

She shot a glance at Webworm's weary party as it trudged closer. "I'm sure the Blessed Sun will be more concerned with sleep after his long journey than he will with me."

"That will probably be the case, Matron." He watched

as she walked across the roof, hips swinging. Her white skirt flashed in the midday sun. The thick black wealth of her hair glistened as it swayed to her step. Back straight, head erect, she walked forward down the ladder that led onto the third floor as though it were a stairway.

He had always admired her perfect balance, be it physical or political. She was well suited to her position as the most powerful woman in the world.

The construction of Sunrise House was physical proof of how their world had changed. Back in Straight Path Canyon, Talon Town had occupied the place of prominence. Dedicated to the sun, and ancestral home of the Red Lacewing Clan, it had been larger, more imposing than Kettle Town. Here, at Dusk House—dedicated to the moon—the Blue Dragonfly Clan controlled the powerful western side of the world.

Dusk House was physically smaller than Kettle Town had been. Instead of Kettle Town's five hundred rooms, Dusk House only had four hundred, but these were newly constructed, open for storage and occupancy. None had been ritually sealed by the Matrons, or filled with refuse. So, in actuality, Desert Willow's people had more utilizable space available to them. When—as would eventually happen—they needed more rooms, additions could be built on to Dusk House as they had to Kettle Town.

Now he looked at Red Lacewing Clan's legacy: Sunrise House was symbolic—a mere shadow of the building Talon Town had been.

The world has changed. Father Sun rides lower in the sky. Sister Moon is in ascendance.

His gaze followed Desert Willow as she left the eastern gate and strode toward Sunrise House. She might have been weightless, so light and airy was her walk. By the blood in his veins, she was a stunning woman. He could feel his pulse quicken. To still it he returned his attention to the party winding its way through the cornfields.

A sudden silence came from the construction site. Wind Leaf noticed that Yellowgirl had stopped fiddling with her strings. She turned her square face and thick-shouldered body to watch the Blessed Sun's approach. The master mason was a middle-aged woman, broad through the shoulders and muscular. Her breasts were small, flat, and wide set; she kept her hair bobbed short.

When she glanced back at the slaves, it was to find that they, too, had stopped to watch. Across the distance, Wind Leaf heard her bark, "What are you doing? Wasting Father Sun's light? We can finish three more courses of stone today!"

How like her.

From habit he turned, looking up the Great North Road where it ran across the flat terrace to the uplands. There another of the large towns had been laid out. The successor to Center Place, it remained nothing but a pattern of sticks driven into the cobble terrace with lengths of string stretched between them to mark walls and rooms. Given the drought, the political unease, the rumors of rebellion, and the other troubles, talk was that not enough workers could be mustered to quarry the stone to build it.

"We may resort to adobe bricks," Yellowgirl had told him sourly.

"You're joking," he'd replied.

"Oh?" she'd asked warily. "I suppose you have a couple hundred workers hidden away somewhere? Or did you just think you'd send your war parties out to round them up at the waggling of the Blessed Sun's finger?"

He couldn't, of course. Even slaves had to eat. And that was the fundamental problem.

He squinted up at the searing ball of the sun. White and hot, the god scorched his face—burned into his eyes. Summer had been brutal. The dryland fields had wilted, the tender young corn stalks now brittle and fit for nothing more than winter fuel. The bean plants, those that still survived, were short, stunted, and well past the date for flowering.

Nor had winter been of much help lately. He could almost believe the stories that circulated about how Old Woman North was withholding the snows, keeping the buffalo from calling them down. She had sent a numbing cold rolling down out of the north last winter, but little in the way of snow. For days the land had been gripped by a deep dry cold, the temperature never above freezing. But instead of drifting snow, the cruel winds had only traced patterns of dust from the friable soil.

What a terrible jest the gods played when a person awakened every morning in midwinter to find his water jar frozen solid, but with a fresh coating of dust across its surface.

He sighed and returned his attention to the approaching party. The weather would change. It always did.

With quick hands he straightened his bright red war shirt, picked up his bow and quiver, and slung them over his shoulder. After tying his war club to his sash he quickly descended the ladder to the third floor, crossed the roofs, and trotted down the ladder to the second. A stairway led him to the first floor and finally the plaza.

Passing between the First People's kiva and the great kiva, his path took him across the plaza and out the southeastern gap in the walls. On the way he saluted the guard perched on the roof above and ignored the collection of colorful Traders who displayed their wares beside the walls. Wind Leaf made his way onto the earthen berm that spread over the floodplain.

Dusk Town, like most of their sacred structures, was a representation in miniature of the Five Worlds the First People believed in. The roof where he had first stood represented the Fifth World in which the people currently lived. The Fourth World, or Feather-Wing World, was represented by the first two stories of the town. The Third World, or Fog World, had its counterpart in the open plaza. Beyond the southern storerooms the flat berm portrayed the Sulfur-Smell World. To reach the First, or Soot World, one had to enter the kiva and seek the *sipapu*, or tunnel, that led down to the land of Power and danger.

People had begun to call back and forth, and now a crowd of onlookers began to assemble on the berm behind him. Happy calls and greetings could be heard. It was quite a collection: Hohokam Traders, local farmers, some of the potters, fletchers, and weavers. But for Yellowgirl's stern nature, half the construction slaves would have been there, too.

As Wind Leaf waited, the Blessed Sun, Webworm, followed by White Stone and the two ranks of red-shirted warriors, climbed up to greet him. The Blessed Sun wore a tan-and-blue shirt that reached to his knees. The hem was still damp from fording the river, but in the arid heat, it would dry within moments.

Webworm was in his midforties, his face wrinkled with worry. He had once had a bland expression, but these days it was perpetually tight; the man's eyes never quite hid an incipient panic. Gray streaked the long hair he'd wound into a bun at the back of his head. He'd pinned it with several gorgeous turkey-bone skewers inlaid with turquoise. Three necklaces of ground turquoise beads hung at his neck, one of them interspersed with polished copper bells. Long earrings of carved jet sported accents of bright red coral. In the light, Wind Leaf could see the small spirals tattooed on the man's chin below his broad mouth.

"Welcome home, Blessed Sun." Wind Leaf bowed, fingertips to his chin in a sign of deference.

"It's good to be home," Webworm granted with a sigh. "Gods, I'm tired." He rocked from foot to foot as he looked back at the rest of the procession. The litter bearers, mostly slaves, looked ragged and footsore. Most of the Made People, dressed in brown coarsely woven tunics, carried large packs or assortments of pots in net bags. They, too, were grimy, sweating, and dust-streaked—but for their legs where the river had just washed them clean.

Webworm raised a hand. "Thank you all for your courtesy and help. Go now to your families and rest. You've earned it."

The column disintegrated, people calling well wishes, or touching their chins as they walked away. Some of the Made People plodded on into Dusk Town in search of their dwellings. They faded into the crowd as hucksters offered Trade, and friends demanded details of the journey.

"Creeper?" Webworm called to the Buffalo Clan leader. "If you would see me later."

"Yes, Blessed Sun." The older man nodded, a dogged loyalty in his eyes as he bowed in respect.

"Walk with me," Webworm ordered Wind Leaf as he strode past.

Wind Leaf matched the Blessed Sun's pace. "Yes, Blessed Sun."

"What is the news? While I was seeing to my mother's funeral, did the elders come to any decision? Am I still to be the Blessed Sun?"

"You are, my Chief. You are Red Lacewing by birth, and the Blessed Featherstone proclaimed you such. Your wife, the Blessed Desert Willow, has been named Matron of the First People. She informed the Council of Elders that she wished you to remain Blessed Sun." He hesitated. "Unless, of course, the pretender, Cornsilk, comes down from the mountains and seeks to have herself declared Matron in Desert Willow's place."

That brought a growl from Webworm. "If she appears, we'll deal with her. Assuming she's stupid enough to try it. Were I in her sandals, I'd rather live into old age up there in the snow than have someone using my skull for a trinket bowl in the First People's kiva." He made a throwing-away gesture. "Gods, I just want to sleep for a quarter moon."

They rounded the southern rooms, passed under the guard, and entered the plaza. People were emerging, waving, calling greetings. Webworm waved back, his mind clearly on other things.

"I will see to it, Blessed Sun."

Webworm gave him a dull, fatigued look. "That was only a wish, War Chief. Unfortunately, I'm sure that as soon as I hear your report, there will be a burgeoning list of things for me to do."

Wind Leaf resisted the urge to speak, waiting as they climbed the stairways and ladders to the fourth floor. At the T-shaped doorway that led into the Blessed Sun's private quarters, Wind Leaf hesitated, but Webworm waved him in.

The war chief ducked through the doorway after Webworm and took a deep breath of the cool air within the compartment.

The room was large, plastered in white, with large colorful drawings of the gods on the walls. Flute Player Danced on the north wall, his pack curving his back; the feathers on his head were bright red. A smaller doorway let out onto the balcony that hung from the north wall, and could be closed with a wooden-plank door. On the east, Spider Woman spun strands of her web into a net. On the west, the Blue God stared with hollow eyes that seemed to engulf Wind Leaf with unnatural longing.

A line of use-polished weapons were stacked below the Blue God, while decorated ollas, seed jars, and corrugated cooking ware lay below the Flute Player's feet. A cleaned-out fire bowl rested in the center of the room. Two wooden boxes were heaped with turquoise, jet, and coral jewelry. A collection of carefully cleaned and polished human skulls hung along one wall in net bags. They watched Wind Leaf through empty eye sockets, their teeth bent in mocking grins.

Through another doorway Wind Leaf could see the sleeping quarters, where buffalo and elk robes were rolled and stacked against the wall. A single pallet made of cattail leaves over plaited willow stems lay on the swept clay floor. Several stacks of clothing, a paint box, and other personal effects lined the walls.

Webworm sighed, kicked off his travel-worn sandals, and sank down on a folded buffalo robe. He looked up wearily as he pulled his soiled shirt over his head, wadded it, and threw it into the corner. The necklaces looked dull against his sweat-streaked skin. He gestured to Wind Leaf, who handed him a bowl filled with corn cakes. Taking one, he bit a hunk out of it, and through a mouthful, said, "Report, War Chief."

Wind Leaf laced his hands behind his back. "The relocation is progressing. Another fifteen families have moved from Straight Path Canyon and begun building a small row of houses up on the terrace. Given the drought in the canyon, they probably didn't have much incentive to stay."

"Yes, I know. We just passed through there. Expect more to arrive as the winter sets in. They'll be desperate after the harvest." Webworm frowned, reached for a ceramic canteen decorated with hatched black-on-white designs, and washed down a mouthful before taking another bite. "What about the north?"

"My deputy, Leather Hand, reports that several small rebellions have been put down. He expects the corn harvest to be spotty. Farmsteads on the rivers are looking pretty favorable, but they have irrigation. Dryland fields are another thing. Some have had rain, but it's been hit or miss. The bottom line is that we can't expect a surplus from the north."

Webworm washed down more corn cake before asking, "Do they have enough to get through the winter?"

"Maybe. In some places. But Leather Hand warns that you should expect raiding by spring. He doesn't think much of our chances for peace. Hungry bellies are going to stir resentment."

"Um," Webworm grunted. "And the reconsecration of the kivas and holy sites?"

Wind Leaf arched his back. "Leather Hand's preliminary assessment is that it will proceed as planned, but there's been a rather curious development."

Webworm's jaw stopped short, his eyes hardening into brown stones. "Such as?"

"The thlatsinas. The barbarians have started to believe in them."

"What do *they* care? They have their own gods. Silly little spirits that live in rocks and springs. Why would they give so much as a thought to the thlatsinas? When Sternlight prophesied his heresy, it was for the First People, not subject peoples. Pus and blood! We've had trouble enough just getting them to respect our gods, let alone accept them." He waved a hand at the images adorning his walls. "They've resisted for years, saying whatever will please us, and then traipsing off to their clan kivas to polish roots, rattle turkey bones, or whisper to their ancestors. Why the thlatsinas? Why now?"

Wind Leaf took a breath. "Because, Blessed Sun, many of the barbarians are starting to believe that the thlatsinas came to destroy us."

Webworm stared at him, bits of corn cake stuck to his chin. "What?"

"After the events triggered by Crow Beard's death, after Jay Bird's raid, the stories of the prophecy—"

"Gods, yes, that accursed Fire Dog prophecy! The rotted fools think that one of theirs is going to destroy the Straight Path Nation." He balled a fist, jaw hard. "You know how I feel about that, being half Mogollon myself. Some of the ignorant fools even say that I am the fulfillment of that accursed prophecy. Well, we've made a prophecy of our own: The Straight Path Nation will be reborn! Here, at Flowing Waters Town upon the Spirit River. We shall build a bigger, better Straight Path Nation. We have consecrated *this* ground. It isn't the end, War Chief, it's the new *beginning*."

"Blessed Sun, I do not disagree with you. I only report what the barbarians are saying."

Webworm relented, waving his anger away. "Yes, yes, and the Made People clans? What do your spies tell you is being whispered in their kivas? Surely they don't have any sympathy for this wrongheaded notion?"

Wind Leaf nerved himself. "For the most part . . . no. There are elements, however, for whom such an idea has a certain attraction. I've had reports that some . . ." He broke off at the wild-eyed look in Webworm's face.

"You will *crush* any such notion, War Chief. And you will do it *by whatever means necessary!*"

Wind Leaf straightened. All it would take would be a spark. Just one tiny little spark, and their whole world could go up in flames.

Seven

His name was Bulrush—after the green plants that grew in springs and seeps. He belonged to the Coyote Clan of the Made People. A thick-witted fellow from Clay Cup Village on the Green Mesas, he had never been attractive to women. People said he was stupid as well as ugly. Perhaps it was because his broad face, bland features, and slow mind just didn't captivate the female imagination. Or maybe it was because his family—dryland farmers by trade—never amassed either wealth or prestige.

Bulrush had been attending the summer solstice ceremonies at Far View Town when he first saw Gourd Pendant. He'd thought her comely. She'd been a thin sliver of a young woman with small breasts, a shy smile, and large brown eyes. Most of all, he'd wondered at her lustrous dark hair. From the first moment he glimpsed it—freshly washed with yucca soap—it had seemed to capture the sun in its blue-black length.

When he had mentioned Gourd Pendant to his mother, she had immediately approached the girl's uncle, Sage. He and the girl were of the Dust People, subsistence farmers who'd traveled in for the festivities. They actually lived in the flats just south of Thunderbird Mountain a day and a half's journey to the west-southwest. Sage had taken one look at Bulrush's full frame, sized up the thick muscles in his arms, and nodded.

To Bulrush's amazement, he was joined to the raven-haired, large-eyed beauty that very night. When morning broke the following day he and his new family were already headed down the steep southwestern trail that descended the mesa side. Two days later he walked into their shabby little farmstead.

It was poor country, windswept and subject to blowing

dust. It baked in the summer, and his teeth chattered through most of the winter. Water—perpetually scarce—was rationed by the cupful. But Gourd Pendant's people said it was blessed. From their pit house rooftops they could see World Tree Mountain where it jutted up from the Underworlds, its lines of lava roots running across the flats. Southwest of that lay the Bearclaw Mountains, from which the Dust People's ancestors had come bearing their *tchamahias*: highly prized triangular stones used expressly for channeling water from canals into ditches that fed the corn and bean fields. More than tools, *tchamahias* were emblems of ownership, each stone tied to a given piece of land and the right to operate the ditches that irrigated it.

Bulrush had looked askance at his new home—so different from the cool verdant heights of Green Mesa. The place, called Saltbush Farmstead, consisted of two pit houses, a couple of ratty ramadas, and several masonry granaries standing in an open and dusty plaza.

"It is Blessed," his new uncle-in-law, Sage, told him as he pointed at the southern tip of Thunderbird Mountain. A rocky pillar of stone jutted up from the timbered slopes. "Thunderbird alights there to rest and look south at World Tree Mountain. From his perch, he can see the place where our ancestors entered this world."

Bulrush hadn't believed it. But for the fascination of his new wife, he would have loved nothing better than to have slipped away in the night and sprinted like an antelope for the fastness of Green Mesa where it beckoned on the eastern horizon.

Nevertheless those first years had been good. Gourd Pendant's family had pitched in to construct a pit house for the newlyweds. He would never forget the night they had moved their few belongings into their new home.

How proud he'd been as he'd taken in the freshly plastered bench, the peeled pole stringers, and the juniper support posts. A mealing bin had been built against the southeastern wall, allowing Gourd Pendant to grind flour inside where the wind wouldn't wick the fine powder away. Uncle Sage had shaped a sandstone slab that could be used to regulate the air flow through the ventilator tunnel so that fire and ash didn't blow around the room. All in all, it was a tight and comfortable new home.

Together they had lit the ceremonial fire, conducted the Blessing of the *sipapu,* and admired their good fortune. Over a meal of corn cakes spiced with beeweed, roasted antelope backstrap, and cactus-tuna pudding for dessert, they had giggled, teased, and finally retired to the grass-stuffed bedding at the rear of the house. He would remember her face, half of it golden in the reflected firelight, her eyes gleaming with love. They were staring into each other's souls at that magical moment when his seed jetted into her fertile loins. Their first child, Blossom, had been born a full nine moons later.

Bulrush liked Gourd Pendant's family well enough. He had always been a good worker, and went out of his way to labor honestly, to do just a little more than they asked of him. They in turn treated him with respect, if not a little patience given his slow mind. All in all, he counted his blessings, left prayer feather offerings to the gods in gratitude, and considered himself extremely lucky.

Over the years, fortune waxed and waned at Saltbush Farmstead. They heard little of the doings of the Straight Path Nation, and cared less. Sometimes on the rare occasions when they traveled to Lanceleaf Village or Tall Piñon Town to Trade, or to watch the ceremonials, they would see the red-shirted warriors and the immaculately dressed Priests.

Then the drought had settled over them like a spectral vulture. Starvation had been staved off through the collection of wild plant seeds and a fortunate spike in the rabbit cycle. From the roofs of their homes they had seen the Rainbow Serpent as it rose against the southwestern sky like dirty smoke. Gritty gray ash had painted a perpetual dusk overhead and fallen in a thin mantle over the dry soil. Stories had come up the trails about trouble in Straight Path Canyon, of murder and witchcraft.

For five summers the rain had been spotty, the runoff in

the wash barely enough to keep the plants alive, let alone allow them to mature for harvest.

This last year had begun even worse. For weeks, Bulrush did nothing but walk, a collecting basket on his back as he gathered yucca, saltbush, stickleaf, goosefoot, cliffrose, ricegrass seeds, wild rye seeds, globemallow, squawbush berries, and cactus tunas. He hung snares for rabbits, burned out packrat nests, and even stole coyote pups from their den. If it walked, flew, or crawled, he killed it for the stew pot.

And day by day, he watched the bellies protrude on his children and saw the listlessness grow in their dull stares. Little Blossom's ribs looked like basket staves over a swollen melon. Worse, he read the desperation in Gourd Pendant's once large eyes—now sunken into her skull.

His mother-in-law wasted, slipping her food ration back into the large corrugated cooking pot. One day when her brother, Sage, awoke, she was gone from the house. They found her two days later, sitting atop a low knoll off to the west, her desiccated body savaged by buzzards.

Summer solstice passed, the heat brutal. Gourd Pendant traveled a half-day's walk each way to fetch home a brownware jug full of water from a spring they shared with the other families in the area.

The night after Uncle Sage buried his youngest daughter, he climbed down into Bulrush's house. His expression had been grim. Tears had left crooked paths on his dusty face. "We can't go on like this. I won't bury another child. Some of us have come up with an idea. We know where there is food, lots of it. But it might be dangerous."

Bulrush heard him out, all the while looking into his dying son's eyes where he lay on the worn split-willow matting. His daughter, too, was giving him a haunted stare, her face little more than a skin-covered skull pinched narrow by starvation.

What choice did a man have? Did he sit and watch his family die one by one as the flames in their souls flickered out?

Or did he act?

Ripple sat with his back to the wall. Through the smoke hole, he could see the familiar patterns of the Star People out beyond the soot-darkened ladder that stuck up through the roof. Three corrugated pots had been placed like points in a triangle around the glowing embers in the fire. Burning piñon mixed with the aroma of bubbling stew. His stomach growled so loudly his sister, Fir Brush, glared her irritation.

She had just passed her first moon as a woman, having been initiated into the Blue Stick Clan's woman's kiva. She wore her hair cut short, and it hung to the corner of her jaw, as was appropriate for a young woman eligible for marriage. When she finally took a husband, it would be expected that she grow her hair long again, befitting her status.

This night she wore a loose skirt belted at the waist with a rope. Ripple was vaguely aware of her as she knelt by the fire, stirring the stew with a wooden paddle.

To his right, his youngest sister, Slipped Bark, sat beside a bowl of piñon nuts. Employing a small stone and anvil, she cracked the hulls and used her thumbnail to pry out the meats. These she dropped into a wooden bowl. Ripple noticed that more than a few were popped into her mouth.

Because she was still a girl, Slipped Bark's hair hung down her back in a tangled black wave. Bits of pine duff, milkweed seeds, and other detritus were stuck in the mass. She wore a virgin's girdle belted around her skinny hips. At ten and one summers, her thin chest hadn't begun to swell with the first hint of womanhood.

"This vision . . ." Fir Brush began hesitantly.

"Why are you so skeptical?" Ripple shifted his back as he studied the interior of his house.

To build a home, his people excavated a waist-deep hole, round, and four paces across. They lined it with a thick sandstone foundation, wide as a man's arm, and then set four posts equidistant into the floor to support the roof. Stringers were set side-by-side leaning from the foundation to the beams; then a thick layer of juniper bark matting was laid over the whole. Finally they packed dirt over the bark matting to seal the structure. A square hole was left in the roof for entry and egress, while a ventilator shaft in the south wall admitted air and provided draft for the fire. Inside, the stone foundation was plastered over to create a combination bench and wall. During winter, the thick courses of stone absorbed heat from the fire and radiated back at night. During the summer, it acted as a cool sink, keeping the lodge interior pleasant on the hottest of days.

"You really saw Cold Bringing Woman?" Slipped Bark couldn't hide the disbelief. She never believed anything, no matter who said it.

Ripple sighed. "Do I have to repeat myself again?"

Fir Brush gave him an uneasy stare, her eyes gleaming in the yellow light. "What we believe isn't the issue, Ripple. What if the First People hear about it? They're scared enough as it is."

"And you can't forget who we are!" Slipped Bark added. "They hate us!"

"They don't hate us," Fir Brush countered. "But if this gets out, they might remember who we are."

Ripple rubbed his face. "They haven't forgotten our family. It's only been what, ten winters?"

"Ten winters," Fir Brush agreed, turning sober eyes on Slipped Bark. Their little sister had only been a year old, still dependent on mother's milk. Too young to remember what happened that terrible day. As Ripple recalled, she'd slept through most of it, even the screams. The miracle was that she'd survived his care afterward.

"I just want you to keep quiet about it, that's all," Fir Brush added. "I'll speak to Wrapped Wrist and Spots. Maybe they'll just forget you said anything."

He watched her, wondering how he'd missed the moment when she had changed from a flighty girl into this new, serious person. She might have been a middle-aged woman the way she talked and acted. But then, life hadn't allowed any of them much leisure for childhood. True, their cousins had fulfilled kin obligations and provided for them when times were tough, but for the most part, Ripple and Fir Brush had raised themselves.

He glanced at the strips of green-bark binding up in the soot-stained rafters, a symbol of their childhood construction. The knots were crude, but they still held. Not bad work for children. In the last five winters, the house hadn't fallen down around their ears. In some places the stringers had started to rot, but they'd last a couple more winters before he had to strip the upper half off and reroof it.

Ripple lifted his hands. "Who cares if they remember who we are? Cold Bringing Woman came to me. She told me what she told me. I can't change that."

"And the meat?" Fir Brush arched a slim eyebrow. "Wrapped Wrist said it really was frozen. Gods, it was still icy when you brought our quarter home. I felt it, but I can't believe it."

He glanced away. "Then don't, Sister. What you believe will not change what happened up on the mountain."

"Are you going to go find the witch?" Slipped Bark asked, voice dropping.

"Yes."

Fir Brush vented a frustrated sound and shook her head. "If this gets out, they'll hurt you, Brother!"

"I was chosen!"

She closed her eyes, expression pained. "Maybe I don't want you *chosen.* Maybe I want you here, alive, hunting and working for us. I still plan to be married, to have children, and continue our line. When I do, I'm going to need you. You're all I have left, Ripple."

"If anyone will marry you," Slipped Bark whispered. She levered another nut meat free of its shell and dropped it into the bowl.

"She'll be married," Ripple said stiffly.

"Will I?" Fir Brush straightened, tossing her head back so her hair bobbed. "Do you think anyone is going to have much to do with me if the Red Shirts come here some night, pull you out, and crack your skull open?"

Before he could speak, she added, "Assuming they don't drag Slipped Bark and me out as your accomplices and murder us, too!"

He closed his eyes and sighed in defeat. "It's not going to work that way."

Fir Brush gave him a piercing look. "Brother, if we'd been with Mother and Uncle that night, instead of sleeping at Cousin's, do you think we'd still be alive?"

He shook his head. The Blessed Sun's wrath was terrible. His warriors didn't just kill the miscreant, but as many members of the man's family as could be found. That, or the truly unlucky ones were hauled off into slavery as punishment for their transgressions.

"I'll bet you don't even remember how you got your name," Slipped Bark added.

Oh, he remembered all right. Fir Brush surely saw that reflected in the set of his mouth. She only nodded, as if to say the subject was closed.

Except it wasn't. He needed but close his eyes—and there *she* was, her pupils like midnight, staring right through to the meeting of his souls. He could see her milky cape swirling around her shoulders as it floated with her long hair. His heart beat with the cadence of her Dancing feet, the turquoise-studded moccasins flashing. Her crimson tongue flicked and twisted like an irritated buffalo's tail while sharp teeth gleamed in her dangerous mouth.

Her words whistled between his souls like a lonely winter wind: ". . . *If you endure.*"

"She chose me," he said stubbornly.

"Gods!" Fir Brush cried in despair. *"Don't do this to me!"*

Eight

Wrapped Wrist had known the woman called Blue Gentian for most of his life. That she was ten summers older than he had never mattered. Nor did it matter that she was married to a Whisper Clan man named Willow Pole. He was a minor Trader, traveling twice a moon down the river to either Flowing Waters Town or Northern Town where he exchanged vegetable dyes, squirrel hides, high-mountain plants, wooden racks, or other goods for luxury items from farther away.

As a result, Gentian often found herself alone for days at a time. Which was good news for Wrapped Wrist, because Gentian liked him—especially when her husband was away.

From Wrapped Wrist's perspective, Gentian was perfect. She cared for her husband well enough, would never leave him in fact, but she also liked coupling. She had made quite a study of it and had a great many things to teach a sturdy young man like him.

Despite the fact that Gentian had borne three children, her body remained firm. Her thick black hair swayed and shone in the light when she walked. She was an attractive woman, but some men thought her breasts too large. Narrow of waist, broad of hip, she had long slender legs that, at the moment, were clamped tightly around Wrapped Wrist's buttocks.

"Shhh! Don't move," she whispered as she clasped her arms around his shoulders. "Bless me, yes." She tilted her head back. Faint starlight illuminated the point of her chin, the angle of her cheekbones. Her eyes were like dark pools, the curl of her hair across the buffalohide a swirl of jet.

His body stiffened as she tightened her sheath around his hard penis and began to roll her hips. She lifted, straining. He pressed against the hard arch of her pubis, rotating his hips ever so slightly, and heard her explosive gasp.

She undulated against him, strangling her cries of ecstasy as waves of delight rolled through her. The tingle that had been building at the root of his penis exploded. She matched her movements to his, her sheath milking each pulse of his release.

When it was over they were both panting, gasping cool air into their overheated bodies. He heard mosquitoes whining and ignored them.

"You're going to wear me out," she finally said.

He placed his lips against her ear. "Give me a couple of breaths and we'll do it again."

She shook her head. "Can't. I've got to get back. I have a cousin coming by to pick up some things for a weaving she's making. I can be a little late. If I'm too late, well, she might come looking for me."

He nodded. "Tomorrow night?"

"My husband is due home." She traced a finger down the small of his back. "If you hadn't spent so much time carrying other people's elk home . . ."

He chuckled. "I'll see that you get some. That's meat for your pot, too."

She unlocked her legs, and he rolled off her, sitting so that the buffalohide cushioned him from the rocky ground. The air on his damp flesh sent a shiver through him.

She dressed in silence, her movements half-hidden beneath the fall of her hair. "You've become very good at pleasing a woman."

"I've come to realize that. At first I thought we were coupling on top of an anthill. Then I realized it wasn't biting insects that were making you jump."

She punched him playfully on the arm, giggling. "Silly. You did a little hopping yourself."

She stood, pulling her hair back and combing it with her fingers. "I'll leave the signal for you."

When she was available she left a broken piece of pottery propped against her wall.

He watched her walk off into the darkness and sighed. A weary ecstasy lingered in his loins, warm and tingling.

He rubbed his face, shivered again, and pulled his hunting shirt over his head. Standing, he was tying his belt around his waist when an unfamiliar male voice from the darkness said, "We must talk, Wrapped Wrist."

For a moment, he froze, horrified, then, heart beating, turned and stared at the dark shadows in the surrounding brush. "Who's there?"

A thin shape moved in the inky recesses of sweet sumac, serviceberry, and scrub oak. Wrapped Wrist could make out a man, older, taller than he. Not that it took much to be taller.

"You *will* come with me."

That voice . . . Wrapped Wrist was sure he knew it. "Who are you?"

"Hmm. If you spent more time with elders, and less driving yourself into other men's wives, you might know to whom you speak." A pause. "Collect your things, then come."

The figure turned, walking carefully on the path that wound through the brushy labyrinth.

Wrapped Wrist hesitated. *If he was here to kill me, he'd have done it before I stood up.*

He bent down and plucked up the half buffalohide, folding it as he followed in the man's footsteps.

The way led west down one of the many trails that crisscrossed First Moon Mountain. When they approached any of the dwellings that dotted the slope, the shadowy figure circled wide, picking his way through the irregular footing. Once, when a dog barked from the shadows of a ramada, the man whispered something.

To Wrapped Wrist's amazement, the cur immediately went silent and lay down.

Who is he that he can command other people's beasts?

"Elder, could you tell me—"

"Hush!"

He puzzled at the shadowy form walking ahead of him. It moved like an old man, making those slow careful steps, almost as if he were feeling his way. The elder's body was thin, slightly stooped. In the open patches of starlight, he appeared to be bent and frail, but while they were passing under the shadows, the old man seemed to grow Powerful and strong, as though drawing strength from the very darkness. Wrapped Wrist experienced the uncomfortable prickling sensation of fear as it danced on his skin.

They had followed the main trail down the mountain for almost a hand of time before they emerged onto the saddle that led to the Dog's Tooth. The old man took the narrow ridgetop trail. Here and there ponderosa pine and juniper still dotted the way. Then they began the slow climb up the northwest side of the Dog's Tooth itself.

A three-sided point of sandstone, the formation jutted defiantly from the foot of First Moon Mountain. It over-looked the confluence of the River of Stones and First Moon Creek. The summit was capped by a walled enclosure that surrounded a two-story building, two great kivas belonging to the Blue Stick and Whisper clans, and an assortment of pit houses. Wrapped Wrist had visited there before—what young man hadn't?—but he had never been there at night, and never under such odd circumstances as this.

Whisper Clan? Could his shadowy guide be one of Willow Pole's relatives? Someone tired of seeing his kin humiliated? Wrapped Wrist winced and glanced back at the shadows cast by the trees. He could just slip away, ghost off into the darkness where no one—

"Stay with me, young hunter. It will go hard on you if you run."

Wrapped Wrist swallowed so loudly the elder had to hear.

"Reading your thoughts is no challenge," the man added. "Keep that in mind when we reach our destination."

They climbed past several more of the square-roofed pit houses and finally scrambled the last little bit up to a gate that pierced the northern wall. The two-story building could be seen rising above the eastern wall, its shape faintly bathed in rose light from a dying fire. Pit houses, like stubby sentinels, crowded around the wattle-and-daub walls of the great kivas. Several stone granaries could be seen, their doorways darker squares in the night.

"In here." The man indicated a pit house; he hitched his slow way up a ladder leaned against the wall. He paused, panting, as he stepped onto the roof. "Oh, and leave that hide outside, will you? It bears the smells—both yours and hers—of rutting humans. I would prefer to breathe less irritating air."

Wrapped Wrist nodded and lowered the hide to the ground. As he started up the ladder, the man added, "Too bad I can't leave *your* stench outside as well."

Wrapped Wrist stepped onto the roof, taking a quick glance at the stars. They frosted the inky sky, giving way to a ragged horizon of blackness where the mountains thrust jaggedly upward.

The old man had already climbed down into the interior. Wrapped Wrist, baited by his last opportunity to run, reluctantly grabbed the polished poles of the ladder and climbed down. The sweet scent of piñon smoke rose around him as he descended into the warm interior.

He hadn't spent much time atop the Dog's Tooth. He knew that the kiva keepers and Priests lived here, ensuring that the roofs were repaired, that packrats and mice didn't invade, and that the weeds didn't grow around. The keepers kept the plaster fresh and made sure that nothing profaned the sacred grounds.

His feet thumped onto hard dirt. A dim red glow came from the fire pit, but other than that he could see nothing but the four roof supports in the reddish hue. Whatever was going to happen wasn't going to be pleasant. But if it turned ugly? Did he dare defend himself? And if he did, where was that going to end? In a clan feud?

Cloth rustled, and a handful of sticks clattered onto the coals. The place smelled like roasted sage leaves. Warmth began seeping into his pores after the night's chill.

Flames, as if alive, suddenly leapt up around the sticks. Wrapped Wrist was facing the south wall, so the first thing he saw was the sandstone slab that deflected the gusts of wind that sometimes jetted out of the ventilator. Next he took in the bench, plastered in white clay. A series of small figurines rested atop it. To either side of the ventilator were Dance masks, one of a buffalo face, the other an eagle's. Large white jars had been placed in a row on the floor. Each was sealed with a juniper-wood lid.

"You are not familiar with such places?" the voice asked from behind him.

Maybe the best defense was to make the first threat. Wrapped Wrist turned, raising a finger in preparation to launch into the old man—and stopped cold.

For a moment, all he could see was the shining white eye. It seemed to glow with a light of its own, like a pebble of frosted ice. That single terrible eye dominated the old man's face. Where the man's left eye should have been, a black pit extended back into the skull. Dark and wrinkled, the man's face puckered around that gaping orbit. Even his long nose appeared warped out of shape, as if repelled by the white orb, and drawn toward the dark socket.

In that instant Wrapped Wrist knew fear as he had never known it. His mouth went dry, his knees weak. A runny sensation loosened his guts.

The old man grinned, the expression pulling the lines of his ancient face into monstrous shapes.

"Old White Eye," Wrapped Wrist rasped through a tight throat.

"Ah, so you do know me. That's something, little though it might be in your case."

Gods, how could he have found me and Gentian? How did he walk across half the mountain, blind as a desert mole?

"There are other ways to see . . . not that a young man with your apparent inclinations would be interested in them."

"You do hear my thoughts!" Wrapped Wrist cupped a hand around one of the ladder rungs, ready to scramble up and out the smoke hole into the safety of the night.

"I find it to be no challenge, simple boy. Now, let loose of that ladder or I'll have that oversized prize you enjoy so much shriveled into a potter's coil before I'm through."

Wrapped Wrist's fingers slipped off the worn rung, and he fought the urge to cup his suddenly vulnerable male parts. "What do you want?"

"What stories do they tell about me?"

His tongue seemed thick in his mouth. "That you are

not really human. That you talk to the dead. Some people call you a witch. It is said that the animals tell you things, and you speak their languages. Some say you were dead yourself once, and after four days, you came back to life."

Old White Eye gave a slight wave of his wrinkled hand, as if dismissing the idea. "Sometimes reputations serve us well, don't they?"

"I—I don't understand."

That horrible white eye fixed on him.

"Your reputation brought you Blue Gentian, didn't it? Wasn't she drawn to you because of the rumors? Hmm? Wasn't she curious to find out if they were true?" The smile was anything but reassuring. "And, fortunately for you, they were. She found herself enchanted by your shaft. It filled her in a way she had always hoped for."

"Elder, please listen. I'm sorry. I'll never touch the woman again. It was a mistake. I know it could cause problems if Willow Pole ever—"

"Quiet!" The glowing white eye pinned him. "The trouble you will make for Blue Stick Clan is nothing compared to what I wish to talk to you about. But, just to show that I am not without a certain pity for the young and stupid, here's how it will go if you persist in slipping your staff into the artful Gentian's willing sheath. Willow Pole will eventually figure it out, as he has in the past. When he does, you, young hunter, will most likely vanish into the forest, and perhaps, someday, your bones will be tripped over by some other hunter." He tilted his head, the movement birdlike. "You see, unlike you, Willow Pole understands the ramifications of clan politics. When he deals with you, it will be quietly, where no one knows. He will not leave a mess for his clan to clean up through expensive reparations in order to keep the peace."

This time Wrapped Wrist's swallow stuck halfway down his throat.

Old White Eye let him stew on that for a long time. The only sound was the slight moan of the wind in the ventilator and the crackling sparks as the wood burned down.

In a gentler voice, the old man finally said, "Very well. Now, let's get to the important matter."

"Yes, Elder."

"Your friend, Ripple."

For a matter of heartbeats, Wrapped Wrist's soul stumbled in confusion. "Ripple? He has nothing to do with Gentian. She doesn't even—"

"It might save everyone a great deal of trouble if you simply walk up to Willow Pole, tell him how his wife is dancing on your manhood, and let him kill you."

Wrapped Wrist's mouth was hanging open stupidly. He snapped it closed.

The old man continued, "You're not very smart. Knowing that, you would be well advised to *listen* before you speak."

Wrapped Wrist nodded vigorously.

"You were on the mountain with Ripple? You carried an elk quarter down for him?"

"Yes, Elder. I still have some. It's good meat, and I'd be honored to bring you a portion of the best—"

"Gods, boy. *Hush!*"

At the tone, Wrapped Wrist lost his ability to breathe.

Old White Eye glared for a moment, then, as if speaking to a simple child, said, "The rumor is that he had a vision. Is it true?"

It took a moment for Wrapped Wrist to find his voice. "Yes, Elder. At least, I think so."

"You think so?"

He nodded.

"Did he or didn't he?"

Wrapped Wrist made a futile gesture. "Well, he says he did. He says that Cold Bringing Woman came to him in the night. That she said the First People could be destroyed. I know Ripple believes it. And the elk, Elder . . ."

"Yes?"

"It was frozen solid. All four quarters. And the plants around them, they were wilted, the way they would be after an early frost."

The old man pondered that. Wrapped Wrist waited, afraid to say anything more.

"What else?" the old man asked.

"Ripple thinks he needs to go find the Mountain Witch. Something about allies in strange places."

Finally, the old man nodded. "Yes, for the first time, this makes sense."

"Elder?"

The old man waved it away and turned his single baleful eye on Wrapped Wrist. "You, and your friends, must see that he reaches her."

Wrapped Wrist frowned in confusion.

"Don't you understand, boy? If I have heard of this vision, it won't be long before the First People up in their abominable great house will hear of it, too. And when they do, they are going to want to have a little talk with you, Ripple, and the rest of your innocent friends."

Wrapped Wrist felt his guts drop.

"The First People are frightened right now," White Eye continued. "Their world is changing. The rains no longer come like they used to. Crops are dying in the fields. The Underworlds are angry. Remember how the Rainbow Serpent rose into the sky just after Talon Town was sacked and Sternlight was killed? The First People certainly haven't forgotten. Now Matron Featherstone is dead." He smiled like a hungry bear. "And soon the First People's Priests will be returning to our mountain for the Moon ceremony."

"Yes, Elder."

"Go. Find your friends and take this vision to the Mountain Witch. When Ripple has spoken to her, send Bad Cast back to me. No one will suspect him, and unlike you or your peculiarly colored companion, no one will notice him."

"Yes, Elder."

That horrible white eye seemed to burn into his very souls. "If there is a way . . . I want to thrust a burning branch right through the heart of the First People. Do you understand?"

Wrapped Wrist nodded as he scrambled up the ladder, missed a rung, and almost fell. He caught himself before leaping the last bit out onto the roof. Heedless of the outside ladder, he jumped to the dark ground and sprinted headlong into the darkness.

It was half a hand of time later that he remembered his buffalohide—but didn't have the courage to go back and retrieve it.

Matron Larkspur understood the effect her body had on men. In the case of the Trader called Takes Falls, it worked to her absolute advantage. He was a member of the Made People's Coyote Clan and had married a local First Moon woman who lived in a village on the west side of the mountain. He imported enough exotic items for the woman's kinsmen that they accepted him for the most part, and he shared many of their confidences, and all of their gossip.

Takes Falls was no one's fool. As one of the more influential men in the community, he had come to pay his respects just after Larkspur had taken over administration of Pinnacle Great House. A Trader who stood in the Matron's good graces had an advantage over his peers—and Takes Falls, being ambitious, was willing to take whatever advantage he could get.

She had seen the effect her beauty had on him during that first meeting, and had made a point of encouraging his attraction over the passing moons.

She was stringing beads when he arrived in the plaza, asking to see her. She let him wait.

The beads she worked with were a present from her cousin, Desert Willow. They had come in a striking black-on-white jar capped with a stone lid that had been sealed to the rim with pine pitch. Inside had been a wealth of tiny stone and shell beads.

The value of a bead was directly tied to its size; the ones Desert Willow had sent were among the smallest Larkspur had ever seen. To craft them had taken a master beadsmith. First the raw shell—Traded from the distant western ocean, carried across the deserts to the Hohokam, thence to the Fire Dogs, and finally to the Straight Path Nation—had been ground into thin sections. The artisan then sifted clean sand through fabric to obtain the finest of grit. A thorn was fitted to the shank of a small bow drill, wetted, and dipped in the grit. Then, with the greatest of care, the hole was drilled. Using that as a center, the next step employed a hollow tube of bird or rodent bone. This, too, was fitted to the bow drill, dampened, and dipped in the fine grit. Consummate skill was required to cut an even circle around the hole.

Mixed among the white shell, a smaller number of beads had been cut out of thin sections of bloodred slate, while others were from black jet. The challenge for Larkspur was to manufacture a single necklace from the thousands of tiny beads in the jar. To augment the value of the beads themselves, it would have to be a single strand that could be looped time and again to hang from her neck. Her contribution included not only the pattern but spinning a single cotton-and-buffalo-wool thread to go the length. That thread had to be small enough to pass through the tiny hole but still strong enough to bear the weight of stone and shell. If it broke at the wrong moment—say, perhaps in a ceremony—the tiny beads would cascade to the ground and be forever lost.

Stringing the beads wasn't a task for the farsighted. She used a flat section of river cobble polished smooth by eons of water. The gray schist contrasted to the white, red, and black beads. She used a cactus thorn to pick the beads off the rock. A tiny dab of pine pitch attached her thread to the base of the thorn and pulled it through the bead.

She finished another repetition of the pattern: ten white, one red, five white, one black, five white, one red, and so on. As she had laid it out, the colors would align when she settled the fifty or so loops of beads around her throat. She had measured the length so that they would hang just below the notch of her sternum and contour to the swell of her breasts.

Laying the needle down, she took a sip of peppergrass and blazing-star seed tea. She used a bone spoon made from a mountain sheep humerus to dip more of the tiny seeds from the jar.

"I will see Takes Falls now," she called as she picked up her needle and bent to the task of spearing the beads one by one from the smooth stone work surface.

She heard his steps on the clay outside before he entered her room. His glance went surreptitiously to her, and then to her belongings where they lined the walls. He was seeing colorful blankets dyed all the colors of a desert rainbow, beautiful dresses adorned with beadwork, feathers, and gleaming shell. A collection of turquoise pendants sat on a polished split-cedar box in the back. Lines of delicate white jars decorated in the fine-lined black patterns of the Blue Dragonfly Clan lined the north wall. The ladder tips extending through the floor opening in the rear of the room marked the way down to her bedchamber. His gaze seemed to stop there, a longing in his dark brown eyes.

"Can I be of service, Trader?" she asked coyly, raising an eyebrow.

"Oh, Matron, yes. I have come with news." He tore his gaze from her bedroom entrance, centering it on the bit of bare floor between his dusty feet. She noticed that he wore yucca sandals with plaited cords at the toe and heel.

"Don't tell me it's that the Blessed Webworm has returned to Flowing Waters Town."

He looked confused, then said, "He has?"

"The period of mourning for the Blessed Featherstone is officially over. We can smile again. The signal went up from Smoking Mirror Butte yesterday."

"Oh . . . good." Now he stared at her breasts, his lips making the smallest of puckering movements.

"Did you just come for my company, Trader?" She flashed him a smile, glancing sidelong from the beads she'd lined onto the tiny cactus thorn.

"Your company is always a joy, Matron, but no. There is news." He seemed to hesitate.

She pinched the beads between thumb and forefinger, running the cactus thorn back and forth through their holes. "News among the First Moon People?"

"Yes. I just heard it last night."

"You seem reluctant to speak."

His gaze was fixed on the cactus spine as it slid smoothly in and out of the beads. "It wouldn't be good if anyone associated me with this—"

"Of course not. I never want anyone to know what you tell me."

"Well, I don't know if it's important, but you always told me that if anything concerning the First People came up, I should tell you."

"Then, tell, Trader."

"Well, it seems that some hunter has had a vision."

The thorn went still in her hand. "A vision? Of what sort?"

Nine

Bulrush had traveled with Uncle Sage and two of their neighbors to this place four days' walk north of Saltbush Farmstead. They had passed along little-used trails by night, slept in thickets and patches of trees during the day. Now Bulrush found himself in a dense grove of darkened juniper at the edge of the rimrock just below Tall Piñon Town.

The night was dark, the moon in its first quarter, and low on the horizon. Bulrush, Uncle Sage, one of the neighbors named Made Clay, and Two Stone, Uncle's cousin, crouched in the darkness and stared at the cluster of buildings on the mesa top. They looked like oversized squares dropped here and there in an irregular pattern. The beaten ground around the settlement appeared pale against the darker mosaic of wilted cornfields. The drought had wreaked its havoc here in the Deep Canyon highlands, too.

"The dogs might be a problem," Uncle said. "But then, people come and go from this place all the time."

Bulrush reached down and grasped the straps of his burden basket. "Which one is the warehouse?"

"That one." Made Clay pointed to the great house on the northwestern corner of the U-shaped complex of buildings. A story taller than the others, it was the largest of the structures in Tall Piñon Town. "The problem is that we've got to work silently. The Blessed Sun's warriors live there, along with the Priests."

"Didn't you say they were all gone?" Uncle reminded.

"War Chief Leather Hand is supposed to have taken most of the warriors to Windflower Village for the reconsecration of the great kiva. There should only be a few Priests, if anybody, guarding the storerooms."

"What if they hear us?" Bulrush asked. A slow fear had lain hold of his heart. That he had to do this for his family didn't make it any less terrifying.

Two Stone touched the war club hanging on his belt. "We silence whoever comes to investigate."

"What if it's one of the First People?" Tension made Uncle's voice shrill.

"What if it is?" Two Stone shrugged. "Look, the important thing is to get out with the food. Once we're off the mesa, we head straight east on the main road. We skirt around the head of the canyons. After we're a day's walk from here, no one will ever be able to pick out our trail. We're just another party of Traders, maybe headed home after the rededication of the great kiva over in Lanceleaf Village. Or we stopped to visit family along the River of Sorrow, and they gave us this food. No one will be able to prove it was us who stole from the First People's warehouse."

Uncle added, "We're not the only ones watching our families starve. If it gets out that someone stole from them, others will try it. Maybe they'll get all the blame."

Bulrush just nodded, wishing that worry would stop chewing at his guts.

It started out well enough. Granted, they were all weak,

their bellies gaunted into knots under their ribs; but they walked carefully up the trail between two of the Tall Piñon clan villages, past the round wall of the great kiva, and up to the First People's great house. Grit scraped on the bottom of their yucca-fiber sandals as they climbed the stone steps to the first level. The night was silent but for the faint sigh of wind and the distant *hooo-hooo* of an owl.

When he was a child, Bulrush had heard a flicker pounding on a hollow piñon out in the forest. Now his heart hammered like that; could no one hear it but him? Every nerve prickled with danger as he stepped out onto the roof. In the dim sliver of moonlight, he could just make out the rising floors of the great house before him.

The great house really was huge, rising three stories in places. He had seen the buildings at Far View, of course, but he didn't remember them being as majestic as this. The stairway Uncle Sage had led them up opened onto the angle of a darkly shadowed ell.

"Which way?" Two Stone asked.

"Here." Made Clay pointed, leading past roof openings that yawned like black death. The ladders poking from their depths might have been the lances of the ancestors. Made Clay continued: "I carried corn baskets here after harvest one year."

"Shhh!" Uncle cautioned as he looked warily this way and that up at the imposing walls that rose around them.

Two painted figures seemed to Dance on the shadowed plaster walls. Bulrush pointed. "Who's that?"

"The Yamuhakto," Made Clay hissed in return. "They're paintings, you simple fool."

Bulrush tried to swallow. His guts knotted painfully, his knees weak. He could see the two war gods staring at him through vengeful eyes.

Made Clay stopped at a doorway in the darkest shadow cast by the walls. A sandstone slab had been rolled in front of the entry. Made Clay got Bulrush to grasp the other side of the heavy stone. It was a measure of his feebleness that it took two tries to move it.

Made Clay ducked over the threshold and vanished into

the black maw. Moments later, he stuck his head out. "This is it. It's full of shelled corn, squashes . . . It smells like a living Dream."

Two Stone ducked in, and then Uncle. Bulrush froze, unable to move.

Uncle leaned back out. "You coming?"

"I . . . I can't."

"Then give me your basket."

Somehow Bulrush managed to slip his burden basket from his shoulder and extend it.

He was panting, staring fearfully at the tall walls that rose on either side. He could feel the implacable stare of the Yamuhakto boring through the gloom. High overhead the Star People glistened in a wash of patterns. Gods, he wished he was up there with them. Nothing had ever scared him like this.

But, if it saved his children, brought them one more season until the rains came again, it would be worth it.

He swallowed hard. And if the First People killed him here? Well, what did it matter? A blow from one of the Blessed Sun's warriors would be more merciful than burying his children in shallow graves and watching Gourd Pendant waste until, like her mother, she walked out to die alone.

No, as he loved her, he would see this through. Nerving himself, he ducked into the dark storeroom.

"Here, feel by the wall," Uncle told him. "Empty these seed jars into your basket."

Two Stone was the first to finish, slipping out through the doorway with his burden basket. Then Made Clay and Uncle followed. When corn kernels pattered on the floor, Bulrush knew his basket was full. He was in the process of hoisting it up to his shoulder when it hit something in the darkness.

A pot shattered on the floor behind him with a hollow pop. It might have been the crack of a lightning bolt so silent was the night.

Bulrush froze, fearing his heart had battered its way right through his chest.

"Hurry!" Uncle's voice came as an urgent hiss.

Bulrush, no matter what his other faults, had always obeyed. He ducked out, thankful for the faint moonlight, terrified that he would find it full of swarming warriors. The dimly lit roof was vacant but for his companions.

"What was that?" Two Stone demanded, stooped from his burden.

"I don't—"

Light flashed to one side, and a strange voice asked something unintelligible.

Bulrush turned, seeing a white-dressed figure as it ducked out of the next chamber. Light speared darkness again as the leather door hanging swung to the side.

Two Stone never hesitated. He turned, his club hissing through the air. Then came the sharp wet snap as the stone head caved in the man's skull. White fluttered as the Priest collapsed, falling so hard he bounced on the packed clay roof with a thud.

"What did you do?" Bulrush squeaked in terror.

"Shhh!" Two Stone swung his basket down. "Help me." He stared back at Bulrush as he stooped over the Priest. "Don't just stand there like a knob on a pot. Help!"

Bulrush swung his basket down. Together he and Two Stone dragged the limp body back through the doorway the Priest had emerged from.

Bulrush gaped in spite of his fear. For a moment he thought they were real, so perfectly rendered were the figures of the old gods who Danced across the walls. Nor was that all. Along one wall gorgeous bowls, white as snow, were decorated in perfect black patterns, hatched with fine lines. And there, beside the hearth, a stew was still steaming.

"Gods," Two Stone said in awe as he looked around the painted walls. "Have you ever seen such a place?"

"Never." Bulrush stared down at the Priest where he lay limp on the floor. Blood leaked down from the crown of the man's head. The eyes were wide, staring, the mouth opened in disbelief. Long black hair, freshly washed, streamed out to glisten in the light. The floor beneath the body was covered with beautifully dyed fabrics woven in intricate patterns. A gorgeous scarlet macaw-feather cloak hung from a peg.

Bulrush started, bit off a cry of fear, and gasped in relief as he recognized that the faces staring at him from shelves in the back of the room were brightly painted masks. He recognized Spider Woman and the Flute Player, but couldn't place the ogre-looking thing with the big mouth full of teeth.

But it was the painting of the Blue God on the wall that obsessed him. She seemed to be staring, the black hole of her mouth anxiously agape, eyes like molten jet pinned on his.

"Here." Two Stone tossed him a leather belt pouch that he'd taken from a wooden shelf. As Bulrush fingered it, Two Stone grabbed another for himself and quickly knotted it to his belt. Then, pulling up the hem of his shirt to create a pouch, he emptied one of the small decorated jars into it and tied it off.

Bulrush glanced at the two ladder tips that protruded from an opening in the floor. He hesitated. What additional great wonders might be down there?

"Forget it. We've got enough." Two Stone grabbed up the stew pot and was on his way to the door, calling, "Let's go."

"What about him?" Bulrush pointed at the dead Priest.

"Do you want to stay and bury him?"

"No."

"Then, by those unholy gods on the wall there, let's get out of here. We want to be far enough away by dawn that they'll never find us."

Bulrush nodded before he ducked out into the night. As he shouldered his burden basket, he could remember the hungry eyes of the Blue God where she'd Danced, her arms extended. In his heart, Bulrush knew she reached out for him. And, should she catch him, starvation would be the much better death.

Ten

The sky glowed with a transparent luminosity. A few faint stars gleamed defiantly against the coming dawn. Ripple had heard Traders say that the sky looked different from the lofty heights of First Moon Mountain, that even the finest quartz would be envious of its crystalline quality.

He quietly climbed the pit house ladder, making sure he didn't rattle his atlatl and darts as he emerged through the smoke hole. With great care he set foot onto his clay-packed roof and felt the timbers give slightly under his weight. When it did, he knew, dirt sifted through the cedar-bark matting to trickle down into the house. This morning he hoped it wouldn't wake Fir Brush. He didn't want to deal with her adamant insistence that he forget this mad venture.

Step by step he eased to the edge of the roof and picked his way down the outside ladder to the ground. Not for the first time did he wish that instead of high on the mountain, his family had built their home lower on the slopes, maybe even in the valley, despite its colder climate. As it was, he had a good hand's journey ahead of him just to make it as far as First Moon Creek. The only good news was that it was all downhill.

People would be up by the time he made the First Moon trail. They'd see him, and eventually the story would get back to Spots, Bad Cast, and Wrapped Wrist.

You didn't come to us first? He could hear their crying protests. *You left us behind!*

No, my friends. There is no reason for you to risk your-selves. I was the one who was called. It falls to me, alone, to make my way to the Mountain Witch.

He shivered at the thought. Making a face, he started for the trees that clustered along the eastern rimrock. The square bulk of the watchtower jutted against the lightening sky. Three stories tall, it overlooked the First Moon Valley. From its heights, a keen-eyed observer would be able to follow his progress as he headed up the valley later that morning. Would Fir Brush be up there, searching for her missing brother when he didn't show up for breakfast?

The Mountain Witch!

A tingle of worry ran through him. As he'd dozed that night waiting for first light, he'd wondered about the Mountain Witch. Why, in the name of the gods, had Cold Bringing Woman told him to go search her out? What could the Mountain Witch do for him that Cold Bringing Woman herself couldn't?

On his back, his pack swung with each step. He'd packed corn cakes, a ceramic canteen, strips of jerked turkey meat, his fire bow, a length of cord, a stone knife and scraper, some hardened pitch, his sleeping blanket, and a container of grease.

How did one go about finding a witch? Worse, when he found her, what did he say? "Good morning, I'm Ripple. I'm chosen to destroy the First People."

Right. And then she'd turn him into a packrat's liver, or suck his souls out through his nostrils, or something equally abysmal.

He thought it a monument to his courage that he could even contemplate searching out such a dangerous being as a witch; yet here he was, bravely walking forth to face her, to look into her eyes.

What if she steals my souls?

Well, Cold Bringing Woman wouldn't allow that to happen, would she?

"She said I have to be tested," he muttered under his breath as he entered the shadows of the trees. His nerves squirmed as he considered the ways a witch could test a person.

"She said I had to endure great suffering." A tingle of fear shot through him. When a person got right down to it, there were a lot of ways a witch could inflict great suffering. He was thinking of curses that made a man's eyeballs

fall out of his head, or that opened oozing sores on his
shins and elbows. What if she clapped her hands and
caused his body to jerk in fits like the ones that had afflicted Bad Cast's great uncle Black Root?

Preoccupied thus, he jumped when a dark figure
stepped out from the trees, asking in an accented voice,
"You are a hunter called Ripple?"

"Yes, I . . ." Squinting, he tried to identify the burly form,
realizing too late just what kind of shirt the man wore.

Ripple hadn't even begun to turn before two strong
arms clamped tightly about his chest from behind. As they
tightened, they drove the air from his lungs. Two more
warriors appeared on either side, one ripping his atlatl and
darts from his hand, the other tearing his pack off his
shoulder.

"We're going to see the Matron," the first warrior said.
The rest laughed as their hard hands trussed him securely
with a braided leather rope.

Ripple opened his mouth to scream, only to have a hard
fist slammed into his kidneys.

The last thought in his head was, *This can't be happening! I'm chosen!*

"Hello!"

Bad Cast blinked his sleep-heavy eyes open. He lay in
the warm comfort of his bed. The familiar furnishings of
Soft Cloth's house came into focus: the support beams,
the faint thread of smoke from the fire pit, the clay-
plastered benches with their lines of ceramic jars, sandal
lasts, and folded stacks of blankets and clothing.

Had it been part of the Dream, or did someone have the
bad manners to wake him from the most peaceful slumber? Through bleary eyes he saw a pale dawn sky beyond
the ladder uprights where they jutted out the smoke hole. A
head, haloed by the light, intruded into the square and
stared down at him. From the dangling braids it was a man.

"Hey! Wake up!" the voice prodded.

"Wrapped Wrist? Go away." Bad Cast settled his head back and felt Soft Cloth's warm body snuggle against his beneath the thin deerhide that covered them.

He was dropping back into slumber's gentle caress, satisfied to have Soft Cloth's sleek buttocks cradled in his crotch. The line of her back pressed against his chest, and he absently snugged his arm around her shoulders.

"I said, wake up!"

"Can't you go find a wasps' nest in need of tormenting?" Bad Cast opened his eye to a slit, seeing that the head was still silhouetted in his smoke hole.

"We've got to go get Spots," Wrapped Wrist continued. "I'd have been here earlier, but for you living halfway across the valley and on top of Juniper Ridge."

"Wazzit?" Soft Cloth shifted away from him, pulling the blanket with her so cool air slipped across his skin.

"I don't believe this." Bad Cast had been planning on rising late, after he and Soft Cloth repeated the languid coupling they'd engaged in the night before.

"Believe it," Wrapped Wrist added seriously. "We're in trouble."

Bad Cast opened both eyes and sat up. The deerhide fell away from his torso, ensuring he knew it was a cool morning. "What do you mean, in trouble?"

Soft Cloth growled, her eyes open now. Curls of her long black hair matted on her cheeks. She propped herself on one elbow, squinting up at the smoke hole through puffy eyes.

Wrapped Wrist shifted on the roof. A fine trickle of dirt sifted down through the still air. "I had a visitor last night."

"Only one? I would have thought you'd have a line by the time you got back."

"Don't joke. You'll never guess who."

Soft Cloth muttered dryly, "Given your reputation, I'd guess the Blessed Matron Featherstone? Or was it that other one? Cornsilk, is it? The one who would be Matron of the First People if she wasn't Outcast?"

"It was old White Eye."

That didn't make sense. Bad Cast grimaced, rubbed a

knuckle in his eye, and said, "What? You mean the old shaman?"

"That's him." Wrapped Wrist's tone didn't leave much doubt.

"Why? What have you done this time? Wait. Don't tell me. He has a daughter, and you just happened to get caught polishing your stick inside her?"

"No! Nothing like that."

"All right, what did you two do?" Soft Cloth demanded, first looking at Bad Cast, then twisting her head to squint up at Wrapped Wrist where he hung like a vulture.

"It's not us . . . I mean me or Bad Cast. It's Ripple."

"Ripple?" Bad Cast reached out and pulled the deerhide so that it covered Soft Cloth's enchanting body. "What's Ripple done?"

"He had a vision," Wrapped Wrist said dully.

Soft Cloth shook her hair back. "This story he's telling about Cold Bringing Woman? About being able to destroy the First People? Is that what White Eye wants to know about?"

"It seems that he already knows."

"So?" she pressed.

"He believes."

Bad Cast winced. "And he wants us to . . . what?"

"Take Ripple to the Mountain Witch."

"Absolutely not!" Soft Cloth cried, bolting upright.

Bad Cast made an appeasing gesture, saying, "Wait. Let's think this thing through."

"There's *nothing* to think through," she insisted. "You're not going near any witch. If Wrapped Wrist and Ripple got themselves into this mess, they can get themselves out of it."

He could see no give in her hard eyes, or in the set of her mouth. He shot an apologetic look up and shrugged.

Wrapped Wrist's expression had gone grim. "You don't have any choice, friend. White Eye named you specifically. He wants you to carry messages from the Mountain Witch's camp."

"Why me?" Bad Cast cried, sensing Soft Cloth's building rage.

"He said that no one would suspect you." Wrapped

Wrist pulled back from the smoke hole, standing as he called down, "I'll meet you at high sun at Ripple's. You'll need a little time to pack."

"Wait!" Bad Cast cried, stumbling up from the bedding. But Wrapped Wrist was already gone. The baby was crying, having been wakened.

From the hot glare in Soft Cloth's eyes, there would be no languid lovemaking this morning.

Eleven

Leather Hand considered his personal empire as he climbed out of the last canyon and onto the ridgeline that would finally take him to Tall Piñon Town.

His domain embraced a landscape of high mountains rising above sandstone, limestone, and shale plateaus. Spruce and fir forests on the slopes of the Spirit Mountains ceded to piñon-juniper woodlands patched with ponderosa, edged by oak, serviceberry, and currant brush on the plateaus. It in turn gave way to scrub oak, sage, rabbitbrush, chamisa, and four-wing saltbush in the canyons and drainages. Finally to the southwest lay desert where the rabbitbrush and greasewood grew sparse, clinging to dunes and sand shadows. Alternating with dirt and rock, a few clump grasses held sway, waiting for the occasional spring, monsoon, or fall rain. In places the open basins consisted of clay, scabbed here and there with calluses of saltbush or the few spears of sickly grass.

It was a land of color, ranging from bloodred sandstone formations to yellow clay and sand, or, in places, gray silt and black shale. The darker greens of juniper and piñon clashed with a brighter verdure of cottonwood, ash, and willow in the stream bottoms.

Above it all was the sky—a vast dome of the most impossible blue, ever in contrast with stone, soil, leaf, or flower. Color was everywhere, and this more than anything else perpetually left him feeling humbled.

He had grown up in Fourth Night House, one of the Straight Path Nation's great houses far to the southeast, where the land's only color was a dull yellow leached from the soil and eroding sandstone. Even the sky there had a pale hue, more brassy with a perpetual haze.

His family, First People of the Red Lacewing Clan, had lived in the compact two-story multiroom great house. Their settlement consisted of three extended families who shared a patchwork of gravel-mulched farm plots. While his mother had been the Matron his father's duty to the Blessed Sun had been to protect and maintain the turquoise trail that led to the mines in the foothills east of the Great River.

On the day young Leather Hand had first traveled westward and entered Straight Path Canyon, he had been awed by the tall buff sandstone walls that contrasted to the pristine white of the great houses. It was as if color had finally burst into his life. Now, as he led his party up out of Deep Canyon, he swore he would never live without it.

The land surrounding Tall Piñon Town was an uplifted plateau cut by deep canyons that ran off to the southwest. The effect was as if a giant bear had grooved an overturned bowl with mighty claws. The flat ridgetops were treed in juniper and piñon, cleared here and there by means of slash-and-burn for agriculture. Thick loamy soil made for productive crops when the rains came. Below the rimrock, seeps dotted the canyon walls, most of them having been exploited for small cornfields. The narrow canyon bottoms themselves were stippled with fields, diversion dams, and rough ditches to capture any summer runoff.

For generations prior to the coming of the First People, the locals had prospered here. Many still lived in the same style of pit house that their ancestors had first cut out of the ground hundreds of sun cycles before. They had cleared plots, grown their corn, beans, and squash, lived and died with the regularity of the seasons. So, too, had they warred among themselves, clan fighting clan, tribe fighting tribe, until the Blessed Sun's red-shirted warriors had enforced the peace.

Now all they had built was in jeopardy. Stories circulated along the trails: tales of the dead Snake Head's witchcraft; of Jay Bird's raid; and of the new Prophet, Poor Singer. Even from here, high atop Tall Piñon Town, everyone had seen the Rainbow Serpent rise into the southwestern sky, its plume of smoke obscuring the sacred mountain.

It was whispered that the First People's Power was broken.

How do I combat that?

Leather Hand let the retinue straggling behind him catch their breath as they entered the shade of a clump of piñon trees. Twenty of his warriors followed in two ranks. Sweat streaked their faces and darkened their red shirts. Round wicker shields hung from their backs, while cane arrows bristled from quivers that rode high on their shoulders. Each carried an unstrung wooden bow, a pack, canteen, and his personal effects.

Behind them came teams of locals bearing the four Priests atop their litters. Seven Stars and his companions had remained immaculately white while their bearers appeared dust-streaked, lines of sweat having traced weblike patterns down their lean brown legs. White crusted under their armpits where salt sweat had dried on their brown tunics.

As he took their measure, he could see uncertainty in the eyes of Priest, warrior, and commoner alike. Each, for his own reason, was upset. It was as if they could feel the threat, like a winter smoke lying heavily upon the air. They could scent its odor, each wondering what it portended for their separate futures.

Yes, news had traveled fast.

The authority and prestige of the Blessed Sun has been violated.

Sucking in a lungful of the hot dry air, Leather Hand

considered his situation. The whole country was talking
about it: Several men had slipped into a storeroom in the
Tall Piñon Great House, filled packs with food, then
killed the Priest called Right Acorn, looted his room, and
made off into the night. The Deep Canyon farmsteads
Leather Hand's party had passed on the trail were abuzz
with the news.

They have defied my authority.

That single thought had confounded him from the moment he'd first heard of the raid. How insolent could they
get? To walk right into his great house, steal the Blessed
Sun's corn out from under his nose? Murder his Priest?

Leather Hand glanced back. Seven Stars had been
brooding since the word had come that his young acolyte
had been found dead in the High Priest's room. Seven
Stars' fine features gleamed in the dappled light, perspiration adding to the effect. His long black hair, freshly
washed, hung in silky waves around his white-robed
shoulders.

*What does it mean to the people when they hear that a
Priest has been killed?* Leather Hand motioned his men
forward and started off at a trot. Tall Piñon lay in the distance. He could see it through the mirage, a cluster of multistory buildings shimmering like a wish.

The way led past several farmsteads: rickety pit houses
rising like earthen pimples beside fields of intermixed
corn and beans—all drought-parched and tan under a hazy
sky. Those few people who watched them pass looked
gaunt and worn. They had a shabby air about them, as
though their bodies were as played out as their dust-
choked fields. He noted the filthy faces of the wide-eyed
children, framed with unwashed locks of black hair. The
adults, however, watched him with sloe-eyed looks that revealed nothing of their thoughts. In the name of the gods,
he hated those weary masks of expressionless anonymity
they managed to adopt at will.

*Do they exalt in the fact that thieves could make us look
like fools? Or do they chafe at the knowledge that someone made off so easily with their hard-earned tribute?*

He had listened when the locals passed him in the plaza and tried to decipher the hushed sibilance of their strange language. It irritated him that he had no clue of the meaning behind their words. They might have been speculating philosophically on the miraculous nature of air, or making rude comments about his mother's lack of morality.

The nature of the danger began to sink in. He shot a sidelong glance at a group of commoners who had stepped off the trail to allow them free passage. Again he noted their stoic expressions. The only acknowledgment he received was a slight nod from one of the middle-aged men bowed under a burden basket containing potsherds to be ground into temper for new pottery.

What would it take to hearten them into action against us? Could it be something as insignificant as the theft of some corn?

It was as if he were seeing the once-familiar terrain surrounding Tall Piñon Town through new eyes. Just within sight were twenty-some pit houses and several scatterings of small masonry room blocks. That meant how many people? Perhaps a hundred? Of them, over half would be children. Estimate it at somewhere around forty adults— and that was just in the short distance between him and the haven of his great house.

How many people actually live around here? He'd never given it a thought. Who cared? The fact was, until today he'd never taken them seriously. He was the strong right arm of the Blessed Sun, governor of a string of isolated great houses that ran from Windflower Village out west on the River of Souls to the Far View community where it stood defiantly atop the high brow of Green Mesa, then to Pinnacle Great House on First Moon Mountain to the east. Each great house had a garrison to ensure the safety of the Priests and Made People. Perhaps two hundred in all? They were so few to cover this vast territory.

Here, at Tall Piñon, his warriors numbered a full thirty. As he trotted, he tapped his fingertips against his callused thumb, counting them out. What a small number when one placed it against the uncounted masses of people living in the huge area encompassed by his administration.

"Gods," he whispered under his breath. A cold shiver crept down his spine. True, his men were trained, elite fighters, but what chance would they have against a raging mob of angry farmers that numbered in the hundreds?

Pestered by the thought, he led his weary command past the southeastern corner of the great house and into the plaza. He took in the flat-roofed cylinder of the great kiva and looked around at the Made People's towns. The blocky buildings appeared dusty in the hot light. Men lounged in the shade cast by the northern walls, some knapping flint, others working with wood, or weaving. But for a couple of extra desultory loiterers, nothing seemed to be amiss.

"Seven Stars?" he called, turning. "Will you accompany me?"

He watched as the litter bearers lowered the High Priest and helped him to his feet. Seven Stars walked forward, his snowy robe flowing about him in swaying folds. People were appearing now, hanging back, or standing on the rooftops across the way, eyes shaded with the flats of their hands.

Leather Hand took the stairs two at a time onto the first-floor roof. As he did a young man stepped out of Right Acorn's room. He wore a clean tan shirt that hung down to midthigh. Freshly washed, his hair was pinned behind his head. New sandals shod his feet.

"Who are you?" Leather Hand demanded.

"I am called Thorn," the youth said in a guttural voice thick with the local accent. "I am servant."

Leather Hand glanced at Seven Stars, who added, "His family sent him to us when they could not make the Blessed Sun's tribute."

So, the boy was a slave. Leather Hand noticed that Thorn wore a fine red coral necklace under the collar of his tunic. A well-cared-for slave, at that.

"What happened here?" Leather Hand shot a glance at the storeroom doorway. The sandstone door slab lay canted to one side. He could see scattered kernels of yellow corn on the packed clay flooring. The pattern seemed to indicate it had leaked rather than been broadcast.

"We have touched nothing," Thorn said quickly. "All is

left as it was. I have only kept the flies off Right Acorn's body."

"Let me see." Leather Hand stepped forward, aware of another spill of corn beside the doorway to the priest's quarters. A smear of blood had baked black in the sun, and droplets marked a path back to the doorway. Unlike the storeroom's, this doorway was T-shaped, wider at the top with a ledge midway along the side so the occupant could swing through on his hands.

He ducked inside, taking a moment for his eyes to adjust. The first thing that resolved itself was the body of the Priest, flat on his back, limbs akimbo. The eyes had dried open, slightly shrunken. Black hair matted with dried blood almost masked the wound.

Leather Hand was aware of Seven Stars as he entered. Together they bent down, studying the body. Looking like a desiccated mushroom, some of the man's brains had oozed out through the cleft in his skull. The open mouth seemed to express surprise.

Leather Hand could follow the spatters of blood where the body had been borne back into the room. "They killed him outside, it would seem."

Thorn added, "He heard them. It was the middle of the night."

Leather Hand looked up. "You were here?"

Thorn nodded, swallowed nervously, and gestured to the rear, where a ladder jutted from the entrance to the room below. "I was there. Sleeping."

"You sleep here often?"

"I am servant," Thorn replied. "I do as told."

Leather Hand glanced at Seven Stars. The Priest gave a slight shrug. Perhaps Thorn provided other services in addition to just fetching and carrying?

"Tell me what you know."

Thorn took a nervous breath. "It was the middle of the night. We heard a crash, a pot being broken. Ri—my master almost ignored it, then on second thought, pulled on his robe, and climbed the ladder. He said that he heard voices and was going out to see."

Thorn closed his eyes, as if seeing it all again. "I heard him call, 'Who are you? What are you doing?' And a moment later, there was a thump as he fell. I started up the ladder, and had just stuck my head up when men came into the room. The first one had his back to me, and didn't see me as he carried my master's body. A second man bore the feet."

With a deep breath, Thorn stilled his nervous fidgeting. "I ducked down, clinging to the ladder. They couldn't see me."

Leather Hand considered. "So you saw them?"

"Yes, War Chief."

"Did you know them?"

"No, War Chief. They were not from here. But I have heard their language before. It was the tongue of the Dust People from down south."

"Conditions are very bad down there," Seven Stars said thoughtfully. "It is said that the drought has led to starvation. Some people have taken to sifting dung for seeds. Whatever they can find." He hesitated. "Starvation drives people to desperation."

Leather Hand lifted an eyebrow. He'd seen the small farmsteads down below Thunderbird Mountain. The Dust People were from a clan that had originally been displaced from the foothills of the Bearclaw Mountains to the south. They had staked claims on the flats below Thunderbird Mountain, using the washes leading down from the high country for a water source. They were called "Dust People" because of their often threadbare appearance, their relative poverty, and the usual condition of their domestic circumstances.

"You're sure they were Dust People?"

Thorn nodded, but the certainty didn't extend to his eyes. "I just had a glimpse, War Chief. They wore filthy rags, and they smelled strongly of sweat and dirt. They had a wild look about them. Like animals."

"Then what happened?"

"They took several bags of jewelry and emptied that pot over there of the ritual jewels Ri—my master wears during the ceremonials. Then they left, went through the door." He pointed. "I heard voices, and then after a while, nothing."

"You didn't walk out and shout the alarm?" Leather Hand asked, eyes on the youth's.

Thorn made a face, obviously shamed. "No, War Chief. I was afraid. I had just watched my . . . my master killed before my eyes. I was terrified, clinging to the ladder, imagining them coming back to kill me. It took a long time before I could nerve myself to climb out and see if he was really dead." A tear leaked out the side of his eye and traced down his cheek.

"I see." Leather Hand took a deep breath, standing. He looked at Seven Stars and gestured to the corpse. "What of the body?"

"He was born of the First People, a distant cousin of the Blessed Matron, Desert Willow. We shall take him to the kiva, prepare for our friend's journey to the Sky Worlds. His breath-heart soul must be propitiated and shown the greatest of respect from this point on." Seven Stars's eloquent stare made the point. "Do you understand?"

He glanced at Thorn, who was waiting, head bowed. *Oh yes, Priest. I understand fully how dangerous this could be for us.*

He stood then, walked to the doorway, and ducked out into the sunlight.

"So, we find the fruit of the Blessed Sun's sowing," a brittle voice said softly.

Leather Hand cast a glance at Matron Husk Woman's shadowed doorway. "I find your tone of voice insulting, considering one of the First People was murdered just down from your door." He fought to keep his face straight. "It should be a warning, Matron."

"Ah, but you will keep us safe? Is that it, Deputy? You will charge forth, raining death and terror on the Dust People? And after that, as you stand over those poor wretches' bleeding bodies, peace, grace, and justice shall have been preserved."

He stepped closer to her door in order to better see her

withered face peering out at him. Her white hair was drawn neatly back over her wide sloped skull, her head having been bound as an infant to give her such patrician features.

"They must be punished or others will try the same. Next time it might be your skull they split."

She grinned at him, exposing the few brown teeth left in her lower jaw. "Go ahead, fool. Fan the flames. I don't know who's the greater danger, you or that incompetent Webworm. Featherstone was a halfwit. Like begets like."

"Your words are treasonous."

"So, what will you do? Come back and punish me?" Her laughter cackled. "You just try it, you homeless half-bred dog of a First Person."

He began to tremble, enraged by the disgust in her voice as much as by the words.

"Go on," she growled, shooing him from the shadows of her room. "Go posture before your warriors. They need a good show."

He stood for a moment, anger running bright along his bones. Taking a breath, he turned away.

Turquoise Fox, his deputy, stood at the head of a knot of warriors and scowled down at the bloodstain on the beaten clay. He was a wide-shouldered man, scarred on the left cheek from a slicing war club. His neck had the thick look of an ancient juniper trunk. Now he turned dark eyes to Leather Hand.

"Turquoise Fox?"

"Yes, War Chief?"

He raised his voice so that it carried across the plaza. "Find the man known as Tracker. Prepare your warriors. It seems the Dust People must learn their place in the world. It has fallen upon us to teach them." He smiled humorlessly, Husk Woman's words ringing in his souls. "We must do it in such a way that no one will dare to repeat this atrocity."

"Yes, War Chief." Turquoise Fox straightened, a crooked smile on his thick lips.

"They have incurred the wrath of the Blessed Sun!"

Posturing? He'd give them posturing. Leather Hand raised a clenched fist high. "We shall show them how such perfidy is repaid." He stared out at the small crowd that had gathered below the great house. "You, all of you! Carry word out from this place! Those who spit upon the Blessed Sun's benevolence shall pay the ultimate price! You shall bear witness. As shall the Dust People!"

As he spoke, he tried to read their eyes, tried to see if they would believe. But their dark stares remained impenetrable, their souls hidden. If he failed now, the entire northern frontier could disintegrate around him like an unfired clay pot in a winter rain.

Twelve

Water Bow, Sun Priest of Pinnacle Great House, knelt at the *sipapu* in the First People's kiva. The air was cool, damp with the odors of earth and faintly spiced with the aroma of sacred herbs. Juniper ash in the fire pit gave off a whiff of perfume. Around him, newly painted images of the gods danced on the wet-plastered walls.

He felt better knowing that Spider Woman, the Flute Player, the Blue God, and First Bear were watching. He had never been comfortable with the thlatsinas, or Sternlight's heresy.

Water Bow had seen more than forty summers pass, and his hair had turned as white as the loosely fitting Priest's robe he wore. Once smooth and muscular, his now-thin body had gone to little more than bone and sinew. He had the wide forehead of the First People, the sharp cheekbones and pointed chin. Three spirals had been tattooed beneath his lower lip.

As he chanted the Awakening Song, he bent down, touching his forehead to the *sipapu*, and felt the hole's cool rim kiss his delicate skin. He tried to ignore the discomfort caused by the awkward position. His knees, bony as they were, speared pain, and his joints ached.

"Where are you, great Ancestors? Can you hear me down there? Come to us. Come in our time of need. Your children call you."

He lapsed back into the chant again, calling it down into the narrow hole just beyond his lips. Again he bent his forehead to the void, listening, extending his senses.

And felt nothing.

In the end, he straightened, relieving the pain in his lower back and hips. Settling on his buttocks, he looked up at the high cribbed roof. The overlapping timbers were sooty, shadowed behind the dim shaft of light coming through the smoke hole. But he could see the masks. They stared at him from where they rested on the pole shelves. Spider Woman inspected him through yellow-circled eyes. Bear's shaggy face looked menacing, rows of white teeth filling his open mouth. Buffalo Above's wide horns had grayed with dust.

Ritual pottery, delicate vessels slipped in white with black hatching and geometric designs, held the sacred colors of cornmeal: blue, yellow, white, and red. Other jars—each stoppered with a shaped stone lid—were full of pollen from each of the different kinds of corn plants. Rendered bear lard filled a large white-slipped jar of local manufacture, while smaller pots clustered around it and contained different colors: red hematite, blue clay, yellow dirt, purple larkspur pigment, and white earth. From the ceiling, net bags hung in the south, each holding a different Spirit Plant. On the west, a jumbled line of soot-encrusted skulls dangled from cords tied to the rafters. Missing their jaws, they seemed frozen in surprise, slightly comic, and disorganized. Three other specimens—miscreants from the past—consisted only of skull caps, cut so that they could be used for cups.

He sighed, rubbing his aching knees, and struggled to his feet. Then almost fell as his blood-starved legs refused to hold him. Knowing what was coming, he hobbled over to the bench and sat while his flesh prickled with renewed circulation.

"Priest?" a voice called from above.

"Yes?" he replied, wincing as he finally managed to stand. He limped to the base of the ladder and looked up to find Burning Smoke, Pinnacle Great House's war chief, staring down. The moon-faced man's skin sagged and seemed to slip off the bone as he bent over the smoke hole.

"We have the young hunter you wanted to see."

"I am coming, Burning Smoke." He climbed slowly and deliberately up the use-polished ladder and into the Fifth World. There, blinking in the morning sun, he squinted at the vista. Pinnacle Great House perched high above the First Moon Valley. Only the sacred spires of rock at the end of the ridge rose any higher.

This was a holy place, more the realm of eagles than of men. It was here that Sister Moon, every eighteen and a half sun cycles, returned home from her journey across the sky. For a single season she rose between the rocks, casting a Blessing light between them to illuminate Pinnacle Great House.

He stopped, as he always did, to take in the view to the north. He could see across the mountains to the high peaks above timberline—some still spotted white with snow. They drew the eyes, especially those of a desert-dweller such as Water Bow had been for most of his life.

Turning to the southwest and looking down the long V of First Moon Valley, the mountains slowly gave way to the mesa land, and finally to the distant desert. He could see the River of Stones shining like a silver thread where the sunlight reflected from its surface. It lay cupped by a gentle green valley dotted with fields. Finally, in the distance, a series of buttes rose in successive layers until on the farthest horizon he could see Smoking Mirror Butte, the last of the heights on the Great North Road, where the Blessed Sun kept watchtowers.

From that vantage point, a signal could be flashed by means of pyrite mirrors, illuminated by means of fire, or sent by means of smoke. In the old days an observer at Center Place Town just above Straight Path Canyon waited to bear news to the Blessed Sun. Smoking Mirror Butte was the relay that held the northern frontier together.

But what of the present? He stared at the distance,

thinking about the new center the Blessed Webworm was building at Flowing Waters Town on the Spirit River. Was it appropriate to move the whole of the Straight Path Nation there? Or were the other voices, those that pleaded for a move farther to the south, the correct ones?

He lifted his eyebrows, wrinkling his parchmentlike forehead. Who knew?

It was only when he looked at the surrounding valley that he remembered their precarious position here. Now, with this unknown hunter in custody, he was more acutely aware of it than ever.

Below the heights that Pinnacle Great House dominated, he could see clusters of houses descending the ridge to the southwest. Here and there, patches of trees obscured yet more houses. The valleys that lay on either side of the rocky mountain atop which he lived were intensively farmed; patchworks of fields used every bit of arable land. The drainages feeding the valley bottom had been dammed, ditched, or diverted in one manner or another. Each flat spot, including the gentle shoulders of the surrounding ridges, had been built upon. Sometimes at night, when the home fires were twinkling around the valleys, it was hard to tell where the stars stopped and the houses began. On days when the air was calm a thick veil of blue smoke hung heavily in the valley, so many were the cook fires.

Now, in midday, he could see the endless clusters of buildings, the sinuous paths that led back and forth between the settlements. A lot of people lived here in this valley oasis, fed by consistent water, frequent rains, and the fertile soil. So very many people.

And most of them hate us.

It was a sobering thought.

But safety lay in Pinnacle Great House's impregnable location. Sheer cliffs fell away immediately to the south, while steep rocky talus and the near-vertical slope to the north made approach from that direction difficult. The only easy access, if it could be called that, lay along the knifelike ridgetop that made an irregular descent to the southwest. That narrow causeway was controlled by a small fortified structure called the Eagle's Fist. It perched across the trail a stone's throw from the great house. Perpetually manned by warriors, it was a formidable barrier past which any assailant had to pass.

Adding to Pinnacle's security, the houses of the Made People—the warriors and craftsmen who served the First People—could be seen clinging precariously to the restricted ridgetop just below the narrow approach to the Eagle's Fist. While the Made People harbored resentments of their own, here, too, they were the outsiders, the interlopers who had come in the wake of the First People's conquest, to help administer, oversee, and ensure the functioning of Pinnacle House. They were the eyes and ears of the Blessed Sun, the strong backs upon whom both the Matron and Webworm relied.

Finally, as the ridge began to flatten and expand, the Made People had constructed a modest, multiroom dwelling with attached kivas. Called Guest House, it was there that visiting workmen, servants, Traders, and other itinerants were housed. The edifice also served as the first line of defense, guarding the bottleneck through which all must pass.

Below Guest House the slope was pimpled with the lumpy dwellings of the barbarians. Following the cliff to the south, the barbarians' square sun tower stood sentinel. It jutted up from the rimrock like an ugly thumb, a combination solar observatory and lookout. For the First People in Pinnacle House, it was a constant reminder that this land had belonged to the barbarians first—that they were squatting on ground held sacred by the First Moon People.

He need only look out at the crowded valley—dotted with so many houses, structures, and towns—to have that knowledge driven home. Finally, at the foot of the slope to the southwest, the formation called the Dog's Tooth jutted up defiantly. A thin haze of smoke rose from the walled compound. He growled to himself, thinking of the kivas there, and of the old blind man who conducted black rituals of sorcery inside them.

One day I'm going to find a reason to send the warriors down there. And when I do, your days of evil and mayhem will be over for good.

Stepping across the roof, he followed Burning Smoke.

The man was thick and heavy the way a ponderosa pine trunk was. Never fast or flighty, the war chief approached a problem in the same manner a grizzly did a log full of grubs. He ripped it apart with one strong swipe after another, never hurrying, never pressed; but when he was finished, only splinters lay in his wake.

Burning Smoke walked down the narrow line of steps that jutted from the great house's southern side and led the way along the buff-plastered wall to the small plaza cupped in the angle of the ell.

It was here, with its southeastern exposure, that Priests for three generations had greeted the winter solstice sun, or reclined in the shade cast by summer sunsets.

The beaten earth had been stained with charcoal, littered with bits of broken pottery and colorful flakes of chipped stone. A line of waist-high water jars rested against the north wall, while several looms were propped on the west.

A red-shirted warrior sporting a half-bored expression stood just behind a young barbarian. The warrior gripped a war club in his right hand, its double-bitted stone head polished to a gleam.

The young hunter was wearing a brown fabric hunting shirt that hung to his knees. He'd belted it with a rope from which hung several hide pouches. Heavy yucca trail sandals covered his feet. He squatted, head down, expression blank with the enforced inscrutability of his kind.

"Blessed Water Bow," Burning Smoke began, gesturing. "This is Ripple, a man of the Blue Stick Clan. We caught him trying to escape from the mountain at first light. My warriors spotted him as he left his sister's house. His pack was filled with the kind of supplies he'd need over a several-day journey."

Water Bow stepped over and studied the young man. Given his looks he might be just on the short side of twenty, muscular, rangy, with long hair hanging down his back.

"Look at me," Water Bow said in the barbarian tongue. He had spent some time learning their language, and it had stood him in good stead. The hunter looked up, his eyes betraying a fleeting moment of fear before he managed to hide it with blankness.

"There are stories circulating about you," Water Bow continued. "It is said that you had a vision on the mountain. It is said that Old Woman North came to you. Is it so?"

The young man's lips barely puckered, the only sign that he might have heard. For several heartbeats, he squatted there, perhaps deciding what to say, and then gave a faint shake of his head.

"So, you had no vision of Old Woman North?" Water Bow pressed.

"No, Blessed One," the hunter finally whispered.

Burning Smoke, hearing the translation, reached down, cupped the man's jaw, and twisted his head around. The war chief had never seen the value of learning a tongue he thought inferior to his own. As a result, the hunter gave Burning Smoke an empty look when he demanded, "Then where did the stories come from?"

Water Bow raised his hand, gesturing for Burning Smoke to desist. Reluctantly, the war chief released the hunter and stepped back, a dark scowl on his face.

"Things would be easier if you simply told us where this story has come from. Did you start it?"

The hunter swallowed hard, shaking his head, a distance in his eyes that began to ebb into fear.

"Does that mean you didn't?" Water Bow pressed. "You did not see Old Woman North? She did not foretell the destruction of the First People?"

The muscles in the young man's jaws were clamped, and the vein in his neck was pulsing.

The guard standing behind Ripple smacked his club into the palm of his hand. "Blessed Water Bow, should I bruise him up a little? Loosen his tongue?"

Burning Smoke shot a questioning glance at Water Bow, one eyebrow lifting. The war chief most assuredly thought it a good idea, but Water Bow remembered another occasion when an overzealous guard had leveled one blow too many, leaving the prisoner suddenly and quite inarticulately dead.

Water Bow fingered his chin as he studied the young man. The look in his eyes erased all doubt but that he was at the bottom of this ludicrous rumor; nevertheless something in that posture communicated that beat, flogged, or tortured, the youth would rather suffer and die than speak.

Still, there might be another way.

Water Bow bent down. "Beating him will do no good." In Ripple's language, he said, "Take him and lock him in the hole until you can return with his kin. Sisters, you said? Sometimes a man will talk with greater facility when someone he loves is doing the screaming." He made a gesture with his hand, then added, "And send warriors to bring in his friends, as well."

An ashen pallor washed over the hunter's face. This time when Water Bow looked into his eyes it was to see outright terror.

Fir Brush was no one's fool. When she had awoken to find Ripple missing, she had feared the worst. Rumors were already passing from lip to lip that the young man seen escorted by warriors just at dawn was Ripple. She considered that as she sat under the low branches of a juniper tree and inspected the contents of the small pack she had assembled. Slipped Bark sat beside her, a corn-husk doll clutched tightly to her narrow chest as she watched the tree-dotted slope between them and Guest House. If the warriors came, it would be from that direction.

The breeze made a soft shushing sound as it played through the piñon and juniper branches. To her left, rain and wind had scrubbed the sandstone bare of soil. A single perfectly round *sipapu* had been painstakingly ground into the solid rock.

The *sipapu*, about three hands across, had originally been higher on the slope, closer to the twin pillars of stone where Sister Moon had emerged from the Under-worlds. It was on that spot that the First People had built Pinnacle House. They had placed their kiva directly over the *sipapu*, thereby controlling that doorway to the Below Worlds.

After much bickering—or so the story went—the First

Moon People had drilled this second *sipapu.* It had been located with precise deliberation where, it was said, First Man had seen the first sunrise after his emergence from the Underworlds.

Nor was that the only celestial event that had ties to this place. The oldest of the surviving elders still talked about how Morning Star had burned so brightly he had outshone Father Sun. It had occurred just after the First People occupied First Moon Mountain. The First People had said it was an affirmation of their authority. To the Moon People, it was a sign that Morning Star had been so incensed he burned for days in anger. During those weeks, there were three heavenly lights that had been visible during the day—and his daily rising had been directly in line between the sun tower and the newly drilled *sipapu.*

Looking east, she could see the high tower of the observatory where it perched on the cliff overlooking First Moon Valley. Twice a year, on equinox, Father Sun rose in direct alignment. His light was cast from the watchtower, over the *sipapu,* and clear across the River of Stones valley to Mid-Sun Village.

The Priests, Healers, and Shamans had conducted secret rituals to redirect the Spirits of the Underworlds to this new *sipapu.* On both summer and winter solstice, the Priests came to conduct their rituals here, calling on the gods of both sky and earth to bring them rain and mild weather, to intercede with the dead, and grant health and fertility to the people.

Just to her left, Fir Brush counted no less than five tens of prayer sticks; *pahos,* or feather plumes; and other offerings made to the spirits of the Below Worlds. These brightly painted, carved, and feathered offerings were left propped on the rock, set on small tripods, or otherwise displayed. People knew that their prayers had been heard when the offerings began to fade, weather, and deteriorate. When they did, it meant the message, or soul, of the prayer stick had been taken, leaving only the corpse of the offering behind, much as a human body deteriorated after its soul flew off to the afterlife.

"Fir Brush?" Slipped Bark ventured softly. "They're coming."

Fir Brush followed her little sister's pointing finger. It wasn't with surprise that she caught sight of the four red-shirted warriors striding purposefully down the hill. They were weaving their way through the pit houses and ramadas of her neighbors toward her house.

"Let's go." She led the way, backing quickly down the slope so that the crest of the hill and old woman Chickadee's house hid her from the approaching warriors.

Slinging the pack over one shoulder, she took Slipped Bark's hand and ran swiftly, her sandal-clad feet whispering on the sandstone slabs she crossed.

The great kiva lay little more than a stone's throw down the slope, and it was there that she paused by the south entrance. Glancing quickly over her shoulder to see if anyone was watching, she touched her head in deference to the spiritual Power of the place and led Slipped Bark up the ladder, over the stone wall, and down into the shadowed depths.

"Should we be here?" Slipped Bark looked nervously up at the roof with its smoke hole open to the morning sky.

The great kiva had been dug down into the ground, its walls built up with thick courses of shaped stones. Four large logs had been set as roof supports, beams laid across, and stringers run down to the thick walls. It wasn't like the massive roofs that the First People constructed to cover their great kivas, but more of a ramada. Something to keep the sun and rain off.

"No one will look for us here," Fir Brush said. "Shhh! Keep quiet." She led the way past the firebox and the rectangular foot drum to the eastern edge of the circular wall. There she stooped and lifted several wooden planks from the small stone-lined pit dug into the floor.

"That's for the Priests!" Slipped Bark said with a gasp. She had her little doll crushed to her chest, her eyes wide with fear.

Fir Brush slung her pack into the depths, surprised to see a field mouse scamper up the plastered rock and scurry across the beaten clay floor. "We're going to be like

Priests for a while. Hurry now, climb down. They'll never look for us here."

"I don't think—"

"Shhh! Go! Or I'll give you to the Red Shirts myself. And if you're not quiet, and don't obey, they'll eat you!"

Terrified, Slipped Bark hoisted herself down into the dark hole. Her corn-shuck doll was nearly bent in two as she worked it back and forth against her chest.

Fir Brush lowered her feet into the hole and slid down, bending around to pull the planks back over the top. The gap between the boards cast slivers of dim light across the cramped space where they crouched.

"What are we going to eat?" Slipped Bark asked.

Fir Brush patted the pack she'd made. "I've got corn cakes and a bladder of water here. That will hold us. But we'll have to wait until after dark to pee."

"I'm scared!"

"Not nearly as scared as you'll be if those warriors catch us."

"What about Ripple?"

Fir Brush took a deep breath. "I don't know. I just don't. Maybe, somehow, he'll get away."

"Mother and Father didn't."

Fir Brush turned her face away so that Slipped Bark couldn't see the tears that trickled from the corner of her eye. "I know."

Thirteen

The day couldn't have been more perfect for the task at hand. Spots shifted on his haunches and poked another length of aspen into the long trench where his low fire burned. He squinted against the smoke rolling out of the trench and decided the position of the wood was just perfect.

Backing away, he studied his creation. Two upright poles about chest high had been planted into the ground and a crosspiece lain between the two to create a drying rack. He'd dug the shallow trench between them, filled it with wood, and kindled a fire. Then had come the laborious process of stripping the elk quarter, cutting each muscle loose and splitting it along the grain into thin flats. These he draped over the drying rack, where the heat and smoke rose to coat them.

Periodically he would walk down to where his sister, Yellow Petal, was washing her family's clothing. After inquiring as to her progress, he would yank some of the rich river grasses out by the roots. These he'd drop on the coals to create thick clouds of smoke in which to bathe the meat.

Satisfied with his smoking fire, he sat back on the flat grass and watched Yellow Petal finish her washing. She'd lain each article of damp clothing across one of the polished river boulders to dry. Now she waded out of the cold water, shaking her hands. Water droplets sparkled as she flung them from her callus-hardened fingers.

She was not a particularly attractive woman, being thick of body, with a broad face. Unlike Spots, only her left arm showed faint patterns of scar tissue. Since the night of their tragic fire she had always kept her hair short, saying that nightmares about it catching fire and burning around her like a halo still haunted her sleep.

None of this bothered her husband, Black Bush, a Strong Back Clan man. His first wife had died in childbirth when the baby wouldn't pass his wife's narrow hips. He'd taken one look at Yellow Petal's broad pelvis, smiled, and sent his relatives to talk with her uncle about finalizing marriage details. To Black Bush's delight, her first child had slipped easily from her womb after but a half day's labor.

Yellow Petal stepped out onto the bank, her strong brown toes curling as if to grasp the thick grass. She cocked her head as she studied him where he sat beside the fire.

"You gonna lay like a lump all day?"

Spots gave her a grin. "I'm making meat. This is serious business. The amount of smoke's got to be monitored, kept just right, or the meat won't cure."

"Uh-huh." She pointed at a large brown ceramic jar that rested at a cant among the rocks. "You see that? That's another really serious bit of business. It's called a water jug. You remember that name?"

"Water jug? As in to carry water."

"Very good, Brother." She pointed at the small cornfield just beyond his drying rack. "And that's where the water goes. One jug per plant." She gave him a mocking grin. "Unless, of course, you can conjure a flood. One just big enough to water that field."

He glanced distastefully at the brownware jug, then at the river, running low in its banks. Next his gaze went to the distant mountains, the peaks clear in the high dry air. Not a single cloud piled against those rugged slopes.

Figuring where to lay out a cornfield was more of an art than anything resembling an exact process. In some of the better floodplain locations people cut ditches to water the corn and beans. This was the easiest way to grow corn. Simply opening and damming ditches ensured that the plants flourished.

Nothing came without a price. Those selfsame floodplain fields could be easily destroyed by a single flash flood if it came rolling down the valley. A wall of thrashing brown water might flatten the field, snapping off stalks of corn, stripping the beans. Ditches would be filled with silt and stone, necessitating backbreaking labor to clear them again.

If that happened, the next hope would be the terrace fields, laid out above flood stage at slightly higher elevation. This was the sort of field Yellow Petal now indicated. The downside was that water had to be carried if insufficient rain fell during the growing season.

Finally, the upland fields higher on the mountainsides were the ultimate hope. Those fields relied on the evermore-capricious patterns of rainfall. Steps had been taken to lengthen the odds on the hillside fields. Every catchment had been dammed or ditched to trickle precious runoff onto the terraced flats when those decidedly unpredictable rains came.

Spots glanced at the corn where it stood in rows, interbedded with bean plants and beeweed. The plants looked healthy, green in the sunlight. "I don't think you want me meddling with that."

Yellow Petal glanced suspiciously at him as she walked over to where Baby hung. She was Yellow Petal's latest, a two-moon-old girl with a round face and a nubbin nose. Her cradleboard hung in the shade of a young cottonwood that grew beside the bank. The infant had fallen asleep earlier, entertained by the flat leaves as they flapped in the breeze.

"Why wouldn't I want you meddling with the cornfield? You'll spend enough time eating its harvest this winter. Seems to me having a little labor spent in watering the crop will make the gleanings that much sweeter."

"Oh, no." Spots shook his head as he watched her lift the cradleboard flap to inspect Baby. The infant wouldn't be named until it had lived at least a year. "Male sweat really sours the taste of good corn."

She shot him a disapproving look as she began unlacing the leather around the infant. Baby cooed, yawned, and stretched her short arms; the pudgy hands knotted into fists.

Before Baby could come awake enough to let out a squall, Yellow Petal raised the infant to her left breast and cradled it with one arm. With her other hand she reached in and pulled fouled cattail-down padding from inside the cradleboard and tossed it into the river.

Spots watched her move with such an economy of motion as she fished more padding from a leather pack and tucked it into the cradleboard. "That's amazing."

"What is?" She continued efficiently about her business.

He chuckled. "Oh, just the way you make it all look as if you've been doing that all your life. Taking care of children, I mean."

"After the first one, the second is easy." She shot him a

smile. "Your part doesn't start for another year or two. I can't wait to see how you deal with discipline, Uncle."

Raising the girls fell to him. They were his family, members of his Blue Stick Clan. Yellow Petal's husband, Black Bush, had little responsibility for the children he sired. Being Strong Back Clan, his concern was the proper raising and education of his own two sisters' offspring. If anything, he'd go out of his way to spoil Fresh Stalk and Baby. After all, if they grew into young terrors, it wasn't his family, lineage, or clan that would be thought ill of. No, people would look to Spots.

He'd heard that some of the Tower Builders traced descent through the men, and wondered what that would be like. Somehow, it just didn't seem as logical. And since when did men have enough sense to see to the management of a family or a clan? Worse, how did they go about keeping land claims straight? Especially since everyone knew a man was more likely to die in warfare, hunting, or an accident than a woman was.

"What are you thinking?" Yellow Petal asked as she came and settled herself next to him.

"About the Tower Builders and the way they trace descent through the men."

She shrugged, then stared thoughtfully down where Baby's mouth was pressed to her breast. "People are different everywhere, I suppose."

He nodded, aware from a lifetime's experience that she was about to say something important. She never liked to rush into these things, but considered her words first. It was a trait she'd adhered to even more after the fire that had killed their parents and other brother.

"What happened on the mountain?" she asked at last. "This story about Ripple having a vision—is there anything to it?"

Spots chuckled, picked up an angular shale pebble, and flipped it out into the river, where it vanished with a plop. "He seems to believe it. You should have seen him: It was like he'd been touched by Cold Bringing Woman's hand. He was so . . . I guess I'd say, different."

"How?" She'd known Ripple for years and had a teasing relationship with him. Probably would have married him but for the fact they were clan kin and such a joining was forbidden.

"Withdrawn, distant, seeing things in his mind. Kind of, well, lost."

"That doesn't sound like Ripple."

"No, I suppose not. I guess after what they did to his parents you can't blame him for taking things too seriously."

"Was the elk meat *really* frozen?"

"How many times do I have to tell you?"

"How do you explain that?"

Spots exaggerated his shrug. "What can I say? Cold Bringing Woman came down and gave a shake of her head. The meat froze and—"

"Spots?"

At the wary sound in her voice, he looked up, followed her hard gaze down the valley, to where two red-shirted warriors appeared out of the willows.

They stopped where Cousin White Nose pulled mustard weeds out of his small bean field. Across the distance, Spots could see them talking, could see White Nose point their direction. A chance flip of the breeze curled the smoke around from the drying fire, hiding the warriors from view.

"Maybe you'd better slip into the cornfield," Yellow Petal added nervously.

"What? Why would—"

"Go! *Now!*"

Spots scuttled around the fire, bending low as he duck-walked his way into the tall corn. Once between the rows he dropped onto his belly, slithering like a snake under the sprawling bean vines. The damp scent of rich earth rose to fill his nostrils. He could barely see through the stalks and leaves, but it was enough when the smoke shifted to see that the warriors were approaching.

Yellow Petal was watching them warily, Baby still sucking greedily on her left nipple.

"Good day," one of the warriors, a bandy-legged man

greeted. His command of their language was rude but effective. He looked curiously around as he stopped. His attention focused on the elk, a slight smile coming to his lips. "Uh, we look for Spots."

"He's not here," she told him. "He's headed back up the mountain."

The second man was younger, thin-faced, with narrow black eyes. He asked, "What did she say?" Spots knew enough of the Made People's tongue to make that out.

"That the hunter's not here," the bandy warrior replied.

"You believe her?"

The bandy warrior asked in their language, "Where he go?"

Yellow Petal pointed up the valley, saying, "He killed a second elk. He's gone for the meat."

From his position, Spots couldn't hear the whispered conversation between the two warriors, or see their faces clearly, but it looked as if they weren't buying Yellow Petal's story.

"When he back?" the bandy warrior asked suddenly.

"Tomorrow." Yellow Petal glared up defiantly, as if daring them to contradict her.

The warriors traded looks, the thin one finally shrugging.

"We need talk to Spots." Bandy Legs propped his hands on his hips. "Not in trouble. Just talk."

Yellow Petal nodded. "I'll tell him when I see him."

"See you do," came the hard reply.

As they turned to leave, the thin warrior reached out, pulling several slices of meat off the rack. He tucked them in the tail of his war shirt, then smiled insolently at Yellow Petal before they walked away side by side.

Spots took a deep breath, wondering when his body had gotten so hot. Nerve sweat slipped down the side of his face.

Yellow Petal stood, Baby still cradled, and walked over to the woodpile. With her free hand she picked up a length of wood and settled it onto the fire. Then, taking a couple of steps closer, she said, "Stay where you are."

"You going to water me to see if I grow like the corn?"

"I wouldn't like the harvest if you did." She stepped

over to the cradleboard and lifted it from the cottonwood branch. Baby had finally given up on the nipple. Yellow Petal raised her to her shoulder, bounced her enough to get a burp, and then laid the little girl on the grass beside the cradleboard.

"They're crossing the stream, turning uphill," she said. "My suspicion is that they'll head up the trail toward the trees. When they get there, one of them will stay and watch."

"Why?" Spots demanded. "What did I do? What do they want with me?"

"Information," she said quietly as she wiped Baby's bottom with leaves.

He gave that some thought. She had always been a little quicker than he about some things. He could spin a joke at a moment's notice, but she seemed to have a better grasp of real things.

"Ripple's vision?" he asked.

"Do you know of anyone else that a god has appeared to with stories about how to destroy the First People?"

"But how did they hear about that?"

"The First People have ears everywhere."

"So, what am I going to do?"

"Stay right there and don't move." She tucked Baby back into the cradleboard, lowering the flap so that the sun didn't shine in the little girl's face. "Gods, it just goes to show you, Spots."

"What does?"

"That you'd do anything to worm your way out of having to water the corn."

Through the stalks, he watched as she stepped down to the water's edge and scooped the brown ceramic jar full. Raising it to her shoulder she strode up the bank and then into the cornfield, the jar held high.

"Hey, I was going to tell you—"

She poured the first jarful right onto the back of his head.

Leather Hand fingered the beautiful pot as he sat beside the fire and stared up at the star-washed night sky. Firelight cast a yellow ring around the juniper and piñon just back from the small spring.

Ages of wind and water had hollowed out this little niche in the sandstone and exposed the underlying shale formation. Water trickled in a mossy seep at the base of the sandstone. People had camped here since the emergence. Bits of fire-cracked rock, charcoal stains, and the refuse of old camps lay strewn about.

Tracker had found the pot here, lying on its side in the rocks up from the sedge-filled spring. He had been waiting when Leather Hand had led his squad of warriors out of the breaks and to this small secluded hollow beneath the gray caprock.

Leather Hand studied Tracker. He was of the Deep Canyon folk, short, thick of body, with a round, somewhat squat face. He wore a breechcloth belted with leather, a ceramic canteen dangling from a strap over his shoulder. His collar-length black hair was contained by a red cloth headband and hung straight, covering his ears and framing his face. He hunkered at the edge of the firelight now, limp hands dangling over his knees, eyes like hard obsidian pebbles as he watched Leather Hand inspect the pot.

Leather Hand turned the vessel slowly. Thin-walled, light as a feather, it was white, painted with black lines in the design of the Red Lacewing Clan. He knew the workmanship. Only the finest of potters were allowed to make ceramic vessels for the First People. He tapped a thumbnail against the thin wall, hearing it ring, the sound almost musical.

"The one stolen from the dead Priest?" Turquoise Fox asked. He sat across the fire, inspecting his arrows one after another, ensuring the fletching was straight on the cane shafts and that each finely chipped stone war point was tight in its bindings.

Lifting the pot to his nostrils, Leather Hand sniffed, catching the faintest odor of stew. "They certainly licked it clean."

"Why leave it?" Turquoise Fox wondered. "They must have known we'd find it."

Behind Turquoise Fox, the other warriors reclined in the flattened grass, many chewing on dried meat, others sipping at corn gruel they'd made. They listened eagerly, knowing full well that the stakes had been raised.

"Why indeed?" Leather Hand wondered. "Were it me, I'd have tossed it off a cliff somewhere. Let it fall to shatter into tens of pieces."

"But you know what the design means." Turquoise Fox pointed with one of his arrows. "Perhaps they didn't. Being barbarians, they might have just thought it was another pot, albeit a pretty one."

"They may not have known this pot bore the Red Lacewing design, but it most certainly would have stood out in their dingy little farmstead out in the flats. They must have known it was a First Person's bowl. Not something easy to explain away to the neighbors."

"Which means . . . what?" Turquoise Fox reached up to run a thumbnail along the scar on his cheek.

"Which means they're most likely just what the boy, Thorn, thought they were: starving farmers. Ignorant barbarians with no realization of what they've just unleashed upon themselves."

"And when we find them, War Chief? What then?"

The warriors in the back perked up, all eyes on Leather Hand.

"We show them what it means to challenge the Blessed Sun."

Turquoise Fox nodded, firelight reflected in his dark eyes. The corner of his lip was quivering in an old and familiar way.

Leather Hand asked, "You have a problem with that, Deputy?"

He narrowed an eye. "I was just thinking, is all. Famine lies heavily upon the land, War Chief. It changes how a man looks at death. Put yourself in their position. What do they care if we come and kill them? If it's a choice between slow starvation or the quick and merciful snap of a war club, which would you pick?"

Leather Hand tilted his head. "What's your point? Either way, they're dead and won't be spreading ideas to others. We want to make examples of them."

Turquoise Fox pursed his lips, then turned to stare thoughtfully at the warriors behind him, as if evaluating their merit. When he shifted back to face Leather Hand, he asked, "What kind of example does a corpse make?"

"The dead kind. The kind that makes others decide not to challenge the Blessed Sun's authority."

"You are still thinking that life is all they have left to lose," Turquoise Fox replied cryptically. "And that's the problem we are going to be facing from this point forward. Unless there's rain, War Chief, more and more people are going to have nothing but misery left to escape. These Dust People have shown those desperate souls that there is a way: Food lies in our storerooms for the taking. A Priest has been killed. The First People are not invincible."

"But we *will* catch these culprits. They will pay."

"Yes. In this case, we will catch them. But others will be thinking they are smarter, skilled at hiding their trails. Someone will club a guard in the night. Or they will storm the great house while we're drawn away, as we are now. It is only a matter of time before someone is successful in stealing from us. It will be like a trickle over the dam, but within a moment it will become a torrent, washing away everything."

Leather Hand grunted, returning his attention to the pot. It felt like an oversized eggshell in his hand. The thieves who had taken it had rubbed most of the soot off the bottom, perhaps passing it back and forth as they chugged down the contents. Yes, half-starved. He remembered the faces of the children they had passed today. The youngsters had stared at him with a hunger-hollow look in their oversized eyes. It had shivered his souls. How much more would it bother a parent?

"The trick is," Turquoise Fox continued, "to make them fear losing something more than just their lives."

"And what would that be?"

"Dying isn't so difficult, old friend. It's the manner of it that strikes terror into the soul." Turquoise Fox was watching him, thinking something he wasn't quite ready to divulge.

"If you have something to say, Deputy, be out with it."

"We know how desperate the Dust People are, War Chief. How desperate are you?"

Leather Hand lifted the bowl so that the firelight caught it. Flickering yellow light played on the beautifully painted sides. "There are pressures on our world." He placed his palms on either side of the thin-walled bowl. "They are pressing in from all sides." He felt the muscles swell in his chest and arms. The watching warriors could see the tendons stand out as his strength built.

"We are under a great strain." Leather Hand looked from face to face, reading their acknowledgment. "And all it would take would be one small crack, one little weakness." He pressed harder, feeling the smooth surface of the clay pot under his hands.

"Like the Dust People killing one of our Priests," Turquoise Fox said.

The pot collapsed with a loud pop—pieces of it flying out to pepper the watching warriors. They flinched, some jerking back.

Leather Hand let the shards that remained fall from his hands into his lap. "That's all it would take. Just like that . . . our world will be gone. We are all that stands between it and destruction."

Turquoise Fox stared from man to man. "Do you understand now how important this pursuit is?"

They nodded, eyes narrowing with resolve.

"Good." Turquoise Fox shot a measuring glance at Leather Hand. "We may all be driven to extraordinary measures in this most dangerous of times."

Leather Hand nodded. *He does have something in mind. Something so terrible he doesn't even want the men to think about it yet.*

Fourteen

Ripple crouched in the corner of the dark room, hugged his knees to his chest, and tried to keep any warmth trapped against his skin. His trembling body was a mixture of numbness and pain.

They had stripped him naked and brought him to this room three floors down in the north wing of Pinnacle Great House. They had withdrawn the ladder that led down into tall, narrow rectangle of a room. When they left, the lamplight had been cut off as they placed something over the hole. Alone in pitch blackness, he had explored by feel, encountering what felt like old dried feces in one corner. In another, his fingers came across what seemed to be fragments of turkey bone. Beyond that there was nothing but the gritty surface of plaster. Jamming his thumbnail into it, he had pried out bits to encounter stone.

A long time later the guard—a man called Horned Lizard—had appeared bearing a torch. He had looked down into Ripple's high narrow room, lowered the ladder, and climbed down in the company of a Buffalo Clan man. The latter was a burly fellow with a face reminiscent of a toad. He carried a curious-looking war club with a small stone head hafted to a whip-thin willow handle.

"Your friends seem to have vanished," Horned Lizard had told him. "Like water under a desert sun, they've dried up and blown away."

"My . . . my sisters?"

"Perhaps they're with them." Horned Lizard smiled down. "You know what that makes the Matron and her war chief?"

Ripple glanced up. "No."

"Mad."

Then the toad-faced man struck. Blow after blow rained

down while Horned Lizard held a pitch-and-tallow lamp high. As he cowered under the blows, Ripple had taken note of his room. The plaster was scratched here and there, ripped by frantic fingers. Several small piles of dried feces lay in the corner. In the flickering light, he thought the stains on the floor might be dried blood.

When it was over, Horned Lizard called out, the ladder dropped, and the two men climbed out. A desperate Ripple watched as the ladder was hauled up into the room above. The light faded with the sound of steps.

This wasn't how it was supposed to be. How had this happened? In the hands of the First People, there would be no future, no testing by the Mountain Witch. Like his parents before him, he would die here.

Cold Bringing Woman? Did you lie to me?

The gritty masonry wall felt rough as Fir Brush ran her finger along it with one hand. Her other arm was around Slipped Bark's thin shoulders. In the hazy night she could see the fires winking at Pinnacle Great House high on the mountain above them. On this night the dry late-summer air was heavy with dust and smoke. Bats flitted through the darkness, their chittering calls barely audible as they whispered their secrets to the Star People.

Ripple was up there somewhere. The distance to Pinnacle Great House seemed insurmountable to Fir Brush. At least here, atop the Dog's Tooth, she and Slipped Bark were safe. It just didn't seem fair.

A man laughed as he stepped from one of the rooms in the two-story clan house that dominated the triangular peak. In the firelight the rounded walls of the two great kivas shimmered like beaten copper. The warm air carried the scent of cooking beans, piñon smoke, and tobacco mixed with kinnikinnick as someone smoked a stone pipe in the shadows.

"What do you think is happening to him?" Slipped Bark asked in a reedy voice.

"Nothing good."

"Do you . . . do you think he's still alive?"

"I don't know."

"He lives," a rattly voice said from the darkness before a pipe bowl glowed fiercely. A soft exhalation preceded the perfumed scent of the tobacco mixture. Then a scuffling of cloth accompanied a grunt as a dark form rose to its feet and stepped toward them. "At least, he lives if Cold Bringing Woman really did come to him."

Fir Brush squinted to make out the ruined face of the white-eyed old man she'd seen when two young men had escorted her and Slipped Bark here just after dusk. "I should know you. What's your clan?"

"Most call me White Eye. I gave up on clans many winters ago. Old Matron Hoarse Caller still had a voice back then."

Slipped Bark gasped and tried to pull free from Fir Brush's arm as she backed away.

"White Eye? The old witch?"

"Some call me that." The old man chuckled softly, then took another pull on the stone pipe. It was little more than a conical stone tube. "If I'm a witch, I'm a poor specimen."

"Why is that?"

"You're an impudent one. Do you always take such a hard tone with your elders?"

"Would you understand if I told you that life has left me little choice but to be direct?"

"Ah, yes, the orphans who raised themselves despite their clan's help and concern."

Fir Brush felt herself bristling. "As I recall, we were trying to decide why you were such a poor witch."

He chuckled dryly and gestured with his pipe. "If I were a good one, there would just be darkness up there on First Moon Mountain, your brother would still be home, and our people would be preparing for Sister Moon's return to our world."

"Why is that?"

He added dryly, "For all the curses I've hurled up there over the years, the First People and their helpers should have been charred to a crisp sun cycles ago. Since they are not, I can only conclude that I'm a hapless failure as a witch."

"Then . . ." Slipped Bark's faint voice asked, "what do you do?"

"I plot," the old man growled. "Just as I plotted to have you brought here. They would have thought of searching the kiva sooner or later. They won't come here looking for you."

"Why?" Fir Brush asked. "What good are we to you?"

The old man sucked at the last of his tobacco, the bowl going dim. He sighed, knocked the hot dottle out of it, and said, "However it works out up there, you are Ripple's kin. One way or another, you are going to be important."

"Someone's coming," Slipped Bark said as she leaned out over the wall and stared down the dark path that led up the north side of the Dog's Tooth.

"Yes," Old White Eye said softly. "Quite a lot of some-ones. We had to wait until after dark, until after the infor-mants were asleep, before they could move."

"Who?" Fir Brush asked.

The old man seemed not to hear, saying, "Your brother is true to his name. The ripples of his vision are rolling across our world."

THE SPIRAL

I trace my fingers across a spiral pecked into the stone. The rock is rough against the soft pad of my finger, the heart of the stone cold and uncaring.

I wonder if the one constant among human beings is selfishness. We see only the center of the spiral. It is there that we struggle to live, oblivious of the outside of the rings. It is in the battle to stay there that we condemn our-selves.

Would it be so bad to live out at the edges? There we still breathe. Our hearts continue to beat. The sun shines with as much brilliance, and to Dance upon the rim is to know absolute freedom.

The center of the spiral is a trap. It is a one-way tunnel into which we fall, dropped forever downward, tighter and tighter until our souls are crushed, our hearts compressed, and our lungs squeezed breathless.

In the deepest heart of the spiral lies the end of hope.

We would destroy ourselves and our world in the mad attempt to gain and be the center. We are like crows that squabble over the pecked remains of a dry corncob when a fresh green ear is but a short flight away.

For this, we are condemned.

Follow me. The center of the spiral beckons.

We will begin at a walk, proceed to a jog, and then rush headlong toward the center. Deeper . . . ever deeper . . .

. . . Into the madness . . .

Fifteen

Ripple placed a hand on the wall behind him. Beyond it was a narrow path and then the sheer cliff that dropped down to the steep fir-and-spruce-forested slope below.

He shivered, puffing in the cool air. Shivering hurt. Even breathing was painful. Horned Lizard's henchman had used considerable skill. He'd pulled his blows to inflict the greatest pain with the least damage. How did a man learn that?

Ripple bowed his head and fingered the splinters of turkey bone he'd found. Could they be used to dig the baked clay mortar out from around the stones in the wall? Were they long enough to reach into the space between the tightly fitted rock? And, once through the expertly laid masonry, could he pull out enough of the rubble fill to allow him to work on the outside wall?

It would take time. Assuming his turkey bones lasted. Assuming they didn't come to check on him. And if they didn't hear him scratching away.

He pressed the sharp end of the turkey bone to his

thumb, testing it, and then turned, beginning the laborious task of chipping off the plaster. In the silence bits of it pattered onto the floor.

Voices!

He turned, staring up at the high ceiling. Faint yellow light reflected from the square opening overhead. He could hear steps.

The First People's tongue sounded like grouse squawkings to him. Then came the higher lilt of a woman's voice. Gods, not Fir Brush!

Ripple lowered his turkey bone to the floor and braced his back against the wall to hide where he'd pried at the plaster. He squinted as the flickering light appeared over the high entry. Then it was lowered, casting its yellow glow into his narrow room. Through the glare he could just make out the faces: Deputy Sunwatcher Water Bow scowled; War Chief Burning Smoke looked stern; and Horned Lizard was smiling with anticipation. The pretty young woman who accompanied them looked curious, her eyes gleaming in the light.

Ripple swallowed dryly, knowing her: Blessed Larkspur, Blue Dragonfly Clan Matron of Pinnacle Great House, cousin to the Blessed Matron, Desert Willow. He had seen her from afar. For the most part she traveled by litter, being carried up and down First Moon Mountain by her Made People porters. She was a beautiful creature, doe-eyed, slender, with delicate bones and round breasts.

Horned Lizard bent and lowered the ladder. He turned, climbing down first, the lamp in one hand. Behind him Burning Smoke followed, a fabric bag over his shoulder. Then came the Priest and finally Larkspur.

Ripple stared up as they crowded around him.

"We no longer have the option of waiting on you," Water Bow said in his accented voice. "Things are happening beyond our little valley that concern all of the First People. Someone has dared to mock the Blessed Sun's authority and goodwill."

Ripple swallowed hard as Burning Smoke said something to the Priest and lowered the bag. Larkspur's musical voice asked a question. When she glanced at Ripple, it was as if she were idly studying a crippled camp dog; pity tempered the curiosity in her large dark eyes.

She was a striking woman, broad-shouldered but thin at the waist. She wore a kirtle belted low. Her navel was a dark shadow in a flat belly. Strings of turquoise, jet, and coral beads hung at her throat, the lowest of them draping the tops of her high breasts. Her face was triangular; four small spirals were tattooed on her chin below full lips. The delicate nose was straight, her eyes like polished obsidian that accented the thick wealth of her gleaming black hair. It hung loose down her back and swayed lightly with her movements.

Burning Smoke lifted something from the sack, raising it so that Ripple could see.

"Do you know this?" Water Bow asked.

Ripple glanced at the soot-crusted thing, fought the urge to recoil, and nodded. "It is a man's skull. Someone has ground off the bottom of it, leaving only the top."

Burning Smoke turned it, showing how it had been so perfectly ground and polished. It looked like someone had cut straight through from the bridge of the nose, through the eye orbits, and around to the far back of the head. Lamplight cast shadows over the inside of the braincase, revealing hollows and the imprint of veins.

Water Bow smiled. "Yes, as I understand, the back of it, just here"—he placed a finger to the swell of Ripple's skull just behind his ear—"was damaged. Broken. Crushed. So they discarded it."

Ripple wiggled away from the Priest's finger, his heart beginning to race.

"This particular skull was used as a cup for a great many ceremonials," Water Bow continued. "I myself have drunk from it on occasion."

Burning Smoke grinned and uttered something in his lilting tongue.

"The war chief," Water Bow translated, "was just telling me that the man's name was Falling Cone."

Ripple's pulse leapt as he stared at the use-polished skull cup in Burning Smoke's hands.

Dear gods! That's my father's skull!

The image flickered in his souls' eye: A war club raised against the blue of a spring sky. Then it began its descent, whistling down through the air in a graceful arc. Like a diving falcon it sliced straight and true. The red-shirted warrior stood with his foot pressing down on Father's neck, pinning him to the ground.

Ripple jerked at the memory of the impact: a snapping smack as the stone crushed the skull behind Father's ear.

Ripple closed his eyes, seeing back to that day. Father had been on his belly, hands bound behind his back. As the body bucked and jerked in death, the warrior had failed to keep his foot atop the straining neck.

"Ripple," Water Bow whispered to interrupt his thoughts. "They called you Ripple because of your threats as a boy."

Ripple turned his head away, wincing. How could they know this?

Water Bow's voice was like a snake's hiss. "Way back then, you, an angry little boy, said you would kill us all." A pause. "They mocked you. Said that such a mouthy brat would have no more effect on the First People than a ripple in a pond. And the name stuck."

Ripple clamped his eyes shut, remembering Cold Bringing Woman, seeing her midnight eyes flashing in bloodred irises. *Is that why she chose me?*

Larkspur said something soft, and Ripple slitted his vision, glancing unsurely at what was coming out of the sack: yucca fiber ropes, a hammer, the sort of thick stone mortar used in cracking nuts, a slender brow tine cut from a bull elk's rack, and long yucca leaves.

Water Bow gave him a sad look. "Why don't you tell us about this vision you've had? Did Old Woman North really come to you?"

Ripple began to pant and tried to huddle into a ball. Was it best just to keep silent?

Larkspur spoke again, her voice half-bored. He shot her a glance, wishing for the first time that he understood the First People's tongue. She was watching him with the same scrutiny she might give a boiling root.

"You should talk now," Water Bow insisted.

"She will destroy you," Ripple whispered in return. For

the first time, he felt sure of it. She had told him he would be tested, even maimed. What a fool he'd been to think it would be at the hands of the Mountain Witch.

Horned Lizard and Burning Smoke laid their callused hands on him, shoving him down onto the floor. Horned Lizard wrenched his right arm behind him, and Ripple cried out. The rope sawed into his flesh as they bound his right wrist to his right ankle, and then the left to the left. The posture was awkward.

Burning Smoke reached down and wrapped a hand in Ripple's hair. Ripple bellowed fear when they jerked him to his knees.

Water Bow said softly, "You could end all this. Just tell us what happened up on the mountain."

Ripple tried to swallow, his heart racing. He could see the bowl made of his father's skull, rocking like an irregular pot on the floor.

The words formed in his throat. "I will destroy you."

"Yes," Water Bow answered absently. "I'm sure you will."

Matron Larkspur gave an order, crossing her arms in finality.

Ripple met her dark stare as Horned Lizard pulled his head up by the hair and slammed him violently against the wall. Ripple screamed when his legs pulled down on his shoulder joints, seeking to pop them loose from their sockets. By rocking back on his toes, he could barely support a portion of his weight. He was still staring into Larkspur's eyes when Burning Smoke picked up the hammer and elk tine. The hammer had a rounded stream cobble for a head, the stone just big enough to cup into a man's palm. It had been bound to the handle by means of wet rawhide sewed to shrink tight as it dried.

Burning Smoke handed the tools to Matron Larkspur. She hefted the hammer in her petite hand, testing the weight. The antler tine rolled between her thin fingers. A smile curved her sensual lips when she knelt in front of him. Gods, how could such a beautiful woman strike such terror?

She raised the tine, holding it like a chisel in her left

hand. With her right, she choked up on the hammer handle. A slight frown marred her perfect forehead as she slipped the point past Ripple's lips.

He tried to squirm, agony eating at his shoulder joints. Trussed like a backward frog, hanging by his hair, and jammed against the wall, he could barely twist his head to the side. She moved with him, the frown deepening.

The quick blow surprised him. A sharp snap traveled up his jaw—was felt more than heard. Stinging pain accompanied the sensation of the loose tooth rolling around on his tongue. Blood rushed warm across his palate, the taste salty and metallic.

Dazed, fighting a ragged scream, he felt the sting as she deftly knocked another tooth out of his jaw.

"You could talk," Water Bow reminded from the side. "Wouldn't it be easier than spending the rest of your life without teeth?"

Matron Larkspur continued to smile as she leaned forward. The chisel was gripped in her small brown fist for another blow.

Sixteen

W̲ho comes?" a voice called from the darkness beside the trail. The way led up the steep sides of the Dog's Tooth. Bad Cast was panting, he and Wrapped Wrist having run most of the way from Soft Cloth's house in Mid-Sun Town atop Juniper Ridge.

The darkness reminded him of the inside of a sealed kiva at midnight. Cool mountain air sighed through the conifers and rattled leaves in the scrub oak and sumac. Overhead, even the late-night stars had vanished.

Bad Cast slowed, unsure of the footing, and not a little frightened by whomever lurked in the darkness. So far, it hadn't been what he would call a stellar day. Most of it had been spent being shuttled from one of his clan's dwellings to another, depending on where the Red Shirts were headed.

Nerving himself, he called out, "I am Bad Cast, of the Blue Stick Clan. With me is Wrapped Wrist, my friend and kinsman."

"Do you know the way?" the voice asked.

Wrapped Wrist called back, "I've been there before."

"Good. Proceed," the shadowy voice called.

"What if the Red Shirts come this way?" Bad Cast asked. "They've been searching for us all day."

A low chuckle came from the dark shadows at the side of the trail. "Let them. By morning they'll be in pieces. Long gone."

Bad Cast suffered an uneasy tingle in his guts. He jumped when Wrapped Wrist placed a hand on his shoulder and said, "Come on. It's this way . . . I think."

"Don't overwhelm me with your certainty."

Bad Cast let Wrapped Wrist lead. Loose rock and dirt slid under his sandals. They climbed through a ragged patch of timber and out into a clearing. He could smell smoke and make out the faint square cast of the masonry wall atop the Dog's Tooth.

Wrapped Wrist led him unerringly to a gate in the wall. Stepping through into the plaza, he looked around. Light came from gleaming coals in a shallow-basin fire pit in the plaza floor. Pit house fires painted the ladder tips protruding from their smoke holes in dull red. The two-story clan house loomed dark and brooding in the night.

Together they felt their way forward. Not even a dog barked. It was eerie, as if people were purposefully staying out of their way.

"Rot!" Bad Cast growled as he stumbled over a grinding stone hidden in the shadows.

"Quiet," Wrapped Wrist warned. "Half the mountain will know where we are."

"What about Spots? Do you think Soft Cloth got a message to him?"

"I hope. Last I heard the Red Shirts didn't have him

yet." Bad Cast placed a hand to his belly. He wanted to be anywhere but here, sneaking around First Moon Mountain under the cloak of night. More than anything, he wanted to be home, playing with his baby, enjoying Soft Cloth's company. Instead he was out stumbling around in fear, hunted by the Red Shirts, in who knew what kind of trouble.

His stomach hurt.

"There," Wrapped Wrist said, pointing at a stubby-looking kiva visible between the pit houses. Like veins of light, cracks in the kiva wall gleamed with translucent red. What looked like brush around the bottom resolved into seated people, most of them young men.

"What is this?" Bad Cast asked, hearing the muted whispers among the seated men.

"I have no idea."

"You are Wrapped Wrist?" A shape rose and detached itself from the fringe of the crowd.

"Yes?"

"Come forward. They've been waiting for you."

"Who?"

"You have been summoned, hunter. They want you and Bad Cast inside." Dark shapes shifted as a path was cleared.

His guts turning sickly, Bad Cast followed Wrapped Wrist to the steps that led up to the kiva entrance. A hanging covered the doorway, effectively blocking anyone from seeing inside.

As they approached, a hand pulled the hanging aside, exposing the square entryway in the curving side of the structure. When Bad Cast hesitated, a rude shove urged him forward. He ducked below the lintel into the interior. From the painted walls, this kiva belonged to the Black Shale Moiety, of which his Blue-Stick Clan was a member.

The interior was spacious, fifteen long paces across the diagonal. The floor had been excavated into the soil to the depth of a man's waist, then lined with a multicourse stone wall and bench. This in turn had been plastered over with a dark clay. Poles set at intervals were lashed together to create walls. These had been interwoven with willow stays, then packed with a coating of clay to create wattle-and-daub walls. Rafters ran from the poles to a square framework of wooden beams supported by thick logs rising from the kiva floor. A large square opening in the middle of the roof provided daytime illumination as well as a place for the smoke to exit.

The First People mocked these local kivas, smiling crookedly at their mud-caked walls and thin roofs. They joked about the giant square openings that allowed rain and snow as well as ample sunlight inside. Compared to the complex heavy-log roofs in the First People's kivas, maybe these were more like ramadas than anything else, but they remained a defiant symbol in the face of the First People's occupation of their lands.

A low fire burned in the stone-lined hearth cut into the center of the floor. Its light bathed the sturdy roof supports and sent a shine over the clay-washed walls.

Bad Cast stopped short at Wrapped Wrist's side, a sudden catch in his throat as he took in the crowded kiva. Expressionless, unfamiliar faces were watching him. The other eerie thing was the haunting silence. Not a whisper came to his ears, not a careless shuffle or snicker. Instead, seriousness, like a large stone, seemed to lie heavily on the people. He could see it in their worried gazes, in the somber set of mouths, or the too-tightly clasped hands. The only sound was the crackle of the burning wood in the firebox.

Along the northern wall, seated on the bench, were four old women and two robe-cloaked elderly men. Sitting cross-legged in a ring spreading out from their feet were numerous men and women, all wearing their best. But for a narrow path through the center of the kiva, every inch of floor was occupied.

Bad Cast had never been the center of so much attention. In his sudden confusion and embarrassment, he froze like a deer before a cougar.

Gods! These were the clan leaders! Along the north

wall sat the lineage elders: the Matrons and their war chiefs sat cross-legged on the kiva floor before them. No wonder so many young men waited outside. Most of the authority in First Moon Valley was concentrated here.

"Come forward," a reedy voice called.

Bad Cast blinked owlishly at the line of withered elders seated on the bench. It took a moment for their identities to sink in. The first to be recognized, of course, was Elder Rattler, the shriveled, white-haired leader of his own Blue Stick Clan. She rarely left her house down in the valley except for ritual occasions. What was she doing here, and in the middle of the night?

Beside her, the legendary Dreamer, old White Eye, sat, his back curved by age, a coarse gray blanket wrapped about his shoulders. His one white eye gleamed like a bit of shell in sunlight, while his ruined face seemed to fall in around his empty eye socket. The old witch was grinning as if he could see into Bad Cast's very heart and was enjoying the queasy terror locked there.

To White Eye's right sat Green Claw. He ruled the Bee Flower Clan of the Soft Earth Moiety in his sister's name. His sharp eyes were taking their measure, glinting like struck obsidian in his round face. Ample of body, but with sagging flesh and wheezing breath, he was still sharp of mind. Few things occurred inside his clan without his knowledge.

On the far right was Black Sage, of the Soft Earth's Whisper Clan. She was a wizened stick of an old woman who crouched under a turkey-feather cloak. Flat flaps of breasts sagged over her protruding ribs. She had a smoky gaze that seemed to be waiting like a wary predator in search of prey.

By Old White Eye's left sat Hoarse Caller, the aged female elder of the Strong Back Clan of the Soft Earth Moiety. She had passed six tens of hard summers and was tall, reedy, like a blue heron that had borne too many burdens. She had a long face, her gray hair pinned atop her head as if to make her appear even taller. The way she sat, her curved back was ever more apparent.

Next sat the Muddy Water Clan's elder, a woman of the Black Shale Moiety named Old Dead Bird. She had received her name when, as a girl, an eagle had fallen from the sky and thudded like a stone at her feet. To everyone's surprise, the bird had been dead when it hit the ground. One of the Priests had cut it open to see if it augured some terrible message, but not a drop of blood had been found inside. Dead Bird had never been large, and over the passing of seasons, she had grown ever more slight of body. Her dark brown eyes now watched Bad Cast with veiled curiosity.

By her left elbow sat the elder Matron known as Red Water, leader of the Green Acorn Clan of the Black Shale Moiety. In her midthirties, she was younger than the others, still attractive despite an odd white streak that started above her forehead and ran through her black hair. She wore a loose deerhide skirt that draped over her muscular legs.

"I said, come forward," the reedy voice repeated.

It took a heartbeat for Bad Cast to realize that old Rattler had spoken. He saw a hardening of her expression as both he and Wrapped Wrist remained rooted, obviously scared stiff.

Unseen hands caught them from behind. The shove was so unexpected that Bad Cast stumbled forward, careening down the narrow aisle. He glanced back to see a hard-eyed warrior—a strung bow hung over his shoulder—pushing them along.

Before he could catch his breath, he was standing in front of the most important people in his world. Try as he might, he couldn't force himself to meet Elder Rattler's hard gaze. It shamed him that the old woman was seeing a trembling young man whose fear shone in his eyes.

Old White Eye stood, raised a hand, and waved it toward the exit. "The rest of you, please leave us. We would talk to these young men in private."

Bad Cast glanced back to see the hard-eyed warrior gesturing with a muscular arm. People slowly rose amidst a rustling of clothing, their sandals whispering on the packed earth as they shuffled back out the entryway.

That beckoning doorway looked impossibly far away.

The people slowly drained away like water through a small hole in a cooking jar. If only he could be going with them. The muscular warrior ducked out behind the last of the people; the door hanging swayed in his wake.

Shouts could be heard outside. Moments later a cowed-looking Spots was ushered into the now-empty kiva. Spots blinked, started to grin, and then recognized the elders seated on the bench. His expression fell like the downdraft preceding a summer thunderstorm.

"Ah, the last of our young cocks has arrived," White Eye whispered, though how the old blind man could know Spots's identity was beyond Bad Cast.

Spots walked hesitantly forward, turning questioning glances from Wrapped Wrist to Bad Cast, who gave him frightened shrugs in return.

The muscular warrior leaned in, calling, "My men have moved the curious away, Elders. You may speak in private."

"Stay, Whistle," White Eye replied. "We may need your expertise."

Whistle? Bad Cast tried to place the name, coming up blank. Tens of hundreds of people lived around the First Moon Valley; no one could know everyone. Still, this muscular man, with his almost feline walk, striking appearance, and gleaming black hair pinned in a warrior's bun would have stood out. The warrior, apparently unfazed in the proximity of so much authority, trotted up and crouched like a waiting cougar beside one of the roof supports, his dark eyes flicking alertly back and forth.

Elder Rattler cleared her throat. "We are here because of the mess you and young Ripple have gotten us into."

Bad Cast swallowed hard; a band of dread began to close around his chest. Wrapped Wrist winced painfully, while Spots turned so pale that the mottling of his scarred flesh looked uniformly white.

"As we speak, that poisonous serpent, Burning Smoke, is torturing Ripple for information." Rattler made a grim face. "But for the distance, and the thickness of Pinnacle Great House's walls, we'd be hearing his screams now."

The band pulled even tighter around Bad Cast's chest.

Elder Rattler studied them one by one. "Whatever Ripple's vision was, it has apparently frightened the First People. We did not act quickly enough to save Ripple, and it was but with the narrowest luck that we've kept the three of you out of Matron Larkspur's grasp."

"What happened up there?" Hoarse Caller asked in the breathy low voice for which she'd been named. "Up on the mountain . . . What did Ripple see?"

Uncharacteristically, it was Spots who found his voice first. "He claims that Cold Bringing Woman came to him and that she told him he could destroy the First People."

Elder Red Water leaned forward, her white-streaked hair catching the light. "The three of you were the first to reach him. Do you believe he really saw Cold Bringing Woman?"

While Spots and Bad Cast shrugged, Wrapped Wrist said, "The elk was frozen solid, Elder. The plants were wilted as if from a frost. We can tell you that Ripple firmly believes it. Were he here, he would swear it was true."

"Why Ripple?" Dead Bird wondered absently. Her callused brown fingers were caressing the loose wattle of flesh under her chin.

"His family has a history with the First People," Elder Rattler answered. "They executed his mother and father ten summers ago. The boy watched both of his parents die."

"His father was Falling Cone, a Bee Flower man," Green Claw added. "A cousin of mine, and something of a hothead. Ripple's mother, Pine Berry, had no siblings, and only several cousins living some distance downstream in the valley. Falling Cone took considerable interest in helping Pine Berry raise her children. He doted on them with the same affection as if they were his own clan kin."

"I remember," Red Water said thoughtfully. "War Chief Ironwood had already left Straight Path Canyon at the head of a war party when Water Bow signaled that the trouble was over."

"Just as well," Black Sage muttered. "It would have gone hard on us had Ironwood come all this way. No telling what might have broken loose. All it would have taken would have been a hotheaded young man flinging a stone, perhaps a shouted insult, and passions could have burned out of control."

"And we don't want that to happen now, either," Dead Bird added. "These are perilous times. People are frightened. Stories are carried to my ears all the time of starvation and drought in the lowlands. The last thing we want is for the First People to make an example of us. We're some of the few who aren't teetering on the verge of starvation."

"Not yet," Hoarse Caller rasped. "But how many more loads of tribute can we watch carried out of our granaries before it's our bellies that grow gaunt?"

"Not to mention some other sort of catastrophe," Red Water reminded. "An early frost . . . a flash flood that takes out too many fields . . . a plague of insects?" She shrugged. "We're working very closely to the edge here, having just enough to see us through after giving the Blessed Sun his tribute."

"And tribute comes first," Elder Rattler reminded. "Webworm won't lose a moment's sleep if his demands leave our granaries empty and our families starve to death before spring."

"We might be able to hide some of the harvest," Red Water suggested. "Make secret caches and store enough to make the difference."

"Sure," Green Claw added dryly, "with the Red Shirts slipping around all winter wondering where the constantly full stew pots are coming from? Don't forget, they have their sources among our people. As long as they perch up there atop our sacred mountain, they see and hear everything."

"Now is not the time to stir things up." Black Sage glanced back and forth among her peers. "This new Deputy, Leather Hand, has been making quite a name for himself. Traders tell me that the troublemakers in Lanceleaf Village are lying headless, sprawled in trash pit graves, their newly polished skulls staring down from the kiva niches."

Old White Eye spoke: "We are losing the purpose of this meeting." He steepled his fingers, the sightless white eye bulging from his ruined face. "Cold Bringing Woman came to Ripple. We didn't act quickly enough to remove the young man from the Blessed Larkspur's enthusiastic deputies. Now he is discovering just how much pain his young body can stand." He turned his head toward Elder Hoarse Caller. "Perhaps, gentle Elder, his voice will be forever broken, as yours was so many summers ago."

Hoarse Caller's whispery voice replied, "Yes, a human throat can only scream for so long before it tears away like a cobweb in a gale."

Bad Cast watched the elders shift uncomfortably, queasiness slipping about in his stomach. He tried to keep his imagination from conjuring images of Ripple, of how his friend's face must be contorting to make screams like that.

"All the more reason to avoid a confrontation with the First People," Black Sage maintained. "Who wants to suffer what Hoarse Caller did? Who wants to see their relatives endure that, let alone live with memories of the horrors?"

"Yes, yes," Green Claw avowed. "And we must not forget, the moon cycle is coming complete. The Blessed Sunwatcher, Blue Racer, will be leading his entourage this way. Perhaps even the Blessed Webworm and Desert Willow will be coming to view the renewal of Sister Moon."

Old White Eye smiled. The satisfaction it communicated brought a shiver to Bad Cast's souls.

"Why do you smile?" Elder Rattler asked.

White Eye chuckled softly. "Because, my old friends, what you wish is no longer at issue."

"And why is that?" Green Claw sounded annoyed, as if his stature had been impugned.

"Because the gaming pieces have already been cast," White Eye added. "And once they were released, no amount of longing on your part can call them back."

"What gaming pieces?" Black Sage demanded, her deeply lined face reflecting skepticism. "We have made no decision here, committed ourselves to no action."

"How arrogant you are." White Eye tilted his head

back, the firelight bathing his damaged face, gleaming redly into the dirt-encrusted socket of his missing eye. "You have no gaming pieces to cast. They were thrown by the gods long ago."

"When Webworm was made Blessed Sun?" Green Claw asked.

"Before that," White Eye replied.

"When the Rainbow Serpent rose from the Below Worlds?" Hoarse Caller whispered.

"Much before that."

"When Matron Night Sun mated with Ironwood?" Dead Bird guessed.

"Long before that, even. No, the pieces were cast the night the Tattooed Raiders stole away the Tortoise Bundle from Talon Town and carried off the little girl who Dreamed with it."

Silence followed.

Bad Cast could see that each of the clan elders was puzzled.

White Eye continued. "From that moment on, the future of the First People began to unwind. Power shifted. But, most curious of all, almost no one in our world marked the moment when the destruction of the First People became irrevocable."

"And when was that?" Elder Rattler asked skeptically. "Surely not when Ripple had this supposed vision."

"Of course not," White Eye chided. "As I said, the gaming pieces were cast long ago. Perhaps Cold Bringing Woman had something to do with it, as did Brother Mud Head, and the katsinas, and perhaps, even, the Flute Player himself." He paused. "Sometimes the most momentous of events pass unmarked by ordinary men."

"Let me guess." Dead Bird snorted. "You're going to tell us that you're not an ordinary man."

"Far from it. I'm as ordinary as the next man," White Eye responded. "Nevertheless, I knew immediately what had happened."

Elder Rattler leaned forward to see the old Dreamer's face. "Knew what? Explain yourself."

White Eye's grin exposed toothless pink gums. "I knew that the First People were doomed the moment the Mountain Witch returned from her captivity among the eastern mound builders."

"What does this have to do with us?" Bad Cast finally nerved himself to ask. He'd begun to feel foolish standing in the presence of elders who were preoccupied with cares far beyond his own.

White Eye swiveled his head. An unseen gaze was piercing Bad Cast's body. "It has everything to do with you. But for a mistake on my part, you would already be carrying Ripple to the lair of the Mountain Witch, which, if we are to survive, is where he must go."

Seventeen

As he sat chewing the last of his corn cake breakfast, Leather Hand watched the sun finally crest the high wooded slopes of the Green Mesa off to the east. He and his men had camped on a rise just below the stone pillar known as Thunderbird's Toes on the southern tip of the mountain. Now the stone caught the first morning light.

The valley between Green Mesa and Thunderbird Mountain still lay in shadow. The drainages cutting the alluvial bottoms created a tracery of deeper purple like veins in the pale soil. He could make out distant farmsteads by their irregular fields.

"There." Tracker pointed off to the south.

Leather Hand followed the man's arm. From their vantage at the foot of the rocky prominence, he could trace the winding drainage channel as it worked out of the juniper-dotted slope and etched the yellow and tan soils that stretched into the broad basin. In the hazy south, World Tree Mountain, a black spear of basalt, thrust up from the pale beds of sandstone and clay.

Leather Hand turned his attention back to the place Tracker indicated. In the trees behind him, a flock of piñon jays trilled and called in long rolling racks that sounded like human laughter.

"Perhaps a half day's run," Tracker replied laconically. "They have already started their morning fires. You can see the faint blue pall of the smoke. It hangs low in the air."

Maybe Tracker could see it. Leather Hand couldn't, but he'd take the Deep Canyon barbarian's word for it. He stood and gave it one more hard look. Then he turned and saw Turquoise Fox staring thoughtfully at distant World Tree Mountain.

"Do you believe it?" he asked his deputy.

"That it's a tree?" Turquoise Fox shrugged, glanced down the hill where the rest of the warriors were finishing breakfast, then turned his keen eyes back to the distant peak. "I don't think so, War Chief. I've climbed around the base of that pillar while hunting desert rams. The kind of stone it's made of looks nothing like wood. Now, you go south, down to the Colored Desert, and you'll find wood that is obviously turned to stone."

"Perhaps the world tree lies deeply inside the rock, Deputy."

Turquoise Fox gave him a sly smile. "What you really want to know, War Chief, is whether I think that peak is actually holy like the Priests tell us. Do I really think it protrudes from the Underworlds into ours, and most of all, do I believe that First Woman sits beneath its roots, spinning out Dreams in World Tree Cave?"

"Do you?"

He shook his head. "If it were a great Spirit tree sticking into our world, it would have branches. Instead, those rocky lines that run out from it look more like roots. If you ask me, whatever it is, it is firmly planted in our world, not the ones below."

"So.you don't believe that First Woman is down there."

Turquoise Fox smiled wistfully and shifted his attention to the distant southwest, where a hazy smear leaned eastward in the pink morning sky. "Now there, War Chief, is true Spirit Power. The Rainbow Serpent rises from the

Underworlds. At the Serpent's base, the earth bleeds. Blood runs from the wound so hot it pours out in rivers that glow. Only when it begins to cool does it scab, crack, and harden. Even then, a man can't touch it. If there is any Power I fear, War Chief, it is the Rainbow Serpent."

Leather Hand stared at the distant pillar of smoke and ash. The slanting sunlight began to turn it from purple to blue.

"War Chief?" Turquoise Fox asked.

"Yes?"

"We will find the raiders today." His deputy had returned his gaze to World Tree Mountain. "Are you serious about driving a stiletto of fear into the hearts of the barbarians?"

"More than serious."

Turquoise Fox glanced curiously at the men downslope, who laughed as they ate the last of their corn cakes. He lowered his voice. "Are you serious enough to make your men comply, even if it means the most severe of discipline?"

Leather Hand frowned. "Is there some reason you won't tell me what you have in mind?"

"Do you remember the stories that circulated during that hard summer drought six years ago?"

"I heard a great many stories that summer."

"Do you remember the stories they told of famine at Deer Mother Village?"

Leather Hand stopped short, frowning. "This isn't a matter of hunger, Deputy."

Turquoise Fox smiled. "Oh, yes. It is, War Chief. It's just that we're talking about a different kind of hunger than the one that lurks in an empty belly."

Stunned by the implications, Leather Hand stood quietly for a moment. Gods, was the man serious? Finally he cupped his mouth to call, "Come! We have important work ahead of us. Today, we avenge Right Acorn and the Blessed Sun!"

He started headlong down the hill, long strides taking him toward the narrow wash that meandered its way toward the Dust People's pathetic farmsteads. Turquoise Fox's proposed "solution" to their problem left him nervous with its possibilities.

*Do I have the courage to order my warriors to do such a
thing? Can I go through with it myself?*

Ripple lay on his side in the darkness. He was vaguely
aware of the gritty floor. It stuck to his cheek where blood
had caked and dried. The chill rising through the clay-
covered stone countered the hot rush of pain that pulsed
with each beat of his heart. He tried not to move his
tongue. Each time he did it was to feel a mouth that wasn't
his. That—more than the throbbing in his jaw—
frightened him. But the misery in his mouth was drowned
by the white agony in his broken hand and the searing in
his genitals.

Thankfully, it was too dark to see the terrible reality of
what they'd done to him.

A droplet of something wet ran down the curve of his
thigh, the tickle of it lost in the fiery pain in his crotch.
Was it blood, or perhaps urine? They had told him to release his water as often as possible.

"It washes out the pus," Water Bow had told him. "If
your penis scabs over, your water has no place to go. It's a
nasty and most painful way to die."

Ripple sobbed, blood and saliva trickling past his bruised
lips. He clenched and unclenched his good right hand. His
left he tried to keep still. The slightest movement shot
agony up his arm.

"You'll have time," Water Bow had told him. "You can
think for a while. When we come back, you will tell us
about this vision. Remember: You have more teeth on the
other side of your jaw. You still have your right hand. Living the rest of your life with one good hand and half your
teeth will be much easier than living with no hands or
teeth at all."

*I want to die! Please, Cold Bringing Woman. Come and
rip what's left of life from my body.*

He heard only silence and felt fluid drip down his thigh.
He remembered the Blessed Larkspur, an indecisive

frown marring her beautiful face, as she took his penis in her slim brown fingers. He'd stared down in horror as she turned his defenseless member with great precision, studying it intently. Then she had reached for one of the dried yucca leaves. Still bound, wrists to ankles, he'd tried to wiggle away, only to be jammed hard against the wall by the guards. She had pulled out on his penis, stretching it. With the sharp point of the yucca she had dimpled the tender skin. She had been looking into his eyes when she pushed it in like an arrow.

He'd wailed like a scalded baby as Larkspur drove the yucca leaf crosswise through the center of his penis just behind the foreskin. She'd had to tug to pull it through, the same as if she'd been sewing a rawhide bag.

Through the burning pain he had been vaguely aware of Larkspur saying something, her voice musical.

The laughter of the guards had followed.

"She says that there's a lot of gristle in there," Water Bow had translated. "But, unlike our own people, your barbarian bitches are probably used to that."

He'd been gasping, half choked on the blood that pooled in his ruined mouth. Crimson drool leaked past his bruised lips and down his chest and stomach. He would remember her large brown eyes—deep pools of curiosity—searching his. The lilting tones of her voice seemed to hang in the air.

"Will you tell us the content of the vision?"

Ripple had whimpered in horror.

Water Bow then said, "There is another way to end this: You could deny that Old Woman North ever came to you. Say it never happened. Tell your people that it was just a story. A way for a young man to impress people. They'll understand."

He doggedly shook his head, only to have it twisted down by the guards so he stared at his crotch. He blinked, seeing Larkspur's fingers, slick with blood as she took a second yucca leaf and placed the hard point against the skin of his penis.

Had he shrieked again? He couldn't remember. He had been sobbing after that. Tears had silvered his vision. But one image—clinging through the blur—had been of Lark-spur, her pink tongue flicking as she licked his fresh blood from her long brown fingers.

I didn't break. By the gods, Cold Bringing Woman, I didn't betray you. The thought rolled over and over in his head.

When he finally threw up, thick yellow bile soaked the broken roots of his teeth and burned like bitter fire through the side of his head.

The ache in Bulrush's bones, joints, and muscles sucked at his exhausted souls. He had never felt as weary as he did when he half stumbled into the dusty plaza in front of his home. His back was bowed under the weight of the burden basket. The food he and his companions had cooked along the way had helped; sweet boiled corn had given him enough strength to tote the load down the wash trail to Saltbush Farmstead.

He looked around, now half afraid of what he'd find. No one sat beneath the tattered ramadas, or lingered in the shadows of the three shabby pit houses. The southwest wind chased little trailers of dust across the packed clay of the plaza, and flipped bits of juniper bark, flecks of char-coal, and other litter around.

Gods, was anyone still alive?

He glanced over his shoulder where Uncle Sage trudged—head down and dust-streaked—his hair batted this way and that by the aggravating wind. The older man's feet shuffled doggedly toward the low dome of his own dwelling.

Over the last couple of days, Bulrush hadn't been sure they'd make it. None of the men who left on the raid had been in good shape to start with. All had been gaunted by hunger, their reserves depleted.

But now we're home. We did it!

A rush, like ecstasy, charged his aching limbs, only to drain away as he swung the heavy basket to the ground and glanced up at the rounded roof of Gourd Pendant's house. The familiar ladder uprights, one side longer than the other, thrust desolately up from the smoke hole into the brassy summer sky.

Bulrush sighed, his mouth too dried from thirst to call out with more than a croak, and, step by step, climbed the notched pole that led onto the curved roof. He crawled across to the ladder and looked down into the shadowed interior. "Anybody here?"

"Bulrush?" Gourd Pendant called.

He squinted down into the dim room. Below him, beneath the ladder, the fire pit was nothing more than a gray stain of ash. He could see the mealing bins in the corner by the deflector. A sandal last, half covered with woven yucca leaves, lay abandoned on the floor as did two corrugated cooking pots, one resting on its side next to the sandstone slabs used to prop it over the fire. Gourd Pendant's prized *tchamahia,* along with the one she'd inherited from her mother, lay flat in the dirt, as though they no longer mattered. Two yucca-fiber dolls looked abandoned on the stained floor.

Swallowing down his dry throat, he turned his gaze to the bedding along the west wall, terrified of what he'd find.

He could see them lying on their willow-mat bedding. Blossom and Lizard were tucked under his wife's right arm. All three of them looked so thin, nothing but sticks of brown flesh, too-round heads black-thatched with filthy mats of long hair.

His children stirred, looking up with hope-filled eyes that sucked at his souls. In unison they asked, "Father?"

"I've brought food." It seemed so difficult to say. He wanted to laugh, to jump around, wave his arms, and shout. Instead, an inexplicable tightness pulled at his throat, and tears—impossible given his thirst-ridden condition—rimmed his eyes, dripping one by one like silver drops of rain into the dark interior.

In the end, he wept, his voice breaking as he repeated over and over, "We will live. We will live."

Eighteen

Deputy War Chief Leather Hand squatted on his muscular brown legs and studied the ground. He cocked his head, reaching down to run his fingers through the pale yellow dirt between his feet. He tightened his fist, lifting the powdery soil and watching it run between his fingers—only to be whipped away by the unforgiving southwest wind.

"What is this place?" he asked as he looked across at the sinuous lines of silt-filled ditches that snaked across the alluvial flat. A series of stones had been carefully placed in the arroyo bottom a stone's throw to his right. A dam waiting for water that had never come.

"This is supposed to be a field." Turquoise Fox blocked the fierce afternoon sun with a hard brown hand. "Those wooden contraptions over there where the ditches radiate, those are the head gates. Each of these little plots is owned by a different woman's lineage. In order to work these ditches, she must have the right *tchamahia,* a symbolic hoe that is Blessed for this piece of land ... for these ditches. To work these fields with any tool but the correct *tchamahia* is thought to anger the ground and cause the crops to fail."

"From the looks of things, I'd say someone used the wrong hoe."

Wind plucked at loose strands of black hair that had come loose from Leather Hand's bun. He squinted in the hot sunlight, wondering at the sere yellow soil, the exposed outcrops of crumbling brown sandstone on the surrounding ridgetops, and the dry-cracked patterns of clay at his feet. Where he now waited a low ridge protected the fields close to the dry wash; it looked like the last place on earth where corn, beans, or squash would grow.

"Why are there holes in the middle of these little mounds?" He indicated the lines of bumps that pocked the field. "Isn't that where they plant the seed?"

Turquoise Fox nodded. "Yes, War Chief. They make the mounds, then use a digging stick to poke a hole in the top when the soil is moist. Mounded like that, the roots get more water when the ditches flood these little fields."

"But there have been no floods."

"That is correct, War Chief."

"Then why do each of these little humps have gaping holes in them? Did rodents do this?"

Turquoise Fox gave him an evaluative look. "Not rodents, War Chief. It was the people who did this. The corn never sprouted. What you see here, the reason each little hump is opened, was so that the people could retrieve the seed corn they had so laboriously planted this spring."

"To save it for next year?"

Turquoise Fox slowly shook his head. "No, War Chief. It was ground, boiled, and eaten."

The notion stunned him. The last morsel of food that a good farmer would allow to pass his lips was one made from the seed corn. A man who ate his seeds was eating his future. Only a fool, or a man touched by madness, would do such a thing.

Leather Hand shifted on his heels to claw at one of the little earthen humps. All he retrieved was dust. As it sifted through his fingers the wind whisked it away in feathery streamers.

"Have you sent the scouts?"

"I have." Turquoise Fox gave him a knowing nod. "They are fanning out, following the tracks of the other raiders."

"I want to recover every single kernel of corn that is left."

"They'll barely have time to get their cooking fires started. We are within but a short walk of the first farmstead. Tracker reports a scatter of buildings, perhaps twenty people."

"Good." He looked up at the low ridge where the man known as Tracker hunched like a squatting coyote, his body silhouetted against the hot, brassy sky. The wind made whips of his black hair, as if trying to pull it loose from the man's head. Tracker, like the hunter he was, kept his vigilant attention on the surrounding flats.

"How many of these 'Dust People' are there?"

"I make it twenty to thirty farmsteads, War Chief. Maybe ten to twenty per settlement. Perhaps three hundred total. Some, those lucky enough to have relatives with food to spare, have moved back to the foothills of the Bearclaw Mountains to the south. The others are surviving by whatever means they have available."

"Our punishment must be swift and sure."

"War Chief," Turquoise Fox hesitated. "Have you given any more thought to the incident at Deer Mother Village?"

"I have."

Turquoise Fox indicated the dusty field where they waited. "Do you understand now why they won't care if we only kill them?"

Leather Hand nodded. *They have eaten their seed corn. How do you terrify a people who have devoured their future?*

Bad Cast didn't know what he feared more, the loose feeling in his bowels and the notion he might shame himself, or the fact that he might be dead before night fell.

As he pondered his dilemma he studied the backside of the man he followed. The warrior's red shirt was dirty; white sweat rings stained the armpits and collar. The travel-worn garment did little to hide the broad shoulders that rippled with slablike muscle. Lowering his gaze, Bad Cast watched the warrior's thick calves, like gnarled juniper, swelling and bulging with each step as they climbed toward Guest House.

Behind them, Father Sun had swollen into a red-gold ball that hung over the northwest horizon beyond Juniper Ridge. The reddish haze that lay low in the sky told Bad Cast that a big wildfire was burning somewhere to the west. All day they had been buffeted by strong southwest winds, that, along with the dry condition of the forest, augured ill for anyone in that distant fire's path. He could smell the smoke, acrid, on the air. The gaudy light made the red-shirted warrior ahead of him appear even more frightening.

"Are you afraid?" Whistle asked over his shoulder.

"I've never been this scared in my whole life," Bad Cast answered. "When you walked out from behind the kiva partition wearing that red shirt, I thought my life was over."

"It may well be," Whistle said earnestly as they emerged from the last of the trees. Ahead of them, Guest House glowed like a hot coal in the red sunset. The multistory structure perched astride the ridge, squatting like an ugly toad. Bad Cast could see some of the Made People enjoying the last light as they occupied themselves with different tasks on the rooftops. Despite Whistle trudging toward them, none bothered giving him or Bad Cast a second glance.

"Where did you get the warrior's shirt?" Bad Cast asked. "I mean, no one will recognize it, will they? You didn't steal it from one of the warriors, did you?"

"No. It's mine," Whistle said softly. A gust of wind pushed them from behind, whipping the long tails of the war shirt around Whistle's legs.

"You serve the Blessed Sun?" Bad Cast asked incredulously.

"Served." Whistle's voice remained calm. "That was a long time ago. At least it seems that way now."

Guest House was looming ever larger as they approached. Bad Cast knotted his fists around the coarse fabric bag that was slung over his shoulder. "You should have picked Wrapped Wrist. He's the brave one. I don't know if I'll freeze like a terrified rabbit, or foul myself."

"Do neither," Whistle replied evenly. "Remember, for this to work, you're supposed to be my slave." He pointed up the narrowing slope, past Guest House and the Made People's pit houses that dotted the narrow ridge. "Look, we're just about perfectly spaced. Can you see your friends?"

Bad Cast glanced owlishly past Whistle's shoulder. On

the ridge trail beyond Guest House he could see two figures, each looking more like a walking woodpile than a human. "That's Wrapped Wrist and Spots?"

"No one will question two barbarians bearing tribute to the First People." He shot a glance back to where the sun was just touching the distant mountains. "And by the time we arrive, it will be dark enough to hide their identities. We rubbed your friend's distinctive skin with soot. In the half-light, no one will notice."

"Elder Rattler and old White Eye just dressed me like this and told me to follow your orders." Bad Cast looked down at the filthy garment they'd given him. It looked more like an upside-down bag with a hole cut in the bottom for his head and one in each corner for his arms. "Why on earth are we marching like mice right between the snake's jaws?"

"I chose you to accompany me because, unlike your friends, you're unremarkable."

"Thanks."

"Not only that, you speak the Made People's tongue. If you're going to play the part of a slave from Flowing Waters Town, you'd know a little of their speech. And, finally, the last place the First People will expect you is right in their midst."

"Oh?" He tried to sound reassured.

Evidently it didn't work, because Whistle shot a glance back, eyes narrowed. "You'd better find some courage down in your guts somewhere, Bad Cast. If we are discovered, I won't live to experience their torture. You, however, don't look to have nerve enough to make them kill you."

"Whistle, I don't understand. Why are you doing this?" He tried to keep the desperation out of his voice.

"Kinship makes a stronger tie than opportunity."

"That doesn't help me understand."

"I am of the Bee Flower Clan. These days I serve my people."

"But you were one of the Blessed Sun's warriors?" Bad Cast lowered his voice as they followed the trail up to Guest House.

"It's a long story. Speak no more for now."

His heart began to hammer, and his mouth went dry. In the Made People's tongue, Whistle called up to one of the women working on a low rooftop, "Is there news?"

The woman looked down at him, not even wasting a second glance on Bad Cast. "News of what? I don't know you, so you must have just arrived. If there is news, you bring it."

"I bring messages for Deputy Burning Smoke. I thought I'd see what the rumors were before I climbed that last bit. I heard some of the barbarians talking about some Prophet."

The woman chuckled. "If that's what he is. A local youth. Claims Old Woman North appeared to him with a promise of the First People's destruction. He's up in a back room in the new section of Pinnacle House." She jerked her head toward the heights. "I suspect they'll pitch his dead body over the cliff in the next couple of days." She frowned. "You speak the local tongue?"

Whistle jabbed a thumb over his shoulder. "This slave does. I borrowed him from a friend before I left Flowing Waters Town. Thought he'd be useful."

As she began to call out another question, Whistle waved it off, saying, "I'll be back. For a hot meal, I'll tell you all the news."

Bad Cast, nearly quaking, kept his eyes down and plodded anxiously after Whistle.

Beyond Guest House, the ridge constricted; the trail snaked its way through the clustered pit houses. The structures had been built precariously on the narrow shelf to keep the occupants safely buffered from the First Moon People below. These were the elite, the Made People who served at the whim of Blessed Matron Larkspur. It was here that Deputy War Chief Burning Smoke's warriors kept their houses. So, too, did Water Bow's assistants and the specialized weavers, masons, and potters who labored for Matron Larkspur.

As they passed within spitting distance of the houses, people looked up from cook fires, their weaving, or other tasks, and called friendly greetings to the unfamiliar warrior. Bad Cast noted that the small storerooms attached to the backs of the houses were bulging with jars of corn, dried meats, and other foodstuffs. Each of the water jars was full, having been packed up from the distant river on one of his people's backs.

Whistle spoke to each person they saw, giving a greeting in the Made People's tongue.

When they passed the last domicile, Whistle drew up and stared at Pinnacle Great House where it stood beneath the two mighty stone pillars that crowned First Moon Mountain. "Quite a fortress, isn't it?"

Bad Cast studied the precarious way before them. Eons of erosion had left a narrow, rugged causeway of stone that fell away to either side. The precipitous trail led up to a small tower called the Eagle's Fist, no more than a bowshot farther up the hill. There, a red-shirted warrior was hanging over the tower wall saying something to Wrapped Wrist and Spots, who simply bobbed before proceeding onward like a clot of two-legged driftwood.

"Good, they're past," Whistle noted, and started up the final approach.

Bad Cast glanced down the sheer cliff that fell away on his right. The heights gave him an eagle's view of the farmland in the valley so far below. Just beyond his left sandal, tall spires of fir, spruce, and ponderosa clung miraculously to the slope.

"Nowhere to run, is there?" Whistle asked.

"Nowhere at all."

"Then we had better succeed."

"Why did you leave the Blessed Sun?"

"I made the mistake of following Webworm just after Snake Head demoted Ironwood. I was there when Webworm murdered my old friend Beargrass. Nor was he the only friend I lost during those days. I saw my old companion, Cone, die when he revealed Snake Head's witchery. Finally, I fought in the ambush Jay Bird laid for Webworm after the sacking of Talon Town. Then, one night after the Rainbow Serpent rose in the southwestern sky, I quietly walked away."

"I know a lot of Bee Flower people. My wife is Bee Flower. But I've never seen you, or heard of you before."

"It's a big clan."

"You're a noteworthy man."

"I've led a quiet life."

At the tone, Bad Cast didn't pursue it. Instead he cast cautious glances at the approaching Eagle's Fist. The warrior standing watch had propped his arms on the high wall of the tower, his head cocked. Finally he called, "Who comes?"

Whistle's rich baritone returned with, "A messenger from War Chief Wind Leaf. I would speak with Deputy War Chief Burning Smoke."

"We saw no signal that a runner was approaching." The guard sounded skeptical.

A huge hand might have tightened around Bad Cast's guts.

Whistle never missed a beat when he responded, "There are times, warrior, when the Blessed Sun would prefer that others did not know his messengers are running the trails."

"Pass," the guard called. Then added, "Good luck to you."

"And to you," Whistle called. He paused to look back down the long valleys, past the layers of evening-purpled mountains, to the distant desert. "But with such a view as this to fill the eyes, I'd say you have all the luck you could use."

"Much better than watching the dust blow down south," the guard replied.

Bad Cast kept his head lowered, but glanced up fearfully at the magnificent squared profile of Pinnacle Great House. Already the sky was darkening. He could just see Spots and Wrapped Wrist as they staggered under their huge burdens of firewood.

Far to the north, the distant high country burned blood red in the alpenglow. Bad Cast hoped it wasn't an omen.

Nineteen

Leather Hand didn't even bother hiding his advance. His warriors fanned out, trotting across the flats like dust-streaked wolves. Their red shirts, sweat-darkened and grimy, jerked with each step. Dust rose under their pounding yucca-fiber sandals as they came in from the north—the Blessed Sun's vengeful beasts.

After today, Leather Hand thought, *the world will be changed. Anyone who considers flouting the First People's authority will tremble down to their bones.*

He glanced sidelong at his warriors, grim men who clasped their weapons, faces hard. Would they obey when Leather Hand gave the order? Were they capable of inflicting this new horror?

And what are you going to do if they refuse?

He turned his attention to the farmstead they approached. Two poorly plastered masonry structures looked to be granaries, or perhaps summer rooms. A ramada sat off to one side. Beyond them he could see the humped outlines of three rounded pit houses, a couple of wattle-and-daub huts, tattered ramadas, and a trash midden. The place was dreamlike, washed out, devoid of the colors of life. Didn't the people feel what he did seeing this desolate place? He was only the final scavenger, come to collect the pale shadows that remained.

They arrived in silence. Two warriors glanced into the first of the square rooms, finding only worn digging sticks, and a collection of firewood—packed from who knew how far—stacked in a back corner.

Leather Hand watched as his warriors paired off, climbed the pit house ladders, and descended like raptors into the depths. The rest of his men charged the mud huts on the southwest side of the farmstead, poking into the doorways, signaling the all-clear.

Screams and shouts broke the stillness. Then only crying children and the hushed tones of his warriors could be heard as they went about their orders.

It was almost over before it even began.

One by one, weeping children began climbing out of the pit houses. Wearing little more than rags, they reminded Leather Hand of brown spiders, so sticklike and spindly were their arms and legs. The children stared around with large-eyed, tear-streaked faces, their hair dust-matted and filthy. They clambered down the rounded roofs to the hard-packed dirt of the plaza and bawled like orphan fawns. Then came the adults, thin women first; they watched with fear-glazed eyes as they called their children to them. The men emerged last, swallowing hard, calling back and forth in their incomprehensible barbarian tongue. Their voices were heavy with fear.

And fear you should.

Leather Hand crossed his arms as his warriors cuffed and prodded the captives into a huddled mass before a low depression in the center of the small village. The women sobbed, reaching out to him with imploring hands.

Leather Hand stepped up, arms crossed, his war club in hand. What a pitiful collection of . . . Wait, what was that? Sunlight glinted on a polished stone bracelet that hung like a loop around a young girl's arm. Perhaps thirteen, she stared up in horror.

"Pretty one, there," Turquoise Fox noted as he took a position on Leather Hand's right.

"What's she wearing?"

"One of these." Turquoise Fox lifted a gleaming abalone pendant. "Loot from Right Acorn's room, I'd wager."

Looking around, Leather Hand noticed more and more bits of colorful shell, polished jet, and gleaming turquoise. A cold rush of anger began brewing.

Turquoise Fox indicated the girl. "You wouldn't mind if I enjoyed her before we kill her, would you? From the looks of her, she's never had a man before."

"Make sure you remove that bracelet when you're done."

Turquoise Fox leaned forward, grabbed the girl by her wrist, and jerked her, screaming, to her feet. A large-boned man—her father perhaps—started forward, only to be clubbed by one of the warriors.

The man fell, shouting, as he cradled his suddenly numb arm. Leather Hand thought he made out the words "We do no wrong!"

Yes, it was the abominable accent common to the Green Mesa villages—coupled with the local Coyote Clan dialect—that made the words almost incomprehensible.

A thin, long-haired woman was crying as she watched Turquoise Fox drag the young girl off to one side. His fist was knotted in the girl's ragged dress; with a jerk the fabric was ripped away. As Turquoise Fox threw the naked girl to the ground, Leather Hand returned his attention to the captives.

The big-boned man was blinking, a stunned look in his dumb eyes.

Leather Hand gestured for Tracker. The scout trotted up, a deep reserve behind his black eyes.

"You speak their tongue?" Leather Hand asked.

"Some."

"Tell them they stole from the Blessed Sun and murdered one of his Priests."

Tracker's voice rose, stilling the babble, even softening the sobbing of the children. The girl under Turquoise Fox made a choking sound as he pried her legs apart and settled between them.

"Tell them," Leather Hand continued, "that by their actions, they have lost their souls."

As Tracker spoke, the big-boned man's expression fell. A distance grew behind his eyes, as if somehow, behind that blocky, dumb-looking face, he had finally come to understand. Despite his expression of confusion, he pulled loose from his wife and began calling out, slapping himself emphatically on the chest.

As the rest of the warriors cast anxious glances in the direction of Turquoise Fox, Tracker translated, "He says his name is Bulrush. He says it is all his fault. He has done this thing, and no other. His wife, his children, his kin, and friends, are all innocent."

Bulrush slapped his chest again, and Tracker translated, "He says that the Blessed Sun's warriors need not punish anyone but him."

The woman at his feet let out a piercing wail, her thin arms reaching up to pull at the man's tattered shirt.

"Bring him," Leather Hand ordered.

Two of his warriors stepped forward to drag the man away from the circle of cowering captives. One had to kick the woman's arms to loosen her grip on the man's garment. Another warrior blocked her, raising his war club.

Bulrush was cast into the dirt before Leather Hand. The man straightened, staring anxiously into Leather Hand's eyes. The corners of his lips quivered, and the vein in his neck pulsed with an insectlike intensity. His desperate eyes had gone glassy.

"You poor deluded fool," Leather Hand told him in the Made People's tongue. "Two men were followed to this village. Two other men were followed to other farmsteads near here. We know who committed the crimes against the First People."

Lowering his eyes, Bulrush mumbled, "My family starves."

"Oh, believe me, none of your people will die from starvation."

At the sudden hope in the man's eyes, Leather Hand smiled. "Get down on your belly."

The man shot a quick look at his wife. The woman was chewing nervously on a knotted fist, her other arm hugging her remaining child.

Bulrush laid himself on the ground, his head turned toward his wife and son. His thick body shivered, lungs rising and falling.

Leather Hand placed his foot squarely on Bulrush's neck and shifted his grip on his war club. The man's breathing grew labored. Through his foot, Leather Hand could feel Bulrush swallow.

"This is but the beginning of the suffering for those who would mock the Blessed Sun's Power!" And with that, he swung his stone-headed war club down, deftly crushing the base of Bulrush's skull.

The woman's scream might have come from some dying night animal.

Leather Hand bore down with all his weight as the man's body convulsed and finally relaxed.

He frowned at the women, curious at his own reluctance for what was going to come next. "Save the women for last. Consider it tenderizing before the meal."

He watched as one of the warriors dragged the woman away from her child. The little girl began squealing, clawing at her mother's leg.

The warrior called Two Needle sliced neatly down with his war club, crushing the little girl's skull. The others waded in, clubs rising and falling. From behind the bulk of the pit house, the sound of ripping fabric could be heard over the woman's sobs.

When most of it was over, Leather Hand gestured to the storehouses out back. "Bring wood. I want them cut up and cooked."

The warriors shot him a surprised look, Black Rabbit asking, "Cooked, War Chief?"

"That's right, warrior. To eat."

"Who's going to . . ." His face lost all color.

"We are going to teach the world a grim lesson here."

As Whistle and Bad Cast climbed the stairs that led onto the Pinnacle Great House roof, Deputy War Chief Burning Smoke emerged from the First People's kiva. He gave Whistle a curious look, taking in his red war shirt and the bedraggled-looking Bad Cast. In the half-light of dusk, he stepped forward and clasped the warrior by his shoulders, a smile breaking his lips.

"It is good to see you, old friend."

"And you," Whistle replied. "I come with a message from the Blessed Sun." He turned, looking at Bad Cast. "You, slave, over there. Against that wall." He pointed at the blocks of rooms that rose in tiers to form the north wall. "You know your duties."

Bad Cast gave him a hesitant nod, clearly showing his fear. Then he shuffled across the plaza, stepped wide around the kiva roof, and lowered himself beside the ladder leading to the upper stories.

"He's worthless," Whistle continued. "A meek chickadee instead of a man."

"They all are," Burning Smoke replied, taking one last look to where the sun's rays burned through the smoke in the west. Already, the Evening Star gleamed in the darkening east.

"Where have you been?" Burning Smoke asked cautiously. "Word is that you deserted us."

Whistle chuckled. "A man thought disloyal has a great deal more freedom in his dealings with the Blessed Sun's enemies."

Burning Smoke fingered his chin. "I see. Didn't Cone say the same thing once?"

"He did. And if you will recall, he was more loyal to his people than the witch Snake Head proved to be in the end." Whistle sighed. "Webworm is no Snake Head."

"True." Burning Smoke was peering in the half-light, trying to read Whistle's expression. "We received no word of a messenger coming."

"Because none was sent." Whistle braced his hand on his war club. "I am here to learn of your plans to ensure the safety of the Blessed Sunwatcher, Blue Racer, and his entourage." He paused. "Is there a place we can talk? I must see the Priest and Matron Larkspur as well."

"Come. This way."

The original Pinnacle Great House had consisted of a V-shaped three-story structure open to the southeast. Later, a second addition had been constructed on the west, giving the building the appearance of an F with its top to the west. It was to the older section that Burning Smoke led Whistle. They climbed a short ladder that led to the old section roof, passed the room block that divided the great house, and skirted the Red Lacewing kiva before

climbing onto the second story. There, T-shaped doorways opened to the third-story rooms on the north wall.

Two old women sat beside a glowing fire bowl as they
shelled corn from dry cobs. They didn't look up as Burning Smoke and Whistle passed.

At the middle doorway, Burning Smoke called, "Matron? A messenger has arrived from the Blessed Sun. May
we enter?"

"Come."

Burning Smoke led the way through the T-shaped doorway. A crackling fire illuminated a white-plastered room
decorated with images of colorful dragonflies. Fine buffalo
robes were piled to one side. Beautiful Straight Path pottery
lined the walls, some brimming with turquoise, jet, and red
coral jewels.

A trim young woman dressed in a bright blue skirt and
wearing a bloodred macaw-feather cloak over her shoulders was seated beside an old Priest dressed in white. The
man's thinning hair looked like loosely blown snow. His
face was thin, hawkish, with protruding brown lips. His
old eyes immediately fastened on Whistle.

"Ah," Burning Smoke said. "Deputy Sunwatcher, you're
here."

"A messenger?" the young woman asked.

Whistle took a moment to study her. A delicate beauty,
she had that familiar triangular face of the First People,
spirals tattooed on her chin. Her eyes were large in her
face and luminous as she took in his muscular frame.

"Matron." Whistle bowed.

"This warrior is Whistle," Burning Smoke said by way
of introduction. "He was once one of the Blessed Sun's
greatest warriors. He tells me he has been doing special
duty for Webworm." To Whistle, he added, "I present to
you Matron Larkspur, of the Blue Dragonfly Clan, and
Deputy Sunwatcher Water Bow."

"What duty is this?" Water Bow asked.

"Put in the simplest of terms," Whistle said, "I'm a spy.
I serve the Blessed Sun by going places, hearing some
things, seeing others. For the moment, I am here to see

what steps are being taken to ensure that the coming Moon Ceremony is safe for the Blessed Sun's servants."

"Do they doubt me?" Larkspur asked, an amused smile on her lips. "Or does my cousin's husband think me simple because of my age?"

Whistle gave her a grim smile. "Neither, Matron."

"What does Webworm wish to know?" Burning Smoke asked.

"What are the feelings of the locals? Can they be trusted?"

"Can you trust a camp dog?" Larkspur asked. "Of course not. Can you keep him at bay and fearful of your presence? Most assuredly we can."

"We have the situation here under control." Burning Smoke clasped his hands together. "The people will be no threat. The harvest looks good for this year. Bellies will be full for the most part, even after tribute is paid."

"How many warriors are under your command?"

"About twenty," Burning Smoke replied. "Most are Made People. They live along the ridge between Guest House and the Eagle's Fist. We haven't had any serious trouble."

"And this visionary youth?" Whistle asked.

Water Bow started. "The Blessed Sun has already heard of this?"

"I am a spy," Whistle returned somewhat arrogantly. "It is my business to know these things. As it is the Blessed Sun's."

Water Bow spread his hands. "He is but a foolish young hunter. He's currently in our custody. We're in the process of breaking him. By tomorrow night, he'll either be dead, his body tossed down the slope, or he'll be so broken we will let him go to whine among the lodges of his people like a clubbed mongrel. Either way, no one will believe his vision."

"If he ever had one," Larkspur added. She was giving Whistle's muscular body a thoughtful appraisal. When she met his eyes, her brow lifted in the slightest hint of inquiry.

"What of Ironwood?" Whistle asked, meeting her questioning gaze with one of his own.

Burning Smoke snorted in derision. "He and his pathetic band of Outcasts are no threat. They lurk just over
the mountains to the east of us. For the most part they hunt
and live like barbarians. Night Sun, of course, being the
former Matron of the First People, has some following as
the legitimate heiress to the Red Lacewing Clan. She
could no more be Matron than that whelp, Poor Singer,
could be a Dreamer. The only real Power up there was
Dune, the Holy Derelict. Recent rumor hints that he's
dead."

"And good riddance!" Water Bow added.

"How many warriors can Ironwood muster?"

"Maybe thirty are still loyal to him or Night Sun,"
Burning Smoke said dismissively. "Assuming they can
take the time from scrounging their next meal to practice
arms. But from the stories, Ironwood is a broken man. He
lost an eye when Jay Bird had him, and, if we are to believe the gossip, his courage is turned to mud. If the
Blessed Sun would just send a force up there, he could end
it once and for all."

Whistle barked a sharp laugh. "He has tried that three
times now. Each time his warriors search the forests,
streams, and valleys, and find nothing. But when the count
is made before heading home, some five or seven are
missing. Never heard from again."

"It's the Mountain Witch," Larkspur said bitterly. "She
sees the future. Warns them."

"The Mountain Witch?" Whistle gave them a mocking
smile. "The mythical Nightshade, supposedly stolen from
Talon Town at birth, carried off to the east, to the land of
the tattooed warriors and their piles of dirt?"

"The last living member of the Hollow Hoof Clan."
Larkspur steepled her slim fingers. "As a child I heard stories of the Hollow Hoof Clan's legendary Powers. How
Yarrow, Nightshade's mother, could climb a column of
smoke, turn herself into an owl, and converse with the
dead."

"Stories," Water Bow said. "Silly stories. Nothing more."

"Instead of a war party, I wish Webworm would send an
entire army to root them out," Larkspur growled. At Whis-

tle's questioning look, she added, "Webworm and Desert Willow sit down there at Dusk House, surrounded by their warriors and servants, feasting on tribute, hearing tales of their own greatness, and have no idea what we face out here on the edge of the world. We are all that stands between the barbarians and them! Don't they understand? All it would take would be a symbol, a leader, someone who provided a spark that set the tinder of discontent ablaze, and we could lose everything."

"Let's not overreact." Burning Smoke shot Whistle a sheepish look. "We've heard good things about Leather Hand since he took command. He has stamped out discontent like a hard yucca sandal."

"Yucca can be burned," Larkspur added hotly, then, as if rethinking, took a deep breath. "Yes, yes, perhaps you're right. But Desert Willow and Webworm aren't here. They don't have to look these people in the face and see the festering resentment."

Whistle adopted a pensive pose. "Upon my return, would you like me to suggest that reinforcement be sent?"

Burning Smoke licked his lips. "Perhaps another twenty? Good men? Not these simpering recruits Webworm has strong-armed into wearing the red. Most of these are callow boys who've never had blood on their hands. Some of the others enjoy the taste of authority only. They wear the red because it makes them into something they aren't: men with courageous determination. Half of my command would panic if things ever looked grim."

"You don't trust them to stand?" Whistle asked incredulously.

"Leather Hand ordered our veterans away moons ago. They've been his strength. I fear the warriors we have left don't have the stomach for a real fight."

"How have you made it this far?"

"Because of that red shirt." Larkspur pointed at Whistle's stained and frayed garment. "The locals think it's more than it is."

Whistle couldn't help but smile.

From outside the door, a surprised voice called, "Alarm!"

Whistle was first out, swinging through the T-shaped doorway into the cool night. One of the two old women was pointing off to the east. There, at the base of the closest pinnacle, a yellow bead of fire flickered, growing ever brighter as it cast its glow on the stone pillar.

"What the . . . ?" Burning Smoke sputtered as he emerged and saw the signal fire. "Who lit that? Who's responsible for that?"

Water Bow ducked out behind Larkspur, blinking in the darkness as he stared up at the signal fire. A mound of firewood was always kept up there, sheltered from the rain, ready to be lit should Pinnacle Great House ever be attacked. Now it was roaring to life.

It was Matron Larkspur who looked up at the starry night and then down the valley to the southwest where darkness cloaked distant Smoking Mirror Butte.

"On a night like this," she said, "the message is already being relayed to Desert Willow that we're under attack."

"Quick!" Burning Smoke shouted. "We've got to put that out! Hurry!"

Whistle smiled crookedly as people rushed for the ladders.

Twenty

Bad Cast hunched in the darkness, his back to the north wall. He tilted his head to stare at the frosting of stars that grew in brilliance as the night deepened. This might be the last evening he'd ever have to enjoy the sky. Within a hand's time, his bloody corpse might be thrown off this very wall to tumble down the sheer slope behind the great house.

There he'd lie, broken and twisted, while the ravens, magpies, and vultures picked at his bloating flesh.

Why did I ever agree to this?

Wasn't it enough that Ripple pay for his folly? Why did the rest of them have to?

He looked up as a dark figure appeared on the steps and climbed onto the roof. It hurried forward past the kiva entrance and toward the ladder.

"Wrapped Wrist?" Bad Cast called to the burly figure. Even in the darkness, he looked short.

"Here!" Wrapped Wrist came at a trot and crouched down to Bad Cast's right. "Blood and dung, my heart's beating like thunder."

"What about Spots?"

"Shhh! Keep it down. He's headed up to the signal fire with his fire kit."

"I want to be anyplace but here."

"So does Ripple. *Remember* that."

Bad Cast swallowed hard, wondering what Whistle was up to. What did they know about him? He'd just appeared as if the katsinas had dropped him from the sky.

"Our elders trust him," Wrapped Wrist said, as if reading his mind.

"Who? Whistle?"

"No, Spots. They thought he was the man to light that fire."

"But why did they ever trust me?"

"How should I know? I'm just here in case Ripple can't walk."

"We could just run, say we couldn't find him."

Wrapped Wrist stared at him in the darkness. "Kinsman, we're in more than just a little bit of trouble here. If we come away without Ripple, your conscience is going to be the least of your worries."

A cry broke the night, an old woman calling, "Alarm!"

Within moments shouts of dismay and frantic orders could be heard. People emerged from the rooms above them, many calling questions in the First and Made People's languages. Feet hammered on the ladders. Dark forms thudded onto the earthen roof and sprinted for the stairway and the eastern plaza.

"That's our signal." Wrapped Wrist stood.

Bad Cast blinked hard. "I think I'm too scared to move."

Wrapped Wrist's strong arm jerked him to his feet. "You can be just as much a coward while you're looking for Ripple as sitting here waiting to be discovered. Come on."

Wrapped Wrist half pulled him up the ladder onto the second story. Two girls, mere forms in the night, were talking excitedly on the third-floor roof, their eyes to the northeast. They barely noticed as Wrapped Wrist led the way to one of the T-shaped doorways.

Ducking inside, Bad Cast was surprised to see a flickering fire in the fire bowl. He stopped short, staring in awe at the white-plastered walls. Dancing figures, so colorful as to seem alive, adorned each wall. The black-on-white pottery—exclusive property of the First People—lined the walls. Fabrics dyed with the vibrant colors of spring flowers were placed in neat stacks. Corn could be seen in the thick round seed jars.

"No doorway leading down," Wrapped Wrist muttered as he took in the grandeur. "Come on."

Bad Cast followed him out, then ducked into the next doorway. A Priest lived here. Probably Water Bow himself. Bad Cast recognized images of the Flute Player, Spider Woman, and the Blue God. They seemed to be glaring at him with a burning hatred.

Bad Cast stopped short, staring into the Blue God's angry eyes.

"Not here," Wrapped Wrist murmured, reaching out to pull Bad Cast back.

Bad Cast tried to stifle the shakes that were making his muscles liquid. "Horribly spooky place, that." His teeth were chattering as he ducked into the last room, finding a plethora of weapons: the long S-shaped war clubs; shields of wicker and buffalohide; several long bow staves, the strings hanging; quivers of arrows; and stone-headed war axes. A line of grinning skulls hung from a cord stretched between the roof poles. The patches of hair neatly lashed to small hoops looked suspiciously human.

"Burning Smoke's room!" Wrapped Wrist stopped short, his throat working. A wide-eyed slave girl wearing a doeskin kirtle stared up from where she was feeding twigs into a fire.

"Where's the prisoner, Ripple?" Bad Cast demanded.

She looked at him as if he were one of the gods freshly set foot on earth. Her eyes were wide, surprise filling her pretty face.

He switched to the Made People's tongue. "We're looking for the Moon People hunter known as Ripple."

"Blood and dung!" Wrapped Wrist cried. "She probably doesn't understand a word you're saying."

"I show you way," the girl said in Made People's tongue. "You take me? Hide me? Protect me?"

"Yes, yes," Bad Cast hissed.

"There." She pointed at a leather war shield lying on the floor in one corner of the room.

"That's the way to find Ripple?"

She nodded.

Bad Cast took two steps across the room, lifted the heavy shield, and tossed it aside. A rectangular hole opened below. The two uprights of a ladder were leaned against the pole frame of the doorway.

"Down there?" Wrapped Wrist asked.

"It's black as a snake's belly." Bad Cast started down, aware of the coolness of the room. "Gods, if she pulls this ladder up while we're down there . . ."

"You need this," the young woman said, plucking a bowl from behind her. White, decorated with fine black lines and the blocky shapes of mountains, it was made in the form of a duck. She lit a twisted yucca wick in the fire bowl and handed the lamp to Wrapped Wrist.

Holding the lamp, he leaned over the doorway to set his feet on the rungs before climbing down to stand beside Bad Cast.

In the lamplight, they could see row on row of large jars, each brimming with foodstuffs. One was heaped high with corn, another with dried squash. Yet another was topped with dried beeweed. Rawhide boxes yielded stacks of desiccated rabbits, and venison and buffalo jerky. Still more pots were filled with beans.

"Tribute?" Wrapped Wrist asked.

"Enough to feed them for a year. This is surplus. It's late summer, little more than a moon before the harvest. The First People keep this for a reserve."

Wrapped Wrist frowned. "We've always thought if it became necessary, we could starve them out."

"We'd best think again." Bad Cast stepped over, seeing a ladder leaned at an angle in the room's rear. "Over here."

"Should one of us watch that ladder?" Wrapped Wrist hesitated. In the lamplight, they stared at each other, well aware of what would happen if the slave girl pulled it up behind them.

"You stay." Bad Cast stepped over and looked at the floor.

Another war shield lay in the open space at the ladder's feet. Bad Cast lifted it aside, then reached for the lamp. He lowered it into the black oblong hole and stared down. For a moment, he couldn't place the broken and pathetic thing as human, let alone the cocky Ripple he'd once known. Black and filthy, the shape tried to curl away from the light.

"Ripple?"

"Go away!" the apparition cried with an oddly slurred speech. "Leave me alone."

"Gods," Wrapped Wrist whispered.

"We've got to get him out of—"

At that moment, the girl came climbing down the steps. "Hurry! Get man! They come back!"

Bad Cast reached for the ladder, wondering how, if they survived, he was going to explain a slave girl to White Eye. When he started down the ladder, the temperature dropped. He could see his breath. When he bent to Ripple, the man's flesh was like ice.

"Gods, it's cold in here!"

Ripple's head rolled back, his breath white in the half-light. "Cold Bringing Woman? I didn't betray you."

"No," Bad Cast agreed, trying to pull his limp friend up. "You did fine." He looked up at Wrapped Wrist. "You'll have to help; he's delirious." *And I'm already half frozen.*

Whistle stood to the rear, behind the crowd that thronged the third-floor roof, and watched as Burning Smoke's warriors did their best to pull the bonfire apart on the high summit.

He turned his eyes to the southwest, wondering what the Blessed Sun's guards on the high promontory of distant Smoking Mirror Butte were making of this. Assuming they had seen the fire spring to life, of course. Their keen eyes weren't always focused on the horizon. Sometimes a game of dice took precedence.

No matter—that was Larkspur and Burning Smoke's problem. Let them explain as best they might.

He was mulling that when a petite shape sidled up beside him. He looked down, aware of her scent: a combination of yucca and wild rose.

"How do you think it got started?" she asked.

"I'd say a fire bow," he answered dryly. "Do they do this to you often, Matron?"

"Never before." She sighed. "I've already sent out runners to stop the war party Webworm or Leather Hand will be dispatching and turn them back."

"It will make an interesting report to the Blessed Sun."

She stiffened; then her cool hand came to rest on the swell of his arm. "Whistle, perhaps we could come to an arrangement? Some way to soften the Blessed Sun's scrutiny?"

"What did you have in mind?"

"Why don't you come down to my rooms? You've been running the roads for a long time. I have warm water steaming over the fire. Perhaps you'd like some of this trail grime washed away."

He gave her a sidelong look. "The last time one of the First People trifled with a warrior below her class, it ended in disaster."

"I'm not Night Sun," she replied. "And I'm not planning on having your child." She hesitated, glancing at where the crowd still watched the fading red glow of the signal fire. "I've spent nearly two years here without a man's company."

"What about your husband?"

"Away in the south. He has his duties to the Blessed Sun. He keeps an eye on the Hohokam and Mogollon who have gathered at the base of the Rainbow Serpent. They're building a ball court there, can you believe?"

"I can."

"Then perhaps you understand long separations . . . and how lonely a person can be." She paused. "Are you an influential man? One who might speak persuasively to the Blessed Sun about the situation here? Let us say, a favor for a favor?"

He was on the verge of finding an excuse to get away, but saw shadowy figures hurrying across the western plaza. They looked as if they carried a heavy burden.

"Yes, Matron, your company sounds most appealing. Assuming it can be shared without complications for either of us."

She tightened her slim fingers around the muscles in his arm. "Believe me, warrior, I have my ways."

She led the way, descending the ladder and walking to her doorway. The two old women were still seated, shelling corn in the darkness as if it were the most normal thing in the world.

"See that no one interrupts us," she told one of the crones, then led Whistle into her spacious quarters.

Leather Hand looked up at the sky, awash with the myriads of Evening People in all their formations. So many of them twinkled—like patterns of souls gleaming against the soot-blackness of night. Wind Baby still blew up from the southwest, his hot breath tempered by night, but his touch remained dry, sucking for any hint of moisture.

Behind him the collection of buildings that composed Saltbush Farmstead formed silhouettes against the sky.

The granaries were dark squares, while the pit houses made rounded humps on the pale plaza. Reddish yellow light painted the ladders protruding from the roofs.

Here, in this place, the world had changed. He could feel it: a brooding that seemed to rise from the drab desert land around him. He cocked his head, listening, trying desperately to hear the wailing Spirits of the dead. He kept turning, looking over his shoulder, as if he could sense a dark presence. Each time nothing but empty desert met his eyes.

What was it? Something dark and Powerful, a malevolence tempered with curiosity, as if it watched him. Recognition lay just beyond the threshold of his understanding.

He shook his head. Nonsense. He was alone but for the wind. Nonetheless he could feel the dead, aware that part of their breath-heart souls were within him—that more than their flesh, he had gorged on bits of their souls.

His men, their bellies full, had turned somber, wondering, as he now did, what they had become.

We have changed our world here, tonight, in this accursed place.

Leather Hand turned, barely able to pick out the shadowy form that lay beside the middle pit house. Black Rabbit's body looked like no more than a broken beast where it sprawled lifeless on the ground.

"Not me!" The warrior's words rang in Leather Hand's memory. He could still see the revulsion on the man's face, the way he shook his head, hands spread before him in denial.

A war chief must command the obedience of his men.

Black Rabbit had seen it in his eyes, had chosen the horror of sudden unjust death over that of eating another human being.

Of all the men Leather Hand had killed, Black Rabbit's execution would cling to him, haunting his nightmares. Over and over, he would relive the whiplike snap of his arm, the cracking of the man's skull. He would see the body pitch sideways, broken brain and blood spilling as Black Rabbit fell headlong to the ground.

The rest of his warriors had watched, owl-eyed, disbelieving. Only then had they followed his orders, casting unsure glances at each other as they bluffly proceeded with the audacious task of chopping through bone and sinew, stripping meat, then breaking the long bones for stewing. How sick they'd looked as they dropped bloody chunks of human muscle onto the coals to roast.

What kind of monster have I become?

Leather Hand rubbed his fingers over the palms of his hands, feeling the callused skin. It remained warm, familiar in a body now grown foreign.

We are a new breed of monsters, not unlike those that walked the earth in the days of old.

How had he ever let Turquoise Fox talk him into this madness?

You had no choice! People without hope have to know that beyond losing just their lives, they can still lose their souls.

The worst part had been the cooking, smelling the curious new odor as the meat boiled. It was knowing what they were about to do that dragged at the souls and sent shivers through a man's stomach. Butchering the men hadn't been so bad. They had been the guilty culprits. It was the memory of the pretty young girl's eyes, of how he had crushed her face with a war club in an effort to prevent the memory. Her slight flesh had yielded stubbornly from the bone as his obsidian knife sliced it free. He recalled that fluttery feeling of setting her head in the coals to roast, and later, after the hair and scalp had burned off, how her brain had sizzled and popped behind her ruined face.

How did one come to grips with what he'd done to the woman? He had taken a turn with her—the long-haired one with the large frightened eyes. He had lain atop her, slid his hard rod into her warm sheath. Her skin had been smooth and firm, her breasts soft against his chest. He had pressed against the unyielding arch of her pubis as his pulsing orgasm shot seed into her and had looked down into her terrified brown eyes. He had *seen* her souls in that instant. Touched her, knew her.

Then, less than a hand of time later, he had helped chop her up into pieces fit for roasting.

She is part of me now as no other woman has ever been.

His hand pressed over his stomach, as if to fix her in place. *Will her souls mix with mine? Are we joined as no man and woman have ever been before? Will she live within me?*

"Gods, what does it mean?" He stared up at the glittering Evening People, desperate for an answer, afraid of what it might be.

"War Chief?" Turquoise Fox called from behind.

Leather Hand turned, seeing his second-in-command approach. "Any trouble?"

Turquoise Fox came to stand beside him, bending his head back to look up at the stars. "No trouble. They are just oddly quiet."

"It isn't every day that men become monsters."

Turquoise Fox sighed. "Now you know why the monsters inspired such terror among the First People when they first emerged into this world."

Leather Hand lowered his voice. "So, tell me, do you think Spider Woman will help the Yamuhakto to hunt us down?"

"Maybe. Doesn't matter. We are expendable, War Chief. As the Blessed Sun's warriors, we do his bidding. Our lives are his. Remember that. We are nothing more than his strong arm, sweeping away those who stand in his way."

Leather Hand grunted neutrally. "No one has thrown up?"

"One or two." Turquoise Fox looked back at the pit houses. "But they will hold fast. We are bound now, all of us, together. We share a brotherhood that few warriors ever have. They know what this means, how it will change their lives."

"They are ready to become shunned among men?"

"From this day forward people will look at us differently. They won't see us as men."

"No . . . beasts, more likely."

"Let them. Myself, I would add to that notion. I would cultivate the image of human wolves. The sort that inspire terror . . . the stuff of nightmares. If we do this properly terror will do what force of arms cannot. No one will dare to cross the Blessed Sun."

"Our actions already reek of witchcraft."

"Then let the people think of us as witch wolves."

"This is only the first of the farmsteads who stole from the Blessed Sun. Will the men be willing to do this again?"

"The first time is always the hardest." Turquoise Fox shrugged. "And, War Chief, unlike other warriors, we no longer have to carry our food with us."

As Leather Hand turned and started back to the warmth of the pit house fire, he glanced up at the stars one last time. The constellation he saw was that of the Blue God. The dark holes of her eyes seemed to be staring right through his souls.

The Blue God? He glanced uneasily over his shoulders, fitting a name to the presence that seemed to lurk in the darkness.

Yes, I become you.

Twenty-one

Light slanted across the sky, casting yellow tones in the tops of the pines. Somewhere close, jays rasped at the morning and a chickaree squirrel chattered shrilly. Grasshoppers were clicking in the dry air.

Cool hands brought Ripple to wakefulness. He blinked, looking up to see Wrapped Wrist dabbing at his face with a damp bit of cloth.

He lay in a small grassy meadow, bounded on all sides by tall ponderosa pines. The soft sweet fragrance of the trees filled his nose as he inhaled. Spots squatted beside a low smoking fire, feeding it sticks.

"Where are we?" Ripple asked, aware that he didn't sound like himself. Not only were the teeth missing in the right side of his jaw, but his vocal cords had a raspy sound. He was too afraid to look down at his body. It was enough to feel the pain and know he was in desperate shape.

"We're headed east."

"Toward what?"

"The Mountain Witch. That's where you wanted to go, isn't it?"

Ripple closed his eyes. It even hurt to nod.

"We're sorry it took so long to get you out."

"Thank you."

"Thank the elders, Ripple. Especially old White Eye."

"White Eye?"

"He seems to think your vision is a sign."

He was happy to feel the damp cloth wiping at his cheek. Then Wrapped Wrist pressed too hard against his swollen jaw and Ripple couldn't stifle the sudden cry.

"Sorry."

"It's all right. I'd endure anything rather than be back in that place."

"Your hand . . ." Wrapped Wrist couldn't finish.

"They used a stone hammer. Held my left hand down on a slab. Each time I refused to answer their question, they'd smash another knuckle." He tried to smile through the pain and swelling. "I can't bear to look. How bad is it?"

Wrapped Wrist hesitated. "I don't know how it can ever be the same. It's . . ."

"Crippled?"

"Perhaps not."

"You lie poorly."

"And your penis?"

"Matron Larkspur drove yucca leaves through it. That hurt worse than my fingers and teeth. You have no idea how loud a man can scream. I can't bear to look. . . ."

"It's bad. Swollen and leaking pus."

"Dear gods." Ripple swallowed hard. "I remember bits and pieces of last night. Did you see her?"

"Who?"

"Cold Bringing Woman. She was there just before you came, told me she was proud, that I had been braver than she could have expected."

"There wasn't any snow in that room," Wrapped Wrist told him. "But it was colder than a winter bear's ass."

"What about my sisters?"

"They're being taken care of. So are our families. The

elders are hiding them from the First People's wrath. Fir
Brush even has a new friend. A slave girl who helped us
get you out. The elders are going to see if they can sneak
her back to her people."

"Where's Bad Cast? I remember him from last night."

"He's back with Whistle."

"Who?"

"A warrior. A man of the Bee Flower Clan. Quite a fellow. Just the kind of leader we need."

Spots asked, "Ripple? Can you eat anything?"

"Soup," he answered. "But, by the gods, don't make it
too hot." He swallowed hard. "Wrapped Wrist, I have to
make water. Is it . . . is it scabbed over?"

After a moment, Wrapped Wrist said, "I guess so."

"I don't know if this is going to be harder on you or me,
but someone has to pull the scab off."

It wasn't reassuring to watch Wrapped Wrist's face go
pale.

Twenty-two

STARLIGHT

*Few people know the Dead. Most of the time I wish I
didn't. They come and whisper secrets to me. Things that
often would have been better unsaid. To truly know the
way of things is to live with constant fear. The end is coming. Will I be able to bear it? I have borne so many end-
ings. How can I stand this last one?*

*Perhaps that was why the Tortoise Bundle caused me to
be stolen away those many sun cycles ago. I was destined
to be taken, carried away into the distant east by my captor, and lover, Badgertail. Power wanted me to learn the
ways of the Dead, of suffering and injustice. Sister Datura*

wanted to seduce my Souls with the Dance. She and Power sought to prepare me for horror.

Sometimes, across the distance of a world, I hear Tharon's angry scream of disbelief and rage echoing into the afterworlds. Let him cry out. Evil chose him for its own ends. But evil, like good, is always defeated by time.

I sit here now, high atop this ridge where Badgertail's mortal remains lie. His body is buried in a log tomb, piled with rock and covered with dirt. It is a small monument to a great man. His ancestors were buried beneath huge mounds of earth cut from the fertile floodplains beside the great rivers that wind through their eastern woodlands. Here, my lover, my husband, lies alone, barely covered by a mound not even chest high to an old woman like me. Already the dirt is washing away, poorly held by the few scrawny high-country grasses that have grown here. I can see one of the logs, exposed and rotting.

Pine makes a poor tomb.

My lover, however, is from another time, another life. I live in constant amazement at the lives I have been chosen to lead. In my first I was a girl in Talon Town—last daughter of the Hollow Hoof Clan, Keeper of the Tortoise Bundle. They expected me to be a great Dreamer, to bear enough children to rejuvenate the clan. Little did they know who I would turn out to be.

Brother Mud Head had plans for me, he and Long Horn, the god some now call a thlatsina.

They reached across the land and spun the Dream around old Marmot's soul—told him that he should send his warriors to find me and the Tortoise Bundle. Oh, and find me they did, in a raid that was only eclipsed by Jay Bird's stunning strike. My second life began that night when Badgertail carried me off to the east. There, in the land of Cahokia, I learned the true nature of Power, of authority, and of empire. In those years I first heard the call of Sister Datura, and Danced in her arms. There I courted Death, wound my arms around it and stroked it with a lover's touch. I was witness to the fall of mighty Cahokia, and saw her Power broken.

Compared to Cahokia with her god-kings, the Straight Path Nation is but a petty chieftainship, its great houses no more than minor vassals. Despite their notions of grandeur, the relentless tide of time is about to sweep them away as if they had never been. Where the singing of slaves now echoes, soon only the wind will moan.

Whistle stopped, staring at the two faint game trails that disappeared into the timber. Around them, towering spruce and fir shadowed the ground, dulling the tones of duff, deadfall, and moldering cones from seasons long past.

"Which way do we go?" Bad Cast asked Whistle as he studied the two diverging trails. "Ripple was always the better hunter. He'd know which way to go. He could track a butterfly across a grassy field."

"To the right. It's the most direct route."

"How do you know that?"

"We're headed for Ironwood's camp, correct?"

"If that's where the Mountain Witch is."

"She's there." Whistle started forward, his muscular legs bunching with each step as he climbed. Bad Cast saved his breath, ducking under low-hanging boughs, stepping over deadfall, and concentrating on the footing. Places where an elk traveled easily threatened a man with constant danger of falling, tripping, or just breaking a leg. On this steep slope, in this thicket of black timber, it would be nearly impossible for Whistle to carry him out.

Within a hand of time, Whistle led the way out onto a narrow crest. They stopped where an old fir tree had been lightning-riven. Blown into slivers, pieces of the tree lay strewn about the forest floor—yellow and stark against the dark needle mat.

"You've been to the Mountain Witch's camp?" Bad Cast asked as he looked down into the black mat of timber that dropped away to either side.

"I serve Ironwood."

"I thought you served your clan?"

"Them, too."

"You actually know Ironwood?" Bad Cast couldn't keep the skepticism out of his voice.

"I'm alive because of him. Every breath I draw is a gift he gave me. Every sunrise I see I owe to him."

"Then you've met Matron Night Sun, and Poor Singer, and Cornsilk."

"Yes, all of them."

"Even the Mountain Witch?"

"Yes."

"What's she like?"

He didn't speak for a moment. "She's the most frightening woman I've ever known."

Bad Cast stopped dead in his tracks. "How is that?"

"When you look into her eyes, the reflection is of places and worlds that no human should see."

"I don't understand." He started hesitantly forward.

"No, I'm sure you don't."

Bad Cast followed Whistle around stone and deadfall, trying to puzzle out the meaning of the words. The tone Whistle used had sent a shiver down his back. He thought back to that morning, remembering how Whistle ducked out of Matron Larkspur's curtained doorway.

"Did Matron Larkspur call for you this morning?"

"This morning? No."

"But I saw you step out of her room."

"That is correct."

"You stayed with Matron Larkspur?" Bad Cast shook his head. "I can't believe it."

"You seem to believe few things." A pause. "She's just a woman."

"She's *Blessed*."

"So?"

"She's one of the First People!"

Whistle stopped short, turning on his heel. He gave Bad Cast an irritated scowl. "Women, all women, belong to some people or another, whether they're First People, Made People, Tower Builders, Fire Dogs, or even, gods forbid, People of the Moon. A woman is a woman, no matter who her people might be. She has the same breasts, arms, legs, and sheath. What's your point?"

"Doesn't the fact that she's Blessed frighten you?"

Whistle rubbed his forehead. "They're not gods, Bad Cast, no matter what they've tried to make you believe. Ah, I can see by your expression that you think bedding her might have called down the wrath of the Blessed Sun himself."

"I'd never . . ."

Whistle raised an eyebrow, waiting for Bad Cast to finish.

"Never share her bed? That's your misfortune. Her coupling was driven by a sense of desperation. Were I any judge, I'd say she'd been without a man for moons now."

Bad Cast gaped. "But coupling with a First Person is forbidden. Look at what happened between Night Sun and Ironwood."

Whistle's eyes rolled. "Have you ever been anywhere outside of First Moon Valley?"

"Well . . . no."

Whistle slapped his arms to his sides. "Gods, I'm saddled with a self-righteous babe. Right, well, think of it like this: She's alone. Surrounded by potential enemies. She can't turn to the Priest. He's too old. Not her type. Burned Smoke isn't a safe partner either. Not only is he her war chief, but he's there, constantly. If she bedded him it would eventually get around, and who knows, they might come to care for each other. As you so aptly noted, look where that got Night Sun."

"But you're different?"

He shot Bad Cast a smile. "I'm a safe gamble—a lone warrior passing through on the Blessed Sun's business. I show up just as she's embarrassed by an untimely fire. Perhaps sharing her bed will make my report to Webworm more favorable."

"That doesn't sound safe to me."

"Oh? And what if I did brag about bedding her? She could order my throat cut just for saying such a thing."

"How do you know she won't?"

"Because she enjoyed herself last night." Whistle resumed his path along the ridge crest. "Come, don't you tell me you wouldn't think fondly of a woman who made you feel like you were still an attractive and potent man."

"How do you know you made her feel . . . how did you put it, attractive and potent?"

"Outside of your wife, how many women have you ever made love to, young hunter?"

"A few."

"Did they pretend enjoyment when that magic instant came?"

"I don't think so. If they didn't like it, they told me." He was remembering some of the times Soft Cloth had derided him for being too rough, too quick, too distracted.

"Just so. Now, do you think the Matron Larkspur would have been under any compunction to pretend? Hmm? She is a woman accustomed to giving orders, to being obeyed. This morning, she asked me to return when my duties allowed."

"You would do that? Go back to her bed?"

"Maybe."

"Why?"

"Because of what I learned about her last night." Then he added softly, "She's no one's fool."

"Can't prove that by me. And, I'm not so sure about you, either." Messing with a Matron—a First Person, no less!

"A spy lives on risk, Bad Cast. She's a lonely woman with no one to rely on but herself. She has only her wits, an aging Priest, and a handful of warriors to protect her. When Spots set that fire last night, he scared her. She could lose everything. They're vulnerable up there, and she knows it."

"Vulnerable! You should have seen the food they've got stored. We always thought we could starve them out if we had to. That or cut off the water."

"They have enough water stored in the rooms along the south wall to see them through until the Blessed Sun's warriors could relieve them."

"Then how are they vulnerable?"

"Work it out. Then maybe you can answer all of the

grouse-stupid questions rolling around in your simple head."

I'm not simple! But he wasn't sure he believed it.

Wrapped Wrist took a deep breath and shifted Ripple's litter in his firm grip. He could feel the strain in his shoulders, and if it was bothering him he knew that Spots must really be smarting.

They walked down out of a cloaking patch of timber and into the lush meadow grasses that grew between the trees and the willow-banked River of Souls. Here, it was a clear mountain stream, unlike to the south and west, where it was a sluggish, muddy current cutting through high desert.

This was known as the Valley of the Hot Water Springs—a place where the River of Souls dashed down out of the rugged high-country canyons. Here its waters were Blessed by the bubbling hot springs—a gift from the Below Worlds—before it drained into the high bluffs and broken mesas claimed by the Straight Path Nation.

His people occasionally traveled this far to look for game, or to bathe in the springs. The elevation in this part of the valley discouraged farming, so few families from any people had tried to settle here. They did come, however, to leave *pahos*—prayer feathers and multicolored prayer sticks—at the bubbling and steaming hot springs. Where the hot springs issued from the rocky earth and spilled into the stream was considered sacred ground—a doorway to the Below Worlds.

Here, too, the Traders passed. Some coming over the high mountain passes to the east, bringing buffalohides from the Great River Valley or jerky from the distant plains beyond the final mountain wall.

This was the last refuge. It was with relief, after bearing the heavy burden of Ripple's unconscious body, that Wrapped Wrist and Spots hoped to camp, to rest, and perhaps to meet up with Bad Cast and the warrior Whistle.

"Think they . . . made it out?" Spots asked while huffing for breath.

"I hope so. Assuming, that is, that Whistle was able to extricate himself from Burning Smoke's rage over losing his prisoner and his signal bonfire all in one night."

Spots was winded, his knuckle-white hands clutching the poles of their makeshift litter. He had started to stumble, his steps hurried and awkward.

Ripple—his sallow skin speckled with perspiration—lay suspended on the litter. Half curled between the poles, he cradled his maimed left hand protectively. Bloody mucus had begun to leak past his dry lips, and whimpering sounds could be heard from deep in his throat.

"How's he doing?" Spots asked between gasps.

"Still fevered."

Ripple had been that way since dawn, as though his inflamed body had chased his souls out to hover loosely in the air. During this dangerous time the souls could simply leave, in which case the body would die.

"I can't believe what they did to him." Spots shook his head.

"You didn't see him down there in that hole. The very sight of him, filthy, bleeding, and frightened . . . It made my souls weep."

"We must do something. Things like this can't go on." He stumbled. "I must rest. Sorry."

"There, down by where those rocks break the willows. They give cover and access to the river. That's a good place."

Spots veered farther downhill, his pace lagging as the thick grass and colorful wildflowers pulled at his feet. The place Wrapped Wrist had indicated consisted of large gray boulders pitched up in some long-ago flood. Between them, water lapped at a narrow pebble beach.

Spots made his fatigued way to the hollow between the rocks and gasped with relief as he carefully lowered the litter. He sighed and walked loose-limbed down to the bank, knelt, and began sucking up great drafts to slake his thirst.

Wrapped Wrist massaged his arm muscles and followed, kneeling beside his friend and drinking before cupping water and splashing it on his face. For a long moment he looked out at the clear stream. Sunlight played brightly on the ripples cast by the current. He could see the wavering outlines of rocks and stones in the shallow bottoms. A sinuous column of insects hovered on wings that glowed silver in the sunlight.

Finally he said, "Hard to believe, isn't it, that this is the source of the First People's strength."

"What are you talking about?"

"This water. From here it runs down the canyon, out among the mesas and into the desert. Follow this stream and it will take you right into the heart of the First People's world. This water feeds their cornfields. From it the bean and squash plants drink." He reached out, cupping the clear fluid and letting it trickle through his fingers. "This is the blood of their life."

"What would you do? Shut it off?"

"If I could."

Spots frowned out at the sun-silvered current. His brow was lined, eyes troubled. "Wrapped Wrist, what's happened to us? In no more days than I can count on my fingers, our world has turned upside down. We were just ourselves—hunters and friends—until we answered Ripple's signal on the mountain. Now look at us: fleeing like packrats from coyotes, scurrying away into the high country, looking for a witch."

Wrapped Wrist nodded, clamping his tired fist to watch the muscles in his arm bulge. "I just hope we can find her. Somehow, I don't think the Mountain Witch is easy to locate. The Blessed Sun has sent several war parties up into those mountains to chase her and the Outcasts down."

Spots looked eastward, past the bubbling hot springs across the channel to the tall granite peaks that rose above the valley head, fit to pierce the very sky. "None of them so much as reported a sighting. And each party went home missing warriors."

"If you ask me, that's Ironwood's doing. He was the greatest war chief the First People ever had. People say that if he had remained as war chief, none of this would have happened."

"I'll face a war chief over a witch any day," Spots avowed. "A war club is quick and sure, but people say the Mountain Witch can draw your souls out through your nostrils, slowly, so that your body wastes and fills with pus."

"Stop it. Why would she want to do that to us?"

Spots shrugged. "What do I know of witches?"

Wrapped Wrist squinted at the water, listening to its crystal music as it flowed past. The wind made a soft sound in the grass. "I just wonder why Ripple insisted that he be taken to the Mountain Witch. Why does a lowly hunter think the Mountain Witch will even speak to him?"

Both Spots and Wrapped Wrist jumped like spooked rabbits when a gruff voice behind them said, "We wonder the same thing."

Scrambling up, Spots clawed at Wrapped Wrist for balance. The two of them splashed about in the shallows, steadying each other as they gaped at the gray-haired apparition behind them.

The man stood behind Ripple's litter, muscular, scarred, with a grizzled and weather-beaten brown face. And what a face it was: stern, with a dominating nose and slanting brows. His left eye was hidden under a patch made from a tuft-eared squirrel hide; the right was probing, smoldering like hot obsidian. A terrible scar ran jagged across his cheek. The war club in his hands fit the man: old, use-polished; the dark stains around the sinew that bound the stone head to the chokecherry handle had the appearance of long-dried blood.

"Who . . . who are you?" Wrapped Wrist was the first to find his voice. It finally registered that the man wore a beautifully tanned deerhide hunting shirt, tall hunting moccasins made of mountain sheephide, and a silver fox-hide cape that was thrown back over his wide shoulders in favor of the warm summer day.

"What if I told you I was an assassin sent by the Blessed Sun to kill nosey Moon People who wander too close to the hot springs?"

Wrapped Wrist edged in front of Spots. If this turned ugly, it was he who stood the best chance of taking the fearsome stranger. The man was *old*, he tried to tell himself, no doubt slow of reaction. Surely the years had robbed those sinewy arms and sapped the strength that those thick legs belied.

But when he looked into that single fierce eye, quailing fear sucked at the bottom of his heart.

"We're just traveling through," Spots sputtered. "Taking . . . taking our sick friend for a Healing."

"Yes," Wrapped Wrist agreed. "That's right. We want no trouble with the Blessed Sun." And then it struck him. "Wait. We don't know you. How is it that you speak our language?"

The grim warrior—and yes, he was a warrior, it was in the set of his shoulders, the way he held the war club—uttered phrases in several languages before he finished in their own. "A cunning warrior knows the tongues of many peoples. In my later years, I've been making a study of it." He slapped the war club meaningfully on his hard palm. "Now, why are you seeking the Mountain Witch?"

Wrapped Wrist hesitated. Gods, did he come right out and say why? Choices, choices—he'd never been good at choices.

Spots spoke first. "We need only to find a Healer for our friend. He . . . well, he was mauled by a bear, you see. The attack fevered him, and his souls are loose while his body fights the evil Spirits the bear put into him."

It sounded lame even to Wrapped Wrist. He glanced down, seeing one of the round cobbles at his feet. It was a little larger than his fist. If he could just reach down, grab it up, it would give him a weapon. Crude, yes, but something he could throw, or use to club the old man.

He stopped short as the man's piercing eye seemed to burn right through to his souls. The lips hardened, the slanting brows lowering. "Don't even think it."

"Think what?" Wrapped Wrist almost squeaked.

The thin lips relaxed the least bit. "Do bears normally crush the joints of a man's fingers? Hmm? And from the watery blood leaking from his mouth, I'd say someone knocked his teeth out." His head tilted. "Why is there blood on the blanket over his crotch?"

"He was pierced with yucca," Spots blurted.

Wrapped Wrist almost growled as he pulled his friend back behind him and strode toward the man. "If you're with the Blessed Sun, either let us go, or try and kill us. My friend, here, needs help and we're going to find it."

The man's thin smile widened, the breeze playing idly with loose strands of the snowy hair. "There, at last I can see your soul, boy."

"I'm no boy! I'm of age. A hunter!"

"Yes, of course." The grizzled stranger turned, placed fingers to lips, and blew a shrill whistle.

Men appeared out of the very grass around them—muscular, dressed in dirt-and-grass-streaked capes that blended with the ground. They held long bows backed with something that looked like horn. Unlike the cane arrows of the Blessed Sun's warriors, theirs were made of solid chokecherry stems, each tipped with a glittering obsidian point. Within a few desperate heartbeats, he and Spots were surrounded.

"What are you going to do with us?" Wrapped Wrist demanded, to cover his building fear.

"We're going to fulfill your wishes, young hunter." The man gestured to the litter. "Firehorn, Yucca Sock, take the litter." To Wrapped Wrist, he added, "You two, walk with me."

"Who are you?" Spots demanded. "Where are we going?"

"I'm the Blessed Sun's worst nightmare. And you young men are going to see the Mountain Witch."

Twenty-three

HEALING

Healers are of two kinds. There are Healers who strive day and night to keep dying people alive for as long as possible. And there are Healers who work as helpers, holding a lamp in the darkness, leading the way.

I have watched the first type of Healer very closely. I call them Deceivers, for they are very much like witches. They try to get the dying person to look the other way while they work their magic. Almost always their magic requires so many Spirit Plants that the sick person's afterlife soul drifts in and out of her body, either floating in a stupor, or shivering in a pain-racked body while she fights to bear the horror reflected in her loved ones' eyes. Most of those patients died in their beds like lost children, abandoned and alone.

My heart shrivels when I try to imagine what they must have been thinking and feeling.

I started out being the first kind of Healer. For many summers, I fought to keep people alive for as long as I could. Then I was called in to Heal an elderly woman that no one else dared to approach. Her name was Little Flower. She seemed to hate everyone. Whenever a Healer entered her house, she threw things at them and cursed them. No matter how much of her dwindling strength it took, she always managed to drive her Healers away.

I was called in at the very end. Her sobbing daughter came to me and begged me to try to Heal her. When I arrived, Little Flower knew it immediately. She began shouting for me to go away even before I entered her lodge. I was standing out in the village plaza when she ap-

parently heard me speaking with her daughter and had a fit.

Nonetheless, I clutched my Healer's bag and ducked beneath her door curtain.

It was very difficult to feel compassion toward a woman who so obviously did not want to be Healed, but I was determined to try. The instant I saw her, however, I understood what her desperate family refused to see: that my efforts would be fruitless. Truly, she did not need a Healer, and Little Flower had known it all along.

As I approached, she gave me an evil look. Her wheezing filled the firelit darkness. But when I sat down beside her, I could tell the rage was a disguise for terror. It was a way of crying without tears, without evoking pity, which she obviously loathed.

"No ... Spirit ... Plants!" she gasped, and her death rattle grew louder. She thrashed weakly in her bed, rolling from side to side as though to stop the liquid from filling up in her lungs.

I nodded in sudden understanding. All of her "Healers" had accomplished but one thing: They had prevented her from participating in her own death, surely the most fundamental right of everything alive.

I said, "If you don't mind, I'd just like to sit with you for a time."

The anger in her eyes diminished, replaced by a kind of exhausted relief. She knew she was dying. She just wanted to be left in peace to be finished with it.

I took her hand, and very quietly said, "I once knew a great holy man named Wanderer who told me that a person's entire life could be read in the pattern of wrinkles on the backs of his hands." I smiled. "Of course he also believed it could be read in shriveled elderberries, on tortoise shells, and anything else with intricate patterns."

Little Flower gave me a faint grin.

As I began telling her what I saw in her wrinkles—a life of joys and travails, of many children, and even more grandchildren—her smile grew. Finally, she sagged against her bedding and closed her eyes.

I began Singing the Death Song, which is a very beauti-

ful lilting melody. As she listened to my soft voice, her terror dissolved. In less than a few hundred heartbeats, her breathing stopped.

The weight of the silence that followed was crushing.

Since that moment I have been the second kind of Healer. I do not deceive my patients into looking the other way. Instead, I encourage them to stare straight down the dark tunnel's throat. As a Helper, holding the lamp and walking as far as I can with them, I let them follow their own way into the darkness. I have never left them alone, but tried to keep vigil and protect them while they stepped inexorably forward.

As I gaze out across the vast deserts, I realize that civilizations have the same needs that dying people do.

I am merely the Helper. If I have hoarded enough Power, I will be able Sing this world into Death. . . .

The great kiva dominated the Dusk House plaza like a huge stone drum. It stood in defiance of the hot summer sun. Constructed with a line of vaults around its perimeter, the kiva was insulated from the oppressive heat that rose from the fields and shimmered the distant horizon into liquid silver.

Inside, down on the kiva's cool subterranean floor, Matron Desert Willow stood with her arms crossed under her high pointed breasts. She had had her slaves braid turquoise, jet, and coral beads into her long black hair, and a necklace of copper bells hung from her slender neck.

War Chief Wind Leaf watched her, making no pains about admiring her athletic body, enjoying the way her smooth brown skin dipped from her sides to a narrow waist and then swelled into the roundness of her hips. The twin globes of her tight buttocks rounded the light cotton skirt she had belted below her navel. Behind that thin fabric lay the glistening thatch of her pubis. He could sense it, as though it called to his manhood.

She must have felt his longing, for she cast a reproving glance at him; warning flashed in her large dark eyes, but her reddened lips hinted at a sensual smile.

The Buffalo Clan Elder, Creeper, seemed oblivious where he sat on the plastered side of the eastern foot drum, his vague stare fixed on the square column that supported the heavy roof to his right.

The elder hadn't been the same since Featherstone's death. It was common knowledge that the old fool had loved her, despite her fits of mindlessness. Nevertheless, Creeper served his purpose. His lifelong friendship with Webworm helped to keep the fermenting Badger Clan in line. They could do nothing until Creeper finally died; only then could the dissenting clan leaders hope to take over.

When that day finally arrives, we're going to be in trouble. The more strident voices were already calling for the First People to share authority equally with the clans. They pointed out, correctly, that there were so few First People anymore that the time had come for them to give up their monopoly on control. Wind Leaf had seen the simmering resentment, had heard the muttered deprecations as his warriors passed. Jealousy, like a festering sore, afflicted the Made People.

"What do you think of this?" Webworm called from behind the decorated screen that concealed the northern entrance. Made from painted fabric stretched over poles set in the floor, the screen was painted with images of the Yamuhakto, the Warriors of the East and West, who guarded the doorway to the Under Worlds. A rustling of fabric preceded his appearance at the masked doorway.

He strode out from behind the screen, head high, majestic in a colorful costume. A panoply of bright macaw, eagle, and blue heron feathers splayed out from the sides of a large wooden eagle mask that he wore. The eagle's head had been painted black, the eye holes rimmed in white, and a hooked yellow beak protruded for half an arm's length. Drapes of the finest white and blue cloth hung from his blocky body. A fan made of thin wooden boards and painted in blood red, sunflower yellow, and charcoal black gave his shoulders the appearance of an oversized butterfly. A giant bustle spread from behind, also of thin wood, and was painted in the shapes and colors of a dozen wildflowers. The flowers framed the cross of Morning Star on his right, and of Evening Star on his left.

Creeper looked, blinked, and then clapped his hands, calling, "Excellent, Blessed Sun. You look like a god."

"Yes," Desert Willow added, "but which one?"

Webworm paced and skipped, turning so that the magnificence of his costume could be seen. The wooden parts had been painted with azurite and malachite along with charcoal, hematite, and plant-pigment-based paints.

"Why, Sun Eagle, of course. We've almost forgotten him in our worship. War Chief? What do you think of this?" Even as Webworm spoke, the lower jaw of the eagle's beak dropped, only to snap shut with a loud clack. Webworm repeated the performance, diving like a bird, snapping his beak at an unimpressed Desert Willow.

"Remarkable, Blessed Sun," Wind Leaf added dryly, clapping his hands in approbation. The sound echoed hollowly within the kiva.

"Sun Eagle is only a god out in the Red Rock country," Creeper said with a frown. "Those people have always had peculiar ideas. They even portray the Flute Player as a cricket, of all the silly things."

Webworm sighed. "Old friend, the idea is to reinforce the notion that we respect all of the old gods. I want to reassure people that we take their heritage seriously, especially in the Red Rock country where the famine is going to be severe. They have to understand that we sympathize with their plight. The last thing we want to do is belittle them, even though they do think Flute Player is a cricket."

Webworm stopped, evidently seeing Desert Willow's distaste reflected in her hard eyes. He spun around two more times, then reached up and lifted the eagle mask from his head. A look of satisfaction lit his round face. "I think it will help, don't you?"

Wind Leaf asked, "Have you discussed this with Blue Racer?"

Webworm made a gesture, the motion pulling on the

string that worked the elaborate wooden beak. "He's down in Straight Path Canyon, sitting atop Spider Woman's Butte . . . doing something with the Sun Marker. But as soon as he comes back I'll—"

"Summer solstice is two moons past," Desert Willow said. "What could he possibly be doing up there?"

"I think he's trying to understand this drought. I told him there had to be some reason why the rains won't come. If it's tied to Sister Moon's homecoming I want to know about it." Webworm waved it away. "But the old gods, I remember how it was when I was little, sitting at Mother's feet during the ceremonies. They inspired me."

"I remember," Creeper said fondly. "Your mother was still young. You should have seen her. She was among the most beautiful of women. Her souls . . ." He winced and looked away.

Wind Leaf caught Desert Willow's roll of the eyes. Her boredom must have rivaled his own.

"It's no wonder our authority is being challenged," Webworm continued. "We've got to go back to the old ways. I half suspect that's why we're afflicted with this drought. We've strayed from the ways of our ancestors."

"What does that weigh?" Creeper asked, pointing to the splayed wooden fan.

"Quite light, actually." Webworm beamed. "And cunningly made. Look here, see how brightly they've painted it?"

While Creeper fingered the wood, Wind Leaf took a deep breath, considering the things he still had to do. Guards had to be posted, reports needed to be made to his deputies. Someone was going to have to do something with old Flat Nose over in the Red Rock country. Too many rumors tied him to the molestation of young girls. Then there were the "Sotol People"—barbarians from the cactus-and-limestone country to the southeast. They were a thorn to the settlements in the southern Great River country. Never a major threat, their raids were more of a nuisance, and no one really wanted to follow them out into their desolate rocky wasteland to hunt them down.

He was so preoccupied that it took a moment to register

the scuffing steps echoing from the southern entrance. He turned, glancing up to see a burly warrior, sandals slapping the sandstone steps as he descended to the kiva floor, made the bow of obedience to the gods, and hurried forward. He wore a warrior's shirt and had the look of a winded runner. Sweat had left a creased path down the scar that marred his cheek.

"Blessed Sun!" the man called as he approached.

"Yes? Who comes?"

"I am Turquoise Fox, Blessed Sun. I serve with Deputy Leather Hand in the north." He bowed and touched his chin in respect.

Wind Leaf nodded. "I remember you. What is the word on the beasts that broke into the Blessed Sun's stores and killed our priest?"

"Dead, War Chief." Turquoise Fox stopped short, as if aware that his sweaty body and dust-caked war shirt carried the odor of a man too long without a wash. And there was something else about him: a sweet, cloying, but not unpleasant odor. The stains on his red shirt looked like grease, and there were smudges of charcoal and soot.

"It's such a shame." Creeper sadly clasped his hands together. "I knew Right Acorn. I watched him grow from a boy to a man. My heart goes out of his family."

"His murderers suffered, I assume," Desert Willow interjected.

"Yes, Matron," Turquoise Fox replied. "In a hideous way."

"And what way was that?" Desert Willow asked with mild annoyance. "Let me guess, their bodies are now feeding ants, coyotes, and vultures. Their bones are bleaching in the sun, their relatives wailing in despair."

Turquoise Fox frowned slightly. "Matron, we had to take *special* measures."

Webworm tossed the eagle mask to Creeper, heedless of the string. It ripped the cloth of his costume before snapping the mouth shut with a clack as the string parted. Creeper barely scrambled forward in time to catch it before it crashed to the floor.

Pinning Turquoise Fox, Desert Willow demanded, "Did

you torture them first? Yes? Did you rape the women, gut the men slowly? I won't have the storerooms being raided by these pesky barbarian thieves."

Turquoise Fox straightened under the barrage, as if to attention. "Blessed Matron, we did worse."

"What could be worse?" Wind Leaf asked. "I take it that Leather Hand understood the severity of the situation."

"Yes, War Chief. He did."

"And?" Webworm demanded.

"We ate them."

For a moment the great kiva was silent. Webworm seemed to be struggling with the notion. Desert Willow, too, looked confused. Only Creeper's eyes widened.

"Ate them?" Wind Leaf prompted.

Turquoise Fox swallowed hard. "War Chief, you must understand, these people, the ones who stole from us and killed our Priest, they had nothing left to lose."

"What of their lives?" Webworm shouted. "Isn't that enough?"

Turquoise Fox shook his head. "No, Blessed Sun. They were dead anyway. The drought, you see. They were starving. They'd eaten their seed corn. All of it. And they had nothing to Trade for more." He looked panicked for the first time. "Don't you see? They had *nothing*!"

"Yes, yes," Wind Leaf waved it down. "They had nothing. So, what did you mean when you said you ate them?"

Turquoise Fox licked his lips, shifting uncomfortably. Wind Leaf wondered if it was fatigue from the long run, or if his nerves were failing. "War Chief, do you remember Deer Mother Village several winters back?"

"Of course, they were starving, snowed in. They . . ." He stopped short. "Wait, you mean you were starving?"

Turquoise Fox was now looking distinctly miserable, as if this wasn't going the way he had anticipated. "No, War Chief. Do you remember the horror among the people when they talked about what had happened at Deer Mother Village?"

He nodded. It had been the talk of the country.

Knotting a fist, Turquoise Fox cried, "Blessed Sun, don't you see? It's the only weapon we had left to inspire terror!

Nothing else would work. We had to teach them that they had something more terrifying to fear than just death!"

Webworm looked stunned, if slightly ludicrous, in his gaudy costume. "You mean Leather Hand ordered his men to eat the thieves? Cook them up like deer and . . . and gobble them down?"

"Yes, Blessed Sun." Turquoise Fox looked as if he, too, had suddenly lost everything.

"And what was the response from the people?" Desert Willow asked, her voice oddly tinted with curiosity.

"Abject horror, Blessed Matron. We brought some of the other Dust People to see the remains. You could see it in their eyes. They melted back from us, avoided our gaze as if we were monsters. I would say that by now there isn't a single occupied farmstead in the whole of the country below Thunderbird Mountain."

"And the warriors?" Wind Leaf was amazed. "They agreed to this?"

"Yes, War Chief." He paused. "Well . . . all but an Ant Clan man named Black Rabbit. Deputy Leather Hand killed him for refusing. A war chief must enforce discipline."

Gods, can this be true? Wind Leaf was trying to comprehend the ramifications, how this was going to change his plans. Then he glanced at Webworm. What if the Blessed Sun ordered him to punish Leather Hand? *Eating* another human being just *wasn't* done. What if half of his forces bolted for fear of being forced to eat human flesh? Gods, this could turn into a real mess.

Desert Willow—heedless of the effect of her words on Creeper—smiled slightly. "Well, we've always said they were no better than animals."

"They ate them?" old Creeper repeated in a mystified tone.

"They ate them," Webworm replied flatly. His face still reflected stunned disbelief.

A bubble of laughter rose in Desert Willow's throat. "They ate them!" She slapped a hand to her shapely thigh and laughed out loud. "They *ate* them!"

The Matron's peals of laughter rolled around the great building like a wave.

Twenty-four

High atop the Green Mesa, Leather Hand sat in the cool recesses of a yucca-mat-covered ramada and sipped at a mug of mint tea. Around him, the inhabitants of Far View Town had turned lazy, taking their ease from the strong midday heat. Most of his warriors had disappeared into the shade of the high-walled buildings or the scattered pit houses to enjoy their well-earned rights to the slave women. The rest of the population was doing its best to avoid them.

There is a price to greatness.

Warm as it was up at this high mountain elevation, Leather Hand pitied the people in the distant lowlands where the heat must be brutal. He sighed, leaning back in a hammock made of tightly knotted cord, his tea perched on the rippled muscles of his belly. A feeling of great satisfaction had grown in place of the indecision he'd felt after the punitive raids on the Dust People.

I have changed things. My men are different. I am different.

By the gods, word had traveled fast. It had been apparent when they came trooping up the mountain, passing the Green Mesa villages on the way to Far View Town. People had watched them pass with frightened eyes, whispering among themselves. No one had dared to so much as call a greeting.

It wasn't just the people; he could see it the eyes of his men. They walked, talked, even seemed to breathe with a sense of otherness, as if by eating the flesh of men, they had become sharper, passing like blades among ordinary folk.

It is well that the Blessed Sun's special warriors are set apart. No one will dare to incite our wrath now.

Here, from the Blessed Sun's holding high atop the

Green Mesas, he could look down over the large multistory buildings and towers that composed Far View. Given the town's importance, each of the major First People clans had their own house: Red Lacewings' was built on the solar line, while the Blue Dragonfly Clan had built along the line of the lunar maximum. The Made People clans had constructed towns of their own. In addition to those, he could see the pimples of pit houses rising here and there in the spaces between the corn and bean fields. The two observation and signal towers stuck up like stubby thumbs above the patchwork of terraced fields. Little squares of single-room granaries stood beside paths and the sinuous ditches that watered the fields. It was a thriving community, not as large as Tall Piñon with its three thousand souls, but large enough to boast nearly half that.

Far View was more than a sprawling center for Trade and ceremony; it was the Blessed Sun's giant stamp of authority over the Green Mesa villages. From here, his prestige and control radiated out over the mesa-top towns and farmsteads. The Matrons who served here felt the stirring of each breath taken by the Made People who called this high broken land home. From this large complex of buildings, they sent out their Priests and warriors to enforce the commands and pull the strings that administered the countless settlements.

The lifeblood of Far View, however, could be found a stone's throw up the slope from his ramada: a large stone-and-clay-lined reservoir. It was fed by winter snows, spring or summer rains, any weather that dropped enough precipitation to cause runoff. The caprock above had been cunningly engineered to divert water into ditches. These in turn emptied into a large canal that flowed through a clever silt trap and into the reservoir. At first light slaves descended the stone steps to fill tall water jars that they carried down to the towns or perhaps to the gardens when the rains were too widely separated. There, in the cool evening, men gathered to splash water on their faces and gossip about the day's events. For the children it was a focal point for play, an opulent wet miracle to amaze a desert people.

Far View had come by its name honestly; its location was strategically perfect. From his hammock, Leather Hand could look south across the settlement, down the sloping mesa, across the broken River of Souls Valley to distant Smoking Mirror Butte where it hulked below the southern horizon. He could see the Bear Claw Mountain uplift, World Tree, and even the distant hump of mesa where Center Place stood above Straight Path Canyon. There, baked by the midday sun, the Blessed Sun's sentries kept watch on the northern reaches.

On the ridgetop a half hand's run to the north, the signal observatory stood. From its top, Thunderbird Mountain, Tall Piñon, and all the northern settlements could be observed. By means of a complex system of mica mirrors, different colored smokes, or signal fires, any of the northern great houses could immediately communicate with the Blessed Sun at Dusk House on the River of Souls. Within moments orders could be given, questions answered, or a party dispatched in relief of whatever sort of disaster loomed.

Lot of good that does. Leather Hand smiled wryly at the notion. Only yesterday had come word that a fire seen at Pinnacle House had been accidentally set. A prank, said the runners dispatched by an embarrassed Matron Larkspur.

The event left a sour aftertaste. With all the potential for trouble looming around them, didn't the Blessed Larkspur have her people under control up there? And worse, was Burning Smoke slipping, losing his ability to inspire the barbarians to obedience?

He let his brooding gaze settle on the faint southern horizon. There the fires at Center Place, the high northern town above Straight Path Canyon, could be seen flickering on a clear night.

The beating heart of my people. He thought about the canyon that lay just below that horizon, considered what it meant to the Straight Path Nation. A thousand souls had traveled there to take the Great North Road in search of the doorway to the Underworlds. For generations the First People had marched out of Straight Path Canyon, their red-shirted warriors and thick-set masons following, to slowly but surely bring order to the surrounding peoples. During those generations, the world had changed. True, the Blessed Suns ruled with a stone fist; but such policies were necessary to ensure that the subjects remained compliant. The cost of peace might have been broken bodies, a couple of fired towns, and occasional bloody massacres here and there—but during the Straight Path rule, the land had flourished. Stories still told how in the old days, people lived in constant fear of their neighbors. How after the coming of the Straight Path peace, they could move out, establish small farmsteads on isolated patches of fertile soil, and know that no footloose party of raiders was going to steal in during the night to murder them in their beds for the crops in their fields.

Why on earth would the malcontents threaten that?

As he mulled the thought he turned his gaze farther to the southwest. In the midday haze, he could just make out the Rainbow Serpent, a dirty smudge rising from the horizon. Why, of all times, had the Powers of the Underworlds picked this moment to emerge? Just what did it mean for them?

He was brooding over that when the Sun Priest known as Moon Knuckle walked down from the reservoir. An old friend—and the only one who apparently refused to shun Leather Hand—he carried one of the tall black-on-white ceremonial Straight Path mugs in his hand. He squinted in the bright sunlight as he approached, nodded, and stepped into the ramada's shade. Sighing with relief, Moon Knuckle settled on a stump beside Leather Hand's hammock and sipped his tea, smacking his lips.

"What a perfect day," the Priest began. "Shade, a slight breeze to cool the skin, and a refreshing beverage." He lifted the tall mug to display the fine-lined hatching design of the Red Lacewing Clan.

"Mint?" Leather Hand asked casually.

"Indeed," the Priest answered. He was a middle-aged man, his face lined and weathered. Gray streaked his hair, now pulled into a severe bun at the back of his head. His flabby breasts hung down like an old woman's, and his rounded sides challenged the belt that kept a white cotton kilt around his hips. "The women have brewed another large batch. I was fortunate enough to dip this from the pot."

"It's still warm?" Leather Hand asked. He'd taken his from a sweaty olla that had cooled in the breeze.

"Better that than just water. The children were playing in the reservoir earlier. It's muddy, and may the Blue God chase them, they're still children. You never know when they might have peed in the pool."

Leather Hand grunted. "We don't have that problem at Tall Piñon. Of course, our reservoir isn't as large as yours, but the Deep Canyon People keep a pretty close eye on it."

The Priest rested his hands on his knobby knees where the brown flesh stuck out from his kilt. "In that case, they let the little boys pee in your water jar before they cart it up to your rooms."

"Should I ever discover that such a thing had occurred, I would skin one of the little brats, gut him, and pour the contents of his bladder down his lifeless throat so that it coated the inside of his gaping gut cavity."

Moon Knuckle chuckled, his brown eyes searching the southern horizon. "Is that how you deal with all of your troubles?"

"I am the Blessed Sun's fist." Leather Hand sipped his tea, letting the taste of mint roll over his tongue. "You, Seven Stars, and the rest of the Priests can be their friends. The Matrons can be their Healers and counselors, but in the end, isn't it reassuring to know that we are here, lurking in the background? We are the lightning bolt behind the rainbow. And, believe me, the people never forget it."

"That is true." He glanced curiously at Leather Hand. "Could I ask a personal question?"

"Of course."

"What did it taste like?"

Leather Hand laughed. "Most are too timid to ask."

"I suppose. I, however, have known you for too long to take your abrasive exterior so seriously."

"You've had the meat of that pig? The one that runs the lower desert where the Hohokam live?"

"Once, yes."

"Like that. Oddly sweet, but with a tang. Perhaps the tang came from the fact that what we ate had no fat on it. Their meat was stringy with starvation."

"I see." He fingered his tall mug, his gaze fixed on the Rainbow Serpent's distant smoke plume.

"You are placing yourself at risk, old friend. People have been going out of their way to avoid me and my warriors."

"Of course." Moon Knuckle waved his free hand at the long flat ridges that sloped off to the south before them. "Even here in the Green Mesa villages, it is the talk of every farmstead, village, and town. 'Leather Hand has killed and *eaten* the Dust People!' It is spoken with a mixture of horror, wonder, and titillation."

He snorted, watched a crow rising and falling on the thermals, and finally asked, "And you, Moon Knuckle, do you think it was a wise move?"

Moon Knuckle squinted, his squat face unsure. "Time alone will answer that. How you go about incurring Spider Woman's wrath is your business. But as to the way it will affect the Blessed Sun's policies?" His sloped shoulders rose and fell. "All I can tell you is that we deal with a tenuous time."

"A fist must remain a fist, even when its target has lost the ability to feel pain."

"Given what happened to Right Acorn at Tall Piñon I don't know what you could have possibly done differently. Order must be maintained. If the Blessed Sun's control is broken, we face chaos. People will turn upon their neighbors. We will become like rats trapped in a jar, having only ourselves to devour."

"On that we agree." Leather Hand sipped his tea, the tang of mint lingering on his taste buds. "To that end, I shall become more than the Blessed Sun's fist. I shall become his hammer."

Moon Knuckle's expression saddened. "Chances are good we may need you in that role before this comes to an end. But this I do know: If we don't get rain, you will need ever harsher measures to keep the people in line."

"My warriors and I understand that."

Moon Knuckle turned serious eyes on him. "I have known you since you were a child. Your father was my good friend back in the days when I oversaw Chief Crow Beard's turquoise mines. I watched you and Wraps His Tail grow up. I wept at your brother's death. Now, my souls worry for yours."

Leather Hand smiled. "Unlike my brother, I have learned not to put my trust in the likes of Ironwood. No assassin will find my back."

"You misunderstand me, Leather Hand, as perhaps you also misunderstand the people."

"How is that?"

"You and your warriors, like the First People themselves, are few. A handful of warriors here, a handful there, cast across so vast a land. Up until now, for the most part, people have been content with their lives. As you so aptly noted, the lightning bolt behind the rainbow was sufficient to keep them in line. It wasn't worth incurring the Blessed Sun's wrath over a petty intervillage feud or a squabble over clan cornfield boundaries. It was to our advantage to only have a handful of warriors, a couple of Priests, and the Matron and her staff at any given great house. There weren't enough of us to become a burden to the local people. What it cost them to support us was made up for by the storage of tribute for the hard times. We were there to arbitrate their disputes, to pray for their sick, and to demand their tribute. They may not have liked us, but they tolerated us. In the event of an uprising, a signal fire would be lit and forty warriors would arrive the next morning to quell the trouble. Communications and mobility balanced our limited numbers."

"I take it you don't think that is still the case?"

"Leather Hand, I said the people were *mostly* content. Today they are anything but. The truth is, we can't feed everyone with the limited number of irrigated fields we have."

"Ah, but I have heard the Priests at Dusk House assure the Blessed Sun that we can. They have counted the number of baskets of corn that can be grown in the valleys. They say that if we dig some more canals, clear some more fields, we can do it."

"Perhaps," Moon Knuckle agreed, "in a couple of select

locations along the big rivers. But how would you transport all that corn? A man can only carry so much. In so many days he must eat so many handfuls of that same corn he bears on his back. As you move out from the major valleys the porters eat more corn than they deliver. Returns diminish over distance."

"It always comes back to that, doesn't it?"

"For exactly that reason Straight Path Canyon is being abandoned. No matter what the Blessed Sun says about making a new beginning on the Spirit River, it's the corn that really necessitated the move. More of the yield along the Spirit River and the River of Souls can be packed into the storerooms of Dusk House and these other towns they're building."

"So, we've moved our world closer to the corn? What do you think, Priest? Is it a new beginning?" He gestured toward the Rainbow Serpent in the distant haze. "Or is that a sign that Spider Woman's wrath is turned upon us all?"

Moon Knuckle fingered his chin. "Let us hope the former. You see, no matter how much corn we can grow in the river bottoms, it still has to be protected. And, as you have just so recently discovered, protecting a resource—even inside a fortified great house—is something of a difficult task, let alone along a winding river valley pocked with hiding places, timber, and endless trails leading off into the hills."

"Which is why we do not want to bring the people to the corn. We would be packing thousands upon thousands into the valley of the River of Souls."

"Where we would be outnumbered by thousands to one. Vulnerable as we are with our widely scattered great houses, the barbarians would drown us were they to be concentrated into one place. That many people, uprooted from their ancestral homes, frightened and unsure? All it would take would be a spark among the multitudes—like a lightning strike in a tinder-dry forest."

"I see what you mean."

Moon Knuckle sipped his tea, a moody expression on his face. "Then you had better pray that the gods send us rain, Deputy. And you, for one, will be a fortunate man."

"How is that?"

"Because if the drought continues, and people turn to raiding for what little corn is left, you will have an endless supply of desperate men willing to do anything to keep their kinsmen and children alive." His lips twitched. "Tell me, 'Hammer,' do you think you can eat them all?"

Twenty-five

Warmth, like a fondly remembered Dream, stole into Ripple's body. It lapped around him, bearing him up and up. He could feel himself rising. His wounded souls began to spin, round and round, as images of clouds slipped past him, soft and white. Upward he was borne, to a place of light, where pain was washed away with the soft stroke of something like warm dog tongues against his skin.

The light was so bright. He squinted his eyes, feeling it sear the inside of his brain. He clamped them closed, thankful for the kind darkness.

"Do you hear me, Ripple?"

"Yes. Who are you?"

"My name is Nightshade. Once of the Hollow Hoof Clan. You know me as the Mountain Witch."

He felt a shiver run through his floating body.

"The wounds you have suffered are not severe enough to have driven your souls from your body. Something else has caused your souls to retreat from the flesh."

"The pain was unbearable. But seeing what they did. Feeling it. That was the worst thing."

"Were you brave?"

"No. I cried. Fear ran through my veins. My water ran down my legs and pooled on the floor. I screamed so loudly my throat remains raw."

"Did you tell them about Horo Mana?"

"Who?"

"Yohozro Wuqti."

"I don't know that name."

"Cold Bringing Woman. Did you tell them about your vision?"

"I told them nothing they did not already know." He sniffed at the wetness in his nose. "But I would have. The next time, I would have done anything they asked me to. They're smart, you see. First they hurt you, but not all the way. They leave you there in the darkness feeling the sharp splinters of broken teeth. You wait with the knowledge that when they return, they will break the rest. They let you run your tongue over them, count them, knowing that they, too, will snap, one by one, from the roots.

"They let you cradle your broken hand, while the pain pulses and leaps. You know that next time they come, your remaining hand will suffer the same. Do you know what it's like to bend your fingers, knowing that soon they will be made useless to you? They leave you knowing that you must make water, or your penis will fester. But they leave you nothing to drink to replenish yourself. You lay there in the darkness, desperate with thirst, your manhood burning with pain.

"Over and over, you ask yourself, 'What will they do to me when they come again?' "

"You believe you failed?"

"I would have done whatever they wished." He wept. "I would have betrayed Cold Bringing Woman."

"Ah, so that is why you wish to let go of life."

"I would have given up."

"But you didn't."

"Didn't, would have, isn't it the same thing?"

"You don't understand what you have learned."

"I learned that I would have failed."

"That may or may not be correct. You learned that success is never guaranteed. Even with the best intentions, the utmost honor, and courage, we are ultimately frail. Knowing how much burden you can bear keeps you from overloading your pack. The arrogance of your convictions has been tempered. You will not demand of others what you yourself cannot withstand."

"How can I trust myself?"

"That is for you to answer. You are being tested, hunter. Your souls are hovering close to your body, unsure of your resolve to live. You were sent to me for judgment."

"I don't understand."

"Cold Bringing Woman asked me to determine if you are worthy. I cannot tell. Your souls are hovering between commitment and defeat. Your body, despite its wounds, craves life. The hunger of its yearning is so great it consumes your souls. If it is your wish to save your body, you may return to it. If you do, you will be desperate to flee as far as you can from the First People and their wrath."

"If I do that, I will have betrayed Cold Bringing Woman."

"She knew the risks when she first revealed herself to you."

"Is there another way?"

"I can set your souls free. Give them time away from your body. Once lost in the darkness of the Dream, they can choose, free from the body's selfish cravings. You will be isolated from the pain, distant from the hunger. But beware! You will be alone in the darkness. Vulnerable. Malevolent things prowl the Dream and prey on the fearful. I cannot protect you. You will have no more safety than you did at Pinnacle Great House. You could lose your souls forever, Ripple."

"But I could keep my oath? I could serve Cold Bringing Woman?"

"If you survive the Dream. The choice is yours."

A different fear—one worse than what he had known in the dark room at Pinnacle Great House—sent clammy fingers of unease through his souls. It would be so easy to give in to his body. He could save himself. Escape. He would never have to feel pain and fear again.

Ripple could see himself, traveling east, walking alone through green mountain meadows as his body healed. A new home could be built in the grassy flats beside the Great River.

A vision formed of his older self, his fingers caressing green corn tassels, smiling at a sun-browned woman who labored beside him in their field. His children were pulling weeds, periodically stopping to pelt each other with dirt clods.

He imagined himself lying beside his wife at night, the warmth of her body soothing his. She murmured as she turned under the blanket. Reaching down, she grasped his hard manhood, drawing his body onto hers as she opened herself to his desire.

In another vision, a soft snow fell outside their dwelling, while inside the plastered walls, a fire crackled. He could see himself, laughing and smiling, his hair whitened with age. Grandchildren shrieked in delight as his daughters dished up spicy corn cakes and handed them to him. He bit down, chewing on the flavorful meal with his remaining teeth.

"You could have these things," the Mountain Witch's voice intruded.

He swallowed hard, feeling the ache in his broken mouth. In the lapping heat, his mangled hand pulsed in misery. The vision promised children, grandchildren—so the wounds in his penis would heal. He would have a legacy.

"The choice is yours, Ripple."

He remembered Cold Bringing Woman, saw again her white face, fierce red eyes, and bloodred tongue as it whipped through the chill air. Her fierce words hung like frost: *Do not disappoint me!*

How do I choose? What can I choose? What is a promise compared to paradise?

Do not disappoint me!

"How can I choose?" he cried, as he had on that fateful night.

In that instant he watched his other life slide away, sadness in his wife's panicked face, his children staring at him in wide-eyed disbelief.

"Gods, no," he whispered. "I can't bear it."

"I am sending your souls away now. Only when you have made your choice can they return."

He could feel gentle fingers massaging the sides of his

head. A cool sensation began to seep through his temples, and he felt himself rising, looking down to see a gray-haired old woman standing waist deep in a hot spring. His body floated before her, bathed by the warm water. He could see his swollen face and winced at the sight of his crushed hand and inflamed penis.

"Go now," a gentle voice ordered.

Ripple turned to see a huge being with round head, tube like eyes, and a circle of a mouth. *Mud Head!* The giant Danced, his feet beating with the cadence of Ripple's heart. Pointing with a rattle he held in his right hand, Mud Head inclined his head. The intent was clear.

Ripple turned, heading into the gray fog before him. Hollow fear and desperate longing were his only companions.

Horo Mana, the one you know as Cold Bringing Woman, calls. She Dances among the Cloud People, her turquoise-jeweled feet stamping out the hail. She twirls and spirals, bringing darkness, chill, and storm. The katsinas scatter before her.

I watch his souls as they disappear into the mist.

Beware the gods that prowl the Darkness, young hunter. Strangle your fear, or you will have no idea that you are lost until She devours you.

"Will he live, Elder?" the warrior called Yucca Sock asked as they lifted the unconscious hunter's naked body from the hot steaming waters of the spring. Evening light sent yellow rays to bathe the high mountains around them. It softened the forest-clad slopes of the valley. Even the breeze had stilled, as if pleased to bask in the perfect afternoon.

"I can't tell yet," Nightshade replied as she waded out

behind them. Her gray hair gleamed in the light. The faded red dress she wore was soaked up to the waist. Her age-lined face betrayed worry and misgiving. She was tall for her age, with spine unbowed, and agile despite her years. "Place him on the grass there. I have sent his souls away. They must decide if they want to return."

She bent down and continued to rub a gray paste into his temples. "I could feel the fear when his souls spoke to mine. There's no telling what might be attracted by such powerful fear and longing. Like the scent of blood on the wind, such emotions will draw predators—and he has no guardian."

"Is it important that he live?"

Nightshade shrugged. "I do not know. We stand in a forest grown thick with old timber. Lightning flashes through the sky. It is up to the gods when or if it will strike."

"And if it does?" Yucca Sock asked.

"Answer that yourself, warrior."

She ignored his stricken expression and glanced down at Ripple's mutilated penis. Water had washed the coagulated blood from the punctures to expose swollen and inflamed tissue. "This must be drained."

Both Yucca Sock and Firehorn flinched and looked away as her bony fingers took the hunter's swollen member. Holding it like a slippery trout, she began squeezing pus through the loosened scabs.

"Perhaps it's just as well his souls are traveling," she added.

Nevertheless, the unconscious Ripple groaned and gasped as she cleaned the punctures and dabbed on an herbal potion of coneflower, mallow, and crushed sage leaves.

Inspecting his hideously bruised and puffy hand, she said, "Bring me willow splints and thongs for binding. They crushed all the joints."

"Can you save the hand?" Firehorn asked.

"He will never have the use of it, but it need not end up looking like a claw."

"And his mouth?" Yucca Sock asked.

"He'll have one side to chew on. As to the broken teeth, well, the remaining roots will fester and fall out in the coming days. They left him enough teeth in front that he won't lisp when he talks."

Firehorn handed her willow sticks cut to length and thin leather laces. He made a face as she straightened the bruised and swollen fingers. The unconscious Ripple stiffened, a cry locked deep in his throat.

"Can you call his souls back if you need to?" Yucca Sock asked.

Nightshade glanced up, eyes dark and large. The effect was like looking into midnight. "I can do nothing for them. They must decide their own fate. When they come back, if they come back, or what they come back as . . . Well, we'll just have to see."

She took a moment to raise Ripple's eyelids, staring into the rolled-back pupils. Then she leaned forward, sniffing at his breath where it came in shallow gasps. "Very well, place a blanket over him and take him up the mountain to Orenda. I have done all I can for the moment."

"Yes, Blessed Elder."

"Time to report to the war chief." Nightshade turned her attention to the conifers overlooking the hot springs and made a gesture with her hand. Immediately a form detached itself from the shadows where it had been keeping watch. A warrior bearing a round wicker shield and carrying a bow and quiver trotted down the rocky slope on slender legs.

The two warriors beside her glanced meaningfully at each other, gently lifting the unconscious man onto the litter that had borne him thus far. With care they tucked the blanket around his body.

Firehorn stepped around to grasp the handles, each made of narrow lodgepoles. He hesitated. "His souls, Elder. What did you mean? You said 'what they come back as'?"

Nightshade barely shrugged. "His body will never be the same, warrior. Why do you expect his souls to be?"

She watched them as they started up the hill, barely nodding to the approaching warrior. Now, closer, the shape was unmistakably female, a striking woman, tall, with a perfect heart-shaped face. She would have been a beauty, but for the flinty anger in her large dark eyes and the hardness in the set of her mouth.

"Yes, Blessed Elder?" she asked as she came to a stop.

Nightshade smiled, reading the woman's stormy gaze. "It is easy to hate, isn't it, Crow Woman?"

"Anything else is weakness, Blessed Elder." The woman's mouth hardened even further.

"Step close. I won't hurt you."

Crow Woman's frown deepened, but she nervously took another step. The flint in her eyes began to ebb as anxiety took its place.

As Crow Woman looked away, Nightshade said, "You do well to fear me."

"Elder?" The woman's throat had tightened, but she stood her ground, back stiff, the breeze playing with the single warrior's feather that stuck up from the tight bun at the back of her head.

Nightshade reached out, the tips of her fingers pressing through the shirt and into Crow Woman's abdomen below the navel. A tremor ran through Crow Woman as though she'd been stuck.

"What are you doing?"

It was barely above a whisper. "Feeling the future, girl. Sensing the energy building in your womb. Don't you hear them? They're crying out to you, knowing the things you refuse to believe."

"Revered Elder, my womb is a withered vine. By the Blessed katsinas, I'll die barren. And the gods help the man who tries to slip himself into me."

"Yes, girl, pour that hate out. Let it run like blood from a vein." Nightshade smiled. "Opposites attract. Now, go. Tell the war chief I am entering the water to Dream the future."

"Entering the water?" Crow Woman looked confused.

Nightshade pointed over her shoulder to the blue-green waters of the hot springs. They steamed, cradled by mineral-encrusted rocks. Beyond them, the river looked cool and refreshing, the willows along its shores bending with the breeze. Nightshade bent and pulled her sodden dress over her head. She dropped it loosely on the grass beside her opened pack.

Reaching in the pack, she retrieved a gleaming black pot. Just big enough to be cradled comfortably in two hands, the vessel was incised with curling designs around the shoulders.

The warrior woman gasped. "It's beautiful."

"It's called a Wellpot, made by only the finest Cahokia potters. Look at the walls, thin enough you'd think they were crafted of eggshell. The slip is so black, so lustrous you can see yourself reflected in it. Look closer, woman of war, and you can see into other worlds."

Unsure, Crow Woman asked, "What do you keep in there?"

"My sister," Nightshade replied laconically as she reached in and ran a fingertip through soft gray paste. She raised it to her nostrils, sniffing carefully. "Yes, my dearest sister. Are you ready to Dance?"

The younger woman watched in awe as Nightshade placed her forefinger to her temple, rubbing the paste around in slow circular motions.

"Go on, Crow Woman," she said softly. "Tell the war chief I'll have his answer by morning."

Crow Woman cast one last worried glance over her shoulder as Nightshade slowly waded into the steaming water. Even as she watched, some gargantuan shape seemed to twist and bend in the rising steam, as if gyrating in some terrible Dance.

Twenty-six

Evening was falling when Whistle led Bad Cast out of the trees and across a grassy meadow toward the river. Bad Cast had figured they were nearing their goal when a voice hailed them from the shadows beside the timbered trail. While Bad Cast had nearly jumped out of his skin, an unconcerned Whistle had answered with a single word: "Orenda."

Orenda. What did that mean? When Bad Cast asked, the stalwart Whistle had just ignored him.

Now, high mountains rising on either side, they walked along the bank of the River of Souls. It murmured and whispered as it poured over rocks and rapids on its way to the lowlands. The first stars were rising above the peaks to the east as Whistle led Bad Cast down to the bank and picked his way across a rocky ford creased with ripples.

The cold water felt good on Bad Cast's tired feet. He paused only long enough to drink and splash some water on his face, then followed Whistle up the high bank and across a grassy flat.

A cluster of small fires flickered at the edge of a rocky outcrop overlooking the river. At each a handful of people sat in the glow, their eyes turned toward Whistle as he approached.

To Bad Cast's surprise, he could see Wrapped Wrist and Spots crouched over a small fire in the center of the camp. Both looked oddly out of place, reminding him of rabbits surrounded by a ring of coyotes. They were wide-eyed, with uneasy stares that added to the stiffness of their postures.

A faint smell of damp sulfur carried down the canyon on the evening breeze. It added to the sense of premonition that burned like a burr between Bad Cast's souls. Overhead, a bat flitted on silent wings, cutting closely beside his ear, as if whispering a warning. Or was the night creature simply after the clinging mosquitoes that followed his movements with a gentle hum?

"Greetings to the camp," Whistle called. "I come with a young man of the Moon People."

"Come," a gruff voice called, and a tall man rose from one of the peripheral fires. "We've been worried."

"All went well, War Chief." Whistle then turned, saying to Bad Cast, "Go and join your friends."

Bad Cast, with more than a little apprehension, picked his way past the squatting warriors to Spots and Wrapped

Wrist's fire. As he did, two lean and muscular men, warriors from the look of them, rose and followed the grizzled giant Whistle had addressed as "War Chief" into the evening gloom.

Spots let out a soft sigh at the sight of Bad Cast. "We thought you were dead."

Bad Cast took a seat beside Wrapped Wrist and glanced over his shoulder at the clusters of warriors. Firelight reflected in their intent eyes and gave them wolfish appearances. "I thought I was, too. But I don't think Matron Larkspur has any idea who set that fire."

"What about Ripple? Did anyone see us take him?"

"No. They hadn't even discovered his escape by the time Whistle and I left." He glanced around. "Speaking of Ripple, where is he?"

"They took him." Wrapped Wrist reached over, offering him a ceramic bowl filled with stewed meat. "Hungry?"

"Who took him?"

"These warriors." Wrapped Wrist made a circle with his finger as if to take in the camp. "Believe me, we weren't in any position to object. That old one-eyed war chief ordered two men to take the litter. They trotted away out of sight."

"Who are these people?" Bad Cast took the bowl, feeling heat radiating through its sides as he placed it on the ground and began plucking out bits of meat flavored with beeweed, yucca flower, and goosefoot seed.

"We have no idea." Spots glanced surreptitiously to the growing darkness and the men who watched them with hawkish eyes. "They come from all over, but most are from the Made People clans. They say they're with the Mountain Witch. There are at least two tens of them. Some are scattered out along the passes and valleys as scouts and sentries. They wear a hodgepodge of clothes, some of Made People design; some have red warriors' shirts. No matter where they come from, they all look pretty mean, and their weapons are cared for and well used."

"Then," Bad Cast added, "that old one-eyed man is probably Ironwood."

"Ironwood?" Wrapped Wrist asked incredulously. "You think that's really him?"

"Whistle said he worked for Ironwood, that the war chief was allied with the Mountain Witch." He smiled at the stunned disbelief in his friend's eyes. "It isn't every day that you meet a legend, is it?"

When Wrapped Wrist found his voice, he asked, "What happened back at Pinnacle Great House? You really think we got away with it?"

"As far as I know." He jerked a thumb toward the darkness where Whistle talked with the war chief and the two warriors. "Whistle spent the night with Matron Larkspur. Shared her bed."

Spots was round-eyed. "Who *is* he?"

"One of Ironwood's warriors. He claims to be of the Bee Flower Clan, but I've never heard of him."

"Bad Cast," Spots asked softly, his eyes on the surrounding warriors, "what's going to happen to us?"

"I don't know." He followed Spots's gaze. One by one, he inspected the warriors who surrounded them. Their postures, the alert eyes, even the air of tension about them reeked of deadly earnest.

Spots asked, "Do you really think that's Ironwood?"

"He's spooky enough to be." Wrapped Wrist rubbed his hands down his muscular shins. "That patch he wears . . . It is said that Jay Bird blinded his left eye. And the scars on his body—they look like those left on a man who was tortured almost to the death."

"His men," Spots added, "obey him with a passion that I have never seen before. Were he to order them to cut their own throats I think they'd just nod and do it right on the spot."

"Spooky," Wrapped Wrist repeated.

Bad Cast chewed the succulent meat, trying to remember how long it had been since he'd eaten. "What did he say to you?"

"He asked us over and over to tell him everything we could about Ripple's vision." Wrapped Wrist frowned. "Unlike the others, he listened very intently, thinking about everything Ripple told us."

"Did he believe it?"

Spots made a helpless gesture. "I don't know, but the content of Ripple's vision is very important to him."

Bad Cast puffed his cheeks out as he exhaled. "What do you think?"

Wrapped Wrist shifted uneasily. "How do I know? But consider this: You didn't get a chance to really see what they did to Ripple. Before the fever drove his souls away, he told us that Burning Smoke, Larkspur, and Water Bow worked on him. They tried to get him to reveal and denounce Cold Bringing Woman's vision. He said he wouldn't do it."

Spots swallowed hard. "Look, we all know Ripple. I'll tell you just what I told that one-eyed war chief. To endure what he did at the hands of the First People, Ripple believes that Cold Bringing Woman really came and spoke to him."

A shiver ran down Bad Cast's spine. "So, when can we go home?"

"Not anytime soon," the gruff voice said from behind.

Bad Cast turned to see the one-eyed war chief leading the others back toward the fire. The patch over his left eye was like a slash of darkness across his weathered face. Despite his age, he still moved with the liquid grace of a bobcat. He seated himself cross-legged; his good right eye fixed thoughtfully on Bad Cast.

Is this really the infamous Ironwood? It was hard to believe that the subject of story and legend sat just across from him. But then, the man exuded a dangerous quality, a sensation that the slightest mistake might let loose a maelstrom.

Whistle dropped with a grunt, reached for the meat bowl beside Bad Cast, then asked, "Is there time to involve the Mogollon?"

The one-eyed man's gaze went to the fire. For a long moment he considered. "I think not. Not only would it be a risk for them without many benefits, but communications through the middle of the Blessed Sun's holdings would be precarious at best. No, if we are to do this, it must be done here, among ourselves."

"Do what?" Bad Cast blurted, and then regretted it as that piercing eye fixed on him.

Instead of a reprimand, the war chief said, "A great many things are in the offing, young hunter." A wry smile came to his lips. "Our world hangs in the balance. One way, we bring it back into harmony and continue to enjoy life as we know it. In the other . . . well, let us simply hope the signs are more favorable."

At that moment, a young woman came trotting in from the dark. She was tall, lithe of body, perfectly proportioned. A warrior's feather curled up from the gleaming black bun at the back of her head. She also wore a red war shirt, faded now, belted as if to emphasize her narrow waist and round hips. Her face was a perfect heart shape; her small mouth was taut. The flinty anger in her eyes seemed at odds with her delicate nose. A bow cased in bobcat hide rested diagonally atop the bark quiver on her back. She carried a large wicker shield on her left arm, and a slim but deadly looking war club was tied to her belt. She barely noticed the others, but her eyes pinned Whistle with a tightly focused fury.

Bad Cast wasn't sure, but Whistle seemed to flinch, and then squirm as he looked everywhere but at the striking woman. Her gaze narrowed the slightest bit; she knelt beside the war chief, her voice barely a whisper as she spoke into the man's ear.

Whatever she said didn't seem to please him. The lines around his mouth hardened. After the woman finished, she stood, and without another glance, strode off to one of the outlying fires.

Ironwood's brow furrowed as he stared into the fire. "Your friend Ripple is on his way to one of our Healers. Nightsh—the Mountain Witch is unsure if he will live or not. She says his souls are no longer with his body."

"He's dying?" Wrapped Wrist asked, his eyes straying to where the woman had joined the warriors' fire.

"That depends on whether his souls decide to return to his body." Ironwood rubbed his callused hands together.

"And if he dies? Is that a problem?" Whistle asked.

The war chief said softly, "I want to hear from his own

lips about Old Woman North's prophecy. We travel a perilous trail. The slightest misstep could send us all to our dooms."

Wrapped Wrist hadn't heard a word; his gaze was fastened on the warrior woman with a longing that couldn't be mistaken.

Bad Cast couldn't decide who was more interesting, the brooding and worried Ironwood, or the black-haired female across the camp. He was comparing the woman's predatory aura with Soft Cloth's maternal gentility when the war chief's words brought him up short.

"No one is to approach the hot springs tonight. Our future is being decided there."

Whose future? Bad Cast started to ask, but at the grim expressions on Ironwood's and Whistle's faces, kept his peace. Spots, looking cowed, ran his fingers across the scars on his arm.

Wrapped Wrist had propped his chin on his palm, eyes on the woman as she undid a wooden bowl from her pack and used a ceramic ladle to fill it with some steaming liquid.

"What future?" Spots finally dared to ask.

The old war chief's single eye fixed on him. "Sister Moon is coming home, young hunter. A holy person, someone I trust, is unsure whether it means the rebirth or the extinction of our world. She has entered the waters, seeking an answer."

To Bad Cast, it sounded silly. Entering the waters? What waters?

"All we can do is hope, War Chief," Whistle said somberly.

"And pray," Ironwood added. "Pray with all of our souls."

A shiver rolled down Bad Cast's back, and for the first time he wondered if he'd ever see Soft Cloth and his little girl again.

A toe pressed insistently into Wrapped Wrist's side.

"You," a voice whispered in the darkness. "Wake up."

"Huh?" Wrapped Wrist blinked, rolled back in his blanket, and stared up into a midnight sky. A half-moon hung over the tree-furred peaks and cast a silvered light on the rocky outcrops. To his right, a dark form loomed in the night, some sort of irregular and monstrous shape.

"I said, wake up!" the voice hissed. "Do you want to have half the camp stirring?"

"Who are you?"

"I serve the war chief. Take me to one of your leaders: the elder named White Eye."

Wrapped Wrist stared up at the apparition. Tall, inky with shadow, the night-backed silhouette reminded him of a kiva wall mural: a round blob with a head and long legs. Perhaps some form of distorted wading bird.

"Go away and bother somebody—"

His words were cut off as a cool stone came to rest against his cheek. He could just make out the long handle attached to the war club.

The looming shadow bent over him, saying in its odd high whisper, "You will obey the war chief's orders and take me to the one known as old White Eye, or I will break your skull on the spot."

A shiver ran through him. "Oh, the war chief. Why didn't you say so." Wrapped Wrist began wriggling out of his bedding, taking but a moment to roll his blanket and wrap his cloak around his shoulders.

"Just let me tell my friends where I'm—"

"Move. *Now!*"

Wrapped Wrist jammed his bedroll into his pack and staggered to his feet. He thought about kicking Spots's blanket where it lay just to his right, but a stiff jab from the war club sent him stumbling into the darkness.

"Hey! Easy! We're not going anywhere if I fall over and break my leg. And why are we doing this now? It's the middle of the pus-dripping night!"

"I need to be in your village as soon as I can."

"Why me?"

"Because the war chief told me to take one of the First Moon hunters, that you would know the trails better than anyone. Beyond that, it was my pick. I chose you."

"That doesn't tell me why."

"Maybe it's because you're short and I'll be able to see over your head the entire way."

"Thanks." Wrapped Wrist yawned, walking carefully as he picked his way past the last of the warrior's camps. He could see Ironwood where he sat beside a solitary fire. The one-eyed war chief looked pensively at the flames as he jabbed at the fire with a flimsy stick. Assuming Wrapped Wrist could read faces, the old warrior looked worried right down to the roots of his souls.

"Doesn't he ever sleep?"

The war club hissed like a snake as it slashed the air over Wrapped Wrist's head. He yipped and ducked.

"Don't talk," the harsh whisper ordered. "Just walk."

He swallowed hard. Gods, he'd been taken by a night-stalking monster.

Twenty-seven

A great house was more than just a building; it was a symbol of the Straight Path world. While the Red Lacewing Clan built their structures according to the movements of the sun, Blue Dragonfly Clan built theirs according to those of the moon. Each of the Blue Dragonfly Clan great houses were aligned to the lunar maximum: the northernmost position of the moon in its eighteen-and-a-half-year trek across the sky. Kettle Town had been built that way, as had Dusk House, and so, too, was the Pinnacle Great House. Each had a long balcony that extended from the top story of the northern wall. There the Priests and Blessed First People congregated on the nights of the lunar standstill to watch Sister Moon when she appeared on the eastern horizon, rising in perfect alignment with the northern wall and the balcony. It was said that those who

were washed by her first light were eternally gifted by the
Flute Player.

As a chill night wind ruffled his hair, Water Bow stood
on the long balcony of Pinnacle Great House and stared
up at the midnight sky. The balcony itself was a clay-
covered platform built upon poles laid across thick beams.
Not only did it provide shade on summer afternoons, but
the view was spectacular. A person could almost feel like
an eagle as he looked out across the valley to the distant
high peaks in the north. To the east he could sight through
the gap between the two pillars of stone.

That gap marked the place where Sister Moon had
emerged into this world. An electric thrill tickled his
nerves. Soon he would see her pass through it, a reenact-
ment of her first birth into the sky. He could feel the holy
nature of it, sense the Power of a daughter seeking to return to her roots.

*Like us she entered this world, passing from the Fourth
World through a womb of stone and squeezing out into a
virgin night sky.*

He imagined how she felt, tricked, alone, rising into the
sky of a new and strange world. What a trauma birth was.

*One from which we cannot escape until death. Does she
feel as lost as we ordinary humans do? Does she age slowly
but eternally with each trek she makes across the sky?*

While he watched, the tip of the half-moon peeked out
from behind the slim right-hand column of stone. Enrap-
tured at the sight, he smiled. For long moments he stood in
silence marking the slanting path Sister Moon took into
the sky.

Once again, you are almost home. How desperate she
must be to forever search for the way back, eternally
doomed to remain here, trapped in the Fifth World sky.

Had Spider Woman sealed that doorway forever? Was
the reality that Sister Moon, Father Sun, the gods and
Spirits, even the First People themselves were all trapped?

Is there a way home for any of us?

"What do you think?" Matron Larkspur asked. She
crouched in the low doorway behind him. In the moon

glow he could see that she wore endless loops of tiny shell ·
beads that left her neck and chest covered with the wealth.
A form-fitting black cotton dress decorated by four-
pointed white stars was pinned over her right shoulder,
leaving her left bare.

. "With her next phase, Sister Moon will have finally
come home." He took a deep breath of the cool night air.
"It is time. Send word to the Blessed Sunwatcher. Blue
Racer will want to know. So, too, will the Blessed Sun."

"Then we must prepare. They will be coming here by
the next time Sister Moon's face is full."

"Let us hope that all goes well with their journey."

"Is there word on the escaped slave girl and the false
Prophet?" Water Bow asked.

Larkspur snorted. "I think Burning Smoke knows better
than to trust a slave, no matter how well his shaft fits her
sheath. What is it about men that they lose their senses
around a woman?"

*Do I dare mention the warrior you kept in your rooms
that night?* Actually he was smarter than that. If she
wanted to maintain the charade that she kept herself only
for her distant husband, that was fine with him. He did
ask, "What has been done to recapture him?"

She was glaring angrily at the moon. "In an effort to redeem their war chief, Burning Smoke's warriors are searching every household, kiva, and storeroom in the valley."

"That will produce nothing, but will add to the Moon
People's anger."

"Precisely." She rolled her shoulders, as if to loosen
them. "Fortunately, I don't even think he's still in the valley. So I've offered a jar of turquoise beads to whichever
of my informants can deliver his head to me should Ripple
ever return. Where Burning Smoke's clumsy warriors fail,
greed will finally prevail."

Nothing had substance. Ripple walked through an endless gray mist. Stamping his heel, he encountered nothing

solid. When he hugged himself, his arms pressed a Dreamlike quality, as though he were there, and wasn't. He couldn't actually feel himself, even if he could look down and see his body. Raising his left hand, he wiggled the fingers, and pawed his hunting shirt aside. His penis hung as it always had, the wrinkled skin whole and healthy. His tongue slipped over the bumpy cusps atop strong teeth.

"I'm whole again!"

A fierce joy rose in his chest. Whole again. As if the pain and misery had never happened. The fear that had left his souls whimpering and paralyzed was only a memory. Relief, like a surging wave, buoyed his spirits.

He leapt, jumping high, trying to remember why he had been sad, why he had been so worried. Leap by leap, he sailed through the gray mist, his weight never crashing down, but sinking softly.

"Quite a sensation, isn't it?" a voice asked.

Ripple stopped short, spinning, wondering how he could have missed the great black raven. The midnight bird perched on a snag of wood that vanished into the ether. It watched him with a piercing, but very human eye.

"Who are you?" Ripple tightened his arms around his chest again.

"Go ahead, Ripple," the raven said amiably. "It helps."

"What does?"

"Hugging yourself like that."

"Why?" Ripple asked, unease stirring again.

"You are pressing your dream soul and breath-heart soul together." Could it be? Did the raven's beak actually curl into a smile?

"Ah, my shape confuses you."

Ripple's vision seemed to blur, and when he blinked, it was to see a handsome young man watching him with amusement. The man had gleaming black hair hanging straight over his shoulders. He wore a silky white cape—a hide the likes of which Ripple had never seen.

"They no longer exist," the young man told him as he fingered the white hide. "A Dreamer, a man called Sunchaser, tried to save them. He chose instead to save himself and a woman he fell in love with." He smiled. "Funny, isn't it? The things that men will choose?"

"Why funny?" Ripple kept his arms crossed over his chest.

"Sunchaser had the opportunity to give himself for the mammoths. If he had dedicated himself to the Dream, he might actually have saved them. Or so my brother claims. Instead, he chose the woman and himself. Love triumphed over saving a magnificent animal. At least for a time."

"What do you mean, for a time?"

"In the grand scheme of things, humans don't live very long. Though to them it seems they manage to hammer a great deal into what is less than a blink."

Ripple began to back away. "Who are you?"

The young man perched on the branch and cocked his head. "In life I was called Raven Hunter. Here"—he lifted his arms—"I have many names: Many Colored Crow, Mocking Raven, Coyote, Trickster, Spider Above, and others. Among many peoples, yours included, I am called the Dark Twin, Evening Star, or Monster Slayer."

Ripple gaped, refusing to believe.

"So, Nightshade has tucked your souls into Sister Datura's wings and sent you into the Dream." Raven Hunter shook his head. "Ah, Nightshade, always preoccupied with Death and suffering. She's one of the greatest of them all, you know. Her Power has changed the world."

"I have to choose," Ripple remembered, and in that moment, memory came crashing back. He winced, remembering the pain, loneliness, and confusion.

"Ah," Raven Hunter cried, leaping from the branch. "I see. Promises to gods, guilt for a mother and father you've almost forgotten, all stirred by a burning hatred. And what's this terrible longing? Yes, the glimpse of what might be."

He waved his hand, and the vision of Ripple in the cornfield returned. His wife was smiling at him with a shared intimacy that pulled at Ripple's heart.

"Now there's a bitter potion," Raven Hunter admitted. "So that's it, is it? A glimpse of a future that could be. How like Power to dangle temptation in front of your nose."

Ripple watched as one after another, images formed. He saw her belly grow full, witnessed the birth of a daughter, then a son, and another daughter. Glimpses formed of a cool house on hot summer days, of shaded afternoons under a ramada as he spun cord with his good hand or joked with his wife as he helped sift rocks from the gravel mulch they created on a terrace. He caught images of feasts, of a still child being lowered into a shallow grave. Of a winsome daughter smiling at a young man, and moments later, presenting Ripple with a grandchild.

"Amazing how life can be compressed like cool moss, isn't it?" Raven Hunter asked.

Ripple clamped his eyes shut, an ache deep within. "Is this really what will come?"

"If you choose it."

When Ripple opened his eyes, Raven Hunter was studying him. "She looks like a good woman: solid, healthy, and pleasant company. Very unlike the capricious fox I loved when I was a man. You could do worse."

Ripple raised his left hand, staring at it, wondering that it was unscathed.

"That's only in the Dream, Ripple." Raven Hunter shrugged. "Some things cannot be changed."

"Why are you here?"

"Curiosity." He tilted his head. "I am waiting to see if you condemn yourself or your people."

"What are you talking about?"

"The burning thorn of individual choice. It is designed into the very cosmos. Saving yourself is saving your wife, those darling children, and those precious grandchildren. Beyond them lie their children, and so on down through time. All that happiness and joy, all those people, looking back to you, remembering the sacrifice you made for them."

My descendants. Somehow the notion had never entered his head that he wasn't the end of his family, that others would live because of him.

"I see where you're headed, Ripple." Raven Hunter smiled sadly. "I cannot tell you all of the future, but I can promise you this. If you choose Cold Bringing Woman's way, you will die on the mountain, in a tearing agony. Your death will be gruesome, the stuff of nightmares."

A cold shock ran through Ripple's souls, seeking to cleave them from each other.

"Think of it," Raven Hunter added gently. "All that pain, your body tossed haphazard onto a pile. No wife to share her smile with you, no warmth under the blanket to stiffen your manhood. Your children will never be, except as a dream of possibility locked away in your dead souls."

Ripple bowed his head, wishing to sob, but unable to conjure tears.

"But what . . . what can I do?" He struggled to hold himself together, arms tight around his two wounded souls.

"So much suffering," Raven Hunter whispered, as if from a long way away. "But it need not be yours. Run, Ripple. Flee as soon as you're able. You have seen your wife. Go find her. Grasp onto that one faint hope of joy. Seize and clutch it to your breast, or lose it forever!"

He felt the stirring of mighty wings, felt the brush of feathers and huddled in the backwash.

Silence.

When he looked up, only the soft grayness of the Dream surrounded him.

His souls howled in anguish.

TURTLE GOES TO WAR

*S*ome *of my favorite stories are about Warrior Turtle. I have heard the story told by many peoples. Each tribe has*

*its own version, but they are basically the same: Turtle
gets angry with human beings because they are hunting
animals and decides to declare war on them. He paints his
face and begins to gather his allies.*

*When powerful creatures like Wolf and Bear volunteer
to join the war party, Turtle stupidly tells them he doesn't
need them. He sends them away, preferring other allies,
such as Awl, Hairbrush, and Knife, or perhaps Grasshopper, Cricket, and Skunk.*

*The story, naturally, ends the same way, by Turtle and his
allies losing at every turn. Skunk gets knocked in the head
when he mistakenly sprays an unsuspecting woman, which
explains why to this day he has a flat head. And slow-moving
Turtle gets whacked so many times his shell is cracked ir-
reparably, explaining the intricate designs he still sports.*

*The lesson taught by the Warrior Turtle stories is clear:
He who makes war foolishly, even when the cause is right,
is destined to fail.*

I lie back in the hot steaming water and heave a sigh.

*Unfortunately, most warriors are Warrior Turtles. There
are but a handful of true Wolves and Bears in the world.*

*The difficulty is telling one from the other before the
battle begins.*

*I think I know which of these young men is a Wolf, but
only time will tell whether or not I have chosen a Hairbrush for an ally. . . .*

Spots blinked awake and stared up at the purple of an incipient dawn. He yawned, startled to see a faint misting of
his breath.

He wiggled around, feeling the stones that had poked
up through his blanket to irritate his sleep. In between
bouts of tossing and turning, he'd had one delightful
Dream after another, most of them about a naked slim-
waisted and dark-haired beauty who had teased him un-
mercifully. After a long chase, he would corner her in a
moss-covered niche deep in a cliff side. There, she would

smile and reach out for him with firm brown arms, her fingers grasping for his flesh.

He would cup her high breasts, rolling the nipples between his fingers as they hardened. White teeth flashed behind her full lips as she threw her head back, spilling that splendor of shining black hair down her back. Then she would sink down, curl onto the springy moss and spread her legs. The moist rosette beneath her dark mound glistened.

Then, just as he lowered himself onto her—his stiff organ throbbing with desire—she would laugh . . . and vanish.

Over and over, the Dream had tormented him until finally he lay exhausted, frustrated, with aching testicles and his loins feeling like a knot yanked much too tight.

The odor of stale sweat rose from his hunting shirt to remind him of how long he'd been on the trail. He looked around as he threw back his blanket and pulled on his thick trail sandals. The fire was down to coals, a faint trace of blue smoke rising from the ash. Here and there the long shapes of men lay rolled in coarsely woven blankets, some with cloaks over their heads as protection against both mosquitoes and morning dew.

Spots stood and draped his blanket over his shoulder, spared the sleeping Wrapped Wrist a glance—and realized his bed was missing. What? Wrapped Wrist up early? That wasn't like him. Bad Cast still lay where he'd bedded down, his face covered with his blanket.

Spots stepped outside the ring of sleepers to relieve himself. As his urine spattered the ground, he tried to work the clammy taste out of his mouth. Images of the Dream clung like cobwebs to his souls. Gods, he could see her so clearly, dark eyes flashing, her white teeth shining as she smiled at him. The very notion sent a tingle through the root of his manhood.

Rising steam from the hot springs over to the east made a violet mist against the morning. He lowered his shirt and started forward, climbing up the stony terraces and into the gap where the hot water bubbled up. He had never seen the hot springs, but had heard stories about them all of his life.

No sense being so close and not looking upon the marvel with his own eyes.

In the semidarkness he picked his way down to the shadowed water. It looked dark, mysterious where the swirling mist revealed and then hid it from view again. A smell of heavy mineral hung in the misty air. Holding his hands out, fingers spread, he could feel the Power, sense it rising with the heat and sulfuric odor.

Some said that if you could stand the heat, you could duck your head beneath the surface and see down into the Below Worlds. Even as he thought it, a swirl of silvered mist blew around his head, and for that instant, he swore he heard the whisper of voices.

Leaping back, he tried not to breathe for fear of sucking some terrible Spirit into his lungs.

Movement! There! Something twisted in the steam. He blinked, struggling to see. Was it his imagination, or had there been a deformed shape, ungainly, with a round head, protruding circle of mouth, and hollow tubes of eyes? The form had flickered there, an arm's length above the water, as if Dancing.

In a half heartbeat the apparition and the voices vanished, replaced by the gurgle of water as it bubbled out of the steaming pool. He could hear it trickle down the rocks into the whispering river.

Silly, it was just the rising steam, the sound of the water.

Spots made himself chuckle, amused at his fear. He should at least touch the water, maybe taste it. People would ask about it. How could he tell them that he'd heard voices and left?

Staying well below the rising steam, he scuttled forward and dipped his fingers at the edge of the pool. At the touch, he yipped and pulled them back.

"Fool," he muttered. "This is a place for . . ." Squinting, he realized the light had changed, growing pinker with the dawn, and in that illumination he could see a form floating in the center of the pool.

At first he thought it a dead tree that some miscreant had tossed into the hot water. Then it slowly began to turn.

What he'd thought to be branches became legs; the roots turned into arms and a head with long trailing hair that floated out like a halo.

"Blessed Ancestors, protect me," the warding came unconsciously to his lips.

"Back, Spirit!" he cried, stumbling over his feet as he tried to stand and retreat. In horror he watched as the floating figure came alive, slowly raised its arms and head, the legs dropping down into the shimmering depths. Water streaked down gleaming flesh like shining scallops of cloud. It rose, dark, menacing, and with each step, emerged from the depths.

Spots crabbed backward, hands catching on rocks, feet clumsy with fear. Someone's old forgotten prayer stick clattered under his foot.

The Spirit rose with the steam, ever taller until it towered over him, blotting the pink sky.

Twenty-eight

Spots cowered on the rocky ground before the spring.

A woman! Yes, it was a woman, broad shoulders narrowing to a slim waist, the rounded curve of her hips dropping to long legs that braced her above him. In the dark silhouette of her form, Spots couldn't see her face, couldn't make out her features.

The faintest image of his Dream replayed.

"Leave me alone, Dark Spirit," he pleaded. "I'm sorry, so very sorry."

"You are sorry?" she asked in a thickly accented voice.

"It was only a Dream," he said weakly. "I don't really want you! Please, go back to your world. Don't hurt me."

Her head went back, laughter, like a distant pain, issuing from the faintest shadow of mouth. "You don't want me?"

"No, Spirit. I . . . I thought you were real in the Dream. Otherwise I never would have chased you into that cleft in the rocks!"

"Ah, a Dream, you say. Tell me, did I entice you in this Dream?"

"Yes! You were beautiful!"

This time her laughter was like a clattering of bones.

"Please," Spots whined, "let me go."

The head cocked, studying him. "What if it turns out that I want *you*?"

Speech froze in his throat, his heart hammering against his chest. He grabbed up the old prayer stick and clutched it like a spear, wondering what good a faded and warped *paho* would be against a malicious Spirit.

Her voice dropped. "You look like a strong, fit young man. Your scars tell a terrible story of fire and pain."

No sound issued from his working mouth.

"I could use a body like yours."

A shiver coursed through him, his breath catching in a half sob.

"Fear is a terrible thing, isn't it?" she asked. "Does it often send its tendrils through your nerves?"

He could barely shake his head.

"How wonderful for you. Me, I Dance and weave with Fear. We circle and dip, rise and twirl, forever locked in each other's embrace. Such close companions are we that we know each other's taste, can Sing to the rhythms of our breathing. Our hearts beat as one, liquid and jetting. Together we are a harmony of blinding black brilliance." A pause. "Does that mean anything to you?"

He swallowed hard, desperate as a fawn beneath a mountain lion.

"Too bad," she whispered wearily. "Until it does, you will never crave Death's honeyed kiss. You will never understand the pounding longing as you wait for it to release you from this captivity."

"Captivity?" The word croaked from his throat.

"Oh, yes. Locked in our frail and failing bodies, we are held like turkeys in their cages. All the while the waste of memory deepens around us. Recollections of joy and ecstasy pile up with those of grief, sorrow, and pain. The frustrations of accumulated failures and dashed hopes mix with impossible Dreams and aspirations. Images of the past rise like a flood: glimpses of faces long gone; voices raised in ritual Song, or the first wail of a newborn. We hear again the clatter, screams, and fury of battle, or see a brilliant sunrise across an endless expanse of forest. A friend's laughter pricks us like a thorn. It's all the debris of life, of the very act of living—a huge mass of it burying you inside the cage of your body. Struggle as you might, there is no way to wriggle out from under its crushing weight until Death whisks you free."

Her cavernous eyes pinned him in place as he tried to squirm away.

"The Dream . . ." Her voice changed stridently. "You think I am the girl from your Dream?"

He sputtered an incomprehensible answer.

"You said that in the Dream I was beautiful?"

He jerked a nod.

"Alluring?"

Another nod.

"You desired me?"

A terrible shiver racked him.

"Tell me, would you have taken me in your Dream?"

He swallowed hard, pinching his eyes shut at the memory of her opening before him.

"Ah, I see. Did you?"

He managed to shake his head, rasping, "You . . . you disappeared each time. I swear it, Spirit."

This time the laughter was light, trickling like dewdrops from her lips. "Oh, yes, I know that Dream of the vanishing lover. How well I do. I live it over and over. It leaves my loins aching with a whirlpool emptiness that sucks at my souls."

At the hollow pain in her voice, he looked up. Light, like fire through the twirling steam, was silvering her hair, softening her shape. In the glow he could see more of her, could make out her nipples like dark dots, could discern the inky triangle between her thighs. Her eyes, no more than holes in the shadow of her face, were fixed on his, but the details of her remained a mystery of silhouette and curling mist.

She reached out to him. "Come with me."

He began to shake. "With you? Back into the Below Worlds? Down . . ." He couldn't finish the rest but gestured at the water lapping at her feet.

He could feel her curiosity. "What are your souls worth, handsome young man? What would you give to save them?"

"Anything."

"Would you open your veins here? Bleed your life away into the water to keep from following me back into those hot depths? Or would you Dance again with fire? Share its searing embrace until this time it finally scorched the life out of you? Would you willingly open your lips and kiss passionately of Death's sweetness?"

He gaped in horror.

"Ah, then perhaps you should rethink your offer of 'anything.' In the future, scarred man, someone more demanding than I am might take you up on it."

Tears began to leak past his eyelids.

"What brought you to this valley?"

Somehow he managed to whisper, "Cold Bringing Woman's vision."

Silence.

He stared at the shadowed features of her face, aware that she was inspecting him as though he were some sort of rare stone. The hand remained outstretched as she added, "I give you back your souls, handsome man. Perhaps you have more need of them than I do." The fingers curled in beckoning. "Come."

It took all of his courage to let go of the weathered *paho* and reach up. He jerked back at the touch. Her flesh was almost hot enough to blister him.

"Too hot?" she asked. "Given time, the body can become used to great heat, just as it can to numbing cold. Ah, but then, you've known the touch of fire. Try again."

He flinched as she pulled him to his feet.

"Do not fear me. At least not for the moment. Though, I

promise, you will have plenty more opportunities to savor Fear's intimate arms before Death finally does place its kiss upon your lips."

She was taller than he, her hand bony. The light spilled over her face as she turned, and he gasped. By the gods, *she was an old woman!* When she'd stepped from the water he'd imagined her as the woman in his Dream, not this . . . this old hag.

Her sidelong gaze slipped to his. "My true appearance surprises you?"

He bit off his answer.

"Darkness can be a Powerful ally, Spots."

"You . . . you know me?"

"I know all about you."

Confusion filled him as he let her lead him up from the water. "What are you going to do to me?"

She threw her head back, damp white hair sticking to her grainy back. "You will attend to your own destiny."

He stopped short as they emerged from the shadow and into the pink light of dawn. She was old, withered. In profile her breasts hung low, lines of flesh sagging around her belly, and wattles beneath her chin. Despite that, he could see the beauty she had been in his Dream, with flashing eyes, shining teeth, and muscular limbs.

"Illusion weaves an enticing fabric, don't you think?" Her eyes caught the dawn, dark and haunted, like wells into a lifetime of midnights. He winced at the swirling dark Power reflected there.

"What are you?" He mouthed the words.

"Everything fate has worked to make me."

"Nightshade!" a rough voice called. "Something has happened that you need to—"

Spots turned to see the one-eyed war chief stop short, apparently surprised to find her naked, holding Spots's hand. His glance slid from her to Spots, pinning him like a thorn. He said awkwardly, "Nightshade, I thought you should know. The situation has changed."

Nightshade? Spots gaped. *The Mountain Witch?*

She raised her free hand. "Our nightmare has come. The music plays . . . the flute notes high and as wavering as our breath. The drums become our hearts and the rattles our blood. Raise your feet, mighty Ironwood, and drive your heels into the dust of Dreams."

Ironwood's jaw hardened. "And my role?"

"Clap your hands, stamp your feet, and drive the thunder of Death through the land."

Spots's heart skipped at the expression reflected on Ironwood's ruined visage.

"I am very sorry to hear that." Without another word he turned and walked back the way he had come, a posture of defeat in the slope of his broad shoulders.

"You see," she whispered, "we all caress our fears, young hunter." A wistful smile played at the corner of her ancient lips. "Some of us just do so with more love and dedication than others."

In the swirling mist behind her, he would have sworn he caught a glimpse of the same giant figure he'd seen earlier. It turned with the mist, rising high, then bending low, Dancing in the rising vapors. Huge, misshapen, round-headed, with bugged-out eyes and ears, it had only a hole for a mouth. The gaudy light of dawn cast it in pink, as if the head were crusted in fresh mud.

For an instant, the giant figure stared at Spots, met his eyes. The effect was like standing before a deep dark cave that exhaled an icy breath of terror.

As dawn cast its glow over the rugged mountains in the northeast, and shot pink light through the high clouds, Bad Cast used a stick to dig through the feathery gray ash in the fire pit. He flipped out several embers, laying bits of twigs atop them and blowing until the flames caught. He added the last branches from the firewood pile and leaned back on his haunches. As the fire crackled, it sent a lean column of blue smoke into the morning sky. Extending his hands, it was pleasant to feel the growing warmth on his cold skin.

Around him, some of the warriors stirred in their bedding; others snored lightly. He considered Spots's rumpled blanket and the crushed space in the grass where Wrapped Wrist had slept, and wondered where the two of them were off to.

Bad Cast rubbed his jaw with sooty fingers and inspected the stew pot. Half full, it was a large corrugated-ware pot that stood knee high. Wide-mouthed, with a rounded rim, it braced on a tripod of three stones at the fire's edge. The contents had cooled during the night, the surface of the deer-and-quail stew congealing into white grease. Using a stick, he scraped fire against one side of the vessel and watched the flames curl around the rough exterior.

As he waited, several of the warriors muttered and climbed out of their blankets. Yawning, they stumbled off to make water, drink from the river, and attend other needs.

Bad Cast breathed deeply of the crisp clear air. The sound of the river was soothing, the air still. It would be another hot day, but here, in the morning-shadowed valley, cool air still drifted down from the peaks.

It was a pretty place, the confluence of a stream from the north meeting the River of Souls before it turned south toward the Straight Path lands. Trees furred the hillside to the south, while brush, occasional pines, and aspens covered the grassy slopes that rose to steeper timbered slopes above the valley.

When this was all over, maybe he'd bring Soft Cloth and the children here. He could see the flowering branches of serviceberry, the greening wild plum, wild rose, and down by the river, mint. Hunting would be good, and after the roots and meat were dried, it would be well worth the trip. Besides, Soft Cloth had never seen a hot spring.

In peace, he sat enjoying the moment. The morning sun burned silver-white in the steam rising from the hot springs. Like an apparition the war chief emerged from it and headed toward the camp. Even at this distance, he was an imposing man, nimble of stride, a war club resting on his shoulder. Something about his posture didn't bode well. A queasy feeling began to boil in Bad Cast's stomach. Then, there, just behind the war chief, came the gangly form of Spots, hurrying along.

By the flying gods, what did you get into this time?

Or was it Wrapped Wrist who'd gotten into trouble? His bedding was missing. Bad Cast winced and remembered the woman from the night before and the way Wrapped Wrist had been watching her. Bad Cast made a face. She was attractive, fit and healthy, and most definitely the sort Wrapped Wrist would home in on like a cougar onto a fawn.

Bad Cast turned, taking a quick count of the bedrolls. Most were lying flat now, their occupants busy with the tasks of the morning. He didn't see any graceful, long-limbed warrior woman.

Blood and pus, Wrapped Wrist, no wonder the war chief looks like a black cloud full of thunder. He could imagine Spots trying desperately to talk Ironwood out of his rage. It was always Spots who stood up for Wrapped Wrist's indiscretions.

Still, Bad Cast did his best to keep the curiosity out of his eyes as the war chief walked up to one of the men rolling his bedding and spoke in hushed tones. The warrior nodded, then went on about his business as the war chief strode on.

Spots—looking like he'd just swallowed cactus spines—stepped around the fire and crouched at Bad Cast's side.

"In trouble already this morning?"

Spots swallowed hard, placing his face in his scarred hands. "You wouldn't believe it. There was this naked woman floating in the hot springs."

"Oh, rat dung!" Bad Cast whispered shrilly. "I figured Wrapped Wrist was at the bottom of it. But, no, it's you. What's gotten into you? You're lucky he didn't kill you for taking liberties with her!"

"Liberties?" Spots seemed to hesitate.

"Well, when you find a naked woman floating in a pool . . . ?"

Spots dropped his hands, confusion in his eyes. "What are you talking about?"

"That woman warrior, the slinky one with all the round curves and the long legs. The one you and Wrapped Wrist were making eyes at last night."

"She wasn't there."

"Then who . . . ?"

Bad Cast followed Spots's pointing finger to a third form that came walking down from the hot springs.

"Her."

Bad Cast squinted into the morning light. "Her . . . who?"

"Nightshade. The Mountain Witch." The tone was shaky. "I think she . . ."

"Go on."

". . . I think she is the most frightening human being I've ever met."

Bad Cast could make out the silver-haired woman now. Tall, willowy despite her apparent age, she walked with a liquid grace so profound she seemed to float across the irregular ground. Even the swing of her hips had a sensual and Dancelike quality.

"*That's* the Mountain Witch?"

"That's her." Spots had clasped his hands to his face again. "And I think she wants something from me."

"Well, given her age, I don't think it's your body," Bad Cast suggested wryly.

"Don't joke. I'd swear something follows her. I could see it in the rising mist, huge, misshapen. It was . . . was Dancing. In the air. I'd swear it."

Bad Cast considered the old woman. She didn't look like much in the morning light, just a thin old hag. Wet white hair spilled down the back of a faded red pullover dress, and a battered pack hung from her thin shoulder.

"Story is," Bad Cast said, "that a mud head follows her around."

Spots looked sick to his stomach. "The thing I saw in the mist . . . I'd swear its head was pink! Like in the stories where it's said it fell headfirst into the mud of the sacred lake."

"What does she want from you?"

"I don't know." Spots swallowed hard. "Where's Wrapped Wrist?"

"I thought he was with you."

"Gone. Before I got up." He fixed his eyes on the old

witch. "I think we're all losing our souls, Bad Cast. I think we're all going to die."

At that moment a jaded-looking warrior came trotting up the trail. His red shirt was splotched with dust and sweat stains. The morning light on his damp skin created a glowing effect. Though exhaustion hung from his frame like an old garment, he plodded ahead, his trail sandals slapping the dew-covered ground.

All eyes turned his direction as he made his loose-limbed way to Ironwood, placed a hand to his heaving chest, and called out, "War Chief. I have news."

Spots didn't lift his head from his hands, but Bad Cast stood, watching the knot of people that grew around Ironwood. Suddenly voices exploded with cries of "No!" "Impossible!" "He *what*?"

Behind the group, the old woman stopped short, her thin voice rising. "It's true, all of it. Can't you hear them?"

Ironwood pushed out of the crowd, asking, "Hear who, Blessed Nightshade?"

"Their voices," she answered. "Screaming, because unlike the rest of the dead, parts of their souls are locked in the living."

"What's this?" Whistle demanded from Ironwood's group.

The old woman raised her finger, pointing it at the clear morning sky. "We shall all scream now, just like the hapless ghosts. Hear me! Abomination is loose on the land. The thlatsinas recoil with disgust. There is only one way out for us. We have to pull this world through itself. Are you ready for that? Ready to turn your world inside out?"

The warriors stared at her in silence.

"Surely there is another way." It was Ironwood who stepped forward.

The Mountain Witch shook her head. "No, War Chief. When Leather Hand and his warriors ate those people, he turned Power inside out. Do you understand? They ate them before the breath-heart souls could escape." She raised her thin arms. "The only way to set it right is to pull our world back through itself."

"How?" Ironwood demanded.

"We cannot re-create what we do not first destroy." She smiled, a shaft of sunlight striking her face. For the moment she looked as beautiful as she once must have. "You have your duties, warriors. Your destiny lies atop First Moon Mountain. When Sister Moon paints her face in blood, follow the path of the Prophet. I've seen his fire in the night."

"What of you?" Ironwood asked.

Her smile was birdlike with fragility. "I have my own destiny, War Chief. Power alone will know which of us has chosen the better path."

Bad Cast watched the old woman as she looked around, a slight frown on her face. "Where is my young man?"

Where he sat at Bad Cast's feet, Spots made a pathetic whimpering sound.

Twenty-nine

The surprise was complete. Wrapped Wrist had had no idea that the misshapen form that had routed him out of his warm bedroll would turn out to be her. The ugly round shape that he'd assumed to be a belly was no more than the silhouette of a large wicker shield. He'd gaped when, in the gray light, realization came that no ordinary warrior followed him, but the hard-eyed beauty from the night before.

He'd made that startling discovery as he glanced back over his shoulder in the gray light of predawn. He'd seen the shield flopping, glimpsed the arcing swing of her most feminine hips. Neither were her shoulders broad like a man's, but, though muscular, they had that compact grace that betrayed a woman.

"What's your name?" he'd asked over his shoulder.

"I have no name but 'Run.' Neither do you, shorty. So, live up to it," she'd snapped.

Wrapped Wrist returned his attention to the trail. After making the westward climb out of the River of Souls Valley, they topped out onto a broad flat consisting of low hills, open meadows, and shallow winding creeks. Game was plentiful on these uplands, and periodic fires had burned a mosaic of timber, brush, and grasslands.

Here, by threading his way through the elk and buffalo trails, he could make fast time. Behind him, the woman followed relentlessly.

A woman! The notion rolled around in Wrapped Wrist's head. Blood and guts, she'd scared the grease out of him. Worse, he dare never let anyone know that a mere slip of woman could have frightened him into leaving his warm bed in the middle of the night.

So, what are you going to do about it? He cocked his head, considering his options. Then a slow smile spread. She wanted him to run, did she?

Since when could any woman keep a man's pace? And he had spent all of his life running these trails.

With that, Wrapped Wrist slowly began to pick up his pace, falling into the easy lope of a long-distance runner. All of his concentration went to the trail, reading it for holes, fallen branches, stones that could turn a foot.

In his head, he kept count. One, two. One, two. One, two. Yes, Father Sun was hot; he'd have her panting with fatigue in less than a hand of time.

In the beginning it was working just like he planned. He could feel the first warm tingling in his muscles, the building dryness in his throat. If he was feeling like this, her muscles had to be burning with fatigue. He kept listening for her first stumble, his ear tuned to the rhythmic pat of her sandaled feet on the trail behind him.

The question came as glorious affirmation of his plan when she asked, "Hunter? Do you think we should push this hard?"

"I was ordered to run," he called back. "However, if you're tired . . ."

"You won't be much of a guide if you end up wheezing your guts out by the side of the trail," she answered sharply. "And you don't have the legs to be a runner. But if you think you can keep it up, we're making very good time."

If I think I can keep it up? Wrapped Wrist grinned happily. The next time she asked anything of him, it would be to plead that they slow so she could catch her wind.

Three hands of time later, his tongue had blown dry, his windpipe afire from the endless sucking of his heaving chest. Behind him, the maddening pat of her sandals on the trail seemed to have no letup.

It was on the way down to a brush-choked stream that he stumbled, staggered, and caught himself.

"Hunter?" she called. "Let us stop at this creek. I think you need a drink and to catch your breath."

He panted his way down a circuitous trail to the shadowed bottom and slowed, feeling the rubbery looseness in his legs. His lungs might have been Wind Baby's laboring to move the very entirety of the sky in and out of his fevered body.

Reaching the creek, he dared to look back for the first time. The only sign of exertion she showed was the slight sheen of perspiration, her chest rising and falling in the even breathing of a trained runner.

To hide his mortification, he bent down and stared at his sweat-streaked face in the wavering pool of water. He drank the water in long gulps, then sucked down some more, only to swallow wrong. Coughing, his entire body convulsed, lungs panicked. He rolled onto his back, body curling as he hacked and fought for breath. His overfilled stomach rebelled, and he threw up the water and what little breakfast remained. When the fit subsided, he blinked through the tears to see her staring down at him, head cocked. She might have been studying a corn weevil.

"Are you all right?"

"Swallowed wrong," he lied.

"I thought you were pushing too hard."

He tried to identify her accent. She spoke his language

with a slight lilt that hinted of the First People. The gods knew she had that same triangular face. But none of the Blessed First People would deign to accept the role of a simple warrior. According to their likes, they were born for better things.

"Catch your breath," she told him as she pushed through the willows upstream and bent to drink. "Then we will go at a pace that is easier for you."

In dismay, Wrapped Wrist rolled over, splashed water onto his hot face, and drank with greater care. Who would have thought that such warped and malignant souls could inhabit such a beautiful body? Somehow, some way, he swore he'd put her in her place.

Spots stared up at the old woman's finger. It thrust out like a gnarled lance—and skewered his very souls. Her dark eyes seemed to swell like openings into a swirling darkness.

"You," she commanded. "Collect your things. We have a long way to go."

Spots's mouth opened and closed, but no sound came. He could sense Bad Cast's dismay, was aware of the war chief and his warriors staring. Time seemed to freeze like a winter waterfall. For one eternal instant, there was nothing but him and her, linked through those Power-driven eyes that sucked him in.

"There's no escape, boy." His souls heard words her lips didn't issue. *"My path was laid out in the beginning time. Come, be my witness."*

As quickly, the spell was broken, and Spots realized he was gasping for air, sweat breaking out on his body. "Leave me alone," he whispered.

"To be alone is the only true peace a person may ever know," she replied, the darkness shifting behind her eyes. "Provided, that is, that your souls don't devour each other in the silence."

Spots was shaking as he gathered his blanket and shoved

it into his small pack. To his surprise, it was Ironwood who handed him a tightly woven burden basket stuffed with dried meat, cornmeal, and a ceramic canteen.

"You'll need these," the war chief told him, a sober scrutiny in his single hard eye. "Obey her orders as you would obey mine."

Spots nodded unsurely, watching the grizzled war chief walk away, several of his warriors in tow.

"Who says we're under his command?" Bad Cast asked. "We're not his warriors. I say we just turn around and leave. They don't control us."

"You have no idea how good that sounds," Spots muttered, a longing like none he'd ever known in his chest. If only he could just be home, hauling water to the cornfields, weaving at the loom, packing firewood. Never had those simple things been so precious and dear to his souls.

"Hurts, doesn't it?" the old woman asked as she stepped closer.

"What?"

"Finding yourself after all of these years—only to discover you had never been lost in the first place."

Bad Cast glanced nervously at the old woman. "What do you want with him?"

She gave Spots a knowing smile. "Opposites crossed: youth and maturity; strength and wisdom; the scars of the flesh mingled with the scars of the soul. Oh yes, we'll draw on each other. Twist and turn like the whirlwind."

"Let me go," Spots pleaded.

"Let you?" Bad Cast seemed to burst. "She has no authority over you! I say we turn around and walk out of here. Now. These people have no right to tell us what to do."

"Tell him, young Spots," she prompted. "Do you want to go with me? Hmm? Or do you want to turn around and walk away into the trees with your friend? Your souls hang in the balance, my strong young man. Which way will you let them fall?"

Spots couldn't help but look into the dark mirrors of her eyes. In that moment, his souls began to slip, to drift toward their magnetic pull. He sensed himself falling, that loose fluttering in his stomach as though he'd cast off into air.

"I . . . I'll go."

"Go?" Bad Cast cried, grasping his arm in a painful grip. "She's a witch! She's snared your souls! By the gods, Spots, can't you see what she's—"

"You!" A sharp voice broke Bad Cast's tirade. Spots turned to see Whistle pointing at Bad Cast. "The war chief wants you. Collect your things and come with me."

"You were saying?" the old woman asked with a breathless whisper.

Bad Cast swallowed hard, glancing back and forth between Nightshade and Whistle. Meekly he asked, "What if I refuse?"

Whistle shrugged and loosened his war club from his belt. "How you go is up to you. It can be painless or with as many broken bones and bruises as you wish—but no one disobeys the war chief."

"Do it," Spots urged. "Whatever they want with us, it won't take long." He slung the basket that Ironwood had given him over his shoulder. Surely this spooky old woman wouldn't need him for more than the afternoon. And anything was better than having her give him that look that sucked at his souls.

Bad Cast blinked, as if somehow the world had gotten away from him. Like a man in a Dream, he bent down and began rolling his blankets.

"Come," the old woman said. "We've a long way to go. Unfortunately, I'm no longer as young as I was the first time I was dragged across the world." In a louder voice, she shouted, "Someone! Hand this strong young hunter my pack!"

A lean-hipped warrior trotted up and handed a ratty-looking brown fabric pack to Spots. To his surprise, the warrior gave him a slight bow of respect.

In a reedlike voice she said, "Hunter? Whatever you do, don't drop that pack. Don't bang it. Don't spill it. If you break anything in it, you will end up being a most unhappy young man."

She turned, selected a long stick from the firewood pile, and using it as a staff, started down the valley.

Spots hefted the pack, finding it remarkably light.

When he slung it over his shoulder, he felt a prickling along his skin, as if ants were trooping over his scars.

Wait, wasn't that a faint whisper, as if hidden lips were just behind his ear? He shot a quick glance over his shoulder, seeing nothing. Then he swore he heard muffled laughter.

When Spots took one last look back at the mountain valley a dazed Bad Cast was walking off in the war chief's wake, Whistle following. His crestfallen friend never looked back.

A long way to go?

As Spots hurried to catch the old woman, the eerie invisible voice whispered, *"Yes, a very long way."*

But when he glanced back no one was there.

How much pain can a person stand? Ripple asked himself over and over, the sensation of loss leeching his souls empty. Raven Hunter's words echoed hollowly, the finality of their import like thunder in the haze.

"He's always like that," a kind voice said.

Ripple lifted his head and stared numbly. A black wolf had fixed its glowing yellow gaze on him.

"Who are you?" Ripple hugged himself, fearing that the last of his will would drain away.

"I have had many names: Runs in Light, Wolf Dreamer, Masked Owl, First Man, Monster Slayer, among others. You would know me as Morning Star, the Warrior of the East.

Ripple blinked warily. "The second of the hero twins."

"Names mean little," the wolf said. His muzzle betrayed a very human smile. "Little more than shape." And as Ripple watched the wolf rose onto its back legs, lengthening, hair changing into a wolfhide coat and long fur-covered moccasins. Where the wolf had been, now a handsome man stood, his brown eyes glowing with Power.

"Go away," Ripple pleaded. "Your brother hurt me enough. I'll do whatever you say. Just leave me in peace."

"Ripple, look at me."

Ripple's gaze met Morning Star's. A radiant warmth spilled through him, a sensation of joy unlike anything he'd ever known. The euphoria built, sweeping him into a wondrous pulsing unity with the earth and heavens. He could sense the world around him, as though sharing the very breath of plants, animals, and people. His souls were the clouds, his breath the wind. The blood in his veins swelled, pulsed, and flowed in the rivers. His bones were rock, solid and thick.

He closed his eyes and let his souls float in the thunderous silence. He opened his arms to bask in the blinding darkness. His breast folded back, and joy spilled from the center of him, rising, twirling like strands of smoke to stroke his tingling skin.

He had become a pool of slowly swirling ecstasy; currents eddied and shifted within him.

In that instant he understood life with a crystalline clarity. As quickly, the euphoria faded.

Morning Star spoke. "That is only a touch of the One."

In its aftermath a sucking loneliness grew within Ripple's breast. He clamped his jaw to keep from weeping at the sense of loss.

Sympathy filled Morning Star's voice. "This pain that you feel, it's only fleeting. It's meaningless. Forget it, Ripple. Let it go."

Ripple gasped as he blinked in the grayness. Had he ever felt so bereft?

"I was like you, once. Lonely, frightened, denied any hope for the future. Then Wolf came and shared a Dream. From it, the world was spun." Morning Star smiled. "The people have strayed, as you yourself so recently discovered."

The image of Water Bow formed between Ripple's souls. He could see the man, smiling, holding his father's skull. The Priest's voice whispered in his ear as renewed pain speared through Ripple's body.

"My brother showed you a way out, Ripple, but he didn't show you the other half of that future."

Morning Star waved his arm in a circle, and within it, Ripple could see a vast wasteland of desert. Wind blew across the sand, piling it against empty towns. Where men had once held sway, now only field mice and rattlesnakes lived.

"They are all gone," Morning Star said. "A whole nation, swept away in war, disease, famine, and hatred."

"But what of the gods? What of Cold Bringing Woman and the katsinas?"

Morning Star's voice was kind. "Do you believe that gods and Spirits cannot die? Nothing lasts forever, Ripple. But there is a way. If we act now, we can save some of the people, broker a deal between the thlatsinas and those old gods who survive. We can make a new world out of the old, one where Priest-chiefs and Matrons serve the people instead of maim them, murder them, and consume them."

Morning Star's hand waved again, and within its arc an abandoned pit house formed. The dwelling was roomy, with excavated recesses where additional rooms had been added—all accessible by means of a crawlspace. A double bench circled the main room. He could see a corn-husk doll, a little boy's bow, toy animals made of bent willow sticks, and a small gourd rattle just big enough for an infant. Hafted stone tools, grinding stones and milling bin, a dark hearth, ash pit, and ripped clothing lay here and there, as did smashed pots and broken wooden boxes. Ripple recognized two *tchamahias* and a sandal last. He could see a *puki*, or concave ceramic form that a potter used to support the coils on a new vessel. The place looked as if it had been turned upside down.

"Where are the people?"

"Look closer," Morning Star said sadly.

Ripple followed Morning Star's pointing finger. There, in one of the recesses, lay a pile of splintered bones—the sort of refuse left after a deer or antelope had been eaten. But they didn't look right.

The image shifted, moving to the stone-cold fire pit. In the ash Ripple could see bits of burned bone and human teeth. Looking toward a small chamber dug into the northeastern wall, he could see charred pieces of human skull, and stripped leg bones.

"Her name was Blossom. She was thirteen. The boy was called Lizard. He looked forward to turning eight."

"I don't understand," Ripple cried. "This is what's left after a deer is cooked."

Morning Star pointed at curled feces that lay in the cold fire pit. "When human beings begin eating other human beings, their souls twist into foul shapes. This is the future that the First People are creating. Will you live it?"

Morning Star's glowing eyes fixed on Ripple's. "Are your sisters' lives and souls worth the life Raven Hunter would have you escape to? I can tell you that if you do not see this thing through, Leather Hand *will* capture them. As a way of discouraging other 'false Prophets' he will rape, murder, and eat them."

The familiar image of his pit house on First Moon Mountain formed. There, on the floor, beside the hearth where he'd sat night after night, burned, shattered, and stripped bones could be seen. In the fire pit ash, a flame-blackened skull rested, its base broken out so the baked brains could be spooned out.

Ripple turned, horror nauseating him. He ran, his feet pounding effortlessly at the gray beneath his feet. An inhuman shriek tore from his lungs.

And then everything turned black. He fled headlong through the darkness. In his panic, he was sure that something hideous and deadly followed, but when he cast a frightened glance over his shoulder, it was to look into an even blacker abyss.

Thirty

Leather Hand ran at the head of his warriors. They followed a winding trail down from the uplands where rugged mesas, capped by cracked sandstone, gave way to the gray clay hills above the Spirit River. They had helped themselves to the best of everything available in Far View. Their war shirts, new and bright red, were now smudged by the two-day run down from the heights of Green Mesa. In the hot air sweat dried immediately to leave stains under the arms, on the chests, and on the backs of the warriors.

Looking back, Leather Hand's heart filled with pride. Despite the ovenlike heat, his men trotted in ranks of two, each with a single warrior's feather jutting from their tight hair buns. They carried round wicker shields on their left arms, right hands bracing the straps that held quivers, packs, and canteens.

The final additions to their wardrobe were sashes made from a stack of tanned wolfhides he'd stumbled across in one of the Far View Great House storerooms. Taking a pelt for each warrior, he'd had them cut into strips and then braided so that the tails hung down at the left side.

Yes, his human wolves. He had wanted some special badge, a talisman that marked these most unique and feared of warriors. Even the Blessed White Cloud Woman, the Matron at Far View, had given them a wide berth. In his previous dealings with her, she had been imperious, distasteful of Webworm, whom she considered unfit, and disapproving of War Chief Wind Leaf and his violent deputy. This time a look of fear and revulsion had settled on her patrician face, and loathing had reflected from her hard eyes.

Now, as Leather Hand led his ranks of warriors down

the road toward Flowing Waters Town, one final worry continued to sting him like a bothersome insect.

The flashing signal from Flowing Waters Town had come as no great surprise. Turquoise Fox had had more than enough time to travel to Dusk House to make his report. One of the signal men from the Red Lacewing tower had come at a run to tell him that he was summoned to the Spirit River settlement by order of the Blessed Sun.

So, what will it be? A scathing lecture by an outraged Webworm, a demand for explanation, or praise for a job well done?

No matter which way it went, he and his men came with the knowledge that since their fateful actions below Thunderbird Mountain, their lives would never be the same. Many were still trying to grasp what had happened to them. A few understood down in that quiet place between their souls. Yet others were floundering, unsure of the fear they had seen in their hosts' eyes at Far View. Most, however, were coming to grips with the distance that others now kept from them.

Sorry, my companions, but you may not go back. You have been changed forever, placed apart.

The challenge to his leadership was to see that it cemented them together like fire-cured adobe so that the pressure they would face might be borne rather than cause them to crack like simple sun-dried mud. The fancy dress and the wolf sashes were but the beginning.

Above and beyond everything else, he must create the example. No matter what the consequences, his projection of unflinching superiority must be seen and emulated. It wasn't enough to think they were different. They must also believe down in their hearts and souls that they were chosen, elite. The horror of what they had committed at the Dust People's farmsteads had to be molded into strength—a brotherhood, admission to which demanded a shared initiation of ultimate bestiality.

They passed the first of the upland farmsteads: a three-room structure with a view of several scraggly corn and bean fields fed by runoff from one of the dry washes. No one seemed to be home, although two scrawny turkeys sulked in a willow-slat pen beside the structure.

Trotting in their loose-limbed gait, he and his warriors threaded their way past the first of the small towns rising on the highest terrace; people stopped work to shade their eyes and watch the warriors' silent passage.

From the dark and somber stares of the Made People, Leather Hand couldn't tell if they had heard the rumors yet, or if to them, they were just a party of well-dressed warriors going on about the Blessed Sun's business.

He led the way around the lines of strings and pegs that marked the proposed foundation of the new Northern House. A party of slaves was busy with hafted stone hoes leveling trenches for the foundations. They looked up soberly as Leather Hand led his men around them and down the defile in the terrace wall. The new capital of the Straight Path Nation spread out before him with its venous pattern of ditches, deep green corn, bean, and squash fields, and the pale lines of roads leading down to the sinuous channel of the Spirit River.

The plastered walls of Dusk House gleamed in the afternoon sunlight. Straight and tall, it dominated Flowing Waters Town where it rose above the floodplain. People sat in shade on the third floor, or moon balcony, that projected the length of the north wall. Some were weaving, others shelling corn.

A long bow-shot to the east, the new Sunrise House was rising; smaller, more irregular in shape. It was skeletal, a series of rectangular rooms exposed to the sky, some already sporting the peeled yellow beams that would support the second floor. A small army of slaves carried stone to masons who fitted the tabular pieces of sandstone into walls. Still others struggled under burden baskets filled with mud mortar as they bore it to the plasterers. In the flat that would become the plaza, a steady industry of woodworkers peeled logs and carefully sanded the chopped ends flat and to length. Amidst the piles of ready stone were stacked huge bundles of willow staves, giant piles of shredded juniper bark, and long lengths of slim lodgepole pine carried down from the mountains. The latter were to be peeled and cut to length as lintels for windows and doorways. The swarming effort of it all reminded him of a kicked anthill.

He slowed and forced his tired body into an erect posture. Head high, his shield snug against the side of his chest, he filled his lungs with the hot dry air and practically pranced the length of Dusk House's eastern wall. A floating market was maintained there. The hawkers, Traders, craftsmen, and artisans who sat there, wares displayed on bright blankets on the ground, watched in awe. Some shouted out greetings, or whooped in delight at the display. Some among the throng who had gathered to dicker for goods, food, and exotic trinkets whistled approbation. Others stood, arms crossed, watching with hard expressions, a cool reservation in their eyes. Most of them, Leather Hand noted, were Made People, not barbarians or foreign Traders.

Ignoring the desire to turn on them, he led his men through the gap at the southwestern wall and stalked across the plaza. Behind him, his men emulated his proud movements, their shields high, the wolf tails at their sides swinging with their long steps.

The plaza baked in the sun. People sat or squatted in the shade of ramadas as they went about their work. Children, dogs, and turkeys dotted the shaded western walls. High above on either side of the Blessed Sun's doorway the freshly painted figures of the Yamuhakto, the Warriors of East and West, dominated the sun-washed fourth story. They carried shields, each decorated with their personal four-pointed star. They stared down at Leather Hand with hard black eyes, as if judging his very souls. He glared back at them in defiance. If any of the deities should understand, it would be these two.

A cry came from the third story, and Leather Hand picked out the figure of War Chief Wind Leaf, followed by one of his deputies, Ravengrass. The two men descended a ladder to the second story, trotted across, and skipped down the stone stairways to the plaza level.

Leather Hand met his war chief as he rounded the First People's kiva in the eastern plaza. Dropping to his knee,

Leather Hand heard the clatter of shields and equipment as his warriors followed suit behind him.

"War Chief," he cried, "your deputy and his warriors arrive in response to a summons by their Blessed Sun. We come from the north, where we have punished the Blessed Sun's enemies, recovered the possessions stolen from him, and avenged the death of his Priest."

"Welcome, loyal deputy." Wind Leaf reached out and took Leather Hand's offered hand, pulling him to his feet. In a lower voice, he added, "You've created quite a stir."

"Turquoise Fox has given his report?" Leather Hand tried to read behind the glint in Wind Leaf's eye, but the war chief betrayed nothing.

"He has indeed. The Blessed Sun has been informed of your arrival. He will see you as soon as possible in the First People's kiva." His lips twitched. "There will be fewer people who might happen to overhear."

"As the Blessed Sun commands." Leather Hand touched fingers to his chin. "In the meantime, my warriors need water, food, and rest. I would consider it a personal favor if they were housed in the finest accommodations possible."

"Third floor on the west side," Wind Leaf said. "I will have Ravengrass attend to it."

"Thank you, War Chief."

Wind Leaf looked at the kneeling warriors in their perfect ranks of two and ordered, "You are dismissed. Deputy Ravengrass will take you to your quarters and see to your needs."

Ravengrass, a thick-shouldered man, stepped forward and called, "This way."

Leather Hand watched his men pass, giving each of them an encouraging smile, and occasionally, a reassuring nod. Only when the last had disappeared around the curve of the great kiva did he match step with Wind Leaf. The war chief followed the curving wall of the First People's kiva, then took a short flight of steps onto the roof. There, a woman was coiling clay in a pottery form and carefully shaping the sides of her vessel. She looked up, caught Wind Leaf's slight jerk of the head, and began gathering her things. Even before Leather Hand stepped onto the ladder leading down into the interior, the woman had packed the last of her clay from the roof.

After descending the polished rungs into the depths, it took a moment for Leather Hand's eyes to adapt from the summer glare to the shadowed interior, but the cool damp kiva air felt wonderful on his sweating skin.

"Tell me, am I better off to drive my stiletto into my heart before the Blessed Sun arrives, or should I wait and let him ritually crush my skull?" Leather Hand asked as he clamped his eyes shut to more quickly adjust to the light.

Wind Leaf hesitated for a moment. "Leather Hand, old friend, I must know. What prompted you to actually eat them? I mean, you did, didn't you? Or was that just some hoax to maintain the Blessed Sun's authority?"

"Oh, we ate them. Just like in the old stories. Turquoise Fox provided the brilliant inspiration for the act." He turned, fixing his gaze on Wind Leaf's eyes. "War Chief, make no mistake. The situation is desperate on the northern borders. What my men and I did was necessary. Do you understand?"

"You truly had no choice?"

"No, War Chief."

"Good, because I think you have made a most curious impression on the Blessed Sun."

"Indeed, War Chief, and what impression is that?" a voice called from above. The ladder juddered under Webworm's weight as the Blessed Sun descended. He wore a white tunic. Belted at his waist was a red sash decorated by black zigzag cloud patterns. His thick legs were bare, and intricately knotted sandals shod his feet. His round bland face was haloed by the light from above.

"That is for the Blessed Sun to say," Wind Leaf added, bowing slightly.

Leather Hand dropped to his knee, offering his hands in a token of supplication. "We received word at Far View that the Blessed Sun required my presence. Summoned, I respond."

"Be welcome, Deputy." Webworm took his hands and pulled him to his feet. "Have you eaten? Had anything to drink?"

"No, Blessed Sun."

Webworm looked around, perplexed. "I think we're fresh out of stewed Dust People to offer you. Perhaps some corn cakes, bean mash, and baked squash instead? I also have a freshly made raspberry drink that is quite refreshing. It doesn't taste like blood, of course, but the color's the same."

"That would be fine," Leather Hand replied, unsure if the man was joking or not.

"Could you see to it, War Chief?" Webworm looked to Wind Leaf.

"Yes, Blessed Sun." The war chief touched his chin and went up the ladder two rungs at a time.

Webworm watched him disappear through the high entry and mused, "He's a very enthusiastic servant. I have convinced myself it's because he's sleeping with my wife." He read Leather Hand's surprise and dismay. "Oh, that surprises you? I suppose that given the disaster that befell Night Sun and Ironwood one would think a Matron would be discouraged from such intimacies with her war chief. Unfortunately what they never tell you, and what you never learn until you finally find yourself in the position, is that leadership is a terribly lonely profession."

"I think I can understand that, Blessed Sun. My recent actions have given me but the slightest glimpse."

"Yes, I'm sure. A runner brought word that Matron White Cloud Woman wants you quietly executed. Would have done so herself had she known for sure I did not order your curious actions below Thunderbird Mountain." His smile carried a multiplicity of meanings.

Before Leather Hand could reply, Webworm added, "Discretion is such a delicate matter, is it not?"

Leather Hand felt his heart begin to hammer.

Webworm turned, walking slowly around the large kiva interior. A weaving, half-completed, filled a ceiling-to-floor loom on the west. He studied the carefully painted blue dragonfly on the east wall and the pole shelves filled with beautifully designed pottery, colorful fabric bags that contained Dance masks, and intricately woven baskets full of turquoise, jet, and shell jewelry. Then he glanced up at the heavy cribbed ceiling, where human skulls dangled from cords.

"You killed one of your warriors," Webworm stated.

"Yes. A man named Black Rabbit. He refused to follow orders." Where was this going? Leather Hand fought the sudden desire to vault up the ladder and out into the light of day. Was it his imagination, or did the dark kiva feel closer, almost suffocating? It seemed as if eyes were staring out of the niches, watching his every move. Webworm was living up to his name, spinning an entangling cocoon.

"Tell me, Deputy, how did the rest of your men react?"

"They were hesitant, Blessed Sun. Eating another human being is not an easy thing."

"Nevertheless, you made them do it."

"Yes, Blessed Sun." Leather Hand drew himself up. If this was going to go badly, he would die a proud man, unflinching in the presence of his Blessed Sun. "The people who robbed Tall Piñon could have cared less if they lived or died. A way had to be found to maintain your authority. My actions below Thunderbird Mountain played upon the people's deepest horror. No other form of retaliation would have created the desired effect."

Webworm ran his finger along the plastered kiva bench and turned. "I have heard that the Dust People—those who survived your feast—have fled the entire area. They call it accursed and pray that your breath-heart soul be sent straight to Spider Woman upon your death."

"So that she might mete out the justice I deserve?"

Webworm cocked his head, looking suddenly unsure. "Does that frighten you? The story is that when the wicked die their soul travels to the Underworlds, there to be beset by monsters. Those who make it past the monsters reach a fork in the trail. The unrighteous are tricked into taking the trail that leads to Spider Woman's fire. There they are revealed for the evil beings they are and burned to ash. It is said that Spider Woman Dances upon that ash, her feet beating it into oblivion."

"Blessed Sun, our world is at stake. If your order and authority are not maintained, we will see warfare break out between villages and the subsequent massacre of thousands. Entire towns will be burned, every man, woman, and child butchered. If Spider Woman cannot understand my responsibilities to the people, perhaps she is not worthy of her own."

"Our world is at stake." Webworm smiled wearily, uneasy thoughts smoldering behind his eyes.

"I do not question the gods, Blessed Sun. You know the sacred stories as well as I do. The gods understand the use of desperate measures in desperate times. Ours is a hard land, a high desert, and I wonder if the Flute Player isn't testing us by withholding the rain."

"Go on."

"I wonder, Blessed Sun, if he isn't punishing us for the thlatsina heresy, and at the same time waiting to see if we are worthy to be his chosen people."

"Worthy how?"

"By being willing to do whatever is necessary to redeem our world."

"Do you think eating people does that?"

"It demonstrates the length to which we will go to save ourselves. It shows the gods that some of us are willing to become monsters in order to keep our world from disintegrating like a dried mud pot in the stream of time."

"I suppose you would be the fire in the kiln? Is that what you are telling me?"

"If you will be the temper, Blessed Sun, I will indeed be your fire."

Webworm walked over to the ladder and stared into the ash-dark eye of the cold fire pit. For a long passing of heartbeats he just stood there, one arm braced on the ladder. When he spoke, it was in a low voice. "Do you know why Desert Willow kept me as Blessed Sun?"

Warily Leather Hand said, "It wouldn't be my business."

"Because she thinks I am compliant. After Chief Crow Beard's death, Snake Head dismissed Ironwood and appointed me war chief because he didn't think I was smart enough to discover his plotting. Then I was made Blessed Sun because the Red Lacewings couldn't bear the thought of losing leadership of the First People. Many of the First People Matrons, elders, and leaders think me a fool." He was watching Leather Hand as he spoke.

Leather Hand forced himself to meet Webworm's eyes. What was this all about?

Webworm took a deep breath. "Our world is at stake. Perhaps you are the only person besides me who really understands."

"Yes, Blessed Sun."

"Being thought a slow-witted dolt can have advantages, Deputy War Chief." Webworm smiled. "It can allow a man like me a certain freedom to take the steps necessary to save our world."

Leather Hand nodded warily.

"Will you work with me? Help me save it?" Webworm's eyes bored into his. Was this the same halfhearted Webworm he'd once known? No, something fierce and desperate lay behind the man's eyes.

"Why do you ask me, Blessed Sun?"

"I've been having Dreams of death, war, and famine. Even in my waking moments, I hear whispers of dire warnings coming from the Spirit World. We are threatened on all sides. Not just by the Tower Builders and the Fire Dogs, but by the barbarians whose lands we control. There are even those among the Made People who speak openly against us. Creeper tells me that many are calling for us to share leadership." His lips bent into a sad smile. "We even have enemies among the First People."

Leather Hand nodded, knowing full well what many of the Matrons were saying.

"Where do your loyalties lie, Deputy?"

"When you sent me north, Blessed Sun, it was under the order that I do anything I had to to keep the peace. I do whatever I must to save our world from chaos."

"Whatever you must?"

"Yes, Blessed Sun. I am yours to command."

Webworm smiled. "And what reward would you seek?"

"My reward comes from service."

"Well spoken, but not very practical, I'm afraid." He paused. "You should know that Matron White Cloud demanded that you be executed; but she would settle for a declaration of your being Outcast." He chipped absently at the ladder wood with a thumbnail. "She is Red Lacewing Clan, you know. She was not well disposed toward the decision the Council of Elders made when they named my mother Matron of the First People."

"Nor is she supportive of you now."

"Quite correct. My agents tell me she is working quietly behind the scenes, sowing discontent." He stepped away from the ladder, pensively tapping his lips with his fingers. "Need I remind you how important Far View is?"

"It's the key to the Green Mesa villages, our visible presence among the Made People clans. I rate it only second in importance to Tall Piñon, which is why I traveled there immediately after dealing with the Dust People."

"Then, you realize the danger a poisonous Matron could pose for us?"

Leather Hand carefully said, "Blessed Sun, dangers come in many forms. A man may fall to a known enemy on the battlefield as easily as to a supposed ally who drives a stiletto into his back."

"Which enemy is more honorable, Deputy?"

"The one faced on the battlefield."

"I think you understand my situation." Webworm paused, his stare going to the brightly colored dragonfly on the wall. "Dissension among the First People could drive a wedge between the Made People, or, the gods help us, incite the barbarians into some lunacy worse than that perpetrated at Tall Piñon."

"Who would succeed Matron White Cloud Woman?"

"Her daughter, Three Corn. She's young and would be more compliant to the right suggestions."

Leather Hand took a chance. "The girl is also considered by many to be sickly. If I could suggest: A strong argument could be made for transferring Matron Larkspur from Pinnacle Great House to Far View after the Moon

Ceremony. She is close to Desert Willow, and best of all, amenable to her cousin's suggestions. Then, should something happen to Three Corn in the coming months, Larkspur would already be there."

"Very good." Webworm raised an eyebrow.

"As you wish, Blessed Sun. I'm sure, given my ability to pass where I will, that these things can be accomplished with great discretion." Leather Hand stopped cold. "Blessed Sun, my men . . ."

"Yes?"

"They give me an idea."

"Go on."

"You have never been able to run down Ironwood, the Outcast Matron Night Sun, or the pretender, Cornsilk."

"No." Webworm gave him a cold scowl.

"Perhaps, Blessed Sun, what could not be done with a large force might indeed be accomplished through silence and stealth by a trusted few?"

"Let us see." Webworm reached into a fold in his white robe. "In the meantime, here, take this. Only those whom I trust will carry this fetish."

Leather Hand looked down at the warm stone resting in the palm of his hand. It took a moment for him to discern that it was a carving made from polished jet, a coiled snake resting inside a broken eggshell. In the triangular head a single red eye stared malignantly up at him.

Thirty-one

"This is marvelous," the red-shirted woman said as Wrapped Wrist led her out on the sandstone rim.

They stood on an overlook in the hills just east of First Moon Mountain. The whole of the valley spread before them. Though night had fallen, the vista was limned in evening fires, like a thousand twinkling stars. The light illuminated the smoky haze, turning the valley into a magical place and dusting its slopes with a reddish orange.

"This is how I imagine the Underworlds to look," she said with awe. "Softly dark like this, with the camps of the dead spread from mountain to mountain. The way the fires gleam and twinkle, it reminds me of shining souls. Seeing this place, it's a way of touching the Ancestors."

Wrapped Wrist shot her an uncertain look. Was this the ogre woman? She had just mistakenly sounded like a real human being. "I'm glad it pleases you. But then, we think it's a very special place to live. Blessed in its own right." *As are we.*

"So many people," she marveled. "How do you feed them all?"

"We have constant water from the rivers. Then, too, the slopes here snag the Cloud People as they run into the mountainsides. From below you can see them trailing rains up the slopes like dragging tails. That makes our land more fertile, our corn larger, and beans more plentiful."

She said thoughtfully, "Looking west from the Green Mesas at night is something like this, but not so dramatic. The little pricks of light are scattered, fainter. They don't dazzle the eye the way this does."

"The Green Mesas, is that where you're from?"

"No. I grew up in Fourth Night House, east of Straight Path Canyon."

"Is that where you learned our language?"

"A friend of mine was a slave from here. She told me of this place, but until now I always thought it was a fantastic story, a wild yarn that soothed the hurt in her souls." She made a motion, as if tossing something inconsequential away. "That was long ago."

"I'm sorry."

She turned, "About what?"

"The pain in your voice."

"Do not worry about me, hunter." The flintlike hardness returned. "Take me to your elder. The sooner I speak with him, the faster we're back on the trail to the war chief."

Wrapped Wrist shrugged, turning and following the

path through a patch of dark juniper, feeling his way in the gloom. Behind him he could hear the woman's delicate steps. Given her surety in the darkness, she might have been half cat.

"You could at least tell me your name."

Silence.

"Unless you give me your name, woman, I will have to introduce you as 'This Woman.' Hardly a title appropriate to a messenger from War Chief Ironwood, don't you think?"

More silence, then: "These days I am called Crow Woman."

"Really, well, what did your clan call you?"

"You needn't be concerned."

"Very well, but why did you choose Crow Woman for a name?"

"I chose the name because when my enemies see me, they know the crows will be picking on them before long."

"That's very . . . interesting." He rolled his eyes in the darkness. "What made you decide—"

"How far to White Eye's?"

"Another hand of time."

"Then let's not waste it talking."

He led her through the trees and down into the broad valley. Coming back to First Moon Valley affected him. He might have been seeing the familiar farm plots and landmarks through a different man's eyes. They seemed more precious to him, somehow vulnerable. For the first time he realized how much this place meant to him.

They splashed across First Moon Creek and crossed a bean field before starting the steep climb up the ridge that separated the Dog's Tooth from the bulk of the mountain. After the hard run it didn't take long before Wrapped Wrist was puffing and sweating.

"Who comes?" a voice called from the shadowed wall that guarded the town.

"Wrapped Wrist, a man of the Blue Stick Clan. I bring a messenger to the elder."

"Pass, but know that you will be watched."

Wrapped Wrist made his way past darkened houses and

rounded the great kiva before he approached the elder's pit house. At the ladder, he called, "Elder White Eye, it is Wrapped Wrist, a hunter from the Blue Stick Clan. I have returned from the journey upon which I was sent. I bring a messenger from War Chief Ironwood."

"Enter this place," the old man called.

Wrapped Wrist led Crow Woman up the ladder, crossed the roof, and climbed down into the familiar interior of the pit house. Nothing seemed to have been moved since the last time he had been here. Even the white pots were in the same order. The old man sat cross-legged on a willow-stave mat in the rear. His white hair shone in the firelight, and he poked absently at the fire with a long willow stick. His single white eye seemed to catch the glow, like a reddened coal in his ruined face. He didn't look up as Crow Woman descended and stepped around to the side.

"Tell me what happened," the old man ordered.

Wrapped Wrist related his journey with Spots and the unconscious Ripple to the hot spring valley.

"And Ripple?" the old man asked. "Is he well?"

"He is wounded, Elder," Crow Woman offered in her harshly accented voice. "Matron Nightshade tended to him, bathed him in the hot springs and dressed his wounds. Ripple has been taken to Orenda. She will try to coax his souls back to his body."

White Eye cocked his head at her voice. "Who are you?"

"I am called Crow Woman. The war chief sent me because I speak your language."

"You are of his clan?"

Wrapped Wrist saw the faintest of frowns on Crow Woman's forehead. After a slight hesitation she said, "No, Elder. I am one of his trusted warriors."

"And because he trusts you, I am supposed to?"

After the trip he'd just had with her, Wrapped Wrist appreciated seeing her expression tighten. Apparently not many people dared to question her reliability.

She responded, "I don't care if you trust me or not. I have come to ask a simple question. You need only give me a simple answer, and I'll be on my way."

White Eye smiled thinly. "Very well, warrior, ask your question."

"What do your people think of Ripple's vision?"

White Eye seemed to ponder that for a moment. Perhaps it was an illusion of the light, but the gaping black hollow where his left eye should have been seemed to enlarge. Finally the old man said, "They might be made to think anything, given the proper direction from their elders."

Wrapped Wrist blinked. *What? Didn't the old man believe it? And if not, why risk Ripple's rescue?* Before he could think, he blurted, "Elder?"

The old man's lips curled into a thin smile. "Does that surprise you?"

Wrapped Wrist glanced sheepishly at the stony Crow Woman. "Excuse me, Elder."

White Eye laid his fire stick to the side and steepled his fingers. "Warrior, this is a time of signs and portents. Sister Moon has almost completed her journey back to First Moon Mountain. The Rainbow Serpent rises in the southwest, and famine stalks the land. In my lifetime I have seen the rise of the katsinas, and now the Blessed Sun has declared war on them, seeking to erase them from our world. The very notion that a man—divine among the First People though he might be—would declare war on Spirit beings is unsettling. People are anxious and frightened. The rains do not come. Children are hungry. A sense of growing desperation fills the land."

"You tell me nothing new," Crow Woman added.

"Ah, but have you heard the latest?"

"What would that be?"

"Off to the west somewhere, live a group called the Dust People."

Crow Woman nodded. "I know of them. Subsistence farmers with ties to the Bearclaw Mountain clans."

"They robbed one of the Blessed Sun's storerooms at Tall Piñon. Killed a Priest and stole food and jewelry."

"Then I pity them." Crow Woman crossed her arms. "I know Leather Hand; his retribution will be swift and sure."

"More than you know." White Eye leaned back. "He not only killed the raiders, he ate them. Ritually executed them, cut them up, and then roasted and stewed their bodies the same as he would a butchered deer."

Wrapped Wrist saw the look of dismay cross Crow Woman's face. "To what purpose is such madness, Elder? It smacks of witchcraft!"

"I believe that is precisely Leather Hand's purpose. Those who dare to defy the Blessed Sun will be hunted down by his witch warriors." A pause. "Word is that it has created quite a stir. Matron White Cloud Woman at Far View has even been bold enough to send a runner to Webworm and Desert Willow demanding Leather Hand be declared Outcast."

Crow Woman frowned. "Highly unlikely. Leather Hand is one of the few remaining deputies upon whom the Blessed Sun can rely. Webworm's rise to authority was tainted by Snake Head's evil actions. The elite warriors of the Straight Path Nation drifted away after Ironwood's dismissal and Webworm's defeat at the hands of Jay Bird. I think Webworm not only needs Leather Hand, but will find a way to use his newly found fame."

"You know this Leather Hand well?" White Eye asked.

"I do. He is a very capable commander, but he harbors a wounded and twisted soul. He believes that all the Straight Path Nation's misfortune can be traced back to Ironwood, Night Sun, and the katsinas. It does not help that twice he led forces into the mountains to hunt Ironwood down and bring Matron Night Sun to the Blessed Sun's justice."

"I heard that twice he was forced to retreat empty-handed and with losses." White Eye nodded. "Yet, at this very time, Cold Bringing Woman appears to Ripple, a common hunter, and tells him that he can cause the First People's destruction? Curious timing, don't you think?"

"Is Ripple a Dreamer?" Crow Woman asked. "Was he up there seeking a vision?"

"He was up there seeking an elk," Wrapped Wrist muttered.

"And for no apparent reason this just happened to

him?" Crow Woman shot him a withering glance. "Why would Cold Bringing Woman appear to some ill-prepared and ignorant hunter?"

Wrapped Wrist began to bristle, but White Eye held up his withered hand, saying, "He was chosen for a reason."

"Which is?"

"His mother and father were murdered by Red Shirts when he was but a boy of ten summers. He was a witness to their executions. Memory of that has haunted him, driven him to the hills, actually. Ripple comes of a prominent lineage in the Blue Stick Clan. His great-uncle led the resistance just after Pinnacle Great House was built upon our most sacred place on the mountain. Even farther back, his great-great-grandmother, a clan Matron, was one of the original captives taken to Straight Path Canyon when the First People conquered us. She was worked to death as a slave." White Eye smiled. "If Cold Bringing Woman had to choose one man to be symbolic of my people's resistance, Ripple would be the one."

"Why did you send him to us?" Crow Woman demanded to know.

"His vision told him to seek the Mountain Witch. Matron Larkspur would have broken and then murdered him. With you, several purposes are served: One, he is safe for the moment. Two, his vision has been brought to the attention of Ironwood, Matron Night Sun, and the Mountain Witch. Three, his presence in your camp increases the chance that my people will seize this opportunity to strike at the First People."

"You're using him for your own ends!" Wrapped Wrist cried.

"Don't be a naive fool," White Eye replied. "With a little manipulation Ripple can serve our purpose."

Crow Woman interrupted. "Do you think your people will have the stomach for a strike?"

"They chafe," White Eye answered. "Matron Larkspur ordered her warriors to search every house for Ripple. That invasion has upset people even more. They know that their granaries are going to be stripped to feed other mouths far beyond our valley. Anger has been brewing here for generations. They need only an excuse, and a chance, warrior."

She nodded thoughtfully. "With cliffs on all sides and only a narrow crest for an approach, Pinnacle Great House is one of the most defensible positions I have ever seen."

"There is always a way."

Crow Woman hesitated, expression pinched; then she asked, "Would your people be willing to attack Pinnacle Great House on the second night of Sister Moon's maximum?"

Wrapped Wrist barely stifled his gasp of disbelief. *Attack the First People atop Pinnacle Great House? Are they mad?*

Then, to his greater consternation, White Eye replied, "I will need to discuss this with the other elders, warrior, but I think, if there is a way to capitalize on Ripple's vision, and if Ironwood were to add his warriors to ours, it would become very tempting."

The last thing Ripple remembered was fleeing into the blackness, the grisly images of his pit house burning in his souls.

Now he felt peace. The darkness swayed, moving rhythmically around Ripple's floating soul. For a moment he was confused by the gentle undulations as they rose and fell. The sensation was like being borne upon warm black water. So soothing, wonderfully peaceful, after his ordeal.

Here in the swells of inky black he could forget the pain and fear. Yes, the terrible fear. In this place was safety, retreat from the horror of what they'd done to him.

"You don't need to go back," a voice whispered from the darkness.

"I don't?" He would have sworn something sniffed at his mouth, like a dog seeking the scent of meat.

"You can let go, allow the last of the light to slip away. You can rest here in the safe darkness. Drift, Ripple. Let the current bear you along. It will carry you like a river, forever away."

He sighed, his souls exhausted and numb. Yes, let the darkness carry him. It was easier, so very soothing and safe.

Light flashed. The effect was like closing one eye, holding a tight fist over the other, and staring at the sun through the clenched tunnel of fingers as they flexed. Then a hole opened into gray and Cold Bringing Woman came striding through, her dusky cloak flying about her shoulders, her wild hair standing on end. She brandished her staff as though it were a war club, the red of her irises glowing around midnight pupils. Her ropelike tongue flicked this way and that.

"Is that all you're worth?" she demanded, leveling her staff at Ripple.

"Leave him alone," the voice from the darkness chided. "He is not for you. Not yet."

A sudden sliver of fear forced itself through the warm haze of his body. "I'm not worthy!" he cried. "I'm sorry, so very sorry!"

Cold Bringing Woman fastened her jet eyes on his. "The First People asked you to reveal my vision and deny me."

"Yes," he answered hoarsely.

"But you did not."

"The next time . . ." He couldn't finish.

"But we don't know that for sure, do we?"

"He was whimpering and weak," the voice supplied from the darkness.

"Ripple, the Hero Twins have shown you pieces of the future. You are frightened."

"I've seen terrible things."

"Things we can change," Cold Bringing Woman said. "Your mother and father acted before the time was right. If you would throw off the First People's yoke and save your sisters, you must act now."

"He was moments away from being mine. I was sucking at his breath, stroking his throat with a feathery caress."

"You intrude where you are unwelcome. I found him first." Cold Bringing Woman stepped close, staring down into Ripple's eyes. "Do you still wish to destroy the First People?"

"Yes," Ripple cried.

"He hasn't the courage," the voice insisted.

Cold Bringing Woman cocked her head warily. "You tempt him, old friend. At the same time, you deceive him. I find this curious and can't help but wonder why when your normal way would be to simply rip his souls from his body and devour them."

The voice did not answer.

"It is even more curious," Cold Bringing Woman continued, "that you do not show yourself, but hide behind a veil of darkness. Oh, you know well enough what the stakes are, don't you? They are high enough that you would seduce poor Ripple out of his souls rather than risk incurring my wrath by simply taking them."

Silence.

"I don't understand," Ripple cried. "What is happening to me?"

Cold Bringing Woman twirled in the circle of gray light. Her turquoise-studded moccasins flashed; the snowy white of her face seemed to emit a glow of its own. "You are being tricked, young hunter. Just as tricked as my old friend apparently is."

"Tricked how?" the angry voice demanded.

"Tell the truth: the Flute Player put you up to this, didn't he?"

Silence.

"You see," Cold Bringing Woman said, "not all would like to see the First People fall. Spider Woman waffles, but the Flute Player, he stands to lose the most. Oh, how vain he is, he and his burden basket of seeds. He wears his three warrior's feathers so proudly atop his head, but he is no warrior. I find him as silly as the image the humans engrave into the rock: a Dancing musician, his stiff penis bouncing before him. Yet he has ensnarled you, old friend. I can only wonder how."

Ripple could feel his heart begin to pound. It had been beating in time with the undulations of darkness; now, as it sped with fear, the sensations splintered about him like a dropped pot.

The silky voice asked, *"What do I gain from the destruction of the First People?"*

"You have lived on the bounty of their wars, drank the blood spilled during the executions of their prisoners. The howling misery of their slaves has lulled you to sleep."

"Yet you think I should allow that to pass?"

"Little will change," Cold Bringing Woman said with a casual shrug. "These are people, after all. It is in their nature to inflict suffering, war, and misery on each other. You need not worry about slaking your unquenchable thirst."

"What of my worshipers?"

"There will always be sorcerers; you need not worry about any shortage of those. As long as men and women lust, covet, and hunger for ambition, your followers will call upon you."

Ripple's fear had continued to grow. "Who is—?"

Cold Bringing Woman silenced him with a flash of the hand and a hiss that sounded like frozen snow blowing across a drift. To the darkness, she said, "Surrender Ripple to me. You, of all gods, have nothing to fear from the future."

"I found him. He is mine."

"You *found* him?"

"His souls were loose, whimpering in the darkness. If he was yours, you should have kept better track of him."

"He wasn't ready."

"If you ask me, he was a poor investment to start with. Look at him: A couple of missing teeth, some broken bones, and a couple of holes in his seed stick are enough to drive his souls loose? What if they had really hurt him? You would bet on a weak wretch like this one?"

Panic seized Ripple's souls. He fixed on Cold Bringing Woman's wintry face, saw the hesitation behind her red-rimmed eyes. The scarlet tongue flicked in and out past her pointed teeth.

"I'm not weak!" Ripple cried. "Don't abandon me!"

Still, Cold Bringing Woman hesitated. Then she asked cautiously, "What would you do with him? Just devour his souls?"

"I would save the future."

"Save the Flute Player's future, you mean. Spider

Woman still hasn't decided. The Rainbow Serpent and I may have to do this on our own."

"What of the Hero Twins?"

"They are divided, of course. Wolf Dreamer sides with me, Raven Hunter with the Flute Player. Harmony against disorder. First Woman is oblivious, since none of the souls have managed to reach her cave."

"Why shouldn't I side with the Flute Player? The thlatsinas could care less about my needs. But among the First People? I have finally found one who shares my hunger. I might have kivas dedicated to me. A place where I can commune with my worshipers."

Cold Bringing Woman continued to hesitate, her tongue flicking this way and that as she considered. When she smiled, it was with bitter acceptance. "Very well, will you Trade?"

The Darkness seemed to pulse, and Ripple felt himself rise and fall in the expectant silence.

"This one for Leather Hand? Why should I? I already have your precious Ripple."

The sound that passed Cold Bringing Woman's lips was the whistle of the north wind; it blew past Ripple, frigid and bitter, carrying a promise of something Ripple couldn't comprehend. In its wake, he shivered, a quavering terror like acid in his souls.

"You wouldn't!"

A long silence passed as Cold Bringing Woman struck a resolute posture, her staff out before her.

"Very well," the voice finally said.

In that instant, Ripple felt himself fall, his surroundings turning a medium gray.

Cold Bringing Woman moved in a blur, her arms shooting out to catch Ripple as his stomach tickled with weightlessness. Her arms dug into him like bars of ice. The staff she clutched in her left hand lay next to his ear. A miserable numbing cold speared through him, causing him to shiver violently.

Cold Bringing Woman turned rapidly, striding toward the circle of light. The gray haze around them began to recede. Once again, Ripple felt the rising and falling, like undulations. This time, however, it was coupled with a freezing agony that knotted his limbs.

"That was close, Ripple. Very close," Cold Bringing Woman whispered.

He managed to crane his head, to look back at the wavering darkness behind him. For the briefest moment, his gaze locked with something malevolent; it speared white fear through his souls. Hideous, a waking nightmare, the mere sight of the *thing* would leave him shaken forever.

Then it smiled at him, yellow eyes burning with violent promise.

His scream burned in his throat.

Thirty-two

Ripple's naked body lay in a low-ceilinged room, the walls made of wattle-and-daub: clay packed over a woven framework of poles and branches before fire-hardening. Several elkhides had been folded, hair out, to make a soft bed for Ripple. His skin was goose-fleshed, every muscle knotted and shivering. He lay next to the wall in the back. Despite the warm summer day, a small fire flickered in the heating bowl just inside the door. Smoke rose to pool against the ceiling before drifting out the single window in the rear.

"Poor Singer, what do you think?" A twenty-summers-old woman asked in a thickly accented voice. "Have you ever seen anything like this before?"

"No." Poor Singer shook his head as he laid a hand on Ripple's chest. "A moment ago he was burning up. Now he's too cold to touch."

They both stared in amazement as Ripple's breath began to frost from his mouth, then to vanish as it rose and mingled with the pleasant summer air.

Poor Singer frowned. "Orenda, he is touched by Power

in a way I've never seen before. As to whether it's good or bad, I can't say. The Spirits alone know what his souls are going through. If only Dune were still alive. He'd know what to do."

"We have to warm him." Orenda turned and pulled a thick buffalohide from the shadows in the back corner. "Otherwise, he'll die."

As she moved, long black hair swung on either side of her round face. She wore a loose blue dress embroidered with the image of a dancing figure that looked part human, part bird, and part snake. Feathers sprouted from the figure's arms, and snakeskin covered the image's back. A human face was topped with a high hairpiece pinned in place.

"He may die anyway." Poor Singer helped her lay the heavy hide atop Ripple. The shivers grew so violent the hide seemed to vibrate.

"I don't see how—"

Ripple's sudden scream scared them both. It stopped just as quickly, leaving them wide-eyed and staring in the deathly silence. Beyond the room, the sounds of the village ceased. Even the evening breeze seemed shocked into silence.

Ripple's panic-glazed eyes were wide and staring sightlessly. His mouth gaped to expose lacerated gums. Puffing white breaths continued to explode from his heaving chest despite the ever-more-violent shivers.

Poor Singer glanced at Orenda. She was staring in surprise. "I know that look. Thank the gods we can't see what he is seeing."

Spots blinked, jerking with terror, and sat straight up in his blankets. Bits and pieces of images, fragments of shredded Dream, spun away from his blurry eyes.

Cool dawn had grayed the sky in the east. Birds were greeting the morning with melodious song from the cottonwoods, willows, and brush that crowded the banks of the River of Souls. He could smell the grass, damp and crushed, and caught the faint acrid scent of smoke and perspiration rising from his hunting shirt. Small flames leapt from blackened wood in the fire pit, and wisps of blue smoke merged with the predawn.

Nightshade sat across from him, a blanket draped over her shoulders; her white hair had been parted down the middle and fell over her shoulders in a mantle. The woman's large dark eyes were fixed on him, as if they'd drilled down into his bones.

"D-Dream," he stuttered hoarsely.

"I find it surprising that they speak to you."

He shook his head. "Wha-What?"

"Have you always sought the ways of Power?"

"No! I want nothing to do with it! My parents did—and look what good it got them! If they hadn't been locked away in Spirit Dreams, they wouldn't have burned the house down around us!"

"Not all people are as sensitive as you. Few could hear so many voices, share so many visions. Did it frighten you when the flames began rising around the funeral pyre?"

"How could you know what I Dreamed?" Images flashed of terrible heat, a shrieking horror of disbelief rising from the ghost's mouth.

A flicker of smile crossed her lips. "They whisper to me. All of them. Tharon, among the worst."

"Who?"

"A dead king from another world."

"How many worlds have you been to?"

"They are beyond count."

"In the Dream, I was carrying a wounded man. He kept growing heavier and heavier."

"And your feet became sodden, your muscles stiffening like grease on a cold day. It was only at the end when the darkness closed in that the dying man slipped away."

Spots frowned. "You shared that Dream?"

She shook her head again.

"Then, how did you know?"

"I hear them just as loudly as you do."

"Hear who?"

She pointed to the pack that sat beside her, the one he had carried the day before. "Some are old friends, others enemies I have encountered. They come and go, as their whims dictate."

"You have ghosts in there?" A shiver ran down his spine.

She took a deep breath. "You should know: It irritates them when you bat at them."

"I keep hearing voices. Like insects that buzz around my ears."

"They wouldn't talk to you unless they thought you might be willing to listen."

He stared warily at the pack. "Are they going to attack my souls?"

"Well, if I were you, I wouldn't anger them."

He rubbed his face, his guts prickling with unease. "What do you want from me?"

"The same thing I wanted from you yesterday."

"Where are we going?"

"To see this world die."

"I beg your pardon?"

She laughed, the sound bitter and lonely.

If Bad Cast had expected Ironwood's camp to be something spectacular, he was wrong. His journey brought him to a high mesa top just south of the hot springs. From there, a view could be had of most of the River of Souls drainage to the west. Best of all, the signal relay for Flowing Waters Town could be seen atop its perch high in the clay hills south of the River of Souls.

"We can read most of the Blessed Sun's messages," Whistle told him. "Somehow Webworm never thought it prudent to change the code. After all, what does he care if Ironwood knows his communications? He doesn't think we can hurt him."

Bad Cast looked out across the vista, and asked, "Well, can you?"

"We will find out." Whistle gave a shrug.

Back in the trees a row of single-story houses had been built of poles thrust into the ground, the sides interwoven with branches, and then mud daubed onto the framework to seal it. Low doorways opened out onto what might be considered the plaza. Here lazy smoke rose from several fires to drift away on the afternoon breeze.

Women rose from where they had been grinding corn, pounding jerky, or crafting pottery. With calls they ran to greet the line of warriors who trotted into the settlement.

Ironwood himself walked with open arms to an elderly gray-haired woman wearing a form-fitting black dress decorated with white four-pointed stars. If she was who Bad Cast suspected she was, age had done little to dim Matron Night Sun's poise or presence. She carried herself as a ruler should, possessed and controlled, even though her smile was for Ironwood alone. He caught himself staring.

"Yes, that's her." Whistle noted his interest.

He just kept staring, thinking, *So that is what a Great Matron of the First People looks like?* Not just a Matron, but the famous Night Sun, no less! This was the woman whose dalliance with her war chief had brought low the Red Lacewings and given Blue Dragonfly Clan the opportunity to take over the Matronship for the first time in seven generations. He stepped closer to see her.

Night Sun had a triangular face with a high forehead. Spirals were tattooed on her chin, and lines had deepened around her mouth. Her cheeks were broad, her forehead wide from the flattening of her skull by a cradleboard as an infant. She walked and moved with a subtle grace, her gestures fluid and stately. Her whole face lit up when she smiled at Ironwood, and love gleamed in her eyes.

"Hard to believe, isn't it?" Whistle asked.

"Excuse me?"

"She doesn't look like a terrible monster-demon from the First Days, does she?"

"She looks like someone's grandmother—a stately but very composed elder."

Whistle laughed. "Oh she's all of that and more. She will want to hear Ironwood's report, but afterward I would be happy to introduce you."

Bad Cast shook his head at the thought. "I still can't believe I'm here." Then he caught sight of a most attractive woman, tall, oddly reminiscent of Night Sun, but with a blunter face, high questioning brows, and a deeply scarred cheek. Two young boys perhaps fourteen and fifteen followed her. She stepped out of the last of the rooms and shaded her eyes to study Ironwood.

"That is Cornsilk," Whistle told him. "The infamous daughter, heir to the Red Lacewing Matronship, assuming she ever wanted to lay claim to it."

She turned sober eyes on Bad Cast, appraising him before passing on to catalog the rest of the warriors, as if counting.

"And the boys?" Bad Cast asked. The elder wore a buckskin hunting shirt that hung to his knees. He carried a bow, and arrows could be seen over his left shoulder. A hawkish intensity lay behind his hard eyes. The younger wore a loosely woven wool pullover; his expression showed happiness as he watched Ironwood and Night Sun.

"Ravenfire is the eldest. She doesn't say much about him. The second, Snowbird, is definitely Poor Singer's son. He was born but a scant ten moons after Ravenfire. Poor Singer's seed is particularly potent. They have a daughter who was born ten moons later. She is named Peppergrass."

"And the Prophet, Poor Singer?" Bad Cast asked. "Is he here, too?"

"There." Whistle pointed across the clearing, where a skinny man with a hooked nose, long face, and surprisingly sad eyes came walking out of the mixed juniper and ponderosa pine. He had a pole over his shoulder from which a brace of rabbits swung with each step. The first strands of gray had touched his temples.

"He doesn't look like a holy Dreamer," Bad Cast noted.

Whistle pursed his lips and snorted. "If you judge all men by their looks at a distance, hunter, your life is apt to be indescribably short, but very, very interesting."

At that, Whistle clapped him on the back and walked off toward the trees. It was only then, with the sun shining at an angle, that Bad Cast saw the low-mounded pit houses back under the branches.

This was hardly the sort of settlement he would have imagined. Most of the peoples who inhabited the Straight Path Nation thought of the worlds as being nestled inside each other, like a small bowl inside a larger one, inside a larger one, and so on until one reached this world. From their pottery to their pit houses, to the kivas, buildings, and towns, each construction mirrored their concept of the universe. At the greatest extreme the First People even built their huge multistory towns as a well-ordered re-creation of their universe. Here, however, was chaos.

The settlement had a wild look, and but for the famous people, wouldn't have amounted to much. In fact, from a distance, due to the lack of bright colors and its irregular outline, the single-room block with its mottled earth-tone plaster disappeared into the background. Even the smoke from the fires was dispersed through the trees.

No wonder the Blessed Sun's warriors never found this place.

He sighed, rehitched his pack on his back, and walked into the center of the dusty plaza, such as it was. It was only then that he realized Poor Singer, the Prophet, was watching him. The man's cocked head, bland expression, and curious smile didn't dispel the intensity of his gaze. He came forward, his rabbits swinging, and asked in a garbled accent, "Have you come to inquire about your kinsman?"

"Ripple?"

"Ah, is that his name? We didn't know. He was delivered to our care with orders to keep him alive. From the gray paste on his temples it's apparent that he's on a Spirit quest, but Sister Datura should have ceased Dancing with him by now. Orenda and I have been worried. We've been having problems calling his souls back. You wouldn't know where they might be, would you?"

"Uh, no." Bad Cast was taking Poor Singer's measure. The man's legs might have been sticks, his knees knobby.

An oversized white cloth shirt, belted at the waist with a length of rope, hung on his skinny shoulders. The fabric was smudged with drying bunny blood and hung down to midthigh. His hair had been pulled into an off center-bun and skewered in place by a slim turkey-bone pin. Fine strands of hair had come loose and wiggled in the breeze. Where Poor Singer's hands clutched the pole, they were bony, long fingered, but looked delicate and unused to hard labor.

It was when Bad Cast met the man's eyes that the world seemed to stop. They had a liquid quality, at once strong but sensitive, and filled with an endless longing. When had he ever seen eyes like these?

"Yes," he heard himself whisper. *"Here is a Prophet."* Louder, he said, "It is said that you called the Rainbow Serpent from the Below Worlds. That you humbled the great Jay Bird, and that Dune the Derelict chose you to succeed him in all things holy. It is said that you're the greatest holy man alive. I'll bet you could call thunder down on the Blessed Sun himself and burn out his heart with a bolt of lightning."

Poor Singer's expression reflected an uncomfortable pain. "You've heard some very wild stories."

"But if you could, your wife, Cornsilk, would be named Matron of the First People. And you, as her husband, could be the Blessed Sun. Think of all the good you could do in the place of Webworm."

Poor Singer shook his head. "These things of which you speak all come at too high a cost, hunter. Once, before I touched the faces of the gods, I thought as you do." A fleeting humor played at the corner of his lips. "I think that to be young is to be deluded."

"You think I'm deluded? Gods, anything would be better than living under the First People."

Poor Singer squinted slightly, asking, "What do you come here seeking, hunter?"

"I didn't come seeking anything, great Prophet. I had no choice. I was ordered to follow your war chief or have my skull caved in."

"Yes, well, sometimes Ironwood can be a stern master, but he carries a great weight upon his shoulders." Poor Singer nodded as if in understanding. "Tell me, what do you know of Ripple's vision quest? What are his souls trying to find?"

Bad Cast related the things he had heard Ripple say and then talked about the frozen elk. "I swear, it was frozen solid. When the story got to Matron Larkspur, it frightened her enough that she sent her warriors out to capture us. They caught poor Ripple, and, well, you've seen what they did to him. Before his souls fled, he told Wrapped Wrist and Spots that Larkspur and Burning Smoke tried to get him to deny Cold Bringing Woman's vision."

In that instant, a smile spread across Poor Singer's lips. "At last, something that makes sense."

"Excuse me?"

"That's why Orenda can't find his souls. Old Woman North has them." He placed one of his long-boned hands on Bad Cast's shoulder. "Thank you, my friend. Oh, here, could you take these rabbits? Please hand them around as far as they will go, and keep one for yourself. I must go and see Orenda."

With that he turned on his heel and walked off, his gait oddly bouncy, as though his bony legs weren't quite under control.

Bad Cast arched an eyebrow, glanced at the rabbits, and shrugged. "And he thinks *I'm* deluded?" He glanced around. "Blood and spit, I'm the only normal one here."

FEAR

I long for that quickening of the blood. How light my limbs become; what a wonder my steps are, so filled with air. If I could choose any companion, it would be Fear. My senses remain sharp, focused on the instant like a hawk's narrow gaze.

When others would prefer to remain little more than lumps of dry wood, senseless, feeling nothing but the dull monotony of health, I would rather thrill at the inevitable shock of heart, blood, and muscle drawn tight. For a time, I lost track of Fear. Bliss, love, and companionship all but scoured it from my long-bruised souls. To forget Fear is to forget life; the longer one exists without it, the more terrible its touch when at last it reappears.

How precious and terrible. The tragedy is that we can escape for those few precious moments. To believe ourselves happy, safe, and beyond danger is incredibly blissful. How shortsighted we are to wrap ourselves in the artful lie of security. In the end, a lover's smile is empty, his embrace but a phantom. Savor that moment of happiness, for it is fleeting, and never so achingly precious as when it has vanished into memory.

Yes, being an insensitive lump of dry wood is comforting, but in the end, the licking flames will always find you. Lovers die. Worlds collapse. Bodies age.

Revel in your moments of joy and love.

They are but a blink of the eye.

Fear—though held at bay for those scant heartbeats—cannot be denied. It will consume your flesh and souls. Scream while it devours you, for once again, you are truly alive!

The camp Spots had picked was on a grassy bench just above the river. Cottonwoods towered over them, the leaves rattling softly in the evening breeze. Off to the north, thunderheads had crowded up against the mountains. Piñon jays laughed and trilled as they flocked through the pines high on the slope in search of cones bearing early nuts. A grasshopper clicked and shimmered in the afternoon light, riding the warm air on silvered wings.

Spots bent to the duty of building a fire while the old woman wearily lowered herself to the grass and took a deep breath. Nightshade looked done in from the day's long walk. In places, where the canyon narrowed, the going had been rough, sometimes necessitating the crossing of downed trees, piled rock, or steep side slopes.

Spots could look over his shoulder and see a huge block of sandstone that had tumbled down from the cracked rim sometime in the distant past. On one mineral-stained panel, someone had patiently carved the spiral shape of the sun, two bighorn sheep, and a human hand. Dominating these, however, was a painting of the Flute Player, done in blood red. He stared out at Spots with a single black eye, his flute frozen to his lips.

"Does he bother you?" Nightshade asked. From the moment she'd seated herself, she'd tipped her head back, eyes closed, as if on the verge of sleep.

"Pardon?"

"The Flute Player. Does his stare bother you?"

"I thought your eyes were closed."

"There are other ways of seeing, hunter. You have not answered my question."

"Elder, I'm carrying a pack full of ghosts, Spirits, and who knows what else. My Dreams are haunted, and I'm scared half out of my wits every time a bird flies out of a bush. You tell me that we're headed off to watch our world die. Why should I worry about a painting on a rock?"

She smiled as he went about picking up sticks, piling tinder, and retrieving his bow drill from his own pack. He glanced sidelong at her as he fitted the pieces of the drill together and wound the shaft into the string. Placing charred grass from a small pouch beside the notch in his drill base, he sawed the bow back and forth until smoke rose. He coaxed it onto the nest of dried grass, shredded juniper bark, and twigs. Blowing carefully, the coals glowed before the first flames leapt up.

He leaned back, hands on his thighs, and looked up at the rimrock high above. Late evening sunlight shot gold across the canyon, bathing the rock, shrubs, and pines in a soft light. High overhead, two golden eagles tumbled on the thermals while their young juvenile—its wings and tail splotched with white—flapped awkwardly.

"Elder," he asked, "where are we headed?"

For long moments, she sat immobile. Spots would have sworn she was unconscious; not even her chest rose and fell.

He had just about given up on it when she said, "To Flowing Waters Town."

"But that's right in the Blessed Sun's own plaza. If someone recognizes you, you'll be in great danger."

A meadowlark raised its lilting song from the berry bushes. Moments later a vole rustled the grass as it scurried down one of its hidden trails.

"Danger lives and breathes, hunter. It surrounds us like a cloak. It hovers over you as you cross the clearing, descends as the great bear catches your scent from the trees. It Dances on your very breath. A young woman can feel its fingers massaging her swollen belly as the first pangs of childbirth burn through her hips. When a man coughs, he never thinks of the evil he might have just inhaled, or how it will nest in his warm damp lungs, grow, and slowly consume him. Danger and I have been entwined since the beginning."

"Yes, Elder. But just because I see a rattlesnake coiled beside a rock doesn't mean I'm going to bend down and tap him on the nose with my finger, either. I'm saying that there are times when being prudent can save a person from grief."

Looking serene, she softly said, "It's too late."

"What do you mean, too late? We're still a day's walk from the trail that leads over to the Spirit River Valley, and yet another day after that to Flowing Waters Town. Elder, we can turn around and go right back to—"

He stopped short, seeing a single tear creep past the corner of her closed eyes. "Elder, are you all right?"

She remained like a statue, back straight, hands in her lap, her head tilted to the sky. The breeze teased strands of her long white hair where it flowed down her back.

"Elder? Can I do anything for you?"

She exhaled, and whispered, "Can you conjure my dead

husbands from their graves, or stop a frightened little girl from being ripped away from all she knew and loved? Can you do any of these things?"

He frowned, aware that yet another tear had started down her cheek. "Elder, perhaps we could find some safe place for you, that's all. If you would come back north with me, I'm sure we could make a place for you at my sister's house. Whatever your plan, you needn't go through with it. You needn't put yourself at risk."

A wistful smile betrayed a terrible longing. "I am the darkness, hunter. Pain and misery walk at my side. I shall be there, winding Webworm's souls out of his body as a weaver does fibers into thread."

"By the gods, Elder, what you say is impossible. The Blessed Sun is surrounded by warriors, Priests, the Made People clan elders. Even his slaves are partial to his safety. The moment you try to witch him, tens of people will rise to his defense. They'll kill you for even trying!"

Her eyes snapped open. Like deep mystical pools, they seemed to swirl and gleam in her head. "Yes, they will."

"Then why are you doing this?"

"Let us have supper, hunter. Your fire is crackling, and my stomach is empty."

Spots gave her a shake of his head before he rose, collected the canteen, and headed down to the water. As he let the clear liquid dribble into the narrow neck, he wondered what it would take to slip away from her in the night. He could wait, listen for her breathing to go deep, and then ease his way down toward the water. By wading for a ways she would hear no step, no branch rasping against cloth. He could fade into the darkness and be long gone by morning.

When he climbed up through the brush and across the loose river cobbles to the grassy flat, she was watching him the way a coyote did a mouse. In a sensual voice, she said, "Yes, you could do that, but a misstep in the darkness might drown you. I can see your body floating in the black water; it twists and turns as it sinks and then bobs. Feel the cold leaching into your flesh? Your souls will be trapped down there, wailing in the silence of the depths. Or you could join with me. That way we'll have the darkness all to ourselves. You and me. Together in the most intimate of ways."

Fingers of ice ran down his spine. "Elder?"

"Yes."

"I wish you wouldn't do that. It frightens me."

"Good."

Thirty-three

The fire crackled and spat sparks toward the dark sky. To see it, warm and yellow, licking at the logs, reassured Wrapped Wrist as much as the warmth it cast against the chill of the night. Though it was late summer, where they camped at the top of the mountain divide, night still had a bite to it.

Wrapped Wrist used one of the dead branches he'd snapped off a fir tree to prod the fire and then watched the sparks as they whirled up. Blinking out one by one, they climbed toward the conifer branches overhead. He watched them, bathed in the flickering yellow light. He and Crow Woman had slipped out of First Moon Valley before the dawn, heading back toward Ironwood's camp. All day they had climbed, forcing one weary step ahead of the other. Crow Woman hadn't agreed to make camp until they had reached the divide just at dusk.

Somewhere, out in the forest, the great horned owls hooted and cooed to each other. In answer, a distant pack of coyotes yipped and barked.

"You should be sleeping."

He turned at the voice, glancing at where Crow Woman lay in her blanket.

"I suppose," he replied with a shrug. "Things are chewing on my souls."

"What kind of things?"

"Worry."

"About what?"

He jabbed at the fire some more. "I keep remembering that view of the valley. You know, the one where we stood on the rimrock and looked out at all the twinkling fires. You said it was magical." He smiled. "Funny, isn't it? I've lived there all my life, watched the shining lights of the towns and houses, and never realized what a precious place I called my own."

She was silent for a while. "What changed that for you?"

"Hearing you and White Eye talk." He thrust his stick violently into the coals and was greeted with a rising taper of sparks. "It isn't as simple as you and White Eye make it sound, is it?"

"Attacking a high fortress is never simple. Great houses are built for defense."

"That's not what I'm talking about."

She sat up in her bedding, threw back the blanket, and squatted opposite him. In firelight her face was somber, her eyes dark. "Then . . . what?"

"Assume that White Eye and Ironwood succeed. They destroy Pinnacle Great House, kill Matron Larkspur, Burning Smoke, and Water Bow. White Eye seems to think that's the end of it. The First People are gone. Everything is as it was before they came and took our mountain away from us. Life will be as it was in my great-great-grandmother's day."

"But you don't believe it?"

"No." He smiled warily, glancing at her across the flames. "It isn't that easy. Neither Webworm nor Matron Desert Willow will stand for it. This deputy, Leather Hand—I heard you say you knew him. How will he take the murder of a Blue Dragonfly Matron, a war chief, and their Priests?"

"It will send him into a frothing rage."

"Doing this thing will be like driving a cactus thorn right through their hearts."

She studied him thoughtfully. "Anytime you drive a thorn into someone's flesh, you will get an immediate reaction. In this case we hope it will cause similar revolts all across the Straight Path Nation."

"Why?"

"What do you mean, why? Yours aren't the only people who chafe under the First People's rule."

"No, I mean why start this?" He waggled his stick. "No one—not you, White Eye, or even the great Ironwood—knows what this will cost."

"If you don't like the idea of a fight, perhaps you should just ask Matron Larkspur to leave."

"Good idea. Why didn't we think of that before?"

"Because," she chided, "the only way you're going to get your mountain back is by driving the First People off of it."

He studied her for a moment. Something deep and brooding lay behind her eyes. He said, "Have you ever stood at the top of a steep slope and rolled a small rock down the hill?"

"Of course."

"And when you did you didn't know if that rock would roll for a ways and stop, or break still more rocks from the soil that in turn knocked still more of them loose until the entire hillside was rumbling in dust and falling rock."

She rubbed her hands together before extending them to the fire. "Wrapped Wrist, the time of the First People is over. They have abused Power too often. Even the gods have denied them."

"You've talked to the gods about this?"

She laughed bitterly. "No, but remember what the First People have always told us: 'If you will follow our commands, pay your tribute to the Blessed Sun, and attend our rituals we will intercede with the gods on your behalf. Only through us can your needs be communicated to the gods. Through us, they will hear your words. Our Blessed Sun is to you as Father Sun is to the sky. Obey us . . . and the gods will reward you.'" She lifted an eyebrow. "Is this a problem for them?"

He considered that. "Most people have obeyed, but the rains do not come. We have heard stories of crops burning up in the fields, of hunger and blowing dust."

"They are not just stories," she said soberly. "I have seen these things with my own eyes. Especially in the south. I know for a fact that the great houses in the west have emptied their storerooms." She raised her eyes. "Even the floors have been swept for stray kernels of corn. A mouse would starve in rooms that used to be filled to the roof with corn, beans, and dried squash."

"So you think the gods have abandoned the First People?"

"I think they've grown just as tired of the First People's arrogance as I have."

"You've had experience with the First People?"

A bitter smile crossed her lips. "Enough to wish the very marrow in their bones would turn to pus."

"Bones to pus? Wouldn't that be nice? But until it happens, my worry continues. You said that Leather Hand would be driven to a frothing rage? Why should my people be involved?"

She took a deep breath. "If I had to choose a place to plan an attack on the First People, I couldn't pick a better location than Pinnacle Great House."

"Why?"

"Well, to start with, its very impregnability creates a false sense of security among the defenders. That in itself is a weakness—a blank spot in the defenders' thinking. Then there is the location, completely surrounded by forest-covered mountains. We can make an undetected approach from almost any direction. Burning Smoke won't have any idea that we're attacking until it's too late."

"Provided his warriors don't catch us first."

"Correct." She smiled grimly. "And with them combing the country for the escaped Ripple and that slave girl, let's make sure we continue to evade them. Another reason for taking Pinnacle Great House is symbolic. This is the place where Sister Moon entered this world. She's coming back, returning from her long journey across the sky. Do you see the symbolism? It's full circle—she'll be in the same place she was when the First People's warriors captured your elders and conquered your people."

"That idea will play well when White Eye and the elders try to convince my people to participate."

"It will." She studied him thoughtfully. "The ceremony

will bring a number of Powerful men and women to Pinnacle Great House."

"If the Blessed Sun comes, you can be sure he'll be heavily guarded."

"True, but as you well know, Pinnacle Great House is isolated—at least two days' hard run from Flowing Waters Town. Second, the counterattacking warriors will have to travel trails that can be easily ambushed. A war chief will have to proceed slowly, cautiously. Webworm's commanders have bad memories when it comes to ambushes."

"But that's the point: Eventually they will come." He watched the end of his branch catch fire and held it up, the feeble flame dying. Curls of blue smoke rose. "The warriors will probably be led by Leather Hand himself. In a frothing rage, as you said. He'll want to teach us all a lesson, and after what he did to the Dust People it will no doubt be very terrible. Then what will happen to my magical valley?"

The loom rose from the kiva floor to the soot-stained logs that cribbed upward from the stone pilasters to the ceiling. At the bottom it was tied securely to pegged hollows in the floor. Nearly three-quarters finished, the weaving it held was as wide as it was tall.

White Cloud Woman looked at her masterpiece as she leaned against the bench on the kiva's north side. A folded blanket cushioned her old bones from the willow-stave matting and kept the chill from creeping out of the flagstone floor. The pole shelves between the pilasters were filled with colorfully painted masks and associated wooden ritual garb shaped like wings and painted in the Red Lacewing Clan's designs. Large jars stood in the bench niches and were white-slipped with black-hatched zones distinctive of the finest Straight Path ceramics. They contained sacred pollen, ground turquoise, tiny shell beads, and polished pebbles of jet and quartz. At the altar behind her head, a tight bundle contained several hundred bright red macaw feathers that she was planning to use in the creation of a dazzling ceremonial cloak.

She glanced up at the unfinished weaving. Rising black squares, indicative of the mountains at the four corners of the world, were offset by the slanting lines of zigzagging clouds that would eventually complete the upper quarter of the design. Mountains and clouds, earth and sky, opposites crossed.

But something had gone wrong in the world. Somehow she hadn't felt up to completing the weaving. If only she could pin down what the trouble was—why the clouds with their life-giving rain were no longer piling up against the mountains—she would have it.

But then, perhaps it isn't the earth and sky. The old sour thought lodged between her souls. How could the gods be induced to call the rains when the human world was just as out of balance?

From the moment the Blessed Crow Beard had taken sick and his firstborn, Snake Head, had grown influential, the rains had slackened and then virtually ceased. Snake Head's poison still leached through the Straight Path world, tainting Webworm, Desert Willow, and their doomed leadership. They had uprooted the Straight Path Nation, pulled it out of the very canyon that had nurtured it. Now they wondered why it was dying in their hands as they sought to replant it in the Spirit River Valley.

"More trouble is coming," she whispered, and stared down at the beautiful white moccasins she was finishing. They would be presented to her cousin at the winter solstice ceremony. He would Dance as one of the thlatsinas in the First People's kiva. No matter what Webworm had banned for the rest of the Straight Path Nation, Far View was under White Cloud Woman's matronage. Here the thlatsinas would Dance—even if in secret.

She ran the supple leather over her callused brown fingers, and punched a deer-bone awl through the flap she was finishing. Drawing her head back, she studied the hole, then used a turkey-bone needle to draw thread through and pulled the stitch tight.

There, almost complete. From beside her she lifted a shining copper bell, Traded up from the far south; it gleamed in the light. With the dangling length of thread, she tied it onto the back flap of the moccasin. She knotted it tightly and waggled the soft leather, hearing the gentle tinkling of the bell.

There, complete. Ready for the ceremony that lay a scant four moons away.

Enough for one night. She yawned and leaned forward, using a stick to separate the largest embers in the fire pit. Then, taking two tries, she climbed to her feet, one hand on a plastered pilaster. As renewed circulation shot needles through her legs, she made a face, then tucked her white moccasins to her breast and climbed the kiva ladder out onto the roof.

The night was clear but hazy, and the faint smell of dust lay heavy in her nostrils. She puffed out a breath in the chill and made her way across the kiva roof, stepped down to the floor level, and walked over to her third-floor room.

"Who's there?" she called, seeing a dark figure on the edge of the roof.

"Good evening, Elder," Moon Knuckle called back. "It's just me."

"Couldn't sleep?"

"No. Perhaps it was a presentiment, but I thought I felt black wings on the night."

She walked over to the edge of the roof and looked down on the first floor. The large First People's kiva made a giant circle, like an oversized mouth beneath the two smaller clan kivas that jutted out of the packed clay beside it.

"Guard?" she called.

"Here, Matron!" a shadow stepped away from one of the walls and bowed.

"Stay awake. It's going to be darker than pitch until moonrise. The last thing we need is a debacle like they had at Tall Piñon."

"Yes, Matron. No one has passed. Sleep in peace."

She grunted to herself, nodded at Moon Knuckle, and walked stiffly toward her rooms. She could see the faint image of the Yamuhakto where they had been painted on either side of her T-shaped doorway. They might have just been painted on the plaster, but somehow knowing the great Warriors of the East and West flanked her made her feel better.

She ducked into her rooms, relieved at the residual warmth that clung to the thick walls. From long practice she made her way past the jumble of her possessions and into the room where she slept. The slaves were evidently being efficient for once. Glowing embers still gleamed redly in her fire pot and warmed the room.

White Cloud Woman placed the beautiful white moccasins atop one of her wooden boxes and pulled her blue cotton dress over her head. Folding it, she laid it beside her bed, drank from her canteen, and used the chamberpot.

Her bed consisted of buffalo wool blankets laid over shredded juniper bark atop reed matting. It seemed as though she'd just pulled the blanket over her and closed her eyes when a voice said, "What beautiful moccasins!"

She blinked awake just as hard hands clamped over her windpipe.

Thirty-four

First came a gradual awareness. A numbing chill. It lay deep in his body. So deep it left his flesh feeling brittle, his bones ready to snap. Ripple gasped and awoke to a world of white. Cold, so terribly cold. *Am I dead? Is this what it feels like?*

How was he going to stand an eternity of this? He blinked, and ice crystals fluttered on his lashes.

With a groan he sat up and stared around the white world, wondering where he was. A thick layer of snow cushioned him. It faded into curtains of cloud and falling snowflakes until one couldn't tell where frost and sky became one.

Here and there, dark angles of rock projected from the windblown crust. His teeth chattered, breath fogging before his mouth.

"Where am I?"

"Safe, for the moment." At first all he could see were her red eyes with their dark pupils. They seemed to hang in the whiteness. Then her blood-colored tongue flicked past the needle teeth in her mouth. The dusk-colored cloak seemed to float among the flakes of falling snow; her moccasins were all but invisible save for the turquoise beads that decorated them. She Danced, stepping and ducking. At her feet, snow twisted about her ankles in whirls and recast itself into sculpted drifts. She thrust with her staff, and the clouds parted, only to drift shut as she withdrew it.

In that instant Ripple realized he sat atop a high mountain peak. But where? How far had she carried him? Memories of the darkness flooded his souls—including that moment of abject horror as he glanced back at the *thing* Cold Bringing Woman had rescued him from. Remembering those eyes, that face, he huddled in the snow, shivers eating his body.

"Do not fear," Cold Bringing Woman assured. "She cannot reach you here."

"C-Cold. My flesh is turned to ice."

Cold Bringing Woman stopped short from her Dance; her wild hair had frosted with white. "It won't be long. They're calling for you."

"Who? Who calls?"

"Someone with Power. Can't you feel the pull?"

He did, as if threads were tugging at his souls. But pulling him where? The sensation was unlike anything he had ever experienced. First, he had to know: "I Dreamed. I was in darkness, being carried."

"That was no Dream."

Ripple slitted his eyes against a wind gust that pelted his face with ice crystals. "Not a Dream?"

Cold Bringing Woman leaned down, her dark pupils enlarging. "The next time you send your souls loose to wander the half-light between life and death, call me first. Even the Hero Twins' plans were upset when she captured you. She is vain, that one, but never to be underestimated. Getting you back has cost me, cost us all."

"Cost us how?"

"To appease her, plans had to be altered. We will settle for a different future, one not so bright. Her wishes are part of the price; it is irrevocable.. Things have changed. She sees the possibilities."

"I don't understand."

"What is to understand? Have you never agreed to something, and then wanted more? Gods are no different than men; they are driven by the same appetites. In the beginning she hoped to feed off the coming chaos. It was enough for her. Now, this warrior, Leather Hand, has piqued her desires the way a lover seduces with a caress."

"What are you talking about?"

"Imperfections. Yours, mine, hers . . . this Leather Hand's." She seemed lost in thought as little whirlwinds of snow pirouetted around her head. "To save you I had to agree to her bargain."

"What bargain?"

"I get you—she gets Leather Hand."

"Leather Hand? I keep hearing his name. Morning Star said he'd eat my sisters."

"He is an abomination in human form." Her tongue whipped back and forth angrily. "The original plan was elegant—a means of putting the First People and the Flute Player in their place. It was a simple reordering, a way to give the katsinas and Made People their turn. Now Grandmother Spider Woman, too, wavers."

"That was Spider Woman? That hideous—"

"No, no. You've yet to meet her. Until recently, Spider Woman could have cared less, but nowadays the First People don't look up to her the way they used to. The Made People, however, still revere her, so freeing them of the First People's crushing heel had a certain appeal. But now, after Leather Hand's abominable acts, she, too, has begun to realize that events are spiraling out of control." A pause. "We may lose it all."

"Lose what?"

"Our world, Ripple. Gods, like humans, can grow obstinate, petty to the point they will destroy all they hold dear to make a point."

"So we should not destroy the First People?"

Her voice sounded sad. "It is too late for them. Their time is over. Soyok and I have made our bargain. We will act, no matter the consequences, or how frightened Spider Woman might be of what will come."

"What consequences?" Ripple asked.

"Chaos. For a time, Soyok and I shall reign supreme while the katsinas scramble to save themselves."

"Will they? In the end, I mean?"

Cold Bringing Woman shrugged. "Probably. They bring fire. I bring ice. Do not worry. You'll be long dead before the chaos sorts itself out."

"But, if the Flute Player and others are against you, how can you win?"

Her white face was featureless as she studied him. "I told you once: I'm so much older than the rest. Flute Player's Power is over the rain, his Blessing is fertility. His anger over the rising Power of the katsinas led him to stop the rains. Now, he sees the error of his ways. I can feel the shift, but in the end, it will avail him naught." She actually smiled. "Learn this lesson well: It is a fool who pushes a dangerous foe beyond tolerance."

"Do you call the Flute Player a fool?" The tug on his souls increased, as if more threads were pulling at him— and more amazing, an ember of warmth had kindled in his chest and seemed to be expanding.

"We are all fools at one time or another."

The pulling sensation grew stronger. He thought he heard chanting, very faint, rising and falling with the chill wind. "What's happening to me?"

"They are calling you back."

"Cold Bringing Woman, I have to ask. When you took me away from the darkness, I looked back. What I saw . . ."

"Yes, frightening, isn't she?"

"Who . . . ? What . . . ?"

"Don't let Soyok catch you again, Ripple. The next time I will not be able to save you."

The pull increased as delightful warmth crept along his bones. Ropes might have been fastened inside his chest. He felt his body slide on the snow, and cried, "No!"

"It is all right," Cold Bringing Woman assured him. "Let go, Ripple."

"I'm afraid!"

She leaned forward, her eyes expanding in the white-gray gloom. "Before you go, I want you to listen very carefully. A great many things will occur. You cannot doubt. Here are the things you must prepare yourself for. . ."

Ironwood's camp high on the mountain had disadvantages. The nearest source of water was a hand's time away by brisk walk. Exposed as it was to the west, the location suffered more than its share of blasting wind chill. The trails leading to it were difficult, and unless a traveler knew his destination, getting lost wasn't even the slightest challenge.

On the plus side, the little settlement was nearly impossible to find. The Blessed Sun's warriors would have had to literally stumble over it. But best of all, the trails were easily defended and enabled the detection of any approaching warriors. The promontory on which it rested had a remarkable view, providing a stunning vista of the basins and buttes in an arc from the west to the south. From this high location nearly half of the Straight Path Nation lay visible in the distance.

Just then Bad Cast had little interest in the Straight Path Nation. He was totally absorbed by the patterns he could see in the land. He had always been fascinated by the way mountains, ridges, and mesas fit together. From high points like this the underlying formations could be seen, sometimes traced for immense distances across the landscape. Bands of sandstone, limestone, and shale could be followed as they rose and fell, were interrupted by valleys and rivers, and then resumed in more distant hills.

His weren't the first pair of eyes to have distinguished the phenomenon. The layers that made up the world were important to the peoples who occupied the land. Tales of the first days when monsters broke and scarred the surface of the world were legion.

The First People took the notion so deeply to heart that they insisted on building their great houses as sacred representations of Mother Earth herself. As the world was made of discrete and often hidden layers, so, too, were their multistory buildings. Each of their gleaming plaster-coated palaces was constructed of layers of carefully fitted stone. In the construction of Dusk House alone it was said that the masons had the slaves haul in slabs of greenstone from a distant quarry more than four days' walk to the north. These carefully worked stones were used to create a band in the outer wall.

Every aspect of building the walls was a sacred reflection of the world around them. As the layers of stone that made up mountains, buttes, and ridges were cloaked with a skirt of soil, so were the walls of the sacred great houses covered with a clay plaster. A great house must be a precise representation of the physical world it re-created. The macrocosm recast in a single structure, and all under the dominion of the Powerful Matron the First People appointed to rule it. For that reason the Ant Clan masons wouldn't allow the use of other stone. At Flowing Waters Town they had *hauled away* readily available river cobbles from the construction.

Bad Cast cocked his jaw and considered the notion as he stared out over the broken buttes and mesas. How intricate it all was. No wonder the First People made so much of it. From heights like this one, he could feel the Power, the sense of majesty that rose from the very rock and soil. But if he could feel it with such great force, did that mean that only the First People deserved the right to partake of it? Were they truly better than he and his people, or the Made People, or even the lately lamented Dust People?

"It's a good place to come and think, isn't it?"

Bad Cast turned at the voice, surprised to find War

Chief Ironwood standing no more than an arm's length behind him.

"I'm sorry, War Chief, I didn't hear you approach."

"Good." The man smiled, the lines of his face deepening. "I try to keep my skills. With age it becomes an ever-more-challenging battle." He gestured with a scarred hand. "Tell me, what do you see?"

"I was studying the patterns in the rocks, seeing how the layers run through the land. I suppose I was trying to see through to Mother Earth's bones. Someone once said if you can see the bones, you can understand the beast."

"Grandmother Earth may not like to hear herself called a beast."

Bad Cast shook his head. "That wasn't what I meant."

Ironwood seated himself on one of the slabs of tilted sandstone that dotted the rim. There the wind tugged at his gray hair and ruffled his knee-length war shirt. He pulled up a knee and locked his arms around it. "I know. Besides, of all the forces that dominate our world, Grandmother Earth is the most forgiving. I think she has a kind sense of humor. The Powers that fill the sky, however—those you must be very careful of."

"The First People fear the wind, have given it a name, haven't they?"

Ironwood nodded. "They call it Wind Baby. A fickle Spirit Being who steals secrets and blows them to distant ears. He follows the rain, sucking the last drop of moisture from the cornfields before the plants can take their nourishment from it. Don't your people think of Wind Baby this way?"

"No. I suppose it's because we live in a mountain valley with a good river." He hesitated, awed by the presence of this man. "If I could ask, what do you see when you look out there?"

Ironwood turned his single eye to the distance. "I can pick out every ridge, every valley. I see places I have been, battles I have fought." He pointed to a distant butte. "I caught a party of Tower Builder raiders there at the north end. They had taken one of Night Sun's cousins captive.

The trick was to free her before the Tower Builders could kill her."

He pointed out toward Smoking Mirror Butte. "Up there, at the lookout, I spent the coldest night of my life. I was thirteen and wanted more than anything to be a warrior. It was the middle of winter, and Wind Baby was blowing snow across the lookout in a terrible howling. It blew our fire away. Not out, but away, if you can imagine. The warrior I was with froze his fingers. They turned black and fell off."

"How did you survive?"

"I sat on the warm rock where the fire had been." He smiled at the memory, then pointed south. "There, on that far rise, is Center Place, the navel of the Straight Path world. Have you ever been there?"

"No."

"It's a remarkable place. The Great North Road starts there, and uncounted thousands of dead souls have journeyed north on it, seeking the *sipapu* where they could descend into the Underworlds and find their ancestors. The first time I was put in charge of other warriors, I was responsible for the safety of the Priests and pilgrims that were constantly arriving and going. I first came in contact with Crow Beard there. We became fast friends."

"I thought that you and Crow Beard . . ." He winced, realizing what he'd almost said.

"It's all right," Ironwood replied softly. "When he married and was made the Blessed Sun it changed him. When I became his war chief, it changed me, too. Life, well lived, is a series of changes, young hunter. The person you were gives way to the person you will become, and he into yet someone else. The important thing is not to lose your humanity in the process."

"Did you?"

Ironwood's expression saddened. "Oh, yes. I became the Blessed Sun's weapon, wielded as he willed. My arrogance grew to match Crow Beard's own. I walked the land as a god, answerable only to my Blessed Sun. People feared my very name, and I marked my path with the blood of innocents and enemies alike. Anything I wanted,

I was given: clothing, jewelry, women, food, authority, and prestige. They were all mine."

Bad Cast saw remorse in the war chief's scarred face, could feel the pain in the man's souls. "What happened?"

"Everything comes at a price—and in the end you will pay it. At the height of my greatness, I had to live without the woman I loved. My daughter through her was raised by others, and we lived under the constant threat of exposure, death, and disgrace."

"But you have both of them now."

Ironwood gently said, "Look at me. Study me closely."

Bad Cast did, taking in the crisscrossing white scars, the cloth wrap that covered the man's missing eye, the scraggly gray hair and weather-worn skin. The lines in his face were the well-marked trails of pain, the hardness in the set of his mouth that of callused souls.

Ironwood spoke softly, his words mingling with the wind. "Back when I sat on the right hand of the Blessed Sun luxuries were showered upon me. Today I am hunted like a beast, a sentence of death laid upon me, my wife, and family. I live each breath knowing that at any moment we could be surprised and butchered by the Blessed Sun's warriors. Some of them were once good and close friends of mine. I have nothing but my name, my family, and what I wear. I lead a handful of fugitives who, for reasons of their own, have chosen to share my lot. I cherish every moment knowing that I could lose it all within a heartbeat."

"Then why do you care about Ripple's vision? Acting further against the Blessed Sun brings you to his attention."

"It does. But you have to understand my priorities. First is finding enough food for my family and people. Second is for the safety of my wife, daughter, grandchildren, and their children after them."

"You could leave, go south to Jay Bird's country, or even north to live among the Tower Builders."

He fixed his single eye on the distance, looking out across the broken mesas to the west. "Perhaps. Poor Singer and Nightshade, however, have assured me that my destiny lies here. I have a chance, hunter. One last chance to save our world. It comes at great risk, but Matron Night

Sun and I have discussed it. If we can do this thing, perhaps we can satisfy the gods and strengthen both the Straight Path Nation and the faith of the people. With the right leadership, I think it is possible to share authority with the Made People clans and the local populations."

"By making your daughter, Cornsilk, Matron of the First People?"

"Cornsilk tells me she would rather subsist for the rest of her life on roots, berries, and insects—live like a barbarian—than spend a single day as Matron of the Straight Path Nation. I respect her wishes; but Matron Night Sun and I also know that the Straight Path Nation is falling apart. Webworm is not the right man to be Blessed Sun in these dangerous times. Nor is Desert Willow the right woman to be Matron. Webworm is small of soul and imagination, best suited to carrying out the orders of others rather than giving them. And, talk about arrogance, Desert Willow lives, breathes, and devours it until its aroma even permeates her sweat. She has never traveled, never talked with a person outside her rank to do more than give an order. She knows only the company of other high-ranking First People; their views are as closed and bounded as the great house walls that surround them."

"I don't understand, War Chief. Why do anything to save the Straight Path Nation? Our people would love nothing better than to see the whole thing crumble like an unfired pot."

Ironwood's lips hardened. "The nation is an alliance that staves off chaos and war. You might curse the Blessed Sun and his warriors, but they keep the peace. You need not worry that one night your cornfields will be burned by foreign raiders. Farmers sleep peacefully in their isolated huts out in the country knowing that no one will sneak in during the night and crush their skulls for the corn in their granaries. Women know they can walk the trails without being raped and murdered by passing marauders." He made a plaintive gesture. "Do you see? If the Straight Path Nation fails, so does the peace."

"But it comes at a price."

Ironwood nodded. "Tell me, is the ability to sleep

through the night without worrying about raiders worth giving up part of your harvest every year?"

Bad Cast frowned as his eyes searched out the vast distance. "I don't think so, War Chief. My people fume under the First People's rule."

"As do others." He pursed his lips. "I would ask you to think about this: Before the coming of the First People's peace, people here only knew war and raiding. They lived in constant fear, and thought that was how life was. In the two hundred sun cycles since the First People's peace began, people have come to know security. Now, though they chafe at the First People's rule, they think that is how life is. Before they had peace, they could imagine no other way of living. Now, after the peace, they can imagine no other way of living. Do you see what I'm getting at?"

"That if war breaks out . . ." He couldn't finish the thought. Gods, it wouldn't go that far, would it?

Ironwood pointedly said, "The bones of my ancestors are here. My people are here. I would like my grandchildren to grow up knowing the things I have known. I don't want to see a rebirth of the world our ancestors lived in before the peace. I don't want our people to live like snarling wolf pups, raiding and killing. In that way lies disaster. It is time for new leaders."

"Did the Mountain Witch say who?"

"No, only that I am the means by which this change shall occur." A sadness filled his face. "But it shall cost me dearly."

"War Chief, leave!" Bad Cast cried. "Don't put yourself at more risk."

Ironwood smiled. "Why should you care?"

Yes, why? Bad Cast gestured his futility. "I don't know, except . . . except I think you're at heart a good man who has suffered too much in his life."

Ironwood had fixed his single eye on the distant horizon. "If it costs me only my life, it will be well worth the bargain."

Thirty-five

Webworm stood atop the highest roof in Dusk House and watched the smoke rise on the signal butte to the south. He shaded his eyes with the flat of his hand, smiling.

"It's from Far View," Desert Willow noted as the smoke rose in three long and two short puffs. She wore only a skirt belted at her slim waist; her skin shone in the sunlight, having been greased with some unguent thick with the smell of rose petals. He admired her firm breasts, wondering how long it had been since Wind Leaf had been working her brown nipples between his lips.

"A crisis in the Matron's household, no doubt." He turned his eyes back to the smoke. Yellow mixed with the white, symbolic of warning, but not alarm. "We can expect their runner in the next two days. I've been thinking of moving Larkspur from Pinnacle Great House to Far View. She's your cousin—what do you think?"

He was aware of her careful scrutiny as he watched the smoke.

"Do you know something I don't, Webworm?"

"Call it . . . a hunch."

Desert Willow took a deep breath before returning her attention to the smoke. "If this game you're playing is as dangerous as I think it is, don't you think you had better tell me about it?"

"A secret for a secret?"

"Yes, let's try that."

"Very well, you go first."

"I noticed that Creeper's young slave girl shared your bed last night. From the stories, she's very good. The secret I would learn is if she was better riding your shaft than I am."

He stopped short, considering. "A great deal better. She

practices, I'm told. Strengthening her grip. The sensations are truly remarkable. But . . ."

"Yes?"

"The poor girl doesn't have a brain in her head. My turn. Does Wind Leaf's brain, coupled with his brawn, make up for my lack of enthusiasm?"

She stood silently, her eyes on the smoke. Finally she said, "Sometimes."

"I'm glad you're careful."

"How is that?"

"You only allow him to share your bed for a short time before and after your moon. Perhaps you have more sense than Night Sun. She conceived, then had a child. Crow Beard, unlike me, would have killed her had he found out."

"You may not be Crow Beard, but neither am I Night Sun." Her voice was stiff.

He turned, facing her, and used his finger to lift her chin. Her eyes met his, black, defiant, unabashed. "Willow, I will tell you once: From now on, your sheath is for my staff, and mine alone. You won't like the consequences if I find out that another man is sliding his rod into you. Things are changing. Do not anger me."

Her eyes narrowed, and in the bright light, he could see her pupils expand against the brown irises. In a cold, precise voice, she said, "You serve at *my* pleasure, Webworm. *I* am Matron of the First People."

He released her chin, smiling. "Yes, and it would be a shame to have to replace you. So few of the First People remain." He glanced at the smoke again. "Apparently, fewer by the day."

With that he turned and walked to the ladder that led down to the fourth-floor rooms.

The farmstead consisted of two pit houses, a granary, and a series of corn and bean fields watered by a narrow and winding ditch. Spots and Nightshade had passed the first of the farmsteads earlier that morning. People had been moving ever higher up into the mountain valleys as the drought progressed. With each new farmstead they gambled a better chance of moisture against the probability of an early frost.

This small farm was located where the River of Souls Valley emptied from pine-covered hills to run between juniper-dotted mesas. Situated on the north bank it occupied three of the river terraces. Corn and bean plots had been hacked out of the sagebrush flats, the crops a vibrant green compared to the aqua of the sage. Four children had been packing jars of water to the higher plots, and now stopped to watch them. Splotched with dust and mud, they had large eyes, unruly thatches of black hair, and clutched the brownware vessels tight against their skinny chests.

"This is risky," Spots noted as he resettled the packs on his back. "Farms like this, all it takes is an early snow in the mountains, and the cold comes flowing down these valleys. They could lose all of this in an early frost."

Nightshade seemed not to hear; her eyes fixed on the mud-packed walls of the pit houses. A man emerged from the closest, took their measure, and waved in a friendly fashion. He called out in the Made People's tongue.

Nightshade answered and lifted her hand in reply. To Spots she said, "He offers us a meal and a place to stay."

Spots glanced at the shallow slant of sun as it kissed the western buttes. In less than a hand of time, it would be dark. "We're not going much farther before we have to camp."

Nightshade turned and followed the narrow trail that wound through the tall sage. That so much brush remained this close to the structures was evidence of how new the small farm was. In another couple of seasons this growth would all be chopped out for firewood.

As he came closer, Spots could see the fresh look of the square-topped pit houses. The beaten soil in the small plaza was only splotched with occasional stains of ash, and no trash pile could be seen out back.

Two brown dogs had been sleeping in the shade. They leapt to their feet, barking, growling, and wagging their tails. The farmer climbed out and leaped nimbly to the ground. He shouted at the dogs, flinging a piece of firewood to make his point. The thin-boned curs went silent, scuttling off to one side where they looked anxiously from Spots and Nightshade to the farmer. He came forward, hands offered in greeting.

A woman poked her head out the pit house smoke hole, muttered something under her breath, and ducked back inside.

Spots caught enough of the Made People words to understand that the man's name was Cricket, and his wife was called Seed. The children, meanwhile, came trotting in, calling to each other in excited voices. Smiles flashed white teeth behind their dirt-smudged faces.

These were people of the Coyote Clan, one of the larger Made People clans. Simple, but friendly, Seed insisted on grinding fresh flour made from her precious stock of blue corn kernels mixed with ricegrass, giant wild rye, and dried mariposa lily root. Her quick brown hands pounded out a thick flat cake onto which she spooned a concoction of mashed piñon nuts, cactus tuna jelly, and beeweed. Rolling these into cylinders, she placed them on a thin sandstone slab set deep in the coals of the outdoor fire pit.

Spots had found a seat with his back to the pit house wall. He sipped a cupful of serviceberry juice that Cricket had offered and watched the last flames of sunset fade from the sky. The fire crackled and reflected on the pit houses, turning them golden. The evening was cool, with a light breeze fingering the tips of the sagebrush as it rolled down the canyon. The river, several stone's throws distant, murmured softly, and the cottonwood leaves rattled.

"Pleasant, isn't it?" From where she sat on a blanket across the fire, Nightshade noted his smile. "Too bad it won't last."

"Too bad, indeed," Spots agreed, thinking about their destination.

"I didn't refer to that," Nightshade said absently, and returned to her discussion with Seed. Spots could catch enough of the Made People words to know they were talking about the Healing qualities of certain plants.

Cricket came and dropped into a squat beside Spots. He was an easygoing man, forever smiling. He had a blocky, muscular body and a guileless face. When he smiled, half his teeth were missing. Now his attention fixed on the four children: three boys and a girl. Ranging in age from four to perhaps ten summers, they giggled and shot sly glances at the visitors. They chased the happily barking dogs, then each other, tossed a hide-bound ball back and forth, and ended up in a wriggling mass of arms and legs as they started wrestling in the warm dust. The dogs leapt and barked, tails wagging at the melee.

"Is good," Cricket said, adding something in Made People tongue that Spots didn't catch.

"I'm sorry. I know very little of your speech."

"Ah," Cricket nodded. "Moon People." He pointed in the general direction of First Moon Mountain. "Good land. Water. Like here."

"Like here," Spots agreed, seeing little resemblance, but willing to be sociable.

Cricket watched his children, his satisfied smile even wider on his face. "First come here . . . spring." He made a circle with his finger to indicate the camp. "Work hard. Make good crops." He pointed to the green corn. It reflected blackly in the deepening night. A bat whispered past the man's head, swooping up some of the mosquitoes that had come to bother them. "Make new home."

"From where?" Spots asked.

"South." He made an arching gesture with his arm, adding words Spots didn't understand.

"Long way?" Spots guessed.

"Yes, long." Cricket sighed with apparent relief. "Good here. No starve this winter." He pointed to the granary. "Store much." He looked to Spots for affirmation. "Good. Very, very good."

Spots nodded. Cricket was right. Here he was at the edge of his known world, with a rich farm, four healthy children, and a happy wife. If they had come in spring, they had indeed worked hard to have cleared the farm plots, built two pit houses, the granary, and cut the ditches.

Spots wondered, "How much tribute you pay?"

Cricket's gaze shifted evasively. He made the circle with his finger, wider this time. "No great house here." Then he grinned shyly. "Not like old place."

Spots bobbed his head in assent. No great house. For Cricket and Seed this upper valley must have seemed like a fantasy come true.

A sparkle lit Cricket's eye as he watched his children playing. "You have?"

"No. Not yet." Spots shook his head. "Soon." And he wondered about that. With his world suddenly turned upside down, the chances for a happy family weren't looking any too good. He glanced warily at Nightshade, and a shiver skipped over his skin. The old woman looked and acted just like a normal grandmother. These poor people had no idea she was the Mountain Witch.

"Good children," Cricket maintained. "You may be so lucky?"

"I may be." A sad smile. "One day. Perhaps." And he couldn't help but envy Cricket and Seed and their little family. They were perched precariously at the edge of a world about to go mad, and they were so content and happy just to have their lives to themselves.

After supper he and Nightshade laid their bedrolls out at the edge of the clearing. His dreams that night were plagued by images of a pretty wife who smiled at him, of children playing, laughing, and wrestling. Only when he looked closely did he notice that neither his wife nor children had more than blurs for faces.

The next morning, after breakfast, Spots shouldered the packs. He and Nightshade waved farewells and turned their feet to the trail that led into the widening valley.

A short time later, he gave Nightshade a sidelong look. "Do you think we should have said something, warned them about what is coming?"

"No." Nightshade seemed sad. "What is a single grain of sand in the desert?"

"Elder, these are people! Not grains of sand."

Her eyes were holes into nothingness. "None of us is more than a grain of sand, hunter."

"How can you say that? You, who are one of the most Powerful women in the world, should know better!"

"*You?* Would tell me?" She gave him a hot glare that melted his bones.

"I'm sorry, Elder. Forgive me."

As quickly, the anger faded, replaced by a weary smile. "You are young. I keep forgetting. By the time I was your age . . . well, I was burying my first husband and Dreaming a mighty sun chief's death. Dancing between the worlds leaves little room for illusions. But pity not those farmers back there. In the end they are the ones who are free."

"How can you say that?"

She walked in silence for a while, eyes on the rimrock that lined the mesas above them. "Do you think Webworm has more freedom than that man Cricket has?"

"Of course. He is the Blessed Sun. He can go where he will, order what he wishes."

"And me? What did you call me? One of the most Powerful women in the world?"

"Elder, you need but command, and people will obey you."

"You think obedience is freedom?"

"No. I meant that a person has a choice."

Wry lines formed around her mouth. "Ah, so you actually believe that I have a choice about traveling to Flowing Waters Town? You think that I could sidestep the destiny that Power has woven into my future?"

Spots gestured back up the valley. "We could just turn around, Elder. Go the other direction."

"You would accompany me?" she asked. "You will go with me to the Great River Valley? Perhaps follow it down to the saltwater gulf? Will you spend the rest of your life with me there, making a living on the beaches, weaving tight green mats from palmettos and boiling cactus tunas?"

He gave her dumbfounded look.

"I thought not." She led the way to the top of a small knoll. From that vantage, they could see a broad bend of the River of Souls. The floodplain was dotted with little patches of green. Here and there, pit houses rose from the trampled sage. She slowed, considering the number of scattered farms.

"Like your friend Cricket, these, too, shall perish," she said sadly. "Only a few will have the courage to reach out, seize the bars, and pull them wide enough to slip out of the trap."

"Elder, we're not talking about the end of the world. Cold Bringing Woman's vision was just the destruction of the First People."

She waved her arm to include the fertile valley with its irregular pattern of farms, pit houses, and granaries. "Look well upon them, Spots. Engrave this vision upon your souls. What you see is about to pass. The storm is brewing, and all this will be swept away. Here are your grains of sand, about to be uprooted and blown hither and yon, most of them never to be seen again."

"And you?" Spots asked.

At that moment, a small whirlwind came skipping down the valley slope. It roared past, whipping the sagebrush and rabbitbrush, and flicked up dust and bits of detritus. Spots ducked away from it, squinting against the flying grit. As it went dancing down the trail behind them, he swore he could see something within it. A massive round head—its face pink like the color of the Sacred Lake—topped a figure that seemed to twirl in the dust devil, rising high and ducking down like a weasel chasing its tail. Then it was gone.

He glanced at Nightshade, her gaze fixed on the vanishing apparition.

She said, "I was chosen for this destiny long ago, hunter."

Thirty-six

The feeling of warmth grew as Ripple was pulled through a fog of gray. He could feel himself traveling, almost flying through the nothingness. The force of it was inexorable, like being at the end of a long cord that was relentlessly wound in by a strong man.

Moment by moment, the warmth grew. He could feel the cold-numbing ache melt in his bones, and sighed with relief as his flesh turned rosy, his blood spurting in every artery and vein. Yes! He lived!

The heat increased until he shifted uncomfortably. Something seemed to bind him, restricting his ability to move. Panting, cool air rushed into his lungs. Trickles of sweat began to bead on his skin; thirst pulled at his tongue.

"He's coming," a voice whispered.

Ripple moaned, then felt a cup placed to his parched lips. The delight of cool water slipped around his dry mouth. Greedily he drank, sucking great gulps of water down.

"Easy," a voice cautioned. "You don't want to choke."

Ripple laid his head back as the cup was withdrawn. Swallowing, his tongue prodded the wreckage in his mouth, explored the missing teeth on the left side of his jaw. The dull ache of pain shot up from his mangled hand as he tried to flex his fingers.

"You are safe," the calm voice told him. "You are among friends, Ripple."

He couldn't place the accent, but knew it wasn't any he'd heard before. Blinking, he realized a whitish film covered his eyes.

"Your souls have been traveling," the voice told him. "It will take a moment for them to remember your body. It is an old friend, a very comfortable and familiar home. Trust me, they will settle in very soon."

A damp cloth was placed on his eyes, rubbed gently, and lifted. He squeezed them shut, blinked, and was able to finally make out the fuzzy image of the woman who bent over him. Above her head, he could barely discern shredded juniper bark roofing behind the parallel poles.

"Where am I?"

"Safe. This place is Ironwood's camp." The woman wrung out the wet cloth and sponged his forehead.

"Hot," he said as he panted for air.

"Let's remove the stones." The woman bent over him, and as she did a thin, narrow-faced man leaned into Ripple's blurred vision. Together they unwound a thick buffalo robe, and from it, took what appeared to be hot stones wrapped in coarse cloth.

"We were worried that you wouldn't return," the man said with a smile. When he leaned close he had large, gentle eyes. "We think you were with Cold Bringing Woman."

"Yes." A sense of desolation grew under his heart. "She told me things."

The woman studied him thoughtfully. "Not everyone has such a close relationship with the gods."

He pressed his good hand to his eyes, rubbed them, and blinked, his vision clearing. Thank the gods, he wasn't blind, just . . . He gaped, seeing her: the wife from his Dream visions. He took a breath, ready to call out to her. But no recognition lay behind her eyes.

"No," Ripple answered, remembering the choice he'd made. Seeing that other future unfold in his head. "No one would want to."

The young man nodded, understanding in his thoughtful eyes. "I am called Poor Singer. This woman is known as Orenda. You are among friends, here, Ripple. Is there anything you need?"

Orenda. Her name is Orenda.

"More water." As they helped him to sit up, his stomach gurgled. "And food?"

"Of course." Orenda turned. "And while I'm at it, I'll

inform your friend Bad Cast that your souls have returned. He's been worried about you."

"Bad Cast? He's here?" He tried to organize his jumbled thoughts.

"He has come by every hand of time to check on you." Orenda smiled and ducked out a flap-covered doorway.

"Bad Cast is a good friend," Poor Singer added. "He helped us know which way to go in the Spirit World to search for you."

"I'm not sure I should have come back."

"I know."

Ripple frowned. "You do?"

Poor Singer studied his thin hands as he flexed his fingers. The way the tendons moved behind the smooth skin seemed to fascinate him. "The ways of Power are not for the timid of heart or soul. It's nothing like the Priests say it is, is it? That's one of the more amusing ironies."

Her name is Orenda. She could have been my wife. Mother of my children.

Ripple nodded weakly. He was just beginning to understand the import and ramifications of what Cold Bringing Woman had whispered to him. Fire and ice. A lonely sense of desolation hollowed his heart. *Orenda. Children. Grandchildren. All that could be.* "They have no idea of the price."

"No," Poor Singer said wistfully. "Neither the price, nor the pain."

Ripple swallowed hard, closing his eyes. "You don't understand what this will cost."

In a hollow voice, Poor Singer answered, "Unfortunately . . . I do."

"Then I have a message for you. And . . . and then I must see the war chief."

Wrapped Wrist winced as he climbed the last steep slope onto the mesa top. The way wound around ponderosa, juniper, and piñon pine. Loose yellow-white soil slipped under his yucca trail sandals, dust rising to coat his legs. The air was redolent with pine and the scent of dry earth. Grasshoppers clicked as they rose and fell on sun-shining wings. A jay rasped in annoyance, and a tuft-eared squirrel seemed to flow along an overhead branch like an undulating wave.

Crow Woman was gasping as she climbed around a tumbled square of sandstone that had cracked off the rim. The stone was taller than she was. Lichens decorated it in patterns of orange, blue, and black.

"Who comes?" a voice asked from above.

"Crow Woman, you blind wretch," she called up the slope. "And with me is Wrapped Wrist."

"Welcome home."

Wrapped Wrist paused to stare up the slope, seeing the man where he poked his head out past the high rimrock. He held a bow in one hand, several arrows in the other. From that vantage he could have skewered as many enemies as he had arrows before they could climb the narrow trail to the rim.

Crow Woman wasted no more effort on the guard as they continued the climb. Here footholds had been pecked into the exposed sandstone. One by one, Wrapped Wrist made his way up. Despite his fatigue, it was well worth it to watch Crow Woman's fine legs, muscles sliding under smooth, if dusty, skin. Her hips swayed with each step she made, swishing the war shirt in a most enticing way. That her waist was so narrow only added to the effect.

For the moment, Wrapped Wrist could almost forget his fatigue. He was grinning as he followed her through a gap in the rock and onto the mesa top.

She was panting, her breasts rising and falling as she took a moment to look around. The guard had reseated himself under a small shelter of pine boughs. "See anything out there?"

"No. Only the tracks of some hunters from down south," she told him before turning to follow a faint trail in the pine duff.

Wrapped Wrist walked by her side, the way winding among the ponderosas. "How far?"

"Not more than a finger's time now." She gave him a measuring sidelong glance. "You did all right."

She couldn't feel the exhaustion in his legs, feet, and back. "So did you."

She only grunted in response.

"Is it just me, or do you hate all men?" he asked.

For a long time she was silent, then asked, "Tell me, do men think of nothing but coupling with a woman? Is that the only notion wedged down between your souls?"

He kicked a pinecone, watching it bounce and curve off across the gray-brown mat of needles. "Actually, there's lots more stuff 'wedged in there,' as you would say. There's vanity, status, prestige, envy, fear, and uncertainty."

"That's unusual honesty to hear from a man."

"I'm an unusual man." He paused. "I noticed how you looked at Whistle that night. Did he try to lay with you?"

"Once." After a moment she looked at him curiously. "So, why haven't you tried?"

"Because you scare me half to death."

"Good."

"A man did something pretty terrible to you. What was it?"

Her only response was a glare.

As they traveled in silence, Wrapped Wrist began noticing scars where people had broken dead branches off the bottoms of the pines. Sticks and twigs had vanished from the forest floor, and the trail was more distinct.

"We're getting close," he guessed.

"In answer to your question, it wasn't a man," she said shortly. "It was men."

"Surely you've known a couple of good men thrown in with all of us bad ones."

She jerked a nod. "There's the war chief."

"And who else?"

"I said: There's the war chief."

"Just one? Out of all the men you've met?"

"Tells you something about men, doesn't it?"

At that moment a youth peered out from behind a tree trunk. He turned, running like a rabbit, weaving in and out of the ponderosa as he zipped away.

Within moments Wrapped Wrist made out the first of the structures. Two women stood, baskets in hand, looking in their direction.

"We've made it," Crow Woman told him. "Go find your friends. I must see the war chief."

Wrapped Wrist made his way through the camp, nodding to women and children, who nodded back. Most of the men he remembered from the camp at the hot springs. They waved, questions in their hooded gazes as they glanced first at Crow Woman where she stood talking to Ironwood and then back at Wrapped Wrist.

Probably wondering how I managed to keep my balls intact.

"Wrapped Wrist!"

He turned, seeing Bad Cast, a smile on his face as he hurried across the camp.

Bad Cast called, "Your timing is perfect. Ripple's awake." He gestured toward Crow Woman. "And I see that you've come back with the most beautiful woman in camp. I supposed you lingered in the robes like usual."

"Not with that one, old friend. Something's bent in her souls. If she offered herself, it would scare the wood right out of my shaft. You've heard the story told about the Stone Desert People?"

"The one about their women having teeth in their sheaths?"

Wrapped Wrist pointed at Crow Woman. "If ever a sheath had teeth, it would be hers."

"Sounds nasty."

"What's the news?" Wrapped Wrist embraced his kinsman.

Bad Cast's smile dropped the slightest bit. "Scary times. The Mountain Witch took Spots."

"She what?"

"Took him. Told him to carry her things and started off for Flowing Waters Town."

"To do what?"

"How should I know? Witches don't usually tell me things. But from what I can gather talking to people here, she didn't tell them, either. I get the impression that she pretty much does as she wants." He arched his eyebrow. "Would you want to question her?"

"I've never even seen her."

"Trust me, you don't want to. Spots said she was the scariest woman he's ever known."

Wrapped Wrist pointed at Crow Woman. "He's never met *that* one."

Bad Cast grasped his elbow. "Did you see Soft Cloth? What's the news from home?"

"I saw no one but White Eye." He lowered his voice. "Ironwood is brokering an alliance with White Eye to attack the First People during the Moon Ceremony."

"I know." Bad Cast led him to one of the stone-and-wattle buildings back in the trees. A dark-eyed woman with gleaming black hair sat outside the door, her long fingers weaving a basket from sumac and yucca. In the bottom was a pattern the likes of which Wrapped Wrist had never seen.

When the woman looked up at him, it was as if her eyes could see straight through him. But for those haunted eyes, he would have thought her charming.

"Be there for her," the woman said in an accented tongue. "She will need you."

"What?" Wrapped Wrist asked. "Who?"

The woman had returned her attention to the basket as if he'd never existed. As she turned the basket, he could see the design in the bottom: some sort of combination of man, snake, and bird. The very sight of it brought a shiver to his spine.

He ducked in behind Bad Cast, blinking in the dim light. It took a moment for his eyes to adjust. He squatted next to a pallet where Ripple lay.

His friend looked pale, the left side of his jaw still swollen, his hand bound in splints. Ripple's eyes, however, were clear, deep and wide, as if having seen the other side of the world's souls.

"How are you?" Bad Cast asked.

"Sore," Ripple said with a slur. "My body hurts, but nothing like my souls do."

"Why is that?" Wrapped Wrist asked.

Ripple whispered, "I've seen things. Been told things. Where is the war chief? I must see him. I have a message. . . ."

"They've sent for him," Bad Cast said gently. "He's on the way."

"Seen what?" Wrapped Wrist asked.

"I didn't know who she was at first."

"Cold Bringing Woman?" Wrapped Wrist asked. "You mean your vision on the mountain wasn't—"

Ripple reached up with his right hand, gripping Wrapped Wrist's arm. "Soyok! She was carrying me away when Cold Bringing Woman came and took me back."

"Who? Who's Soyok?" Bad Cast looked confused.

"That's her Spirit name," Ripple whispered, looking away. "We know her as the Blue God." He shook his head. "Odd that I didn't recognize her."

Bad Cast cried, "You *saw* the Blue God?"

Ripple nodded. "If Cold Bringing Woman hadn't found me . . . Gods, I hate to think about it. As it is, I've changed things. My fault. A new bargain has been struck. I have to see the war chief. Where is he?"

"He's talking to Crow Woman about attacking Pinnacle Great House," Wrapped Wrist told him.

"I *must* see him. A weasel creeps in our midst. I have to make sure he doesn't waver. He has to believe . . . it's just my word."

Wrapped Wrist asked, "What are you talking about?"

"Fire and ice," Ripple said numbly. "Opposites crossed. Black flakes of snow . . . falling from a gray sky."

"Black flakes of snow?" Wrapped Wrist glanced uneasily at Bad Cast.

Bad Cast muttered, "He's still delirious."

"He's speaking plainly," the woman at the door called, her basket still in hand. "It is your hearing that is confused. The gods have chosen you. It is through your eyes that the story shall be told."

"Does that mean we're somehow special?" Bad Cast asked skeptically.

"No," Ripple rasped. "We are cursed."

The scream sounded so close, as if someone in abject terror were just above Spots's head.

He bolted upright in the night, a cry stifled in his panicked throat.

The thin blanket fell away to leave him gaping in the darkness. He blinked, staring up at the sky. Spider Woman's constellation was just rising, telling him that it was still several hands of time before dawn. In the stillness of the night, crickets chirped, a distant owl hooted, and a slight breeze stirred.

He rubbed a callused hand over his face and stared around. Their camp sat atop a low saddle ridge that separated the River of Souls from Spirit River. The pale loamy soil was dotted by inky blotches of juniper. Even in the faint light, he could see well enough to determine that no one was close. So where had the scream . . .

He squinted at the Spirit bag Nightshade had given him to carry. It lay just an arm's length beyond his head. Far enough away to dim the whispers and mute the wailings.

"Gods, what's in there?"

"Things you don't want to know." Nightshade's voice was little more than a sibilant whisper. "Heard that, did you?"

"The scream?" He looked this way and that, finally seeing her, her form hidden in the shadow of a sandstone boulder. She was sitting with her back straight, legs crossed; her hands lay on her knees, palms up. Even in the night, he could see her wide-open eyes, feel her presence rasping against his souls.

"Soyok prowls the night."

"Who?"

"You know her as the Blue God. She has run amok through the thlatsinas, sending them scampering among the clouds. They have taken refuge on their mountain."

"The one that used to be called the Rain Spinner?"

"Sternlight renamed it for the thlatsinas," she said

softly. "Names, like all things, have their times. Rain Spinner is gone."

"But the mountain remains."

"Did you think it odd that the Rainbow Serpent rose at the foot of the Thlatsina Mountains?"

"I, uh . . ."

"The Spirits of the sky are joining with those of the ground." A pause. "Your friend, Ripple, has returned."

"Returned? From where?" Gods, what was she talking about? The subject of conversation seemed to dart around like a water skipper on a still pond.

"Soyok almost had him. Horo Mana saved him."

"The Blue God almost caught Ripple?" Who in the name of the sage was Horo Mana?

Nightshade whispered, "Opposites crossed. We shall see them Dance together across the sky."

"You talk in riddles! Where did that scream come from? I'd swear it was from the bag." He pointed at the dim shape.

"It came from a place you don't wish to travel to."

He stared first at her and then at the worrisome bag where it lay on the pale soil. She was right: He didn't want anything more to do with the thing. But for his intense fear of her, he might have just sneaked away in the night to be rid of both of them.

"You'd not get far," she told him. "They have latched their claws into the margins of your souls. The Dreams would pull you back."

"Get out of my head!" He placed his hands against his ears, flopping down in the bedding and pulling his blanket over his head. There he lay panting, smelling the warm mustiness of his blanket, eyes pressed closed.

*T*he hunter is cowering, trying to close his souls to the calls and questions of the Spirits. I suppose I could speak to him as a mother does to her child, tell him of the things

I have seen while in the arms of Sister Datura. I could tell him of the new bargain sealed by Soyok and Horo Mana. Could he withstand the knowledge, or would it send him shrieking away in the night to escape the future that continues to wrap around us?

Do I do him any favors?

I sense Brother Mud Head as he Dances around our small camp. I can feel his heavy tread, a weightless tremor that puffs dust around his bare feet. The time is coming near. He revels in the knowledge that soon we shall both be free.

It is only a matter of time until all the players are in their proper position. When the last of them is in place, the end will be irrevocable.

How do I tell Spots that the scream he heard was mine?

Thirty-seven

"Let me see." Webworm leaned forward to stare at the cloth bundle Leather Hand laid upon the great kiva floor. The room was cool, dimly lit by the shaft of sunlight that streamed through the smoke hole. It shone in a square centered on the *sipapu*. The symbolic entrance to the Underworlds was dug into the floor in front of the decorated screens that masked the northern entrance.

On this day Webworm wore the most extraordinary bright blue shirt dyed from a thousand larkspur petals. He had used mourning dove grease in his hair and pulled the shining warrior's bun tight at the back of his head, sticking three eagle feathers into it.

Leather Hand crouched, untying a yucca cord that bound the cloth and unfolding the layers. The innermost were caked and blackened with old blood. With a hard tug he freed the last wrapping from the shrunken flesh.

Webworm bent, unconcerned with the ripe odor rising from the old woman's head. Her features had been mashed by the cloth, the nose bent, lips twisted and pushed out of shape. The eyes had sunk deep into the skull, and streaks of gray could be seen in her matted hair.

"Greetings, Matron," Webworm said. "Far View is in turmoil wondering where your head has gotten off to. They're running around like turkeys in a cougar's shadow, not knowing which way to turn, let alone what happened."

Leather Hand stepped back, crossing his arms. "It wasn't any trouble, Blessed Sun. The few guards she had on duty were expecting nothing. Slipping past them was child's play."

Webworm reached out, shoving White Cloud Woman's head with his toe. The gruesome orb rocked back and forth like a macabre child's toy. "What of her daughter, Three Corn?"

"I whispered at her doorway that it might be better for her health if she were to leave Far View and never come back."

"Do you think she will?"

Leather Hand shrugged. "The people there, of course, will beg for her to take her mother's place as Matron."

"If they do, and if she becomes, shall we say, recalcitrant, can you repeat this triumph?" Webworm indicated the pathetic head.

"I have my ways of getting around Far View."

"You're sure that no one saw you?"

"Only one person, Blessed Sun. And I trust him implicitly."

"Implicitly?"

"Should I discover that he has betrayed me in any way, I'll have his head for my own."

Webworm stared at the grisly trophy, lost in thought. "Take it away. Bury it where no one will ever find it. Oh, and be sure that you smash it first. Preferably with a very large and heavy rock."

"Yes, Blessed Sun."

"Then I want you back here. Blue Racer arrives later tonight. I will meet with him here, tomorrow morning. I would have you present."

"Yes, Blessed Sun."

Webworm turned, then looked back, admiring the pristine white moccasins on Leather Hand's feet. "Those are very nice."

"A gift from the late Matron." Leather Hand bent down and began replacing the cloth around the head. "Something to remember her by."

Webworm smiled as he turned away. "Memories are such sweet treats, aren't they?"

At that moment Ravengrass descended partway down the steps. "Blessed Sun? A runner has arrived from Matron Larkspur. He has urgent news for you."

Webworm nodded. "Deputy, depending on what this is, I may want your input."

A long moment passed after Webworm and Leather Hand's steps faded. Finally the silence was broken when a sigh was uttered from behind the decorated screen. The Buffalo Clan elder, Creeper, stepped out from where he'd been hidden; a Dance mask he'd been repairing was still clutched in his pudgy hands.

He stared at the few dark spots of blood that had leaked onto the floor.

"Blessed Featherstone," he whispered, "what has become of the man we used to love?"

Thirty-eight

Clouds had rolled in from the southwest. In silence Bad Cast and Wrapped Wrist watched them from the high mesa promontory. In contrast to the First People's belief that Flute Player brought the rains, Sternlight had preached that the thlatsinas Danced them from the Cloud People.

Bad Cast rubbed his chin. He wished for rain, a gentle shower that would wash the premonition of disaster from their world. Rain, however, never came.

Could it be that the Cloud People were so disgusted by the strife between Flute Player and the katsinas that they brought rain for neither?

Or was it something else? Was it that neither the Flute Player nor the katsinas called out to the Cloud People for fear that the rival would be given credit for any beneficent rainfall? Either way, most of the crops were gone in the dryland farms. The question was, could the irrigated valleys produce enough to feed the hungering masses?

Bad Cast and Wrapped Wrist walked to the open space that served as a plaza for the little settlement. People kept looking up at the gray skies, turning their cheeks to the hot dry wind, and wondering if rain would follow.

Gods, how they all missed it. Around him, the forest was dry, the duff crackling underfoot. When he plucked living ponderosa needles and bent them between his fingers, they barely bruised, so dry were they.

Overhead, the dark clouds seemed to brood, and distant thunder carried on the pregnant air.

"What do you think?" Wrapped Wrist asked as he matched step.

"I don't know. It should rain. It's the season for it."

"It's been the season for it for the last two moons!" Wrapped Wrist gestured futilely. "And what have we gotten? Blue skies."

"Drought skies," Bad Cast corrected. "Pale and white around the horizons. I heard a joke today. Poor Singer said he appreciated the drought."

"How's that?"

"He said that with all the grass gone, he could see the rattlesnakes coming."

"He worries about rattlesnakes?"

"Not anymore. He says he can see their canteens sticking through the dust before they crawl close enough to bite him."

Wrapped Wrist frowned. "A holy man should know that rattlesnakes don't have shoulders."

"What do shoulders have to do with it?"

"Without shoulders what keeps the canteen from sliding off the snake?"

They had reached the outskirts of the fire. People sat in a ring around the blaze, turning their eyes to the trees where Ironwood, Night Sun, Poor Singer, and Cornsilk were talking. The war chief had called this meeting no more than a finger's time after he'd left Ripple's bedside.

As the gloom deepened, Bad Cast could see lightning flickering among the high peaks to the north. The wind teased them as it alternately puffed and died, as if trying to make up its mind whether or not to blow.

Most of Ironwood's warriors were present: Yucca Sock, Crow Woman, Firehorn, Right Hand, and Whistle among others.

Bad Cast noticed that Wrapped Wrist had fixed his gaze on Crow Woman. Seated, she had laced her arms around her slim legs and was talking to Yucca Sock. A glittering hardness lay behind her eyes, something sharp and cutting. From the pinching of Wrapped Wrist's mouth, the faint lines on his brow, Bad Cast knew his friend was puzzled.

"I thought you didn't like her."

"I don't. Pus and blood. What a waste. Two bent and wounded souls, captive to that entrancing body."

Bad Cast noticed that Whistle, too, was watching her from his place across the circle. His intent stare indicated a shared obsession with the woman.

At that moment Ironwood turned, leading his small party to the open circle. He and Night Sun remained standing while Poor Singer and Cornsilk seated themselves.

Ironwood looked around the ring of faces, nodding to some, smiling at others. Bad Cast could see the strain behind his expression, knew that his souls were screaming at him, tearing with fear and uncertainty. The war chief might have been stone for all he betrayed of the turmoil within.

Ironwood cleared his throat and began, "Many of you know that something is happening. We have initiated contact with the Moon People. Soon the Sunwatcher, Blue Racer, will be journeying to First Moon Mountain to welcome Sister Moon home from her passage across the sky. Webworm and Desert Willow may even accompany him for the opening ceremony. We will never have another opportunity like this to strike at the very heart of the First People."

Night Sun stepped forward. Firelight was shining in her silvered hair. She wore a black dress decorated with four-pointed white stars. "For the first couple of days after the First People reach Pinnacle House they will be wary, alert for any sign of trouble. We will wait until they grow careless. As soon as their guard drops, we will be in position to strike."

Ironwood continued, "A great many pilgrims have already begun leaving their homes, journeying northward. These people—many of them desperate because of the drought—hope to see the miracle of Sister Moon returning home after her eighteen-and-a-half-summer journey. They want to see her when she rises at the same place for days on end—right between the pillars of First Moon Mountain."

Night Sun raised her hands in supplication. "The pilgrims serve us well. With so many people flooding into First Moon Valley, we can move with ease, hide among them."

Ironwood thrust his thumbs into his belt. "The trouble, of course, is that many of us once served the Blessed Sun. Our faces are known. Beyond that, the approaches to First Moon Mountain will be well guarded." A pause. "But there are other ways. Back ways. Trails that only the First Moon People know."

Night Sun continued. "If we are to take Pinnacle Great House from the First People, it will be through stealth and audacity."

As if in emphasis, distant thunder rolled across the mesa tops.

"I suppose that's where we come in," Wrapped Wrist muttered.

Night Sun raised her hands even higher. "You should know this, too. We have recently received word that Matron White Cloud Woman was murdered in her bed. The assassin cut her throat, removed her head, and left her corpse lying in its blood. Although guards were posted, no one knew anything was amiss until late the next morning."

"Tower Builders?" Crow Woman asked.

"They would have been spotted," Whistle interjected. "Someone would have seen the strangers. An alarm would have been raised. Her guards—who were loyal kinsmen— heard nothing."

"Clan feud?" Yucca Sock speculated.

Ironwood shook his head. "Unlikely. None of White Cloud Woman's rivals claim credit—even those happy to have her gone. Word is that in Far View it's a great mystery, and there is considerable unease at the manner of it."

Night Sun had been watching the fire with pensive eyes. "We must accept that this might be an extremely adept move by one of her enemies. White Cloud Woman was a forceful critic of Webworm's policies. As long as confusion reigns in Far View Town, Blue Dragonfly Clan stands to gain."

"Was anything taken?" Whistle asked.

"From what we hear," Ironwood replied, "only a pair of white moccasins that she was working on. The assassin left nothing of his own behind. The stories circulating around Far View claim that a witch flew in on a rawhide shield, cut off the Matron's head, and flew back out again."

"So we're to be on the lookout for a witch wearing white moccasins?" Crow Woman asked. "We do see a lot of them flying around here."

A chorus of chuckles rose from the circle.

Ironwood grinned. "If any witch wearing white moccasins flies close, you're welcome to shoot him down. Just be sure he's within bow range."

Crow Woman extended her left arm, drawing back her right, and mimicked loosing an arrow at the cloud-black sky.

It was at that point that Ironwood looked straight at Bad Cast and asked, "Hunter, what are the chances that White Eye can build an alliance among your clans to attack the First People?"

Bad Cast shot a worried glance at Wrapped Wrist as all eyes turned upon him. "I—I don't know." He swallowed hard, suddenly flustered. "We're not warriors. I mean some of the elders, Green Claw and Black Sage, won't want to. They would much rather pacify the First People. Others, like Hoarse Caller, will probably vote for it. It's hard to say, War Chief. My people have never been asked this before."

Night Sun was giving him a thorough appraisal. "Let me ask you this: If the clans do vote to attack the First People, what are the chances that someone will betray us to Matron Larkspur?"

"If you wish to defeat the First People on First Moon Mountain, you will do as I say," Ripple insisted as he walked out of the night and entered the firelight. He looked around, eyes like crystals. "Cold Bringing Woman has told me how this can be done, War Chief. You must place your trust in me, and in your warriors here. Can you do that?"

Night Sun's quick eyes took in Ripple's worn hunting shirt, the garment apparently donated by someone. Her gaze lingered on his maimed hand in its splints and his swollen jaw. "What do you have to tell us, Dreamer?"

Dreamer? The words caught Bad Cast by surprise.

Ripple turned to Ironwood. "What is coming will demand a terrible price. We stand on the threshold. I have seen." He walked up to the war chief, firelight casting his body in bronze. His crushed hand was held before his chest. "I have looked into the face of the Blue God. She taught me terror and revulsion. Now, she is loose on the land."

"What would you have me do?" Ironwood asked.

"Are you willing to take one extraordinary chance to save your world?"

Ironwood narrowed his eye, glanced uneasily at Night Sun, and said, "I am, Dreamer."

Ripple's lips twitched as if the words elicited some painful memory. "Are you willing to pay what the gods demand?"

Ironwood's expression lined, pulling the patch taut over

his missing eye. "I cannot give you an answer until I know more about what you've seen, Dreamer."

In a hollow voice, he said, "I have seen you standing atop Pinnacle Great House, War Chief. Your body is bowed, the shape of it illuminated as the morning light shines through the great stone pillars. In that vision, you are victorious. But it comes at a terrible cost to you."

Ironwood stiffened. "If you have seen this, and know the way of it, I will pay that cost."

For a long moment Ripple watched Ironwood, and sadly shook his head. Then he said, "Your allies are fire and ice. Send word now. Tell White Eye that only the strongest threads of silk tether the web. If he would see the First People fall, he must call the elders to council. Spider Woman wants all of the flies in the web before we strike."

"Fire and ice?" Whistle asked. "Webs, silk, flies? What is this?"

Ripple looked to the heavens; flashes of heat lightning silently lanced the clouds. "The fire is loosened; flames rise high. The Dance is begun. In days drawing nigh, a web is spun. Sister Moon is caped, veiled, and hidden beneath a midnight cloak. Strike, great War Chief. And furl the frozen smoke."

Then he turned his gaze on Night Sun. She gasped at something deep in his expression and placed a hand to her chest.

Ripple gave her a respectful nod, turned, and walked back into the darkness.

Ironwood looked pensive as he fingered his chin. "What do you think, wife?"

Night Sun's eyes were like hollows in her face. "Is he another Sternlight? Perhaps a Dune? I don't know what to think or whom to trust."

"I do." It was Poor Singer who stood. "A messenger must be sent to White Eye. If this web is to be spun, it must be done as Ripple says." He studied Ironwood with sober eyes. "War Chief? Are you ready to pay the price?"

Ironwood's cheek muscles bunched. In a soft voice he said, "Yes. Of course."

Poor Singer glanced meaningfully at Cornsilk. "If that is your decision, Cornsilk and I must pack. Our destiny lies in the south among my mother's people."

"Are they involved?" Night Sun asked, placing a thin hand on his shoulder.

Poor Singer took her hand from his shoulder, raised it to his lips, and looked into her eyes as he kissed it. "Only in the future, my Matron."

Bad Cast felt it, a bristling in the air, as if something of great import were happening. He could see the reverence, almost worship, in Poor Singer's eyes as he held the older woman's hand.

She smiled bravely. "Take good care of my daughter, Dreamer. We shall do what we must for our people."

With that Poor Singer nodded, released her hand, and touched Ironwood on the shoulder, as if in reassurance. Then he reached down to pull Cornsilk to her feet. Together they walked off toward their lodge, heads close as they whispered.

Ironwood was watching Night Sun, a frown lining his forehead. His single eye desperately sought an explanation. She shrugged but moved to stand beside him as he faced the circle of witnesses. He pointed to Crow Woman. "Can you and Wrapped Wrist make the trip back to White Eye and relate these things?"

"Yes, War Chief." Crow Woman stood, searched the circle until she spotted Wrapped Wrist, and jerked her head before starting off.

"Here we go again," Wrapped Wrist muttered.

"I might as well go with you. There's nothing more I—"

"Bad Cast?" Ironwood called. "If you would meet with Whistle and me, we have things to discuss."

"You were saying?" Wrapped Wrist asked.

"I was saying, tell Soft Cloth that I'm well—that I love her and miss her and our daughter. Tell my family I'll be home as soon as I can." Bad Cast pointed to where Crow Woman had disappeared. "I wouldn't make her wait. She doesn't strike me as the forgiving kind."

"You take care."

He slapped Wrapped Wrist on the shoulder. "I'm not

the one traveling off this mountain in the middle of the night."

"We'll have light." He indicated the flashes of distant lightning that strobed the sky.

They shared a smile, and then he was gone.

Bad Cast walked through the standing people, hearing caution in their voices, feeling the growing tension. He placed himself at the edge of the circle that had gathered around Ironwood in time to hear Night Sun say, "From this moment on our fate rests with the gods." Then the Matron walked off in the direction of her lodge.

Ironwood turned, expression serious. "It appears that we have an attack to plan."

"War Chief?" Whistle asked. "If what Ripple said is true, we will be attacking in conjunction with the combined clans. How do we coordinate so many forces?"

Ironwood's smile turned wary. "Did anything the Dreamer said make sense to you?"

"No."

"Then, Whistle, as the Matron said, we must trust ourselves to the gods."

Thunder rolled, banging and crashing across the land.

W rapped Wrist was bent on one knee, tying his pack together. He lifted his ceramic canteen, sloshing it to judge the contents: at least half-full.

"Wrapped Wrist?"

He looked up to see Ripple's dark silhouette against the lightning-white clouds. The form vanished as the heavens went black.

"Ripple? What was that? What were you trying to say back there at the fire?"

"The pieces are being moved into place, old friend. I won't be seeing you again. Not like this. Not just the two of us."

"What are you talking about?"

"I've come to say good-bye, and to thank you for being my friend."

"I'll always be your friend. Don't be silly. When this is all over and—"

"I never thanked you for not telling old Half Eye that I was the one who stole her pot."

"I didn't know you knew I knew."

"I shouldn't have taken it in the first place. It was the only thing she had left of her mother's."

"She shouldn't have called you a shiftless thief. That was uncalled-for. You weren't. Because you were on your own, everyone who ended up missing something thought you'd taken it."

Ripple chuckled. "We weren't very good farmers. Fir Brush got better as the years passed."

"You made up for it with meat. No one hunts better than you do."

"I did steal, sometimes, when no one was around . . . Well, it was that or starve."

"People understood, Ripple. No one really cared because you always did something to make up for what you took. You'd bring a ground squirrel or rabbit, or even just a shiny stone if you thought it would please someone."

"I just thought you should know that I'm sorry I took that pot. Then Half Eye died and I never had a chance to make it up to her."

Wrapped Wrist grunted. "She was a bitter old woman. No one liked her."

"You always took my side. For that, I thank you."

Wrapped Wrist stared up in the darkness. A distant flash haloed Ripple's form, betraying the worried hunch to his posture. "You sound like this is good-bye forever. Ripple, we'll make it through this. You'll see. A couple of cycles from now—"

"When your trial comes, remember this: Swallow your fear. It is meaningless—illusion meant to keep you from what needs to be done. You have never understood that your souls are even stronger than your body. Without death, there is no life, no future. You know that, don't you?"

"Sure, what hunter—?"

"You *know* that, deep down between your *souls*! Tell me you *understand*!"

What was this passion in his voice? "Of course I understand."

Ripple reached down in the darkness. The instant he touched his finger to Wrapped Wrist's forehead, lightning arced in jagged patterns across the sky. From Wrapped Wrist's perspective it might have leapt from his friend's silhouetted head like a tracery to burn through the heavens.

"If you would be happy, you must save her."

"Save who?"

"Farewell, my friend."

"Don't say—"

When lightning flashed again, Ripple was gone.

Thirty-nine

Morning cast a blue light through the low-hanging smoke. It rose from the breakfast cook fires to hang lazily in the trees. For as wild as the night had been, the morning air barely stirred. Voices carried as mothers talked to children. The deeper murmurs of warriors leavened the clatter of wooden dishes and ceramic spoons.

Whistle, Yucca Sock, and Firehorn knelt to either side of Bad Cast and stared thoughtfully at a drawing he had scratched into the dark earth with a sharpened stick. Bad Cast rubbed his face. Was that good enough? Had he managed to get all the details right? He wasn't sure but that the final rendition didn't look more like a too-many-legged spider than First Moon Mountain with its twin spires and sheer cliffs.

Ironwood was chewing absently at his lower lip as he studied the image. "Can they see down the slopes on every side?"

"They can." Bad Cast used his finger to point out the slopes. "These cliffs can be climbed in many places. Any young man who has spent time in rough country has the skills to scale them. The guards will be fewer, but the chances for discovery higher. A climber will be vulnerable to something as simple as a dropped stone." He indicated the north slope. "This route is the best. The approaches to the mountain are timbered with spruce, fir, and ponderosa. The slope is steep, the footing treacherous. They won't know you are close until you are clambering up the rimrock."

"Just as we won't know where the lookouts are until we appear at their feet," Whistle noted. "What conceals us, also hides them."

"We'll be moving in force; their sentries will be standing quietly," Yucca Sock added. "It's like building a disaster block by block."

Ironwood raised an eyebrow. "Only if a guard is still there when we come. Whistle? What is your opinion? Would Matron Larkspur allow you within the walls again?"

Whistle's expression was pensive. "I think that might be arranged."

Bad Cast remembered the man's words concerning his night with the Matron. Blood of the gods, if Whistle was that bent on suicide he could just throw himself headlong off a cliff.

"If you could silence the guards along that northern slope, it might make all the difference." Ironwood took a deep breath, as if his lungs were starved. His fingers were fidgeting with the fur patch that covered his missing eye.

Bad Cast indicated the northwest slope. "Climbing here puts you behind the farthest pillar. The slope is loose, difficult, but screened by the bulk of the mountain and both pillars."

"And it's a lot tougher to traverse the slope under the pillars," Whistle pointed out. "Any body of warriors crossing there is going to make noise as their feet knock the rocks and scree loose."

Firehorn asked, "War Chief, suppose we take Pinnacle Great House? What then? How do we hold it?"

"We don't. We take our captives, set fire to the great house, and retreat back down the mountain."

Bad Cast was as surprised as the others when Night Sun calmly said from behind them, "Taking captives is not a good idea."

Bad Cast turned on his heels, staring up at the Matron.

"No captives, my wife?" Ironwood asked.

She took a breath. "Husband, am I to assume that you will take the chance of Larkspur, Desert Willow, or Webworm escaping to hide out in the mountains and foment their poison? Have you forgotten that the Blessed Sun's warriors are *eating* their enemies, or that White Cloud Woman's head was cut off her body inside her own quarters?"

Ironwood looked at her with an intensity that Bad Cast could almost reach out and feel. "Killing them will set a terrible precedent. In the past we have always let the Council decide the fate of prisoners."

"The Council consisted of the First People," she said reasonably. "We're hoping to build a new Council, one composed of the Made People clans as well as the last of the First People's clans. The room must be swept clean, husband. Webworm is already ahead of you on that account."

"You are assuming that he ordered White Cloud Woman's death."

She gave him a kind smile. "You still see him as he was. In your memory you are sharing campfires, remembering raids when you laughed together and enjoyed a bond of camaraderie that only a beloved war chief can share with his trusted deputy. In the years since he became the Blessed Sun, he's changed."

Ironwood stared wistfully at the drawing. "He wasn't the right man for leadership."

Night Sun continued without relent. "He is desperate. Disaster is looming before him. If we can remove Webworm, Desert Willow, Larkspur, and—gods grant us— Leather Hand all at once, the serpent will writhe without a head. We can call an assembly of the Made People clans, the last of Red Lacewing Clan, and those of the Blue Dragonfly Clan that might be called upon to effect reason over revenge. With luck we can still mend our world."

Ironwood sat paralyzed, his single eye fixed on some point beyond their seeing. His · hard face revealed nothing—not a twitch of the lips, not the least tightening around his single eye. In a listless voice he finally said, "You're right."

Bad Cast watched the warriors around him shift nervously.

"When do we go?" Whistle asked.

"When we hear that Blue Racer's party is close." Ironwood's single eye locked with Night Sun's.

She said, "Discovering if Webworm is coming will be more difficult."

Ironwood considered. "Nothing would have stopped him from taking his mother's body south in the funeral procession. But Jay Bird's attack still burns in his memory. Before the Dust People stole from his larder, he might have been lured away from Flowing Waters Town, stripping the place of warriors. What if in his absence, one of the Made People clan elders—knowing his relatives are starving down south—slips a couple of basket loads of corn out of Dusk House?"

"Others might be tempted to try," Whistle added.

Night Sun knelt beside them. "Quite a problem for him, isn't it? He's squatting on a wealth of food that he dare not leave. Yet he needs to have the prestige of being seen at the lunar maximum."

Bad Cast asked, "What about Leather Hand? Anyone who got caught stealing might be smacked in the head and eaten. Wouldn't that be a deterrent?"

Night Sun shrugged. "Not for someone like Creeper. Creeper has a soft heart, and Webworm knows it. In Webworm's absence, Creeper might give in to a desperate plea by one of his kinsmen. In Creeper's mind, no minor infraction like the theft of food would justify more than a severe reprimand from Webworm."

"Creeper never has been a deep thinker," Ironwood agreed. "For that reason alone, Webworm might be enticed into staying within the safe walls of Dusk House."

"If he does," Whistle noted, "that will create a compli-cation for us. He will be at the center of his strength, and quick to dispense it against us."

"Or will he?" Yucca Sock was stroking his chin. "When he hears news of the attack on Pinnacle Great House, will the Webworm you've been describing launch an attack against us? Won't he want to solidify his power?"

Firehorn scoffed. "If he does send warriors against us, we'll run them ragged in the forests just like before. They can chase our ghosts among the trees while we pick them off one by one. Eventually they will tuck their tails and scamper back to the walls of Dusk House."

"He can't send many warriors after us." Whistle glanced from face to face. "His warriors are already too thinly spread. Why do you think Leather Hand ate those Dust People? He's doing with terror what he can't by force of arms."

Night Sun patted Ironwood on the shoulder. "This is warrior's talk. I'll go and tell the others that they should begin to get their things together. We'll be ready to leave when—"

"No," Ironwood said firmly. "I'm only taking warriors."

Night Sun stopped short, a frown lining her forehead. "We will appear more like pilgrims if women and children accompany the men. Somehow I don't believe you're go-ing to blend in bristling with bows, arrows, and war clubs."

Ironwood's smile was warm. "No, I suppose not, but I want you to stay, wife. You and the rest. Something about the way Poor Singer said good-bye to you last night wor-ried me."

"And?" she asked softly, love in her eyes.

"He wouldn't tell me when I searched him out later. He just gave me that irritating smile, and told me what a Blessing I had been to his life. What was that supposed to mean? Me? A Blessing?"

Night Sun relented. "Oh, very well. If you would feel better, the women and children will stay."

"They'll never find you here. Among the Moon People

villages, someone might recognize you. You know what a triumph Webworm would have, parading you down the Great North Road bound and disgraced."

"Plan this raid." She ran her fingers through his hair. "I'll be waiting when you finish."

Bad Cast watched her leave, wondering at the love that had shone from her eyes.

Ironwood sighed. "Now, Bad Cast, once we have filtered into First Moon Valley, I'm assuming you have houses where we can stay? Kinsmen who would keep us out of sight until the night of the attack?"

"Of course."

Yucca Sock stood up, stretching. As he looked off to the north, he said, "Did any of you notice? There's a smoke plume up in the Spirit Mountains."

"Compliments of the lightning last night," Ironwood muttered as he studied the drawing. "And that's another thing. As dry as it is, we don't want to let a fire get away from us. When we camp, cook fires are to be treated very carefully. If we set the forest on fire, everyone will be looking our direction. We want to arrive at Moon Valley in secret."

Webworm wore a resplendent yellow war shirt that hung to just above his knees. Black four-pointed stars had been painted onto the cloth, and a startling purple sash was belted at his waist. For the occasion he had chosen a wooden headpiece that mimicked sticky geranium flower petals. The effect was as if his head were the center of the flower. In his right hand he carried a solid stone war club Traded up from the south.

Desert Willow was waiting when he walked through the opening created by the painted walls that masked the northern curve of the kiva. He smiled as he met her dark eyes.

She had actually tried to respond to his caresses the night before. That she had done so was a mark in her favor. When he had slid into her warm sheath and let his weight settle onto her slender body, he had found himself oddly excited. War Chief Wind Leaf had lain thus just days before him. Where his hard rod now rested, so had Wind Leaf's. Did her sheath know the difference? Did it care? Was one man's stiff shaft as good as another's?

He glanced next at Wind Leaf, seeing his war chief's reserved expression. The man wore a bright red shirt, his feet shod in intricately knotted yucca sandals, his use-worn war club hanging from the belt at his narrow waist. Behind him, Leather Hand was dressed in a dark scarlet war shirt, his feet in the resplendent white moccasins. He had a flint-like quality that Wind Leaf lacked these days. But then, the man and his companions had set themselves apart.

He cast a smile at Creeper, wondering. From his old companion's expression, one might have thought that his best friend were mortally ill. When the time and circumstances were right, he'd ask.

Sunwatcher Blue Racer was an ascetic-looking man in a spotless white breechcloth. He had a thin white cotton shawl over his narrow shoulders. The color accented his dark tan. He bowed his head and touched fingers to his forehead, calling, "Greetings, Blessed Sun."

"Greetings, Sunwatcher. You had a pleasant journey here?"

"Yes, Blessed Sun. The porters were both stout of heart and strong of limb. They bore me here in record time, and without so much as a single misstep."

"I shall reward them well. War Chief?"

"Yes, Blessed Sun?"

"See to it when we are finished here."

"Yes, Blessed Sun."

Webworm walked up to Blue Racer and stared into his dark eyes. A question lay there, as if the man were wondering something. "Yes, Sunwatcher?"

"You will be coming to the Moon Ceremony?"

Webworm glanced sidelong at Desert Willow and then Wind Leaf. "I am not sure. I have a question of my own. You are the greatest of the Priests. Alone among them you have been charting the path of Father Sun across the sky, following the trail of Sister Moon as she inches her way toward her northern home."

"Yes, Blessed Sun."

"You have been marking the paths of the stars, following the constellations through the night sky."

"That is correct, Blessed Sun."

"Good. Then my question for you is a very simple one. It should have a simple answer."

"I would suppose so, Blessed Sun."

Webworm smiled as he leaned forward, his voice sibilant with threat. "Where is the rain?"

Blue Racer swallowed hard. "I cannot answer that, Blessed Sun. None of the signs have changed. No comets have appeared to distract the Cloud People. They still—"

"But they do *not bring rain!*" He narrowed his eyes. "Are you aware that most of the crops in the dryland farms are brown and dead? Are you aware that many of my people have eaten their seed corn?"

"Blessed Sun, I assure you, we have done all that we can."

Webworm glared at him, a thick black anger rising around his heart. "Sunwatcher, have you heard of the kings down south?"

"Kings, Blessed Sun? I do not know the term."

"Kings. Call them chiefs of chiefs, the Blessed of the Blessed, or so they style themselves."

"Ah, yes." Comprehension filled Blue Racer's eyes. "Far to the south, where a few of the bravest Traders venture. The stone pyramid builders. Yes, I have indeed heard of them, and the wonders of their great calendars that chart the—"

"Then you know how they feed their god. I believe they call him Chak, or some such thing."

"Feed him?" Blue Racer looked confused.

Webworm smiled in a disarming fashion. "Those tall stone temples they build?"

"Oh, yes." Blue Racer nodded. "I've heard that they take captives atop them, cut their very hearts from their bodies, and tumble them down the . . . Oh, my. Yes, I see. Feed the gods."

Webworm shot a quick glance at Leather Hand to read

his face. "I am wondering, Sunwatcher, what would happen if we fed the gods here."

"Fed the Flute Player?"

"He calls the rain, doesn't he?"

Blue Racer considered that. "I'm not sure what the Flute Player would make of a man's heart, Blessed Sun. The Blue God, on the other hand—"

"Yes, yes, but the Blue God has never been one to involve herself in the conjuring of rain." Webworm waved a hand. "My problem, Sunwatcher, is drought. Without rain, there will be famine in the villages. Do you understand?" He gestured at Wind Leaf. "My warriors are barely keeping the pot from boiling over as it is. Do you have any conception how precarious our situation is?"

Blue Racer was reading the rage stewing behind Webworm's eyes. "Yes, Blessed Sun."

"Good." Webworm clapped his hand on the man's back, feeling his bones through his skinny shoulders. "Because if anyone can call the rain, it's you, correct? You're the one responsible for the rituals. You oversee the prayers and chants. You know, better than anyone else, how the thlatsina heresy of your predecessor has hurt us."

"Yes, Blessed Sun."

"Good!" He gave the man a rictus of a smile. "Since you know it all so well, you'll be perfect."

"Perfect, Blessed Sun?"

"If we don't have rain by the end of the Moon Ceremony, I shall feed you to the gods. Give your heart to the Flute Player, to be more precise. We don't have one of those tall white stone pyramids like they have down south, but I hear that they do have rain."

Blue Racer's dark eyes began to look moist and soft. His jaw worked as he tried three times to swallow. "Yes, Blessed Sun." It came out a whisper. Behind him, Creeper's eyes had gone wide, disbelief in the set of his old round face.

"That will be all." He turned, heading for the northern stairs. "Deputy Leather Hand, I have been giving a great deal of thought to Matron Larkspur's report. If you would accompany me, I have something for you and your special warriors to attend to."

"Yes, Blessed Sun," Leather Hand called as he fell in behind Webworm, followed him past the dividers and up the steps to the Priests' chamber.

"What do you think? Did I make an impression on the Sunwatcher?"

"You did."

"And?"

"Will you go through with it?"

"Feeding his heart to the Flute Player?" Webworm shrugged. "The people have to know we're trying, Deputy. Which brings me to my next problem: If I have to feed my Sunwatcher's heart to the Flute Player, I may need other hearts should his fail. There is one in particular that I would love to cut out." He glanced at Leather Hand. "I think you would like to have a crack at him, too."

"Ironwood's?"

"You seem to have a way of getting things done, Deputy War Chief. I have a plan. If it works, we will down two birds with one cast of the stone. Make this happen and you shall be amply rewarded."

Leather Hand nodded agreement. Then said, "Just one thing, Blessed Sun."

"And that is?"

"Don't ask me to make it rain."

Forty

Ripple lay with his belly on a cool stone and watched the water boatmen as they stroked up to the water's surface, caught a breath, and dove, their two frondlike legs driving them down into the depths.

In the ponderosa that overhung the spring, cedar waxwings tittered as they searched the spreading pine for bugs. A nuthatch scampered up and down the scaly brown bark. The gray-and-white bird cocked its head, hunting for a stray grub with its keen eyes.

I have this one moment of peace.

Ripple took a deep breath and tried to carve it into his souls, hoping to savor it in the coming days. Turning his eyes back to the clear depths of the pool, he looked down into that small world and wished he could be part of it. Some other insect skittered between the pebbles in the bottom. Bees came one by one to drink at the pool's edge; and flies, moths, and butterflies lit, dipped their proboscises, and lifted into the hot dry day. Water dripped musically from wet stones where the seep trickled out of the moss-covered rock.

"Are you feeling well?" Orenda's harshly accented voice intruded on his thoughts.

"Did you know that water boatmen can fly?"

"They can?" He heard her as she came to sit on the stones above him.

He rolled onto his side and looked up at her. "I never knew that. I just watched one swim to the surface and fly away. I had always thought they were born of water."

"Born-of-Water?" She smiled. "Do you know him?"

"I don't understand."

"Nightshade and I brought him here with his brother Home-Going Boy. Born-of-Water is a white-hair. He has no color to his skin; his eyes are pink. He can't see very well, and Father Sun's light does terrible things to him. He sees the future and currently lives on the Green Mesa with his wife."

"And the other one?"

"Home-Going Boy was eaten by Grandfather Grizzly. He was born without arms." She shrugged. "A person without arms can't run very fast. Trees were close, but he couldn't climb them. Badgertail killed the bear. He was buried in the hide."

"Did Home-Going Boy have Power, too?"

Orenda nodded. "He saw the past. They were quite the pair. Forever a handful. When they learned to speak, Born-of-Water would tell of burning towns, masked Dancers, bearded white-skinned men, and silver birds trailing smoke across the sky. At the same time, Home-Going Boy would tell of Raven Hunter and Runs in Light, of Bad Belly and White Ash, and great animals with noses like elongated hands, and others with long white teeth. He'd draw them with his stubby little fingers: beasts like you've never seen. He liked one little boy in particular. He said his name would translate into our language as Tusk Boy."

"I've never heard of these things."

"Me either, but they must have existed."

"Or did he make them up?"

She studied him thoughtfully. "Did you make up your vision of Cold Bringing Woman?"

He slowly shook his head, seeing the god's white face in his souls' eye. "I wish I had."

She looked north, as if to see through the trees. "Have you seen the smoke plume?"

"Lightning started it last night." He pulled himself into a sitting position. "Once again I would like to thank you for Healing me." He searched her eyes, seeing her reserve, her desperation to reach out to him.

"Healing." She smiled. "It's what I do best."

He studied her profile, aware once again what a haunting woman she was. "Why haven't you married?"

"There are reasons." She stared up at the branches where the nuthatch leaped magically up the rough bark. "For one thing, most men fear me. They think that, like Nightshade, I'm a witch."

"Are you?"

"I can't make a piece of rawhide fly, and believe me, I've tried. The mere thought of eating a dead baby's flesh makes me sick. I'd die of starvation before I'd touch it. I've tried cursing some of Ironwood and Night Sun's enemies, but none of them ever seem to keel over dead from hideous weeping wounds or fevers." She smiled at that. "What I do know are the herbs. With the right Spirit Plants, I can cure or kill."

"And the other reason?"

For a long time she sat in silence. "Something happened when I was a child, Ripple. Men see it in my eyes."

She was watching him, waiting for revulsion to mar his expression.

"Then you were meant to live," he said simply. "Power had other things in store for you."

. Her laughter was laced with irony. "Power never chooses a person for anything easy."

"No, it doesn't."

"I should be going. I'm sorry to have bothered you."

"You need not leave."

She gave him a skeptical look, the sort she would if his fever had broken out again.

"I just . . ." He shrugged it off. "I just want you to know that I don't fear you."

"Perhaps I only scare myself." She smiled wistfully. "Nightmares keep rising out of my past. I can't ever seem to outrun them."

He turned his head, as if to see through the screen of trees to the plume of fire burning high in the Spirit Mountains.

What I would give if all of my nightmares were behind me!

"**W**hy do you keep staring at me that way?" Crow Woman gave Wrapped Wrist a sidelong glance as they wound down out of a patch of lodgepole pine and approached a small stream. "Is something bothering you?"

"Nothing." Wrapped Wrist tried to wave it off. He dropped to his hands and knees, touched his lips to the cool water, and drank. Wiping his lips, he stood and stepped across the creek.

Even from this low spot he could still see the blue-brown plume of smoke that rose above the northern peaks. As they had traveled that morning they had caught periodic glances of the fire through the trees. It had grown, the plume widening and blowing off to the east.

Crow Woman knelt on the stones of the crossing and placed her lips to the water.

He admired the sleek lines of her, wondering how such a magnificent woman could be such a bitter thorn.

She stood, water dripping from her firm chin. She wiped it away on the shoulder of her war shirt, her flinty eyes boring into him the entire time. "The look in your eyes has changed."

"Changed?" he asked. "My eyes are the same."

"It used to be you only looked at me with lust."

"I don't lust after you."

"You do . . . or I should say you do when you don't fear me."

"I don't fear you."

"Apparently you just lie a lot."

"I don't think you want to hear honesty."

She considered him, as if seeing him anew. "I'm not used to honesty from a man's lips."

"What about the war chief's? There must be some reason that you ran off to join his warriors."

"You need not concern yourself about that."

"But you think he's honest, don't you?"

She started up the trail, her eyes casting about the grassy valley bottom as if in search of any dangers. "He is the only honest man I know."

He chuckled. "Now you know two."

She resettled the pack on her shoulder, leaving him to watch her slim brown calves as she strode up the trail. He liked the way her hips moved.

"You're not honest." She said it so simply.

"I'm not?"

"If you were you would tell me why your eyes have changed."

"Back to that again? All right, you said I look at you with lust or fear. What's changed?"

"Now you watch me with worry. Not for yourself, but for me. Why?"

He considered his reply as he forced himself to match her long-legged pace. She did it so easily; he was always at a half jog to keep up. Did he dare tell her what Ripple had said?

As if she heard his thoughts, she chided, "Honest?"

Throwing caution away, he said, "Ripple told me something."

"And that was?"

"He wanted me to save you."

Her laughter was melodious. "I saved myself long ago. I did it when I ran away and learned to fight. Know this, hunter: You can only save yourself. No one else can do it for you."

"I wasn't looking for a lecture. You asked for honesty. I gave it to you."

They walked along in silence; Wrapped Wrist studied the surrounding valley, seeing how the grass up the slopes had already gone tawny. The leaves on the trees had a wilted look about them. The sky above was brassy, as if filled with fine dust. Blood and bones, the world was dry.

"Do you trust this Ripple?" she asked suddenly.

"He is an old friend."

"He has always been a Dreamer?"

"He used to be just a hunter."

"But now people call him a Dreamer. I would understand what happened to him. Did he just become a Dreamer with the snap of the fingers?"

"He had a vision, one frightening enough that the First People tortured him for it."

"The Mountain Witch believes in him," she added. "You, who have known him, what do you think?"

Wrapped Wrist considered that as he watched dust puff around his sandaled feet. "He changed that night on the mountain. I don't know. Why would Power choose Ripple? He was never like most holy people. He was happier stalking the black timber for elk rather than seeking Power like a holy man. He never had that empty look in his eyes like a Seeker has."

"What did you see in his eyes last night?"

"Fear." Gods, yes, that's what it had been.

"For me?"

"For himself, I guess. For all of us."

"Why do you fear me? That is, when you're not lusting after me."

She wanted honesty? "I don't trust your anger. Maybe it's because I don't know where it comes from. I understand that some man hurt you, but that hard edge in your eyes can cut like obsidian."

"Good."

"The thing about obsidian," he continued as if he hadn't heard, "is that it'll slice magically through a man's flesh. Nothing is as sharp; but bend it the slightest bit and it snaps and shatters." He lowered his voice. "As I am afraid you will at the wrong moment."

She whirled, her hand going to the war club at her belt. Fire burned in her dark eyes as she whipped the weapon up to strike. "I am not that kind of woman. I refuse to be a victim. Not for them, not for any man . . . let alone you!"

Wrapped Wrist backpedaled to escape her wrath. Raising both of his hands, he cried, "Easy! Pus and maggots! No wonder you don't think men are honest. If a man is, you want to break his head!"

For a long couple of heartbeats she stood there, mouth working, eyes narrowed. She finally sighed, lowered the club, and started back up the trail. He could tell from her stilted posture that she was tense as a deadfall trap.

For the rest of the day he trotted along behind her, forcing his stubby legs to keep up. *What did I do? Which of the gods did I offend? How is it that I—who draw willing women with just a look—get stuck with this foaming she-weasel?*

Forty-one

The dusty trail led down from the gray hills, winding through desperate-looking juniper trees. Here and there along the way small shrines had been built, many with little painted wooden flowers and prayer sticks laid at their sides. During the day they had passed farmers, Made

People mostly, who trudged with packs on their backs, or pots riding in net bags across their shoulders. Round ceramic canteens had swung at their hips. All looked dusty, bestowing smiles as they nodded greetings to Nightshade and Spots.

"They seem like friendly folk," Spots ventured. The sack over his shoulder had been ominously silent, as if smoldering with some terrible presentiment.

"For the moment they hide their worry," Nightshade said as they rounded a bend that looked out over the Spirit River Valley. She stopped short, her attention fixed on the far floodplain across the river. "There it is: Webworm's rebirth of the Straight Path Nation."

Spots followed her gaze and saw the buff four-story building. Even from this distance, it was huge: an imposing square surrounding a plaza dominated by a great kiva and its smaller clan sibling. To the east, another, more irregular structure was rising. The construction swarmed with tiny brown bodies that labored on the walls. The buildings dominated the terrace behind the shallow Spirit River floodplain.

Like so much of the valley topography they had traveled, the Spirit River bottom was verdant and green. In this continuing year of drought, ditches meant life for the corn, beans, and squash.

Spots couldn't take his eyes off the grand structures. "They make our largest buildings seem like huts."

She said, "This isn't a pimple on Straight Path Canyon. Talon Town, Kettle Town, Streamside, Center Place, and High Sun Town dwarf this place. There the paths of Father Sun and Sister Moon are written in the stone. The canyon inhales with the breath of the gods. This place is like a rain-filled playa, appearing to be an oasis. One day, not so many sun cycles from now, you will see it differently."

"How is that, Elder?"

"Learn this: All things have their time. The wisest of men, my young hunter, are those who reach out to grasp each moment of happiness to their breasts. The richest among us are those who can taste the present. Such events are rare in life. When they come to you, sink your teeth into them, savor them to their entirety. When some young woman folds you into her arms, *be there* with your entire body and souls. Drown in the instant, and surrender yourself to it."

"Because it will not last." An empty sensation sucked at the bottom of his heart.

"Learn that at your age," she called over her shoulder, "and you shall be among the wisest of men who have ever lived."

"No young woman has ever folded me into her arms."

"Have you never seen a sunset that shot gold, orange, and purple through the clouds? Have you never savored an exceptionally cooked meal on a cold and hungry night? Gods, hunter, have you never just sat on a spring morning, listened to the birds, and felt yourself *breathe*?"

He frowned. "Yes, I have."

"But you cluttered it up with thousands of worries, didn't you? You fretted about what your friends said, why your elders were upset with you, perhaps you even spent that moment brooding about your scars and how they made some pretty young woman's eyes slide past you."

The emptiness in her voice sobered him.

"Ecstasy and terror await us, hunter. Let's not keep them waiting."

If that is the least of her knowledge, what is the worst of it?

As they walked ever closer to Flowing Waters Town, he could feel the Spirits in her bag: They shifted uneasily, whispering among themselves.

The way Desert Willow had been acting made no sense to Wind Leaf. He squinted under the hot slant of the afternoon sun and took stock of the activity in the plaza. There, between the great kiva and the west room block, bundles, packs, and burden baskets had been laid out. Some contained corn flour, others dried root breads. Ritual clothing could be seen protruding from other packs. This was only part of the heavy load Blue Racer was accumulating for his journey northward to Pinnacle Great House. He might have been outfitting a party of warriors for a raid on the distant Stone Temple Builders that Webworm had suddenly become so infatuated with. As if people who believed in jungle gods had any merit for the Straight Path Nation. Which brought him back to Desert Willow.

She stood on the edge of the second-story roof, her arms crossed below her breasts. A frown lined her perfect forehead as she watched the slaves and Made People milling among the packs and baskets. A babble of voices rose as questions were called and commands given.

Wind Leaf stepped over beside her, saying, "Do you think they can make order out of it?"

"Probably not. I suspect the Sunwatcher will order it all loaded onto as many backs as he needs and carted off to the north. Blue Racer seems particularly anxious to start. He spends a great deal of time rubbing his breastbone."

Wind Leaf casually glanced around, taking note that no one seemed particularly close. "What has happened?"

"Webworm threatened the Sunwatcher's life. You were there, if you'll recall."

Wind Leaf lowered his voice further. "What happened between us? Have I offended you?"

"He knows."

"About us?"

"What happened to White Cloud Woman? I mean, how was she really killed? Who did it? One of yours?"

"I don't know. My scouts report that it remains a mystery. I have asked Leather Hand. He just shrugged."

"Webworm ordered it."

"You're sure?"

"Very. He let me know in no uncertain terms that if I continued to bed you, it would go hard on me."

"You are the Matron. You could remove him."

"And put you in his place?" She glanced sidelong at him, a slim eyebrow arched inquisitively.

"No, not me. Some other more compliant—"

"I don't think I would live long after that."

"How could he get to you? With a simple command you could surround yourself with guards."

"Matron White Cloud Woman was well guarded." She shook her head. "No, I enjoyed you, Wind Leaf. I shall cherish those memories. For now I shall wait, and act as a Matron should. Webworm will grow tired of me again. In the meantime, I intend to learn his secret."

"He has changed since he became the Blessed Sun." Wind Leaf frowned down at the chaos in the plaza below. "Much of his old insecurity has been replaced with arrogance."

She looked up at the sky, yellowed with the haze of dust. Then she looked off to the distant north, where a flat plume of smoke vanished into the northeast. "If Blue Racer can't convince the Flute Player to call the rains, we are going to see a much more insecure Blessed Sun."

"My men have been checking the harvest, Matron. Most of the irrigated fields are doing better than expected. The corn is eared out; we should have an above-normal harvest."

She sighed. "Bless the Flute Player. Your warriors will have to be particularly vigilant during the harvest. We want as much packed into the great houses along the rivers as we can. People are going to want to hoard, but as refugees trickle in from the dryland farms, we're going to have to give them something."

"It won't be enough to feed them all."

"It won't have to be. The critical thing is that we must give them a portion large enough to carry. Enough to send them home with. It won't be our fault that they can't pack enough for several days' journey back to their starving villages."

"Many of the outlying great houses have already emptied their storerooms. There will be no harvest to refill them."

"I know, War Chief." She gave him a hard appraisal. "If there is insurrection, your warriors must be fierce, brutal, and immediate in their retaliation. I will not tolerate any abuse of our Priests or our Matrons and their families."

"Yes, Matron." He wondered at the hard set of her jaw. Didn't she understand that his warriors were going to be just as hungry trying to hold isolated great houses? Or did she think she could have runners bear packs full of corn to those distant warriors? How did she think those packs bulging with corn would ever make it through a land gone thin with famine?

She was giving him a hard look, trying to pierce his stoic expression. "You seem unconvinced of my will."

"Not of your will, Matron. I was just wondering . . ." The old woman caught his eye. She was walking through the opening below the east room block. Tall and thin, silver hair gleaming, she wore an oddly fashioned faded red dress. Behind her a young man in a barbarian's hunting shirt was bearing several packs, his wide eyes almost disbelieving as he stared around at the bustling plaza.

It was the woman, though, that drew his eye. Something about her—crone that she might be—hinted of a ruler's poise. She carried herself as if she might own this place rather than just having entered it for the first time.

"Wondering what?" Desert Willow asked, then followed his gaze. "Who is that?"

"I have no idea, Matron. I don't think I've ever seen her before."

"Some Matron from a distant great house? She carries herself like one."

The old woman's gaze lifted and fixed. Wind Leaf had seen such an expression when a falcon spied a cottontail. He followed her gaze, seeing Webworm as he stepped out of his fourth-floor rooms. The Blessed Sun appeared nervous, as if something had upset his stomach. He glanced around this way and that, and finally saw the old woman. Across the distance, Wind Leaf would have sworn he felt the very air crackle.

"I think I'll go down and see just who—"

Shouts broke out below him, and he stepped forward. Two slaves were beating each other about the head and shoulders with digging sticks, yelling, "You took it!" "You're a liar!" "Give it back, dog!" "I'll kill you!"

"You!" Wind Leaf boomed, pointing at the miscreants. "I'll have your livers roasted and thrown to the dogs! Stop that at once."

The slaves desisted, stared up, went pale, and immediately scurried away.

"Vermin," Wind Leaf muttered. He glanced back at Webworm, seeing the Blessed Sun, looking shaken, his eyes blinking. When Wind Leaf turned back to where the old woman had been, the plaza was empty. He craned his neck, looking this way and that, but nowhere did he see her tall form. She might just as well have been a ghost.

Wrapped Wrist had never understood the simple pleasures of anonymity. Fearing he might be recognized, he and Crow Woman had waited until dark in a copse of piñon pine before crossing the fields in the First Moon Valley and climbing the Dog's Tooth. During the day, she had said nothing more than was absolutely necessary. So be it. Once he'd delivered her to old White Eye, he full well knew the route back to Ironwood's.

The walled enclosure atop the Dog's Tooth reassured Wrapped Wrist when he led Crow Woman through the gap in its walls. As he'd climbed, he'd looked out across the valley. The familiar sights, sounds, faces, and places all served to comfort his anxious souls. Never would he have been so happy to simply retire to his uncle's house, watch the fire as he shared a meal, and enjoy the company of his cousin's children as they romped on the floor, playing with cornshuck dolls, rolling little carved wooden animals across the packed dirt, and guessing which hand held the carved ball Uncle had made for them.

"It is Wrapped Wrist," he called outside White Eye's pit house.

"Enter," the old man rasped.

Wrapped Wrist led the way up, glanced inside at the old man, and found him seated on his mat below the northern bench. His fingers cupped a small figurine. Behind his head a stone feather holder bristled with the feathers of eagle, buzzard, red-tailed hawk, and kestrel.

Wrapped Wrist climbed down the ladder, thankful to squat off to one side as Crow Woman scuttled down behind him. She seated herself, hard eyes on the old man.

His odd white eye seemed to gleam in the firelight. "What is the word from the war chief?"

"He sends his greetings, Elder," Crow Woman said. "Along with a warning from young Ripple."

White Eye heard something in her voice. "But you do not believe?"

Crow Woman shrugged ineffectively, though perhaps the keen-eared old man heard her clothing shift. "My beliefs have no importance. Ripple interrupted a council to speak with Matron Night Sun and Ironwood."

"And what did Ripple say?" White Eye turned the little stone figurine. Wrapped Wrist finally identified it as a crudely formed eagle with its wings spread.

"He said that if the First People were to be defeated, it had to be done according to what Cold Bringing Woman told him." Crow Woman appeared to fidget under that blind eye.

"How many warriors can he bring?"

"Perhaps thirty, Elder."

"Thirty." White Eye sat quietly for several heartbeats.

"We are trained, Elder. Not like the anxious young men you can recruit locally."

"The young men I will pick shall have hearts strong enough for our purposes."

"I didn't mean to imply they weren't courageous, Elder, just that the Blessed Sun will send many of his best warriors to hold Pinnacle Great House. The movement of large numbers of warriors will alert them to an attack. Knowing the war chief as I do, I can imagine that he will seek to avoid—"

"What were Ripple's precise words?"

A pause.

Crow Woman closed her eyes, speaking precisely, as if she were pulling the words straight out of her memory. "I have seen fire Dancing with ice. Send word now. Tell White Eye that only the strongest threads of silk tether the web. If he would see the First People fall, he must call the elders to council. Spider Woman wants all of the flies in the web before we strike." She paused. "The fire is loosened; flames rise high. The Dance is begun. In the coming days, Sister Moon's veil will be spun. When she is finally draped in a smoke-black cloak it will be time for us to strike."

"And after that?" White Eye asked.

"Nothing. He walked away."

"And Poor Singer? Did he hear these words?"

"He did."

"What was his reaction?"

"Poor Singer began to pack his family's belongings in preparation of leaving. I did hear Poor Singer say that we needed to trust the gods. That wasn't encouraging to those of us who have little use for gods."

"Sister Moon's veil will be spun," White Eye mused. "Fire and ice." He nodded. "At last the pieces begin to fit."

"Fit how?" Wrapped Wrist asked.

The old man ignored him. "How does Ironwood plan on coming here? Surely he isn't going to try and sneak in among the pilgrims. The Red Shirts will be watching for him and his people."

"That I do not know, Elder."

White Eye rolled the stone eagle between his fingers. "Like you, perhaps he should arrive in the night. Bring me word, and I shall have places to secret his warriors. First Moon Valley is big, with a great many towns, villages, and houses. We can find places where the Blessed Sun's warriors cannot weasel you out."

Wrapped Wrist asked, "Do you believe we can do this, Elder? I mean, can we take Pinnacle Great House while the Blessed Sun holds it with his best warriors?"

The old man smiled wistfully. "What did Ripple say? Fire and ice? The key lies there."

"But what does it mean?" Crow Woman asked, and glanced at Wrapped Wrist with a camaraderie that surprised him.

"We shall just have to wait to find out." White Eye smiled. "And trust to these gods you seem hesitant to accept, Crow Woman. They have their own needs here."

"So do our clans." Wrapped Wrist stared thoughtfully at the fire. "I was there that night of the meeting when you decided to rescue Ripple. Some of our clan elders won't want to participate."

"No, I suppose not." White Eye tilted his head back. "We will have to be very discreet."

Crow Woman yawned, the warmth of the fire obviously playing upon her fatigue. She shook it off, adding, "What message do you wish me to take back to the war chief?"

White Eye said, "I will have an answer for you in the morning. Meanwhile, I must think."

"I need to take a message to Soft Cloth." Wrapped Wrist rose to his tired feet.

"Take Crow Woman with you," White Eye ordered. "See if you can find her another dress to wear while she's in the valley. That war shirt stands out like a burning brand in the dusk. Rest at Soft Cloth's. I will send Fir Brush and Yellow Petal to see you. They have been wondering about their kin. Then return to me tomorrow night. Should anyone show interest in you, you are a husband and wife visiting from down valley."

Wrapped Wrist knew he looked just as horrified as Crow Woman.

"Your lives may depend on it." The old man's voice snapped like a whip. *"Act like it!"*

It was only after they had climbed back out into the cool night that Crow Woman asked, "How could he know I wore a war shirt?"

Wrapped Wrist shivered, dreading her presence. "Oh, you wouldn't believe the things he knows."

"Act married? To you?"

"I think he's still punishing me for leaving my buffalo-hide at his doorstep."

She pointed her finger. "If you so much as touch me . . ."

"Go ahead and kill me. It'll be a Blessing."

Forty-two

MONSTERS

*T*he stories about giant rattlesnakes, man-serpents, fly-ing spiders, deer-antlered men, and all the other creatures of evil and darkness have filled my imagination from the beginning. I know them all: blood-sucking, meat-eating creatures that lurk in darkness, prowl the Underworlds, and hide in springs. They are tied to rivers, deep forests, and hidden places below the earth.

In Dreams I have battled them. While soul-flying, I have escaped their clutches or outwitted them while in search of the dead. I have enchanted some, lured and baited others, and even brought a few into my embrace.

I have little fear of monsters, demons, or evil Spirits. For the most part, they seek only to tear the heart from a person's breast, or perhaps devour his soul. In any event, their strike is quick—usually without warning. An instant of excruciating pain, a heartbeat of terror, and then . . . Nothing. Blackness. Void.

While Dancing in Sister Datura's arms I have looked into the darkness and seen the monsters staring back. The first time, so long ago, an abject fear almost paralyzed me. I survived by the barest chance of fate.

Knowledge is Power. As I came to understand the mon-sters, my fear ebbed and drained away like a muddy pond in a drought. Familiarity with their ways taught me to re-spect and understand them, as a hunter knows and avoids the great bears, cougars, and poisonous reptiles.

I have watched the unease grow in people's eyes when I describe the monster beasts that inhabit the Spirit Worlds. I've seen them shiver in mindless terror at mention of a *cannibal owl. For days after, they cannot sleep, their Dreams filled with images of huge monsters.*

How can they be such fools? Those selfsame individuals who toss and turn in terror of a Spirit Beast will fawn over some soul-twisted chief who just pulled the intestines out of an infant in a futile attempt to scry the future. Tell people that a certain spring is inhabited by underwater witches, and they will flee in screaming panic. Mention a giant winged scorpion, and they will cower in their houses until they starve. But show them a great chief infected with evil and watch them flock to his side. They will compete to curry his favor, mindless of the demented gleam in his eyes as he turns his smiles upon them.

Do I fear monsters? Oh, yes.

Spots glanced nervously at Nightshade as he busied himself about their small camp. Nightshade had picked this place in the thickets beside the river after she had slipped away from Dusk House that afternoon. She had said she needed time to think. He had cooked their supper of steamed cornmeal and lily root over a handful of fire. Fuel had consisted of sticks, rabbitbrush, and bits of driftwood he'd found lodged in the riverbank willows.

Nightshade seemed oblivious to the water lapping just beyond the yellow-brown stems, or the star-speckled night sky above. The whining mosquitoes that plagued Spots seemed to ignore her as she sat, back straight, hands neatly folded in her lap. Her wide eyes stared, unblinking, at something beyond this world. Periodically her lips moved, as if speaking. Her black cloak with white stars gave her the appearance of a night creature.

Spots used river water to wash out their little round brownware pot and replaced it in his pack. Then he squatted, limp hands dangling from his knees. He snorted at a mosquito that had flown up in his nose, and shook his head to keep them from whining in his ears.

"Elder?" he whispered. She might have been dead but for the occasional twitch of her lips. Watching closely, he couldn't even see her breathe.

Grunting to himself, he shot a nervous glance at her pack. The faint whisperings carried to his souls with greater clarity. He'd sensed their disturbance growing from the moment they'd crossed the Spirit River and walked across the cornfields to Dusk Town. They'd positively shrieked when he'd borne them into the plaza that afternoon, only sighing with relief after Nightshade had suddenly turned and led them away.

He was sure he didn't hear them with his ears—not that such sibilance would penetrate the incessant whining of mosquito wings. No, these were voices who spoke to the souls. The whispering was interrupted by a new nervous chattering—the sort that might have been made by tortured bats.

How could this happen to me? I never wanted anything to do with Power; now it falls around me like ash from a forest fire.

Something inky and unseen flapped through the night over his head. He caught just the faintest shadow passing across the stars. A shiver ran down his spine. He could *feel* things shifting and watching from the surrounding willows.

He tossed the last of their scanty firewood onto the dying flames. In the renewed light he unrolled his blanket and pulled the coarse weave through his fingers, wondering what protection it would give from the wavering cloud of mosquitoes, let alone the occasional soul-craving Spirit that might reach out of the darkness.

"Tomorrow," Nightshade said suddenly, "you need to be very careful. No matter what you see or hear, do not interfere. Do you understand, Spots?"

"Do not interfere with what, Elder?"

"In the morning, when I enter Dusk House, you are free to go. I thank you for your help on this journey. You have been a brave and worthy companion."

He frowned. "Elder? Aren't you going back to Ironwood's? Won't you need me to carry your pack? Cook for you on the return journey?"

"I am not going back."

His anxiety grew as his souls heard the Spirits in her pack crying out.

"No!" he cried, unsure about what.

She cocked her head. "You have responsibilities to your family and clan. In appreciation for your help and company, I will tell you this: Take your relatives—all that you can convince to accompany you. Go from this land. Save those you can, and run."

"Elder?"

"This is your chance to break free. You have very little time. Just enough to run back to your home and try to persuade your closest kin to leave."

Spots frowned. "That man you looked at in the plaza today. I saw your eyes meet, felt the change in the air. I heard the voices of the Spirits I carry cry out. Who was he? You wouldn't say. You just came straight here."

She almost smiled as she said, "Webworm."

"That was the Blessed Sun?" The notion stunned him. He had actually *seen* the Blessed Sun? The man hadn't looked like a magical figure; his body hadn't glowed in golden rays of light. He'd been average, overweight, and somehow soft. When his attention had turned to the fighting slaves, Nightshade had stalked away—walking with vigor he hadn't suspected the old woman capable of.

"I have come for him," Nightshade said simply. "It is between him and me."

"What is?"

"The future. The past. What might have been. And what might not."

"I don't understand."

"But for a choice made by a far-off Dreamer many sun cycles ago, I would have become Matron of the Straight Path Nation, the last of my clan, and the most Powerful. Would it have been better or worse for our peoples, I cannot say."

"It must be a terrible thing to have such responsibility placed on your shoulders."

"My shoulders?" She laughed. "That morning you decided to climb the mountain to help Ripple with his elk, did you think about it first?"

"Well . . . no."

"Choices. Who knows how decisions you make here will change your life and the lives of thousands of others?"

"Elder? I can't leave you alone."

"Go with the sunrise, young friend. Save yourself and your family."

Spots stared at her, trying to fathom what she was up to, how she would defeat Webworm in the safety of his lair.

The voices in her pack whimpered in fear.

At the sound of people talking, Crow Woman blinked awake, startled to find herself in a pit house. Morning light slanted through the smoke hole to illuminate the inside of a mud-daubed wall. Several white-slipped pots, corrugated-ware cooking vessels, and plain brown seed jars occupied the bench beneath the rectangle of light. Folded clothing rested on a willow mat next to them. The four roof supports had a honeyed look in the morning. Beside her, Wrapped Wrist still slept. With dismay she realized that his chest was pressed against her back, her buttocks neatly formed into the angle of his crotch.

Panic clutched at her heart, a fist squeezing her lungs. She willed herself to take a breath.

It's all right. This is Wrapped Wrist. He's safe . . . inconsequential.

Her heartbeat slowed as cool air entered her lungs. It was just an accident of the way they were sleeping that they'd ended up this way. It had been cold in the night. That's all.

How long had it been since she'd felt comfortable near a man? She swallowed nervously at the memory of his soft voice, cooing as he climbed on top of her and looked down into her eyes.

Snake Head. A witch. He'd eaten whole pieces out of

her souls—left them a patchwork that she'd sewn back together with the greatest difficulty.

"He's here," a woman's voice said from outside. "He arrived last night." A pause. "With a woman." Another pause as she tried to make out the second voice. "I don't know. She's some woman. She was wearing a war shirt, carries a war club, bow and arrows. And she's tall!" Laughter. "You should see her. She *towers* over him like a ponderosa!"

Crow Woman rolled her eyes.

"When I left they were moccasined."

Moccasined? What did that mean?

Crow Woman eased away from Wrapped Wrist's warm body and sat up. Loose strands of hair fell about her face and shoulders where it had come loose from her bun. She reached back, pulling the deer-bone stiletto and spilling the whole mass of it down her back.

"I'll see if he's awake," the voice called. "Or if you're interrupting anything."

The tone in the woman's voice left no doubt what she might be interrupting. Crow Woman balled a fist and thumped Wrapped Wrist's thick muscles with a hard punch. Gods, the man was solid steak. He slitted an eye, mumbling, "I never touched you."

"Someone's coming. I think it's a woman."

Wrapped Wrist sat up, rubbed at his eyes, and stared at her as if he'd never seen her before. "Gods, you're absolutely . . ."

"Yes? What?"

The walls were trembling as someone climbed up and stared down the smoke hole.

"Absolutely—"

"Wrapped Wrist?"

Crow Woman looked up as a young woman clambered down the ladder. She wore a brown skirt woven from some fiber or other, her bare breasts small, the nipples smoothed by the indirect light. She stopped short to give Crow Woman a hard measuring assessment.

"Fir Brush?" Wrapped Wrist asked as he smiled. "Blood and dung, it's good to see you! I see you've kept out of the First People's grasp."

She gave Crow Woman a meaningful jerk of the head. "It looks like you haven't. Who's she? *Another* one of your conquests?"

"Uh, my wife," Wrapped Wrist muttered.

Crow Woman slitted her eyes just long enough to promise retribution, then cleared her expression in time to say, "I hope worms infest your hair, little forest imp," in First People's tongue.

"She doesn't speak like a human," Fir Brush said in amazement. Then her brow furrowed. "Are you sure you're married? I mean, without approval from the clan? No one even knows! And if you've married in opposition to the clan, you'd better hope the Blue God has mercy on you. Old Rattler sure won't."

Wrapped Wrist grinned sheepishly. "I'll tell you . . . but only because you're being hunted by the First People, too. We're only supposed to act married in case the Red Shirts come by. No one is supposed to know she's here."

Fir Brush nodded, then smiled at Crow Woman, saying, "Welcome to First Moon Valley."

In First People tongue, Crow Woman replied, "I hope locusts eat your crops down to stems." Then she smiled politely.

At that, Wrapped Wrist leaned forward, hugging Fir Brush to his breast, eyes closed, a smile on his face. She returned his ardor, clasping him awkwardly as she tried to encompass those broad shoulders.

"I'm glad you're safe," Fir Brush whispered. "I've been sick with worry." She backed away, staring into Wrapped Wrist's eyes. "How's Ripple? I've heard . . . well, terrible things. He's alive, isn't he? Does he need me? I can have Slipped Bark packed, ready to go. We could meet you along the trail."

"He's fine. Fine." Wrapped Wrist made a face. "Gods, how do I explain? He's not Ripple anymore."

Fir Brush tensed, expression hardening. "Because of what they did to him? His hand, his mouth?" She winced. "I heard they cut him. Took his . . ."

"He's healing. As to whether it will ever work, who's to say?"

"Who cares for him? The Mountain Witch?"

"She's with Spots."

"Is he injured, too?"

"No, she's traveling with him."

Fir Brush's eyes widened. "Why?"

"How should I know? I was running messages when she took him. Bad Cast says that he Dreamed her, or she Dreamed him, or some such thing."

Crow Woman arched an eyebrow. How long had it been since she'd seen people act so normally? The scene touched something she'd thought long dead inside her.

Fir Branch shook her head. "This Dream thing will pass. When's he coming home?"

"I don't know." The mood faded, turning serious again. "He may be in Ironwood's camp for a time."

"The war chief?" Fir Brush's eyes widened again. "You've seen him?"

Crow Woman couldn't help but smile at the young woman's awe.

"He's . . . well, impressive," Wrapped Wrist said. "Scary when you first see him, scarred, and his one remaining eye cuts through you like a knife. Then you watch him with his wife, or children, and he's just like anyone else. But sad. Maybe the saddest man I've ever known."

"And Night Sun, you've seen her?"

"Yes."

"What's she like?"

"A stunning woman," Wrapped Wrist answered. "I think she's the greatest lady I have ever seen. She walks with perfect grace, and when she looks at you, a deep serenity lies behind her eyes."

Fir Brush sat back, an expression of amazement on her face. "And Ripple's in the middle of this? Our Ripple? I just can't believe it!"

The walls vibrated again, another face poking into the smoke hole. "Wrapped Wrist? Is that you?"

He looked up. "Yellow Petal?"

Another young woman, this one scarred, thickset, but self-possessed, came climbing down the ladder, followed in turn by Soft Cloth with baby at breast. They both beamed, smiles as if for Wrapped Wrist alone.

Gods, what did he do? Collect young women like a flower drew butterflies?

She sighed; her stomach was empty and her bladder full. She had never had the chance to share a normal woman's society. Had never had female friends like these. Watching them was like observing some strange and distant people. The inside of the pit house looked like a potter's circle.

It was going to be a long day.

From where he lay in the willows, Spots watched the long procession wind out of Dusk House. Like a huge multicolor millipede, it marched down from the first terrace onto the floodplain. At the front strode a thin figure in bright blue robes. He bore a tall walking stick, his eyes thoughtfully on the ground. Behind him came a double line of Priests, dressed in white, their long hair hanging down past the middle of their backs. Then came the warriors, ranks of them wearing red war shirts, their weapons packed in bundles on their backs, most bearing round wicker shields that made them look like bulbous figurines. Four parallel ranks of Made People marched in turn, and finally, at the end, came the slaves with their backs bent under full burden baskets. Warriors trotted along their flanks, calling orders, raising yucca-leaf scourges to swat at any who would tarry.

At the ford, the party waded across and took the eastern trail Spots and Nightshade had come down. East? And he knew: It had to be Blue Racer and his party. They were on their way to First Moon Valley to prepare for the Moon Ceremony.

Spots propped his chin on his right fist and scratched a mosquito bite with his left.

Travel in safety. The words echoed between his souls.

Nightshade had wished him well as he stuffed his blanket into his pack that morning. She had given him the little round brown pot to cook his meals, and had ordered him to take the last of their food.

He had touched his forehead in respect, then wound through the willow trails to this last stand of leaf-green stems. Here, he had stopped, suddenly unsure.

Rot it all, he could still hear the plaintive voices calling from her Spirit pack.

Just go! He knew what few others did: Their world was about to shatter into mayhem and conflict. Nightshade had given him leave to save himself.

Not just myself. Yellow Petal and her baby. Perhaps as many as I can talk into it.

He grimaced as he imagined Yellow Petal's response: "What? You want to leave? Spots, the corn is a moon from being ready to harvest! Do you really think we'd be stupid enough to walk away from our fields? Just leave an entire winter's supply of food? To do what? Go starve in the mountains? All on the word of a witch?"

He chewed his lip, stomach churning in a battle of indecision. The voices in Nightshade's pack were calling.

"We all have choices," he whispered to himself. "Choices on one hand, and the cages that bind us on the other." Yellow Petal was so completely ensnared in the cage of her responsibility that he would have to bind her, gag her, and carry her away from First Moon Valley.

"I should go and try to warn them." He could feel the warp and weft of his own responsibility to his people closing around him.

Of course they would listen to him. Just as they had listened to Ripple? Old White Eye had been the only one who understood, the only one to act.

Yellow Petal's voice chided, "Don't be a fool, Spots! This is our home. Nothing's going to happen to us."

To her, to the majority of his people, it was inconceivable. Generations of the First Moon People had lived there. How could they comprehend that their world was coming to an end? *Gods, but for having lived what I have in the last half moon, how could I?*

He still wasn't sure he believed it.

As he watched the last of the procession splash across the river and begin the winding climb up the silty gray trail, he listened to the grinding of his teeth.

Nightshade's expression that morning haunted his memory.

She knows she might not win, the unified voices whispered to his soul.

Spots frowned as he clawed at another of the mosquito bites. It was sobering to think of what it would take to frighten Nightshade.

Choices.

He groaned, climbed to his feet, and slipped back through the willows. Twice he had to stop, crouching, as women from Flowing Waters Town followed trails through the brush to fill water jars. Only after they had balanced the heavy jugs on their heads and turned back did he proceed.

He approached the little camp he'd shared with Nightshade, using all of his hunter's skills to sneak up on the place.

Nightshade sat there, back straight by the dead fire. He could see a thin gray paste drying on her temples, her eyes glazed and black in her slack face.

She made no move, then smiled slightly, blinked, and reached for her pack.

Spots heard the voices sigh as she shouldered the pack. He almost nodded with the sense of inevitability.

Like a fox he crept along behind her.

Once in the open, she took the shortest trail through the cornfield.

Spots hesitated. Then, throwing caution to the wind, he ran, taking one of the paths through the willows until he crossed the major trail the women followed to get water. Turning, he trotted out into the open, approaching Dusk House from an angle to Nightshade's path. Through occasional openings in the corn he could see her, walking ever so stately in her red dress and black cloak.

Gods, I must be mad.

Forty-three

To avoid the hot morning sun Webworm had seated himself in the shady angle created by Dusk House's eastern and northern walls. Back braced in the corner, his butt rested on a comfortable triple fold of split turkey-feather blanket. A tall mug of berry juice stood by his side; he whistled and scraped at the little stone carving he was making.

Wind Leaf glanced up at the morning; despite the early sun, the sky was already pale, the air hot. A single buzzard could be seen—a portent of the bounty drought could provide. When Wind Leaf looked south, beyond the green band of the river fields, the hills were scorched. The grasses had gone dormant before spring ever began. Even the stones looked thirsty. Slowly dissipating dust marked Blue Racer's path to the east.

Wind Leaf considered the contrast between the spare world around him and the Blessed Sun. The man's round belly was beginning to bulge out over his hips. His light summer shirt had been spun of fine white cotton; it stretched around him like a toad's sides.

The Blessed Sun was whistling softly to himself as he proceeded with his carving. Having seen Blue Racer's procession off, he might not have had a care in the world.

"The last of them have vanished into the hills, Blessed Sun." Wind Leaf shuffled as he waited for some response.

"Good." Webworm finally looked up from his carving. Wind Leaf could see that it was some sort of snake curled inside an egg-shaped jet pebble.

"I've detailed runners to keep us informed of the Sunwatcher's progress, especially once they have reached First Moon Valley." He cleared his throat. "One of my deputies, Leather Hand, hasn't reported to me."

"I'd be surprised if he had. What? Did I forget to tell you?" Webworm cocked his head. "I've given him and his men a special project."

Wind Leaf's stomach tightened. "Did you send him off with a packet of seasonings? I hear that chilies and squash blossoms add a delightful sweet tang to boiling meat."

At that Webworm threw his head back, laughter bubbling from his belly. "Quite so, War Chief. I should have thought of that on my own."

Gods, the man hadn't even caught the irony? "I've begun the process of collecting supplies for your journey, Blessed Sun. I wish, however, that you would tell me why you countermanded my order for another twenty warriors to accompany us to First Moon Valley."

"I am planning on going in secret," he replied. "A large party, as I'm sure you could see with Blue Racer's passage, raises too much dust." He glanced up, smiling. "When we go, it will be quickly, with no warning."

Wind Leaf took a deep breath. "You expect trouble, yet will not allow me to prepare to meet and destroy it."

"There are too many places along the trail where a party can be ambushed. Were we to follow the river bottoms, a smaller force could inflict terrible damage in the canyon narrows. If we were to take the ridges, we would be vulnerable again, either when we climbed up onto the caprock, or when the mesa tops narrowed." He gestured with the stone graver he held. "I learned my lesson well, War Chief."

Wind Leaf exhaled his frustration. After Jay Bird's raid, Webworm had been in charge during the pursuit. His war party had climbed through a treacherous canyon, then out onto an easily defended rim. As they passed into the open—and what should have been relative safety—they'd found a dead captive left behind by Jay Bird. It had been a cunningly devised ambush that had sent Webworm reeling back to Straight Path Canyon in staggering defeat.

"So you will go with a small party? If Ironwood should hear—"

"He won't. That's why I will decide on my own exactly when to leave and which route to take."

"But the additional warriors—"

"I want them here," he declared emphatically. "They must protect the corn!"

"The corn? I'd rather that you not go than waste warriors protecting corn."

"War Chief, a little more than eighteen sun cycles pass between Sister Moon's homecomings. I didn't see it last time, and at my age, it's a sure thing that I won't be here to see it next time. This is my opportunity."

"But the extra warriors, Blessed Sun!"

Webworm looked up expectantly. "They must patrol the river fields. The farmers already have their hands full just battling the raccoons, worms, crows, and other vermin."

Wind Leaf scuffed the packed clay under his feet. Webworm could read displeasure in his expression.

"People are hungry out there." Webworm gestured randomly toward the south. "What good does it do me to travel to Pinnacle Great House to watch Sister Moon come home if the country is starved into revolt over the coming winter?"

Wind Leaf winced, thinking, *I'd rather fight a disorganized hunger-weakened rabble than one better fed, led by a resurrected Ironwood, and goaded on by the murder of a Blessed Sun.*

Webworm gestured with his chert graver again. "I've had some of the Priests out counting."

"Counting?" The change of subject surprised him.

"Yes, counting the number of fields, looking at the corn, beans, and squash plants. We have a chance to avoid calamity. That is to confiscate as much corn as we can, carry it here under guard, and parcel it out throughout the winter. I'll pack every room in Flowing Waters Town, Northern Town, and the rest of the great houses. People may starve this winter—some obviously will—but the First People *must* be seen to help. Everyone must know that their Blessed Sun is working for their good."

"What you are hoping is that something will be better than nothing. That you can buy the goodwill of the people."

Webworm went back to his carving. "The Priests think

that the harvest from the irrigated river fields will be substantial. At least enough to feed people within a seven-days' walk of the valley great houses. Meanwhile, we have another problem."

"And that is?"

"Protecting the harvest. Most of the storerooms in the great houses are depleted. Some, in the dryland areas, have already been stripped bare. By harvest, the Matrons will have no more corn left to distribute. All those hungry people will be looking our direction. If they should descend on these northern river valleys during harvest, it will be like a swarm of locusts."

"Then, what is the choice?"

"I will need patrols of warriors to guard the roads, War Chief. The choice is, Do we pull the warriors away from the Moon Ceremony to guard the harvest?"

Wind Leaf cocked his head. "Absolutely not!"

"You need not worry about the harvest," a soft voice said.

Wind Leaf turned. The old woman wore a black cloak decorated with white stars over a faded red dress. Then he saw her eyes: large and glassy, as though seeing things beyond this world. They dominated her once-beautiful face. Long gray strands of hair fell over her shoulders. She was slim, nearly as tall as he; a worn pack hung over one shoulder.

Something about her sent a shiver down Wind Leaf's spine, as if he could feel prickly insect feet slipping about his skin. Of the verge of dismissing her, he remembered having seen her the day before.

"Who are you?" he asked.

Evidently the Blessed Sun felt the same stirring unease. "The Witness."

"Witness? What witness? To see what?" Webworm glared at her. Even Wind Leaf noticed that he was suddenly rolling the little carving around in his hand.

The woman's eyes had fixed on it. "Curious, isn't it? Only now can you feel its Power."

Webworm looked down at the carving. "This? It's nothing. Something I saw once. I think the design came from the Hohokam."

"It's called a basilisk: a snake born of a cock's egg. A perversion of Power. You are getting ready to inlay a red coral eye into the serpent's head," she told him. "Do you remember the first time you looked into the snake's loathsome eye?"

"It was years ago, just after I became Blessed Sun."

"That was the moment the slithering evil entered your souls."

"You will address me as Blessed Sun, old woman. And unless you tell me your name and your clan, I shall have your tongue pulled out by its roots."

Delicate mocking laughter rolled out of her. "A few sun cycles in charge and already you are hardened by selfish authority. You really don't know me, do you? Your souls have grown so full of you that they cannot see past themselves."

"Drag her away from here," Webworm muttered, returning to his carving.

Wind Leaf took two steps toward the woman before she fixed her dark eyes on his like a slap. In that instant, his thoughts swayed and a weakness ran through his blood. He stopped short, shaking his head to clear it. He blinked, confused.

Webworm gave Wind Leaf a glare. "I thought I told you—"

The old woman spoke slowly, each syllable perfectly enunciated in the formal address of the First People. "I am Nightshade, Matron of the Hollow Hoof Clan, Keeper of the Tortoise Bundle, daughter of Matron Yarrow. My father was Red Crane, Sunwatcher of the Red Lacewing Clan. In fulfillment of a long-ago promise, I have returned to the Straight Path Nation."

"What promise?" Webworm asked.

"One given my mother . . . long ago." Her odd eyes enlarged. "Brother Mud Head has seen to the dead. My concern is with you, Webworm."

"Nightshade?" he asked, thinking. "I'm supposed to believe you are the Mountain Witch?"

Wind Leaf swallowed hard. Gods, what was she doing

here? He reached down, his fingers caressing the handle of his war club.

"The stories they tell about you"—Webworm sounded bored—"you just wouldn't believe them. Did you really get carried off to the land of the distant Temple Builders?"

"I was called to be a witness there, too."

He studied her from under heavy lids. "Are the towns of the forest kings as great as ours?"

She never even hesitated as she said, "The entirety of the Straight Path Nation could fit into the province of one lesser chief. Some of their cities are surrounded by walls forty hands high. Their rulers derive from bloodlines that go back to the beginning of the world."

"What about their warriors? Could they be a threat?"

"You can muster a large war party. The Great Sun can dispatch armies. In battle they are invincible."

"Then why don't they ever come here?" Webworm had begun to smile, as if he'd caught her in a lie. "They took you—never to return."

"Why should they?" Nightshade tilted her head back, staring down her fine nose in disgust. "We have nothing they want, or need. Don't you understand? They are old. Their traditions go back to the beginning of the world. While our ancestors were moving from camp to camp, theirs were already building temples to the sun. It was their Trade that awakened the Stone Temple Builders in the south hundreds of sun cycles ago. To the forest kings we are nothing more than curious barbarians living somewhere out in the dimly perceived desert wastes."

"Barbarians?" Wind Leaf snorted.

She spared him a quick glance. "The sort—barely above animals—that eat other human beings."

Webworm made an irritated sound and continued scraping on his little snake effigy. "Go on back to Ironwood and Night Sun. Tell them their days are numbered."

"The patterns are cast, Webworm. I've come to Dance with you."

"What? Dance with me?" He looked up, taking in her

age and smiling at the insanity of it. "It might strain you too much."

Her voice dropped to a conspiratorial whisper. "I can send you to them."

"Them? Who?" Webworm demanded.

"Cloud Playing and Matron Featherstone. I can free you."

His face had gone white. He looked at Wind Leaf. "You know the bear cage? The one we kept the young grizzly in? I want it placed in the plaza. Put her there, stripped naked, where everyone can see her. It's time the myth of the Mountain Witch is finally put to rest."

Nightshade laughed, turning, and as Wind Leaf hurried in pursuit, she called over her shoulder, "I can *free* you, Webworm."

"That's quite a family you've got," Crow Woman said as they followed the path that led across the valley bottom.

Wrapped Wrist glanced over his shoulder at the sunset. The sky was glowing red and orange over the ridges. To the north, the smoke plume was cast in evening bronze by the slanting light. Compared with that morning, the plume was larger, puffing like a giant mushroom over the high peaks and trailing off into the east in a dirty smear.

"They're clan kin. Surely you grew up with the same."

"No, Wrapped Wrist, I didn't."

Gods, did everything he said have to set her off?

Then she seemed to relent, saying in a softer voice, "I had no relatives."

"*Everybody* grows up with family, cousins, lineages, and clans, although I hear some of the Tower Builders up north don't have moieties."

"No," she replied shortly, "not everybody does."

Cautiously he asked, "What about your mother?"

"Why do you want to know?"

"We travel together. I'd like to know something about who I'm traveling with."

"She died when I was little more than five."

"And your aunts and uncles?"

"I never knew them."

"How could you never know them?"

"Do you have granite for brains?"

Giving her a sidelong glance, he could see her pinched expression. "Well, you surely weren't a slave. You'd have . . ." The bitterness in her face was all the answer he needed.

As the light fled, he tossed the revelation back and forth between his souls. What must her childhood have been like? How on earth had she ever escaped to become one of Ironwood's most trusted warriors?

"What incredible courage," he whispered.

"Courage?" she whispered softly. "I've been scared all of my life." As if she realized what she'd said, she hissed angrily at herself.

After a time he asked, "Where did you grow up?"

"I don't want to talk about it."

The red ember of sunset faded in the west; gloom settled around them as they entered the trees. A party of hunters, packing deer, turkeys, rabbits, and several porcupines, passed, calling greetings.

"Someone's going to be happy," Wrapped Wrist noted. "The dryer it gets, the harder the hunting is."

She said nothing.

"It'll be a long dark walk to our divide camp. There's a little meadow ahead that would make a good camp."

Silence.

"Are you always infuriated?"

"Don't worry about me, stumpy."

Stumpy? He hadn't deserved that ember being stuck between his blankets.

"You must be the most unhappy person alive."

A hand of time later, Crow Woman agreed to make camp. They ate in silence the corn cakes that White Eye had provided for their return trip.

Wrapped Wrist rolled into his blanket, listening to the crickets and hearing the occasional cry of the nightjar. The night lay heavily on the land.

She surprised him, saying, "I grew up in Fourth Night

House—a town on the Turquoise Trail east of Straight Path Canyon. It's a dismal place, dry and dusty, constantly windblown. The land is dull yellow—the soil, the rocks—even the sky takes on that color.

"As a girl I carried water, removed ash from the heating bowls, emptied waste pots, and trapped rodents. I helped prepare and cook food, mixed plaster, carried stone and timbers, and sweated in their miserable excuse of a cornfield."

She paused for a while.

"The thing was, the other slaves treated me differently. So did my Made People masters, and even the First People who lived there. I got more to eat than the others, and was allowed to sleep in the Matron's storeroom." She hesitated. "The rumor was that I was Crow Beard's daughter. That he'd taken a liking to my mother on his trips through." She shrugged. "I never allowed myself to believe it."

Wrapped Wrist kept his peace.

"I only had one friend. The girl who taught me your tongue. She was sleeping with the Matron's oldest son at the time. On occasion he would sneak into our room after dark and lay with her."

Wrapped Wrist wondered if he should say anything.

"I was in love with him, too. I used to listen to them, hear the kindness in his voice as he whispered into her ear, and muffled cries of delight from their fierce coupling." She sighed. "Then his younger brother came to my bed just after my first moon as a woman. Everything his brother was, he was not. I bled for days after he jammed himself into me."

An owl hooted in the trees.

"My friend and her lover left for Straight Path Canyon. The younger brother had always been considered something of a nuisance, never having his brother's courage or talent at doing things. He took out his parents' displeasure on me."

In the long silence that followed, Wrapped Wrist could well imagine the ways a spoiled young man could abuse a woman under his command.

"I ran off," Crow Woman continued. "It was a spring storm. Wind Baby had blackened the sky with blowing dust. In desperation I charged off into the middle of that. Gods, the sand felt like it would scour the skin right off my face. It plugged my nose, ground in my teeth, and burned in my eyes, but I continued, walking into the wind, following the road to Straight Path Canyon. It was the only place I could think of to go, since my friend and her young lover had gone there."

"Did you find them?" he asked softly.

"Oh, yes. She was glad to see me, and while he understood my reasons for running away, he was a new warrior in the Blessed Sun's guard. It was his 'duty,' he said. He took me to Talon Town to ensure that I was taken back to Fourth Night House when . . ."

She tossed in her blankets, unable to finish.

Wrapped Wrist waited for a moment before asking, "Did they ever take you back to Fourth Night House?"

In the dim darkness, he thought he saw her shake her head.

"Snake Head," she whispered, "wouldn't let them."

"The one they said was a . . ." He wouldn't utter the word 'witch,' afraid of what if might do to her.

"By the gods," she almost whimpered, "he was a monster. The things he . . ." Her dry swallow was audible.

In a reasonable voice, Wrapped Wrist said, "He is dead, his souls howling forever. You are alive."

In a half-frantic voice she said, "Why am I telling you this?"

"Have you ever told anyone else?"

"No."

"Then maybe you needed to tell someone. I've heard from the Healers that sometimes just speaking the words can start the souls on the way to Healing."

"If you ever speak of this to anyone, I swear . . ."

He chuckled at the fury behind her words. "Yes, yes, I know. My death will be painful and long."

She sat up in her blankets. "Do you mock me?"

"Quite the contrary, I honor you."

For long moments she hovered in indecision before lying back in her blankets. "Good night, Wrapped Wrist. In the morning I don't want to be reminded that I said any of this."

He rolled over onto his side. *No, of course not.*

Still, sleep wouldn't come. His fertile mind kept conjuring the images of things that she might have endured at the hands of various evil and violent men.

When he finally awoke, morning was breaking; dawn looked bloody and dull as sunlight fingered the smoke-blackened eastern horizon.

When he glanced over, only flattened grass marked the place where she'd laid her bed the night before.

Forty-four

To think about walking unafraid into the middle of the First People's world by himself was one thing; to actually set foot inside Dusk House without Nightshade's protection was something else.

Terrible stories were told of the First People late at night by crackling pit house fires. Tales of their evil deeds, of the hideous rites they practiced, and of how their heartless cruelty knew no bounds. Of course, they had enslaved many of Spots's people over the years, and those few whom fate had spared often broke into tears as they related their experiences in the quarries, or of building the great roads, ramps, and stairways that tied the Straight Path Nation together.

"I should be on my way home," Spots mumbled as he stared at the massive buildings. The symmetrical perfection of Dusk House contrasted to the thriving activity as tens of tens labored to raise Sunrise House. He could hear the distant clattering as the masons used stone hammers to true sandstone slabs for the walls.

His attention kept going back to that immense construction. One wrong move and that's where they would put him: just another slave to build their great house. Assuming, that is, that they didn't just crack his skull and toss his body out to rot in the cornfields.

We all have choices to make. Nightshade's words echoed hollowly within him.

Gods, did a choice have to include the runny feeling of fear that coursed through his guts?

Did Nightshade really need him? Surely, if she had, she would have kept him at her side. On the other hand, he remembered that clear look of fear and resignation behind her eyes as she'd dismissed him.

Something terrible is going to happen to her.

"Then don't let it happen to you," he growled to himself as he watched the dawn light grow brighter.

He stood, throwing his pack over his shoulder. That's it: Be gone. Back to First Moon Valley. He had obligations to his kin. Yellow Petal had to be warned—for what little good that would do. He made a face as he imagined her mocking eyebrow as he told her to pack her things and leave. And what about his kiva? He owed it to his brothers to warn them. And then there was his clan. His duty was to take Nightshade's warning straight to Elder Rattler. Tell her to prepare for disaster.

He nodded, his mind made up. He made no more than four steps toward the Spirit River ford and stopped.

Who did he think he was? Worse, who would his people think he was? A young hunter? Bearing warnings from the Mountain Witch?

They would brand him a fool.

He groaned aloud as he fingered the rough fabric of his sack. Placing himself back in time, to the person he had been before Ripple's vision, he knew how he would have reacted to hearing another young hunter give such a warning of disaster: He'd have dragged him kicking and screaming to have a Healer return his lost Dream soul to his body, for this was obviously the ranting of a sick man.

Choices.

He looked back over his shoulder, turned, and started forward. As he broke the cover of the willows and set foot down the path toward Dusk House, he glanced at the corn. The immature ears were thickening, the kernels green within them. It would be a good crop.

Enough to keep them from stripping First Moon Valley bare? he wondered. As he walked, the smoke plume in the north could be seen. The entirety of the northeastern horizon had turned murky. It matched the Rainbow Serpent's smudge to the southwest.

Fire on two corners of our world.

That notion kept repeating itself as he tried to figure out what he'd say if one of the guards stopped him.

"I'm a Trader."

"Oh, and what did you bring to Trade?"

"Well, nothing. I thought I'd see what they needed here."

He wrinkled his nose. This was Flowing Waters Town. They needed nothing. They *took* everything.

"I'm here looking for my brother."

"What might your brother's business be here?"

"He's a stonemason."

"Then you'd better go down, put on a slave's work shirt, and join him."

Spots didn't like that one, either.

"I'm here with a message for the Mountain Witch."

This time, the guard didn't respond; instead his wrist flicked and a war club caved in the side of Spots's head.

"Gods," he muttered as he left the cover of the cornfields and stepped out onto the Great North Road. He stopped for a moment, looking at the wide thoroughfare.

He imagined it, running straight as a stretched cord southward, across high desert to Straight Path Canyon, and from there on down in the distance. How far south? To the end of the world? It was said that the souls of the dead were released at Center Place to travel this road northward to the *sipapu* that allowed them to descend into the Underworlds. There they would find the Land of the Dead and their ancestors. Did Spirits walk this way even as he stood here?

Did they pass him, wondering at the poorly clad barbarian hunter with his pack?

"Are you planning to be a tree?" a voice asked in Made People tongue.

Spots jumped, heart racing as he turned. The dark-haired Trader had a medium build, three pack dogs at his heel. The man was looking him up and down. "Sorry, didn't mean to scare you."

"I—I was thinking about the Great North Road."

"Glad to see you speak a little of my tongue." He cocked his head. "You look like you're straight out of the hills. Come down to see how real people live?"

Spots swallowed hard and nodded. "I can't believe it. I'm actually standing on the Great North Road?"

"Of course you are. The gods know I've trod it long enough," the Trader added wearily. "What people are you from?"

"First Moon."

"They about ready for the ceremony up there? The Sunwatcher left yesterday." A question lay behind the man's eyes.

What do I say? "Among my people, a great many stories are told about this place. I just thought . . . Oh, it's probably silly."

At that the Trader smiled. "No, not silly. Me, I left the Green Mesas so fast the pollen from my kiva initiation was still sifting out of my hair. Sometimes the people at home don't understand those of us who have to see the rest of the world."

Spots gestured at Dusk House. "Can I go in there, or will they take me prisoner, or something? I can't just walk up and say, 'I want to see inside,' can I?"

The Trader chuckled. "Sure. No one will care unless you climb up the ladders onto the second floor. That's only for the First People and those others who have reason to be there. If you stay in the plaza, no one's going to say a thing. You can poke your head inside the south entrance to the great kiva, but stay off the First People's kiva. Lastly, don't touch anything that's not yours."

Spots nodded. "Thank you. I won't."

The Trader narrowed his eyes as he took in the scars, along with the smooth muscle in Spots's body. "I'd say you had a close call with that fire."

"It changed my life. When you come that close to your end, you see the world differently."

"Interested in traveling down to the Mogollon country?" He pointed at the pack on his back. "I've got some fine First People pottery here. The Fire Dogs will Trade their redware, two for one. I could use the company on the way south. Introduce you around, teach you some of the tricks of the Trade."

Spots grinned, genuinely liking the man. "I thank you from both of my souls, but no. After I see this place, I must get back."

"Ah, yes, Moon Ceremony and all." He puckered his lips, brow lined in thought. "You know, I've never seen . . . No, no. That doesn't make sense. As much as I'd like to see Sister Moon come home, I don't think I can Trade my pots to the First Moon People for anything anyone else would want." He reached around to pat his pack. "Me, I specialize in luxury goods, not that bulk stuff."

"May your travels be safe."

"Yours, too." The Trader passed him, calling, "See you on the trail someday."

Spots turned, taking a deep breath, and headed straight toward Dusk House. *Stay in the plaza. Don't touch anything that's not yours. Stay off the First People's kiva.* That wasn't so hard, and the last thing he was going to do was linger there any longer than it took to have a good look around and see if Nightshade's situation could be discerned.

Still, his heart refused to obey his head's instructions as he approached the huge building. It was a wonder how much courage Nightshade's mere presence had given him the last time he'd strode up to the tall walls.

Like last time, people were squatting outside the walls, many sitting on blankets. Some wove baskets in the morning sun; others knapped stone tools from blanks. Two old women were hawking Spirit Plants, bundles of herbs laid out on white cloths.

Another old man saw him coming and cried, "Charms! I have charms! Young man, for a pittance you can free your souls from fear! Ward off the evil eye!" He waved something that looked like a dried raccoon's foot on a thong.

A little girl ran up to him, asking, "Do you have corn? Please? I haven't eaten in a week! Mother is dying."

He smiled uncertainly at the little waif, avoiding her grasping hands as she pulled at the bottom of his pack.

"Didn't expect this," he told himself. No one had bothered Nightshade that first time she'd approached.

A young man in a white tunic spread a black blanket on the ground and laid out lines of turquoise, jet, coral, and polished shell jewelry. The pieces literally shone in the sunlight. It was more wealth than Spots had ever seen in one place.

He thanked the gods he was smart enough not to meet their eyes, hoping desperately that they wouldn't take him for the naive barbarian he was.

The tall wall before him curved ever so slightly. To his unease, a red-shirted warrior stood on the southeastern corner. Spots battled with the urge to turn tail and run. He wasn't sure his legs weren't shaking as he passed around the end of the wall past a young woman offering corn cakes for Trade and looked up at the high east room block of Dusk House. Yet another guard stood there, his bored eyes noting Spots, lingering for a moment on his scars, and passing on to the slave who walked past with a stinking pot of night earth in his hands.

Spots swallowed hard and hurried past. The plaza opened before him, and he stopped. To his right, the First People's kiva rose waist high above the ground. To its left the huge cylinder of the great kiva gleamed in the morning light. But it was the splendor of Dusk House—rising four stories high and cupping the plaza like a mother's arms—that took his breath away. For long moments he just stared, trying to comprehend what he was seeing. Last time the size of the place hadn't sunk in. Nightshade had been in a hurry—coming and going.

"Surprised?" asked a young woman who appeared at his elbow.

"I never suspected."

"You have a strange accent."

He spared her a glance. She was a little shorter than he, an odd weariness in her eyes. Her breasts stretched her too-tight dress, and her hips seemed to struggle for liberation against the restricting cloth.

"Tall Piñon," he lied. "I'm of the Deep Canyon folk."

Her knowing eyes fixed on his. "No, you're not. First Moon, or somewhere up there in the north, if I don't miss my guess."

"Does it make a difference?"

"No. You just here for the day?"

"I don't know. I just came to see."

"I'm called Cactus Flower." She smiled. "I could guide you."

"You could?"

She indicated his pack. "Depends on what you've got in there. I Trade for services. Let's say for a jar of corn, I can take you around the plaza, show you the great kiva, point out the Blessed Sun's quarters—"

"Up there." He pointed to where he'd seen Webworm while in Nightshade's company.

"You've been here before."

"Once."

Cactus Flower added, "For a shell comb, I could put you up for the night. I have a farmstead up on the terrace. The bed is nice, no fleas or lice. An abalone pendant? Well, I could make your stay most memorable." She swished her hips in a suggestive way.

He tried not to gape. "Thanks, but I don't have any of those things."

"I'm always around." Cactus Flower shrugged, took two steps, and matched stride with a Trader who entered between the walls. He laughed and shook his head, waving her off. She gave a saucy flip of her long black hair and retired to the shade of the wall to await new prey.

Spots felt his heart begin to settle into its normal rhythm. He'd just take a turn about the plaza, maybe look inside the great kiva, and slip out, assured that wherever Nightshade was, he didn't need to . . .

He stopped short, seeing the stout wooden cage. The thing was as tall as a man. Lengths of wrist-thick lodgepole pine had been used for bars. These had been fitted into holes bored into larger ponderosa logs. Thick willow stems had been woven between them for strength. Through the bars, Spots could see something crouched inside. A group of small children were staring in, one little boy whacking at the bars with a stick. Others were making faces.

Spots followed the walls around, glancing up at the upper floors. Nowhere did he see Nightshade among the visible people. While some comfort came from the fact that no one gave him a second look, he could feel the faintest sense of something.

"Must be the Spirits of this place," he muttered as he walked along under the west room block. A most notable man dressed in a bright red war shirt stopped to give instructions to a warrior who stood with a shield over his back. Then the fellow proceeded at a fast clip for the ladders leading to the upper stories.

"War Chief?" Spots wondered. What was his name? Wind Leaf? Or might that have been the dreaded Leather Hand?

At the thought, he whispered, *"Check the kiva, and get your skinny self out of here."*

He turned, approaching the great kiva. The big cage squatted no more than fifteen hands before the kiva entrance. Spots took long enough to lean his head in, marveling at the huge timbers that made up the roof. The painted images between the illuminated vaults dazzled him. A smoldering fire sent fingers of smoke toward the massive ceiling.

"Witch!" a child spat in Made People's tongue. The stick clattered on the wood again.

Spots turned, shaking his head at the magnificence of the great kiva. Just imagine the spectacle of the gods as they came Dancing into . . .

He frowned, watching as a young man, a short slave limping on a bad ankle, hesitated long enough to dash the contents of a night pot onto the bars of the cage. He smiled crookedly as the children scampered away, holding their noses.

Spots frowned, giving the cage a wide berth. Nightshade was nowhere to be seen. It was time for him to start home.

The voices! He cocked his head, hearing them. Instinctively, he wanted to shift the pack on his back, only to remember that Nightshade had taken it with her.

He stopped short, listening.

Yes, a desperation lay behind their urgent plea.

"Gods," he whispered. Something made him look closer at the cage. His very body willed itself to walk up to the bars.

"Elder?" he muttered, seeing her in the shadowed interior. Her long silvering hair draped her shoulders, apparently her only protection outside of the bars. She sat naked, legs crossed, her hands palm up on her knees.

He stepped around, calling louder, "Elder?"

"All things in their time, hunter." Her voice was emotionless. "Mine has not yet come. No matter what choice you have made, do not tarry here."

He glanced back and forth between the bars. "Do you have food or water?"

"For the moment, I am still a novelty. They are watching. Do not let them see you. Go now. If you would help me, it must be through stealth and cunning."

"Where is your pack?"

"The Blessed Sun kept it." She looked up, her eyes boring into his. "If you do not go now, all will be undone. I am just where I need to be. Go!"

He backed up, and must have had a funny look on his face as he started for the gate.

"See!" the urchin with the stick cried. "She's just an old woman. She's no witch."

Spots surprised himself when he pointed at the little

boy's chest. "If you torment her again, your stomach is going to hurt. In four days, your bowels will be passing bloody stools. Unless you seek her forgiveness, you will die screaming."

The urchin's eyes widened, and in an instant, he was gone, little feet pounding.

Gods, why did I do that?

Or had it been the Spirit voices speaking through him?

"Oh, Spots, what are you going to do now?"

Forty-five

Where he lay on Orenda's bed, Ripple jerked awake, sweat trickling down his sides. He gasped and ran his hand across his face. To his relief it was late morning, a muted light angling through the door. Gods, had he slept half the morning away? Or had the Dream—so very Powerful and haunting—refused to free him from its grip?

Images were still wheeling around his souls, so clear, the colors so bright: High atop First Moon Mountain, Cold Bringing Woman was Dancing in the darkness. As she wheeled, her cloak sailed through the night sky. She would lean close, eyes glowing red. Her cold breath blew a numbing frost over the burning building. Ripple had looked up through the flames leaping yellow around him. He could still hear the screams and piteous wailing. An odd tingle remained in his legs where the Dream fire had burned them.

It was with amazement that he looked at the clear morning air inside Orenda's small room, surprised not to see sooty flakes falling around him.

Beside him, Orenda sat up on the narrow bed, the blanket slipping from around her shoulders. "Are you all right?"

He nodded, running his tongue over the ruination of his teeth. Several of the jagged roots had loosened and come free the day before. He'd spit them and the bloody pus they'd produced onto the hard ground.

"Dream?" she asked, eyes widening.

"Yes. I was atop Pinnacle Great House. Standing in the middle of a raging fire. People were screaming. Terrified women clawed at my legs, trying to climb them to safety." He closed his eyes, reliving the details. "Blood was running down my legs, trickling out in pools that fed the fires. As smoke rose from the burning blood, it turned black, falling as flakes."

Orenda laid a hand on his shoulder. "Are you all right?"

"I have to be there."

She narrowed her eyes. "Ripple, you don't need to go back. Your message has been delivered. We know Cold Bringing Woman's vision. Ironwood is already plotting how he will take Pinnacle Great House. Leave it to the warriors."

He reached up, placing his palm against her cheek. Her skin was soft and warm. "I must be there. It's my blood, you see."

She stared into his eyes, trying to read his souls. "Your blood is better off in your body. If Pinnacle Great House must burn, let the fire feed from its wood and matting. You're not even fully Healed yet. You need to stay here where I can tend you."

Trying to find the right words, he said, "I am part of this. A circle. A beginning that must become the end. Without me, I can sense that there will be a wrongness. Some part of this will be incomplete. I am part of the pattern drawn by Power. I must weave myself into the final fabric." He paused. "Does that make sense?"

She nodded, a weary acceptance in her eyes. "Yes, yes. I know the ways of Power. Oh, do I ever. And I'm tired of it, Ripple. Tired of being at the center of great events. By Birdman's sacred mace, I'd break free if I could. I want to go away somewhere, build a house by a stream and grow corn and squash. I want to lie with a man who won't hurt me, and learn what love is. Can't I be left alone, have the chance to conceive and have children? I want to watch them grow, and play, and smile at them as they sit by the fire. Why is it impossible for me?"

He stared down at his left hand where it rested in a mass of splints. The bones were itching, most of the swelling gone. Through gaps he could see scabs crusted and loose atop pink skin on what had once been knuckles.

"Answers are always hard to find," he said mildly. "From the day I watched my mother and father die I have wanted nothing but the First People's destruction. I had not thought to find anything I would want as much." He smiled sadly. "I haven't told you before, but Raven Hunter gave me a vision. In it, I saw your face."

"Then don't go."

"I made a promise to Cold Bringing Woman."

She said nothing. Perhaps Orenda of all people knew what came of breaking promises to the gods.

Oh, the gods, what capricious beings they are. As woven into the ways of Power as humans, but with the ability to use it for their own purposes. Once I feared the gods. That was such a long time ago, before I realized that they, too, were as mortal as I. True, the lives of gods are longer, and the Spirit World in which they live has more twists and turns than the earth that people walk; but in the end, they, too, shall die.

I have yet to truly understand how gods harness the Power they use. I think it resembles the whirlpools and eddies along one of the great eastern rivers. Power is the current, constantly flowing through time. Somehow the gods concentrate that current for their own, holding it for a time, using it for their petty aims. But in the end, they can no more hoard Power than any of us can hoard life. As a god's Power drains away, he wilts, fades, and finally whimpers into a memory. Memory as we all know is ephemeral as a summer rain.

As I sit in my cage, I ponder the irony. In the beginning, people depend on gods for their survival; and in the end, it is the gods who desperately depend on people for theirs. Time will defeat them both.

I cock my head, listening. The faint whisper of the Tortoise Bundle carries from Webworm's room. By now it is sending its tendrils down into his souls. What a fool he is, inviting Power into his Dreams.

All the while he carves another basilisk.

Meanwhile, I sit in my cage. I have heard them say I'm harmless.

Let them believe.

"**F**ool! Fool! You stupid fool!" What on earth had gotten into her? She'd told him things she'd never said to anyone. What was it about him that had conjured such idiocy?

Crow Woman trotted down the sinuous trail, winding her way between patches of pine and lodgepole. She had crossed the divide into the River of Souls Valley. The ford that would take her to Ironwood's camp lay no more than three hands' journey ahead. As she hurried along, her shield, bow, and arrows clattered on her back; with a willow switch she slashed angrily at the brown grass.

She had awakened in the night, morning still hands of time away. Shivering from the nightmares that had haunted her, she'd stared over to where he slept so peacefully. Regret, like a thing alive, had been twisting in her breast.

How would she dare face him in the morning? She'd never be able to look him in the eyes again, knowing that he *knew*! By letting her words run like a brook, she'd given him bits of her souls, pieces he could use against her.

And he would.

He was a man.

Maybe he wouldn't.

She viciously squashed the voice that tried to wedge its way into her thoughts. Of course he would. What man hadn't tried to harm her, humiliate her, bend her to his purpose?

The war chief.

Very well, there had been one. But his respect for her hadn't been shared by his warriors. Her lip lifted in disgust as she remembered the night Whistle had caught her in the willows. How his hands had groped her breasts, how his hot breath had purled across her neck. Or the look of surprise on his face when she'd dimpled his throat with a deer-bone stiletto she used to pin her hair.

Yes! By the gods, that's how you deal with them!

Through a patch in the trees she glared up at the brown pall that cloaked the east. Jays screeched in the trees. The morning smelled of dry grass and dust.

On top of everything else she was an escaped slave with Dreams of something better. She could make no claim on family, kin, clan, or tribe. Her only defense lay in her ability with weapons and in the cold aloofness she maintained with her comrades.

So why had she confessed so much to Wrapped Wrist?

She shook her head, deluged with self-disgust as she stormed down the trail. Around her, muted light gave the ponderosa and lodgepole pine a ruddy tone as it filtered through the smoke-hazy eastern sky. Through patches in the trees she could see the distant plume. With each passing day the pall grew larger as it was carried off to the east.

If the sky was a bowl—as some people maintained— eventually it should fill up. But for days now, the smoke had just vanished over the eastern horizon. That being the case, just how big was the world? Not even Nightshade had seen the eastern edge of it, and she had lived out there for years.

A memory of Wrapped Wrist smiling, eyes sparkling as he talked to his kinswomen, lingered down in her souls. Was that it? She'd seen him so at ease, watched the warmth as he talked to Yellow Petal, Soft Cloth, and Fir Brush. They had genuinely enjoyed each other's company. It had touched some part of her souls she had long thought cold and dead. The very notion of a man at ease with women had confused her.

Enjoyed? In her experience, no woman had ever enjoyed a man's company. If he wasn't ordering her around, working her until her fingers bled, or trying to ram his rod into her, he was asleep.

Wrapped Wrist had thought his relationship so normal;

that had confused her even more. *"They're clan kin. Surely you grew up with the same."* He might have been saying, "The sky is blue."

It's not blue, you fool.

If only it had been. She thought back, way back. She'd accepted the beatings and humiliation that came with being a slave. She'd never known any different. As a girl she had come to admire Wraps His Tail, the Matron's son. For a brief instant when a hard warm body slid into her bed that first night, she'd thought it was he. Only to discover it was his brother who clamped a hand over her mouth, groped her breasts, and jacked her legs apart with his knee.

She'd started to cry out when his hard shaft began prodding at her, but a hand had closed like a rawhide clamp over her throat. He hadn't even forced himself inside when he stiffed and groaned, his seed trickling hot across her skin.

Cursing under his breath, he'd slumped. For long moments she'd lain in fear, taking shallow breaths, feeling his semen soak into the blanket beneath her buttocks.

"Put your hands on me," he'd finally growled into her ear. "If you don't, by the Blue God, come morning, they'll never find your body."

Somehow she'd managed to overcome his ineptitude, contributing to her own rape that night.

So she'd run away—right into worse trouble.

Leather Hand had been nothing compared to Snake Head. She remembered his face, triangular to the point that his cheekbones seemed to stick out of the side of his head. That first night the firelight had glowed red on one side of his face; he was grinning down at her as he twirled a greased stick painfully inside her. The worthless weasel had been absolutely gleeful as she chewed on her wrist to keep from screaming. And all the while, his guards had remained oblivious just beyond his door.

She looked down in the morning light and could still see the faint scars marring her skin. Generate enough pain, burn with a hot-enough anger, and she could endure anything—even Snake Head. Even the memories, and the bits of her souls he had ripped out of her.

"I *saved* myself!" She knotted a fist, feeling familiar anger come bubbling up from inside. Anger had been her ally. It had nerved her when Whistle grabbed her in the willows. He'd seen it burning behind her eyes, felt it in the stiletto tip she'd pressed into his throat. The knowledge was in his eyes every time he looked at her: *I made him fear!*

So why should she think Wrapped Wrist was any different? Perhaps he did treat his kin well, but they were off-limits, family, and thus safe. But let him have a vulnerable woman in his control, and yes, the beast would come out.

She was thinking of Wrapped Wrist, her souls seeing that sparkle of good humor in his eyes, when the trail entered a thick patch of serviceberry. Her thoughts were on his smile, on his unassuming manner, so different from the men she had known.

Gods, yes, he watched her body with the same desire other men did, but not with that covetous need to possess. No, he watched her with something akin to worship. When had a man ever looked at her that way?

She couldn't help but smile as she remembered the first day when he'd tried to run her into the dirt. A stubby sawed-off chunk like him shouldn't be trying games with a long-legged distance runner like her.

Still, he'd given it a—

Two hard hands clasped her from behind.

She'd just raised her hands to claw free when another body exploded out of the brush. Then another, and another, until she was driven down into the dusty trail, pinned by the weight of hard bodies.

"A woman, by the gods," a man cried. "Look what a prize we have here."

She tried to struggle as they stripped off her shield, her bow and arrows, her war club. A pinning knee jammed painfully in the small of her back. Hard hands groped her, ripped the stiletto out of her hair bun, and invaded her clothing. They found her obsidian blade and tossed it away.

She fought as they bound her hands behind her and tied a short length of braided leather between her ankles.

As they stood, she rolled onto her back, ready to kick out, and looked up at the four hard-eyed men. They were muscular, fit-looking, their bright red shirts and weapons proclaiming them to be the Blessed Sun's.

"Now," one said, "before we take you to the deputy, where might you have been headed?"

"Eat pus, maggot!"

Funny how I'm always carrying firewood these days. The notion amused Spots as he picked his way down the dusty trail out onto the high terrace. Evening was darkening the east, sunset having turned the smoke plume up north to deep lavender mixed with splashes of ruddy orange. Meanwhile in the southwest, the Rainbow Serpent had risen in a high column of blue-black backlit by the sinking sun.

Smoke. The skies were full of it. To the chance eye, it brought a quickening of the heart, only to crumble with the realization that it wasn't cloud, that it bore no promise of rain.

Spots trudged down the trail from the uplands and onto the flat terrace. Straggly rabbitbrush speckled the flat. Here and there the powdery soil had been blown away to expose old river cobbles.

Farmsteads dotted the land as if cast out from an irregular hand. The fields around them were barren, nothing more than plots of disturbed soil. As he passed the households, he could see a faint glow in fire pits as the occupants attended their evening meals.

Thank god for the fires. People always needed wood, and Spots was prepared to serve that need. The closest source was a hard day's run to the northwest. Wood for Flowing Waters Town was at a premium; with each load he could not only Trade for food, but it gave him a reason to linger around Dusk House that the guards could understand.

He was approaching a low mounded pit house that stood just off the trail. The thing looked like an oversized swallow's nest, more mud than anything else. The style was different than he was used to, the doorway being a covered arch in the side instead of in the roof. Someone had built a ratty ramada to one side, and a couple of brownware water jars were propped near the wall.

Spots was passing when a woman called, "Hey! You!"

He turned, staring out from under his load of wood. A woman ducked out of the doorway. She wore a white skirt belted at her hips, her top bare. Her long black hair was pulled up into maiden's buns on either side of her head.

"Yes?"

"I need some wood."

She stepped forward, and in the half-light he said, "Cactus Flower?"

She squinted at him as he swung his heavy load down. The blanket he'd used to pad his shoulders fluttered away, and he straightened, gasping with relief.

"Do I know you?"

"We met at Dusk House. You wanted to Trade for favors."

She shrugged. "I meet a lot of people I want to Trade with for favors. Right now I want to Trade for firewood."

"My name is Spots. I'm from the First Moon villages."

"With all the scars. I remember." She cocked her head. "What are you doing with the firewood? Going to try and burn the place down?"

"I intend on Trading it. You know, for food. And maybe some kind of special thing to take back home. A copper bell, perhaps. Or one of those Hohokam pots. Something to remember the place by."

She nodded, eyeing the firewood. "Do you have any food?"

"A little." He indicated the pack Ironwood had given him.

He could see her sucking on her lips. "I'll cook it for half of your load. You can stay the night for all of it."

"Thanks, but I'll go on and camp by the river. Tomorrow I should be able—"

"I'll cook and you can stay for half of your load."

Spots shook his head, looking down the trail. "Thank you, but I think I'll—"

"A quarter?"

"A quarter? You wanted an abalone pendant the other day."

She shrugged. "Trade hasn't been so good recently. Not with this drought. Things have tightened up. Who'd have ever thought a Trader with a painted seed jar would rather Trade for a sack of corn than a night with me?"

He shrugged. "I've never given it much thought."

"Come on, a quarter's not much. Not for a bed and a hot meal. And you can drink all the water you want. I just packed it up from the river."

Spots chuckled to himself. Besides, he wasn't going to get in and see Nightshade at this time of night. "All right. A quarter."

"Good!" She stepped forward, grabbing the length of rope he'd used to tie the bundle together and dragging it possessively toward her house.

Spots followed her to the ramada, where she bade him sit. "Want a drink?"

"Yes. It's a long day's journey. I was looking forward to making the river." He produced his cup, and she filled it from the brownware jar.

As she busied herself with a fire bow and kindling, he sat and sipped. The water was cool, kept that way by evaporation as it permeated the clay sides of the water jar. The evening was quiet, only broken by a dog barking in the distance. Every muscle in his body felt tired.

She rose from the fire pit in front of the ramada as flames crackled up. "There. Now, what did you have in that pack to eat?"

"Rabbit and corn cakes. The rabbit I stunned with a throwing stick today while I collected wood."

She was in his pack in an instant, pulling out the stiff rabbit.

"So, how did you get those scars all over your body?" She glanced up at him as she placed her foot on the rabbit's head, grasped it by the back feet, and jerked the head off. The latter she tossed into the flames.

"House fire." Spots watched her peel the rabbit out of its hide. "Only my sister and I escaped."

"Must have hurt." She hesitated only to use a sharp obsidian flake to cut the feet free as she turned the rabbit inside out.

"More than I could ever tell you."

She sliced the gut cavity open, slinging the intestines, stomach, and lungs into the fire. The rest she dropped into a corrugated cooking pot she produced from just inside the door. Adding water, she placed it in the fire, wiped her hands on her skirt, and dropped all of his corn cakes into the pot.

"Hey! That's all of my corn cakes!"

She stared at him, irritation on her face. "Well, what do you expect? You don't think I'm just doing this for you, do you? Not for just a quarter load! I'm hungry, too!"

Spots opened his mouth, then shook his head as she refilled his cup with more water. Instead of complaining, he asked, "What happened at Dusk House today?"

"Nothing much." She settled herself cross-legged on the ramada matting and added another stick to the fire. "With most of the warriors headed to First Moon Mountain, the place is dead. Matron Desert Willow cut War Chief Wind Leaf off. He's fuming."

"What do you mean, cut him off?"

She gave him the same look she'd give an idiot. "They were lovers. Every other night he was slipping himself into her sheath. Well, just before and after her moon."

"Why only then?"

The "you're an idiot" look returned. "She didn't want his child growing in her belly. Remember what happened to Night Sun?"

"Oh."

She was squinting at him in the firelight. "You don't know much, do you, forest boy?"

He shrugged, embarrassed.

"Do you have a wife back up in the hills?"

He shook his head. "Uh, I'm not very attractive to women. I've never pushed my clan to find a wife. At least, not yet."

She was sucking on her lips again. He was starting to think it was something she did when she was thinking. "But you've been with a woman?"

"Of course."

"Bleeding gods, you're lying!" She laughed at the horrified expression on his face.

"I am not!"

Her laughter increased. "Oh, don't worry." Then she seemed to consider. "Of course, for the rest of your firewood, I could change that."

"No." He raised his hands. "No, thank you. I'm fine. In fact, after dinner, I'll just take the rest of my wood and make my way—"

"I see," she said with a smirk. "Afraid, huh?"

"Well, I wouldn't be any good."

"You're sure? For the rest of your wood I'd—"

"No!"

She stared at the fire, sucked at her lips, and sniffed as the first tendrils of steam rose from the pot.

"Desert Willow and Wind Leaf," Spots said to change the subject. "Who would have ever thought?"

"Anyone with eyes in their heads." Cactus Flower used a stick to stir the stew. "But then, the First People are as blind as moles."

"How's that?"

"Their world is about to catch fire, and they remain oblivious."

"Catch fire how?"

She gave him that "look" again. Curiosity overcame his irritation. "Listen, I'm not from here, all right? Tell me about this fire. Does the Mountain Witch have anything to do with it?"

"Gods, no. She's just an old woman in the wrong place at the wrong time." Cactus Flower shifted, laying her hand on his thigh. She didn't seem aware of the scar tissue. Her touch felt cool on his skin. "You have to understand, the First People have dominated the Made People for years, just like they've controlled everyone else in the world. The Made People clans have built their buildings, farmed their fields, fought their wars, and done their errands. Then Night Sun and Ironwood have a child?" Her eyes glowed. "Think about it! If they can have a child, the First People aren't any better. They aren't any different from the Made People. It's all been a sleight."

"A what?"

"A sham, a trick. A way the First People have kept themselves above everyone else. When Cornsilk was born it was proof that she had souls."

"I don't get it."

"Cornsilk is Red Lacewing Clan. She's alive. A person can't live without a soul. The First People have always said the rest of us have *animal* souls. She is half Bear Clan from Ironwood. A First Person's soul can't live in a Made Person; a Made Person's soul can't live in a First Person. Put it together."

He nodded, seeing the dilemma. "You say the Made People are full of resentment?"

"The clan leaders are having secret meetings." Cactus Flower rose and checked the stew. "They're planning what to do if the harvest fails. So far, only Creeper is keeping them in check."

"Who's he?"

"The Buffalo Clan elder. He practically raised Webworm. It's a measure of how worried he is that he hasn't said anything to the Blessed Sun."

"Why doesn't Webworm do something to appease the Made People?"

She shrugged as she walked to the doorway and returned with two bowls. "I really don't think he has the slightest idea that anything's wrong. None of them do. They're so involved with themselves, they consider no one else important."

Did Nightshade know this? He pondered the notion as he ate the hot stew. If she had truly gone to Flowing Waters Town to destroy Webworm, she must know the ramifications.

"You seem to know a great deal about the Blessed Sun."

Cactus Flower grinned. "All it takes is eyes and ears.

Most of us know these things. The First People don't even see us anymore. To them, we don't exist."

Later, after they had eaten, she set fire to a pinecone on a stick and led him inside her house. Four posts supported the roof, while two concentric benches were crammed with different Trade items. A fire pit had been dug into the floor behind the deflector—the night much too warm to merit its use. To either side were rush-mat pallets covered with soft deerhides.

"That's mine." She pointed in the flickering light. "Yours is there." She glanced at him. "Assuming you insist on keeping that last quarter of firewood."

"I said you'd get a quarter for cooking and a bed."

She grinned. "You've got a good memory."

"And don't forget it."

He had no more than lain down, sighing at the feel of the soft hides cushioning his body, when the little cone torch burned out. In the darkness he could look up at the small smoke hole and see stars.

"You've really never had a woman?" she asked.

"I agreed to a quarter of my wood for dinner and a bed." Silence.

He closed his eyes, thoughts on what she'd told him about the Made People. Could he really believe they were plotting against Webworm and Desert Willow? If that were the case, then what did—

Fingers picking at his hunting shirt brought him bolt upright.

"What are you doing?"

"Trying to get you to sit up and take this shirt off."

"What?"

"I've never been anyone's first before. That's a pretty good Trade, if you ask me."

Forty-six

Making a miniature was a stroke of sheer genius. The notion of building a small copy of First Moon Mountain would never have occurred to Bad Cast, but Ironwood had said, "Can you make it for me?"

"What? The mountain?"

"And the valleys as well."

"I don't understand. Make it?"

"Re-create it. Here, in the plaza, with stones, dirt, and grass stems for trees. The way a potter makes a representation of the world when she forms a clay bowl. Pile up the rocks in as close a representation of the mountain as you can. Draw in the streams in the valleys. Make it so that my warriors can study it, know it, as if they were giants looking from above at the actual mountain."

Bad Cast, with Whistle's help, had gone to work, stacking rocks, laying a sandstone slab at a cant, and dumping soil over it along the slopes. Two round stones replicated the pillars. He used broken potsherds to indicate the villages, scratched lines marking the major trails, and stuck pine needles into the dirt to indicate trees. Making the model took him most of a day, for he had to portray Juniper Ridge, the mountains to the north and south, as well as their major villages.

When it was finished, Whistle fingered his chin, standing back. Afternoon sunlight cast shadows from the waist-high peak, and the lower rendition of Juniper Ridge.

The warrior said, "I think that's it. Even the orientation is correct."

Bad Cast nodded, arching his back and wincing at the pain from being bent over most of the day. "I think we should stick more pine needles into the slopes."

"It doesn't have to be perfect," Whistle reminded. "Just good enough."

"And you think that's good enough?"

Whistle chuckled. "It's a war map, not a sacred offering."

Ripple's voice surprised them from behind. "Sometimes they are one and the same."

Bad Cast turned. Ripple stood silhouetted by the reddish light that filtered through the smoke-hazy sky. His skin might have been copper burnished with blood. Gods, how he had changed: Something about his eyes—they seemed larger, darkened by sadness. A pinching around his once-youthful face expressed an incalculable sense of loss. Before his vision, his frame had been bulky, flesh smooth; now it was composed of bone and fibrous muscle that slid under too-tight skin.

"What is this?" Whistle asked. "One or both?"

Ripple's lips quivered. "That is for you to decide, warrior. Will you give up First Moon Mountain? Or your souls?"

"I don't understand." Whistle looked suddenly nervous.

"You will. Soon you must choose between your life and your souls. The only thing left to be discovered is how you will justify it."

Whistle's frown darkened, and then he waved it away. "I serve the war chief. If doing so costs me my life, so be it."

Ripple nodded with the sagacity of one who knew more than he let on.

Whistle seemed to shiver, saying, "If you will excuse me, I must see to some things."

Bad Cast watched him walk away, steps hurried and jerky. "Why did you say that to him?"

"So that he may prepare himself."

Bad Cast stared at his friend. "Ripple, come on. If you know something, tell him. He's Ironwood's deputy. The war chief is sending him to meet with White Eye as soon as Wrapped Wrist and Crow Woman return with their report."

"Events are moving faster than you would think." Ripple inclined his head toward the room block back under the dull green ponderosas. The mud-splashed line of stone dwellings had taken on the reddish hue of the sky. Protruding roof poles were hung with net bags full of dried corn, chilies, and squash.

Ironwood and Night Sun had emerged from one of the rooms and were talking to Whistle and a dust-covered runner who had appeared out of the trees. The latter was a skinny youth in a brown pullover shirt. He talked hurriedly, arms waving in excitement. He carried a bow and a quiver of arrows.

Ironwood listened to the runner, expression growing stern. He turned and said something to Whistle. The Bee Flower Clan warrior jerked a grim nod, pivoted on his heel, and, with the runner, trotted off toward his shelter back in the trees.

Ironwood spoke tersely to Night Sun, then started across the beaten plaza. Night Sun followed at his heels, a determined look on her face. The tall war chief and formidable woman made for a provoking image: he resplendent in a red shirt and feathered kilt, she in a black dress, strings of gleaming beads at her throat. Her gray hair was twisted and pinned atop her head.

"Bad Cast?" he called as he approached. "Is it ready?"

"Yes, War Chief."

Ironwood shot Ripple a wary glance. "Good evening, Dreamer. We have just received word: Sunwatcher Blue Racer is on his way to First Moon Mountain. He is traveling slowly because of the size of his party, but should be there in another four days."

Night Sun added, "We have just ordered Whistle to travel to the First Moon villages. Perhaps he will intercept Crow Woman on the way; if not, he will give White Eye our proposed plan of attack."

Bad Cast frowned. "We have a plan of attack?" He indicated his piles of stone and dirt, so laboriously crafted. "I thought you'd make that based on my re-creation of First Moon Mountain."

Ironwood gave him a cunning smile. "Actually, I've had the plan in my head for some time. That's why I wanted you to build this copy of your mountain as faithfully as possible. I want my warriors to study it intimately. We will begin as soon as I can have them assembled. We are going to learn your mountain front and back, every drainage and crack, every village, forest, and cliff."

"But what about Whistle?" Bad Cast said in confusion.

"Whistle knows."

"But he didn't say anything about it while I was working on this. Only that it had to show all the mountain's features."

"I'm sure he didn't." Ironwood was inspecting the panorama, squinting as he walked around. "He will tell White Eye what I need from his First Moon clans. With their help, I can crack Pinnacle House like a piñon nut in a mortar."

Ripple's face blanched. "Then it's begun."

Night Sun had a flinty look in her eyes. "It has, Dreamer." She stepped over to the miniature and pointed to the steep northern slope of First Moon Mountain. The loose dirt bristled with needles that Bad Cast had carefully planted to indicate forest. "Our warriors will scale this side in the darkness of the second night after Sister Moon comes full." She bent pointing to the flat incline of the southwestern slope. "The First Moon clans will assemble their warriors here. Whistle will tell White Eye to make an attack toward Guest House at first light. They need only draw the attention of Webworm's warriors to the slope."

Ripple's voice had a singsong lilt. "No matter what plans are made, success eludes us until blood is paid."

"What does that mean, Dreamer?" Night Sun demanded.

"We shall succeed, but we will each, in our own way, pay a terrible cost."

Ironwood stepped forward, demanding, "What price? I must know."

Ripple raised his hand. "Ask yourself, War Chief, do you really want to add my burden to your own? Are your shoulders that wide and strong? No, I thought not. I can see it in your eyes. You have accepted your destiny; now allow me to accept mine." With that he turned, walking slowly, head down, toward the forest.

"Ripple?" Bad Cast called, starting in pursuit. "Is there anything I can do?"

"No, old friend. But soon. Very soon."

Bad Cast slowed to a stop and would have sworn Ripple's shoulders were heaving with sobs, but it might have been caused by his friend's stumbling pace.

Wrapped Wrist puzzled over what to do next. He hurried from tree to tree in the darkening forest. Dry needles crackled under his feet. The ponderosa had turned gloomy and dark; their thick boles barely hid his wide frame. The pungent odor of smoke from the distant forest fire carried on the wind.

A chickadee chattered. Some of the evening birds warbled in lonesome melody. The first of the night creatures were stirring.

He had always liked this time of day—the quick transition into night—because of the stillness that leached from the trees, rocks, and soil. Even the air seemed to grow heavy, lethargic. In silence, the shadows swelled, encompassing the world. He'd always felt at peace.

This time as darkness settled around him, he dared not. His heart hammered, skin hot and sweaty. Nerves made his guts squirm. Fear was proving an uncomfortable and unwelcome companion. He wondered how the heroes in the stories dealt with this sense of incipient panic. All he wanted to do was run away.

Instead he continued creeping from tree trunk to tree trunk, each time hoping that none of the warriors would look back in his direction.

In the gloom they had become slinking shadows, and worse, the forest floor here was littered with old cones, crackly duff, and fallen branches that could snap underfoot and give his presence away.

Four of them! The notion rolled around in Wrapped Wrist's head. Four dreaded Red Shirts, trained warriors! What in the name of the gods was he going to do?

Since he'd been a babe on a teat, it had been beaten into him that Red Shirts fought like Spirit Demons unleashed. They trained for war, perfecting their arts the way hunters perfected the stalk, or potters their vessels.

I'm just a hunter. How can I hope to prevail?

They were armed with bows, each carrying a full quiver of arrows. He had only his atlatl and three darts. A good bowman could have six arrows in the air before the first landed. The atlatl allowed him but three casts, each demanding that he stand, step, and release. Atlatls were weapons suited to hunting, not war. If they discovered him, he'd have no better chance than a rabbit caught on sandstone slickrock.

"Maggot!" Crow Woman's voice was filled with loathing. One of the Red Shirts laughed.

Wrapped Wrist ground his teeth. Whatever they were going to do with Crow Woman, it wouldn't be nice. He knew what Red Shirts did with captive women, had seen the aftereffects among his own people when a Red Shirt fixed his attention on a young woman. Her clan might protest to Matron Larkspur. Sometimes some small offering might even be made in restitution depending on how egregious the warrior had been; but in cases of simple rape, without a beating or disfigurement, rarely was a word of consolation even granted.

Not so long ago a young woman's brother had taken matters into his own hands, attacking the warrior who had raped his sister. The retaliation of the Red Shirts was rapid and remorseless: they burned the young man alive, killed his closest clan kin, and gutted the young woman who had had the temerity to complain.

What can I do? Wrapped Wrist wondered as he sneaked quietly after the warriors. *How can I hope to set her free?*

Frightened, but unwilling to give up, he continued creeping through the deepening gloom. Step by careful step, he followed, hope draining away with the last of the light. What if he lost them in the darkness? Worse, what if he blundered on top of them? They'd kill him without a second thought. The image of whistling war clubs sent a quiver through his guts.

Why am I doing this? He wasn't even sure he liked her. Just thinking back to her caustic comments was enough to give him pause. Stumpy? That had hurt! Maybe this was the gods paying her back for her arrogant attitude?

Then her confession in the night returned to haunt him. She probably didn't even know that hidden in the tones of her voice had been a desperate longing for simple friendship.

Why does it have to be me? If she hasn't been able to trust another human being up to now, I'm not going to be the one.

Nope. Fact was, her souls had been wounded and scarred long ago. Far be it from his responsibility to try and fix them. The mere notion of damaged souls scared him half to death. She'd made her way this far, she could see to herself. This was lunacy! A smart man would veer off from the trail and vanish into the night.

Wrapped Wrist hunched and hurried forward, his darts grasped between his fingers so the wood wouldn't rattle. He could barely make out the shadows of the warriors ahead.

Don't be a fool! Leave!

Down between his souls, Ripple's last words burned like cactus under the skin: *"You must save her."*

HUMMINGBIRD

The Fire Dogs who live in the south have a wonderful story about Hummingbird. It is said that one hot summer day lightning struck the mountaintop where Hummingbird had her nest, and a great fire roared to life and began devouring the forest. All of the other birds flew away. The animals raced down the slopes, and the lizards and snakes crawled into holes trying to find cover.

But Hummingbird refused to leave her eggs. Day and night, she soared to and from a high mountain lake, carry-

*ing water in her tiny beak to drop on the enormous flames
sweeping toward her nest.*

*Her courage so touched the hovering Cloud People, their
tears poured down in a great flood and drowned the fire.*

*The Fire Dogs say Hummingbird proves that even the
smallest efforts of a selfless heart can bring about salvation.*

I see another teaching in the story.

*Hummingbird teaches me that the tiniest act of courage
can draw the most powerful allies.*

Firewood was a lucrative business. The environs around
Flowing Waters Town had been stripped of fuel. Spots was
on his second load. He'd laid it out on his blanket just before dawn, and now watched the sun rise over the eastern
horizon. Its light cast long shadows from the rising walls
of Sunrise House.

The hucksters were still arriving, claiming the best places
along the eastern wall for their blankets of Trade. Cactus
Flower and Spots had arrived in the half-light, getting a position close to the southeastern gap in the Dusk House wall.

The world was just beginning to stir. The guard above
them on the first-floor roof called lazily to a farmer leaving for her day in the fields. Spots grinned. He liked this
place and the odd people who made their living bartering
with travelers.

Squinting into the sun, he could see someone emerging
from a newly completed room in Sunrise House a dart's
cast away. He recognized the form. Though just first light,
the Ant Clan elder Yellowgirl was already on-site, planning her day's work.

"She has no other life," Cactus Flower said from where
she'd laid out her own Trade. Her trinkets consisted of
several pieces of raw clam shell, a couple of Green Mesa
pots, four ears of blue corn, and three rabbits. "She just
lives for her building."

"Oh, I think not." Spots pointed as a rotund figure
stepped out of the room Yellowgirl had just left. The man

glanced this way and that, hurrying past Yellowgirl. He said something as he passed, and Yellowgirl gave a curt nod.

"That's interesting," Cactus Flower agreed. "I'd know that shape anywhere. It's old Creeper. Normally you can't get him out of bed until midmorning."

"Maybe Yellowgirl gave him a warm bed last night?" Spots raised an eyebrow. He'd stayed at Cactus Flower's for a second time last night. She'd been alone when he arrived with his load of wood, and happy to Trade a night for a quarter of his load.

As he watched Creeper approach, he wondered yet again about his relationship with Cactus Flower. He liked her. Apparently clanless, kinless, and irreverent, she made him laugh. Her wry sense of humor, cynical disbelief in anything sacred, and earthy appetite left him completely charmed. Or was he just ensorcelled by her enthusiasm when she tightened her sheath around his shaft? The memory of her face in the fire's glow, gone slack, mouth open as she gasped and stiffened, would be with him forever. Nor had he anticipated that coupling could go on all night. His penis stiffened just at the memory.

Creeper came plodding past, head down, expression dark and brooding. He never even glanced Spots's way as he pounded by in a stiff walk.

"Good Morning, Elder," the guard called from above.

"Yes, yes," Creeper called back absently. "Clan business. It's never done." Then he was inside the walls.

Cactus Flower lowered her voice. "Something's happening."

"Oh?"

She pointed. "That's not how Yellowgirl usually acts."

The Ant Clan Matron had been standing, head bowed as she kicked at the dirt with a sandaled foot. Now she shook her head, as if at something distasteful, and seated herself on a pile of stacked stone, her head in her hands.

"She looks worried."

"All the Made People are. You can feel it." Cactus Flower pursed her full lips, the sunlight casting her smooth face in bronze. "It started three moons ago, clan elders sneaking around in the night, attending meetings in other clan kivas. Not only that, they leave watchers, sentries, to see that they're undisturbed. Once, when the Blessed Sun walked out from his rooms to look up at the stars, one of the sentries pitched a stone into the kiva where they were meeting. It went silent as a log. Just like that."

"I thought you stayed at your farmstead."

She shrugged. "Sometimes a Trader asks me to stay here with him."

Which left him wondering. How was he going to feel the first time he came in with a load of firewood and found her occupied by another man?

"Do you ever think you'll want to stay with just one man?"

She gave him a hard look. "Don't start."

"Start what?"

"Do you know how many times I've heard that?"

"I was just asking. It wasn't—"

"No! And it isn't going to be, either." She chewed her lip, glaring at him. "I like you, Spots. Just don't get any ideas about becoming the one man in my life."

"Sorry. Don't yell at me. I was just curious about—"

"Gods." She sighed. "It's all right. You're young."

"No younger than you."

"I wasn't talking summers. I meant in living. It's different. Time means different things to different people." She shrugged. "Besides, I'd never get attached to you anyway."

"Why not?" He winced. "Because of the scars?"

"No, fool." She jerked her head toward Dusk House. "Because of her. You keep sneaking her food and water, and they're going to catch you. *Any* man who's best friends with a witch isn't headed for a long and happy life. You're just lucky I'm brave enough to lay my blanket next to yours."

He thought about that. "She's my friend."

"Make friends with something safe next time, like a rattlesnake or scorpion."

Spots ground his teeth, frowning at the distant figure of Yellowgirl. She looked as miserable as he felt.

Cactus Flower relented. "Sorry. It's just that they put

her in that cage for a reason. When the Blessed Sun gets tired of her, he'll haul her out, have her whacked in the head, and buried under a big rock. That's all."

Spots shook his head in disbelief, voice lowering. "It won't happen that way. Trust me."

She gave him a sidelong appraisal. "Is there more to her than I know?"

He gave a brief nod of the head.

"What?"

He bit his lip, refusing to answer.

"Oh, come on, give it up, Spots. What?"

He kept his gaze locked on Yellowgirl. Was it the distance? Or was she crying?

Forty-seven

A fire crackled. Yellow light illuminated the camp the warriors had chosen. Thick scrub oak, sumac, and wild rose was interlaced with nightshade vines, the latter rich in black berries. Overhead, smoke from the distant fire damped most of the stars. From this ridge, distant flames could be seen as they sparkled on the high-country slopes.

Crow Woman swallowed hard and fought the urge to tremble. They had tied her feet, waist, hands, and neck to a slim pine pole. She couldn't bend without tightening the thong at her neck. She could barely shift her feet and wiggle her arms. Trussed like a hunter's carcass she could only stand, her back to a sandstone boulder, and hope she didn't fall over.

The four warriors watched her from the fire, eyes like ferrets' in the hot yellow light. They were muscular men, wearing new war shirts. One, a narrow-framed man, kept giving her an oily smile. After they had stopped for the night, he had donned a pair of spotless white moccasins.

Something about him, the way he looked at her, scared the breath right out of her.

She had watched as they fixed a stew of corn, yampa root, chokecherries, and goosefoot seeds. Two had emptied their canteens into a small corrugated pot after the ingredients had been added. They had watched her in silence while it boiled. One by one they dipped from the steaming pot using spoons crafted from mountain sheep bones.

Silence. They just ate, savoring each bite, their eyes fixed on her. She wanted to squirm, to hiss and spit, to curse their mothers as camp bitches, but fear had a stranglehold on her voice.

It would have been so much better if they'd cursed, leered, tormented, and threatened. They just watched, jaws chewing, eyes eating into her courage.

Silence. It left her trembling. She couldn't stop the sudden shiver that racked her. It was as if they weren't men, but some kind of feral predators, wolves gone into men's bodies. Or worse, mute evil that watched from those gleaming eyes.

The narrow-framed man scraped the bottom of the jar, tilted it, and scooped the last of the stew. He lifted the polished bone spoon, letting it slip past his lips as he sucked the last of the liquid from the hollow.

In silence they replaced their spoons in their packs, retied their canteens, and wiped out the stew bowl with grass before packing it away.

Why don't they speak? She swallowed hard to keep her breath from catching in her throat. Her mouth had gone dry, her knees weak.

They stood, stepping around the fire, each inspecting her with eager stares. The narrow-framed man was smiling. Not a leer, just a lilt to the lips. A hint of expectation in his expression. He *knew* how terrified she was.

"What do you want from me?" Her voice came out as a croak.

They might not have heard.

The narrow-framed man raised his hand, and she was

surprised to see a long, hafted obsidian blade. She winced, almost toppled, and caught herself as he slipped the sharp blade across the skin of her cheek. He didn't press hard enough to cut, just to tickle.

"Get it over with, maggot!" she cried. "Kill me, and have done with it!"

Silence, but the men smiled, two showing missing teeth. Another laughed with silent mirth.

The only sound was the crackling of the fire.

"If you want me, take me," she said between pants of fear.

The narrow-framed man leaned close. She could smell his sweat, the smoky tinge to his hair. His breath carried the faint scent of stew. Lips to her ear, he whispered, *"Where's Ironwood?"*

She jerked back, teetering, falling. But one of the men caught her, holding the pole she was bound to upright.

"I—I don't know." Her voice was catching. They could see her shivering now. Blood and spit, if they'd only beat her, give her the pain to cling to! Anything but this slow silent promise. She leaned her head back, throat straining at the thong, and screamed her terror into the smoky night.

It echoed in the quiet air.

With slow deliberation the narrow-framed man inserted his obsidian blade beneath the neck of her war shirt and carefully severed the fabric. He worked his way out, over her shoulder, and down her arm until the cloth fell away, exposing her arm and right breast.

"What are you going to do?"

"Shhh!" He placed a finger to his lips, leaning forward to add in a whisper, *"We follow Leather Hand. He has sent us to find Ironwood."*

"I don't know where he is!" she insisted doggedly.

"Oh, yes," he whispered. *"You do. But we have time."*

She had trouble taking a full breath. "I said, if you are going to take me, get it over with. Come on. Untie me. You're men, aren't you? Your staffs aren't made of wet clay, are they?"

He nodded, and the rest followed, as if at some unseen signal. "Time." He mouthed the word. Inserting his knife on the other side, he began the process of slitting the fabric over her left shoulder.

Crow Woman watched in fascination as the faded red fabric parted and fell away to expose her smooth brown skin.

They're peeling it away. And when they had removed her clothing, what then?

I will no longer be a warrior. She clamped her eyes closed, insisting, *Yes, yes I will!*

That was when the blow caught her. A smacking impact that blasted her kneecap sideways. She would have fallen but for strong hands fixing her pole. The thong cut into her neck, causing her to stiffen, gasping for breath.

She blinked, seeing them, each male face leaned close, peering, as if to see her fear from a hand's breadth away.

"Where is Ironwood's camp?" Narrow-frame whispered.

"I don't know," she insisted. "In these mountains somewhere."

"*Good,*" came the whispered reply.

For a moment they watched; then Narrow-frame reached out and cupped her breast. His touch was light, little more than a caress of her nipple. Nevertheless the hard callus on his hand made her stiffen.

He lifted the knife. "You heard about the Dust People?" She jerked a nod.

He ran the keen blade in a circle around the swell of her breast; the sharp edge left a white scratch on her dark skin. "If I cut this off, we will eat it. And you will watch us." His hand went to her other breast. "Then we will eat this one."

She tried to speak, to deny it, but a croaking came from her throat.

He was playing the obsidian blade up and down her stomach, following the line from her sternum down to the navel. The rope at her waist parted, and the remains of her dress fluttered down to wad around her ankles. She stared down in horror as the obsidian blade traced around her abdomen, then patterned a spiral above the black thatch of her pubic hair.

"I will eat your womb when I cut it out," another of the

warriors whispered. This was a thickset man who was missing two of his incisors.

She tried to shrink away from the gliding blade. Faint white scratches on her smooth skin marked its course.

"Tell," Narrow-frame whispered, his voice barely audible above the wind in the distant pines.

She leaned her head back, screaming, *"By the gods, just kill me!"*

"Oh," the sibilant whisper assured, *"it won't be that easy."* A pause. "Unless you tell us where Ironwood—"

"If . . . if I do . . . you'll just kill me?"

Narrow-frame nodded, voice rising. "After we enjoy you, yes. You will make it good for us? You won't just lie on your back like a sack of corn?"

"No." She tried to nod through the shivers. "I'll make it good."

He smiled, eyes glittering. "And you won't lie about Ironwood? If you did, well, we can eat you slowly. A piece at a time until you die."

Gods, kill me now! "I . . . I won't lie."

"Good." He reached up with the knife, slicing a line across her chest just above the swell of her breasts. Then he severed the thong at her neck. Two of the warriors stepped back, pulling their war shirts over their heads, grinning. One already had an erection that bobbed as he tossed his shirt to one side.

The hiss might have been the exhalation of the gods—the meaty slap, a clap of thunder.

Crow Woman tried to make sense of the image. The two naked warriors jerked up and down like Dancers, their muscular bodies writhing back and forth, out of step. When one moved, the other twisted. She could see the point protruding from the thickset man's side like a misplaced second erection.

"What in . . . ?" The narrow-framed man stepped back, his knife in hand, ready to attack. His darting gaze took in the brush, and he blinked, night-blinded by the fire.

The last man leapt for his weapons as the first two warriors staggered and stumbled, then fell to the ground. The thickset man had lost his erection, his hands clutching the spearhead that stuck out of his side. A wild scream broke from his mouth, only to be cut off by a bubbling froth of blood.

Another hiss ended with a thud as the final warrior stood, his war club in his hands. He stared down stupidly at the dart point that extended half a body length from his chest. He grabbed it with his left hand, sagged to his knees, and gasped out a hoarse rattling cry.

"Show yourself!" Narrow-frame cried. "Come fight like a man!"

Something warned him. He threw himself sideways, a long dart cutting the air where he'd been standing but a heartbeat before.

Narrow-frame lunged for his dying companion, plucked the war club from his hand, and backed quickly to where Crow Woman balanced precariously, her pole held only by her hands and the rope at her ankles. Her knee was an agony of pain.

"Show yourself!" he cried. "Or I kill her!" He jabbed the knife at Crow Woman.

She tried to squirm away; the pole slipped sideways, toppling her onto the grass. Her knee wrenched, but she bit off the shriek.

Narrow-frame grinned as he placed his foot on her neck and pressed down. She could see him lift the war club, knew how warriors practiced this stroke: the death blow for executions.

"I am a White Moccasin! Come and get me, you cowardly filth! This woman is dead! I will eat her flesh!"

From the corner of her eye, Crow Woman watched the stone-headed club rise in the firelight.

A sense of peace filled her. It would be over now. A sharp pain, and then her souls would be free. Free. It wasn't so bad.

The blur came from the sandstone boulder. She felt the impact, heard her neck crack, and then the white moccasins flashed before her eyes. The warrior was driven into the grass before her, his breath making a *whuff* as he hit. It might have been wild animals given the howls and screams that tore from the men's throats as they rolled and kicked.

Crow Woman gasped for breath, watching as a bulky form emerged from behind the warrior. She caught the firelight on a litter-matted hunting shirt as thick hands grasped the warrior's throat.

"You are no stronger!" the apparition bellowed. "Without death, there is no life! No future!"

Narrow-frame made a gagging sound as Wrapped Wrist's hands tightened on his throat. The warrior was flailing his arms, the obsidian knife flashing this way and that, whipping backward in an attempt to find Wrapped Wrist's body.

Wrapped Wrist threw his head back, away from the blade, and a wild *"Aaaragh!"* broke from his lips.

Crow Woman watched as Wrapped Wrist's legs tightened about the warrior's waist. She saw the muscles swell, knot, and strain. The crackling sounded like breaking pottery. Wrapped Wrist heaved again, and a final pop carried on the still night.

Wrapped Wrist tossed the twitching body away. For a moment he stared at his hands, perhaps seeing them for the first time. A shudder racked his body; then he turned, seeing her where she lay trussed. Blood streaked his right cheek.

He asked, "Gods, why am I so scared?"

Bad Cast watched with a curious reluctance as Ironwood held Night Sun in his arms. The war chief cradled her to him like a precious and delicate bird; his face was a reflection of pained love.

Bad Cast would have walked away, but he had to wait his turn by the cleft in the rimrock where the trail led down the slope. Faint morning light filtered pink through the pall of smoke that masked the north and east.

Most of the warriors had already started down the narrow defile. Bad Cast shifted from foot to foot beside Ripple. Oddly, his friend had a sad look on his face as he turned to Orenda and said, "I need you to do something for me."

She gazed thoughtfully at him. "Yes?"

"In three days, I need you to pick mint from the river

just below the hot springs where the Mountain Witch tended my body."

Bad Cast expected her to say something like "What? That's silly," but she didn't. She just nodded, as if this was the most ordinary of requests despite the fact it meant a half-day's journey for her.

Bad Cast glanced back to where Ironwood's powerful arms were wrapped around Night Sun.

"I'll see you soon," he promised. "Remember, each breath I take is for you."

"You stay safe for me, my love." Her smile carried the warmth of the sun as she reached up and stroked the side of his scarred face.

Bad Cast swallowed hard and looked away. Were the roles reversed, would he and Soft Cloth have had that same Power of affection between them? Or was this something born of a different trial? The worship reflected in Ironwood's and Night Sun's eyes would cling to his memory for a lifetime.

Ripple had turned away from Orenda, noticed Bad Cast's attention, and pushed him toward the trailhead, whispering, "He knows. Just not the way of it."

"The way of what?" Bad Cast took his turn, easing himself down through the cleft, oddly reassured by the rock closing around him.

"The sacrifice he has to make for the world," Ripple added. "I wish I had her courage."

"Whose? Night Sun's?"

"Her love is greater than mine."

Whatever Ripple might be talking about, Bad Cast could agree. When had he ever seen devotion like that reflected in lovers' eyes?

Love. Just what was it? Oh, granted, he missed Soft Cloth something terrible, and he had always thought he loved her. But did what he felt in his heart mirror what he'd just seen shared by Ironwood and Night Sun?

"Gods," Ripple whispered behind him. "It hurts."

Bad Cast glanced over his shoulder, seeing the hollow expression of loss on his friend's face.

"I'd think it was you leaving something behind, rather than the war chief."

"I am." Ripple smiled sadly. "I wish I'd never gone up after that elk. If I could, I'd go back, change it."

"Does that mean you'd deny Cold Bringing Woman's vision?"

"No, not at all." Ripple placed a reassuring hand on Bad Cast's shoulder. "Don't mind me. I'm just complaining. Cold Bringing Woman came to me, and I made my choice. What's different now is that I know what the alternatives would have been. Had she not come, I wouldn't have known. So most likely in that other life I would never have met Orenda. Might never have shared what little time we've had. So I live with my decision."

"You and Orenda?" Bad Cast asked. "You still don't know that in the end, after this is all over—"

"Yes, I do. From this moment forward, lips will never smile, children will never laugh, and hearts will remain empty. Promise dies today. The future won't even mourn over its corpse."

"Ripple, don't be so sure. Anything can happen." In that moment, missing Soft Cloth became an even greater need.

"Will you promise me something?"

"Of course. Anything."

"When you've finished your duty with the war chief, find Soft Cloth and your daughter and go as far away as you can."

"What about you? Can't you come with us?"

The smile Ripple gave him was bittersweet with longing. "I've made my bargain with fate."

"What kind of talk is that?"

"The kind that speaks of the death of Dreams."

"**Y**ou're going to have a wonderful scar," Crow Woman said gently.

Wrapped Wrist flinched and hissed as she slipped another cactus thorn through the cut on his right cheek. Narrow-frame's blade had made a neat but deep slice. To bind it, Crow Woman squeezed the flesh together and pierced the skin through both lips of the incision with a long cactus spine. Next she looped thread from her war shirt around the thorn ends so that it pulled the skin together. The process was incredibly painful.

Wrapped Wrist shot an uneasy look at the scrub oak; broken branches could be seen where he'd dragged the bodies out of the little clearing. He could imagine them there, sprawled among the stems and leaves, limbs akimbo, expressions slack as flies crawled over their eyes and into their open mouths.

He gasped again as Crow Woman's steady fingers lanced his cheek with another of the long thorns. The sting was terrible, burning as cactus always did.

A stew was simmering on the fire, the last of the warrior's goosefoot, corn, and water. Knowing that they were Leather Hand's men, Crow Woman had opted to burn the dried meat she found in one of the packs rather than take a chance it might be human.

"Are you feeling better?" she asked, concern in her voice.

"I still feel shaky." He took a breath as she pulled her make-do suture together. "I guess a real warrior wouldn't have thrown up afterward."

She laughed, the sound of it nervous. "A real warrior?"

"Someone like you," he added. "You wouldn't have been a trembling mess. Pus and blood, you should have seen me. I was shaking so bad. That first cast had to be perfect. I had three darts, so I had to wait until I could get two with the first throw. They were close. I was scared. I had to wait." He tried to glance away. "I'm sorry it took so long."

She grabbed his chin, turning his head to see his eyes. "A warrior is smart first, Wrapped Wrist." Then it was she who looked away. "I was shaking pretty badly myself. If you hadn't come . . ."

"You'd have escaped, killed every last one of them," he told her positively.

"Shut up."

He clamped his jaws as she finished pinning and binding his cheek. Her capable fingers tied the knot off, and she sat back, legs crossed.

He dabbed at the binding with his fingertips. His chin

and neck were stiff with blood. It had soaked into his
hunting shirt. "Where did you learn this?"

"It's an old warrior's trick. Be careful and don't snag it
on anything, or you'll break the cactus spines. They're going to soften anyway. It's going to make pus, so I might
have to redo it tomorrow."

"Thank you." He could see the places on her ankles and
wrists where the binding had chafed her skin. Her knee
was swollen, and she held it out stiff before her. She wore
a blanket over her shoulders, the ruins of her war shirt tied
about her waist like a double-flapped skirt.

"Why don't you let me sew your war shirt back together?" He indicated the folds of red cloth hanging at her
waist.

"I'm no warrior," she replied dully. "I am unworthy of
this shirt. When they cut it off me, it was as if I lost myself." She leaned her head back, her hair spilling loose
from the bun at the back of her head. "Nightshade was
right. There was nothing but anger inside me. I became the
shirt. When I lost it, I didn't know who I was. I never knew
I was such a coward."

From his memory the words came: "'Swallow your
fear. It is meaningless—illusion meant to keep you from
what needs to be done. You have never understood that
your souls are even stronger than your body. Without
death, there is no life, no future.'"

She gave him a disbelieving smirk. "Words, Wrapped
Wrist."

He frowned, wincing at the pain in his cheek. "Ripple . . . the Dreamer told me that last time I saw him. He
said I had to know it down between my souls. That I had to
understand."

"What else did he tell you?"

"That you would need me." He made a gesture. "Who'd
have thought? Ripple. My old friend." He glanced up
skeptically. "Did he really see the future?"

She stared vacantly at the fire where the stew boiled.
"Maybe, like Nightshade, he knew I was hollow."

"You're not hollow." Wrapped Wrist reached for his

pack, recovered his little clay cup, and dipped up the hot liquid. "You going to eat?"

"Not hungry."

"Well, you'd better eat. We lost a half day when they started back toward First Moon Mountain."

She shook her head. "I'm not going."

Wrapped Wrist made a face. "Ironwood is depending on us."

Crow Woman said wearily, "I would have betrayed him. Wrapped Wrist, I've got to think about this." At that she got awkwardly to her feet and limped away.

Wrapped Wrist watched her go, the ruined war shirt swaying around her long legs. Sighing, he turned his attention back to the fire and sipped the hot stew. If only he could get the memory to go away, but all night long he'd relived the fight. He could still feel the warrior's neck as the bones popped. Could feel how the man had twitched, how the head had flopped, a dead weight in his hands.

The queasy sick feeling tickled his stomach again.

Forty-eight

Soft white light shone through the small window in the north wall; Leather Hand knew that morning had come. He looked down into her dark eyes, seeing them widen as he slid into her warm sheath. She locked her legs around his hips, pulling the blanket lower on his back. The morning chill prickled his skin.

A satisfied purr came from deep in Larkspur's throat as she tightened and arched her hips against his.

This was a delightful way to awaken. He'd been lost in Dreams when her fingers had found him under the blanket. Only after she'd awakened his manhood had she pulled him onto her warm body and opened herself to him.

He surrendered himself to the moment, tried to concentrate on the sensations. Unlike the slave girls he emptied himself into, she moved with him, grinding her hips against his. The stifled gasps in her throat were refreshment for his soul.

His loins exploded with an intensity that left him breathless. The muscles in his legs and buttocks cramped and locked as he rammed himself into her and stiffened. Her body thrashed under his as she dug her fingers into his back, a scream locked behind clenched teeth. She ended, arched against him, panting, her eyes blazing as she tightened her grip on his shoulders.

"You have to learn to be quiet," she whispered. "Only the slaves would have heard, but at the wrong time . . ."

"I made no sound."

She laughed, digging her nails painfully into his back again. "Really? A rutting bull elk doesn't bray with that much passion."

He rolled off of her, aware that his sweat was drying in the cool air. She stood, the pale light lovely on her smooth skin, her nipples like hard thumbs as she stepped over and squatted above the chamber pot.

He gasped and threw his arm over his head, the nerves in his body still quivering.

"I hope your warriors are getting as much relief," she told him as she reached for a blue cloth dress that hung from a peg. She slipped it over her tawny body and belted it at her slim waist. Pulling her long hair out, she fluffed it by running her fingers through it.

"Your orders were explicit. They were to be granted every request." He grinned under the weight of his arm. "I saw the looks in the eyes of the Made People. What your authority does not dictate, the wrath of my men does."

She was watching his face closely when she said, "News arrived last night. Matron Husk Woman was found in her sweat bath. Her head was missing. Tall Piñon has been without a Matron for over a week."

Leather Hand allowed no reaction to cross his face. "Too bad. She and I might not have agreed, but she served her people fairly."

Larkspur cocked an eyebrow. "Rumors have begun to circulate. Traders carry the most outrageous stories."

"Oh?"

"They say that witches fly past the guards in the dead of night, murder the Matrons, and quietly fly away with their heads again."

"Clever witches." •

"Yes," Larkspur agreed. "Odd, isn't it, that these witches are so clever they only seem drawn to the Blessed Sun's enemies?"

"Curious indeed."

Larkspur's voice dropped. "Then perhaps it's lucky that I serve the Blessed Sun as faithfully as I do."

Leather Hand looked at her from under his arm. "You need fear no witches here, Matron."

A faint smile played at the corner of her lips. She gave him a slight bow, took a feathered cloak down from the next peg, and climbed up the ladder to her top-floor room.

He drew the blanket back, used the chamber pot himself, and pulled on the coarse-woven hunting shirt he'd wadded beside the sleeping pallet the night before. His red shirt was tightly rolled inside his pack, as was his war club. He'd dressed thus, looking like just another hunter, since he and his men had filtered into the First Moon Valley by ones and twos. Like him, they, too, kept out of sight, lodged in certain Made People's pit houses where they were fed, bedded, and sheltered.

He walked around the long room, fingering her dresses, examining her turquoise, jet, coral, and shell jewelry.

Matron Larkspur. The title intrigued him. *Heiress of the Blue Dragonfly Clan.* She was in line to inherit the clan Matronship should anything happen to Desert Willow. Not only that, from what he'd seen, she was smart.

He lifted one of her dresses, a beautiful black thing with white four-pointed stars, sniffing at the fabric and filling his nostrils with her scent. The future was an uncertain place. There were so few of the First People left, and he was Red Lacewing Clan. If something happened to her husband? An accident, maybe?

Voices could be heard from upstairs. He froze, aware that a man was speaking in low tones. He couldn't quite make out Larkspur's cautious reply; then he heard her say, "Stay right there."

Her body darkened the hatch as she climbed swiftly down the ladder, shot him a warning glance, and grabbed up a small turquoise brooch from a cedar box. As quickly, she was back up the ladder, saying, "Well done. This is for special service. Come back when you have more."

Leather Hand heard sandals scuffing as the man left. Moments later, Larkspur leaned into the hatch, one eyebrow lifted. "One of my little songbirds just arrived. He tells me that a messenger has arrived from Ironwood. All of the clan elders will be atop the Dog's Tooth tonight. They are going to have some sort of meeting."

Leather Hand matched her smile with his own. "Tonight. On the Dog's Tooth?"

Larkspur nodded. "That nest of vipers has been a thorn in my bed for long enough."

"What of the Moon People?"

"Do this right, Deputy, and they won't dare try anything."

War Chief Wind Leaf found the Blessed Sun absently wandering Dusk House's plaza. He had just taken Deputy Ravengrass's report and had been on his way to find Webworm.

"Good day, Blessed Sun."

"What's good about it?" Webworm wondered.

"Excuse me?"

"Oh, nothing. I didn't sleep well last night. Hideous Dreams. Smoke, fire, people screaming." Webworm gestured with the basalt graver he held. "And voices, whispering, all night long. Can you believe, War Chief, I even got up and checked the Matron's quarters on one side, and Blue Racer's on the other to see if people were hiding there?"

"What of my guards? Did they hear anyone?"

"No, nothing. I asked." Webworm waved it off. "I could see by the man's expression that he had no idea what I was talking about."

Now it's voices? Wind Leaf squinted up at the sky. A hot sun burned down on them, baking the packed earth. As they followed the wall of the great kiva, he took note of the few hucksters who had placed their wares in the shade of the single-story rooms on the south. Others would have retreated to the greater shade of the north wall behind Dusk Town.

He grimaced as Webworm worked on his hideous little carving. Each scratching sound seemed to resonate, grating clear down to Wind Leaf's bones. The malignant thing was clearly defined now; a coiled serpent inside a broken eggshell. Webworm was using his basalt graver to detail the triangular head.

In an effort to keep from staring at the loathsome fetish, Wind Leaf looked out across what vista he could see through the gaps on either side of the southern wall. The land baked in the heat, waves of it rising off the cornfields and the distant uplands. The southwest wind seemed to suck at his very souls. It carried a cloud of ash from the Rainbow Serpent that settled atop them; at times he could catch its foul breath: sulfurous and noxious.

He said, "I have everything in readiness, Blessed Sun. Supplies are packed. I have detailed a handful of scouts to precede us along the route. Five of my best warriors will accompany us dressed as slaves. If Matron Desert Willow goes with us, I will detail another eight warriors to act as her litter bearers."

As he talked, they rounded the great kiva. Webworm seemed not to hear, carving as he walked. Nevertheless he said, "Oh she will go. She won't want to miss Sister Moon's homecoming. I don't know if she wants to attend the opening ceremonies at equinox or pick a time during the next three moons to travel up there."

"Fire and ice!" The cry came from the bear cage several paces beyond the great kiva's southern entrance.

Webworm stopped suddenly. Did his face go pale?

Then the Blessed Sun shook himself, pacing up to the wooden cage. He peered into the shadowed interior. "Are you enjoying your stay, witch?"

Wind Leaf could see the old woman. She sat cross-legged, naked, her aged skin hanging in loose wrinkles. She should have been half-delirious from thirst by now, let alone famished. Instead her eyes gleamed with an other-worldly intent as she studied Webworm.

"You don't look like you've been sleeping, Webworm." Her voice carried more conviction than a prisoner's should.

Wind Leaf frowned. No, she couldn't have heard. They'd been on the other side of the great kiva.

"My sleep isn't your concern." Webworm snorted, shook his head, and continued with his carving. "Were I you, I'd be contemplating my journey to Spider Woman's fire."

She smiled, her gray hair hanging in ratty strands. "That's a curious thing for you, of all people, to say. I'm not the one carving a serpent born from a cock's egg."

Webworm held the carving up.

As quickly, the old woman had turned her head to the side, refusing to see it. "I know it very well. Didn't you hear the voices warning you? Just having it in the same room with the Spirits sends them into a frenzy. I'd be careful, Webworm."

"You'll be dead," he growled.

"Not just yet. You and I still have business between us."

Webworm looked mystified. "What business?"

"I have come to free you of evil, Webworm. I am the Witness."

Wind Leaf thought it was all rantings, but when he looked at Webworm's face, he could see a deeper worry. "Free?" the Blessed Sun whispered under his breath. "What good would freedom do me?"

"If I kill you without freeing you from the serpent, your soul will never find Cloud Playing. She's waiting for you."

To Wind Leaf's amazement, Webworm nodded slightly,

frowning. Blood and pus, he wasn't believing this, was he? "Blessed Sun? About traveling to First Moon Mountain?"

"Hurry," the old woman added. "The sooner you get to First Moon Mountain, the sooner the people can rise against you."

"What have you heard?" Wind Leaf demanded. "Speak, or I shall have your tongue stretched and pierced with cactus thorns."

She glanced at him as if seeing him for the first time. He couldn't help but gasp as her eyes met his.

"So, you've heard the rumors? Reported it to your Blessed Sun, have you?"

Wind Leaf flinched.

"Rumors?" Webworm asked.

Wind Leaf waved it away, uneasy at the old woman's manner. "It's nothing. Talk, is all. The story is that the Made People are ready to revolt. Supposedly even the clan leadership is conspiring against you. I haven't been able to prove any of it."

Webworm chuckled at that. "Nor will you. Rest assured, Creeper would tell me at the first hint of trouble."

"You are indeed your namesake," the witch said. "A worm caught in your own web. A treat for the robins, kingbirds, spiders, and wasps. I wonder, which will get you first?"

"You could be dead at a moment's notice, witch!" Wind Leaf pointed a hard finger. "Let me kill her, Blessed Sun. We don't need to put up with her spreading her poison."

"Not yet," Webworm said, frowning.

"Hurry," the old woman whispered. "Away with you. Go, Webworm. The sooner you reach First Moon Mountain, the sooner the world will be rid of you. Go, before the Rainbow Serpent snatches you for fouling his realm with your little carvings."

Webworm stepped back. "You couldn't know . . ."

"It was a Powerful Dream, wasn't it?" The old woman put her head back and laughed. "You call for me when the nightmares become too real. Then, and only then, will we Dance, you and I."

At that, Webworm turned, hurrying away. He almost

kicked over a pile of firewood that a young barbarian had packed in to Trade.

"Blessed Sun?" Wind Leaf called as he hurried after.

"Stupid old hag," Webworm growled under his breath. "Thinks she can scare me, does she? I'll show her." To Wind Leaf he said, "Unpack. If she thinks she can drive me out of my own great house, she's sadly mistaken."

Wind Leaf slowed to a confused halt. Behind him in the cage, he heard the witch chuckling.

A southwest night wind had blown the smoke pall away. Powerful gusts moaning through the trees had awakened Bad Cast. He blinked after rolling in his blanket, and looked up at the midnight sky. The stars were haze-grayed, Sister Moon nearly full. He could see a ring around her, as if some sort of storm were coming.

Bones and stones, it was a storm indeed. He made a face, sitting upright in his blankets. If this went wrong, the Red Shirts would take it out on his family. Somehow he had to get word to Soft Cloth and his kin.

Several paces away a single fire still burned, the flames whipped this way and that by the capricious winds. Iron-wood sat like a bowed god, his scar-filled face illuminated by the flickering light.

Bad Cast unwrapped from his blanket, picked his way past sleeping men, and squatted opposite the war chief.

"You should be sleeping," Ironwood said softly. The wind pulled at his hair, slapping it around in a wild display. The patch over his eye made a black streak across his deeply lined features. The shadows cast by the fire lent him a terrible expression.

"So should you."

"A great many things are on my mind."

"Mine, too."

Ironwood's single eye gleamed in the light; his scars interrupted the lines on his face. "Oh?"

"My family. If the First People discover who is leading

you up the mountain, they will hunt down my brothers, sisters, mother, and uncles. They will find Soft Cloth, and my daughter, and who knows how many others."

Ironwood reached out, dropping another broken pine branch into the deeply dug fire pit. "That is a possibility."

Bad Cast waited, watching the war chief as he stared into the flickering fire. His broad shoulders sagged.

When he finally spoke, he didn't meet Bad Cast's eyes. "I will make a bargain with you."

"A bargain, War Chief?"

"Once you lead us up the back side of First Moon Mountain, you may go. Find your people, and warn them. Tell them not to take part in what's coming, but to pack and leave. Personally, I'd take them east to the Great River. There's good land there."

"But what if you need me?"

"If we do not completely surprise them, Bad Cast, my warriors and I will have no need of anything." A faint shrug of his shoulders. "Your presence will not affect the outcome."

Bad Cast frowned. "Somehow, it doesn't feel right just leaving you, Yucca Sock, Firehorn, Right Hand, and the rest. I would always wonder if my being there might have made a difference."

"Ah, so you're a man with a conscience. It's a terrible thing to have." He rubbed his face with his large bony hands. "But in your case, I am going to play on this conscience of yours, and ask you if you will do something for me."

"Of course, War Chief. It will be my honor."

"When I dismiss you before the attack, go and warn your people. Then, when the fighting plays out, I want you to return to my settlement and tell Night Sun and Orenda what has occurred. I need you to make sure they are safe."

"I don't understand. Why won't you send one of your warriors for them?"

He ignored the question. "Your people know this country; you have kin that you can count on to hide them, keep them safe. If the worst happens and we are all killed, the Blessed Sun may have warriors searching under every bush. You might have to move them around, travel by night until Webworm gives up. When things finally quiet down, please promise me you will take Night Sun down to Cornsilk and Poor Singer. Chief Jay Bird will know where they are."

"You can take care of her yourself."

Ironwood turned his head, looking where Ripple had lain his bed. Bad Cast followed his glance. He would have sworn Ripple's eyes were open, that he was listening. "When you bargain with the gods, they expect you to keep your word. From the things both Nightshade and Ripple have told me, I know that I must suffer something terrible. No, don't protest, Bad Cast. I've done unspeakable things during my life. Being granted the few summers I've had with my wife and daughter are more than I deserve."

"War Chief, you can't—"

He reached out, taking Bad Cast's hands in his strong grip. "Do I have your word that you will take care of my wife?"

Bad Cast swallowed hard, and nodded. "Yes, War Chief."

From where he lay in his bedding, Ripple made a soft whimper and turned onto his side.

Forty-nine

Throughout the afternoon Leather Hand's men had filtered down off the mountain. In ones and twos they had made their way, packs over their shoulders. Some had dressed in hunting shirts, others in farmer's kilts. The patches of trees that surrounded the base of the Dog's Tooth became their lair. There, they secreted themselves, burrowing into brush, hunkering under duff-covered blankets among the rocks.

In the last fingers of light, they had emerged, opened their packs, and removed their bright red shirts. They strung their bows, counted the arrows in their quivers, and practiced swinging war clubs to loosen their muscles.

Leather Hand himself had taken the scout's position, secreting himself beside the trail. Motionless as a snake, he had covered himself with a gray blanket and watched as five slow processions of the elders made their way no more than two arm lengths from his hide. He had heard their soft barbarian speech, listened to the tension in their voices.

Matron Larkspur's informant had been right.

He waited for a half hand of time, watching the stars slowly rise on the southern horizon. Then, the moon appearing, he rose and took up his weapons. The only sound he made was a hooting, the sort one of the cliff owls would have made. Another hoot answered. And then another.

Step by careful step, he began the climb up the Dog's Tooth. The first sentry was a mere boy, the lad so stupid he asked something in his incomprehensible tongue. Leather Hand's whistling war club thudded into his neck, snapping the spine.

He could see the walled enclosure, now little more than a dark blot against the moon-bright sky. There would be other sentries, some perhaps smarter than this one had been.

Whistle, still caked with trail grime, stood tall, a war club in his hand. The central fire in the Black Shale Moiety kiva cracked and popped, sending sparks toward the wide opening in the roof. Firelight reflected amber off of the support posts as well as the ring of watching faces. The elders sat on the kiva bench as was their due; the war chiefs, such as they were among his people, sat on the floor—ten young men of dubious valor and experience.

Old White Eye sat in the preeminent center of the bench, his snowy eye cast red from the fire. "How will we know when the war chief is in position?"

Whistle said, "We will have runners, people you delegate to us. As we prepare our assault, we need you to make a demonstration lower on the mountain. If each of our clans deploys their warriors and begins to ascend toward Guest House, Burning Smoke will mass his warriors there. Given the narrow approach to Pinnacle Great House, he'll want to concentrate his forces."

"You're sure?" Hoarse Caller of the Strong Back Clan asked through her rasping voice.

Whistle gave her a nod. "Burning Smoke is no fool. The clans will outnumber him. His strategy will be to narrow our front of attack. He knows his fighters are better than ours. His warriors are trained. Ours will be made up of hunters and farmers. Most of our people still use atlatls. Knowing this, Burning Smoke's warriors will be close to cover, far enough away that they can duck and dodge. His goal will be to hold us back, or induce us to charge. If the latter, he's counting on the effectiveness of his bowmen. In the time it takes for our fighters to close, his men can send a hail of arrows down. Then, our ranks weakened, morale lowered from the casualties, his warriors attack with war clubs. They need only to break our attack and send our fighters fleeing back down the hill."

Rattler, of the Blue Stick Clan, said, "And that's the one thing we cannot allow to happen."

"Correct," Whistle replied. He looked at the uncertain war chiefs. "It is imperative that we hold back. Do you understand? This will be a game of nerves. We must keep the threat up, but never allow ourselves close enough where they can rain arrows upon us."

One young man said, "We have to tease them."

Whistle nodded. "That's right. You may allow some of your most fleet young men to dance in and out of the danger zone. Burning Smoke's warriors will be anticipating this, so don't expect them to draw many arrows." Whistle steepled his fingers. "You see, they, too, will be playing the game. They will try and tempt your young men farther and farther into the killing area."

Wizened old Black Sage asked, "How long does the war chief expect us to keep this up?"

"As long as it takes," Whistle replied. "Now, here is the final thing: On the day before the attack, each of the clans needs to send a small party of fighters around the base of the cliffs below Pinnacle Great House."

"Why?" Red Water asked. Firelight gleamed in the white streak in her hair. "They'll be able to see us from above."

Whistle clapped his hands. "Precisely." He turned to the war chiefs. "You are to order these scouts to retire immediately after being spotted. Do you understand?"

"No," Dead Bird muttered. "That's as crazy as a stone-struck grouse. They'll know we're coming."

Whistle said, "Of course. Pay attention. We want them to know that we know the rim is guarded. We want them to think that because of those guards, we have no other option but to try and force our way past Guest House and onto the ridgetop."

White Eye asked, "Does the war chief really think this will work?"

Whistle spread his hands wide. "Elder, in war no one can know."

"Precisely!" a voice called from the kiva entrance.

Whistle turned, seeing a familiar figure enter. It took him several heartbeats to realize this man spoke in First People's tongue. And then the red shirt, dark in the firelight, sent a stab of fear into his heart. As the man approached the stunned elders, his face caught the firelight.

"Leather Hand!" Whistle's heart skipped, his gut sinking. He raised his war club, dropping into a crouch. He had a fleeting glimpse of the elders, the war chiefs, all frozen as if thunderstruck, expressions of panic on their faces.

Even more warriors were pouring into the kiva, spreading out, bows drawn, arrows nocked and held for release.

Leather Hand's white moccasins flashed in the firelight. "No one need die here," he said in Made People's tongue.

One of his warriors repeated the words in First Moon language. "You may leave this place, alive, and accompany my warriors up to the great house. There you will remain for the duration of the Moon Ceremony."

"What then?" Whistle's voice cracked with sudden understanding.

"Well . . ." Leather Hand shrugged. "We will see. Your futures will depend upon the obedience of your people." He grinned. "If the Moon Ceremony proceeds peacefully, you may be allowed to return to your clans. If it doesn't, who knows? Perhaps my warriors and I shall toss your bones down the slope after we roast your bodies." He made a face as he inspected wizened old Black Sage. "Much too tough. We might have to seek out some of your younger kin to fill our pots."

The grim red-shirted warriors chuckled at that.

"So?" Leather Hand asked. "What will it be? Live, or have your souls devoured by my human wolves?"

Whistle leapt, bringing his war club up.

He wouldn't have believed it. Leather Hand blocked his blow, pivoted, and before he could recover, hammered a blow into Whistle's rib cage.

The pain was agonizing. A second blow smashed his hip, tumbling him to the dirt. Then Leather Hand dropped, his knee spearing the center of Whistle's broken chest.

"Now," Leather Hand said softly, "let's you and I talk about Ironwood."

He bounced his weight on Whistle's sternum. The resulting scream might have split the sky.

From the screen of the trees, Ripple stared out at First Moon Valley. The twin pillars of rock dominated the great mountain. From this angle, Pinnacle Great House remained hidden behind the mountain's shoulder. He could feel the place, like a darkness on his souls. The First People waited there—waited for him.

"Smoke," Bad Cast said as he walked out of the trees.

"What's on fire?" Ironwood asked as he led the rest of the warriors to the tree line.

"The Dog's Tooth," Ripple replied, seeing it in the Dream. "The kivas are gone; bodies lie broken and mutilated on the slope."

"What?" Bad Cast cried, stepping beside him, a hand on Ripple's arm. "You *saw* this?"

Ripple nodded sadly. "It is as it must be."

"Must be?" Bad Cast cried, grabbing his other arm, shaking him violently. "Why didn't you *warn* us?"

Ironwood's hard hand clamped on Bad Cast's shoulder, tightening, fingers digging into the nerves. "Let him go."

Bad Cast's hands fell away, but he kept his frantic eyes on Ripple's.

"I'm sorry," Ripple whispered. "Bad Cast, do you think this is easy? It's not! It's tearing me apart, wounding my souls, but it's got to be this way!"

"In the name of the gods, *why*?"

Ripple took a breath, slapping his hands to his sides. "In the name of the gods. That's exactly why. It's a *battle*, Bad Cast. You're a hunter; you know that it's one thing to bait a trap, but the game has to be reassured before it will walk into the kill pen. There are things going on that you don't know . . . *can't* know!"

Bad Cast's expression pinched in the old familiar way. He nodded, shooting Ripple a submissive glance. "All right. I think I understand."

Ironwood glanced back and forth; the warriors were muttering among themselves.

"What's next, Dreamer?" Ironwood asked.

"Would you let the trap spring before you act?"

Ripple watched the conflict behind the man's eye, could see his souls struggling, writhing with indecision. In the end, desperation won out. "Yes, Dreamer, I would."

Ripple swallowed hard, hearing the man condemn himself to the path of the gods. "Then you must follow my orders." He paused, aware that every warrior was listening. "Will your men follow you?"

Ripple was aware of cautious nods as the war chief

said, "I'm sure they will," with more authority than he felt. The old warrior's single eye was rife with indecision.

"All is not lost," Ripple said quietly. "As it was planned, you'd never have won. Now our victory is assured."

"How?" Bad Cast demanded. "If the Dog's Tooth is burning, Matron Larkspur found out about Whistle and White Eye! For all we know, they're up there waiting for us!"

Ripple nodded, seeing the confusion in his friend's eyes. "Oh, yes. The Flute Player has moved his pieces. He thinks he has won the game. Now we must wait. Be patient."

"For what?" Ironwood demanded, his resolution beginning to fray.

"For Cold Bringing Woman and the katsinas to move theirs." He stepped close to the old warrior, staring into his eye. "Will you trust me, War Chief? Trust Cold Bringing Woman's vision? I promise, allies are coming from unusual directions."

He could feel the tension, see the struggle as if it were smoke that rose from each man in the party.

"Yes," Ironwood said angrily. "Tell me what you will have of me."

"A place to wait." Ripple turned to the surrounding warriors. "And a patience worthy of your greatness."

"What are you doing?" Bad Cast demanded.

"Fulfilling a promise to a god," Ripple said hollowly.

In the evening light, Bad Cast sat with Soft Cloth. They perched on the sandstone rim and looked out over the River of Stones. Juniper Ridge cast a deep blue shadow over the fertile fields in the floodplain below. Across from them, First Moon Mountain rose, the twin pillars touched with the last strokes of orange. Even as they watched, shadow slipped up the rock, as if their world were drowning in darkness.

In the north, the sky was black, yellow, and red, billows of smoke rising as the northern mountains continued to burn.

Bad Cast tightened his grip on Soft Cloth's hand. "There they go."

On the other side of the valley, in the dip below the blackened ruins of the Dog's Tooth, the first white specks of Blue Racer's Priests emerged onto the trail that would take them the rest of the way up to Pinnacle Great House. Like a slow snake the column of men emerged, winding its way upward.

"It can't be that bad," Soft Cloth said.

"How bad can it be?" Bad Cast was past reassurances. "I'll tell you." He pointed at Pinnacle Great House where it squatted on the peak. "Leather Hand will kill and eat Elder Rattler, White Eye, and the rest of the clan leaders. The war chiefs will be gutted and tossed over the cliff. We are back where we were when the First People came here. They'll take many of the lineage elders off as slaves; the rest of us, well, we have to punished. Expect our harvest to be confiscated. All of it. Every last kernel."

She shook her head. "They wouldn't do that. If we starve to death, who will they find to farm this land next year?"

"Dust People," he said quickly. "Yellow Soil People, people from the Green Mesas, refugees from the lowlands. The Blessed Sun can offer it to anyone he wishes."

Soft Cloth frowned, a rebuttal rising.

"No," Bad Cast said firmly. "You haven't seen the things I have. You don't understand." He tightened his grip on her hand. "Look at me, and listen very carefully. I want you to think about leaving this place."

"What?"

"You, me, our baby, and any of our relatives that we can talk into it."

"That's crazy! We have property here, fields." She pointed to Mid-Sun House, the two-story building where even now Ironwood and Ripple sat with her lineage elders. "This is where my family is. Our house is right over there."

He nodded. "Soft Cloth, our world is coming to an end. Ripple and the Mountain Witch have seen it." He gestured at the winding column of worshipers climbing First Moon Mountain. "Equinox isn't that far away. A matter of days." He pointed to the distant watchtower that perched on the high rim of First Moon Mountain. "How far north is the sun?"

"Less than a finger. But that's the point. Harvest will begin soon. You don't expect me to just walk away from my responsibilities, do you?"

Bad Cast sighed. "I was afraid of this."

"Afraid of what?" She shook her head. "What's wrong with you? You're not the same man who left here."

He chuckled bitterly, looking down the slope. "Remember when you caught us gambling down there under that tree?"

She nodded.

"Gods, Soft Cloth, what I'd give to be that man again. What I'd give if only I could go back and keep Ripple from going after that elk."

"You really believe this, don't you?"

He met her eyes. "I want a chance to love you. I want to watch our children grow up and marry and have children of their own. Do you understand? I want to *love* you. Not just now, but forever."

"Bad Cast?"

"I have things to do, responsibilities I must see to. But if I ask you to leave with me, I need you to say yes."

He could see the deep confusion in her eyes. Perhaps it mirrored his own. Pus and blood, what was he going to do if she said no?

Spots saw the northern sky as he walked up from the river. A deer bladder full of drinking water hung in one hand; a thin net bag from his other. Seven baked corn cakes were within.

"Some fire," Cactus Flower greeted him as he approached the southeastern gate. She stood up from her blanket and stretched.

"It is. Must be spectacular from home."

She considered him. "You miss it?"

"Well, sure. My sister must be half-crazy without me to do my chores in the fields. This is the critical time. The corn is headed out, starting to mature. This is when the raccoons, worms, deer, and human thieves get ready to raid our fields. As dry as it's been, she's been working sunup to sundown carrying water."

"But you'd rather run back and forth like a Trader, packing firewood so you can Trade for *her*?" She inclined her head toward the gate.

Spots chewed his lip, aware of Cactus Flower's wary arch of brow. "It's just something I have to do."

"Oh, yes, sneak food to a condemned witch. You know, if they catch you . . ."

"That's why it's got to be done right at dusk."

She frowned at him. "Well, if you're convinced you need to have some warrior stand on your neck and smack your brains out, go ahead. If you escape getting caught again tonight, I don't have anyone staying over."

He cocked his head. "As you well know, I'm out of firewood."

"You've got a string of shell beads. White Lizard gave them to you."

"I'd better get this inside." He lifted the bag, glancing up at the roof where the bored guard watched the south-eastern gate.

"Oh, just come by," she said huffily.

"Trade or no?"

She shrugged coyly. "Sleeping with you is fun. I'm starting to like it."

He thought about that as he walked through the gate, nodded at the guard, and called, "I'm just going back for my blanket."

He received a wave in return.

Evening light had softened the interior of Dusk House. It had masked the hard lines of the great kiva, gloom filling the doorways. Here and there people went about their evening activities. Most would be leaving soon, headed back to their farmsteads. For all of its massive size, few people actually lived here—only the Blessed Sun, the Made People clan elders, Priests, warriors, and the slaves who served them.

He found his blanket where he'd left it, to one side of a doorway leading into one of the southern rooms. He glanced surreptitiously around as he folded his blanket. No one seemed to be watching.

He stretched, flopped his blanket over his shoulder, and walked toward the great kiva. He could hear singing from within. The entrance had a soft yellow glow, and several people crowded at the doorway, watching the events inside.

He felt his heart lurch as he angled past the bear cage. Every time he did this, it scared the liver out of him. He always expected shouts of alarm and red-shirted warriors charging to capture him. The interior was dark in shadow, Nightshade a mere representation of her name.

"Food and water," he said softly, reaching through the bars as he passed slowly by. To an onlooker, it would just seem that he'd barely brushed the cage.

Nightshade said, "Bring me a hafted chert knife the night before equinox."

"Yes, Elder." He passed on, a feeling of relief filling him. The night before equinox? Good. That would be what, four days? Maybe three?

He paused, peering over the shoulders of the onlookers. Down the long rectangular stairway he could see masked Dancers, their bodies festooned with green cornstalks. They swayed and bent to the Song, each step of the sacred Dance made to assure the fruitfulness of the coming harvest.

If the Full Corn Dance was tonight, equinox was four days away.

He turned then, waving at the guard as he passed out through the gate. From the wall shadow, Cactus Flower appeared and took his arm. She had a canteen hung over her shoulder, and it bounced on her round hips.

"So," she teased, "you live another night."

"It would seem."

"Good." She tightened her grip on his arm. "I don't know what it is about you. You're certainly not handsome with those scars all over. You're not smart, or you wouldn't be feeding the witch. You're not even a very good Trader."

"Thank you," he muttered dryly.

She shoved him playfully sideways. "Have you had your witch put some sort of spell on me?"

"No! Why are you asking all these questions?"

"Because my sheath has been itching for you all day long, and I can't figure out why."

Fifty

Orenda bent to pick another mint plant and glanced up at the sky where the drifting haze of blue smoke spread from the north across the entire eastern horizon. Through it, Father Sun's face was a huge ruddy smear of red-brown light.

Ripple had been so intent when he'd asked her to come pick mint. Why? Had it been some curing he wanted her to do? The desperation in his eyes hadn't allowed her any response but to agree.

Ever since he'd asked, she'd been puzzling over it. His simple gaze affected her in a way that left her forever uncomfortable.

One by one she stripped leaves from the stem and dropped them into her coarsely woven collecting bag. Discarding the stem, she was about to reach for another when a flash of red caught her eye. She eased down to one knee.

They were some distance away, just emerging from the trees on the other side of the valley. Even from this distance she could see it was a party of warriors. And, no, this was not the war chief returning. These war shirts were too bright, and two of the men wore white moccasins. They came on at a trot, heading for the river just below her.

She sank slowly to her belly before she began wiggling her way like a salamander for the stand of willows that stood just below the hot springs.

Once she had slithered into the concealing stems, she waited and watched. Hopefully they wouldn't see the trail where she'd crushed the grass, mint, and daisies.

Her view was obscured as they stopped, drank, and then trotted into sight traveling in single file. She watched them work their way, panting, up and into the trees.

By the Long Nosed God, they couldn't know where the village was, could they? Fear began to pound brightly.

What could she do? They were between her and the settlement. Were she to run with all her might, she could never circle around them in time to warn Night Sun.

The tall ponderosa cast slanting shadows as Leather Hand led his warriors across the mesa top. Dry pine needles crackled under his tough yucca trail sandals. He carried his bow at the low ready, an arrow nocked in preparation to be drawn and released.

To either side he could see his White Moccasins. Like the human wolves they were, they slipped from tree to tree, only the faint crackle of the pine needles audible.

Faint trails crisscrossed the mesa top, and here, for the first time, he found a tree where someone had just recently broken the dead branches from the lower trunk. A slow smile crossed his lips.

The young man was oblivious as he came walking down the trail. In his midteens, he appeared on the verge of manhood. Smooth brown skin covered a triangular face, his large brown eyes fixed on the ground before him. A load of firewood had been slung over his shoulder, and the perplexed frown on his forehead betrayed his preoccupation.

Leather Hand raised his right hand in the "ready" signal, and his men shifted silently behind the nearest cover.

Leather Hand stepped behind the thick trunk of a ponderosa, his heart quickening with the fever of war. He could hear the youth's footsteps before he made out the muttering under the young man's breath.

"Pick up firewood. Take out the ashes. Clean up after your brother." A pause. "I hope lightning strikes them all dead."

Leather Hand kept the tree between him and the youth, then stepped out, no more than half a body-length from the youth. "Stop right there! And if you scream, this arrow goes right through your heart."

The youth halted, wide-eyed, mouth dropping open. He blinked as Leather Hand's warriors surrounded him.

"Who are you?" Leather Hand demanded.

"Ra-Ravenfire," the youth sputtered, his head turning this way and that as he took in the hard-eyed warriors around him.

"Cornsilk's get," Turquoise Fox growled from behind the lad.

"Cornsilk's get," Leather Hand repeated.

"What—What are you going to do with me?" Ravenfire's fear sent beads of nervous sweat to shimmer on his skin.

"Why, kill you," Leather Hand said easily. "Just like we did the Dust People."

"You?" Ravenfire's throat worked. "You're Leather Hand?"

"The very same. In less than a hand of time, we'll be carving those tender muscles from your bones. Then we will deliver your head to your mother."

"She's—she's not here!"

"Where is she?"

"Gone south with Poor Singer to Jay Bird's village."

"But Ironwood is here?"

Ravenfire shook his head vigorously. "Gone to First Moon Valley."

"With how many warriors?"

"I—I'm not telling."

"Hold him." Leather Hand glanced at Turquoise Fox. He laid his bow to one side as he pulled a long obsidian blade from his belt pouch. Several of his warriors had grasped the youth, holding him while he kicked, and one clapped a hard hand over his mouth to keep him from screaming.

Leather Hand stepped close, using the keen blade to

sever the belt at the young man's waist. "See how easily the rope parts?" He traced the glittering blade along the base of Ravenfire's throat. "Your neck will cut just as easily. Now, how many warriors did Ironwood take to First Moon Valley?"

"Th-Thirty." It was hard to hear, mumbled against the gagging hand.

"Not enough to threaten Burning Smoke," Turquoise Fox said with relief. "When Ironwood hears that the First Moon elders have been taken, he'll retreat like a whipped puppy."

Leather Hand nodded. To Ravenfire, he said, "You would like to live, wouldn't you?"

Ravenfire swallowed hard, jerking his head in affirmation.

"Then you will tell us where Ironwood's village is?"

The terrified Ravenfire nodded again.

"You won't scream?"

He shook his head.

"Good." Leather Hand fingered his chin. "When you approached, I heard you. So you're tired of running errands and doing chores like a common slave?"

He might have been young, but Ravenfire was quick of mind. Leather Hand saw the calculating behind his eyes. Good, he could still think, even when frightened half out of his skin.

"Help us, prove your worth to us," Leather Hand encouraged, "and your rewards could be greater than anything you have ever hoped."

Ravenfire's cunning eyes narrowed. "How great?"

"I want Ironwood. I'll Trade your life for his."

Ravenfire took a deep breath. "All right. Night Sun is over behind those trees. Once you have her, you can lure Ironwood anywhere you want him to go." He glanced around. "But if I were you, I'd grab her, and run for someplace where you can control all the approaches. The longer you stay here, the more vulnerable you are."

"Is it that easy for you?"

Ravenfire actually smiled. "They've never recognized my talents. I can do a great many things for you. After all,

I'm Red Lacewing Clan—and I deserve a better life than scuttling around like a wood rat in the forest."

For years Night Sun had lived the nightmare. In it, she imagined red-shirted warriors popping out of the trees, charging, their war clubs lifted. She had imagined the expressions of surprise and terror as people looked up from their chores, turned, and bolted in all directions.

That fateful moment when it finally happened, she stood, stunned, staring in disbelief as the warriors appeared out of the trees. Unlike her nightmares, however, they made no sound. The only thing she heard was the patting impact of their sandals on the hard dry ground.

It took her a moment to find her wits. In that instant, as she watched, Cedar Loom was struck down from behind. Then Night Sun turned, willing her old legs to run. She had made no more than six steps before she heard Raven-fire scream, *"Grandmother! Help!"*

She slid to a stop, turning, hesitating as she saw him running toward her. "Come on!" she cried. "This way!"

To her great surprise, he ran up to her, and hugged her with his strong arms.

"Let me go! We've got to run."

"Sorry," he told her with a smug smile. "But I've made a better deal."

She struggled, confused, unable to understand. She was still beating at his confining arms as he plucked her off her feet, carrying her back toward the grinning warriors.

"I wish you would just run ahead," Crow Woman complained as Wrapped Wrist led the way down the trail. "You needn't fuss over me like a hen turkey over her chicks."

Wrapped Wrist perched precariously on the slope to hold a low-hanging ponderosa branch to one side. Crow Woman hobbled past, leaning on the makeshift crutch he'd made.

"Good thing they didn't whack both knees," he said as the branch whipped back in place.

"Too bad Narrow-frame didn't cut straight down the center," she muttered. "If you had a split nose and four lips maybe you wouldn't talk so much."

Wrapped Wrist trotted around and ahead of her. They followed a game trail that wound down the side of the slope. Through gaps in the conifers, he could see the broad River of Souls Valley. It wouldn't be long now before they broke out of the timber. The footing would be better, less chance that Crow Woman would turn her swollen knee.

She cried out as she stepped over a log and jammed her leg. "Bloody pus! Why does that have to hurt so?"

"Knees are funny that way." He stepped around, taking her hand, helping her over the obstacle. Was it his imagination, or did she hold onto him for a moment longer than necessary?

He shot her a wary glance. Had to be his imagination. This was Crow Woman, after all. Even subdued by her run-in with the Red Shirts, he didn't trust her to remain that way. What would it take? A sideways glance? A wrongly inflected word? And then she'd be her old prickly self again.

"What?" She'd realized he was thinking about her.

"Nothing."

"Must be something."

He kicked the remains of a rotten log out of the way, and held another branch. A red squirrel chattered above them, which set off the jays. She was shooting him pensive looks. "Gods, am I really that bad?"

"Kind of like one of those macaws the Traders bring up from the distant south. Really pretty, but I like you with your claws tied and a string around your beak."

He caught the slightest bit of smile at the corner of her lips. "Good."

She continued hobbling down the trail. The slope was gentler here, and she made better time, slowing only to clamber over a deadfall.

"It's just that we've lost so much time. First they made us backtrack, and took us off the main trail. Then this knee." She shook her head. "My fault. All my fault."

"Stop it." He wanted to scratch his face where the makeshift stitches itched and burned.

"If I hadn't been so bullheaded. Gods, I can be such a buffalo sometimes."

"You do all right."

She bit her lip and said nothing more.

Wrapped Wrist kicked a stone out of the trail and craned his neck. Yellow sunlight could be seen between the branches. Good, another couple of paces and they'd be out of the trees and into . . .

Wrapped Wrist raised his hand, stopping short. Yes, those were voices. He dropped to a crouch, trying to peer under the branches.

The timber below them gave way to scattered rabbitbrush, patches of sumac, and tall grass. In the bottom, the River of Souls coursed between willow-bounded banks. Several stands of cottonwoods clustered along the river.

He scuttled forward, taking a position behind one of the last pines. Leaning out from the trunk he could see them: red-shirted warriors. They seemed too well dressed. A line of them, perhaps thirty, were leading a small group of women and children. And there, on a pole litter, he could see a woman being borne along on six of the warriors' shoulders. Worse, they were headed right down the valley. Given their route of travel, they would pass no more than fifty paces in front of him.

Wrapped Wrist eased back up the slope, motioning Crow Woman to get down. He took position behind yet another of the trees.

"Who are they?" Crow Woman whispered.

"Warriors."

"Ours?"

"I don't think so. They've got women and children."

Crow Woman made a face as she crawled down beside him to peer through the screening branches of the pine. "I can't see much."

"Shhh! They're coming this way."

He felt his heart begin to pound and anxiously reached around for the war club he'd taken from one of the dead warriors. It had a good feel to it. He considered his options. He'd left his darts in the bodies of the dead. The one that had missed Narrow-frame had shattered on a stone. Now he cursed himself as a fool, but at the time the thought of pulling them out of human flesh had been too much for him.

If I live through this, I promise, I'll never be squeamish again.

With the appearance of the lead warrior all other thoughts were stillborn. He was a tall man resplendent in a bright red war shirt; gleaming necklaces hung at his throat. Three jaunty eagle feathers had been thrust into his hair bun, and striking white moccasins clad his feet. They rustled in the tall grass.

Crow Woman gasped before she clamped a hand to her mouth.

For a second Wrapped Wrist thought the warrior had heard, for his head snapped to the side, his fierce eyes searching the forest. But his step never faltered, and he continued on his way.

Behind him came two ranks of warriors, bows unstrung, quivers packed with perfectly fletched cane arrows. Some carried the long curved wooden war clubs the Blessed Sun's warriors favored. They talked in low voices, some laughing. The light of triumph seemed to Dance over them as they smiled and nodded amidst animated talk.

The litter jounced into view, and Wrapped Wrist gaped. The expression of disgust on Matron Night Sun's face might have been chiseled in stone. She wore a dark blue robe, strings of beads at her throat. Bejeweled and decked out, she might have been heading for some great house ceremony. She rode with her back stiff, head forward, imperious of posture; but even from this distance, Wrapped Wrist could see fear glitter in her eyes. The leather binding on her wrists betrayed her true status.

Several of the camp children followed; they were being herded by Ravenfire, Cornsilk's firstborn. He carried one of the thin wooden war clubs, and walked with a jaunty attitude. Nor were his hands bound.

"Ravenfire?" Crow Woman hissed under her breath. "Gods!"

Wrapped Wrist recognized several of Ironwood's warriors' wives. All were naked from the waist up, wrists bound, lengths of thong tied between their ankles to keep them from running. The bruises on their faces, legs, arms, and breasts had that new cherry color. Each one had a bloody pack slung over her shoulder. To Wrapped Wrist's practiced eye, it looked like they carried freshly butchered meat. One woman held her arm as if it was broken. Several were crying, while others looked tear-streaked, eyes dull.

A squad of warriors brought up the rear; mindful of their charges, they lashed out at any who tarried.

After they passed, Wrapped Wrist remained as if planted. Gods, what had happened? Who were these terrible warriors? He glanced over, seeing Crow Woman's expression. She looked on the point of tears.

"What in the name of the gods has happened?" Wrapped Wrist asked in a whisper, still unsure whether to trust his voice lest the terrible warriors hear despite the distance.

Crow Woman exhaled wearily. "How?"

Wrapped Wrist waited, his heart beating anxiously.

"That warrior in front," Crow Woman finally said. "That's Leather Hand. Somehow, some way, they've captured Night Sun."

"What about the war chief? Orenda and Ripple?"

"I don't know." She swallowed hard. "We've got to go after Night Sun and Ravenfire."

Wrapped Wrist reached out, clamping her arm as she

started up. "No. Think, Crow Woman. They have thirty warriors. There's just the two of us, and you're half-crippled. Before we do anything, we have to find out what's happened. See if any of the others survived." He hesitated. "And I'm not sure, but Ravenfire looked like he was one of them."

She shot a hot glare his direction, started to struggle, and bent her leg. She bit off the groan of pain, and relented. "Yes, you're right."

Leather Hand! Wrapped Wrist took a deep breath. He'd looked right into the eyes of the cannibal! "I pray the gods guard Matron Night Sun."

The climb up the slope to Ironwood's mesa seemed interminable. Wrapped Wrist chafed, loose soil and pine duff slipping under his feet. Crow Woman, her face a mask of dismay, levered herself up, step after painful step. The way was marked by disturbed ground, churned needles, and tumbled stones.

Wrapped Wrist noted a spot of color: a little boy, his body wedged around a tree trunk. He'd been smacked in the top of the head with a war club, blood having spattered the dirt as he rolled limply down the slope.

Crow Woman shook her head, taking a moment to catch her breath as she leaned on her crutch. "People called him Kit. He wanted to be a warrior like his father, Yucca Sock. He must have angered them."

At the cleft in the caprock, Wrapped Wrist reached back and bodily lifted Crow Woman onto the top.

They found Orenda at the village. She sat in the center of the plaza, a little dead girl in her lap. Her absent gaze was fixed on the smoke plume that hung over the mountains to the north. Her hand moved like a delicate bird as she fingered the girl's limp hair. Tears streaked her dusty face, the corners of her mouth trembling.

"How did they find us?" Crow Woman demanded as she hobbled forward.

Orenda shook her head, mystified. "They came straight here, as if they knew. They didn't even search."

Crow Woman sighed and seated herself on a stump, her stiff leg out before her. "We saw Ravenfire. He was armed and seemed to be guarding the prisoners."

Orenda nodded, looking stunned. "I saw him. They were treating him like he was one of them! Clapping him on the back. *Thanking* him for capturing Night Sun! He was strutting and bragging. Night Sun herself spat on him."

"I always thought he was a worm," Crow Woman said in disgust.

For Wrapped Wrist, the sight in the plaza was ghastly. Several women could be seen, partially naked, limbs askew, hair loose and tangled with dirt and detritus. He stepped over, curious to see that some had long sections of leg muscle cut from the bone. One woman's entire leg was missing, neatly cut off at the hip.

Then he got a close look at the children. He'd last seen them alive—bouncing, smiling, and squabbling as children do. Could these broken bodies be those same expectant little people? Flies were already swarming to the wounds.

"Where is the war chief? Where are our warriors?" Crow Woman asked. "I see no men here."

"Gone. They left three days ago for First Moon Mountain."

"So they could have been captured, too?" Wrapped Wrist asked.

Orenda shrugged.

"We've got to find out." Crow Woman hitched herself back to her feet. "Get anything you need."

Orenda blinked. "What about . . . ?"

"Their souls have already fled," Crow Woman said gently. "This is just flesh. When it's all over, when we know what's happened, we can come back for the bones. The living may need us more."

Just flesh. Wrapped Wrist glanced again at the stripped bones. How could such an evil have entered the world? Worse, what could they do about it?

In the sky above, the smoke plume had shifted, curling around in the sky and pointing off to the southeast.

Leather Hand pushed his warriors and captives until full darkness obscured the trail. They would camp for several hands of time, and then when Sister Moon rose in the northeastern sky, he would order them on. Or so he hoped. When he looked up at the east, smoke had blotted the stars. Would Sister Moon be able to pierce the darkness with her glow?

At his feet the River of Souls flowed, water lapping under the bank. The current was calm here, though he could hear the faint roar of rapids in the distance downstream. Overhead, cottonwood leaves rattled with the breeze blowing down the canyon.

He walked back under the trees to the place where Turquoise Fox had kindled a fire. In the leaping yellow light, he could see his captives. Night Sun sat cross-legged, her bound wrists before her. Back straight, face forward, no expression crossed her stern features.

The other captives, bound together in a line, were overseen by four of his warriors. They, in contrast, looked broken, heads down, shoulders slumped.

Turquoise Fox stepped close, voice lowered. "What do you think? Could Ironwood be close?"

Leather Hand avoided night-blinding himself on the flames as he looked out at the darkness beyond the cottonwoods. "I have no idea. If we are to believe the things Whistle told us, he's camped somewhere outside of First Moon Valley, waiting for the elders to send him word."

Turquoise Fox grinned. "Then he'll wait a long time."

"Without his allies, he won't dare to attack. What can his little band of warriors do against Pinnacle House? No, he's nothing without the Moon People clans. Even Whistle agreed with that."

"Whistle." Turquoise Fox shook his head. "I thought

he'd have been tougher than that." Turquoise Fox glanced at Night Sun, sitting like a wooden statue.

"We didn't get everyone," Leather Hand reminded. "Someone will have escaped. Perhaps a boy out hunting rabbits, some woman picking berries. Ironwood will know soon enough."

"And when he does?" Turquoise Fox asked.

"He will abandon First Moon Valley and come looking for his wife and young Ravenfire." He looked toward where the youth was talking with the warrior called Fast Fist.

"Do you trust him?" Turquoise Fox asked, lowering his voice. "He betrayed his people. What would it take for him to betray us?"

Leather Hand rubbed his fingers together, as if sampling the air. "I don't know. He did grab Night Sun for us like he said he would. And he captured her *alive*. He ate his share of meat tonight."

"He told Fast Fist he's never had a woman before."

Leather Hand chuckled. "Well, he'll have plenty tonight. And he says he knows how to lure Ironwood into our grasp. As long as he continues to be a benefit, he lives. The second he seems to waver, don't even think about it. Just kill him."

"And Ironwood?"

"I expect him to try and sneak into Flowing Waters Town. I'll send you with a warning for the Blessed Sun when we get closer. With any luck War Chief Wind Leaf will round him up before he has a chance to make trouble. It's not like he's hard to miss. How many towering gray-haired men are missing their left eye and covered with scars?"

"Night Sun," Turquoise Fox said softly. "By the gods, I never would have thought we'd take her alive."

Leather Hand smiled his satisfaction. They might not have, but for Ravenfire's deception of Night Sun. The raid had been perfect. In less than a finger's time, those not captive were dead. Some of the women who had fled were run down and dragged back. On his orders they were beaten and raped before they were killed. His men had cut steaks from the bodies.

When Ironwood returned, saw what Leather Hand's

men had done, he would be coming. *Yes, old enemy, feel your blood boil. Know that Leather Hand and his human monsters have your wife and grandson. Lose your senses to rage and desperation. I shall be waiting.*

He walked over, squatting to look into Night Sun's eyes. She stared back with an unexpected serenity.

"Well, Matron, it appears that you have been brought low."

In a firm voice she replied, "This is not the first time I've been taken captive. The only difference is that last time, my captor was a great man, not a piece of walking two-legged filth."

"He's your grandson. It must run in the blood."

"I was referring to you."

With a lightning strike, he slapped her. The force of it stung his hand and nearly knocked her over.

"Do not use that tone with me, Outcast."

She righted herself, working her jaw. He could see the red rising on her cheek. Her necklaces, the ones he'd placed on her as a symbol of her rank, were askew.

"Unlike you," she said angrily, "I was declared Outcast. You have placed yourself beyond the society of honorable humans by your own outrageous actions."

"Do not mock me. I hold your life in my hands."

She snorted derision. "You hold nothing. Our world is coming to an end, and you are but a symptom of the last days. Look at you, one of the First People, a monster who chooses to eat human flesh. Leather Hand, when I see you, I see the rot that the First People have become."

Glaring into her eyes, he said, "I can make your death particularly ghastly."

"Just take me before Webworm. In the end, we shall see who makes whose end ghastly."

He could see no fear behind her hard black eyes, only revulsion to his proximity. He leaned closer, whispering, *"My dear Matron, I'm not taking you to Webworm. Far from it."*

"Stop playing silly games. Your Blessed Sun is far too vain to miss an opportunity to preen and brag in front of me."

Leather Hand rubbed his hard palms together. "Sorry, Matron, but you could become a symbol within the walls of Dusk House. Some of the Made People might foolishly rally to your cause. Even members of your Red Lacewing Clan might attempt something stupid. No, we have a safer place to hold you. You are going home."

At her slight confusion, he added, "I'm taking you back to Talon Town. It's deserted. A huge hulking warren of empty rooms. And when I get you there, you will scream, Matron. And then you will scream some more."

Only then did he see the quickening of her fear. "That's right. And unlike at Flowing Waters Town, where Ironwood might find allies, I will lay my trap for him in Straight Path Canyon. In that abandoned valley, we'll have ample warning before his arrival."

Satisfied, he nodded as he straightened. She'd betrayed herself under his gaze. It was as if he'd seen into her very souls. Down deep inside, she was seeing Ironwood's death.

Fifty-one

The hubbub broke midmorning. Spots was standing in the shade of the south wall. His firewood pile had been halved by the morning Trade, during which he'd obtained a sturdy gray quartzite knife hafted on a chokecherry handle. Cactus Flower's trinkets lay on the blanket next to his. He caught various glimpses of her as she led a Hohokam Trader around, pointing out various sites, taking him through the great kiva. Spots leaned back against the cool wall, shoulders and one foot braced against the plaster.

"I can't imagine what it's like down south." He was talking weather with a Trader from the Deep Canyon country. "The trails I take leading up to the forest are ankle deep in dust."

The Deep Canyon man, with a display of finely

crafted black-on-white drinking mugs on a red-and-brown blanket before him, shook his head. "In all my days I've never seen a fire like that up in the Spirit Mountains. The night sky glows orange. Thank the gods we're upwind."

Spots crossed his arms, watching a squad of red-shirted warriors pass, nodding politely to them. How funny, he'd become a fixture. They had come to consider him part of the landscape. "Smoke in the north, smoke in the south. Between the fires and the Rainbow Serpent, it's enough to make you wonder."

"I tell you, it's the Priests' doing. They've angered the katsinas to the point . . ." He didn't finish, staring instead to where one of the guards atop the fourth floor began shouting, pointing off to the northeast.

"I wonder what that's all about?" Spots saw Webworm, Wind Leaf, and Desert Willow emerge from their high rooms, climb the ladder, and stare off to the northeast.

"If you'll keep an eye on my Trade," the Deep Canyon man said, "I'll step out the gate and see what I can."

"Yes, go." Spots waved him away. More people were climbing out onto the roofs, staring off into the distance.

He frowned. Yesterday news had come that Blue Racer and his party had arrived safely at First Moon Mountain. So, too, had rumors circulated that all of the First Moon elders had been taken captive by Leather Hand.

Spots wasn't sure he believed it. But, if true, some Trader would no doubt arrive today with confirmation. That begged the question of how it had happened. He remembered the night he'd been escorted to the Dog's Tooth and seen the gathered elders. How, in the name of the Blue God, would Leather Hand have learned of their meeting?

Cactus Flower emerged from the great kiva, bowed to the Hohokam, and received a beautiful cotton shawl from him in payment for her tour. She almost skipped as she passed the bear cage and stepped into the noontime shadow beside him.

"Look! Isn't it magnificent?" She had the fabric laid out over her arms. It was indeed striking, the red, blue, yellow, and green colors lifelike, so good were the dyes.

"Something's happening." He pointed where Webworm had begun leaping from foot to foot on the high roof. Wind Leaf was nodding vigorously, slapping his thigh. Even Desert Willow threw her head back. The laughter carried faintly.

"In the northeast?" Cactus Flower wondered. "More news from First Moon Mountain?"

Spots shrugged. "Anything that might be good news for the First People is probably bad news for me."

The Deep Canyon man came trotting back through the gate, his expression neutral. He nodded to Cactus Flower, having already avoided losing any of his ceramic mugs to her wiles. "It's a signal fire, a black smoke. One of those warriors who passed earlier, he said it was a message. War Chief Wind Leaf called down that it was the prearranged sign for Night Sun. Evidently she's been taken prisoner."

"Night Sun?" Spots asked, stunned. "Someone captured the Matron?"

"Apparently." The Deep Canyon man returned to the shade beside his mug-covered blanket. "It has to be Leather Hand who did it. That's why no one's seen him recently. When he's around, people talk."

"You know him?"

"Seen him. That's bad enough. He spent quite a bit of time at Tall Piñon. I'd rather stand on a high peak in the middle of a lightning storm than be close to him."

Up on the rooftop, Webworm was clapping his hands and Dancing with joy.

"Excuse me." He walked forward, stepping around behind the bear cage. He could see Nightshade seated inside. The old woman gave him a curious glance.

"The word is that Night Sun has been captured." Spots made sure that no one was within hearing distance as he kept his back to the cage, his attention on the roof of the great kiva.

"The Flute Player is lulled," Nightshade replied.

"Lulled?" Spots asked, trying to keep his voice low. "Gods, what if the rumors about the First Moon elders are true? My people won't risk their elders' lives by attacking

Pinnacle Great House. If Night Sun's been captured, can Ironwood be close behind?"

Her laughter had a hollow echo. "Live well, Spots. These are the last days."

With unerring precision, Turquoise Fox kept them on secondary trails that followed ridgetops and avoided the more heavily traveled valleys.

Leather Hand held a hand up to block the last shafts of reddish gold as he stood on bare caprock and watched the sunset. The light set the northern horizon ablaze as it bathed the smoke-filled skies.

He cast a final look into the valley below, seeing the scattered farmsteads where isolated farmers kept their fields. Here, so close to the River of Souls, the flood-plains were watered by ditches, or were so close to the river that water could be carried in jars and fed to the corn plants.

With a final glance at the distant horizon he turned and walked back along the wind-smoothed sandstone to the tree line. He could smell the juniper fires as he walked through the trees to rejoin his little band of warriors. Several of his men were already taking their pleasure of the captive women. He could see Ravenfire's bare buttocks gyrating as he took his turn. The children watched from the side, wide-eyed, disbelieving.

Turquoise Fox had been amused to discover that Ravenfire had never lain with a woman. Now the boy was making up for lost time.

"What do you think that does to a child?" Night Sun asked as he walked up to her fire and seated himself.

"Pardon?" He glanced up, pulling out a piece of fine leather he'd been working on.

"Watching their mothers being treated like receptacles," Night Sun elaborated, jerking her head toward the grunting men.

"The children do not worry me, Matron." He chuckled, using his rabbit-bone awl to poke a hole into the soft leather. He was carefully beading the strip with patterns of chevrons; Larkspur had given him a supply of the finely crafted beads. A token, she had said, of their future alliance.

"They do not worry you?" She had lifted an eyebrow.

In the beginning, it had irritated him that she looked at him as though he were some sort of loathsome parasite, perhaps similar to a tick or gray louse. He'd considered beating it out of her, but thought better of it. She'd travel better in good health.

He smiled. There was always the future. Until Ironwood showed up, he'd have all the time he needed to hear her scream.

"The children," he told her, "are temporary. They are a lure, like a stuffed rabbit placed atop an eagle trap. When we have drawn Ironwood and his warriors into the trap, they will be of no further value. He glanced at them, snot-nosed, filthy-faced, their skinny arms bound behind them.

And then there was Ravenfire. "Your grandson, however, has turned out to be an unexpected prize. While I have you, and will soon have Ironwood, I still need to deal with Cornsilk. The young man assures me that he has no problem sending the sort of frantic message that will draw her into my web."

"I'd worry more about Poor Singer than my daughter."

"What's another silly Dreamer? Jay Bird might take him seriously, but the old chief isn't long for this world. He's elderly Matron. Just like you. Somehow I can't see skinny Poor Singer rallying warriors to accompany him north in search of me."

"You have this all thought out, have you?"

He nodded at Night Sun as he strung another chevron of beads onto a flax thread and stitched them down. "Something happened to me the night that we ate the Dust People."

"Yes, you became a walking abomination."

Ignoring her, he continued. "I felt a presence in the night. I'm fairly sure it was the Blue God herself. She was watching me, but I didn't sense that she'd come to devour me."

"I'm sure she has better taste than that," Night Sun agreed. "Given a choice between you and six-day-old carrion, I'm sure she'd choose the latter."

He gestured with his awl. "I've felt her since then. The last time was atop First Moon Mountain. I'd had a most enjoyable night with Matron Larkspur. It's the oddest thing, but I just knew that my future was being decided."

"Spider Woman's fire might be closer than you think," Night Sun said coldly.

He chuckled. "Ah, you do tempt me, Matron. But I can be patient. It's a necessary virtue for a man in my position. So as much as I'd like to hurt you now, we'll consider it a future obligation. No, what I was saying is that I could feel the Blue God's presence that night. She heard Larkspur and me making plans, and I have to tell you, I'm sure she's on my side."

Night Sun's expression hardened. "Any normal human being would burn himself alive before surrendering himself to the Blue God."

"You're probably correct, but I'm nowhere near a normal human." He gestured to his men where they sat at their fires, slabs of meat from the bloody packs extended over the coals. "Nor are my men normal. You've seen the white moccasins?"

"Of course."

"To be granted a pair, the warrior in question must not only have eaten man-meat, but must have eliminated one of the Blessed Sun's enemies by stealth."

"Matron White Cloud?"

"These are her moccasins." He indicated his footwear. "I took them as a trophy, but the Blessed Sun really made the idea stick."

"What will you do when he no longer thinks your services are necessary?" she asked.

Leather Hand met her distaste with a warm smile. "I've always liked the sound of 'Blessed Sun,' haven't you?"

"A wise man wouldn't be telling me such things."

"Why, Matron, what on earth makes you think that you'll ever live to tell anyone?" He finished the last row of beads, and stepped around behind her. The piece was done in chevrons of alternating colors.

She went stiff at his touch, but he was very careful as he placed the beaded slave collar around her throat. "There," he said proudly, and quickly stitched the ends snug. "It's very becoming, but I wouldn't advise swallowing a large bite of food. It could end up choking you."

She was seething as he stepped away.

"Matron, I want you to remember, I made that from untanned leather. If you should anger me, or cause me to pour water on it, it will shrink as it dries. It would be a pity. As it slowly strangles you, the beadwork will be distorted. You wouldn't want that, because, well, it's absolutely magnificent just as it is."

She hawked and spat in his direction as he walked off to take his pleasure from one of the captive women.

A stillness lay in the air as Wrapped Wrist paused on the outcrop where he'd first looked out over First Moon Valley with Crow Woman. This time, Orenda accompanied them.

The day had turned to dusk, sunlight fading into red. Muted light cast the blue-shadowed valley with a golden rime. The smoke from hundreds of fires softened the hard edges and darkened the green of junipers, pines, and agricultural fields. Overhead, in a huge curl, the smoke plume from the high-mountain fires was painted in gaudy red, orange, and black.

Looking to the north, he could see entire slopes denuded and charred, pale feathers of smoke rising into the larger mass.

"By the gods," he whispered, awed at the contrast of his peaceful valley and the distant conflagration.

"How would you ever describe that? Words don't have the ability to make it real." Crow Woman leaned on her cane. "I've never seen such a huge fire. People wouldn't believe it if they couldn't see it. The whole north is in flames."

"I've already seen too many terrible things," Wrapped Wrist said softly, images of the warriors he had killed mixing with those of brutalized and broken women and children at Ironwood's camp. "Let's just pray those flames stay north."

"I guess we're just lucky for these southwestern winds," Crow Woman agreed. "It would have gone poorly for us if they'd shifted while we were up on the divide."

Orenda was staring soberly at the fire, and then down at the valley. "Ironwood is down there? It's so huge. So many villages. How will we find him?"

Wrapped Wrist tightened his grip on the war club. The feel of the wood reassured him. "The elders will know. We'll go find White Eye. He'll tell us what to do."

Crow Woman pointed. "Look at the Dog's Tooth. Is it the shadows, or has it been burned?"

Wrapped Wrist squinted into the fading light. "Gods, I think you're right." A sinking premonition grew in his gut. "What's happened here?"

"I have the feeling this homecoming is going to be particularly painful for you," Orenda said soberly.

Ripple walked slowly through the night. He picked each step, setting down one foot and then the other. The dark climb wasn't particularly hazardous, but he feared what he would find when he reached the crest. The vision Cold Bringing Woman had given him hadn't been explicit about this part.

The trees waved around him as the breezes changed direction, teasing the piñon and juniper. The night air remained warm, carrying the fragrance of dust, pine, and cook fires. A cold breath danced across his cheek as an eddy carried cooler air, trapped from the bottomlands. As quickly, it was gone.

He could see the walls now, dark and straight where they topped the Dog's Tooth. No head broke the silhouette. He could feel Power in the air. Unseen eyes watched as he climbed the last bit and entered the unguarded gap in the wall.

The smell of charred wood still lingered here. Ripple walked past the collapsed remains of smoldering pit houses, feeling the heat that radiated from their ovenlike interiors. The two great kivas were flattened piles of rubble. In the darkness, he could see gleaming red eyes: coals that refused to die as they ate into the incompletely consumed roof supports. Inside the eastern wall, the upper story of the clan building had collapsed when the roofing burned through.

Broken pottery cracked and popped under his weight. Bits of torn matting, cloth, split baskets, drying racks, and other household debris were scattered about.

Curls of smoke rose around him, the acrid odor clogging his nose. He closed his eyes, inhaling the stench of destruction into his souls. When he opened them and looked north, he could see the distant forest fire: a thousand winking eyes that vanished and reappeared in the smoke palls.

Those were the mountains of his youth. He had traveled every trail, scaled every peak. He'd known them as intimately as this valley he called home. The clearing where Cold Bringing Woman had appeared to him was now turned to ash. Had the great bear survived? Or had that shared meal of elk been among his last?

He blinked at smoke-induced tears and remembered the cool forests where he'd hunted. The mice and voles wouldn't have escaped. Many of the deer and elk would have been trapped in the blind valleys. How many of the stately trees now existed as burned snags?

The time has come. He threw his arms wide, aware of the heat that radiated from the burned buildings to warm his skin.

In the vision he had seen the River of Stones running black with ash; then that afternoon, it had been as he had seen. The image was burned into his memory. The farmers he had overheard were discussing how it would help finish the corn, the added nutrients sure to guarantee full kernels and large ears.

"What an empty promise the gods have made." He let the first sob rise from his chest. Hot tears trickled down his cheeks.

Cold Bringing Woman? Can I cancel my bargain? Can I just go away and save this world? Will you allow me to escape with Orenda? Can I have my children? Can I die of old age, having lived a ripe and full life?

He felt rather than saw or heard the dark rasp of wings in the smoke-laden air. Smoke and tendrils of ash whirled about him.

No, the bargain was long since struck. Only now, as the immensity of it was brought home, did he wish that he'd been left to die in his prison deep inside Pinnacle House. That end, painful as it was to his body, was preferable to what his souls were about to suffer.

He heard the crunching steps behind him. Then Ironwood said, "You asked me to meet you here."

"In the vision, Cold Bringing Woman said I would face you in the smoking ruins of my people's house. I didn't know what that meant. But here I am, and here you are."

"Face me?" Ironwood cocked his head. "Does this have anything to do with the signals we've seen flashed from Pinnacle House?"

"Cold Bringing Woman said you would have to decide if you would save one, or many. Tonight you must choose if you are a husband or a chief. Will you save your souls, or your people? Power awaits your decision."

Ironwood was silent, a towering dark form in the night. "My souls or my people? I don't understand. I have always chosen my people."

"As you did the night you lay with Night Sun and conceived a child? As you did when you refused the temptation to kill Snake Head before he could become Blessed Sun? How many times have you ignored your responsibilities to salve your heart?"

"Many," he said reluctantly. "What are you trying to tell me?"

"That when the time comes, the choice of the heart will oppose the choice of leadership. You may choose either way, War Chief. There is no wrong answer."

"I still don't understand. What you are trying to get me to choose?"

Ripple turned, pointing up past the dark pillars of First

Moon Mountain. There, behind the billowing black of the smoke-filled night, Sister Moon appeared for the briefest of seconds, her round shape but a faint reddish disc in the murky sky. She shone for less than a heartbeat before she faded into nothingness.

"Sister Moon has donned her smoke-black cape, War Chief. By this time tomorrow, we must commit ourselves to the Dance."

Fifty-two

The wind brought Bad Cast awake. He lay curled against Soft Cloth, thankful for her warmth under the thin blanket. Another gust whistled through the ladder uprights where they protruded from the roof.

He sniffed, aware that the odor of smoke was stronger. Outside a basket tumbled across the plaza, pushed by the wind. He hoped nothing fragile or important had been inside. Something wooden was blown over to an accompanying clatter.

"Storm?" Soft Cloth asked.

"Sounds like."

She sniffed. "That's not our fire, is it?"

"No. Sure is strong." He glanced around, assured that no flames were licking at the inside of their pit house. House fires terrified his people, especially because escape was through the roof smoke hole. Just ask Spots; he could testify to the terror of a burning house.

Now that he'd thought about burning to death in his sleep, any kind of meaningful repose was out of the question. If he tried, it would be to constantly crack one eye, sniff for smoke, and worry.

As he threw back the blanket, Soft Cloth asked, "What are you doing?"

"Taking a look."

"Don't wake the baby."

He climbed up the ladder and stuck his head out. The wind was from the north, the smell of smoke worse. His first glance took in the plaza they shared with Soft Cloth's two sisters. Everything was inky black. Blood and pus, it was one *dark* night.

Then he looked into the wind and froze. From Soft Cloth's pit house, there was no clear view of the northern horizon. The shoulder of Juniper Ridge and the tree line obscured it, but a dreadful reddish orange glow could be seen.

"Snake's blood," he whispered.

"What?" Soft Cloth rustled the bedding below.

He climbed back down, reaching for his clothes. "The whole northern sky is glowing. It's like nothing I've ever seen."

To his surprise, she checked the baby, dressed, and followed him out into the night. Hand in hand, they felt their way along the trail that led past the Mid-Sun Village great kivas and up to the rimrock.

At the rim, Bad Cast stopped, heart leaping. Flames dotted the entire northern horizon. Yellow at the bottom, they raced upward, illuminating the smoke in orange, red, and then a dull crimson that faded to black.

Another gust of wind shook them, powerful, tearing down from the north.

"Maybe it's a rain cloud," Soft Cloth said over the gale. "You know how it can blow under a thunderhead."

Bad Cast sniffed again. All he could smell was wood smoke. "Do you smell rain?"

She sniffed. "No."

They staggered under another gust.

"If it's not rain, it's unusual for the wind to blow out of the north this time of year. You'd think it was winter solstice instead of coming up on equinox."

Bad Cast felt something pattering on his skin. Reaching up, he expected it to be rain, but it was dry to the touch, powdery.

"I hope that wind doesn't keep up. At this rate, it will push that fire right up to the edge of the valley."

"Come on, let's go back to bed. I'm scared."

Another gust pattered the invisible specks against him. When he rubbed his finger over his skin and touched it to his tongue, he tasted ash.

Wrapped Wrist led the way to Yellow Petal's house, figuring she was a kinswoman; and after all, Spots was his best friend. Yellow Petal had built a large, tight, two-room dwelling. The bigger main room contained the hearth, two stone benches, containers, and ventilator. The smaller chamber was separated by a wattle-plastered wall and accessed through a hide-covered door. It was there that Spots kept his bedding, tools, weapons, and personal possessions.

To his surprise, the place was empty. Food, however, was plentiful, and he felt no guilt as he pawed through the jars. In a wood-lidded white-slipped jar he found cornmeal. A net bag produced smoked turkey meat. He lifted the lid off of a globular brownware jar to find hulled pine nuts. Pulling the stopper from a canteen, he sipped, delighted with the taste of chokecherry juice.

"Are you sure this cousin won't mind us eating her food?" Orenda asked skeptically.

"Sure. What's the point of having kin if they can't help you when you're in need?" He mixed cornmeal, pine nuts, some dried rose hips, and the turkey in a corrugated cooking pot. Then he went about stoking the coals in the fire pit to life. Yellow Petal had stacked a liberal supply of firewood along the south wall.

"What are you smiling at?" Crow Woman asked as she awkwardly lowered herself onto one of Yellow Petal's blankets. She had her leg stuck straight out in front of her. Wrapped Wrist was hard pressed to keep from jarring it as he prepared the meal.

Orenda looked worried as she removed the wrapping she'd placed on Crow Woman's knee. The bruise looked black and ugly, but the swelling had gone down.

"What's wrong?" Crow Woman asked cautiously.

Orenda prodded the knee, eliciting a gasp from Crow Woman. "Nothing. You're healing fine."

"That's a relief. From the expression on your face I thought maybe I was crippled."

Orenda failed when she tried to produce a smile. "It's not you. First Nightshade walks away, who knows to what purpose or fate. Then this Leather Hand . . . Well, I can't do anything about the dead, but I'm sick at the thought of what they'll do to Night Sun and the others."

Crow Woman's eye narrowed. "The war chief will see to it. But, by the Blue God's soul, Leather Hand will rue the day if he so much as yanks a hair out of that woman's head."

Wrapped Wrist kept his attention on his cooking, wondering all the while what Ironwood's handful of warriors could do against the might of Flowing Waters Town.

To change the subject, he said, "I was thinking of what a good worker Yellow Petal is. She's always after Spots to do this, or do that. Fortunately for us, she's laid in a goodly supply of everything we need."

"I'd say she's going to skin a piece out of your hide if you don't replace what we use," Orenda told him. Too worried to simply sit, she pushed him out of the way, busying herself with the corrugated cooking pot on the coals.

"I wish she were here," Wrapped Wrist replied as he sat back. He was aware of Crow Woman. She'd been watching him with a peculiar intensity all day long. Whatever motivated the penetrating interest in her eyes, Wrapped Wrist was sure it boded him no good. He'd probably said something during the last day that she'd been stewing on. The thing was, she didn't look mad at him. And twice, he'd swear she'd been on the verge of smiling at him.

"Stop that!" Crow Woman snapped as he started to pick at the cactus thorns holding his cheek together. It itched like a thousand lice were under his skin.

"Sorry." He lowered his hand, unsettled by the concerned look that Crow Woman gave him. "I'd sure like to know what's happened here since we left."

"Tomorrow," Orenda said, "I can go around and ask. No one will recognize me. To them I'll appear as another pilgrim."

They ate in silence, but Wrapped Wrist was acutely aware of Crow Woman. She was watching him, a veiled speculation in her eyes. Whatever it was, he tried to avoid her as he attended to the task of filling his belly. Odd, though, that she hadn't just lit into him with her usual vigor.

After they had cleaned the pots, Wrapped Wrist retired to Spots's room. There, to his satisfaction, a bundle of darts had been stacked. He fingered each of the long shafts and wondered where Spots was, and how he was faring. Wherever he was, Wrapped Wrist figured Spots wouldn't begrudge him this cache of desperately needed darts. Given the change in affairs, he swore he wasn't going to be unarmed again if he could help it.

He flopped out on Spots's bed, careful to lie on his back so as not to snag his stitches. What an odd sensation to be home, safe for the night in a kinswoman's house. As he thought about it, the last half moon might have been lived inside a whirlwind.

I killed four men. And after what he'd seen at Ironwood's village, he'd have no hesitation to kill more.

Who have I become? Until this one moment of peace, he hadn't had time to ask.

As the fire died, he watched the light fade, then heard Orenda's deep breathing. Well, at least one of them was sleeping well.

Then the wind began to blow. He heard it whistle around the ladder uprights, felt it stirring inside the house as it sucked through the ventilator shaft.

Crow Woman surprised him when she slipped through the entry and carefully sat on the bedding beside him.

"What's wrong?" he whispered.

"Nothing." A pause. "Everything."

He waited.

"Wrapped Wrist, I have a sense . . . a premonition."

"Good or bad?"

"Bad. Is there any other kind these days?"

He remembered the mutilated bodies in Ironwood's camp, the look of fear in Night Sun's eyes as she was borne past their hiding place.

He started when she lay down beside him, and was surprised when she placed a hand on his chest to push him back down.

"Can you hold me tonight?" she asked.

"What's wrong?"

"I think I'm going to die soon. It would be nice, just once . . . Rot and blood, how do I say this? I've been alone all of my life. And then, for the last quarter moon . . ."

"I know. Sometimes it's hard to remember what life was like before you started to make me miserable."

"I'm sorry. I'll go now."

He tightened his arm around her shoulders. "Don't. Maybe it turns out I like having you make me miserable."

"That day I was captured?"

"Yes."

"They caught me because I was thinking about you. I was imagining . . ."

He waited. "You seem to have trouble finishing phrases."

She sighed in frustration. "Look, I don't know if I'd be any good at this. I'd never be a normal wife. Nothing like your adored kinswoman, Yellow Petal. Snake's blood, I don't even know what you want in a woman."

He smiled, feeling the tightness in his stitched face. "How about a simple friend and companion?"

"Is it ever simple between a man and woman?"

"Absolutely positively never."

She tensed, taking a deep breath. The wind hammered at the house. "This coupling business. It's always been an unpleasant experience."

"Doesn't have to be."

She hesitated, then sat up in the dark and pulled her brown shirt over her head. "If you hurt my knee doing this, I'm going to rip those stitches right out of your face."

"Sometimes your charm leaves me dazzled."

He wriggled out of his own hunter's shirt and stretched out beside her. Every muscle was rigid, as if she were primed for combat instead of love. She spread her legs, whispering bravely, "I'm ready."

"For the moment," he said softly, "let's just hold each other. I want to feel your heart beating against mine, and your breath against my neck. Then you need to touch me, gently, as I touch you. We have plenty of time, you and me.

"Careful of your knee." He reached out, pulling her tense body onto his. Sighing, he hugged her to him, her hair falling around them like a veil.

After tonight, you'll never call me Stumpy again.

As the wind moaned past Cactus Flower's little house, Spots lay awake. She was sleeping with her head on his shoulder, her arm draped over his chest. Her firm brown thigh lay atop his groin, her right breast soft against his ribs.

Angry gusts pattered sand against the north wall of the house, and he could smell dust on the wind. Outside he could hear the matting on the ramada flapping, and something rattled as it blew away.

He breathed deeply, taking in the scent of her hair. He had watched her turn down a Trader's offer that afternoon when the man offered her an abalone pendant in exchange for a night at her place. It seemed that every time he was around, she was mysteriously unoccupied. Even more odd, she no longer even hinted that he Trade any of his goods in exchange for her bed.

He found a lock of her hair, running it around his finger. By the bloody gods, he'd come to enjoy this. It was more than the wondrous sensations she conjured from his shaft. He enjoyed the sparkle in her eye, the anecdotes she told about the Fire Dogs and First People, the Hohokam, and the Tower Builders. She just seemed to *know* so much.

From the moment they returned to her little farmstead, they talked—and talking was remarkably easy with her. He had learned that her father had been a Trader and that she'd grown up in a town down along the border with the Fire Dogs. She'd just passed her tenth summer when a mysterious coughing disease sickened most of the inhabitants. Cactus Flower's mother had asked her father to take her north, away from the miasma. When they'd returned the next spring, her entire lineage—mother, aunts, and uncles—had perished.

"So I just traveled with Father from then on."

He smiled at that, amazed at the differences between his upbringing and hers. He'd never been more than three days' travel from his mother's house. Cactus Flower had been from one end of the world to the other. Had seen the Rainbow Serpent where it belched out of the ground, had visited the Hohokam cities with their ball courts and river-wide canals. She had followed the trails north into the land of the Tower Builders, and had tried her hand at their ceremonial game of divination: They rolled stone balls across their pit house floors as they Sang and prayed.

"Then Father was killed," she'd said simply. "It was a river crossing. Among the Hohokam, I learned to swim. He didn't."

As he stroked her hair, he could almost sense the presence of the sharp quartzite knife where it lay hidden in his pack beside the door.

Tomorrow would be the day. He would slip it to Nightshade when the opportunity presented itself.

And then what? He swallowed hard, hearing the patter of wind-driven gravel against the house walls. A fine filtering of dust hung in the air, muting the scent of her hair. It ground between his teeth, and he could feel it on his face.

Choices. Nightshade's benediction and curse balanced between his souls. He could slip her the knife, and then come home with Cactus Flower. Together they would kindle the dinner fire, make a meal, and then she would take her clothing off and entwine her soft brown body around him.

And Nightshade? Was she really a witch, or a madwoman?

What makes her think she can defeat Webworm?

Fifty-three

A howling wind ripped over the weathered sandstone cliff behind Talon Town, whirled past the column of rock called Propped Pillar, and made a low moaning, as though the very stone was tortured.

Leather Hand stood atop Talon Town's fifth-floor roof and stared up at the black sky. He ran his fingers over the smooth stone of the serpent-in-egg carving Webworm had given him. His souls were slithering around inside him—as if his gut were mimicking the carving. It was an eerie feeling, perhaps stimulated by the snake's head he rubbed under his thumb. Or perhaps his souls were hearing the cries of the dead. The First People had been living in this canyon for hundreds of years; their Spirits called from the stone, log, and soil that composed Straight Path Canyon.

He shifted, feeling the chill in the night air. In the room below his feet, Night Sun lay securely bound. She was back in her old quarters, the ones she'd lived in before her exile. What was it like to return to that very room where she'd bedded Crow Beard, borne her son, Snake Head, and betrayed the Straight Path Nation when Ironwood crept into her bed? Was she reliving those days, unbidden memories drifting up from her souls?

Wind Baby tugged at him, whipping his hair this way and that. The prickling in his souls continued.

"War Chief?" Turquoise Fox asked as he climbed the rickety old ladder onto the roof.

"Yes, Deputy?"

"I have seen to the warriors. They are in place just in case Ironwood is closer behind us than we think. I will rotate the men three times a day to ensure that everyone stays crisp and vigilant."

"Excellent."

"We are home," his deputy said softly. "It's almost as if we'd never left."

Leather Hand frowned, thinking. "Home. The souls of the dead Dance here. It is to this place that the Dreams of our people return. From this dry canyon, the plant that would become our nation sent down its roots, sprouted, grew, and flourished." He sighed. "Deputy, I first entered this canyon in awe, my heart literally beating in my throat. I remember the sense of disbelief when Webworm and Featherstone decided to move north."

"Many of us couldn't believe it."

"By abandoning this place, we left the essence of what made us ourselves." Wind Baby pushed him again, trying to shove him backward off the roof.

"How do we find ourselves again, War Chief?"

"To whom does your first loyalty belong?"

"War Chief?"

"If you had to choose, would you serve the Blessed Sun, or your companions?"

Turquoise Fox was silent, searching for the trap, aware that the wrong answer could kill him. "I would have to say, after the most careful consideration, that I serve my companions, War Chief. It is they who serve the Blessed Sun."

He let Turquoise Fox stew in suspense. Finally he said, "I can feel the Blue God tonight. She is stirring, driving Wind Baby across the world as a warning."

"A warning of what?"

"That a mighty change is coming. There is a reason we've had no rain."

"Yes?"

"The Blue God is in ascendance, my friend. Webworm, Blue Racer, and the rest—they don't understand her cravings and appetite. I can imagine her sniffing around the Flute Player, mocking his music, fingering the pack he carries on his back. What is seed and fertility compared to blood and terror?"

"I don't know, War Chief. My concerns are not with gods and chaos, but with obedience and service."

"Did you check on the boy?"

"I did. Fast Fist tells me the youth has done nothing to incite his suspicion."

"What do you think?"

"Ravenfire wanted me to ask you something."

"And that is?"

"Is there a way to blame this on the Made People?"

"Ravenfire asked you that?"

"He did." Turquoise Fox squinted into the wind. "It would have to be done carefully: a rumor planted here, a Trader bribed there. There are those in the Made People clans who dislike Night Sun and Ironwood even today. Those individuals would likely brag about it. Before long, people *will* believe that what happens here was the work of the Made People."

"I notice that you gave the youth one of your war feathers."

Turquoise Fox nodded. "I told him he's a man now. He participated in the raid, captured Night Sun, and has bedded his first woman. You should have seen his face when we first approached Talon Town. 'The home of my ancestors,' he said."

Another gust blew out of the black night. Leather Hand turned his back to it. "He's right. We stand on the same spot where the rulers of the Straight Path Nation have stood for generations. Look out there. The canyon is black, deserted. From here they would have seen thousands of lights gleaming up and down the canyon. Now only darkness remains."

"Would you bring the lights back?"

"Yes." He slapped Turquoise Fox on the back. "Come, let us sleep. Tomorrow, Night Sun is going to have a very, very long day."

In his high room, Webworm sat on his sleeping pallet. Wind Baby howled out of the north, whistling and moaning as it savaged Dusk House's balcony. His door hanging jumped and jerked as though alive. Embers flickered in the fire bowl he'd ordered a slave to bring him. In the ember's blood glow the paintings of the Flute Player, Spider Woman, the Blue God, and Father Sun seemed to pulse on the plastered walls.

He lifted a tall ceramic pitcher and sipped at the black-berry juice. Grit grated on his teeth. Dust. It was every-where: blowing on the wind, leaving its scent in his nostrils.

A hollow moaning was spun where Wind Baby howled through doors, around corners and protruding roof poles. Spirits were out. He could feel them, hear them as they slipped about in the dark wind. Yes, a dark wind indeed.

He peeked out and found the night stygian despite the promise of a full moon. He wondered how Blue Racer was going to fare up on First Moon Mountain; thousands of people would be watching, and Sister Moon was nowhere to be seen on the equinox of her homecoming.

Something whispered behind his ear and he turned, staring. He heard them all the time now: chittering little voices. Or he'd hear a shout; but when he turned, only the echo remained, hollow between his souls. The laughter was the worst. Just that afternoon, he'd spun around and shouted, "Stop it!" at Wind Leaf. His war chief had looked at him with shocked eyes, and quietly asked, "Stop what?"

Did no one else hear the voices?

Chortles of delight fluttered around his ears, and his eyes were drawn to the witch's pack where it hung from a peg in the corner. He'd looked through it, found the Tor-toise Bundle, and inspected its worn leather. The beautiful black bowl was like nothing of local manufacture. He'd sniffed the gray paste it contained, and supposed it was datura. Other items had included a thin copper man-snake-bird image he'd never seen before. A huge shell gorget had been decorated with a spider effigy circled by a snake that was eating its own tail. Small sacks made of colorfully feathered bird skins held various powders and potions. Bits of bone, dried animal feet, and other amulets defied any explanation of their purpose.

Fact was: He hadn't had a good night's sleep since he'd gone through the pack. As he stared at it, he wasn't sure but that he ought to set fire to it. He'd picked it up the day before with just that intent, but at the last moment, rehung it before pacing back and forth. Then someone had called that a black signal fire burned in the north. Black, but not white. Leather Hand's signal that he'd only captured Night Sun.

Night Sun. I've got her. Where Night Sun goes, Ironwood will follow.

An image formed: Ironwood, years ago. Webworm had been his deputy back then. What fine friends they'd been. Life had been so simple. Ironwood gave the orders, and Webworm carried them out. Ironwood's youthful words clung like cobwebs in Webworm's memory: *"Be strong, my friend. Never forget your warriors in arms. Your life is theirs, theirs is yours."*

The corners of his lips quivered. How had they lost such a perfect friendship? He would hate to see Ironwood's body, to have to remember how it had been between them. Gods, how he missed that life. He'd been so happy back then. But for a twist of fate he would have married Cloud Playing and been happy for the rest of his life. A man could only love like that once.

"Webworm?"

Was that his mother's voice? He cocked his head, struggling to make out the words, but they faded right out of the air.

Voices, voices. Where do they all come from? It hadn't been this bad until the Mountain Witch had walked into his room.

Yes, Nightshade.

He glanced over at the corner where Nightshade's bag hung from its peg. Even as he did, the voices grew louder. Some spoke in a tongue he'd never heard. The language of the Mound Builders, he supposed.

"I really ought to burn you," he muttered.

Whisperings and rustlings made him whirl and stare owlishly at his bedding. Something had been there, hadn't it? He'd just caught movement from the corner of his eye. Jabbing at the blankets with a nervous hand, he found only cloth atop the cushioning layers of buffalohide.

Webworm muttered under his breath, sipped more of the berry juice, and scratched beneath his arm. Was that smoke he smelled on the wind? If only he could sleep.

No, he dared not. When he drifted off, it ended in disastrous nightmares.

He blinked, yawned. A child began to cry, sadness and grief in the driven sobs. He scrambled to the doorway and pulled the hanging back. Nothing.

"Did you hear a child?" he asked the dark shape of the guard who huddled in the wind-blown dark.

"No, Blessed Sun." The warrior sounded wary.

Rot it all, that was the third time he'd asked the guard if he'd heard anything. Maybe the man's ears were plugged with the thrice-accursed blowing dust.

He crawled back to his bed and slumped onto the blanket. Blinking, he forced himself to stay awake.

Gods no, you dare not Dream. When he did, it was more than just voices.

He was just drifting off when he heard the serpent's Powerful hiss.

Jerking up, he spilled berry juice over the floor, crying, "What was that?"

From outside his door, the guard asked, "Blessed Sun? Are you well?"

Webworm winced, blinked, and stared down where his hand was planted in the berry juice. Thoughts. Scattered thoughts.

I have Matron Night Sun. With her for bait, I will have Ironwood. "And then I will have murdered the last of my friends."

In the light of the glowing coals, he could see his latest carving. The serpent lay curled within its eggshell, a black hole where the eye should be. Tomorrow he would set that eye. Perhaps he would make a little gift of the carving to Desert Willow.

He lifted his hand and began licking the sweet juice from his palm.

Fifty-four

In the course of a night, the world had changed. The knowledge lay deep down between Bad Cast's souls. When he and Soft Cloth had returned to their house after watching the fires, it had been with a sense of some great portent. After she had fed the baby, they had coupled with a tender violence that left them both limp and drained.

He had awakened to the stench of smoke, still entwined in his wife's arms. The light through the smoke hole was a dirty gray. Outside, the wind alternately roared and eddied, and bits of ash, like flakes of snow, drifted down from the skies.

Bad Cast kissed Soft Cloth's shadowed cheek and rolled out from under the blanket. She murmured in her sleep and rolled over.

To his relief, the baby was still asleep. He pulled on his hunting shirt and climbed up the ladder and out into the day. He coughed, hawking up black phlegm. Looking to the sky, he was amazed to find the heavens blackened with smoke. He could see the stiff north wind rolling patterns of darkness across the skies.

Making his way through the gloom, he walked up the path to the rimrock and looked out over First Moon Valley. Wind gusts pushed at him, relented, and pushed again. Was it his imagination, or did the gusts have an unaccustomed bite to them? Through the haze he couldn't even make out First Moon Mountain.

Someone coughed on the trail behind him, and he turned to see Ripple as he emerged from between the juniper trees.

"What a morning." Bad Cast squinted up into the soot-filled air. "I've never seen it this bad."

"No, I suppose not."

Bad Cast waved. "Look—you can't even see across the valley. Everything's blue-brown. Even my spit's black."

"It's the Dance."

"What Dance? No one's Dancing." He looked out into the haze. "Equinox is coming. They should have started the first ceremonies up at Pinnacle House last night. Our elders should have been at the *sipapu*. With this wind, I'll bet Blue Racer couldn't even keep his costume on."

"They Danced," Ripple assured him, his thoughtful eyes on the gloomy valley. "Tonight, they shall Dance again."

Bad Cast took a breath, wanting to cough. "This is part of Cold Bringing Woman's vision, isn't it?"

Ripple nodded.

"Can you tell me about it?"

Ripple smiled softly. "Do you remember the trail that leads up the north side of the mountain? The one that passes the old lightning-riven tree?"

"Sure. It passes through the trees on the north side. Ah, I recall. You're thinking about the time that the four of us climbed up that way to spy on the First People's solstice ceremonies."

"They never knew we were there." Ripple smiled. "Spots wouldn't let me climb onto the top. He was afraid I might go in search of my father's skull."

"We climbed up that crack in the rocks," Bad Cast remembered. "You couldn't climb over the rim because Spots was holding your ankle." He smiled at the memory. "You know, he probably saved your life."

"Could you find that trail again?"

"Sure. I just have to look for—"

"Can you find it *in the dark*?"

Bad Cast frowned. "I don't know." He glanced at Ripple, seeing his friend's sad expression. "Why?"

"They will be depending on you tonight."

"Ripple? What's wrong? You know something, don't you?"

He seemed not to hear, but smiled, as if seeing something in the distant past. "We had some times, didn't we? Remember when you made that willow-bark doll for Slipped Bark? And the time when Wrapped Wrist was coupling with that Strong Back Clan girl down by the river?"

"We stole their clothes." Bad Cast laughed. "They had to wait in the willows, swatting mosquitoes until midnight before they could dare to sneak home without anyone seeing them." A pause. "When I was courting Soft Cloth, we coupled in the willows once. She thought I was demented because I insisted on keeping one fist balled in our clothing the entire time."

"We have all been so jealous of you."

"What?"

"Spots and I—and even Wrapped Wrist—thought you were the luckiest man we knew when you married her."

"Why?"

"We imagined you going home to her every night. You have what we all wanted: a capable and caring wife. The two of you just fit together. That's how I want to remember you. Not pulling pranks, not sharing the hunt, but with her. I want to imagine you in the future, not the past."

"What's to imagine? You'll share our fire for years to come. Maybe you and Orenda."

His smile was wistful. "Orenda will travel over to the Green Mesa after this. There, she'll live for a while with Born-of-Water. Then she'll marry one of Cornsilk's sons."

"That's no way to—"

"I *know* these things, Bad Cast. And it's all right. I made my decision. I'm at ease with it. I have one last responsibility to my people; and, after that, well, the ghosts will rest easier."

"Ripple, why don't you just take Orenda and go? You've already made a difference."

"Funny, isn't it? I spent my life hating the First People.

Now, with their end looming, I'm just tired." He placed his good hand on Bad Cast's shoulder. "Deeply and soul-weary tired. Do not mourn me, dear friend. As much as I hated the past, I couldn't bear the future. Take care of Wrapped Wrist and Spots. They will need your sober counsel even more in the days to come. And whatever you do, make sure Soft Cloth and the baby travel with you when you leave for the Great River Valley."

"You're talking as if you won't be there."

He shrugged. "I told you: I'm tired, Bad Cast. Our world is about to be cleansed. I would rather rest than en-dure the storm—but if I am to serve my purpose, I have one last duty to perform. I promise, tonight, finally, you will understand."

"You are talking nonsense." When Bad Cast stared out at the roiling smoke where his pristine valley should have been, it looked anything but cleansing.

"It only seems that way now." Ripple tightened his hand on Bad Cast's shoulder. "I just wanted a moment with you. Thank you for always being there for me. I know what risks you took on my behalf. I will be forever grateful."

"We have always been there for each other."

"Go now," Ripple added gently. "The war chief is meet-ing with some of the lineage leaders in the Soft Earth Moiety kiva. He's going to need you before this is all over."

Bad Cast gave Ripple a furtive inspection. His friend was staring thoughtfully into the north, eyes squinted against the smoke and blowing ash.

Coupling, Crow Woman decided, had definite therapeu-tic value. Her limp was decidedly better, the pain nowhere near as intense. She followed close on Wrapped Wrist's heels, placing her feet in his footsteps.

In the smoke-thick morning, they climbed a well-traveled trail, each step something of a trial for her, but nothing like yesterday's trip. The smoke, however, burned the eyes, nose, and throat. She coughed periodically. Between wind gusts bits of ash filtered out of the murky air.

Wrapped Wrist nodded to the people they encountered coming down the hill, many burdened with hoes, baskets, or water jars. Everyone looked worried and nervous, usually pausing long enough to ask if he had news on the fire.

Gusts of wind still batted at them, and the whirling flakes of gray-white ash reminded her of perverted snow. It coated everything: hair, cloak, her pack. The merest touch left gray-black streaks on her skin.

Orenda coughed as she followed them up the steep trail. The woman seemed more subdued than ever, expression pinched, worry behind her soft eyes.

"It's up to me to tell him," Orenda had said over their breakfast in Yellow Petal's house. She had been so preoccupied with what she would say to Ironwood that she hadn't noticed the secret glances and smiles Crow Woman and Wrapped Wrist had shot each other.

Flashes from Crow Woman's experiences during the night before kept popping up in her memory. The first surprise had come from his tender hands, the way he'd brushed his lips lightly across her skin. The sensation of his tongue on her nipples had charged her with excitement. His sensitive fingertips had sent pleasure through her sheath.

At his urging, she had touched him back, fascinated by the feel of his hard shaft in her hands. By the time he had gently shifted his weight onto hers, the fear of his imposing organ had vanished. She couldn't believe that she was literally *aching* for him. She'd sighed with relief as he slid into her, and miracle of miracles, it hadn't hurt.

She'd moved with him, eyes closed, arms around his muscular shoulders. He'd been slow, patient and careful, his breath purling on her chest as his hips rotated against hers. If only she could have kept those honeyed sensations forever.

So this is what it's all about! The thought had barely formed when her loins exploded. She was panting, hugging him to her, when the sensations faded.

"Shhh!" Wrapped Wrist had whispered. "Orenda is trying to sleep."

She'd swallowed hard. "I've heard women talk. . . . It's just never happened to me before."

"Well, let's see if we can do it again."

When she'd awakened in the predawn, his muscular arms had been around her, his body sending its warmth into her night-chilled flesh. She had turned, finding herself face-to-face. He'd looked her in the eyes and given her a happy smile. After he brushed his lips across her cheek, his hands began smoothing her sides, rounding her hips, and stroking her legs.

His touch lit the fires inside her pelvis, and they were at it again. Not once, but twice before she had to dress, leave his bed, and find her way outside for the purpose of relieving herself.

Gods, what has happened to me? She ached to be alone with him, to ask him about what had been kindled between them. Did he share the same mad desire she felt for him? Was his memory as filled with her as hers was with him?

Snake's blood! What if he's planted a child in me? Dumbstruck, she wondered what the consequences of that would be.

They stepped out onto the crest of Juniper Ridge, and Wrapped Wrist took the moment to catch his breath. A biting chill was rising, and she shivered against it. Two pit houses stood back in the trees. First Moon Valley was masked by the thick haze.

She caught his eye. "I have to speak with you."

He nodded, a reassuring smile on his lips. To Orenda, he said, "We'll be back."

She nodded, granting them a wistful smile before returning to her gloomy thoughts.

Wrapped Wrist walked several steps down the ridge. "It's hard when there are three people, isn't it?"

"There are so many things," she began. "I'm confused.

Delighted. I'm half-scared. What happened to me last night?"

He took her hands, grinning. "I'm hoping you fell in love."

"It's impossible!" She dropped his hands, limping off and crossing her arms as she stared out at the smoke and falling ash. The wind gusted, whipping the trees. The cold seemed to intensify. "Wrapped Wrist, you have a life here. I have duties to my war chief."

"Crow Woman, I've lain with a lot of women, but last night my souls were Singing." A conspiratorial grin crossed his lips. "And yours were, too. You're anything but quiet when your moment comes."

"I wasn't that loud."

"Orenda didn't get much sleep last night."

"She *knows*?"

"Well, it was pretty hard to miss."

"She didn't say anything, didn't stare at us."

Wrapped Wrist raised his hands to calm her. "Because what we did is normal for two people who really like each other."

She swallowed hard. "Do you really like me?"

He nodded.

"Why? Most men, and nearly all women, think I'm unlikeable."

"You never let men see the souls you keep locked inside that wonderful body of yours. As to the women, you'll have to find your own answer to that." His voice dropped. "When this is over, I want to go away with you. Just you and me, where we can be alone with each other."

"Why?" she almost cried. His words kept stirring feelings she'd thought long dead. Hope, longing, and dread all mixed together. By the gods, she hated being confused—especially by herself.

His grin was contagious. "I like you. I think I love you. But I want to know that you and I can love each other forever. It will take time for both of us, but I want to try."

"What if you made me *pregnant*?"

"We will deal with it," he replied reasonably. "If, for some reason, you don't want me to help raise the child, that's fine. On the other hand, if your life precludes raising it, my clan will be happy to adopt. I'll raise it." He arched a teasing brow. "Who knows? Maybe we'll decide to raise it together."

She stared at him in disbelief. "It can't be that easy."

"It's not." He turned deathly serious. "There's nothing harder on earth than a relationship between a man and a woman. It'll even be harder between you and me because of what fate and other men have done to you."

She sighed. "I'd swear you put some sort of charm on my souls. For the moment all I can think about is you and what happens when we lay together."

"Good." He stepped close, pulling her head down and brushing his lips on hers. "Trust me; we'll work it out."

The problem was, they were heading into a war; and the last thing she needed was to have her thoughts constantly distracted by either his smile or his body.

A long-legged man could cross the Soft Earth Moiety kiva in Mid-Sun Town in eight paces. The roof with its large opening was rattled by the wind, and bits of ash drifted in. A fire had been lit in the central fire pit, a concession to the growing chill. Bad Cast had slipped inside after returning from his meeting with Ripple. He'd found his wife seated on the corner of the foot drum and had taken a seat beside her. Her expression was grim, her brow lined. She'd taken his hand in hers, grip tight.

Around the walls, lineage leaders sat cross-legged, eyes thoughtful. Ironwood stood in the north, a grim expression on his thin-lipped face. His single eye had fixed on the fire.

"Ironwood has asked for help in attacking Pinnacle House," Soft Cloth whispered into Bad Cast's ear. "Without the elders, it's up to the lineage leaders."

Under normal circumstances, the kiva would have been the preserve of the Priests and Shamans who were preparing for the equinox, a most special time this year since it coincided with Sister Moon's homecoming. Now, however, with the presence of the war chief, the captivity of the elders, and Ripple's looming vision, a special meeting had been called.

A Strong Back Clan man, Black Bush, who had married Yellow Petal, held the floor, a long dart in his right hand. "I have talked with my opposites," he said forcefully. "My own inclination is to attack Pinnacle Great House according to the war chief's plans. It seems, however, that others in my clan do not share this conviction." He shot the war chief a sad smile. "It is their fear that if we help you attack, our Clan elder, Hoarse Caller, and War Chief Rose will be put to death by the First People. I must, therefore, respectfully decline your invitation, War Chief."

Ironwood nodded. He'd obviously heard enough of this already.

Black Bush relinquished the long dart, symbol of a speaker during a war council, and returned to his seat beside Yellow Petal. She nodded encouragement to her husband and took his hand as he seated himself.

Bad Cast looked around, waiting for someone else to come forward. No one did. An uneasy silence spread through the room.

Someone, do something. Bad Cast glanced over his shoulder to where the Whisper and Muddy Water clan leaders sat. Most of them looked down at their hands, or anywhere but toward Ironwood.

Bad Cast nerved himself. Gods, he'd never done anything like this, but he took a deep breath, winked at Soft Cloth when she gave him a questioning look, and stood. His heart was hammering as he picked his way between the seated people and walked up to Ironwood. His hand was trembling as he took the long, fletched dart and turned.

He froze as every eye fixed on him. Words stuck in his throat. The carefully rehearsed argument vanished into air. For long moments he stood petrified.

"Bad Cast?" Ironwood said gently. "It is traditional to introduce yourself."

A chuckle came from the floor, and Bad Cast grinned

sheepishly. "I am Bad Cast, of the Blue Stick Clan." His mouth was dry. "I am not a lineage leader. I'm a hunter, not a leader."

He happened to glance at Soft Cloth, and saw the surprise and amazement in her eyes. As their eyes met, she smiled, nodding her encouragement. He stiffened his spine, planting his feet. "What I wanted to say here is that I was one of the first to hear Ripple's vision. I was one of the men who rescued him and took him to the Mountain Witch. She believed his vision, and took it as a sign. In the meantime, I have lived with Ironwood's people, and talked to the Dreamer, Poor Singer. He believes Ripple's vision."

He glanced at Ironwood, and drew strength from the slight nod. The dart shaft was slick in his sweaty hands. "Cold Bringing Woman told Ripple that the First People could be broken. I know it is difficult to decide what to do when our elders' lives are at risk, but I think in my heart that we must support the war chief and Ripple."

Was he making any impression at all?

"I cannot speak for my clan, not even for my lineage. I can't even speak as a warrior. I speak only as a man. But I want every person in this room to understand that when the war chief and his warriors move against Pinnacle Great House, I will be with him." He paused, looking out at the faces. "I do not ask you to come and fight with us, only that you be ready to do what your souls and honor ask of you. That is all."

The room was silent.

Bad Cast tightened his grip on the dart and tapped it against the kiva floor before handing it back to Ironwood. "That is all."

He knew that Ironwood's single eye followed him as he went back and seated himself beside Soft Cloth.

Ironwood pursed his lips as he stared thoughtfully at the floor. "Well, at least I have one of you with me. Thank you, Bad Cast."

A voice from the door called, "Whatever Bad Cast has gotten himself into, you can count on me, too." Wrapped

Wrist ducked through the entryway, followed by Crow Woman and, most surprising of all, by a worried-looking Orenda.

Ironwood jerked a curt nod. "Thank you, Wrapped Wrist. Your support is deeply appreciated." To Crow Woman, he said, "Good to see you, warrior. We've been worried."

He stiffened when Orenda said, "War Chief? Might I have a word with you outside?"

Ironwood addressed the room. "If you would excuse me for a moment, I'll give you time to digest Bad Cast's words." Then he followed the others as they stepped out.

Bad Cast stood, retraced his way through the crowd, and ducked out into the smoky day. Behind him, voices rose in sudden bedlam, although a voice shouted, "Order! Order! One at a time!"

Bad Cast slapped Wrapped Wrist on the back. "Good to see you. Where've you been?"

Wrapped Wrist gave him a sober grin. "Having interesting times. What happened on the Dog's Tooth?"

"Leather Hand surprised the Council of Elders up there. He captured White Eye, Whistle, and the elders, and burned the place on the way out. He's taken them up to the great house. No one has seen him or them since."

Orenda had led them several paces into the center of the small plaza. She turned, looking Ironwood in the eye. "I have no way to tell you this, but the camp has been attacked. Leather Hand killed many, took others." She drew a breath. "Night Sun is his captive. He and his troops have taken her south. Perhaps to Flowing Waters Town."

Ironwood's flinty expression began to sag. "How long ago?"

"Three days now." Orenda wrung her hands. "They went straight to the camp, Ironwood. It was as if they knew exactly where we were."

Crow Woman asked, "You said they caught Whistle?" A pause. "That's how they found us."

Orenda threw her hands up. "One other thing: Ravenfire was with them. It was he who captured Night Sun. I swear it, War Chief. He gave her up to them."

Ironwood looked stunned.

"We saw her," Wrapped Wrist added. "They were carrying her on a litter. Some of the other women and children were walking. Ravenfire was with them, walking freely and carrying a weapon."

Crow Woman cocked her jaw. "You should also know they butchered some of the bodies. Took the flesh with them for meat."

Ironwood's face was as ashen as the sky. "By the gods."

Bad Cast fought the urge to reach out and steady the man.

"War Chief?" Crow Woman asked, stepping forward.

Aware of Soft Cloth as she walked up behind him, Bad Cast said, "Come. My house is but a stone's throw from here. Let us have some tea and consider what to do."

"We can save her," Crow Woman insisted. "It will have to be done quickly and carefully. They'll most likely have her in Dusk House. We can sneak most of our people inside, then, with a good diversion, break her out."

"Do that," Bad Cast said, "and we'll lose any element of surprise here."

Crow Woman shot him a withering glare. "Who are you, *hunter,* to advise the war chief?"

"He's *my* husband," Soft Cloth said, stepping forward.

"Well, woman, our Matron has been taken, and that supersedes any attack on First Moon Mountain. Besides, the situation here has changed. If the First People took Whistle, they know everything." Crow Woman turned to Ironwood. "He would have talked rather than endure Leather Hand's torture." Even as she said it, her face blanched, and she turned away.

What was that all about? Bad Cast wondered.

Soft Cloth, fuming now, started forward, lifting a finger to launch into Crow Woman. Bad Cast held his breath as he interposed a warning hand. One could never predict results when dealing with enraged women. Fortunately, Soft Cloth stopped short.

"Easy," Wrapped Wrist said in a calming voice. "We're all on the same side here. The smartest thing that's been said is that we go somewhere and think this through. Hasty action now could lead to disaster, whatever action is finally chosen."

To everyone's relief, it was Orenda who took Iron-wood's arm and started him in Bad Cast's direction.

"My choice," Ironwood said woodenly, as if speaking to himself. "Oh, how bitter the gods have made this."

"What choice?" Crow Woman asked.

Ironwood said hollowly, "The Dreamer asked: Do I serve my heart, or my people?"

"Your people," Crow Woman rapped.

"Your heart," Orenda countered, concern on her face as she looked up at Ironwood.

Soft Cloth leaned close, whispering, "Whatever you must do, husband, I am behind you."

Bad Cast anxiously took Soft Cloth's hand, feeling blessed by her love and camaraderie. As much as he loved her, how much more painful was this for Ironwood?

Ironwood stopped suddenly, shaking off Orenda's arm and staring off into the smoke. There, between the trees, stood Ripple, a phantom figure in the haze. Then, as suddenly, an eddy in the wind obscured his form.

"Yes, Dreamer," Ironwood whispered miserably. "I know. My pride and arrogance have at last come home to curse me." He looked about, face working. "I need no tea, Bad Cast. Let us go back to the council and tell them this news."

Crow Woman asked, "War Chief?"

"Sister Moon's cloak is no blacker than the one around my heart," he said, waving at the smoky heavens. "Prepare yourself, Crow Woman. Our souls and our world hang in the balance."

"You will save the Matron?" Orenda asked.

"She knows the depth and extent of my love. Perhaps someday the world will know what this decision has cost me." Ironwood straightened. "Come. We've a rescue to plan."

Ripple could sense Ironwood's decision. Once again Cold Bringing Woman had gambled well. He smiled wearily to himself as he turned and walked through the trees. They surrounded him like shadows, ghostly gray wreaths of smoke blowing past.

The temperature was dropping, and when he turned his nose to the wind, he could smell the blowing fire as it raced and raged through the rocky mountains to the north.

My beautiful world. He had spent most of his youth up in those thick-forested slopes. The dark trails that had known his sandal-clad feet were ash now. The creaking trees but black spears that smoked and smoldered against a flame-streaked sky.

Fire was clearing the way for Cold Bringing Woman.

He remembered cool springs, places he had bent and touched his lips to. The once-crystal waters would still be flowing, choked with ash. He could imagine the streams where trout slipped over the brown mottled rock. They'd be turgid and black, much of the water boiled away. Did anything live there anymore?

My world is dying.

One thing left to endure now.

He glanced over his shoulder, seeing a dark form slipping from tree to tree.

Yes, only one thing.

Fifty-five

The morning had dawned gray. Spots and Cactus Flower walked down to Flowing Waters Town with the wind howling from behind. It whistled through the heavy load of firewood that bowed Spots's back and kept trying to blow Cactus Flower's pack around in front of her. Grains of sand stitched their backsides with stinging effect. The combination of wind, the smell of smoke, and the dropping temperature had combined to ensure that few Traders had displayed their wares around the Dusk House walls;

and those who did had chosen the lee of the south wall, where they could huddle in the wind shadow.

Only in the far west did any blue remain, while to the southwest, the Rainbow Serpent rose into the sky, curled south, and then merged with the thinning smoke plume.

Spots just had a feeling that it boded ill to see the fires of the north and south merged into one. The eerie feeling that had ridden his Dreams and dogged his bones deepened.

"Must be a terrible fire," Spots muttered. "I hope it's not too close to home."

Cactus Flower staggered under a wind gust. She'd done her hair in twin buns on either side of her head to designate herself a maiden. A split-turkey-feather cloak slapped and floated about her shoulders. "We don't usually have this kind of wind at this time of year. You'd think it was winter."

"Tomorrow's equinox." He glanced up at the sinister heavens. "Sister Moon's coming home. Maybe it's the end of the world?"

"Maybe." She shrugged. "Spots?"

"Yes."

"Why were you so quiet this morning? Every time I tried to get you to laugh, you just stared at the fire. Did I do something?"

"No."

"You're sure?"

He nodded, dread thickening around his heart. "It's not you. Well, yes, it is."

"What did I do?"

"Nothing. Everything." He glanced her way, only to have the wind whip hair around his face. "I want you to know: I have something to do tonight. I have to do it alone, so I'd like you to go back to your house and wait for me there. I'll come if I can."

"This doesn't sound like you. What are you doing? It involves that witch, doesn't it?"

"No." He hoped she didn't hear the lie. "It's safe, I promise. And don't even ask if it's another woman. You know better than that."

She pursed her lips in that familiar way, then said, "I

never did believe you were here just because. You arrived just after the witch. In fact, I'd swear I saw you walk in with her the day before. I see most everybody who comes through the gate."

"Will you promise to wait for me at your house?"

"Why should I?"

"Because I want you to." He sighed. "That's the problem. I want you to be away from this. Safe."

"Safe? You're not going to kill anyone, are you?"

"No!"

"Are you going to steal something?"

Only the Blessed Sun's souls! "No one's property is in danger. I just have to give something to someone and then see that she's safely out of Flowing Waters Town. That's all. After that, I'll do whatever you want me to. Perhaps go off to Trade with the Hohokam. I don't care."

"I want to help you."

"I'll Trade you. A week's worth of firewood. Whatever you want, for as long as you want it. Just promise me you'll stay home tonight."

"This thing must be very important to you."

"It is." Besides, if doing this got him killed, it wouldn't matter what he'd promised. *Choices.*

She was silent until they dropped down the hill to the earthen berm behind Dusk House. He could see the high balcony that ran the length of the third floor. This day no people lounged there. The doorways were blocked off. Only a few water jars stood on the clay-packed surface.

"I'll be there for you," Cactus Flower said. "But you worry me. What if someone finds out what you're doing?"

He made a face. "I might have to leave for a while. Go home. I wouldn't want you to get blamed."

She'd pinched her lower lip, eyes wary. "You're not going to bring the Red Shirts down on top of you?"

"No, nothing like that." He hoped.

"Gods, Spots! What kind of trouble are you in?"

"Helping an old friend, nothing more. It's not like I'm declaring war on the First People." Or was it? "I just have to attend to a duty, that's all."

She gave a toss of her head that he'd come to know as irritation. "Sure. Well, pay no attention to me. It's none of my business."

"That's right," he added somewhat coldly, hoping she'd be so angered she'd ignore him for the rest of the day.

"Rat dung!" she spat. "You're as cold as this wind. You'd think it was winter instead of equinox."

He sniffed, smelling the wind-blown smoke that streamed down from the north. What was happening up there?

They waved to the guard as they entered the southeastern gate. On this day, Spots wouldn't have much trouble selling firewood.

Mid-Sun Town had been precisely located atop Juniper Ridge. It lay in direct line between the watchtower, the *sipapu,* and the spot where Father Sun rose on the equinox horizon. The town should have been a hive of ceremonial activity. On this day, with the clan elders imprisoned atop First Moon Mountain, with blowing smoke and rapidly falling temperatures, it was a gloomy and depressed place.

Normally people gathered on the rim, watching for the equinox sunrise as it gleamed over the distant watchtower and then onto Mid-Sun Town's mud-plastered buildings.

Few had ventured out into the choking smoke to leave *pahos* on the high rimrock.

Then the meeting with Ironwood had been called in the Soft Earth kiva. Those people who could had congregated there. From where he sat Wrapped Wrist could cock his head and hear the shouting and argument inside the kiva. He longed to be there, to hear what the clans were deciding.

Instead he stood just outside the Black Shale kiva, keeping an eye on the door as Ironwood met with Yucca Sock and Crow Woman. The big kiva had been the only place large enough for Ironwood to assemble his warriors. Now Wrapped Wrist and Bad Cast strolled casually around the perimeter, ensuring that no one intruded.

"You saw Ripple this morning?"

"I did." Bad Cast gestured off toward the rimrock. "He was out there at dawn. Wrapped Wrist, I'm worried. He wasn't himself."

He snorted irritably. "Are any of us? Look what's happened to us, where we've been."

"No, perhaps not." Bad Cast shook his head. "And where has Spots disappeared to? For all we know, the Mountain Witch has stolen his souls, left his dead corpse by the side of the trail."

"Who knows?" Wrapped Wrist coughed, and sniffed in the smoke. "What was it about Ripple? I need to see him, ask him things."

"He was . . . I don't know, wistful and sad. Resigned to his fate. It wasn't anything he said, just a sense."

Wrapped Wrist nodded. "Whistle and the elders have been captured. The First People know our plans. Leather Hand has taken Night Sun." He glanced uneasily at the Soft Earth Moiety kiva. "The way they're arguing in there, our people are fraying about the edges. Everything that could has gone wrong. Ripple knows it. Now Ironwood's gone into council with his warriors to plan this rescue?"

Bad Cast nodded. "So, Cold Bringing Woman was wrong? What are we going to do?"

"Try and survive, just like Ripple is going to have to." He glanced at Bad Cast. "You know, don't you, that neither one of us can stay here now. After the First Moon Ceremony, the First People are going to come down off that mountain. They're going to be looking for us. All of us. Anyone that had anything to do with Ripple's vision and Ironwood."

Bad Cast missed a step, shock registering on his face. "That's what he meant. Ripple, I mean. He said I had to take Soft Cloth and leave."

Wrapped Wrist took a deep breath. "I want you to think

of something else. What if Cold Bringing Woman was working with the Flute Player all along? What if her vision was meant to bring us all to disaster?"

"You mean she used Ripple to destroy us?" Bad Cast made a face. "But *why?*"

A scream was followed by a smacking impact in the trees just east of the plaza.

Wrapped Wrist wheeled, turning to run, his darts gripped in his left hand. He rounded a ramada and dodged through the trees. The gloomy smoke obscured anything more than a couple of body lengths away.

Bad Cast was off to one side, keeping him in sight as they hurried in the direction of the rim. Yes, the shout had come from here, somewhere. He could hear questions being called back and forth in the plaza behind them.

Bad Cast made a questioning gesture, and Wrapped Wrist pointed. A wreath of denser smoke blew past. The effect was eerie: warm smoke mixed with cooler, clearer air. He might have been in a Dream land, the trees ghostly, somehow unreal.

He stopped just in time to hear clothing rasp on rock ahead of him. Dropping to a crouch, he started forward, nocking a dart in his atlatl.

Bad Cast had matched his pace, eyes searching the trees.

At first the shape didn't register; it looked like a hunched beast. Then the man straightened from the body he bent over.

Wrapped Wrist stepped forward, lifting his atlatl and dart. "Stop where you are," he called, closing the distance.

To his surprise, the man spun, and in that instant leapt for him.

Wrapped Wrist's release was instinctive. The hurried cast drove the dart through the assailant's shoulder, causing him to whirl. The man staggered, raised a war club, and bellowed.

Wrapped Wrist dropped his atlatl, catching the man's upraised arm. He grabbed a handful of fabric, lifting with his considerable strength, and threw the fellow over his shoulder.

The assailant arched, then slammed into the unforgiving rock with a jarring thud.

"You all right?" Bad Cast asked as he ran up.

"Fine." Wrapped Wrist realized he'd started to pant; his arms were shaking. "What is it with me and people?" He gestured to the moaning man. "Keep an eye on him."

Then he stepped over to the prone form, squinted, and bent down.

Ripple's skull leaked blood from the crown. More blood seeped from the jagged slash in his neck.

"By the gods!" Black Bush cried as he arrived, panting. "What's happened here?"

"It's the Trader," Bad Cast said, retrieving the man's war club. "The one called Takes Falls." He drove the head of the war club into the man's shoulder. "Why? Why did you do this?"

The man screamed as Bad Cast's blow landed on the broken dart shaft. He grabbed his bleeding shoulder, crying, "For turquoise, you fool! The Matron will pay anyone who can deliver his head!"

Wrapped Wrist stood, a feeling of despair rising in his souls. "Ripple's dead. The Trader was trying to cut his head off."

Word passed like from lip to lip as people hurried to the scene. "The Prophet is dead!" "They've killed the Dreamer!"

In the dim gloom of evening, Priest Water Bow stepped up onto the third-floor roof of Pinnacle Great House and squinted into the north. The Sunwatcher, Blue Racer, stood there, his long form wrapped in a blanket against the bitter chill. He, too, watched the flames. They could see spot fires burning on the other side of the valley.

Throughout the day, runners had come bearing news about the fire. At first it had blown southward, forming a long and sinuous front. Reports came in of walls of flame that literally blasted down the mountain valleys. High winds carried burning ash and glowing cinders that lit more fires in advance of the flames. By the time the wall of fire caught up, they'd been fanned into conflagrations of their own.

One runner reported the fate of a colleague. He had observed the man fleeing down a mountain trail on the next ridge. A fleet runner, the fire had proved faster, engulfing him and even a small band of panicked elk. The runner had never seen fire move so fast; he'd sprinted from the area, powered by a panic of his own.

"Will it stop?" Blue Racer asked.

"It should," Water Bow replied with a certainty he didn't feel. "This cold will help. The fire will slow, burrowing deep into dry wood. Perhaps by morning the winds will cease. If they do, the valley will protect First Moon Mountain. We have water on two sides, and exposed shale on the other."

"I cast the auspices four times atop Spider Woman's Butte. In none of the auguries did I see this. From the alignment of the Star People as well as the casting of the bones, Sister Moon's homecoming should have met with fair weather." Blue Racer puffed his irritation.

Water Bow could see the condensed breath. "This feels more like snow than anything."

"How would you tell?" Blue Racer asked. He indicated the blowing ash that slowly spiraled out of the darkening night sky. "As it is, Sister Moon will rise between the pillars this night, but no one will see her. Not with a murky black sky like this. Even sunset has been cloaked."

"Will you conduct the welcoming ceremonies?"

Blue Racer shrugged. "I haven't decided. If we can't see Sister Moon, she surely can't see us. What's the point of welcoming her if she remains ignorant of our greetings?"

Water Bow wasn't sure how to reply to that. He glanced down the slope, where the Eagle's Fist was just barely visible. Beyond that, people crowded the slopes. Most were Made People, relatives of the ridge inhabitants whom the warriors had allowed to pass Guest House. As the temperature dropped, their numbers had declined in favor of warm fires in accommodating pit houses.

"Blazes," Burning Smoke muttered as he climbed up from below. He squinted into the wind and wrapped his cloak around his body against the bitter cold. "You'd think this was winter solstice instead of equinox."

"I've been hearing that all day," Blue Racer said caustically.

"We having a ceremony?" Burning Smoke asked.

For a long moment, Blue Racer considered, then shook his head. "I'm not sure if we should or not. I hate having to wait. The Blessed Sun has expressed his strongest interest that we ensure the ceremonies are a success."

"That's assuming we're not battling fires on the slope below us tomorrow night." He looked down at the thick forest on the northern slope. Gods, if that caught, it would roast anyone on the summit like a rabbit on a stick.

Burning Smoke wiped a hand over his face, smudging the soot that had accumulated there.

Hands, faces, clothes—ash and soot coated everything. Water Bow's once snowy white robes would have to be sent down and thoroughly washed in the rivers, assuming the waters ever ran clean again. Just that afternoon Matron Larkspur had poured a cup from a freshly obtained water jar, only to find the water dark with ash. For the next while they would be drinking from the storage jars.

The war chief turned his attention to the stone pillars. In the faint light, they loomed as mere shadows in the thick haze. "As the night darkens, I'm not sure your Priests will be able to see each other. It's going to be black as pitch. And with this wind, torches will blow out. If we light bonfires, the gusts will blow the fire sideways."

Blue Racer hugged himself for warmth. "Nevertheless we shall Dance tonight. But the last thing I want is for one of my people to be blown over the cliff, or to fall just because he couldn't see in this miserable gloom."

Burning Smoke jerked a curt nod. "Very well, I'll alert the guards." He turned, stocky frame disappearing as he descended the ladder.

"Time for a hot drink," Blue Racer said. "I'd better warm my heart as often as I can these days. If it keeps up like this, the gods alone know how soon the Blessed Sun is going to want to cut it out."

Water Bow nodded, thankful to escape the cold. How could the fire keep burning when it felt ever more like freezing? "The gods pity those poor guards on a night like this."

"They're the lucky ones," Blue Racer rejoined. "They can just cover themselves in their blankets and doze."

Gods, it was cold! In the darkness beneath the trees, Bad Cast could barely make out the seated forms of Ironwood's warriors. Everyone crouched under his blanket and wore his warmest clothes. Yucca Sock, Firehorn, Two Teeth, and Right Hand sat close to the war chief, their heads bent. Warriors were looking uneasily at Ironwood in the gloom. Conversations were whispered, everyone in a dark mood after Ripple's death.

No one was sure what to believe, or if this was just more madness driven by the end of the world.

Off to one side, Wrapped Wrist sat close beside Crow Woman. They way they huddled, it seemed to be more than just preraid camaraderie. Bad Cast had seen more than one speculative glance cast their way, at least until Crow Woman shot back with a hot glare.

The other warriors waited, some shivering, as they fingered their bows, checked arrows, and hefted their war clubs.

What am I doing here? Bad Cast had to wonder. He carried his atlatl and an ax. He had never considered himself a warrior. Truth be told, he barely made it as a hunter. Sneaking around in silence had never seen him at his best.

"All right," Ironwood said, rising. "I need you to hear my final orders. This is a rescue first and foremost. The

Moon People elders wouldn't have been taken were it not for my initiating contact. They are *our* responsibility."

The warriors shifted, some nodding, others watching with wooden expressions. They would follow their war chief, no matter what they thought of his motives.

Ironwood continued. "Bad Cast knows a trail that will lead us up the slope. When we reach the rimrock, we will stop. Bad Cast will climb up first, making sure of the route. Yucca Sock will follow and take care of any guard he finds up there. At his signal, we will climb one by one. The place we've chosen isn't that difficult, but taking shields will be too cumbersome. Leave them here. Those of us who live will return for them."

Ironwood reached out. "Friends, companions, we have shared so much. Now, like yours, my heart is worried sick. We don't know if your wives or children are alive or dead. Tonight, we will strike a blow in retaliation for them.

"I want you to think." He smacked a fist into a hard palm. "Our first goal is to free the captive elders. Our second is to take *First People* for hostages. If you kill all of the First People, we will have nothing left to bargain with. Do you understand? We can Trade Matron Larkspur, or Blue Racer, or Water Bow for Night Sun and our women and children."

Grunts of assent were muttered around the dark circle.

"Good." Ironwood clapped his hands together. "Next thing: We have no support from the First Moon People. I can't blame them. Their Prophet is dead. They can't take the chance of having their elders killed, or even face the Blessed Sun's retaliation." He paused. "We are on our own. We have no one but ourselves to depend on."

More grunts sounded, and Bad Cast could just make out the shadowy warriors as they touched hands and thumped each other's shoulders, a physical demonstration of their solidarity.

"This night," Ironwood's voice dropped, "is a gift from Cold Bringing Woman. I still believe in Ripple's vision. I think it is she who has blown this dark wind down from the north."

"As long as she doesn't blow the fire into this forest," Yucca Sock added warily. "We could be burnt to a crisp before we reach the summit."

"On your feet," Ironwood ordered. "Keep the noise to a minimum. If they hear us, if someone has betrayed us . . . well, fight like the fury—but run faster."

Nervous chuckles broke out.

"Bad Cast?" Ironwood asked. "Can you lead the way?"

"Follow me." A terrible weight had settled in his chest. Step after step, he placed his feet and started up the dark slope. Behind him, Ironwood tried to place his feet in Bad Cast's tracks.

Find the trail by the lightning-riven tree! Bad Cast hadn't expected the blowing smoke, the inky darkness of the gloom. Behind him, warriors coughed, their throats smoke-tight and lungs clogged.

Overhead, the trees waved and thrashed as the cold north wind ripped through the timber. Bad Cast muttered under his breath. Any fear of the coming fighting vanished as he waged his own battle with dark branches, slanting deadfall, and treacherous footing. Worse, what if he lost his way?

"Here," he said, indicating a handhold, or, "Watch your foot. Step inside of the log here."

It seemed an eternity later that he found himself panting, half-winded. He stared up into the black tangle of fir, pine, and spruce. How far had they gone? Where was the summit? It seemed they'd been climbing all night.

"Bad Cast?" Ironwood asked, a darker question in his voice.

"It has to be above us somewhere, War Chief." He wiped his face, feeling the dryness of soot, the grit from the forest. Then he resumed his climb, testing his footing, pulling himself up with branches, scrambling ever upward. Behind him, the line of warriors kept climbing.

Over the wind in the trees, Bad Cast could hear them, wood knocking on wood, the rattle of arrows. Sometimes a person slipped, a curse under his breath. Sticks snapped under misplaced weight. The warriors kept coughing from the smoke.

They couldn't hear that up above, could they?

Bad Cast's dire imagination filled the heights with armed Red Shirts, each with a nocked arrow or a perched boulder, just ready to rain death down on the foolish little band that dared to scale the impregnable heights. He kept seeing Ripple's expression, one of longing, his dead eyes wide, blood dripping from his head and neck.

Did you see that coming? Was that why you looked so resigned this morning? He blinked away a sudden tear, wondering at the grief that threatened to flood his breast.

A stone broke loose, and someone gasped in pain before the rock crashed down into the trees.

"Who's hurt?" Ironwood hissed over his shoulder. The question was whispered down the line.

"Thorn Petal," came the whispered reply up the line. "The stone knocked him off his feet. He's fallen into a tree."

"Go." The hissed command went back down the line. "Thorn Petal will catch up if he can."

Ironwood tapped Bad Cast on the back, and the relentless climb continued. A branch slapped him in the face, and painful grit smarted behind his eyes.

If I could just see! Instead he worked his way up, making his way by feel. When he couldn't brace his foot on a stone or fallen log, he had to dig his sandaled feet into the thick duff. Needles pricked and pierced the tender skin between his toes. Often his first foothold collapsed, and more than once Ironwood stopped him from sliding down atop the others.

More to the left.

Bad Cast hesitated. The voice had sounded like Ripple's, merged with the wind in the trees. He began edging to his left.

Onward they climbed, the slope getting even steeper, more dangerous. When his foot slipped, and he skidded down onto Ironwood, the war chief braced him. "Easy. Don't rush. If we start a landslide, they'll know we're coming."

Bad Cast filled his lungs, puffing in the cold air. His fingers were growing numb. Once again he put himself to the task. Hand, foot, hand, foot. Test the toehold, step. Feel around for sticks. Check for loose rocks that could roll underfoot. Hand, foot, hand, foot.

Something wet landed on the back of his neck. Water? Gods, it couldn't be raining, could it?

He glanced up at the blackness; the wind was still slashing through the trees. They were creaking and grinding, covering the sounds of the climbers. Well, for that, at least, he could be thankful.

She comes!

Bad Cast swore he heard Ripple's glad cry.

Something else cold and wet spattered on his shirt. He could smell it now: the damp scent of soot. Snake's blood, they had to hurry. If it rained, every piece of wood would become slick; the rocks, already treacherous, would make each handhold precarious. Fingers growing numb from cold would add to the danger.

He pulled himself past the thick trunk of a fir tree and felt the wind twirling in the night. And what was this? He tilted his cheek, aware that something light pattered down around him. He caught one on his tongue, tasting water and soot.

"Snow!" he whispered in disbelief.

"Snow?" Ironwood asked, confused.

"It's snowing," Bad Cast affirmed, and scrambled up on all fours before his fingers encountered wet sandstone. He felt his way up, could see the blacker rock against the night sky.

The rimrock!

He bent down, whispering, "Shhhh! They're right above us." But where was he? How close to one of the cracked chutes that could be scaled to the ridgetop?

"Fire and ice!" He barely heard Ripple's call over the storm. *"Cold Bringing Woman has come for us."*

Bad Cast started along the rim, feeling his way, hearing dirt and stones as they periodically rolled down into the trees. He could feel the snow as the wind swept it around him. The cold had increased, and he could hardly feel his wet fingers.

He stopped, exploring a crack in the rock. Yes, here he could find a foothold. "Rope?" he whispered. Moments later

Ironwood passed him a coil of braided leather that he hung around his neck and shoulder. Bad Cast began to climb.

He levered himself up, searching for a handhold. His wet, numb fingers clawed at the rough stone, found purchase, and he muscled himself up another half body length.

"Well?" Ironwood whispered, his voice hidden in the wind.

"Wait." Bad Cast grimaced as his sandal slipped off the rock. In desperation, he kicked it off, using his toes, and gained another half body length. A strong gust of wind plastered his back with snow and almost tore him from his hold.

He reached up, grasped the rim, and pulled. Sandstone crumbled in his hand. At the last moment, he saved himself, but heard a soft thump, and a grunt as the rock dropped onto whomever waited below.

"Are you all right?" he called softly.

"I'll live," a hoarse growl answered. "Climb. Then toss the rope down."

He stuffed a fist into a vertical crack, lifted, and swung a bare foot onto the rim. He toppled onto his side, blinking and panting. Snowflakes pattered onto his face, melting, and trickling down his skin. To the north, half-hidden in the storm, a wicked red gleam marked the fire.

Fire and ice. He shook his head. Ripple *had* been shown the future. Bad Cast pulled himself upright, unslung the rope from his shoulder, and tossed one end down. He felt a hand give a tug, and braced himself.

Dearest gods, don't let my grip slip. Everything depended on him.

Fifty-six

They had taken Night Sun to the old Red Lacewing kiva, a large cylindrical room built into the third story of Talon Town. Turquoise Fox had preceded him, having a large bonfire kindled in the fire pit. The floor and benches had been plastered in a deep red, the upper walls in white. On the pilasters between the pole-shelved niches, images of the thlatsinas had been painted. Rendered by Sternlight's own hand, they had graced the walls since Crow Beard's day.

Leather Hand studied one—the Long Horn thlatsina—and stepped up to it. He gave Night Sun a sidelong glance, then spit on the image.

She just continued to stare at him as if he were some detestable insect.

To his men, he said, "Destroy these."

He stepped back, watching as his warriors attacked the images, raining blow after blow onto the hated thlatsinas with their war clubs and stone-headed axes. He had found a room full of snowy white capes, which, given the frigid temperatures, his man had adopted with appreciation. In the process, he had allowed them to ransack some of the storerooms, decking themselves with jewelry the likes of which they would never have been allowed otherwise. Loyalty deserved to be rewarded.

"Your gods are dying, Night Sun," he said evenly. "As they go, so, too, shall you."

She looked around. "Where is my grandson?"

"He came to me earlier today, saying that he had heard of a special room. A place here in Talon Town where the most wondrous treasure had been hidden."

"Anything in this building belongs to the Red Lacewing Clan."

"I am Red Lacewing; you are Outcast." He smiled, hearing steps on the kiva roof. He looked up as a large fabric bag came tumbling down the ladder. It clattered to a stop over the *sipapu* in the northern floor. Ravenfire's sandaled feet came stamping down the ladder.

"I found them!" he cried. "Just where Poor Singer said they'd be." He leaped the last three rungs to the floor, grinning maniacally.

Leather Hand watched the tightening of Night Sun's expression. He'd purposely kept the two of them separated while he and Turquoise Fox worked on Ravenfire. The young man was desperate for special recognition. When he'd asked to go in search of something he'd heard tell of in Ironwood's camp, Leather Hand had immediately dispersed Fast Fist to accompany him.

"So, you found them?" Leather Hand asked. He glanced around; his men were finishing the job of mutilating the wall paintings. The timing was perfect.

Ravenfire had a smug look on his face as he untied a cord that bound the bag and upended it. A pile of wooden masks clattered onto the hard-packed floor.

They were beautiful, painted in bright colors with striking eagle, macaw, and hawk feathers. Some had long noses, others white-rimmed eyes or gaping toothy mouths. One—covered with fitted pieces of turquoise, coral, and jet—gleamed in the light.

"Blessed gods," Turquoise Fox whispered. "Look at the wealth they represent!"

Leather Hand made a face, his gut crawling as the obscene masks stared up at him. Then he glanced at Ravenfire. How committed was the young man to his new life and friends?

"Burn them," Leather Hand ordered.

He caught the look of horror on Night Sun's face, the sudden reservation on Ravenfire's. Even Turquoise Fox hesitated, saying, "But War Chief, the turquoise alone—"

"I said burn them."

He turned, his white cape whirling. He pointed at Night Sun. "Tonight we dedicate ourselves to the task of destroying the thlatsina heresy. You, woman, were as much responsible as anyone. And since I don't have Sternlight here to atone for this blasphemy, you will."

"I will do nothing you ask of me." Night Sun lifted her chin defiantly.

"Cut the cords that bind her," Leather Hand ordered as several of his warriors bent and began pitching the gorgeous masks into the central fire. "She no doubt Dreams of escape, of slipping away in the night." He was watching Ravenfire's expression as he said, "Tonight, *Matron* Night Sun, you will Dance atop the burning thlatsinas. After this night, you will never walk again."

Ravenfire only swallowed. He looked slightly ill as two warriors prodded Night Sun forward; then one shoved her into the fire pit, her bare feet stumbling over the burning masks.

She tried to flee, but with each step she took, the ring of warriors pushed her back.

Even when the smell of her burning flesh began to fill the air, Ravenfire's expression remained strained, but not sympathetic.

Perhaps he is suited to be one of us?

Through it all, Night Sun locked eyes with his, as if her souls were untouched by the pain she had to be feeling.

Very well. He could always raise the stakes.

Dusk bore down on Flowing Waters Town, the sky black and cross. The smell of smoke had intensified while tiny black flecks of ash drifted down from the surly sky.

Spots crouched, his blanket around his shoulders, and wondered if it was the end of the world. A couple of sticks of firewood remained. His pile would have been gone by midday but for the horrendous return he asked for each piece.

People had been wary. He'd seen it in their eyes, felt that sense of foreboding as the wind sawed at Dusk House's tall bulk, prodded at the doorways, and whistled around the square-cornered rooms.

Each time he glanced over at Nightshade, her dark eyes were fixed on his. No expression crossed her impassive face, but he could feel her anticipation. The question lay deep behind her eyes.

Yes, I'm here for you.

Spots exhaled worriedly, and realized his breath was white before his mouth. Gods, how cold was it going to get? Worse, the old woman was still naked, her thin bones having no protection against the increasing chill. People were staying inside, walking quickly, with wraps around their shoulders when they had to travel outside.

The circular bulk of the great kiva resembled a big head, vaults like eyes, the entrance a square muzzle with a yawning mouth. Atop the southeast gate, the guard huddled under his blanket, looking particularly glum. His expression left no doubt about his misery. The guard on the southwestern gate looked similarly preoccupied as he shivered in his war shirt. When he'd come to take his place, he'd been poorly dressed, having given no thought to the fact the chill would intensify.

"It's almost dark," Cactus Flower said from where she huddled in the next doorway. "Let's just go home, Spots. Whatever you have to do, wait until the weather's nicer."

"I can't." He stepped out, shivered, and walked to where she'd taken shelter. Wind Baby had flipped up the corners of her blanket, mostly covering her pile of shells, jet bracelets, and locally made ceramic jars with their pretty black-on-white patterns.

She shook her head, a sober reserve in her eyes. "It smells like snow. You don't want to be out in this."

He smiled. "Would you do me the greatest of favors?"

She tilted her head. "In return for what?"

"Me."

"What do you mean, you?"

"Will you go back to your farmstead, fix a warm dinner, and eat it? Then I want you to go to bed, and have the covers warm for me when I show up. I don't know how long I will be, but when I do finally get there, I will be yours for as long as you want me."

"You will be mine?"

He nodded. "To do whatever you want. To stay here and farm if you wish, or to go on the road, Trading where we will. I would be happy to continue fetching firewood for Trade here just as we've been doing. You decide, and I will agree to it."

"Assuming you live through this?"

He shrugged.

"You know," she told him, "the Blessed Matron suspected a young man and his dog of aiding a witch who was cursing people using bits of buffalo fur soaked in menstrual blood. She had him walled up in one of the interior rooms. People said they could hear the little dog scratching at the walls for days."

"I'm not cursing anyone."

"Can you imagine what that must have been like?" Cactus Flower asked, looking past him to Nightshade's cage. "Slowly dying of thirst in the dark, all the sound deadened by the thick floors and walls." She paused. "Do you think in the last days he clawed at the walls? It's been said that people will rake their fingernails off in desperation."

"Go home, Cactus Flower." Spots smiled gently. "I will be there as soon as I can. Then, well, you decide. You may even grow tired of me and decide to go back to your old life."

She gave an irritated shake of the head. "You're not going to be talked out of this, are you?"

"What good would my word to you be if it weren't good to anyone else? Oh, and take my Trade. I got a nice piece of turquoise today."

He helped her pick up her things and fill her pack. When she was ready, he gave her a final hug, relishing the feel of her cold body against his. In a last act, he brushed his lips across her forehead.

"Take care, Spots," she said with resignation, and he watched her walk through the southeast gate. The guard didn't react to her wave.

Spots took a deep breath, picked up his blanket, and

folded it into a square. Taking the knife from his belt pouch, he slipped it between the folds of the blanket and had a final look around. Both guards seemed completely oblivious to anything but shivering.

Spots walked forward, passing by the side of the cage as if on his way to the kiva entrance. He hesitated beside the thick poles only long enough to slip the blanket inside.

"Cold Bringing Woman comes," Nightshade said from within. "It's our night, Spots. Wait for me in the kiva entrance."

He continued on his way, the gloom of evening darkening around him. Several of the remaining Traders had packed their goods and were walking out of the plaza, tossing waves to the guards.

Did they keep track? Were they aware that Spots had remained? He'd never seen them keep a count of who went in and out, and besides, the numbers of people passing was large. Who was to say if someone came in one way, and left through the other gate?

He could see Nightshade's dark figure as she sawed at the ropes that secured the door to her cage. Moments later the old woman stepped out, the blanket over her head. She hobbled toward him, ducking into the shelter of the kiva entrance.

"I swear, my joints have stiffened during my days in there."

He sniffed, wincing at her odor.

"Come," she said evenly. "There will be water in the Priests' room behind the altar."

"We can't go there! It's forbidden!"

She snorted derisively. "Who's going to notice? It's equinox. All the Priests are out Blessing the fields in preparation for the final moon before harvest. None will be back within the walls for another hand of time."

Heart in his throat, Spots followed Nightshade down the stairs, across the great kiva floor, past the altar, and behind the screens. She made her way slowly up the northern stairs into the Priests' room.

Spots peered around in the gloom. Large cedar boxes

held different costumes. Masks hung from pegs on the wall. It seemed to Spots that the black eye holes were watching his every move with displeasure.

"Here." Nightshade removed a wooden lid from a large water jar. She used a piece of cloth taken from one of the boxes and began sponging herself. The air picked up the odor of damp excrement.

"I'm sorry, Elder," Spots whispered. "There was nothing I could do. It was hard enough to sneak you food and water."

"You did just fine, young hunter. More than I would have hoped for. The filth is only on the outside, and the body but a husk." He could see her smile. "What counts is in the souls. Look at yourself. That pretty young woman has seen past your scars. Your courage, humility, and kindness spoke to the longing and loneliness in her life. In you she found a part of herself that was missing. You made her whole, as she made you."

"She wasn't lonely," he pointed out. "She had men there all the time."

"Is that what you think? That a warm body beneath the blankets is company? For her it was only illusion, the image of what life should be. Then you came along with the real thing and she'll never be happy until she finds it again."

He wasn't sure he believed that.

Nightshade continued sponging herself and asked, "Could you pick that jar up? I want you to pour it slowly over my head so I can rinse all of me clean."

He picked up the heavy jug and hesitated. "It will splash all over!"

"After this night, that will be the least of the Priests' worries."

He did as directed, feeling the water splattering against his legs and feet as she washed her hair and wrung out the last of the water. A long white robe served her for a towel before she dropped it to the floor to dry her feet. Then one by one she picked through the robes, finding a short white tunic. In a box she discovered buffalo socks and yucca sandals that fit her feet. Fingering through the garments she took down a beautiful macaw-feather cloak that hung down almost to her knees. Finally she picked a particularly gruesome mask from the wall. She held the piece at arm's length, staring at the white-rimmed eye holes, at the long muzzle and wicked-looking teeth. Stringy gray hair had been pasted to the domed skull.

"That's hideous," Spots said, backing away.

"Soyok is meant to be hideous."

"Soyok?"

"You call her the Blue God."

"You'd better put that back."

"Oh, no," she whispered. "The gods of terror and I go way back. For tonight's purposes, the Blue God is just right." Then she bent, rummaging through several more boxes for items Spots could barely make out in the gloom.

She straightened, head back, eyes closed, and took a deep breath. Was it his imagination, or did she swell, expand, a renewed vitality radiating from her?

He could imagine her as she once had been: a raven-haired beauty, eyes flashing, Power like lightning crackling from her fingertips. No wonder the Mound Builders had stolen her away. And who knew how the world would have been changed had she stayed to rule the Straight Path Nation?

"Come, Spots. The time has come to begin the Dance." She didn't look back as she walked regally toward the doorway that led out onto the plaza. "Let us unleash the Power of the Blue God!"

Deputy Sunwatcher Water Bow sat on his most beautiful rug: a piece woven with yellow, black, red, brown, and white interlocking diamonds. The thick wool cushioned his old bones from the hard floor of the First People's kiva. Fortunately for him, he'd managed to stay warm for the most part. It had been Blue Racer and his Priests who'd born the brunt of the storm as they'd called the Blessing to Sister Moon. Most of it had been torn away as Wind Baby howled over First Moon Mountain, pelting the procession first with ash and cinders, then with brutal cold that numbed the bones, and finally finished the ceremony off with driving flakes of soot-encrusted snow.

Even as he stared around the brightly lit kiva, the effects of the weather were obvious. Everyone's clothing was blackened; some, who'd been afforded less protection by their robes, had black-streaked faces where they'd rubbed at the wet soot sticking to their skin.

No one had been happier to beat a retreat to the warm kiva than Blue Racer. The Blessed Sunwatcher sat before the crackling fire, his hands out, long face pensive and worried. And well he ought to worry. Who had ever heard of such a terrible storm so early? The Sunwatcher had chanted less than half of the Blessing before people broke and ran for shelter. The four lines of Priests behind him didn't look any too happy either.

Matron Larkspur was sitting to the side, War Chief Burning Smoke just behind her shoulder. She was one of the ones who'd smeared soot when she wiped away the melting snow. To her right, Deputy Ravengrass had a dour look. He was responsible for the security of the First People's party while at First Moon Mountain.

"The storm worries me." Blue Racer placed another piece of firewood into the blaze. "I cast the auguries four times. The weather was supposed to hold. I can't believe that the Flute Player would allow this to happen to us."

"The gods have their own ways," Water Bow reminded. "And do not fear for the weather. At this time of year it is not uncommon for a storm to blow through. Tomorrow it will be warm, sunny, and all shall go well. You will see. And do not chide the Flute Player. But for this storm, the fire might have jumped the valley, and had it done so, we would now be fleeing the fire's wrath, not just enduring a little snow."

"The flakes are black," Ravengrass said in amazement. "In all of my life, I have never seen black snow."

"And with luck," Larkspur added, "you never will again. My concern is the harvest. The valley is literally bursting with corn."

"It will not last," Water Bow predicted. "And what we

feel here, atop the mountain, is much colder than the valley bottom. When snow blows here, it falls as rain below."

"You don't seem concerned," Blue Racer said warily.

Water Bow kept his mocking smile in check. After all, it behooved Blue Racer to worry. His heart was on the line if the weather didn't break. "Blessed Sunwatcher, you bear too many responsibilities on your weary shoulders. We have asked for rain, and this storm is a good one. You forget you are atop a tall mountain. Were I you, I would send the Blessed Sun a message telling him the Flute Player has brought moisture. If anything this is a further affirmation that the Flute Player has forgiven his people."

"We have neutralized any threat," Larkspur added. "Even as we speak, Leather Hand should be leading Matron Night Sun into the safety of Straight Path Canyon. He will be laying his trap there, awaiting the arrival of Ironwood. The Outcast war chief's warren of vermin has been cleaned out. Neither can we forget the other service that Leather Hand has done us: We have the First Moon elders locked away under our guard. The local population dares try nothing against us. Everything is going our way."

Water Bow couldn't stop his dry smile. Fortunately, no one interpreted its true nature. He'd been out at midnight the night before Leather Hand left to hunt down Ironwood. Unable to sleep after hearing Whistle's screams, he'd gone to check the moonrise. He'd walked in the shadow cast by one of the stone pillars, and had approached the signal fire when he heard a woman's panting.

On the verge of calling out, he'd heard a man grunt and the rustle of cloth on stone.

Water Bow had stopped, unwilling to intrude on what was a private moment.

"Gods." Larkspur's throaty whisper had barely carried to Water Bow's straining ears. "I miss a man's hard staff."

"There is always opportunity in the wind."

"How is that?"

"You and I work very well together, Matron."

"Is that ambition, Deputy?"

"You have Desert Willow's confidence, and you are in

line to be Matron of the First People should anything happen to her."

"She's young."

"So are you."

"I'm married."

A pause.

"Do you love him?"

"How could I? I haven't seen him for seasons on end. He's not an imaginative man. There's a reason Webworm sent him south. He follows orders, but thinking is too trying for him."

"I see."

"And?"

"You think a great deal, and you long for more."

Larkspur had shifted. Peering around the tall pile of wood, Water Bow could see her arms where she tightened them around Leather Hand's back. She said, "Tell me, Deputy, if we were to work together, do you think we could achieve more?"

"If our bodies are this good together, think of what the mating of our souls could bring."

"I would like to explore that," she'd whispered, "assuming I was to find myself suddenly without a husband."

Water Bow had eased himself away before Sister Moon could rise high enough to reveal his presence. The next morning he'd seen one of Leather Hand's warriors sneaking out of Pinnacle Great House, a large travel pack on the man's shoulders. To Water Bow's surprise, the man hadn't been wearing his red war shirt, preferring to travel unrecognized.

I wonder how long it will be before Larkspur's husband is found lying in his blankets, his head mysteriously missing?

Now, as he sat in the kiva, he knew Matron Larkspur's cunning smile was based on more than just the weather. For her, things were looking very good indeed.

"We are more secure than we have been in quite some time," Burning Smoke agreed. "With the elders in captivity, any threat from wild prophecies and possible attacks by Ironwood are nullified. With this moisture, the crops should be abundant. First Moon Valley can contribute even more to the famine relief in the south."

Water Bow watched Larkspur's growing smile. Apparently she was already imagining pack after pack of corn as it was borne out of the valley, headed for Flowing Waters Town. She was seeing another feather for her hair, and an even higher status in Desert Willow's eyes.

Beware Matron Desert Willow. Let us hope that the serpent you have created in Leather Hand does not strike you sometime in the night.

It would, of course. Leather Hand's ambition would only be rivaled by Larkspur's.

"We still have no idea where Ironwood is," Ravengrass said as he looked from face to face. "I first served under him. It doesn't pay to underestimate the man."

"I think we can be assured that he'll be headed south as soon as he hears of Night Sun's capture." Larkspur's eyes had narrowed. "He has surrendered his ambitions for Night Sun before; there is no reason to think he is a different man today than he has always been."

"You must admire him," Water Bow said, curious to elicit her reaction. "It's hard to condemn a man who would sacrifice so much for the woman he loves. Such an undying love is hard to find, and should be appreciated."

Her smile was wooden. The kind she'd give a doddering old fool.

"I've half a mind to call the guards in," Burning Smoke said. "In this weather, they're not going to be able to see an arm's length in any direction. And the Matron's right: With the First People elders in our hands, no one will try anything."

"Do not delude yourself," Ravengrass said. "Until we hear that Ironwood is spotted in the south, we must remain vigilant."

"I have twice the number of men on the ridge below us." Burning Wood insisted. "In this weather, no one could find their way up the slopes. Not even Ironwood is that crazy. Besides, he'd lose half his command to treacherous footing. Those who didn't slip and break bones would be lost within moments of entering that thick timber."

"You're probably right." Ravengrass steepled his fingers, eyes on the leaping fire. "But I'll take a chance on the sentries just in case."

Burning Smoke had a big smile on his face, and said, "Oh, you won't have any worry. Matron Larkspur's right. The Flute Player is on our side. Nothing could go wrong now."

Fifty-seven

Wrapped Wrist waited his turn in the dark and leaned close to Crow Woman. "How's your knee?" Around them, the trees swayed and thrashed as the storm intensified under the First Moon Mountain rim.

"Stiff and sore," she growled back. "But I'm not missing this."

"Can you climb?"

He heard her swallow hard before she admitted, "I'm not sure. Whatever happens, I've got to get up there. I won't let the others down."

"Wait. When I go up, I'll pull you. All you have to do is keep your grip on the rope and keep from banging your knee on the rocks. No one will know."

He got a quick squeeze from her hand before he turned to the rock face and scrambled up. Like Bad Cast, he'd been climbing since he was a boy. It was just part of growing up in the First Moon Valley. Ready hands pulled him onto the caprock.

"Here," Wrapped Wrist told Yucca Sock. "Let me do this." He handed the man his atlatl darts, took the braided leather rope, and shook it. He felt Crow Woman take her grip and give him a ready tug.

He stood, bracing himself against the wind, which blew snow and acrid smoke. Gods, the stench of it: wet ash and slush. He knotted his grip and flexed his muscles. Crow Woman wasn't light by any means, but he pulled her up with ease. She caught herself as he lifted her past the rim-rock. She swung to the side, getting her feet under her. For a brief instant, she put her arms around him, hugged him, and then vanished into the dark.

"Which way?" Ironwood asked.

Wrapped Wrist squinted in the blackness. Trickles of water from snowflakes stung his eyes. When it ran into his mouth, he could taste soot. Gods, it was cold up here, the wind blowing a blizzard.

"We're but a stone's throw," he said. "Pinnacle Great House is just above us, the Eagle's Fist below."

"I will attend to the Eagle's Fist," Yucca Sock said. "I have business with the First People." He turned, vanishing into the blowing snow.

Wrapped Wrist had bowed his head, letting his shoulder take the brunt of the blizzard. Snow was packing on his side. Amazed, he realized he could see faint images.

"Sister Moon has risen by now," Crow Woman said, voice hollow. "She stares down at the cloud and smoke. She is come home to watch the destruction of our world."

"Let's go," Ironwood ordered. "Pairs of two. First group take the building's west wing; second group with me attacks the east. Remember, we want as many of the First People taken alive as possible, but your first concern is the rescue and safety of the elders."

Wrapped Wrist stayed close to Crow Woman, trudging against the wind. The big flakes of snow pattered against the side of his face. Any trace of heat had vanished from his claylike flesh. Gods, how could the warriors manage to wield a bow in weather like this? Their fingers had to feel as wooden as his own.

He tapped the atlatl darts he had taken from beside Spots's bed. Thank the Spirits his people remained some of the last holdouts for the atlatl. He could nock and cast no matter how numb his fingers became.

The wall loomed out of the night, dark and foreboding. In the faint storm glow, Wrapped Wrist could see snow beginning to crust on the rocks. A shivering fit left him shaken and miserable.

Then, from the night, a sudden cry: *"Alarm!"*

Crow Woman hissed. "Hurry up! We're spotted."

Wrapped Wrist pounded his way forward and followed Two Teeth up the stairs onto the first-floor roof. Dark figures were spilling out of the kiva as well as from the lower-floor rooms.

He charged forward, nocking a dart. Before he could use it, a man seemed to rise from the very roof. He heard the whistle of the war club, turned, and took the blow meant for his ribs on the shoulder. At the impact, his entire left arm went numb.

Wrapped Wrist staggered, gasping with pain. He heard the warrior laugh as he stepped in, bringing the war club high. In that instant, a dark shape twisted out of the night; a smacking slap came as Crow Woman drove her war club down on the warrior's suddenly lifted arm. In lightning movements, she literally danced around him, slashing, chopping, and finally crushing the enemy's skull with a snapping blow.

"Thanks," Wrapped Wrist said through gritted teeth.

"Broken?" she asked, crouching beside him, eyes on the wavering figures who fought around them. Was it just Wrapped Wrist's inexperience, or were there a lot of warriors emerging from the rooms?

Wrapped Wrist flexed his elbow and raised his arm. "I don't think it's broken."

"Stay behind me. Watch my back."

"Glad to." It was sobering to think how close he'd just come to death. The fight became a melee of whirling figures, screaming men, and hissing arrows.

Spots could have turned and run—should have bolted like a panicked jackrabbit—but something had kept him walking obediently at Nightshade's heel as she climbed up the tiered levels of Dusk House, into the forbidden territory of the First People.

No one seemed to give her a second glance as she walked regally in the macaw-feather cloak, the hideous mask tucked beneath one arm. She crossed the second-floor roof and climbed to the third. She never hesitated as she turned and walked straight past a guard, the poor fellow huddled under a deerhide cape. He stared out from under his blanket. "Elder? Excuse me. That's the Blessed Sun's room. Do I know you?"

Unconcerned, Nightshade ducked into Webworm's personal quarters.

The guard muttered, stared uncertainly at Spots, and stood while he fumbled for his war club.

The action was instinctive. Spots stepped close, ripped the man's stiletto from his belt, and drove it straight into the warrior's breast. At the same time he clamped his left hand over the man's throat, squeezing his cry short in his windpipe.

Hot blood spilled over his hand. Within moments the guard's flailing ceased, his body limp in Spots's arms. The man sank, tremors running down his legs and arms.

Spots's own breath came in fast gulps. He shivered, and stumbled toward the doorway.

What did I just do? What came over me?

In the Blessed Sun's ornate room, coals glowed in the fire bowl. Spots stared in amazement at his blood-slick hand.

"Come sit," Nightshade whispered.

Spots staggered forward, still in shock. Looking around, he recognized several of the pieces of wood he'd Traded that day in the Blessed Sun's woodpile. Who would have thought? Then, to his amazement, he realized that the form under the blankets was none other than Webworm himself.

He must have looked like a gaping idiot when Nightshade motioned him to be seated atop a pile of buffalo-hides that had been stacked against one wall.

I've got to run! I just killed a Red Shirt! But his muscles had frozen.

Moving quietly, Nightshade retrieved her familiar pack from where it hung on a corner peg. She reached inside and withdrew several pouches. Her long fingers took a pinch of something from one. This she sprinkled atop the glowing coals. A faint but pungent smoke rose from the hearth.

Nightshade lifted a narrow pitcher from beside the bed and poured water into a striking white cup decorated with thin black lines and patterns of dots. Into this she poured yet another potion from one of her little bags. After she removed her shining black bowl, she dipped a thick dab of paste onto her fingertip. This she touched ever so lightly to Webworm's temples. She made a faint grunt of satisfaction.

Spots just stared, wondering what had possessed him to follow her here. Nightshade was inspecting the line of pots and jars. She picked one—a wide-necked black-and-white Green Mesa design with a wooden lid. Raising the lid, she dumped the red cornmeal it contained onto the floor and set the open jar by her side.

Finally she gave Spots a warning look. "No matter what, say nothing. Do nothing." Then she sat back, donned the hideous mask, and began to chant.

How long they sat there, Spots couldn't say, but periodically Nightshade would reach out to dab more of the datura-laced paste and rub it with ever more vigor onto Webworm's temples. Meanwhile, the wind howled outside, and Spots grew ever more frightened.

Someone will come and find me here. When they do, I am going to die.

In all of his wild nightmares he would never have believed that he would be seated like an idol, terrified to the point of jumping out of his skin, across from the Blessed Sun's bed.

Webworm tossed and turned, mutters and moans coming from deep in his throat.

"That is Sister Datura wrapping her souls around you, Webworm." Nightshade spoke gently. "Let yourself go.

Rise and twirl in her arms. Surrender yourself, Webworm." She paused while Webworm mumbled, swallowed hard, and groaned. "Yes, tell Sister Datura what you desire more than anything."

"*Cloud . . . Playing . . .*" Webworm whispered.

Spots made a face. Power was loose in the room. He could hear the subtle whispers and hisses as the voices from the sack began to tease the deep recesses of his souls. It seemed that each time the voices grew louder, Webworm's mutterings increased.

"Free yourself," Nightshade repeated as she reached forward and rubbed the datura over Webworm's lips.

"Elder?" Spots barely mouthed the words. "Are you trying to kill him?"

Spots jumped when Webworm screamed, "*Gods, no!*" The man sat bolt upright. "Night Sun! Don't burn! *Stop the fire!*"

Webworm blinked, eyes fixed on the distance. He rubbed his face, smearing the gray paste over his skin. With fumbling fingers he reached for the white cup Nightshade had filled and sucked down large swallows. As he finished the drink he froze, eyes sliding sideways to take in Nightshade's masked form. The now-empty cup sagged in his nerveless fingers.

"Who—who are you?" The words came with difficulty. His glazed eyes were wide with fear.

"I have come for your heart," Nightshade said in the formal tongue of the First People.

"My heart?" Webworm blinked, his eyes glassy from the drug. Sweat was beading on his skin, trickling down around his loose gray-streaked hair.

"You are no longer using it. Only the serpent lives there now. It is black, polluted by your actions. Your orders are reaping the storm, Blessed Sun. Your world is dying. If you doubt, go out and look to the north. See the wrath of Cold Bringing Woman. Feel the bitter flakes of snow that she blows out of the north."

"Snow?" he asked stupidly.

"Your harvest is freezing, Webworm. The Flute Player has been caught by surprise. The thlatsinas are Dancing even now. With each beat of their feet, they drive snow from Cold Bringing Woman's storm. The old gods never saw them as they left Cloud Maker Mountain, climbed the Rainbow Serpent, and crossed the smoke pall to help Cold Bringing Woman Dance the storm out of the north. By this time tomorrow, the ripening corn will be frozen solid on its cob. The beans will blacken in their pods, and the sunflowers will turn dark and wither. Some of the squash may be saved, but the immature gourds are lost."

"What snow?" he repeated, then crawled on wobbly hands and knees to the rear of the room. There he fumbled for the handles, and pulled down a wooden door that had been carefully fitted into the north wall.

A gust of wind immediately blew through the room, and with it came a chilling brace of winter air. Spots could see snowflakes as they blew into the room, landed on the floor, and melted into damp spots. Webworm stared out into the stygian night, sniffing at the damp smells of smoke and snow.

"Fire and ice," Nightshade said with an empty voice. "Opposites crossed. You sit at the crossroads of the old world and the new."

It took Webworm three tries to fit the doorway back in place. As suddenly the fire died down to a gleam. Nightshade added another piece of wood.

Webworm collapsed onto his butt, one leg crossed, an anxious look on his drug-slack face. "I can't lose the harvest. Thousands will revolt. They will blame me."

"You are too late." Nightshade's voice echoed from inside the mask. "The cock-hatched serpent cares only for itself. The only way to save yourself is to surrender your heart."

"Who are you?" He shot her a glassy glance. His voice began to slur. "Is that you, Seven Stars? Wait, you must be Blue Racer. But no. You're supposed to be atop First Moon Mountain. Yes, that's right, and if you don't bring the rain, I'm taking . . . taking your . . . heart." Even as he said them, the words choked in his throat. He shot a fearful glance at Nightshade's mask, eyes bulging, sweat popping out on his face.

"The time has come, Webworm. Your tortured Dreams must end. I've heard you crying and moaning in the night. You want to be free of that, don't you?"

"Yes." His head wobbled as he stared at her mask.

"I can save you from the serpent in the egg. He possesses your souls, and as long as he has them, your breath-heart soul will never escape to travel to the Sky Worlds. You will never see your beloved Cloud Playing, never hold her in your arms. You will never fly up toward Father Sun in the company of your mother, Featherstone. She has so many things to tell you now that her wits have returned."

"I can't give you my heart!" Webworm cried.

"You looked into the serpent's eye," she told him. "That was the moment it entered your body and wound its way into your heart."

His eyes had lost their focus, and he blinked in confusion. "I don't understand."

"Tell me," Nightshade asked. "Are you happy?"

"Happy?"

"Are you? Do you ever awaken, glad to be alive? Do you ever finish the day, thinking, 'I have a good life'?"

Webworm's face went from slack, to squinting, to slack. "My life stopped when Cloud Playing . . . my precious Cloud Playing . . . was . . . was murdered by Swallowtail. He took my Dreams away. . . ."

"And you took his evil fetish," she hissed. "You looked into its eye, and your souls, like his, were swallowed by the serpent. It coils inside you, Webworm. Only I can take it out, relieve the pain."

He nodded slowly, crawling back to his bed. "You swear? If you do this thing, I can go to Cloud Playing?"

"You can."

To Spots's amazement, Webworm began tugging at his shirt. The effort to pull it over his head was tremendous and came perilously close to defeating him. The fabric fell from his senseless fingers, and he sank back naked on his bed.

"It won't hurt?" Webworm slurred.

"Do you feel yourself flying?" Nightshade asked as she leaned forward.

"I'm floating. Lighter . . . lighter."

"That's Sister Datura, bearing you aloft. She can't take you all the way to the Cloud People until I remove your heart."

". . . The Serpent . . . stays with . . . ?"

"It will."

"I will . . . be free?"

"You will be free."

He yawned. ". . . Sleepy . . . now . . ."

"That's the morning glory powder you drank filling your veins. Let go, Webworm."

Spots gaped as the Blessed Sun closed his eyes, breathing deeply. His left arm skipped off his belly, landing on the bedding like dead meat.

"Elder?" Spots whispered.

"Shhh!" Her masked head swiveled, and he found himself staring into the Blue God's hard eyes.

His breath locked in his throat.

The terrible face swung back to Webworm. The man's breathing had slowed, his head lolled to the side. Spots could see his eyes rolled back in his head. His tongue lay in the side of his gaping mouth.

The curious chant rose on the air again as Nightshade reached into her pack and carefully laid out a spindle whorl, a length of thread, and a long obsidian blade.

"Elder, you can't—"

"Do not meddle, boy!"

He started, as if slapped. The voice issuing from behind the mask hadn't been Nightshade's.

The Blue God extended her bony hand, and the glassy blade glittered in the red light. With one swift motion, she cut a long slice that followed the V of Webworm's ribs.

The man jerked, air hissing as the blade sliced the diaphragm. Without effort, Nightshade batted his flailing arms aside, leaning over him as her hand disappeared under his breastbone.

Spots watched in disbelief as the old woman worked the blade this way and that. When she withdrew her blood-slick hands they gripped the quivering heart. Webworm's mouth worked like a fish's in air. Bug-eyed, he stared into eternity.

"Yes," the old woman said solicitously. "I hear you in there." Turning, she laid the heart inside the wide-necked jar, slapped the lid down, and sat back, sighing wearily. "Go, Webworm. You're free now. The serpent is safely removed."

Spots rose off his seat to stare into the slit in Webworm's chest. He could see pooled blood in the cavity where the man's heart had been. The Blessed Sun's feet were kicking weakly, his hands grasping at air. A gurgle sounded from his throat.

Nightshade was stringing thread around the spindle whorl. "Go now, Spots. Take the heart with you. No matter what, do not remove the lid until you are in the great kiva. The Priests will have returned from the fields and kindled a bonfire. Tell them you come with the offering of an elk heart. Cast it into the flames yourself. Stay only long enough to see that it is indeed burning, and then leave. Once outside the walls, smash the pot." She glared at him, and once again he was staring into the Blue God's eyes.

"I understand." His voice sounded weak.

He took the vessel, a beautiful thing, white-slipped and painted in the striking Green Mesa mountain-and-cloud designs.

He wasn't prepared for the weight. Gods, a man's heart couldn't be that heavy, could it?

"It's the evil inside," Nightshade told him. "Now, go. Your duty to me is finished, Spots. When you have smashed the pot, find your woman, but speak nothing of what you've seen here."

He almost stumbled, legs gone curiously awkward and stiff; he stepped out into the cold night. Snow twirled down to melt on the roof. The guard lay sprawled, a darker stain of blood on the wet roof.

The gods help me! Gods, please *help me!*

In the silent night, Spots made his way down the combination of ladders and stairways to the plaza level. With each step, the pot seemed to grow heavier. He skipped sideways as a serpent hissed from the night.

"Silly, in this temperature, a snake would be as slow as a stick." But he kept a hand atop the lid, clamping it in place as he rounded the great kiva. At the southern entrance several people waited, taking their turns one by one. Each carried a package, jar, or bundle of cloth: all equinox offerings tied to some sort of prayer for the coming season.

When his turn came, Spots carefully entered, bearing the beautiful pot. He made his way down the stone-and-pole steps and crossed the floor to the great crackling bonfire.

"You come to do honor to the season?" a white-robed Priest asked.

"I—I have an elk heart."

"We receive your offering," the Priest intoned. "Place it in the fire. Let the smoke rise and bear it to the Star People."

A swallow stuck in his throat as Spots grasped the bowl, tossing the lid and bloody heart into the center of the flame.

Even the Priest stepped back as the heart exploded in a loud hiss.

"You'd think it was a snake." The Priest laughed.

"Yes," Spots agreed absently. "You would."

He was turning to go when, to his amazement, he swore he saw a bloodred serpent come slithering out of the big severed artery. It whipped and twisted in the flames, growing smaller until it was but a flicker of red leaping this way and that over the coals.

"Gods," Spots breathed.

"Tell the next to enter," the oblivious Priest told him.

Once outside the Dusk House walls, Spots lifted the beautiful vessel high. As he smashed it on the hard-wet ground, he heard a faint cry in the snow-thick night.

Blessed Gods, what did I witness this night? Then, in panic, he ran as he'd never run before.

Fifty-eight

As wind-whipped snow whirled out of the night, Bad Cast kept to the shadows below the Pinnacle Great House wall. The sound of fighting rose above the moaning of the storm: wood clattering on wood; screams that tore from wounded throats; shouts of anger and insult; the meat-smacking sounds of war clubs hammering home.

The war chief had given him permission to leave after he'd guided the warriors to the mountaintop, but Bad Cast lingered. His heart pounded in his chest. His mouth was fear-dry, and his breathing came in gasps. Every muscle was charged to the trembling point.

A body sailed off the roof, thumping loudly as it landed in the snow a hand's length from Bad Cast's foot. The dying man issued a rasping gasp, twitched, and went still.

Peering, Bad Cast was able to determine that the face belonged to a stranger. A well-crafted war club lay beside the man's limp hand.

Bad Cast grabbed it up, surprised and awed that the handle was so warm. He hurried to the stairway that led up to the first floor. As his head cleared the wall he could see knots of warriors surging back and forth. They twisted, leapt, dodged, and slashed at each other, mere shapes in the falling snow.

A sprawled figure was alternately screaming and weeping as it kicked and bucked on the packed clay. Bad Cast stepped onto the roof, bending to see one of Ironwood's warriors. Was it Thorn Petal? The man had two feathered arrow shafts protruding from his chest. Even as Bad Cast extended a hand, the man uttered a croaking rasp and went still, his eyes staring into the falling snow.

Something hissed through the air beside Bad Cast's ear, and he leapt for the shadow of the dividing wall.

I'm not a warrior! That fact repeated down in his souls as he crept along the wall.

At that moment one of the white-robed Priests emerged from the Blue Dragonfly Clan kiva in the plaza floor. The man carried a pine-pitch torch in his hand as he emerged like some bizarre worm from the smoke hole. He stood on the ladder, torso protruding, waving the torch as he peered at the melee.

Bad Cast saw Crow Woman turn and hammer the man in the crown of the head; she skipped away. Wrapped Wrist trotted behind her, jabbing this way and that with a handful of hunting darts.

The Priest toppled, his robe snagging on one of the ladder uprights, and there he hung. The torch, pinned by his robe, set the cloth on fire. Yellow light leapt, illuminating the tumbling patterns of snowflakes where the wind whipped them in and out of the fighting.

Bad Cast suffered a sudden shiver. Ironwood's warriors were most definitely outnumbered. Six of them had been crowded back toward the western room block.

Where are the elders? Bad Cast forced a swallow down his tight throat and ran for the ladder leading up to the third-story roof.

Yes, that's where they'd be. Outside of Wrapped Wrist, he was the only one who knew the way. Assuming, that is, that the elders were being held in the same northern room where they'd kept Ripple.

On the third floor, he ran to Burning Smoke's room, hesitated at the doorway, and glanced back at the kiva. The dead Priest's robes flared as the man's hair caught fire. The corpse had a gruesomely black char to the skin. Then, the cloth burning through, it fell, one leg across a ladder rung, the body half in and out of the smoke hole. Smaller flames were licking on the dry wood of the entry.

Bad Cast ducked inside, ran to the shield, and tossed it aside. He clambered down the ladder into the darkness, felt for the second cover, and tossed it aside. Leaning his head over the dark hole in the floor, he called, "Anyone here?"

"Who comes?" a voice answered in his First Moon tongue.

"Bad Cast, of the Blue Stick Clan. Stand back. I'm lowering a ladder."

He felt around, located the ladder close to where they'd found it before, and lowered it into the depths. No sooner had the rungs thumped onto the floor than someone began climbing.

"What's happening?" the first young man asked as he emerged.

"Ironwood's warriors are fighting the First People," Bad Cast said. "It doesn't look good. There are weapons in the room above. Hurry."

Bad Cast assumed the young men who climbed out were the clan war chiefs. In the darkness he couldn't really tell. Then, bracing the ladder, he helped the elders as they climbed one by one from the lower level. They were old and frail, and he wasn't sure how they'd make it past the fighting, across the perilous ridge crest, and through the storm to safety.

"Bad Cast?" a raspy voice asked.

He helped an old white-haired man off the ladder. "Elder White Eye?"

"Has Cold Bringing Woman come?"

"Yes, Elder."

"And the fighting?"

"Not good. We are outnumbered."

"Then let us not waste time. Lead me to the way out."

In the confusion of the dark room, he wasn't sure, but he thought Elder Rattler, Green Claw, and Red Water climbed out before he led White Eye to the ladder. He followed the elder up into Burning Smoke's room. A wavering shaft of yellow light illuminated the doorway.

One hand on White Eye's arm, Bad Cast led the old man to the doorway and looked out. Fire still licked around the dead Priest's corpse. But how could a freshly dead man's . . . And then it came clear. The cedar-shake packing in the kiva roof, after moons of dry weather, had caught fire. He could hear people screaming from inside the kiva.

Bad Cast winced, wondering how many might be trapped there, watching helplessly as the fire burned around the plugged exit.

He had helped the old man onto the second level by the time the war chiefs charged into the fight. For long moments, they took the pressure off Crow Woman's little band of warriors where they'd backed against the room block.

Even as Bad Cast watched, the Blessed Sun's trained warriors parried blow after blow, ducked and dodged, and clubbed down their opponents. One red-shirted warrior caught Elder Rattler by the arm, threw her down, and crushed her skull with a single blow.

In a matter of moments, the other elders were likewise struck down.

Bad Cast stared in horror, and dragged White Eye back into the shadow cast by the second floor.

"What's happening?" the elder asked.

"The others, they're dead. Killed by the Blessed Sun's warriors."

"And Ironwood's people?"

Bad Cast raised his head to see. "Crow Woman led them into one of the rooms. They can't be attacked, except through the doorway."

"But they can't escape, either."

"No. They're cut off."

White Eye sighed. "Then it's only a matter of time."

A sensation of sudden despair sent an ache through Bad Cast. "So it would appear, Elder."

"The Blessed Sun's warriors need only to hack a hole through the roof of the room where Crow Woman's people are hidden. Through it, they can shoot arrow after arrow."

Bad Cast sat back, heedless of the thick flakes that fell around him. "Then we are all dead."

Wrapped Wrist hadn't meant to become separated. One minute he was behind Crow Woman, and the next an enemy warrior came charging up. Without time to nock his dart, Wrapped Wrist used them as a cluster of short spears, jabbing them into the man's belly. The warrior shrieked, trying to backpedal. By the time Wrapped Wrist jerked his darts loose, Crow Woman was gone, and what seemed like a flood of red-shirted warriors were flocking between him and the other warriors.

As First Moon war chiefs emerged from Burning Smoke's upper room, Wrapped Wrist clambered up the ladder that led to the eastern plaza.

There, too, the battle swirled, Ironwood leading his warriors forward as they fought their way into the plaza. His men seemed to draw from the great war chief's very presence, their actions heroic as they crouched and loosened flight after flight of arrows into the warriors who emerged from the rooms that lined the plaza. The screams and shrieks of wounded men mingled with the falling snow.

"Ironwood!" someone cried. "Leave him to me!"

Wrapped Wrist turned to see a muscular warrior start through the press of the Blessed Sun's warriors. At mention of the name, the red-shirted warriors began to fall back.

"Ravengrass?" Ironwood strode through his ranks of kneeling warriors. As he approached, an arrow drove into Ravengrass's throat. The man clutched at the quivering shaft, turned, and wilted onto the packed clay.

Goaded by shouts of rage, the Blessed Sun's warriors charged. Wrapped Wrist bent, staring down into the kiva. He could see worried Priests picking up ritual clothing, bagging sacred masks, and staring up with fright.

Arrows hissed past his ear as he laid his darts and atlatl aside and grasped the heavy ladder. No ordinary man could have lifted the heavy weight; rung by rung he pulled it from the depths. Below, the Priests were dumbfounded, and in the time it took for them to recover their wits, one of Ironwood's warriors ran up. As the first of the Priests reached to pull the ladder back down, an arrow sliced down through the man's chest.

Wrapped Wrist muscled the teetering ladder into the wind, letting it drop atop the milling enemy warriors.

Ironwood's men shouted, and threw themselves on the disorganized foe.

"Form up!" came the stern order as War Chief Burning Smoke descended the ladder from the third-tier rooms. "We outnumber them! Fight like you've been trained."

Gods, I am no warrior. So what can I do? Diversion, that was it. Something to take the pressure off Crow Woman and Ironwood.

Wrapped Wrist ducked into one of the plaza-level rooms and almost tripped over a coal-filled fire bowl. This he dumped into the neat stack of firewood. Room by room, he made his way around the plaza floor; in each he set fire to the woodpiles, or dropped the coals in rush matting. He poured grease onto cloth bedding and propped it where the oily flames licked at the dry roofing.

When he emerged again, it was to see Ironwood's men being pushed relentlessly back. Burning Smoke had restored order and spirit. *So many warriors.*

Wrapped Wrist sucked cold air into his hot lungs. Smoke was billowing from the rooms along the northern wall. Each of the doorways was outlined by a red-orange glow.

What is happening to Crow Woman? Could he set fire to the other side, too? He crouched, sneaking behind the battling warriors to climb atop the dividing line of rooms.

Flames were rising from the western kiva. Red-shirted warriors lurked to either side of the western room block, bows curved as they periodically released arrows into one of the room doors. He studied the bodies illuminated by the burning kiva. None of the sprawled corpses looked like Crow Woman. So, had she taken refuge in the room?

We are losing. He suffered a sinking sensation and dropped to his knees. Wild flakes of snow came whipping past, and in the firelight he could see that they were black, tainted with ash and smoke.

"Ripple, you saw it so well." And a knot formed in his throat as he remembered his dead friend's face, and the blood that had pooled under his head and dripped down the half-severed neck.

He raised his hands to the sky, crying, "Ripple? Where are you?"

When he looked back at the high third-floor rooms, it was to see Matron Larkspur as she stood imperiously beside Water Bow and a finely dressed Priest he assumed was Blue Racer.

The battle must have turned enough that they felt safe enough to watch, heedless of the fires that grew one floor down, beneath their feet.

The voice seemed to come from the blowing snow. *"We come, good friend. Fire . . . and ice."*

Larkspur stood before her room, a buffalo robe over her shoulders. She was heedless of the dirty snow that swirled and twisted from the night sky. Smoke was boiling out of the lower rooms, but she was unsure of its origin. As soon as the fighting was stopped, she'd have her warriors retrieve the big water-storage jars from the south-side rooms to douse any flames.

When she looked at the western kiva, however, her heart sank. Even over the shouts and fury of battle, she could hear the screams of the Priests trapped in that inferno. Smoke and flame rose in a huge curling torch that defied the storm. The doomed inside were no doubt huddled where the ventilator drafted cold air into the blaze.

"Kill them! Kill them all!" she shouted, stepping forward and raising an angry fist.

"Who are these people?" Blue Racer asked, stepping up by her side. He raised an arm protectively as hot air came curling up from the room beneath his feet.

"Ironwood's Outcasts," Waterbow said distastefully. "Matron, we're going to have to consider leaving this place."

She whirled on him. "Why? We're winning." She gestured to where Ironwood's warriors were retreating, their arrows slowed from a shower to a trickle as they backed away from her advancing warriors. Her people needed only to charge, close, and finish them with war clubs.

"We'll put the fires out. Then, you can bet, we're going to

take our revenge on the Moon People. I swear, by the time we're done with them, they'll wail for the days when . . ."

They came from the darkness and storm. The first Larkspur saw was a woman who emerged from the darkness carrying only a stone-headed hoe. Behind her came the rest: farmers with stout digging sticks, hunters with atlatls and hunting darts. Some of the men carried stone-headed axes, others sharp-edged adzes.

Larkspur's warriors stared at them in disbelief, then foolishly waved at them to go away. For so many years, their mere wish had been the barbarians' bane. This time, the Moon People were heedless.

"No!" Larkspur shouted. "Kill them! They, too, are the enemy!"

In the light of the fire, her warriors made perfect targets for the barbarian hunters. The heavy hunting darts, powered by atlatls, sliced through the warrior's shields meant only to stop cane-shafted arrows. Within moments, half of her warriors were screaming as they lay on the plaza, arms, chests, and legs pierced by the long darts. Ironwood's remaining warriors whooped and charged.

Larkspur stared in amazement as her warriors broke and ran, some clambering up the ladders, followed by screaming Moon People. On the roofs they were battered down, and she saw more than one of her warriors leap from the third-floor roof to certain death on the slope so far below.

More and more farmers appeared out of the blizzard night. The Moon People began to identify their dead elders where they lay sprawled on the packed clay. In a wave, the people rushed forward.

"Kill them!" Larkspur screamed. *"Kill them!"*

She was standing on the edge of her roof, aware that the floor beneath her feet had grown hot. Snowflakes whirled down and exploded in steam.

She stared, dumbfounded, as Moon People flooded across the plazas, picking up her warriors, tossing them alive and screaming into the burning kiva.

"Matron?" Water Bow reached out, placing a hand on her elbow. "It's time for us to leave this place."

"No, I am not about—"

She gaped as the woman with the stone hoe appeared on her ladder, leaped onto the roof, and hammered Blue Racer across the back. The Sunwatcher ran, screaming, leaping onto the lower second-floor roof in the western section. Water Bow scurried in his wake; he tripped and fell as he tried to scuttle down the ladder.

The hoe-wielding woman emerged from Larkspur's room, waving Larkspur's feather holder with its glorious plumage in triumph. In the light, she was a short stocky woman with scars on her forearms.

"Oh, no you—"

She didn't hear him coming. Hard hands grabbed her from behind, and she felt herself lifted. A man was carrying her toward the ladder as she shrieked and kicked, battering at his muscular arms with her fists.

"Shut up," the man growled in a Made People dialect. "I'm tired of Matrons, of Priests, and First People."

"Let me go!" she squealed. "I'll pay you. I can help you."

"We killed your assassin," he growled in her ear. "Takes Falls wasn't worth a jar of turquoise. He told us what you'd paid for the Prophet."

"It's yours. If you'll let me go!"

He'd borne her to the western plaza, where a crowd had formed. She had a glimpse as the Blue Dragonfly Clan kiva roof collapsed inward. Sparks and belching smoke rose as the flames leaped into the swirling snow. A growing roar could be heard as fire jetted from the depths. People screamed in delight as they Danced in the light of the maelstrom.

An image froze, caught between Larkspur's souls. She watched as Blue Racer was tossed high, his body seeming to hang for the briefest of moments before it dropped into the raging flames.

The people cheered.

Then it was Water Bow, his form sent arching into the air. His arms and legs windmilled futilely as he fell into the glowing depths.

A desperate voice called, "No! In the name of the gods, *No!*"

Larkspur saw Ironwood, pulling at the crowd, trying to drag them back.

"Don't kill them!" Ironwood begged, his one-eyed face a mask of horror. "We need them alive! They are the way—"

Larkspur never heard the rest. The brawny man who carried her, slung her around. More hard hands clamped onto her legs and arms. She felt the strain as they swung her back and forth. Then she was flying, her body arching high.

Her scream tore as she fell into the scorching heat. Her body hit the angle of the collapsed roof. She tumbled down into pain and flames. Her hair exploded. When she drew a breath, it was filled with searing fire.

Fir Brush stood at the edge of the roof, one hand on Bad Cast's shoulder as she watched the great house burn. White Eye stood on Bad Cast's other side, partially supported by Soft Cloth.

"Another roof just fell in," Soft Cloth told the elder. "The sparks are whirling up into the air. The snow is falling in a red veil that fills the sky. It looks like bloody feathers as it swirls out of the night."

Fir Brush watched mute. It had no form, no shape in her souls. When they had left the kiva that afternoon, they had had no order, just a quiet desperation. The council had disintegrated without the leadership of the elders. So many individuals had insisted on speaking. Some had argued for war, others for peace.

Some called for revenge for Ripple's death. Others insisted that he was obviously a false Prophet, or no assassin could have killed him.

In the end, they had trickled away by ones and twos to climb First Moon Mountain. They had watched the great forest fire as it burned down from the north, felt the change in the wind, and stopped to borrow blankets and clothing from relatives who lived on the mountain.

By the time the first flakes of snow had been whisked across the mountain by the whistling wind, the words,

"Cold Bringing Woman's promise" and "Ripple's vision" were passing from lip to lip.

As the temperature dropped, they had crowded toward Guest House, creeping up in the dark, filing past. When one of the Made People stepped out to protest, he was clubbed down. For the most part, the other Made People just watched them pass, like wraiths in the storm.

What amazed Fir Brush was how quiet they had been. Even when they approached the Eagle's Fist, no one had spoken.

"Who comes?" Yucca Sock had called, and Orenda had answered, "The people come, Yucca Sock. Let them pass."

As Fir Brush led the first of them up the ladder, it was to find the western plaza kiva shooting a yellow column of flame into the night.

Later Fir Brush would only remember images, nothing particularly coherent. She would remember the shrieks of rage and horror as the elders were discovered dead. She had seen Crow Woman and Wrapped Wrist as they ran into each other's arms.

She remembered Yellow Petal, shrieking and Dancing as she clutched a red-painted feather holder she'd taken from Larkspur's room. She clutched it to her chest, the eagle, hawk, and macaw feathers waving back and forth. She was leaping as she cavorted with Black Bush and his teenage sister, Red Thorn. They weren't the only ones. Everyone was looting the place, racing the flames as they burned through roof after roof.

Finally she remembered Ironwood shouting, pleading, as her people found Matron Larkspur, Burning Smoke, and Water Bow. They were dragged kicking and screaming from the smoking rooms.

He was frantic, trying to stop the howling Moon People, as one by one, they threw the First People, screaming, into the burning kiva.

In the end, Ironwood had collapsed onto his knees, Pinnacle Great House burning around him. He knelt there, sweaty skin shining in the firelight, head bowed, shoulders slumped in defeat. He might even have died there, consumed with the rest, but Crow Woman and

Wrapped Wrist braved the heat and dragged him from the growing inferno.

"What terror have we wrought?" Bad Cast asked.

"The end of our world," White Eye answered. "Come. Someone needs to get me off this mountain before I freeze. The storm is intensifying. We need to seek shelter."

"There is no shelter," Fir Brush said. "Not for my brother, or me, or any of us."

Fifty-nine

THE UNBROKEN CIRCLE

Oh, yes, at my age I know exactly what life is.

Life is the flash of a raven's wings in the sunlight. It is the white breath of the buffalo in the wintertime. It thrives in the glowing bellies of the Cloud People as they sail across the sky to melt into the sunrise.

And Death?

Death is no mystery.

It is merely the raven's dark wing.

It reflects from the buffalo's black hooves, stamping out eternity.

It is the crackle of a thunderhead flashing lightning.

Do you really believe there is a difference between a raven's wing and a raven's wing flashing sunlight? A raven is still a raven. Or between a buffalo's white breath and those terrible churning black hooves? It is still a buffalo. Or a glowing cloud and a roaring thunderhead? Both are manifestations of a cloud.

No matter what foolish holy people try to tell you, there is only one animal.

It lives to die.

And it dies to live.

No other truth is as simple.
Or as complex.

Cold settled on the land, deep and unforgiving as violent winds blew the storm on to the south. In its wake, a crystal sky gave way to the promise of sunrise.

War Chief Wind Leaf climbed onto the fourth-story roof and stared out in disbelief at the blue world around him. His breath froze before his face, his eyes on the fields. Snow draped the corn as if carefully laid. Icicles hung sparkling from the long green leaves. Bean plants bowed under the white weight, and the larger squash wore hats of snow.

The harvest! Wind Leaf could feel his heart slow, each beat sodden in his chest as the realization came home. But how far had the storm extended? Was it just here, localized to Flowing Waters Town?

In every direction he looked, the hills leading up to the horizon were a crisp white.

He shivered in his cloak, staring with glum disbelief. He barely heard Matron Desert Willow as she climbed up beside him. This morning she wore a buffalo coat, her arms held snug around her slender body.

"How could this have happened?" Her voice was small in the morning.

"We must tell the Blessed Sun." He couldn't help but take one last look at the end of Dreams. "After that, we need to recall as many warriors as possible. Maintaining order is going to be a problem."

He led the way, taking careful steps on the frozen ladder. He stopped, staring at the guard who sat before the Blessed Sun's door. The man had frost on his hair, streaks of ice where water had melted and then frozen on his clothing or run down into his neck.

Wind Leaf reached out, shoving him. The fellow sprawled dead on his blanket.

"Well, he didn't shirk his duty," Desert Willow murmured. Her voice was oddly detached, as if she, too, were beginning to understand the enormity of the disaster facing them.

"No." Wind Leaf fingered the frost. "This is blood." Panicked, he ducked into Webworm's quarters, calling, "Blessed Sun, are you . . . ?" He stared at the figure who sat beside the Blessed Sun's bed. She looked regal, a macaw-feather cloak about her shoulders. Long white hair tumbled down her shoulders; he'd have sworn her composed face actually glowed. She raised dark eyes to his, and his heart skipped. He might have been staring into an endless midnight.

"Blessed Sun?" Desert Willow snapped. "Who is this? Why is she here?"

"It's the Mountain Witch," Wind Leaf said, finally catching his breath. He glanced at Webworm's naked body. "And I don't think the Blessed Sun is going to be answering any more questions."

Desert Willow stepped over, her buffalo coat dragging on the floor. She gasped as she saw the slit in her husband's chest, realized that the dark stains were blood.

"Where is his heart?"

"Gone," the Mountain Witch said in formal tongue. "I have drawn it out, sent it away. His souls have been purified, and are already on the way to the Blessed Cloud People. By now he is with Cloud Playing and Featherstone. I have finished my duties here."

"Your duties?" Wind Leaf demanded. "What have you done with the Blessed Sun's heart?"

The old woman smiled. "I have purified it." She inclined her head slightly. "A serpent hatched of a cock's egg is the worst kind of evil. Webworm, despite his faults, deserved better than that. Now, with the coming of this morning, my work is finished."

"Your work?" Desert Willow demanded hotly. "Is your work assassination and witchcraft?"

"I am the Witness," the old woman said simply. "Your world is ended." Her dark eyes seemed to swell in her face. "May the gods have mercy on the people."

"Get her out of here," Desert Willow snapped. "Drag

her down into the plaza and break her neck. No, burn her alive. Anything, as long as she screams and wails."

Wind Leaf grabbed the old woman's pack, upending it, finding a bloody spindle whorl, little bags of powders, a gleaming black pot full of paste, and several hide-wrapped bundles that sent prickles up and down his arms. He found nothing that resembled a human heart.

"What if she's going to use his heart to witch us?" he growled, emptying pots, searching the rolled hides. Through it all, the Mountain Witch sat, perfectly composed as they ransacked the Blessed Sun's quarters.

Wind Leaf checked outside, looking carefully. The only steps in the frost were his and Desert Willow's.

He ducked back inside, thrusting his face close to hers. "Where's the heart?"

"Where you'll never find it."

"We'll see about that."

Desert Willow raised a restraining hand. "No, we probably won't. There are a thousand things she could have done with it. Perhaps tossed it out the back window to an accomplice, or even sliced it up and eaten it." She pointed. "Look, there's a bloody spindle whorl. You know what witches do with those."

"If she's going to use it to witch us, we have to know, Matron. We have to be able to protect ourselves."

Desert Willow nodded, a new fear in her eyes.

Wind Leaf grabbed the old woman's hand. She didn't resist as he thrust it into the hot coals in the warming bowl. No expression crossed Nightshade's face as her skin burned and her nails began to curl.

It was the odor of cooking flesh that made him relent. "Where is the heart?"

"Gone," she said simply.

He stared, sharing Desert Willow's disbelief. What human wouldn't howl in agony as their hand was subjected to such heat?

Desert Willow frowned, thinking. "You remember the witch boy?"

"The one with the little dog? The one we walled up?"

"Take her down to one of the lower rooms," Desert Willow ordered. "Stake her there so that her souls can't escape, but do it in a manner that doesn't kill her immediately. Then leave her in the dark. Each day, you will go down, ask her what she did with Webworm's heart. When she tells you, she can finally die. Quickly, without more suffering."

Wind Leaf stared at his Matron, envisioning the kind of death this would be. "Stake her?"

Desert Willow was fingering her chin, eyes narrowed as she glared into the witch's eyes. "I'm not in a forgiving mood, War Chief. Stake her to the floor. Drive it through her pelvis, right down through her womanhood." A pause. "She'll talk in the end."

Wind Leaf felt suddenly hot, as if on the verge of sickness, but he nodded. "As you order."

"And do it yourself," she added. "This, I don't want you to delegate."

"Come," Wind Leaf said. "But leave your poisons here. And take off the Priest's robes. You'll die naked."

He watched as the old woman shrugged out of the beautiful cloak, then pulled the white tunic over her head. How she did it with a half-cooked hand was miraculous, but no expression of pain crossed her face.

When they stepped out into the cold, Wind Leaf glanced at the dead guard. Gods, how Powerful was this old hag?

Seeing one his guards on the second floor, he called, "Bring me a heavy stone-headed mallet and a thick wooden stake. And hurry!"

As his guard hastened to his task, Wind Leaf took one last look at the morning, purple and violet now. The final stars were vanishing from the west. "Take a good hard look, witch. It's the last sunrise you'll ever see."

She lifted her eyes to the sky, smiled, and then cast one glance down at the plaza. For a moment her gaze lingered on the wood Trader and Cactus Flower, who had arrived early that day. No wonder—the demand for firewood would be huge.

Wind Leaf shoved her violently into the gloom of the third floor. He had a room in mind, one where no one would hear her scream; and in the end, it would be easy to rock up and seal forever.

Leather Hand climbed wearily up the ladder that led out of the Red Lacewing Clan kiva. His eyes were gritty, his nose burning from the smoke. Time had gotten away from him. Night Sun, by the gods, what motivated that woman?

He stepped out onto the kiva roof, cold hitting him like a wave. He blinked, seeing the dusting of soot-grayed snow that had settled on the curving walls of Talon Town. It frosted the high sandstone cliffs, and occasional flakes, mostly white now, still drifted down from the clearing skies.

Snow? This early in the year? For a moment the incongruity of it left him stumbling. Only then did the implications begin to sink in. *What does this mean for the harvest?*

He shook his head, blinked his eyes, and plodded to the ladder that led up to the room he'd chosen. Once it had belonged to the Blessed Sun. And it would again, when he and Larkspur led the Straight Path Nation back to this canyon.

Snow?

A shiver of unease ran through him, and he puffed a breath into the cold air, watching it frost before him. Gods, it was cold. Not just chilly, but frozen cold. He could see ice where the first flakes of snow had melted and trickled down the cracked plaster walls. Ice was slick underfoot, too.

Ice meant a deep frost.

A premonition of disaster festered between his souls. *No, shake it off.* He was tired, exhausted, after a day and night of battling with Night Sun. That look she had given him would mock his memory for the rest of his life.

Next time, I shall gouge her eyes out. Then she

couldn't project that haughty arrogance that drove him half-insane.

She'd almost won, almost driven him too far. But at the last minute, his wits had returned, buffering the anger that had driven him. He had caught himself on the verge of murder, and relented.

Dead, you are of no more use, Matron.

He yawned, rubbed the back of his neck, and allowed the terrible cold to seep into his hot body.

Snow? What did that mean for the future? For his future, once he had destroyed Ironwood, claimed Larkspur, and brought his people home?

He bent his head back, feeling light snowflakes as they landed on his face. "Blue God? Am I only to be a ruler of the dead?"

Night Sun's knowing gaze burned in his memory.

"Tomorrow," he promised, "you will beg me to end it."

Yes, tomorrow. And after that, he would discover the extent of the frost. Webworm would be needing him more than ever.

He reached into his pouch, pulling out the carved fetish Webworm had given him. The little serpent coiled inside the broken eggshell. In the storm light, the coral eye seemed to glow with an internal illumination.

Bad Cast made his way past the Eagle's Fist. Fresh snow covered the bloodstains. He had spent the night at Fir Brush's, and had taken Ripple's winter moccasins as well as a blanket for the climb. He nodded to several people who were headed back down the mountain. People were torn, as desperate to see the burned great house as they were to inspect their fields.

Clusters of people hunched in the cold predawn. Their breath hung in frost around their heads. They talked, voices low, as they watched the blue smoke rise into the still air.

Bad Cast found Ironwood standing atop the western plaza by the stairway. The war chief was staring down into the smoking ruin of the kiva.

Heat from the fire had melted the snow here; Bad Cast climbed up beside him.

For long moments he stared down in silence, seeing the black timbers scabbed by white as coals ate into the remaining wood. Dirt and debris had fallen into piles. Heat radiated out in waves that rippled in the cold air. In the gaps between sections of still-burning roof, the corpses could be seen. Where the fire had been hottest, ash and cindered bone remained. A black mass of tangled limbs clustered beside the ventilator shaft. The upthrust arms, twisted legs, and pulled-back heads could only hint at the agony of their last moments. Open mouths exposed blackened and cracked teeth. Noses were mere holes, the flesh turned to ash, eyes but pits of darker black. When the breeze changed, the odor of charred flesh stung his nostrils; smoke brought tears to his eyes.

"The First People are finished." Ironwood's stare remained fixed on the macabre and grotesquely distorted dead.

"Perhaps we are all finished. My people are trying to save what they can of the harvest. Some are shaving corn from the cobs, seeking to dry it before it rots. Others are cooking green beans and frozen squash, or trying to rig drying and smoking racks."

"It won't be enough," Ironwood said.

"No," Bad Cast agreed.

After a long silence, Ironwood asked, "What will you do?"

He glanced to the north, where patchy snow could be seen on the gray slopes of the hills. Burned timber looked like black fuzzy hair. "There's no hunting up there. The game will have fled. Our crops are frozen. Ripple told me to head to the Great River Valley. He must have seen this, too."

Ironwood continued to stare down at the corpses. "I was going to exchange them for Night Sun. Now, I don't know. I suppose I'll take my warriors, see what can be done at Flowing Waters Town. If the frost went that far south, there may be enough confusion that my people can sneak in and free her."

"I pray that the gods go with you, War Chief."

"And with you," Ironwood answered wearily.

"Oh, I think I've had enough of the gods for a while," Bad Cast said. "Their company comes at too high a price."

Sixty

Wrapped Wrist led the way, picking a trail that wound down through the thinning timber. The route kept to the brushy valleys where lookouts wouldn't be apt to spot them. The Blessed Sun would send any retaliatory war parties up the River of Souls Valley to its confluence with the River of Stones, and north into First Moon Valley. Ironwood's small band of warriors hoped to avoid that main force.

If Webworm attacked First Moon Valley, so much the better. Wrapped Wrist's people had already dispatched more than enough scouts to give fair warning. So, too, had hunters gone, bearing their atlatls, to ambush the trails. Those who knew the bow had taken to making war arrows. Everyone expected a terrible retaliation, but this time, the red-shirted warriors would have to fight for every step. Feelings in First Moon Valley were running high. Storage of surpluses from previous years—food that would have tided the people through the current disaster—had been emptied for the Blessed Sun's tribute.

People who faced starvation didn't fear much from a quick death in battle.

Wrapped Wrist glanced behind him, seeing Crow Woman where she trotted warily along. Behind her, the warriors of Ironwood's surviving band carried their round shields, both wicker and leather-bound. Arrows bristled from quivers, and war clubs hung from belts. Yucca Sock and Firehorn brought up the rear, often checking the back-trail to make sure that no one followed.

Ten. That's all we have left. When, he wondered, had he begun to think of himself as one of them?

The way led down out of the timber, into a broken upland filled with sandstone-capped mesas and juniper-dotted slopes. The drainages here remained damp with runoff from Cold Bringing Woman's storm. Overhead, the midday sun beat down, the temperature pleasant. As was their way, the desert plants were blooming, the sagebrush and rabbitbrush having received enough moisture to flower. A heavy frost might be disastrous to food crops, but it didn't kill the drought-resistant brush.

Topping a rise, Wrapped Wrist caught sight of a man. Immediately he raised his arm, stopping. Behind him, he knew that Ironwood and his warriors were melting into the trees.

The lone figure in the trail was bent under a huge load of sticks and branches. The wood was all gray and sun-bleached, tied into a bundle with a thick leather thong about the middle.

Wrapped Wrist looked around, seeing only the solitary traveler. Assured the man was alone he trotted over the rise, calling, "Greetings!"

The figure turned, shadowed by the heavy load. "Greetings yourself."

"You have no one to help?"

"Unfortunately. Otherwise I could share this burden. You want to carry half?"

Wrapped Wrist thought the voice familiar, but had to trot closer to squint at the shadowed face. He noticed the patterns on the fire-mottled left arm. "Spots?"

"Wrapped Wrist?" Spots swung his load off his shoulder and let it clatter onto the ground. He grinned, winced as he straightened, and walked into Wrapped Wrist's warm embrace.

"Gods, it's good to see you." Wrapped Wrist patted his friend's back, holding his darts in his left hand. "We thought you were dead."

"Hunting?" Spots asked, indicating the darts. "Bit far to

carry meat, isn't it? And wait a minute, aren't those my darts?"

"What are you doing here?"

"I'm a wood Trader." Spots's smile faded. "It's been an interesting moon, let me tell you. We've heard terrible stories about what happened in First Moon Valley. Yesterday morning the first fleeing people passed. They said that Ripple was dead, that all the First People were murdered, that Pinnacle Great House was burned."

"All true." Wrapped Wrist shrugged, wishing he could forget the horrible images in the kiva bottom. "I was there."

"And Bad Cast?"

"He's coming to meet us at Flowing Waters Town. He's traveling with Soft Cloth and the baby. We thought it would be safer that way. Yellow Petal is trying to hang on. You should see the feather holder she has. Black Bush is urging her to go south. There are stories of a valley that didn't freeze. Fir Brush and Slipped Bark might go with her." He looked around. "Where's the Mountain Witch?"

"Captive in Flowing Waters Town. I'm trying to figure out how to free her."

"And Night Sun?" Wrapped Wrist asked.

"The Matron?" Spots shrugged. "The rumor was that she was captured, but I haven't heard of her in Flowing Waters Town."

Ironwood's voice called, "That doesn't mean that Leather Hand didn't take her there." He emerged from the brush at the side of the trail, other warriors rising here and there as if by magic.

Spots smiled weakly. "War Chief. It is good to see you again."

"A Trader?" Ironwood asked. "Does Webworm know you're associated with Nightshade?"

Spots narrowed an eye. "Webworm doesn't know much these days, War Chief."

"Oh?" Ironwood's expression intensified.

"He's dead. No one knows. Desert Willow is keeping it quiet until she can call in enough warriors to ensure Flowing Waters Town's safety."

"Dead?" Ironwood asked. "How?"

Spots went grim. "Nightshade cut his heart out of his body. Nothing could ever have prepared me for the way of it. He lay down, Dancing with Sister Datura, and she cut it, still beating, from his chest. I carried it myself to the equinox kiva fire, and watched the serpent crawl out of it as it burned."

Ironwood's expression fell. "She cut out Webworm's . . . ? A *serpent* was in his heart?"

Spots said soberly. "It had taken possession of his souls. He'd been witched years ago."

"Did he say anything?"

"He wanted to find someone named Cloud Playing."

Ironwood's eyes fixed somewhere in the distance, and he stepped away, shoulders slumping. "Yes, of course he would."

Wrapped Wrist wondered at the man's reaction. He'd swear that watching the First People being burned alive at Pinnacle Great House had taken something out of Ironwood. Or was it just worry about his wife?

"What are the chances of sneaking into Flowing Waters Town?" Crow Woman asked as she walked up. "Are the guards vigilant?"

"Very," Spots answered, studying her intently. "I remember you."

Wrapped Wrist suffered a slight twinge at the interest in Spots's eyes. *Gods, I'm not jealous, am I?*

Spots continued. "A guard was . . . I killed him the night of Webworm's . . . Since then, Wind Leaf's been a terror on guards."

"But you can get in and out?" Crow Woman asked.

"I'm a Trader. I can get into the plaza, but it's not worth my life to try and climb onto the second floor."

"Night Sun would be somewhere deep in the interior rooms," Yucca Sock said, glancing unsurely to where Ironwood stood. The war chief had a hand pressed to his heart, as if it bothered him. Softness lay behind the war chief's eyes; a faint expression of pain pinched his lips.

"We've got to try," Crow Woman replied. "And we have

to do it in a way that doesn't expose us. Wind Leaf and Desert Willow will have everyone watching for us."

Spots cocked his jaw, thought behind his eyes.

From long habit, Wrapped Wrist asked, "You know something?"

Spots gave him a serious look. "I might. For the most part, Traders in Flowing Waters Town are invisible."

"Which means?" Yucca Sock asked.

"Have you ever heard of anyone named Creeper?"

At the name, Ironwood turned, alert again. "Just what would you know about Creeper?"

Leather Hand knelt, his hand on Night Sun's tangled gray hair. Mad rage coupled with a curious respect. He let his fingers smooth her gray locks. They'd gone stiff with age, but he could imagine how sleek they must have been when she was still young and beautiful.

He stared up at the square of sky visible overhead. It beckoned, a deep and crystalline blue.

"I'm so sorry, War Chief," Turquoise Fox said. He stood, a cape over his shoulders, staring down uneasily at the old woman's corpse.

"No, it's all right." Leather Hand stood, head cocked. "I put that slave collar on her as a means of humiliating her. It was to break her spirit." A pause. "It takes a most clever adversary to turn a weapon back upon its wielder."

In the night, she had thrust her fingers under her slave collar, twisted it, and choked herself to death. As consciousness slipped away, the weight of her arm had kept the strangulation tight.

"So dies a Matron," he mused. Even in death her half-lidded eyes had a Power over him. "With her dies the last of her world."

He patted her head one last time, feeling the skull beneath her aged skin. When he rose to his feet, it was with a purpose. "Dead, she is no longer a lure for Ironwood. We need, however, to keep this news from the other captives. I want you to arrange to let the young woman escape. The strong-looking one. She must think she has managed this thing on her own."

Turquoise Fox grinned. "And of course she will run straight to Ironwood!"

"Precisely." He rubbed his hands together. "You know, there's a chance that Ironwood doesn't know where Night Sun was taken. Or perhaps Webworm already has him locked up at Flowing Waters Town. Meanwhile, take what's left of her and find some interior room to stick her in. Preferably an out-of-the-way place. Wall it up, or throw some matting over her. I don't care."

"Yes, War Chief." Turquoise Fox bent to pick up the old woman. A dot of blue caught his eye as a little carved wolf swung loose, dangling on a thong. He considered taking the talisman, then thought better of it. Perhaps she'd earned her guide to the Land of the Dead.

He climbed the ladder into sunlight and looked out at the dawn. The cold air had a bite to it.

Around him, Straight Path Canyon gleamed in the morning. He could see Kettle Town to the east, its squat tiers outlined by snow. To the west, Streamside Town caught the first rays of the morning sun. Across Straight Path Wash, several fingers of smoke rose from the few remaining settlements in the valley. The handful of farmers would have lost what few pitiful crops remained. Leather Hand suspected that within days, they, too, would have left the canyon behind.

He was turning to head for his room when a man climbed the south wall and jogged wearily across the plaza. He wore a woven buffalo-wool cape, a heavy shirt, and thick socks covered his trail sandals, the latter caked with frozen mud.

"Deputy War Chief," the man called, waving. "I have news. Matron Desert Willow and War Chief Wind Leaf order you to come to Flowing Waters Town immediately."

"They have captured Ironwood?" Leather Hand called, propping his hands on his hips.

"No, great Deputy. Ironwood has burned Pinnacle Great House. All the First People, including the Sunwatcher and Matron, are dead. They were tossed into the Blue Dragonfly kiva, burned alive, Deputy. The harvest is lost. People are on the verge of panic. The Matron has re-called all able-bodied warriors to Dusk House. You are to report immediately!"

He stood in shock. *Burned alive?* "You are telling me that Matron Larkspur is dead? That all of the First People at Pinnacle Great House are dead?"

"That is correct," the man answered. He'd stopped on the roof below, chest rising and falling as he panted for breath. "Word is that raiding has broken out all over the land. Farmsteads are burning up and down the River of Souls Valley. Neighbors have turned upon each other. The Matron believes that within days people will begin gather-ing around Flowing Waters Town hoping for food. She will need all the warriors she can muster to defend the stores."

Leather Hand closed his eyes, swaying as if from a blow. In the eye of his souls, he saw Larkspur, remembered her warm body against his. He had seen the interest in her eyes, fallen in love with her daring smile. *She would have been Matron of the First People. I would have made her so.*

Now he was going to have to find another way to be-come Blessed Sun.

The Blue God's hollow laughter seemed to echo in the thin air, reverberating from the silent canyon walls.

Yellowgirl glanced warily out the door as Creeper came sauntering down the southern wall of Sunrise House. The first level of rooms, freshly plastered, had a clean smell of earth, cedar, and pine. The packed dirt floor was unstained with ash, broken pottery, bits of fiber, or the other detritus that accumulated in a room.

It was a good time for a meeting. Creeper had no fear of them being interrupted. As a result of the frost, all work on Sunrise House was halted, the slaves' efforts dedicated to saving what they could of the harvest.

In the room's rear—partially illuminated by the midday light that angled in the doorway—sat Copper Ring, Matron of the Coyote Clan, and Wooden Flower, elder of the Bear Clan.

As Yellowgirl stepped inside, Creeper took one look back the way he'd come. No one followed. Four roughly dressed men, trail-worn and streaked with soot and ash, stood talking by the southeastern corner of the building. One tall man seemed oddly familiar, but his back was to Creeper. Out in the fields, people were salvaging the wilting plants.

Creeper entered, a weary weight on his heart. He wasn't prepared for what he would have to say today. He just knew of no other way to save themselves.

"Greetings, Creeper," Yellowgirl said solemnly. "No one saw you come?"

"No," he murmured, nodding to the others. Copper Ring was old, walked with a cane, and had a face like sundried leather. Her toothless jaw was undershot, and a mushroom might have admired the shape of her nose. She looked frail, bones like sticks inside her thin arms. Her hair, snowy white, had been wound into a bun and pinned at the back of her head. It may have been a male fashion, but at her age, what did she care?

Wooden Flower, nearly sixty summers old, still had an eaglelike glare in his eyes, though his right arm was withered, the result of some long-ago wound. He wore a tan hunting shirt, yucca socks, and sandals. A gleaming abalone pendant hung on his chest. Distaste—no doubt at the subject they had come to discuss—lay in the set of his mouth.

Together, the four of them spoke for the Made People clans. Just the fact that they were meeting in secret would have had Webworm and Desert Willow shivering at the implications, had they known.

"It is a grim day," Yellowgirl began. "The slaves are in the fields, still trying to pack what they can salvage into the storerooms. No one should bother us."

Copper Ring smacked her brown lips. Being toothless, she had a slight lisp. "It's not good. My lineage elders report that maybe a tenth of the seed jars will be filled. Sometimes the lower ears didn't freeze all the way. The kernels are still green, but better than nothing."

"Thousands of people will be dead or dislocated by spring," Wooden Flower said flatly. "There is no other way of it. Entire villages will be filled with corpses."

"And those who survive will be raiding each other," Yellowgirl added. "People will attack their neighbors for whatever scraps they might be hoarding rather than watch their children slowly die of starvation."

"Remember the Dust People? That was a measure of desperation," Copper Ring added. "And that was before the freeze."

"How did this happen?" Wooden Flower wondered.

"Webworm," Creeper said sadly, and a wound that had opened in his soul began to bleed. "I watched him grow up. He was my closest friend in the world. I loved him. But since he became Blessed Sun, he has become a stranger. Something inside him changed. I do not know this new Webworm. He . . . he is the fulfillment of the Fire Dog prophecy. I didn't believe it, as you all know. Now, however, after the things I have seen . . ."

"He changed," Yellowgirl agreed. "Once, he was so likable."

"Bad seed leads to a bad harvest," Copper Ring muttered.

"I have tried to see him for four days now," Creeper added. "Each time Wind Leaf has prohibited it. Desert Willow only walks between her rooms and her clan kiva. She goes nowhere without Wind Leaf and a couple of warriors as guards."

"They are afraid," Copper Ring added. "Pinnacle House has been burned, the holy Sunwatcher murdered. Runners sent by my people say that the bodies were burned in the kivas. Many of the Made People were killed after the attack, others driven out. The fugitives are on the way here, spreading terrible stories of the Moon People's wrath as they come."

Creeper took a deep breath. "I never thought I would be the one to say this, but it is time that we take action." He knotted a fist, his face a mask of despair. "How did we end up here? What did we do wrong?"

"Nothing." A voice came from the door as a tall man ducked into the room.

Fear's fingers tightened on Creeper's heart. Gods, were they found out? He turned, taking a moment to recognize the big man who blocked the sunlight. The patch over the left eye only fooled him for a moment. "Ironwood? Is that you?"

The old war chief nodded, then bowed to Wooden Flower, who looked shocked, his good hand clasping his abalone pendant. "Greetings, Clan Elder. I hope the Matron is well."

Creeper thought Ironwood didn't look well, a grayness about him, a slump to his shoulders.

Yellowgirl bobbed her head in greeting, but asked, "What are you doing here? You're declared Outcast. If Webworm hears that—"

"Webworm is dead," Ironwood said firmly. "The Blessed Nightshade, whom you know as the Mountain Witch, cut his heart from his body the night of the storm."

"But we haven't heard this," Wooden Flower insisted.

"Desert Willow doesn't want you to." Ironwood stared from face to face. "She's deathly afraid of what the people will do when they find out."

Yellowgirl asked, "Is that why you're here? Come to lead the Moon People to destroy Flowing Waters Town?"

He shook his head sadly. "I couldn't stop what happened up there. I wanted only to take Blue Racer, Larkspur, and the rest captive. I could have exchanged their lives for Night Sun, used them as pawns while the Made People clans bartered for shared authority. I hadn't counted on the rage of the Moon People."

"Then," Creeper asked, "you didn't attack with the purpose of killing the First People?"

"No." Ironwood gave a faint shake of his head. "The gods, however, had other plans. I have come here only for Night Sun. If you will help me recover her and the rest of the people Leather Hand took, I will leave you to make your own way in peace."

Creeper spread his hands wide. "They are not here."

Ironwood's single eye narrowed. "Not here?"

"Not that we've heard," Copper Ring corrected. "The rumor here is that angry Made People have taken her as punishment for her crimes against them. We have sent out runners to determine if this is indeed the case, but have heard nothing."

"Leather Hand captured her. I know that for a fact." Ironwood was frowning. "Why would they want the credit to go to the Made People? What is the purpose of this lie?"

"Things are unsettled," Wooden Flower said. "But then you walk in here claiming the Blessed Sun's been dead for four days, too. And we've heard nothing of that."

Yellowgirl grunted her assent.

"How did you find us?" Creeper asked. "No one knew of this meeting."

"I have friends here." Ironwood smiled. "For the most part they pass invisibly. The least among us are sometimes the greatest."

"However you found out, we must decide what to do about the First People. Perhaps the gods sent you to us as a sign that they must be removed from our lives." Creeper raised his hands, making a decision that deepened the wounds in his souls. "I have come here to recommend that we throw them out of Flowing Waters Town."

"Then do it, old friend." Ironwood nodded. "Their time is past. If you will save Flowing Waters Town from destruction, you must act quickly, and with resolve."

Sixty-one

THE MOMENT OF SUMS

I Dream . . .

Dark clouds are passing; veils of rain trail the mountains behind them. In their wake, the air is clean, crisp.

I sit alone on the starlit mountaintop, listening to Wind Mother rustling the wet pines as she climbs the slope. The fragrances of damp trees and grass scent her trailing hem. As she passes I breathe them into my lungs and hold them for as long as I can before I must let them go; then I turn and reluctantly gaze southward. Far out in the distance, a great darkness swells, pricked only by the winking campfires of the dead.

Am I strong enough for what comes?

I cannot move. What was excruciating pain has become a throbbing ache. Reaching back I can run my fingers over the smooth sides of the stake they have driven through my hips. It pierces my center, running down through flesh, bone, and my womb. My souls writhe around it.

I am an old woman, maybe too old to endure this final trial.

My first teacher, the great Priest Old Marmot, told me that the price of old age was Power. I recall once when he opened his skeletal hands to me and told me he could feel it draining away through his fingers like water through a poorly woven basket. At the time, I was young and so full of Power that it nearly tore my souls apart. I didn't understand. But I believed him.

For more than fifty summers now, I have been hoarding Power, trying to prepare myself for these final heartbeats. It has cost me more than I can tell you. I often left

*my family to vanish into forest or desert where I could
Dance with my Spirit Helpers, or spent days on a lonely
hilltop praying until my voice was gone. The people I
loved most paid the price. I barely saw my adopted children grow up, and the man I loved with all my heart always had sad eyes.*

Only Brother Mud Head's grin widened.

*Soon, I will know if it was worth it. The Moment of
Sums is almost upon me.*

*Everything I am, everything I ever hoped to be, is about
to be tallied, and when the darkness drains out of my
heart I will know the total of the Light that is left, the
Power that I have accumulated. I only pray the sum is not
too small to do what must be done.*

*I rub my face against the dusty floor. We all strive to do
so much in life—yet manage so little.*

*I have spent a lifetime acquiring the following single
truth: Spiritual knowing is more a process of unlearning
than it is of learning, and I would think it time poorly spent
if I did not realize that it is through "unlearning" that I
have managed to hold onto the meager dusting of Power
that I possess.*

*Death, Sickness, and Sorrow—my holy trinity of Spirit
Helpers—have taught me the only valuable lessons I know.*

Because of them, I unlearned what I saw with my eyes.

I unlearned that life is the sole cause.

I unlearned that strength is a virtue.

*Were it not for the terrible sacrifices of the weak, the in-
nocent, the infants, death would be meaningless.*

*I will do well to remember that in the terrifying instant
ahead.*

Death's meaning—that is the Moment of Sums.

The load of firewood bowed Spots's back as he trudged
through the southeast entrance to Dusk House. He looked
up, seeing the guard wave him through.

Behind him, Cactus Flower walked with her pack over

her shoulder. She shot him a worried look as they made
their way to their traditional place across from the great
kiva. A party of slaves had carried the bear cage off.
Now the space acted as a haunting reminder of the old
woman's presence. He dared not guess what Wind Leaf
had done to her. He'd seen some terrible knowledge in
her eyes when the war chief had led her into the third-
floor room. Moments later a warrior had carried a large
hammer and pointed wooden stake into that same entrance.

They must have her tied to a pole like a dog.

Well, soon now, he would know, one way or the other.
As he laid his wood on the ground, he saw Creeper and
Yellowgirl walk through the entrance. Creeper shot a look
at the Buffalo Clan guard and gave him a terse nod. The
man swallowed hard, glanced nervously around, and nodded in return.

Crow Woman, Yucca Sock, Wrapped Wrist, and others
entered single file, what looked like heavy packs slung
across their backs. Despite their bowed heads, they were
shooting wolfish glances at the walls, taking stock of the
situation.

In the southwest, old Copper Ring came hobbling in,
her cane tapping the hard ground. Wooden Flower
walked behind her, nodding to the Coyote Clan guard at
the gate. Behind them came more warriors, all wearing
smudged shirts and bearing sacks of this and that over
their shoulders.

Spots turned his gaze to the fourth floor. None of the
First People could be seen. So far, they had no idea.

Wind Leaf cupped a corn cake in his callused hand as he
scooped bean paste from a corrugated cooking jar beside
the warming bowl. He lifted a thinly sliced strip of turkey
breast from a warm stone platter and placed it over the
beans before he took a bite. As he chewed he watched
Desert Willow. The Matron was occupied with dressing

for the day. She had just finished drawing a bone comb through her long glistening hair until it shone. Now she was going through her cedar box, lifting dress after dress, holding it against her naked body, and discarding it to try another.

"I like that one," Wind Leaf told her as she held up a white cotton dress decorated by four-pointed black stars. He liked the way it molded to her body.

"You think?" She smoothed it against her flat belly.

Wind Leaf chuckled. Yes, she was vain. But given the pressure that was brewing around her, she deserved any relief she might find. When he'd taken his final survey the night before, it was to find a hundred new camps dotting the flats above Flowing Waters Town. His warriors reported that refugees by the thousands would be trickling in, looking for food, protection, and salvation.

All things we cannot provide.

He should have been out at first light, checking on his guards, ensuring that the morning bore no threat. But knowing the magnitude of the disaster they faced, he preferred to watch as Desert Willow slipped the dress over her head and wriggled into it like a larva into a cocoon. Who was to blame him for taking a moment to enjoy the sight of this beautiful woman when the whole world would be turning ugly in the coming days?

"What should we do with Webworm?" she asked. "He's starting to stink."

"Our runner should have reached Leather Hand yesterday. He will be on his way as we speak." Wind Leaf finished his corn cake, reached for another, and dipped it in the beans. What a luxury to eat such a delicacy while people picked among the spoiled crops for mere scraps.

"Can you trust him? He was, after all, Webworm's creature."

Wind Leaf rolled the flavor of the smoked turkey over his tongue. "I think he can be persuaded to serve us, provided I approach him correctly."

"And how do you propose to do that?"

"That depends on you."

"Me?" She turned, flipping her shining hair over her shoulder. "I don't even like him."

Wind Leaf arched an eyebrow. "Did you enjoy having me back in your bed?"

A smile curled her full lips. "I have never had to pretend when your staff sends shivers of delight through my sheath."

"Then I propose that Webworm 'die' while fighting to protect some isolated village from raiders. No one need see him leave here; no one but Leather Hand need witness his 'heroic battle' to maintain order and calm. No one need view his corpse until after it is carried back to Dusk House several weeks from now. By then he'll be dead so long no one will be able to tell. His funeral will be a symbol of the sacrifices we must make to maintain the peace."

"Why would Leather Hand agree to this charade?"

Wind Leaf gave her a flat stare, placing it all on this one cast of the gaming pieces. "Because after you name me Blessed Sun, I will name him war chief of the Straight Path Nation. If we name Seven Stars as Sunwatcher, it will give us a unified command." A pause. "And Matron, you are going to need loyal warriors and Priests as you've never needed them before."

She took a deep breath, brow lined with thought. "I will consider this. Not that I have a lot of choice. There are so few First People remaining. In the meantime, how many warriors do you expect to arrive today?"

He shrugged. "Perhaps another ten or twenty."

"When they arrive," she said, "I want you to arrest the Made People clan elders."

"Arrest the . . . Why?"

"I don't like the looks they've been giving me. I'd swear they're up to something. Their manner worries me. I see the anger behind their eyes. They'll blame me for the early frost, you mark my words." She shot him a challenging look. "I want them taken care of. Quietly. Perhaps with the same mysterious efficiency that was demonstrated when White Cloud Woman was removed?"

"I can take care of the Made People Matrons. We can use this rumor that they have captured Night Sun as part of the excuse. I have a few trusted warriors. They can apprehend them in the night and bring them here where we can quietly dispose of them."

A hard voice behind him said, "I think not."

Desert Willow gasped, eyes large. Wind Leaf twisted, seeing two brown-shirted warriors, bows drawn, as they ducked in. A hardness glittered in their eyes. They were followed by a tall gray-haired warrior, and then Creeper and Yellowgirl ducked into the room.

Wind Leaf scrambled to grab his war club, only to hear the old one-eyed warrior snap, "Don't! Or you'll die."

He froze, staring at the old man. "Ironwood?"

"The very same, Wind Leaf." He shook his head. "You never were very smart."

"Get out!" Desert Willow screamed, finger pointing.

"There will be no more getting out," Creeper said gruffly. "Webworm's body is already being borne to the great kiva for all to see. And you are right: You should have feared the Made People."

The man's frigid smile sent a shiver through Wind Leaf. "Creeper? You know me. I wouldn't have carried out her order."

"No," the old man said sadly. "I'm sure you wouldn't. We all know what lies are worth these days."

A tall woman warrior stepped past Yellowgirl and grasped Desert Willow by the arm. "Come on, Matron. We've a special room for you: One where no one will hear you shouting."

"What are you going to do with me?" Wind Leaf watched a short muscular man in a hunting shirt kick his war club out of reach.

"Whatever I'm ordered to," the man said through a thick barbarian accent.

When Wind Leaf tried to struggle, the man's great strength bore his arms back. Ironwood tied them tightly. Then, bound like a captive macaw, Wind Leaf was carried away.

The torch in Spots's hand cast guttered yellow light on the room walls. He knew which doorway Nightshade had been taken through, but once inside, rooms led to other rooms; openings in the floors led down to dead ends. Slanting passages with pole-supported roofs led down in different directions. The place was like a giant rabbit warren.

One by one, he and Ironwood made their way, passing through storerooms filled with dried turkeys, stacked jars of corn, net bags filled with squash.

"It's like following a tree root down to a buried stone," Spots said. "How do you know which way?"

"Nightshade?" Ironwood cupped his hands and called.

The echo reverberated as the war chief seemed to stagger, placing a hand against one of the buff-plastered walls.

"War Chief?" Spots asked. "Are you all right?"

"Just a little dizzy," Ironwood answered, blinking. Sweat popped out on his chest and face. He took a couple of deep breaths. "All right. Let's go down. They like putting prisoners as far down as they can."

Spots lifted his torch, the pine sap hissing as it burned. He had two more in his pack for when this one flickered its last. As he climbed down a tunnel stairway to the next floor, he shot an uneasy glance at Ironwood. The man didn't look well. A gray pallor had crept into his complexion, and his movements were those of a man heavy with fatigue.

The room he entered was empty, four bare walls each cut with a doorway. He cast his light into one, finding nothing but rush matting on the floor. In the next, he found scattered trash, cloth rags, broken baskets, and several smashed pots.

When he inspected the third, he stopped short. Several burials had been placed against the walls. Some of the dead were wrapped in matting, split-feather blankets, and the like. Painted jars, seed pots, and cooking ware had been placed close to the corpses to ease their journeys to the Land of the Dead.

At sight of the blanket-covered form in the back, his eyes widened. Gods, they *hadn't* tied her like a dog.

"Nightshade!" Spots ducked through the door, rushing to the old woman's side. A mug of water had been placed just beyond her reach, as had a small bowl filled with dry cornmeal. Her upended pack lay beside its contents. The Wellpot from Cahokia gleamed in the light as if it were a mirror. Bits of stone, animal parts, and Spirit Plants were scattered about, as if trampled upon.

"Brother Mud Head?" she asked groggily. "Have you come to Dance at last?"

"It's Spots, Elder. I came as quickly as I could."

Her eyes were dull as she opened them, a faint smile on her lips. "My young hunter." She barely whispered the words. "Come . . . too late."

"Nightshade?" Ironwood sank to his knees on the packed clay floor. He was laboring, his breath coming in shallow gasps as if he'd run instead of walked into the room. His hand trembled as he reached out to touch the long stake they'd driven through her pelvis.

"Oh, it's real, War Chief," she told him, smacking her lips. "They didn't want my souls to slip out of my body just yet. I was supposed to confess to witching them with Webworm's heart. If I called back the curse, they would let me die."

"We have to get you out of here," Spots cried, staggering to his feet.

"No," she told him simply. "Leave me like this. All debts are paid." She glanced at Ironwood. "Our world is ended, isn't it?"

He nodded, shoulders sagging. "It is."

Spots sank back to his knees again, reaching for the cup and placing it to her lips. She drank, spilling water down the side of her face. "Thank you."

"Where is Night Sun?" Ironwood asked. "Is she here, in a room close by?"

Nightshade shook her head. "No, War Chief. The cannibal, Leather Hand, took her to Talon Town. Laid a trap for you."

"Talon Town?"

Spots heard the hope in the war chief's voice. He could see the sudden glitter in the man's eyes.

"Yours was a great love, Ironwood," Nightshade whispered. "Mythic."

"What can I do to help you?" Spots asked as he wrung his hands.

"The Wellpot," she said weakly.

Spots carefully lifted the shining bowl.

"Scoop out a handful," the old woman told him. She watched as he mounded the gray paste on his fingertips. "That's it. Place it on my tongue."

"Elder, you can't survive that much datura."

"It will free my souls from the stake, Spots," she whispered. Her eyes went to Ironwood.

Spots extended his fingers, letting the old woman suck the gob of paste from them. He swallowed hard, watching her roll the concentrated datura seed from side to side in her mouth.

"Elder?" Ironwood asked. "Is there anything you want me to do afterward? Perhaps take you back to Talon Town with me? Or back to the mountain to be with Badgertail?"

"My bones will be fine here, War Chief," she said with a sigh. "Fear not for my breath-heart soul; it is already halfway loose of the stake. Brother Mud Head awaits us."

"Us?" Ironwood made a pained sound as he rubbed his left shoulder. He kept wincing, as if against pain.

She glanced at Spots. "Take the Wellpot and my pack. The Spirits say they like you. Treat them kindly and they will serve you well." She looked at Ironwood. "Do you want Mud Head and me to take you to Night Sun now?"

"You'll take me to her?" Ironwood asked. He sounded confused, his breathing labored. He blinked, shaking his head. Sweat made a sheen on his skin. He looked curiously gray, even in the torchlight.

"She is calling from the Land of the Dead. We can take

you to her now, or you can live out the rest of your natural life. The decision is yours."

"She's dead?" Spots asked incredulously. "How can you know?"

Ironwood gasped and closed his eyes, his breath sounding like a great weight was on his shoulders. "If you can hear her . . . Yes, I understand. Take me to her now, Nightshade."

"Then come, War Chief," Nightshade whispered weakly. "Reach out. . . . Take my hand. . . ."

Spots glanced uneasily at Nightshade. Her eyes had rolled back in her head, her breath exhaling slowly as her souls slipped away.

"Let go, War Chief. Embrace the Moment of Sums. . . ."

Ironwood's breath caught, his shoulders hunching as if a hard blow had been dealt to his breastbone. He stiffened, whispering, "Night Sun?" then slumped loosely to the floor. His right eye was half-lidded and dark, and Spots heard him whisper the words, *"Oh, my love . . ."*

"War Chief?" Spots grasped his shoulder, shaking the limp body. *"War Chief?"*

In shadows cast on the walls by the flickering torchlight, he would have sworn he saw Mud Head's ungainly round form Dancing away hand in hand with two human shapes.

Sixty-two

Bad Cast and Soft Cloth had arrived in Flowing Waters Town amid a stream of refugees. Only by demanding that they be allowed to speak to Crow Woman had they finally made it past the barricades that had been thrown up at each gate. Squads of heavily armed warriors kept the crowd at bay and defended the precious food stores.

Once inside, Bad Cast had been taken to Spots and Wrapped Wrist. There, he'd delivered the message that Fir Brush and Slipped Bark were traveling south looking for food. They had left in the company of Spots's sister, Yellow Petal, and her baby, Fresh Stalk. Her husband Black Bush and some of his friends thought they could make it across the mountains to a valley that was rumored to have been frost free. They were traveling light, carrying only a water jar and cooking pot. Yellow Petal had taken her feather holder, swearing it would grace the mantel of her new house.

On the day of Ironwood's funeral, fires were burning in the great kiva. People watched from the galleries, the benches were packed, and outside, guards kept a firm watch on those of the refugees that had been allowed into the plaza.

Ironwood's body had been painted in red ocher and dressed in the finest red war shirt that could be found. A bracelet given him by Night Sun was placed on his wrist, and then he was wrapped in feather-cloth and colorfully dyed matting.

Bad Cast was given the honor of helping to bear the ceremonial ladder—emblematic of the climb into the next world—upon which the corpse had been laid. With Crow Woman in the lead they bore the war chief out of the great kiva, across the plaza, and up to the third floor. Bad Cast heard the whispers of "Ironwood, Ironwood, Ironwood" chanted by the mournful crowd. Then they entered Dusk House, following a route deep into the interior.

They laid Ironwood to rest in a room not far from Nightshade's. The Bear Clan, under Wooden Flower's direction, had shown him a hero's respect. They had dug a shallow trench in the floor into which Bad Cast, Wrapped Wrist, Crow Woman, and Yucca Sock shifted the body. Ironwood's shield, war clubs, arrows, and fending sticks were placed atop him. His kit for making stone tools, his bone stilettos, awls, and other personal goods were laid ready at hand.

Five bowls, one offered by each of the Made People

clans and one from the Moon People, were left full of food to help him on his journey to the Land of the Dead. A mug of water and a basket of sacred cornmeal were left close to his head.

"He was the greatest of us," Creeper said.

"Had the rest of us not been looking into the past," Wooden Flower added sadly, "we would have seen that he was the future."

Bad Cast bit his lip, remembering Ironwood's expression that day on the high point—how he'd known that a price would have to be paid. What would he have done differently had he known it would be Night Sun, not he, who suffered?

It was Spots who said, "Do not mourn. Last night I Dreamed. He and the Matron are together."

"You know this?" Wrapped Wrist asked incredulously.

Spots just smiled, Spirit Power reflecting from his large brown eyes. With one hand he patted the pack that hung over his shoulder.

Leather Hand watched from the crowd as Ironwood's remains were carried from the great kiva. Wrapped in finery, the body was borne on a ladder perched on the shoulders of strong warriors—members of Ironwood's little band of fugitives. One tall woman walked proudly, head high, as she led the procession up the successive tiers of Dusk House.

Around him, people stood in silence, some with tears streaking down their faces.

"Ironwood!" The name was whispered from lip to lip, people touching their heads or breasts with respectful fingertips.

Leather Hand struggled to keep his expression neutral. He could feel Turquoise Fox's hand tighten on his shoulder, urging restraint.

So, you, too, have eluded me, old enemy? Just the

thought of it left his stomach sour. The reverence and worship in people's eyes sickened and disgusted him. They would pay. He could feel it. The Blue God would be coming for all of them—may she find their stinking souls wanting.

Turning, he made his way slowly through the crowd, watching as they swarmed after the procession, knotting around the stairway as Ironwood was borne upward and into one of the upper-floor doorways.

"What now?" Turquoise Fox asked.

They were both dressed in poorly woven shirts, the hems ratty and frayed. They'd smeared mud on their faces and left their hair loose in the manner of barbarians. Not even their own men would have recognized them. They had only gained entry by bribing the guards at the southeastern gate with pieces of turquoise.

Leather Hand stopped just short of the southern room block. With the crowd's attention on the funereal procession, no one was paying much attention to the bear cage where it stood less than five paces south of the great kiva entrance. Inside Wind Leaf and Desert Willow crouched, looking miserable and forlorn. Two guards, both Made People, stood to either side of the cage, ensuring both the safety and security of the prisoners. Rumors were already circulating that throughout the land, Made People had risen in revolt and anger, murdering First People in their beds, running them down and battering them to death with axes, hoes, and digging sticks.

When the guards looked the other way, Leather Hand motioned Turquoise Fox inside one of the storerooms across from the bear cage. In the dark room, he crouched down and took a deep breath.

"Tonight," Leather Hand whispered, "when it's dark, we will slip out. The guards won't be expecting an attack from this close. Tomorrow morning the Made People will find only Chief Wind Leaf's headless corpse within."

Turquoise Fox said, "What if Desert Willow won't cooperate?"

"Do you think she would rather share my bed and bear

my children in hopes of regaining what is rightfully hers, or remain as a prisoner of the Made People?"

"I think by tomorrow morning, I will be proud to call you Blessed Sun," Turquoise Fox said knowingly.

Yes, I will be Blessed Sun, and may the Blue God show mercy on the Made People, for I shall not.

He was at war with the Made People. Terror was his weapon. He and his men could walk among them, and they would never know. His fingers smoothed the egg-hatched serpent that Webworm had given him.

Something stirred in his heart, as if tightening and coiling.

Sixty-three

Sister Moon's first rays consisted of a pinprick of white light softening the gap between the great stone pillars of First Moon Mountain, then brightening as she peeked through. The shaft of pale white light grew brighter as she cast her glow on the ruin of Pinnacle Great House.

When her round disc filled the space between the pillars, cold luminescence shone off the standing walls, turned the blackened timbers into gray, and cast inky shadows across the skeletonized rooms.

Did she see the corpse of Dreams the same way he did? Spots couldn't help but wonder. He stood at the lip of the collapsed Blue Dragonfly kiva, watching Sister Moon rise between the pillars.

So, you are home.

But where was he?

He stared down into the kiva's midnight depths. Only silence and blackness remained. This place was as empty as his heart, as the hopes of his world.

He and Cactus Flower had detoured here against the

advice of Bad Cast, Wrapped Wrist, and the rest of their heavily armed party. But he'd wanted to see this place one last time. He needed to know, and most of all, to mourn.

This plaza should have been crowded with Priests in costumes, masks, and feathers, offering their prayers to the rising moon. *Pahos,* drums, and flute music should have been lifting in the still night. Fires should have been blazing, bathing the great house with their own warmth and light. Children should have been laughing, the smell of boiling corn, squash, and beans heavy on the air. Meat should have been roasting in pits, women tending them to ensure the mouthwatering feast was cooked to perfection.

He sniffed, catching only the tart scent of the conifers on the slope below.

In the days after the attack, the First Moon People had removed much of the roof fall, carted the bodies to the edge of the slope, and laid them just below the cliff. There they remained, each with a basket-load of dirt dumped atop it. Other corpses, those of the dead Red Shirts, had been pitched to tangle in the black timber: hideous, flaking caricatures of people, intertwined, with hollows for eyes, noses, and mouths. The snows would come and cover them, and over the years duff and dust would drift down and softly entomb the remains. Charred flesh did not rot, so they would Dance there, frozen in motion.

He turned, staring out at the valley. His people had thought to reclaim this place, rebuild it in their own image. They hadn't lasted a week before the food was gone. Fights broke out, and by the hundreds they had fled, scattering to the north, south, east, and west in search of a place where they could scratch out enough to feed them through the winter.

But where would they go? The deep frost had ruined the entire harvest across a drought-stricken land. Only Yellowgirl's iron control of Flowing Waters Town had kept the place from being sacked.

Across the land was chaos. He had passed Cricket and

Seed's farmstead on the River of Souls and found the swollen bodies of a man, a woman, but only three of the children among the burned and looted ruins. He had heard that half the great houses had been attacked, stripped, and set aflame. Terror stalked the land. Traders had been attacked. Bodies lay unburied along the trails where entire parties of individuals had starved to death in search of food. The rumored valley toward which Yellow Petal and her party had fled for sanctuary was nothing more than a fantasy.

Even wilder stories circulated that Night Sun had been seized by angry Made People who blamed her for the drought. Other rumors said that Ironwood had watched as she was stoically tortured to death. Still other accounts had them alive, traveling in the south with Poor Singer and rallying Fire Dogs to invade the Straight Path Nation to install Cornsilk as Matron. It didn't seem to matter that hundreds had witnessed Ironwood borne to his grave in Dusk House. What was it about people that to believe the impossible seemed more important than to know the truth?

Darker rumors were whispered from lip to lip. Two days after Desert Willow's mysterious disappearance from the bear cage, Creeper had been found dead in his bed, his head missing. In dark places it was whispered that Leather Hand had fathered a child in Desert Willow, and that Night Sun's own grandson, Ravenfire, had eaten Night Sun's flesh. By some reports, the white-moccasin-clad cannibals were building secret kivas where they ate wombs freshly cut from murdered maidens and Danced to the honor of the Blue God.

Upon one thing, all agreed: While the katsinas and the Flute Player were locked in mortal combat, the Blue God was left free to prowl the land.

Whatever the risks and dangers, tomorrow Spots and Cactus Flower would take the trail east to rejoin Wrapped Wrist and Bad Cast. They would winter in the Great River Valley, and later perhaps their children could return here to reestablish their roots.

He heard the sibilant whispers of the Spirits in Nightshade's pack. They reassured him that coming here had been right. He needed their assurance—he, Spots, who had fled from all that was spiritual.

"Our world is dead," he told Sister Moon. "I only have you to share this night with."

Bibliography

Acatos, Sylvio. 1990 *Pueblos: Prehistoric Indian Cultures of the Southwest*. Translation of 1989 edition of *Die Pueblos*. Facts on File, New York.

Adams, E. Charles. 1991 *The Origin and Development of the Pueblo Katsina Cult*. University of Arizona Press, Tucson.

Adler, Michael A. 1996 *The Prehistoric Pueblo World A.D. 1150–1350*. University of Arizona Press, Tucson.

Allen, Paula Gunn. 1989 *Spider Woman's Granddaughters*. Ballantine Books, New York.

Arnberger, Leslie P. 1982 *Flowers of the Southwest Mountains*. Southwest Parks and Monuments Association, Tucson.

Aufderheide, Arthur C. 1998 *The Cambridge Encyclopedia of Human Paleopathology*. Cambridge University Press, Cambridge.

Baars, Donald L. 1995 *Navajo Country: A Geological and Natural History of the Four Corners Region*. University of New Mexico Press, Albuquerque.

Becket, Patrick H. (editor). 1991 *Mogollon V*. Report of Fifth Mogollon Conference. COAS Publishing and Research, Las Cruces, New Mexico.

Billman, Brian R., Patricia M. Lambert, and Banks L. Leonard. 2000 Cannibalism, Warfare, and Drought in the Mesa Verde Region During the Twelfth Century A.D. *American Antiquity* 65 (1):145–178.

Boissiere, Robert. 1990 *The Return of Pahana: A Hopi Myth*. Bear & Company Publishing, Santa Fe, New Mexico.

Bowers, Janice Emily. 1993 *Shrubs and Trees of the Southwest Deserts*. Southwest Parks and Monuments Association, Tucson.

Brody, J. J. 1990 *The Anasazi.* Rizzoli International Publications, New York.

Brothwell, Don, and A. T. Sandison. 1967 *Diseases in Antiquity.* Charles C. Thomas Publisher, Springfield, Illinois.

Bunzel, Ruth L. 1984 Zuni Katcinas. Reprint of Forty-seventh Annual Report of the Bureau of American Ethnography, 1929–1930. Rio Grande Press, Glorietta, New Mexico.

Cameron, Catherine M. 2002 Sacred Earthen Architecture in the Northern Southwest: The Bluff Great House Berm. *American Antiquity* 67 (4):677–696.

Charles, Mona C. 1991 Chimney Rock Barrier Free Trail Mitigation. Contract No. 43-82CS-1-0346. Paper on file at USDA Forest Service, Pagosa District Office, Colorado.

Colton, Harold S. 1960 *Black Sand: Prehistory in Northern Arizona.* University of New Mexico Press, Albuquerque.

Cordell, Linda S. 1975 Predicting Site Abandonment at Wetherill Mesa. *The Kiva* 40 (3):189–202.

     1984 *Prehistory of the Southwest.* Academic Press, New York.

     1994 *Ancient Pueblo Peoples.* Smithsonian Exploring the Ancient World Series. St. Remy Press, Montreal, and Smithsonian Institution Press, Washington.

Cordell, Linda S., and George J. Gumerman (editors). 1989 *Dynamics of Southwest Prehistory.* Smithsonian Institution Press, Washington.

Crown, Patricia, and W. James Judge (editors). 1991 *Chaco & Hohokam: Prehistoric Regional Systems in the American Southwest.* School of American Research Press, Santa Fe, New Mexico.

Cummings, Linda Scott. 1986 Anasazi Subsistence Activity Areas Reflected in the Pollen Records. Paper presented to the Society for American Archaeology Meetings, New Orleans.

     1994 Anasazi Diet: Variety in the Hoy House and Lion House Coprolite Record and Nutritional Analysis. In *Paleo-nutrition: The Diet and Health of Prehistoric*

Americans, edited by Kristin D. Sobolik. Occasional Paper No. 22. Southern Illinois University at Carbondale, Illinois.

Dodge, Natt N. 1985 *Flowers of the Southwest Deserts.* Southwest Parks and Monuments Association, Tucson.

Dooling, D. M., and Paul Jordan-Smith (editors). 1989 *I Become Part of It: Sacred Dimensions in Native American Life.* A Parabola Book. Harper, San Francisco; Harper Collins Publishers, New York.

Douglas, John E. 1995 Autonomy and Regional Systems in the Late Prehistoric Southern Southwest. *American Antiquity* 60:240–257.

Dunmire, William W., and Gail Tierney. 1995 *Wild Plants of the Pueblo Province: Exploring Ancient and Enduring Uses.* Museum of New Mexico Press, Santa Fe, New Mexico.

Eddy, Frank W. 1977 Archaeological Investigations at Chimney Rock Mesa: 1970–1972. Memoirs of the Colorado Archaeological Society No. 1, Boulder.

Ellis, Florence Hawley. 1951 Patterns of Aggression and the War Cult in Southwestern Pueblos. *Southwestern Journal of Anthropology* 7:177–201.

Elmore, Francis H. 1976 *Shrubs and Trees of the Southwest Uplands.* Southwest Parks and Monuments Association, Tucson.

Ericson, Jonathan E., and Timothy G. Baugh (editors). 1993 *The American Southwest and Mesoamerica: Systems of Prehistoric Exchange.* Plenum Press, New York.

Fagan, Brian M. 1991 *Ancient North America.* Thames and Hudson, New York.

Farmer, Malcom F. 1957 A Suggested Typology of Defensive Systems of the Southwest. *Southwestern Journal of Archaeology* 13:249–266.

Frank, Larry, and Francis H. Harlow. 1990 *Historic Pottery of the Pueblo Indians: 1600–1880.* Schiffler Publishing, West Chester, Pennsylvania.

Frazier, Kendrick. 1986 *People of Chaco: A Canyon and Its Culture.* W. W. Norton, New York.

Gabriel, Kathryn. 1991 *Roads to Center Place: A Cultural*

Atlas of Chaco Canyon and the Anasazi. Johnson Books, Boulder, Colorado.

Gumerman, George J. (editor). 1988 *The Anasazi in a Changing Environment.* School of American Research. Cambridge University Press, New York.

1991 *Exploring the Hohokam: Prehistoric Peoples of the American Southwest.* Amerind Foundation. University of New Mexico Press, Albuquerque.

1994 *Themes in Southwest Prehistory.* School of American Research Press, Santa Fe, New Mexico.

Haas, Jonathan. 1990 Warfare and the Evolution of Tribal Polities in the Prehistoric Southwest. In *The Anthropology of War,* edited by Jonathan Haas. Cambridge University Press, Cambridge.

Haas, Jonathan, and Winifred Creamer. 1993 *Stress and Warfare Among the Kayenta Anasazi of the Thirteenth Century A.D.* Field Museum of Natural History, Chicago.

1995 A History of Pueblo Warfare. Paper presented at the 60th Annual Meeting for the Society of American Archaeology, Minneapolis.

Hatch, Sharon K. 1994 Wood Sourcing Study at the Chimney Rock Archaeological Area. Paper presented at the Second Chimney Rock Archaeological Symposium, Anasazi Heritage Center. Paper on file with the USDA Forest Service, Pagosa District Office, Colorado.

Haury, Emil. 1985 *Mogollon Culture in the Forestdale Valley, East-Central Arizona.* University of Arizona Press, Tucson.

Hayes, Alden C., David M. Burgge, and W. James Judge. 1981 *Archaeological Surveys of Chaco Canyon, New Mexico.* Reprint of National Park Service Report. University of New Mexico Press, Albuquerque.

Hultkrantz, Ake. 1987 *Native Religions: The Power of Visions and Fertility.* Harper & Row, New York.

Jacobs, Sue-Ellen. 1995 Continuity and Change in Gender Roles at San Juan Pueblo. In *Women and Power in Native North America.* Edited by Laura F. Klein and

Lillian Ackerman. University of Oklahoma Press, Norman, Oklahoma.

Jeancon, Jean Allard. n.d. Archaeological and Ethnological Research During the Year 1924. Unpublished manuscript on file, Colorado Historical Society, Denver.

1922 Archaeological Research in the Northeastern San Juan Basin of Colorado in the Summer of 1921. The State Historical Society of Colorado and the University of Denver, Denver.

1923 Further Archaeological Research in the Northeastern San Juan Basin of Colorado, During the Summer of 1922. *Colorado Magazine* 1:11–28.

1924a Excavation Work in the Pagosa-Piedra Field During the Season of 1922. *Colorado Magazine* 1 (2):65–70.

1924b Further Archaeological Research in the Northeastern San Juan Basin of Colorado During the Summer of 1922. Pottery of the Pagosa-Piedra Region. *Colorado Magazine* 1:213–224.

Jeancon, Jean Allard, and Frank H. H. Roberts. 1924 Further Archaeological Research in the Northeastern San Juan Basin of Colorado. *Colorado Magazine* 1 (2):65–70, (3):108–118.

Jernigan, E. Wesley. 1978 *Jewelry of the Prehistoric Southwest.* School of American Research, University of New Mexico Press, Albuquerque.

Jett, Stephen C. 1964 Pueblo Indian Migrations: An Evaluation of the Possible Physical and Cultural Determinants. *American Antiquity* 29:281–300.

Kamp, Kathryn A. 2002 *Children in the Prehistoric Puebloan Southwest.* University of Utah Press, Salt Lake City.

Komarek, Susan. 1994 *Flora of the San Juans: A Field Guide to the Mountain Plants of Southwestern Colorado.* Kivaki Press, Durango, Colorado.

Lange, Frederick, Nancy Mahaney, Joe Ben Wheat, Mark L. Chenault, and John Carter. 1988 *Yellow Jacket: A Four Corners Anasazi Ceremonial Center.* Johnson Books, Boulder, Colorado.

LeBlanc, Stephen A. 1999 *Prehistoric Warfare in the American Southwest*. University of Utah Press, Salt Lake City.

Lekson, Stephen H. 1988 The Idea of the Kiva in Anasazi Archaeology. *The Kiva* 53 (3):213–234.

1990 *Mimbres Archaeology of the Upper Gila, New Mexico*. Anthropological Papers of the University of Arizona, No. 53. University of Arizona Press, Tucson.

2002 War in the Southwest, War in the World. *American Antiquity* 67 (4):607–624.

Lekson, Stephen, Thomas C. Windes, John R. Stein, and W. James Judge. 1988 The Chaco Canyon Community. *Scientific American* 259 (1):100–109.

Lewis, Dorothy Otnow. 1998 *Guilty by Reason of Insanity: A Psychiatrist Explores the Minds of Killers*. The Ballantine Publishing Group, New York.

Lipe, W. D., and Michelle Hegemon (editors). 1989 *The Architecture of Social Integration in Prehistoric Pueblos*. Occasional Papers of the Crow Canyon Archaeological Center No. 1. Crow Canyon Archaeological Center, Cortez, Colorado.

Lister, Florence C. 1993 *In the Shadow of the Rocks: Archaeology of the Chimney Rock District in Southern Colorado*. University Press of Colorado, Niwot, Colorado.

Lister, Florence C., and Robert H. Lister. 1968 *Earl Morris & Southwestern Archaeology*. University of New Mexico Press, Albuquerque.

Lister, Robert H., and Florence C. Lister. 1981 *Chaco Canyon*. University of New Mexico Press, Albuquerque.

Lomatuway'ma, Michael, Lorena Lomatuway'ma, and Sidney Namingha Jr. 1993 *Hopi Ruin Legends*. Edited by Ekkehart Malotki. Published for Northern Arizona University by University of Nebraska Press, Lincoln.

Malotki, Ekkehart. 1985 *Gullible Coyote: Una'ihu: A Bilingual Collection of Hopi Coyote Stories*. University of Arizona Press, Tucson.

Malotki, Ekkehart, and Michael Lomatuway'ma. 1987 *Maasaw: Profile of a Hopi God.* American Tribal Religions, Vol. XI. University of Nebraska Press, Lincoln.

Malville, J. McKimm, and Gary Matlock. 1990 *The Chimney Rock Archaeological Symposium.* USDA Forest Service General Technical Report RM-227.

Malville, J. McKimm, and Claudia Putnam. 1993 *Prehistoric Astronomy in the Southwest.* Johnson Books, Boulder, Colorado.

Mann, Coramae Richey. 1996 *When Women Kill.* State University of New York Press, New York.

Martin, Debra L. 1995 Lives Unlived: The Political Economy of Violence Against Anasazi Women. Paper presented to the Society for American Archaeology 60th Annual Meeting, Minneapolis.

Martin, Debra L., Alan H. Goodman, George Armelagos, and Ann L. Magennis. 1991 *Black Mesa Anasazi Health: Reconstructing Life from Patterns of Death and Disease.* Occasional Paper No. 14. Southern Illinois University, Carbondale, Illinois.

Martin, Paul S. 1936 Lowry Ruin in Southwest Colorado. *Anthropological Series* 23:1. Field Museum of Natural History, Chicago.

Mayes, Vernon O., and Barbara Bayless Lacy. 1989 *Nanise: A Navajo Herbal.* Navajo Community College Press, Tsaile, Arizona.

McGuire, Randall H., and Michael Schiffer (editors). 1982 *Hohokam and Patayan: Prehistory of Southwestern Arizona.* Academic Press, New York.

McNitt, Frank. 1966 *Richard Wetherill Anasazi.* University of New Mexico Press, Albuquerque.

Minnis, Paul E., and Charles L. Redman (editors). 1990 *Perspectives on Southwestern Prehistory.* Westview Press, Boulder, Colorado.

Mitchell, Douglas R., and Judy L. Brunson-Hadley (editors). 2001 *Ancient Burial Practices.* University of New Mexico Press, Albuquerque.

Morris, Ann Axtel. 1933 *Digging in the Southwest.* Doubleday, Doran & Co., New York.

Morris, Earl H. 1917a The Ruins at Aztec. *El Palacio* 4:3: 43–69.

1917b Discoveries at the Aztec Ruin. *American Museum Journal* 17 (3):169–180.

1918 Further Discoveries at the Aztec Ruin. *American Museum Journal* 18 (7):602–10.

1919a The Aztec Ruin. *Anthropological Papers* 26:pt.1. American Museum of Natural History, New York.

1919b Further Discoveries at the Aztec Ruin. *El Palacio* 6:17–23. Santa Fe.

1921 The House of the Great Kiva at the Aztec Ruin. *Anthropological Papers* 26:pt.2 American Museum of Natural History, New York.

1924 Burials in the Aztec Ruin. *Anthropological Papers* 26:pts.3 & 4. American Museum of Natural History, New York.

1928 Notes on Excavations in the Aztec Ruin. *Anthropological Papers* 26: pt.5. American Museum of Natural History, New York.

Mullet, G. M. 1979 *Spider Woman Stories: Legends of the Hopi Indians.* University of Arizona Press, Tucson.

Nabahan, Gary Paul. 1989 *Enduring Seeds: Native American Agriculture and Wild Plant Conservation.* North Point Press, San Francisco.

Noble, David Grant. 1991 *Ancient Ruins of the Southwest: An Archaeological Guide.* Northland Publishing, Flagstaff, Arizona.

Ortiz, Alfonzo (editor). 1983 *Handbook of North American Indians.* Smithsonian Institution, Washington.

Palkovich, Ann M. 1980 *The Arroyo Hondo Skeletal and Mortuary Remains.* Arroyo Hondo Archaeological Series, Vol. 3. School of American Research Press, Santa Fe, New Mexico.

Parker, Douglas. 1994 Chimney Rock Pottery: The Identification of Chaco Ceramics by Petrography and Their Comparisons to Samples from Chaco Canyon. Paper on file with the USDA Forest Service, Pagosa District Office, Colorado.

Parsons, Elsie Clews. 1939 *Pueblo Indian Religion. Vols.* 1 & 2. Bison Books reprint, Lincoln, Nebraska.

1994 *Tewa Tales.* Reprint of 1924 edition. University of Arizona Press, Tucson.

Pepper, George H. 1996 *Pueblo Bonito.* Reprint of 1920 edition. University of New Mexico Press, Albuquerque.

Pike, Donald G., and David Muench. 1974 *Anasazi: Ancient People of the Rock.* Crown Publishers, New York.

Reid, J. Jefferson, and David E. Doyel (editors). 1992 *Emil Haury's Prehistory of the American Southwest.* University of Arizona Press, Tucson.

Renaud, Etienne B. 1924 A Pit-House Skull from the Piedra District, Archuleta County, Colorado. Paper on file at the State Historical Society of Colorado, Denver.

Rice, Glen E., and Steven A. LeBlanc (editors). 2001 *Deadly Landscapes: Case Studies in Prehistoric Southwestern Warfare.* University of Utah Press, Salt Lake City.

Riley, Carroll L. 1995 *Rio del Norte: People of the Upper Rio Grande from the Earliest Times to the Pueblo Revolt.* University of Utah Press, Salt Lake City.

Roberts, Frank H. H. 1925 Report on Archaeological Reconnaissance in Southwest Colorado in the Summer of 1923. *Colorado Magazine* 2:2.

1930 Early Pueblo Ruins in the Piedra District, Southwestern Colorado. *Bureau of American Ethnology.* Bulletin 96.

Rocek, Thomas R. 1995 Sedentarization and Agricultural Dependence: Perspectives from the Pithouse-to-Pueblo Transition in the American Southwest. *American Antiquity* 60:218–239.

Schaafsma, Polly. 1980 *Indian Rock Art of the Southwest.* School of American Research, University of New Mexico Press, Albuquerque.

2000 *Warrior, Shield, and Star.* Western Edge Press. Santa Fe, New Mexico.

Sebastian, Lynne. 1992 *The Chaco Anasazi: Sociopolitical Evolution in the Prehistoric Southwest.* Cambridge University Press, Cambridge.

Simmons, Marc. 1980 *Witchcraft in the Southwest.* Bison Books reprint of 1974 edition. University of Nebraska Press, Lincoln.

Slifer, Dennis, and James Duffield. 1994 *Kokopelli: Flute Player Images in Rock Art.* Ancient City Press, Santa Fe, New Mexico.

Smith, Watson, and Raymond H. Thompson (editors). 1990 *When Is a Kiva?: And Other Questions About Southwestern Archaeology.* University of Arizona Press, Tucson.

Sobolik, Kristin D. 1994 *Paleonutrition: The Diet and Health of Prehistoric Americans.* Occasional Paper no. 22. Center for Archaeological Investigations, Southern Illinois University, Carbondale.

Sullivan, Alan P. 1992 Pinyon Nuts and Other Wild Resources in Western Anasazi Subsistence Economies. *Research in Economic Anthropology* Supplement 6:195–239.

Tedlock, Barbara. 1992 *The Beautiful and the Dangerous: Encounters with the Zuni Indians.* Viking Press, New York.

Trombold, Charles D. (editor). 1991 *Ancient Road Networks and Settlement Hierarchies in the New World.* Cambridge University Press, Cambridge.

Turner, Christy G., and Jacqueline A. Turner. 1999 *Man Corn: Cannibalism and Violence in the Prehistoric American Southwest.* University of Utah Press, Salt Lake City.

Tyler, Hamilton A. 1964 *Pueblo Gods and Myths.* University of Oklahoma Press, Norman, Oklahoma.

Underhill, Ruth. 1991 *Life in the Pueblos.* Reprint of 1964 Bureau of Indian Affairs Report. Ancient City Press, Santa Fe, New Mexico.

Upham, Steadman, Kent G. Lightfoot, and Roberta A. Jewett (editors). 1989 *The Sociopolitical Structure of Prehistoric Southwestern Societies.* Westview Press, San Francisco.

Varien, Mark D., and Richard H. Wilshusen. 2002 *Seeking the Center Place: Archaeology and Ancient Commu-*

nities in the Mesa Verde Region. University of Utah Press, Salt Lake City.

Vivian, Gordon, and Tom W. Mathews. 1973 *Kin Kletso: A Pueblo III Community in Chaco Canyon, New Mexico,* Vol. 6. Southwest Parks and Monuments Association, Globe, Arizona.

Vivian, Gordon, and Paul Reiter. 1965 *The Great Kivas of Chaco Canyon and Their Relationships.* School of American Research, Monograph no. 22, Santa Fe, New Mexico.

Vivian, R. Gwinn. 1990 *The Chacoan Prehistory of the San Juan Basin.* Academic Press, New York.

Waters, Frank. 1963 *Book of the Hopi.* Viking Press, New York.

Wetterstrom, Wilma. 1986 *Food, Diet, and Population at Prehistoric Arroyo Hondo Pueblo, New Mexico.* Arroyo Hondo Archaeological Series, Vol. 6; School of American Research Press, Santa Fe, New Mexico.

White, Tim D. 1992 *Prehistoric Cannibalism at Mancos 5MTUMR-2346.* Princeton University Press, Princeton.

Williamson, Ray A. 1984 *Living the Sky: The Cosmos of the American Indian.* University of Oklahoma Press, Norman, Oklahoma.

Wills, W. H., and Robert D. Leonard (editors). 1994 *The Ancient Southwestern Community.* University of New Mexico Press, Albuquerque.

Woodbury, Richard B. 1959 A Reconsideration of Pueblo Warfare in the Southwestern United States. *Actas del XXXIII Congreso Internacional de Americanistas* II: 124–133. San Jose, Costa Rica.

1961 Climatic Changes and Prehistoric Agriculture in the Southwestern United States. *New York Academy of Sciences Annals,* Vol. 95, Article 1, New York.

Wright, Barton. 1975 *Katchinas: The Barry Goldwater Collection at the Heard Museum.* Heard Museum, Phoenix, Arizona.

Look for the next chapter in North America's Forgotten Past

PEOPLE
of the NIGHTLAND

Available in hardcover in March 2007 from Forge Books

Chapter 1

The Winter of Icebacked Mammoths . . .

Ti-Bish huddled in the lee of the snowdrift and stared out at the bare oak, hickory, and walnut trees. Wind Woman howled over the peaks of the Ice Giants and thrashed the dark forests, whipping the branches back and forth. Nine Pipes village, down the hill in front of him, lay quiet and still. The people slept warmly in their conical lodges, made from pole frames covered with hides. Several people snored. Somewhere on the far side of the village, a baby whimpered. He didn't see any dogs. It was cold, very cold. The people must have brought the dogs into their lodges for the night.

"They're asleep," he murmured to himself. "It's all right. No one will see you."

A tall gawky man with a boyish face and two long black braids, he had seen ten and nine summers. He pulled his bearskin cape more tightly around his skinny body, and clutched his atlatl in a hard fist. The atlatl, as long as his arm, was a mammoth ivory throwing stick he used to catapult long stone-tipped darts; it felt light as a feather to his fear-charged muscles.

On the wind, he heard wings flapping.

He craned his neck to look up. He didn't see any night birds, but Horn Spoon village, the largest village of Star People, had climbed high into the sky.

Surely no one would be awake at this time. No one would come outside, even if they heard a noise.

He rose and walked down the hill, carefully placing his snowshoes, made from willow hoops laced with rawhide. If he slipped on ice beneath the dusting of snow, he would tumble down the hill like a thrown rock.

The entire village would wake and come looking for the intruder.

He eased into a walnut grove. Amid the dark filigree of branches, a few old leaves rattled. Snow had piled around the trunks. The shadowed hollows of the drifts gleamed dark blue, while the cornices shone purple.

He listened for ten heartbeats, then continued down the slope toward the shell midden.

The people of Nine Pipes village collected freshwater mussels from the nearby creeks and rivers. He lifted his nose and could smell the new shells they'd thrown on the midden tonight after supper.

"No one will care," he whispered. "They've already eaten what they want from the shells."

He crept closer and heard beaks pecking at something. Talons skittered.

Ti-Bish cocked his head. It must be night birds scavenging the shell midden, just as he wished to do.

He pulled a dart, as long as he was tall, from his quiver and nocked it in his atlatl. Blessed with the blood of caribou and giant buffalo, the shaft had Power. The light of the Blessed Star People reflected from the snow with blinding intensity. He might be able to see well enough to dart an owl. The thought of warm meat made his empty belly moan.

Wings flapped again.

He crept downwind of the shell midden, praying Wind Woman would keep his scent from Owl. When he reached the edge of the midden, the shells glittered wildly in the starlight. He got down and crawled forward with the silence of a dire wolf on a hunt.

A caw erupted, then several more.

He frowned. A raven? Out at night? He'd never seen it. Perhaps the bird, too, was starving.

He fought the urge to rise up, rush around the midden, and cast his dart in one desperate gamble for food. But it would fly away if he did. Ravens were very smart.

He slid forward on his belly until he could see the bird feasting on the fresh shells at the base of the midden. It was a big bird, black as night, with eyes that glowed silver in the stargleam.

Raven stood on a mussel shell, then used his beak to tug out a stubborn bit of meat, which he gobbled down, and went back for more.

Ti-Bish took a deep breath, rose on his knees, judged the distance, and lifted his nocked atlatl.

Raven stopped eating.

Ti-Bish froze.

Raven cocked his head, and scanned the midden for predators.

Ti-Bish waited, hoping his belly would not moan again and give away his position.

For long moments, he waited, not even breathing, listening to Wind Woman batter the forests . . . until Raven's fears eased and his black beak lowered to tug at another bit of meat. His feet skittered on the frozen shells.

With the noise as cover, Ti-Bish drew back and hurled his dart with all his strength. The white quartzite tip glittered as it arced toward Raven. Raven saw it at the last instant, let out a sharp cry, and tried to fly, but the dart struck him squarely through the middle, pinning his wings to his sides. He flopped over, and cawed in terror. A frozen puff of breath hung in the air before it was swept away by the wind. Ti-Bish raced forward and grabbed him.

"Forgive me, brother," he said as he snapped Raven's thin neck.

The shells forgotten, Ti-Bish took his prize back to the forest, where he nestled in the lee of snowdrift.

"I'm sorry I had to kill you, Raven," he whispered as he petted the feathers. "But I'm starving, too. Thank you for your meat."

Drawing his stone knife from his belt pouch, he slit open the bird's belly and cut out the internal organs first. The heart, liver, and kidneys went down in single gulps.

Ti-Bish drank the blood that had pooled in the stomach cavity and then peeled back the skin, feathers and all, and gently laid it to the side. Using his teeth, he tore the meat from the bones as fast as he could and swallowed it.

When he'd finished, he tucked Raven's bones into the empty skin and carried it to a nearby tree, where he placed them in the crook of a branch. His People, the People of the Nightland, never allowed the bones of animals they'd hunted to touch the ground. It was disrespectful. If animals were killed with reverence, the creator, Old Man Above, would send a new body for them, and their spirits would enter it and fly away again.

"Thank you, brother," he said softly.

He leaned his forehead against the trunk of the tree and took a deep tired breath. He'd been scavenging this shell midden for several days, but had found little to chase away his hunger. Yesterday, one of the village women had brought him food. She'd been kind and beautiful. He'd been hoping she would bring him more today, but she hadn't. He would stay here for perhaps another day, then move on.

He felt suddenly too tired to return to the lean-to he'd constructed far back in the forest.

He walked out into the oak trees, found a big drift, and began scooping it out to create a snow cave. When he'd finished, he crawled through the narrow doorway and curled up on his side. Beyond the entry, snow whirled and gusted across the ground.

He pulled his weapons close, just in case Grandmother Sabertooth Cat or Brother Short-faced Bear also came to scavenge the shell midden tonight. With the strength of Raven's blood warming his belly, he fell into an exhausted sleep.

The Dreaming crept up from the cold ground and twined icy fingers around his body. . . .

In the Dreaming, he and Raven flew side by side over jagged ice peaks that seemed to go on forever. Deep crevasses rent the ice in places and long cracks zigzagged away from the crevasses like dark lightning bolts. Here, in the Dreaming, he was no longer a weak man. He flew behind Raven with his own black glittering wings.

"Look!" Raven said and tucked his wings, plummeting downward toward a huge gaping hole in the ice. "Do you see it?"

Ti-Bish soared toward the hole and floated beside Raven on the warm currents that blew up from the darkness. The air smelled of moss and algae. Water gushed from the mouth of the tunnel, carrying sand and gravel out in a black stream. From the hole, groans and squeals came, as though the Ice Giants that lived inside were being born in pain and blood.

Raven tucked his wings and dove again, getting closer to the hole, finally diving right through the mouth into utter darkness.

Frightened, Ti-Bish followed.

Deep in the belly of the Ice Giants, light glowed, pale and flickering, but there.

"This is the way," Raven said. "Follow me."

He flapped over a great dark lake streaked with a phosphorescent brilliance, as though the fish themselves left sinuous trails of light through the water.

"Through there," Raven said and flew up the shore. "Do you see it?"

Raven sailed along the lakeshore, swooping down occasionally to examine the gigantic bones of monsters that eroded from the ice. A trail wove around the ancient skeletons—*a Monster Bone Trail*—and here and there, Ti-Bish saw the desiccated bodies of dead humans.

Raven soared to where a wide river spilled out into the fiery lake, then flew straight through the hole in the ice from which the water flowed, and vanished.

Ti-Bish, squealing in fear, sailed after him.

Only the sound of Raven's flapping wings led him through the blackness. All around him the Ice Giants chittered and cackled. Often their deep groans were loud enough to scare Ti-Bish's Spirit from his body. He flew harder, trying to catch up with Raven.

For a long, long time, they flew through a quaking,

moaning world of darkness, then a twinkle of light appeared.

"This is the way," Raven said. "You can now be the Guide. You must lead the People this way."

The Ice Giants split wide open, and they flew through the opening into a dark sky filled with thousands of Star People. Far beneath them, herds of mammoth, long-horned buffalo, and caribou grazed together along the shore of a vast ocean.

Fear slipped away like elk's winter coat in spring, and Ti-Bish flew wild and free, darting and diving after Raven, until he flipped over on his back and plummeted straight down toward a long-horned buffalo.

Raven alighted on Buffalo's hump and Ti-Bish landed beside him. The animal's massive shoulders rolled up and down as it walked through the belly-deep grass.

Buffalo broke into a gallop, heading straight toward the huge gaping cavern they'd just flown through to get here. Ti-Bish tightened his talons in Buffalo's thick fur to hold on.

Raven said, "Buffalo shows you the way, also, Man. Just as I have. If I'd flown here to the Long Dark where there is plenty to eat, I wouldn't have needed to scavenge the shell midden, and you wouldn't have had to dart me. You must use the gift of my life to grow strong so that you can find the hole in the ice . . . find the hole in the ice."

Ti-Bish burrowed down into Buffalo's thick fur and sighed. It was so warm and soft. In the distance, he saw mammoth calves running and trumpeting, playing in the starlight. Caribou stood in the ponds, moss hanging from their antlers, and high overhead, crimson waves of light rolled across fluttering curtains of green and blue, the brilliant fires of the Monster Children's war that never ceased.

"This is the way," Raven said. "This is the way you must lead The People."

The flight had been long and tiresome. Ti-Bish worked his beak deeper into Buffalo's silky undercoat and closed his eyes to sleep.